Sophie Green is an author and p  has written several fiction and other am In her spare time on he will holiday by the ocean in pyddu'r

Inaugurual Meeting of the Fairvale Ladies Book Club, a Top Ten bestseller in Australia, was shortlisted for the Australian Book Industry Awards for General Fiction Book of the Year 2018, longlisted for the Matt Richell Award for New Writer of the Year and longlisted for the Indie Book Award for Debut Fiction 2018.

ALSO BY SOPHIE GREEN

The Inaugural Meeting of the Fairvale Ladies Book Club

THE SHELLY BAY LADIES SWIMMING CIRCLE

SOPHIE GREEN

sphere

For Jen, my Shelly Bay friend

SPHERE

First published in Australia in 2020 by Hachette Australia
First published in Great Britain in 2019 by Sphere
This paperback edition published by Sphere in 2020

1 3 5 7 9 10 8 6 4 2

A CIP catalogue record for this book
is available from the British Library.

ISBN 978-0-7515-7824-9

Printed and bound in Great Britain by Clays Ltd, Elcograf S.p.A.

Papers used by Sphere are from well-managed forests
and other responsible sources.

Sphere
An imprint of
Little, Brown Book Group
Carmelite House
50 Victoria Embankment
London EC4Y 0DZ

An Hachette UK Company
www.hachette.co.uk

www.littlebrown.co.uk

SPRING 1982

CHAPTER 1

Theresa screws up her nose as she approaches the water. She knows it's going to be cold. It may be spring but the ocean will still be feeling the effect of Antarctic currents. Are they from Antarctica? Someone told her that once. And they're cold enough to be. Or maybe they're from Bass Strait. Or South America or something. She can't remember exactly, but she does remember what it was like all those years ago when she was a Nipper right here at Main Beach, learning how to read rips and run down the sand and swim fast so she could save lives in the water. She never did grow up to be a surf lifesaver but the memories of the water being cold in November have lingered.

She breathes in deeply and clasps her hands behind to stretch out her arms and shoulders. That's what you're meant to do before exercise, isn't it? Stretch? She's seen swimmers do it on the telly, during the Olympics. Lisa Curry, in Moscow. Theresa isn't kidding herself: she's never going to be able to swim like Lisa Curry. But she's here. She's stretching. Small steps.

As she feels the tug around her chest and shoulders she looks towards the horizon, where shades of yellowy-orange are starting to appear. The sun isn't quite up yet but there's

3

enough light for her to see the long stretch of beach to the left of where she stands, all the way to Kings End.

Behind the beach is the concrete that forms the wall and the walkway, and pine trees that are far older than she is but don't belong here anyway, because they're Norfolk Island pines and this beach is a long way from an island that's closer to New Zealand than Australia. Out of sight to her now, but just around the corner, is Little Beach. That's her goal – to swim to Little Beach. Not today. Some day. Soon. She should probably set herself a more realistic goal for today. Maybe swim from this end of the beach to halfway along, then back. That's not too far. Not as far as she used to swim when they went to the pool for school sport. She was all right at swimming back then.

You're stalling.

Ah, yes – there's that little annoying voice she's been fighting all week, ever since it told her she had to start *doing something*. To get fit. To lose weight.

She knows she needs to – it isn't healthy to be overweight and no man would find her attractive if she was. Her mother had told her that each time Theresa had walked into the kitchen in her school uniform and reached for a piece of cake.

Her mother had liked to bake cakes but hadn't eaten them, and had expected Theresa to follow her example. 'You can never be too rich or too thin,' was her constant advice, cadged from the Duchess of Windsor. Theresa's brothers, on the other hand, could eat as much cake as they liked. In fact, the cakes were baked *for* them.

So Theresa knows she needs to lose a bit. She just didn't need her husband to add his voice to the one in her head. But he did anyway.

Andrew – Andy, Ando, Ands to his mates – had sat on the couch a few weeks ago, his newly burgeoning beer gut spilling over the top of his King Gees and out the bottom of the dirty white Bonds singlet he wore around the house, a tinny in one hand and the other idly flipping through the form guide in the paper while he ogled Delvene Delaney wearing a bikini on *The Paul Hogan Show*. He'd looked Theresa up and down as she'd entered the room carrying his dinner on a tray so he could keep perving at Delvene while he ate.

'You're puttin' on a bit,' he pronounced, then looked appraisingly at the food she was offering. 'What are those – cutlets?' Then he'd made a face like he didn't want cutlets, although she knew, because she's been married to him for a while now, that he loves them.

She'd glared at him and slammed the tray down near enough to his testicles to be a threat. '*Yes*, they're cutlets.'

He'd grinned, then winked at her. That grin and the wink had worked better when he used to be handsome. Of course, in his own mind he still was.

She'd spun away from him only to feel his hand grabbing her wrist. 'Hold yer horses,' he said, putting his tinny down on the card table next to him. That's how she knew he wanted to have a serious conversation. 'I didn't mean to upset you.'

Perhaps. But she knew he'd meant what he said. Because he'd said it before, and not just when Delvene was on the screen.

Theresa can't say he's wrong. She's a little plumper than she used to be, but she's had two kids, and they cut the second one out of her, so what does he expect? Still, she's resolved to do something about it. Not because she doesn't like the way she looks, but because she's sick of feeling the way she feels: slow, stodgy – and old. She's only thirty-eight but she feels a hundred most days. She wants to have – *needs* to have – more energy to run around after her children, whom she loves even if they get on her nerves.

She should be more grateful for the kids: her cheeky boy, Oliver, and her sweet girl, Sasha. She almost lost Sasha. When she was born the cord was wrapped around her neck and Theresa saw the end of her dream of having a daughter named Alexandra and nicknamed Sasha. She'd always wanted that, ever since there'd been a Russian girl in her class who was known to all as Sasha – then Theresa had found out her real name. It had seemed so cosmopolitan to have a 'diminutive' name, as she'd also learnt to call it. And she wanted to be cosmopolitan. Still wants to be. She wants to have a racy life. To zip around the world without any cares. Maybe with that dishy Tom Burlinson she's just seen in that new film *The Man from Snowy River*. It wasn't much like the poem she loved so much in school but that doesn't bother her, because sometimes, when she's alone, she thinks about Tom riding that horse straight down that mountainside . . .

So she's decided to take her inspiration from Olivia Newton-John and get physical. Just not the way Livvy did it, with a leotard and sweatband worn like John McEnroe's. Swimming is the only sporting activity Theresa liked as a kid, so it was to swimming she decided to turn two nights ago, when the voice of conscience had a small victory and she made her big decision and hoped she could stick to it. From now until the end of summer she's going to have a sunrise swim. Every day, she's decided. No backing down – not unless the conditions are truly unfavourable.

Andrew and the kids will sleep through the whole thing, up in their little house on the ridge between Kings End and the next beach, Sunrise. And if the kids wake up, Andrew will just have to deal with them. For a change. It's not as if she doesn't have to deal with them most nights of the week when he stays out drinking with his mates after work and comes in smelling of beer and, mysteriously, Brut 33. She's never seen a bottle of it in the house.

This morning she almost decided to make swimming a New Year's resolution instead, but she knows that if she delays until January summer will be almost half gone and she might lose her nerve. This way she has a few weeks of getting in the water and seeing just how fit she can become.

For a second or two, she'd wondered if she should invite a friend to join her – then she'd remembered that all her friends are as wrapped up with their children as she is. None of them has time for each other any more. She's planning to hold on until the kids are in high school and then they can all reconnect. Her mum told her that's about how long it takes for everyone to 'get past the worst of it'.

'G'day, Tess,' she hears from her right, and doesn't need to look to know it's Trevor King, the unelected ruler of the Shelly Bay Surf Club. He's run the Nippers programs for years, and even taught Theresa herself how not to drown in a rip. She doesn't mind him. He's just a bit narrow in his thinking, the way Andrew is. The way she worries she'll become if she keeps hanging around with narrow-minded people.

'G'day, Trev,' she says, making an effort to sound friendly, even though she wants to tell him – the way she always wants to tell him – that she can't stand being called Tess. She is Theresa, like her grandmother. He, on the other hand, has always been Trev, not Trevor; just like Andrew is never Andrew to anyone but her.

'Nice day for it,' Trev says.

It's the same thing he says every time she sees him. Even when she was standing on the sand watching her own kids go through their drills and it was bucketing down, he'd say it was a nice day. But she supposes he's cheerful. Maybe that's not a bad thing.

As he draws close Theresa averts her eyes from his Speedos, which she suspects he's bought a size too small so he can make the most of his crown jewels. Because it isn't the Koh-i-Noor diamond he's got stuffed inside his cossie.

'Too right,' she says with a tight smile and a tighter wave, hoping he'll leave her alone now. She doesn't want to chat. She is standing here in her old one-piece, which has gone threadbare underneath her boobs and won't withstand close inspection. *She* won't withstand close inspection. But all that is going to change. She will do this swim today, and then she's going to get a new cossie at the mall later this afternoon and it will help her feel more positive about this mission she's set herself.

Theresa takes a step into the foam and realises she's holding her breath.

Another step in and the white water brushes against her shins. It isn't as cold as she feared. Not yet.

She watches the waves building. She has to time it right – she doesn't want to get out there and meet the biggest wave of the set. She might never have become a surf lifesaver but she learnt about the water. How to be watchful. How to be cautious. Lessons she sometimes thinks she should have applied to her life.

There's the break in the set she's looking for, so she wades in quickly and dives under. At this depth the water is indeed as cold as she feared and she gasps. Still, this is the price she has to pay to be gorgeous in a bikini. *Cleo* and *Cosmo* tell her that she has to suffer to be beautiful. Which is why she reads the *Women's Weekly* instead and makes biscuits from their recipes.

Nevertheless, she is here now, and she's going to swim a few metres and see how she gets on. She isn't going to transform into an athlete overnight. But if she just keeps thinking about Tom Burlinson on that horse, she's sure she'll have enough motivation to get there soon.

CHAPTER 2

Marie rubs a towel through her hair as she gazes at her unruly back garden. Every day, after she's had her swim and her shower, she dries her hair looking at this garden and she really doesn't know why. Despite the lovely flowers – frangipanis in summer, camellias in autumn, azaleas in winter, plum blossom in spring and hibiscus year round – it's not a pretty picture. The weeds are taking over and she has never learnt to prune the trees properly. Norm used to do that, and after he died there was no one else. Just like there's no one to swim with her any more. Her habit of a lifetime became his too; became theirs. Now it's hers alone once more. As is the garden.

She's thought about getting someone in to tidy it up but she can't afford it. She can't afford much of anything now that she's on the age pension with no savings. Which is her fault. Hers and Norm's. They didn't really plan for the future.

'Charlie Brown, what are you doing?' She bends down to scratch behind the ears of her Sydney silky terrier as he snuffles between her feet.

Marie's best friend, Gwen, brought Charlie Brown into her life. Gwen's daughter had bought a puppy from the breeder who owned him. Charlie Brown was meant to be a show dog but the breeder had decided he wasn't good enough for that. Marie didn't want to know what the breeder had planned for a dog who wasn't show-worthy, so she swooped in and offered to take him. Even offered money, but the breeder refused it, saying that Marie was doing him a favour by removing a problem. Ever since then Marie has counted herself as the lucky one, although she gives Norm the credit – from somewhere beyond he looked after her, she's sure of it. That's why she gave Charlie Brown that name: *Peanuts* was Norm's favourite comic strip.

'I'm going to the shops,' she tells the dog. 'Will you be a good boy while I'm away?'

He looks up at her, his hair – it's too thin to be called fur – flopping near his eyes, and she knows that he will not be good. He'll curl up on her bed even though he's not allowed to, and she will forgive him, as she always does, because he's her only companion now.

Gwen and Marie have lived within walking distance of each other their whole lives, but several months ago Gwen moved into a retirement village a few too many suburbs to the north. Norm's been gone for five years now, and their daughter, Nicole, lives on the other side of town, across the harbour. So Marie's most regular conversations are with the dog. He doesn't seem to mind.

Marie quickly eats her hard-boiled egg on toast and gulps down her tea, wanting to get to the greengrocer when it opens. That's when the fruit and veg will be straight off the truck from the markets. She knows that because Norm used to be the greengrocer in the very same shop. His shop. He sold it seven years ago; two years after that he was gone. So much for a leisurely retirement.

She picks up her string bags from the kitchen counter and tries to stop herself waddling towards the front door. Once she hit sixty her joints started to tighten up, to her dismay. She's been swimming almost every day of her life since she was a child, right here in Shelly Bay, and still her body is ageing. Getting cranky with itself. She's not sure what else she's meant to do to keep it happy. She eats well, she exercises, and she's still getting thick and stiff, just like her mother did, and her mother before her. Maybe she shouldn't bother with the swimming since her genes are lapping her anyway.

Except she loves it. The ocean has always been there for her, on the good days and the bad. There have been a few bad ones in the last five years. And some very bad ones further back in her life. Days she wishes she could forget but which she needs to hold on to, because they are part of her story. Part of who she has become.

Back then, as soon as she was able, she'd returned to the water. Each kick, each stroke, had brought her back to herself; and a couple of years later Nicole arrived in the world and made the sun shine again. She still does that.

'Stay here, Charlie Brown,' Marie says as she gives him a little nudge with her foot and closes the front door on him. He can't come with her because he's not allowed in the shops, and she never likes to tie him up on the footpath. Instead he can have the run of the old sandstone cottage Marie grew up in and inherited from her father because he, too, didn't get the son he dreamt of.

She ignores the out-of-control lavender bushes in her small front garden, closes the gate and sets off down the hill to the village, as the locals call it. She waves to Mrs Morrison on the other side of the road. The older woman's spine makes a C shape but she's still out there, pruning her roses. Putting Marie to shame.

Livingstone Road has been Marie's lifelong artery into the village: it takes her down the hill to the beach and the shops; past the home of the first boy she ever had a crush on; past the playground of her primary school; past the spot on the corner where there used to be a café. She and Norm had their first date in that café. She smiles, thinking of them sitting in the window, him with his big head of dark curls and the scar over his right eye. His brother did it, Norm said, with a cricket bat. He was never sure if it was on purpose or not.

For a while after Norm died Marie couldn't bring herself to go into his old shop, even though it's the closest green-grocer to home. She didn't understand why so she prayed on it, which made her feel better even though she never worked out the reason for her resistance. She went back, and will always remember how happy the new owner was to see her.

As she steps inside today he's organising the peaches.

'Hello, Vince,' she says.

He looks up. 'Marie!' He comes towards her with his arms outstretched, as he always does, as if she's his favourite aunt or something, and gives her a hug, like he's grateful she's in the shop.

What he doesn't know – because it would be too strange to tell him – is that she's grateful he's kept Norm's business going so well.

'What's it going to be today?' he says when he releases her, in that accent he's told her is 'Australian suburbia by way of Calabria'.

She's never told him that she thinks it's taken a detour via dreamy, because what young man wants a crone giving him compliments? She wouldn't want to make him uncomfortable, plus she's never been the flirty kind. She just misses the company of men. Of one man.

'Half a dozen oranges, please,' she says, and he starts to pick them up and put them in a basket.

'You been for a swim this morning, *signora*?'

'Every morning, Vince.' Which he knows, because he always asks her. She appreciates the banter, though.

He smiles and shakes his head. 'I don't know how you do it. Even in winter?'

'Even in winter.'

He shakes his head again. 'It's too cold for me *now*, *signora* – and it's almost summer!'

'The water will warm up soon. You should give it a try.' She nods towards the end of the street, where pine trees guard the beachfront at almost exactly the spot where she starts her swim each day at sunrise. 'It's so close. You could run down there after work. Daylight saving.'

He raises his eyebrows at her.

'Four bananas,' she says, and he nods as he selects them carefully.

'Two tomatoes.'

'Only two?' He frowns. 'What kind of pasta sauce can you make with only two?'

She laughs. It feels good. And rusty. She doesn't laugh much these days. No one to laugh with. It's another reason to be grateful to Vince. Although that doesn't mean she can afford more than two tomatoes.

'You know I'll never be able to make a proper sauce,' she chides gently. 'I'm not your nonna.'

He winks. 'She makes the best sauce.'

'I know. You always tell me.'

She's almost at the end of her list, after which she'll turn around and go back up the hill, wearing out that short track her life runs on. Her world has become smaller these last few years. If only she'd learnt to drive a car, but she never needed to; Norm took her everywhere she wanted to go. Now it's too late to learn, even if it meant she could drive to see Gwen. And Nicole. Her daughter doesn't live far away as the crow flies, but it takes an unreasonably long time to get there when Marie has to take the ferry then the bus then walk a few hundred metres. It uses up the whole day, going to see Nicole and her kids. Marie knows she has whole days to spend – she has all the time in the world – but she's still not visiting. She should make herself, before she gets stuck further in the sludge she sometimes feels is building up around her feet, holding her in her old ways, not letting her move on.

'Thanks, Vince,' she says as he loads her purchases into her string bags.

'It's lovely to see you, Marie.' He pecks her on the cheek. 'I'll look forward to the next time.'

He's such a charmer, and he knows it, but he's made her day. Little points of light are what she lives for now. She gives him a last wave as she steps onto the street.

She can just make out the glint of the sunlight on the ocean, past those pine trees, and for a second she contemplates having another swim today. She might just do that. Or she could go for a walk up to the headland. Give her hips something to really complain about.

She has time. So much time. She should start doing something with it.

CHAPTER 3

'**K**eep your head down. That's it. That's it! Now kick. Kick!'

Leanne can hardly hear the swimming instructor yelling to her. She has cotton wool doused in lanolin stuffed in her ears and a cap over her head, and the water is rushing past her face as she tries, clumsily, to pull her arms through the water and move her feet at the same time. Freestyle doesn't feel so free when you're still learning how to do it.

She thinks Matt says something like 'Breathe' but she still can't hear him. Then she feels his hand on her shoulder and she stops.

'You're not breathing,' he says when she lifts her face from the water. 'You'll pass out if you keep that up.'

'Sorry,' she says, feeling abashed. She forgets to breathe every single time she's in this lesson, but never when she's practising on her own. Perhaps she's concentrating so hard on what he's saying that she forgets. Or perhaps in his presence she's just more self-conscious about doing things right or wrong.

'No worries,' he says, his grin wide, his sun-darkened skin looking as though it might crack. His shaggy brown hair hangs almost in his eyes, and he has what appears to be encrusted salt on his eyebrows and eyelashes. He's like so many of the young men she sees in the area, although they're usually nearer the beach than this council pool.

It took Leanne many months to get used to how different life in Shelly Bay is to where she grew up, in a landlocked suburb far from the sea where she wasn't the only child who never learnt to swim. Her mother didn't swim either. Her father and brothers did, but they were expected to; her father told her brothers that they'd never grow up to be lifesavers if they didn't. Which was a strange statement, because he wasn't a lifesaver, they never went to the beach and her brothers showed no interest in learning how to save anything. But that's what Aussie blokes did, apparently: they became lifesavers. It was important to her father that her brothers became Aussie blokes. Sometimes Leanne wonders if that's how they turned out, but it's been several years since she has seen any of her family.

'Let's try again,' Matt is saying, although through the cotton wool it's hard to make it out. 'You're doing really well, all right? We just don't want you to drown.'

He laughs and it sounds almost like a honk. She's grown used to his laugh over the past few weeks. He's been her only instructor for the lessons she decided she needed.

As she pushes off the wall and tries to time her strokes properly, she thinks he's probably being kind about her progress. But she's not going to stop just because she's not Shane Gould. She lives in a beachside suburb now and if she can't swim she's not making the most of it. Half of the residents of Shelly Bay are in the water each morning, it seems; each time she goes for a run she can see them ploughing up and down offshore. She wants to try that too. All her life she's been active, and never baulked at a challenge; swimming the length of the beach seems like something she should try. And it will make her a proper local.

Shelly Bay is as different as Leanne could imagine from the place where she grew up. Home was full of streets tightly packed with dark-brick houses and gardens of English plants that usually weren't tended to. There were parks that were mostly patches of dirt with the occasional swing; playing fields that were teeming with rowdy boys on weekends; and streets that were quiet enough for her and her brothers to play cricket on without worrying about cars.

In Leanne's suburb, people mostly stayed inside their houses. It was hot in summer and cold in winter, and those dark bricks were meant to keep everyone's temperature even. In Shelly Bay, the residents seem to be outside all the time. The streets are wide and the houses are set further apart than she's used to, creating a sense of airiness that makes the whole place feel relaxed. And there is so much light: the houses are built of sandstone if they're old, or weatherboard if they're not. Where there's brick, it's blond. The gardens are full of trees and flowers that look like summer: frangipanis with their yellow and white faces; strelitzias, lavender, and freesias on the nature strips. There is scrubby bush nearby, covering the headland and encroaching into people's lives; eucalypts are on every street and there's the occasional stray native plant in front gardens. Leanne grew up with kookaburras and magpies and miners, but here there are more colourful birds too – cockatoos and rainbow lorikeets and king parrots. They obviously prefer the seaside.

Leanne's move to Shelly Bay happened when she took a job at Northern Hospital up on the hill – her first after she finished her nursing degree. She liked paediatrics the best when she was training, so getting a position in the paediatric ward was a dream. And she was glad to move out of the dense city-bound suburbs near the university to the roomier Shelly Bay. She took a flat on her own and still enjoys the freedom it brings her, to make decisions for herself and how she wants to live.

This place has changed her perspective on life. Before, she felt hemmed in by the past and the decisions she'd made that shaped it. The further away from it she has moved, the more she has begun to believe that she can be a different person – the sort of person who lives in a bright, happy place filled with friendly, open people. With Matt as a prime example.

'Right!' he says, tapping her on the shoulder as she reaches the wall. 'That was pretty good. How are you feeling?'

'Fine,' she says, sniffing water up her nose and tasting the chlorine as it trickles down the back of her throat.

He honk-laughs. 'You don't say much, do you?'

'Not really.' She half smiles but is sure it looks like a grimace.

'I think that's enough for today,' he says. 'But it would be good if you could get some practice in before the next lesson. Okay?'

She nods once, definitely. 'Okay.'

He grins. 'See you next week.'

As Matt heads in the direction of the office Leanne wades to the steps, avoiding a more vigorous swimmer whose freestyle is smooth and swift. She wants to swim like that one day. Soon. Or even just a bit like that, so by the time summer starts she can swim in the ocean and be one of those locals churning their way through the surf.

Maybe then she'll feel like she's really home.

CHAPTER 4

Thwack. The ball hits the net and Elaine winces. Another double fault. She risks a glance at her doubles partner and can see how unimpressed she is. As she should be: they've lost two games already because of Elaine's serving.

If Elaine could only work out what she's doing wrong she'd fix it, except she was never this lousy when she used to play at home. Since she and her husband moved to Australia a few months ago, she's lost . . . something. Not her abilities: she refuses to believe that. She's been playing tennis since she was a child and her game is automatic now. Perhaps that's the problem: it was automatic *in England*. A change of country has changed all the parameters she's used to. She's not so much a fish out of water as a mermaid marooned on dry land. Or so she'd like to think. It's a more glamorous idea than the truth, which is that she's wretchedly miserable living in the southern hemisphere and the deficit in her tennis game is the least of it. Yet it's the most tangible part of it, so it's what she's working on. Even if there's been no improvement since last week's ladies doubles round robin.

'How about I serve from now on?' Marguerite says with a pinched look on her face, and although Elaine wants to protest, and make it clear that she's not usually this hopeless *really*, it wouldn't be fair. Because she's hopeless right now.

'Sure,' she replies breezily and forces a smile that she is sure looks as fake as it feels. 'I'm clearly having a bad day.'

Marguerite sniffs and Elaine thinks she can translate: in short, Marguerite doesn't believe that she ever has good days.

It gives Elaine no satisfaction that while Marguerite can serve the ball over the net, she isn't much good at hitting it thereafter, so they lose the match anyway.

'Thank you,' Elaine says as she shakes hands with their opponents over the net, then with Marguerite. 'Next week?' she adds.

She really doesn't want to play with them again, but she hasn't managed to find another group activity that suits her, and if she doesn't play tennis she will have absolutely no one to talk to apart from James, who works all day and half the night. Not that she isn't used to it. He did that in England, too, and she didn't expect that returning to his homeland would change him. A surgeon's work is never done, or something like that. His wife's wait is never over.

'Um, well . . .' Marguerite exchanges looks with the others. The sorts of looks normally seen on cruel schoolgirls in a play-ground. 'The thing is, Elaine . . .'

Marguerite pats her on the arm, a gesture that Elaine finds both patronising and intrusive. Playing tennis together does not confer a level of familiarity that allows for patting. She wonders if shifting away from Marguerite will look rude.

'We have a friend who wants to play with us,' says one of the others – Cheryl, Elaine thinks it is.

Cheryl and Beryl. Elaine thought it was a joke when they told her, but apparently not, and ever since she has rarely been able to remember which one is which – a predicament not helped by the fact that they are both bottle blondes, both play tennis wearing, improbably, boob tubes in combination with tiny ellesse skirts and socks with pink pom-poms on the backs, and both have husbands called Barry. They go to 'the Services' on the weekend – a club, Elaine believes, on the bluff at Sunrise Beach – where the Barrys play 'the pokies' and bet on 'the dogs' and 'the trots'.

Marguerite's husband is known as Bluey. This, Elaine has learnt, is because he has red hair. James tried to explain it to her but she felt too overwhelmed to understand; the steep cultural learning curve she has found herself on ever since moving to Australia has generally had the effect of making her feel simultaneously stupid, tired and resentful. But she's persevered these last few weeks, despite not having anything in common with these women apart from the fact that they have all played tennis since childhood, and now here they are turfing her out of their foursome. She wishes she felt more relieved because she doesn't want to play with them again, either, but being rejected is never pleasant.

'Is that so?' she says, trying to sound nonchalant but instead sounding like she's swallowing a plum.

'Yeah.' Cheryl – or Beryl – inspects her chipped fingernail polish. 'Kel. You met Kel. She plays mixed doubles sometimes.'

Elaine recalls a tiny woman with a perm growing out and a faded navy-blue Lacoste T-shirt. 'Right. Kel.' She smiles quickly. 'So I imagine that leaves no room for me?'

'We'll call you if we have a spot,' Marguerite says, and Elaine steps away as she sees another pat coming.

'Fine.' She tries to smile brightly but feels she probably looks startled instead. 'Thank you for letting me play with you.'

'No worries!' says the other Cheryl/Beryl. 'See you round.'

You will never see me round, Elaine wants to snap. She has never been round in her life apart from her two pregnancies. Well-brought-up young ladies aren't supposed to eat. That's why they drink instead – the calories have to come from somewhere.

It's a drink she's thinking of as she almost trots away from the courts. Her daily gin-and-tonic ritual that she never used to let herself start before six o'clock. It's been creeping in earlier – only because she's lonely, and bored despite the plethora of novels she's been ploughing through; and so many nights she's already asleep by the time James gets home, which means he's not likely to find out that she's drinking more than she used to. Unless he's checking the bottle she keeps on the sideboard. She'll have to start using a decoy bottle.

She walks back up the hill to Francis Street, wishing that she'd brought the car. But that would make her lazy: the courts are only ten minutes' walk from home. Not that their proximity matters any more. She's hardly going to look for another group to play with.

Perhaps there are other courts nearby . . . But then she might face the same problem: women who don't really want her there, and her game not up to scratch. There's more entertainment to be found at home with her books. Maybe she should get a dog. They haven't had a dog since the boys were little.

As she reaches the top of the hill she sighs and turns around so she can look past the rooftops of the village shops and flats, past the spire of the church, St Mary's Immaculate, to the ocean. Today it is a rich blue and, given the warmth of this November day, looks incredibly inviting.

She can take up swimming. It was her favourite sport at school, and she was good at it. Not a group sport, true, so she's not going to make friends by swimming on her own. However, she hasn't made friends trying to be part of a team. She was always a better singles than doubles player – she should have remembered that.

Tomorrow morning she's going to get in the water. Or maybe the day after, because she'll need a cap and goggles if she's going to take this seriously and that requires a trip to the shops.

This afternoon, the only thing she's going to take seriously is that gin and tonic. She sets off in strides towards home, with quinine and slices of lemon on her mind.

CHAPTER 5

The water looks murky this morning with the sky closing in. Those aren't rain clouds up there, Theresa tells herself, just those humid puff balls that promise a lot and deliver not much. The sea isn't its usual appealing blue. She just has to talk herself into going in. She's made it down here, after all. Now she just has to get in the water. It's not so hard! Really, it's not!

The cool air on her shoulders tells her otherwise and her resolve wavers yet again. She was cosy in bed, even if Andrew managed to turn triple somersaults in his sleep and kept her awake half the night.

'G'day, Tess.'

'Hi, Trev,' she says, keeping her eyes on the water as he draws up next to her. It looks cold and she's still wondering if she can talk herself out of going in.

Not that she can say that to Trev, because he's proud of the fact he swims year round, 'even when it's so cold me apricots turn into peanuts!' he said the other day, chortling while she blushed. Theresa's no prude but she doesn't know him well enough to talk about his gonads. She's still trying to work out how to talk to Oliver about his, and that's *after* he came home from school one day asking her what 'balls' were.

'Watcha lookin' for, Tess – Jaws?'

Trev laughs as if he's said the funniest thing ever. But Theresa doesn't think it's funny. It took her more than a year to get back into the ocean after she saw that bloody movie.

'Have you ever seen a shark out there?' she says.

'Nah.' Trev shakes his head. 'Not often.'

'Not often?' she squeaks.

'You'll be right.' He sucks in his belly and hikes up his Speedos before turning to look over her shoulder. 'G'day, Marie.'

'Trev,' comes the response.

Theresa turns to see an older woman with a strong jaw and thick grey hair cut in a bob. She looks like a swimmer: broad shoulders atop a muscular frame, even if some things are sagging. Not that Theresa should judge.

Marie steps away from them before she slowly takes off her T-shirt and shorts.

'Swims every day of her life,' Trev says quietly with a note of admiration. 'Been doing it since she was a little tacker.' He nods slowly. 'Her husband was taken by a shark.' He jerks his chin. 'Out there.'

'What!'

Trev starts with a small laugh that develops into a roar. 'Geez, you're gullible, Tess.'

Theresa feels an urge to punch him, because she knows she isn't gullible, just trusting. It isn't always the same thing.

'Nah, he died of a heart attack or somethin'.' Trev looks almost misty-eyed. 'Five years ago, I think. She's been alone ever since. Swimming alone too. They used to come down here together. She was always better than him, but. Anyway,' another sucking in of the belly, 'I'm off. Gotta train for the surf comp. Cheerio.'

Theresa is glad she isn't required to speak because she really wants to scream at him for letting her think, for even a second, that a lethal shark attack happened right here, where she swims.

She glances over to Marie and sees she's being observed.

'Morning,' Marie says, raising a hand.

'Hi!' Theresa says, quickly putting on her cap. She's been stalling long enough, and if this Marie can swim every day of her life *for years*, through all the seasons, Theresa should be able to manage to get in today.

'I'm Marie,' says the other woman as she comes a little closer. She pronounces it 'Mah-*ree*', the French way, not '*Maah*-ree' like Trev.

'And I'm Theresa.' She smiles broadly.

'Not Tess?'

Theresa laughs. 'No. Trev likes to call me that, and I guess I can't blame him when I've never corrected him.'

Marie nods. 'People can be too familiar. Anyway, I'm going in.'

Theresa smiles again, hesitantly, wanting something but not wishing to seem too forward about it.

'May I follow you?' she says. 'I mean – if you don't mind. It's just a bit lonely out there.'

So what if she's also thinking Marie can be shark bait instead of her? She has a survival instinct just as much as anyone. Besides, she might learn something from Marie, who is likely to be a much better swimmer.

'Sure,' Marie says, and offers Theresa a cautious smile.

'Thank you!' Theresa hurriedly tucks in her hair. 'I'm really bad so I'll be slow. I won't even try to keep up. It's just nice to, um . . . nice to have someone else there with you, isn't it?'

'Rightio,' Marie says with a nod.

Maybe Theresa has pushed her luck – she's foisted herself on this stranger who's probably too polite to tell her to get lost. 'Do you really not mind?' she asks as she folds her sarong and puts it under her towel.

Marie gives her a quizzical look. 'Why would I mind?'

'Okay!' Theresa beams and follows Marie to the water. Marie strides in almost with a swagger while Theresa wobbles on the uneven sand. How embarrassing – Marie has about twenty-five years on her and she's so much stronger.

You just have to keep it up, Theresa. Keep coming down here every day and swim as hard as you can, and you'll get good.

The motivational speech to herself doesn't last very long, because once she's flailing along in Marie's wake, trying out freestyle because her breaststroke is too slow, all she can think is: *No sharks. No sharks. No sharks.*

Of course, she could ask herself why she's in the water at all if she's so worried about sharks – and the answer might be that she's trying to use the sharks as a reason not to swim when she knows she needs to. Even though she's been swimming for only a little while, she's feeling better already. When she arrives home afterwards she's in a good mood and less likely to get upset that Ollie has managed to crease his school uniform again. She's sleeping more soundly too. Andrew is still getting on her nerves, but that's married life, isn't it?

As she nears Little Beach – which she reached on her fourth day of swimming by breaststroking slower than a turtle – the water becomes shallower and she can see the fish she's noticed before. There are quite a few little silvery-white ones with yellow fins on the bottom and a black ridge on the top fin. They like to dart around. And longer silvery-white ones with yellow tails. She wonders if they're related. Even though she had goldfish as a child Theresa has never been as interested in fish as she is now she's sharing their world.

She jerks as she sees a small brown stingray. It's harmless – and nowhere near her – but it still looks a bit creepy. It's territorial, always in the same spot each day. Maybe that's a characteristic of stingrays. She should go to the library and find out.

As her feet find the bottom she decides to take a breather on the beach. She's surprised to see Marie standing on the sand.

'Thought I'd wait for you,' Marie says, looking at her curiously.

'That's nice! Thank you.'

Theresa is conscious she's a little breathless. Over time that will improve. She'll swim this far with ease and be so fit she'd be able to carry on conversations if only she could talk underwater. Which is what her mother used to say about her: *Theresa could talk underwater.* Then her father and brothers would snigger.

'I'm not holding you up?' she says as she positions herself next to Marie and admires the view back to Main Beach, the blond sand sweeping up to the wall, little dots of people already visible on it, walking and running. She wonders, sometimes, about the people she sees at the beach. About their lives. Did they grow up here? Are they new? Do they travel to the city for work? Most of her own adult life has been spent in and around this beach. If it were a forest perhaps she'd have worn a path in it; instead, the waves make sure there's nothing to suggest she was ever here at all.

She can't see her house from here, but she knows the kids will be waking up soon and Andrew will be grumbling about making their breakfast. But he'll do it because he knows the kids' hungry whingeing will be more punishment than getting their food. Then, if he's in a good mood, he'll make coffee for Theresa's nonna and take it to the granny flat.

'From what?' Marie says. 'My dog's the only one waiting for me.'

Theresa feels stuck in the kind of moment that happens sometimes: when you know something about someone but you're not sure whether to reveal that you do. Because what if they want to tell you themselves? Or they don't want you to know at all? Just because Trev likes to gossip on the beach doesn't mean that Theresa should know that Marie's husband is dead.

'Oh?' is the response she decides on.

Marie puts her hands on her hips, and for a second Theresa thinks of Yul Brynner in *The King and I*: his proud stance, feet astride, bare chest . . . She has to stop herself giggling.

'I used to swim with my husband,' Marie says with a quick, sad smile. 'But he's gone. Dead, I mean.' She pauses. '"Gone" is a bit too soft, isn't it?'

Theresa starts a reflexive reply.

Marie frowns. 'Don't say you're sorry. You didn't know him. I don't expect you to be sorry.'

Theresa opens and closes her mouth, feeling like a guppy. She doesn't know what she can say if 'sorry' isn't available to her.

Marie exhales. 'Sorry. That was tough.' Her laugh sounds dry and unpractised. 'Now *I'm* the one saying sorry. I'm just not used to meeting people who don't know that Norm's dead. A consequence of doing the same thing every day and never leaving the suburb.'

'My husband's not dead,' Theresa says, thinking that at least they have husbands in common. 'But he's hardly around.'

Marie raises her eyebrows.

'He's out a lot. With his mates.' Theresa shrugs. 'All the blokes seem to do it.'

She doesn't know if all the blokes sit around the house doing nothing useful while their wives cook and clean and do the washing and watch the kids, but she suspects so. The going-out-drinking and the doing-nothing-at-home seem to be a matching pair.

'Do you have children?' Marie asks.

'Two.' Theresa can't help smiling when she thinks of them. 'Oliver, he's eight. Sasha's five. My nonna lives with us too.'

'Nonna, eh? You Italian?'

'Yep. She's a bit of work, but it's great for the kids to have her around. She speaks to them in Italian sometimes.'

'That's the best age to learn a language.' Marie glances towards Main Beach. 'We should get back. You probably have to take those children to school.'

'I do.' Theresa's skin has dried while they've been standing there and she's not relishing the idea of the sting of the cold again.

'I swim from Main Beach every day at sunrise,' Marie says as they walk into the water.

'So do I. You can probably tell I haven't been doing it very long, though.' Theresa feels the nervousness that comes with trying to make a new friend. It's hard when you're an adult. So hard she rarely tries it, and it usually doesn't stick anyway.

'Well . . .' Marie stops and turns to look at her. 'If you don't want to keep swimming alone, how about we swim together every day?'

Theresa feels the way she used to in primary school when she was given a certificate for being the neatest or the kindest or the most helpful with other children. 'I'd love that!' she says and it comes out almost like a squeal.

Marie winks. 'Great. See you back on the beach.' She pulls her goggles down and dives out.

Theresa knows she won't catch her on the way back – and she also knows she doesn't need to. Because Marie is going to be there tomorrow, and the next day. That's all the motivation Theresa needs to keep turning up.

CHAPTER 6

When Leanne wakes up she can't work out if it's Tuesday or Wednesday. The alarm pulled her out of a dream that she wanted to stay in, and it takes her a while to orientate herself. Finally she makes out the familiar lines of her small bedroom in this small flat. She's never needed much space. She doesn't have knick-knacks; she doesn't hang on to books after she's read them. The kitchenette and cramped bathroom aren't ideal but she's not much of a cook and she takes quick showers, so they're not too great an inconvenience.

She thinks about going for a swim – maybe in the ocean. Then she feels the hesitation. No, it's stronger than that: it's fear. What if she's not good enough? What if she struggles or fails without Matt there to keep an eye on her? Practising in the pool is one thing; swimming in the actual ocean is another. She's not ready.

When she was a child – even as a teenager – she didn't know this kind of fear. She would climb trees and swing off branches; climb rocks and jump off them. She used to win running races too. She was fast back then, accustomed to racing her older brothers through the streets, used to them egging her on half out of love and half out of spite, the way most brothers would. 'C'mon, Lee!' they'd call as they sprinted ahead of her, their spindly legs disappearing around corners as she tried to keep up. They didn't make any allowances for her because she was younger or a girl, and she never cared. In fact, she loved it. She loved the challenge. Not that she had ever managed to catch them, but she grew strong and fast in the trying.

As she moved deeper into her teens, she lost that comfort in her body. Then one day it was gone for good. Taken from her.

Now she's twenty-five and she thinks of her body as a foreign land for which she doesn't have a passport. She should get one, though. It's been a long time since she's moved her body just to feel it move instead of trying to control it – or forget it. For years running has been her way of keeping it in check, and she's used that time and the kilometres to travel away from the past.

Swimming is bringing back some of that childhood exhilaration of using her body to go further and climb higher. She's pushing herself, even though sometimes she thinks her swimming prowess is coming along too slowly. But learning something new requires courage – she knows that. It's the same courage she needed to start her life over, to go to university, to move to this suburb where she knows no one.

She still doesn't think she's ready for the ocean, though, so this morning she goes for a run instead, then eats her one piece of toast and Vegemite, and drinks her black tea with half a sugar, before she puts on her nurse's uniform and walks the ten minutes up the hill to Northern Hospital.

Leanne goes into the bathroom for one last check that her hair is neat and tidy, and her uniform as it should be. Matron likes her nurses to be just so and tells them if anything isn't right. In front of the mirror, Leanne pulls her uniform down a little and tucks some stray hairs into her bun. The problem with fine, dead-straight hair is that it slips out of bounds easily.

As she pats it down at the sides she sees flashes of her mother in her face and feels a tug in her heart.

The door opens and bangs against the hand-towel dispenser, and a breathless, bustling figure comes into the bathroom.

'Hi, Leanne!'

'Hi, Theresa.' Leanne smiles tightly, not wanting to encourage chit-chat. They're likely to be here a while if Theresa gets started.

Not that Leanne dislikes Theresa – no doubt she's perfectly pleasant – but she likes to ask questions that Leanne has no intention of answering. *Where did you grow up? Did you always want to be a nurse? Have you lived in Shelly Bay long?* Theresa likes to get to know people and Leanne isn't ready to be known. She's spent the last few years actively trying to not be known. Luckily Theresa only volunteers a couple of days a week so Leanne doesn't have to avoid her too often.

Theresa smiles as she drops her handbag on the counter and starts rummaging through it. 'I rushed here. Had to get the kids to school. Didn't do my make-up.' She rolls her eyes. 'I'm always playing catch-up.'

Leanne glances quickly at Theresa's face and doesn't know what she is worried about. Theresa has thick, long, wavy brown hair, big brown eyes and long lashes; her lips are naturally a deep pink and she has olive skin. She doesn't need make-up. Whereas Leanne thinks her own black hair, black eyebrows, small eyes, small nose and small mouth make her look severe and mean if she doesn't at least use a bit of blusher.

'I have to start my shift,' she says with a small smile. She may not be willing to chat but she wants to be polite.

'Oh!' There's a flash of something that looks like disappointment on Theresa's face, then her big smile is back. 'Before you go – did I see you running on the beach this morning?'

Leanne isn't always conscious of the routes she runs – her legs take her where they want to go – but she remembers thinking that she needed to push herself and run in the soft sand. She didn't think she'd had a witness, however; the idea isn't welcome.

'I was on the beach,' she says.

'I knew it! I told Marie it was you.' Theresa pulls a lipstick from her handbag. 'A-ha! There it is. It's my favourite. They discontinued it. Don't you hate it when that happens? You should join us,' she adds through stretched lips as she applies the hot-pink colour.

Leanne, about to turn to go, feels the peril of having to consider an invitation she doesn't want.

'Me and Marie,' Theresa continues, blotting her lipstick with a tissue. 'We swim every morning at sunrise, to Little Beach and back. It's great!'

Leanne thinks of the swimmers she's seen off the beach; how naïve of her to never consider that she might know one of them, given how many local people she encounters at the hospital.

Then she thinks of the lessons she's been taking just so she can be one of those swimmers. Now Theresa is giving her a chance to put her plan into practice. If Leanne were an ordinary person, the kind who talks easily to people who aren't her patients and who, therefore, aren't children, she'd probably leap at it.

'No pressure,' Theresa says with a note of uncertainty, her smile slipping.

Leanne's silence seems like a rejection, no doubt, but she just can't say yes straightaway. That once-spontaneous person doesn't exist any more.

'I'll – I'll think about it,' she says. 'I'd better go. Matron gets upset when we're late.'

Theresa nods quickly. 'I know! She can be a bit of a dragon, can't she?'

Leanne smiles, and emerges into the corridor. She can hear the high-pitched hum of children talking. It's nice when the patients get to know each other. She was talkative as a child, once she started. Her father said she didn't talk for so long they thought she might have a problem, then she talked so much they just wanted her to shut up. That was a long time ago.

She walks towards her station, priming herself for the day ahead. She loves her work, but she can find it overwhelming too. There are some children who take so much of her time that she feels like she's neglecting others. There are some who, after spending weeks here, go back to places where she knows they won't receive the care they need. But she didn't get into this job to be comfortable. If she'd wanted to be comfortable she could have chosen a nice, quiet job in a bank or an office, a job she could leave behind when the working day was over. One that didn't involve witnessing hurt and pain and sadness. But comfortable isn't what Leanne wants. Comfortable isn't who she is.

'Good morning, Sister,' Matron says.

'Good morning, Matron.' Leanne hurriedly puts her handbag on a shelf, and tucks up another stray hair she can feel tickling her neck.

'I can't seem to find the night nurse so I'll take you through handover. If you're ready.' Matron gestures with her hand for Leanne to follow her.

'Yes, Matron.'

The young voices grow louder as they approach the first room. Leanne has no idea what to expect from these children – she never does, and that is part of what keeps her job interesting. But she knows there will be the chance to help them, to make their lives better, just as she has wished someone would do for her. Except she would never ask for help, and she has become so good at hiding her need for it that she can't blame others for not noticing.

As Leanne walks through the door behind Matron she sees five faces – some with teeth missing, some with hair like a bird's nest, all with eyes bright – and she remembers something else she loves about this job: the chance to start over, for these children, and for her. Each day anew. Each hour an opportunity for things to be different. Better.

One day it will come true.

CHAPTER 7

'Are these your famous Anzac biscuits, Marie?'

Father Paul gives her a wink as he picks up another biscuit from the plate. That's his third, and Marie can't help feeling chuffed that he's enjoying them.

'I don't know if they're famous,' she says, wishing that false modesty wasn't a quality she'd been taught to cultivate from childhood. 'And I haven't made them for a while, so they probably aren't.'

'I've heard talk at the church.' Father Paul smiles as he bites into the biscuit. 'Dulcie even sounded somewhat annoyed that she hasn't been able to guess your recipe.'

Marie picks up a biscuit for herself. 'It's all in the sugar, Father. I don't use the same sugar as everyone else.'

She closes her eyes as she takes a bite and remembers her mother churning out Anzac biscuits by the dozens. Her mother once confessed that after Marie's father returned from the Great War the only way she could cope with his long silences was to bake. It was also the only way she could show him that she loved him; saying it back then wasn't really acceptable behaviour.

Marie's parents never told her they loved her either, although she knew they did. Just like she never told Norm too often, although she loved him. Still does. Nor did he say it to her, yet she knew how he felt by the way he looked at her and took care of her.

Marie regrets not saying it more, but it simply wasn't done. The fashion these days for verbal declarations of affection stems, she is sure, from those ridiculous television shows everyone is watching. Those soaps. Nothing wrong with a good book, and it lasts a lot longer and gives more comfort than an episode of *Days of Our Lives*. She has to be careful about expressing that opinion, though, because she knows some of the ladies at the church are fond of the shows.

Not that she sees those ladies as often as she used to. Morning service at St Mary's Immaculate, twelve minutes' walk from her house after she showered off the salt water, used to set her up for the day. But she's fallen out of the habit. She's been trying to work out if it's laziness, old age or something more sinister that has her stuck in this position of wanting to keep doing what she's always done but feeling less willing to expend the energy required.

Going to church means talking to a lot of people who aren't friends – people who say all the polite things but aren't genuinely interested in her wellbeing. She used to care about them – when she said, 'How are you?' she meant it. Although it doesn't come back in the same measure; and she no longer has the inclination to give it out when it's not returned. She's not cut out to have a bottomless well of compassion and regard for her fellow man – and she knows that means she's letting down her faith. Her God. That requires a reckoning between her and Him, but she doesn't want to do it with an audience. So she doesn't go to church every day any more.

There is also the fact that, most days, going for her swim is as much as she can manage. Gwen once told her that grief would track her down, just when she thought she'd outrun it. Gwen's first husband died suddenly, so even though her second is still very much alive Marie takes Gwen as an authority on the subject of being a widow. She wants to ask her friend if grief feels like a weight you drag around, a weight that holds you back – holds you under sometimes. But she hasn't been to see Gwen in too long and it doesn't feel like the sort of conversation you can have over the phone. One day, maybe, she'll get herself to Gwen's retirement village and ask her in person.

It's the dragging around that Father Paul has noticed. As well as her absence in the mornings. He took her aside last Sunday and told her that he was always available for her if she wished to talk. 'I may not be a doctor but I can make house calls,' he said – and here he is, doing just that and taking another bite of the biscuit.

'I suppose you're not going to tell me which sugar you use?' he says, and smiles at her in a complicit way.

Marie smiles back. 'Only if you can get me into Heaven.' She's grateful he's made the time to visit her: she feels better already.

'I'll put in a word.'

Father Paul sits deeper in the armchair that Marie keeps telling herself she'll throw out. It was Norm's favourite, and even though it's seen better days she likes the memories attached to it.

She hears the scratch of doggie claws on the floorboards in the hallway.

'Charlie Brown,' she says sternly, 'you know you're not allowed in here while I have visitors.'

The scratching stops.

'I don't mind if he comes in,' says Father Paul, leaning out of his chair towards the doorway, where one of Charlie Brown's paws is visible. 'I like dogs.'

'It's good for him to have a bit of discipline,' Marie explains. 'He has the run of the place usually. I can't let him think he can get his way all the time.'

Father Paul looks amused. 'You don't think it might be too late for that?'

Marie thinks of Charlie Brown sleeping on her bed, sitting on her lap when she's on the couch and standing next to her while she cooks.

'Probably,' she concedes, smiling sheepishly.

'It's good to see you smile, Marie.' Father Paul puts his cup and saucer on the coffee table and sits back, crossing one leg over the other and brushing his hair out of his eyes. He has a good, thick head of hair – like John F Kennedy's. Irish hair. Presidential hair, you might even call it.

'It's good of you to visit, Father.'

They sit looking at each other, and she's aware that she doesn't know how to have a conversation with him like this. He's never visited her at home; they've only ever talked at the church. She's not sure if she's meant to treat this like a casual confessional or chat about the weather.

'I haven't heard you mention Gwen lately,' he says.

'That's because she . . .' Marie stops, surprised to find herself feeling emotional. And embarrassed about it in front of the priest. He may be here because he's concerned about her but it feels impolite to fall to pieces.

'She and her husband moved away,' she goes on, collecting herself. 'To a retirement village in the northern suburbs.'

Father Paul nods slowly. 'Life continues to change, doesn't it?'

This doesn't appear to be an existential statement so much as a personal acknowledgement – or maybe that's how Marie wants to take it.

'It does,' she says, her voice catching.

As he picks up the teapot Father Paul looks at her enquiringly and she nods. He fills her cup just enough to allow her room to splash milk into it. What a thoughtful man.

Marie hasn't known that many men – there was Norm, of course, but she didn't have a brother. There was one boy cousin, but she lost touch with him years ago. She went to a Catholic girls school on the other side of St Mary's. Fraternising with boys was discouraged there, and at home. She barely spoke to young men her age, so when she met Norm she didn't know how to talk to him. Her mother had sent her down the road to buy fruit, and there he was in his shop. He was tall, and she didn't mind that he had a little stoop. Tall men do sometimes. He asked her name, and she told him. He said he recognised her from church, and she couldn't believe, first, that he was Catholic – that seemed too easy – and, second, that she had never noticed him. He told her, well after it was too late to matter, that he'd never been confirmed; he went to mass because he liked the ritual. She'd never seen him because he sat up the back and never came forward to take the sacrament.

'You must be lonely in this house sometimes,' Father Paul says, sipping his tea, 'even with Charlie Brown.'

She nods quickly. It's the first time since Norm died that anyone has acknowledged what has become her natural state.

'I know all this loss has been hard,' he continues, 'but I fear that Gwen's departure might have been one loss too many.'

'She hasn't died,' she says, almost too sharply.

'No, but you have known her longer than you've known your daughter, or your husband. She's – what did you call her? Your bosom friend.' He smiles. 'Like Anne of Green Gables and her friend Diana.'

'Yes,' Marie says. She and Gwen had both loved the book and seen themselves in it: young women fancying themselves headstrong and bright. She isn't sure, now, if that assessment was accurate but she enjoyed it at the time.

'I know how *I* would feel if my bosom friend left and I wasn't able to see her easily. Especially if my other loved ones are far away.' His eyes hold hers and are full of understanding.

Marie has let herself grieve for Norm, even on days when the grief felt like it might consume her. She's let herself miss Nicole, and she knows her daughter isn't too far away. What she hasn't done is allow herself to feel what Gwen's absence really means for her day-to-day life. They saw each other almost every day from childhood, and spoke on the phone in between. She was more honest with Gwen than she was with anyone else – including Father Paul. They'd shared all the ups and downs of a normal human life.

'Have you been to visit her since she moved?' Father Paul asks.

'No.' She sighs. 'That's bizarre, isn't it? That I haven't visited my best friend. I mean, she hasn't moved to Mars!'

Her levity is false, and she can tell that he knows.

'Perhaps you're angry at her for leaving you, in a way you don't feel you can be angry at Norm and Nicole.' Father Paul's eyes search hers. 'But I think it's more likely that you simply need to find a new way to stay in contact with her,' he continues. 'Communicating with Gwen was a matter of course for you when she lived nearby. It was part of your routine for decades. It makes sense that you're having trouble adjusting to life without it.'

This is a kindness he's offering her: letting her off the hook for moping around because her friend has done a perfectly reasonable thing in moving to a different place.

'Don't you think she may feel the same?' Father Paul says. 'She may be having trouble adjusting to life without you.'

'I doubt it!' Marie says, but she doesn't really know. She presumed that because Gwen made the decision to go, she would be fine with whatever resulted from it.

'What makes you think you're so easy to forget, Marie?' Father Paul's face relaxes into a smile. 'I'm sure she misses you just as much as you miss her. Why don't you visit her?'

Marie feels something stuck in her throat. An admission, perhaps, that she's scared to see Gwen in case Gwen's new life is just wonderful without her.

'I should,' she finally gets out.

'Yes, you should.'

As he looks at her she wonders how he became so wise at such a young age. He can't be older than forty, yet he is more understanding and compassionate than she believes she will ever be.

'You're still swimming, I take it?' he says.

'Yes.'

She thinks of this morning's swim, with Theresa attempting a faster freestyle and instead looking like the Tasmanian Devil in a Looney Tunes cartoon, arms and legs thrashing around and hardly any progress being made. Marie had laughed so much she swallowed water, and her body hummed with the joy of it as she walked home up the hill.

'You're smiling,' Father Paul says. 'I take it that means you're enjoying it.'

Marie nods. 'I am. I have someone to swim with. For now.'

'For now?'

'Who knows how long she'll last? I see a lot of people who are very keen for a couple of weeks each spring or summer, then you don't see them again until next year.'

She can't understand why that happens – why anyone would drop a new habit so quickly, especially when it's so beneficial – but she hopes Theresa won't be amongst their number. She is finding her to be good company.

'I have faith,' Father Paul says, gazing at her. 'I'm sure she will enjoy swimming with you so much that she'll have no trouble continuing.' He takes another biscuit. 'Now, are you sure you won't tell me what sugar you use in these?'

They smile at each other. Yes, he is a thoughtful man. Thoughtful and kind.

And Marie has learnt at least one thing today. While Gwen may not be down the road any more, she still has a friend nearby.

CHAPTER 8

The children are still asleep when Theresa checks on them: Ollie lying on his back with his arms and legs flung out, Sasha curled around her favourite teddy bear. It took ages to get them to this point – they each wanted two stories read and to have their backs rubbed. Theresa understood: she'd like to have someone rub her back too.

They're always like this on the nights when Andrew doesn't arrive home in time for dinner. They never say anything about him not being there, yet they cling harder to her. They want all of her time, and they'll fight sleep to get it. It eats into the time she has to potter around before bed but she finds herself thinking that she *should* mind that more than she actually does. She is lucky to have her children, and doesn't take them for granted. One of her sisters-in-law has been trying for years to get pregnant and it hasn't worked; and someone Theresa knew at school had a baby who only lived for a few weeks. There are reminders everywhere that motherhood is not always easily come by or kept.

She pushes open the kitchen's screen door and steps down to the path that takes her to the granny flat. Everyone they know in Shelly Bay has a house like this: one storey, three bedrooms, half brick, half fibro, with a reasonable back garden and some room out the front for rose bushes or whatever else people like to plant to make their place look nice from the street.

When she and Andrew bought the house, not long after they married, the granny flat was a shed. Andrew had liked the idea of a place to store the lawnmower and his surfboard, and it was somewhere to keep the gardening equipment. On weekends he'd disappear into the shed and do god-knows-what. Once Theresa found some girlie magazines, some empty tinnies and three packets of Benson & Hedges. She threw out the tinnies, and the next time she came looking for a trowel the girlie magazines were gone.

Three years ago the shed became a flat when Nonna came to live with them.

Andrew had protested when Theresa said that her grand-mother would have to move in.

'Why do I have to support your family?' he'd said, in a way that made her wonder if he even resented having to support their children. 'Why can't she live with your parents?'

Theresa had pointed out that Nonna was an elderly woman who had lived on the northern beaches for decades; her friends were here, and she knew no one on the Central Coast, where Theresa's parents lived. Nonna could no longer be at home alone but that was no reason to uproot her entirely.

'Besides,' she'd said, 'she can watch the kids after school while I'm—'

'Getting your nails done?' he'd said, and she'd wanted to burst into tears.

'No, Andrew. While I'm shopping and cooking and cleaning.'

'That's your job.'

'I realise that, but you don't have to do your job and also look after the children.'

47

He had looked momentarily stumped. 'You could give up volunteering. Then you'd have more time to do everything else and watch the kids.'

Volunteering at Northern Hospital was the only thing in Theresa's life that was just for her – until she started swimming. She feels competent at the hospital, and gets to talk to people who have ages in double digits. Yet she knew Andrew wouldn't understand; and she also knew not to say anything that might sound defensive because she wanted something from him.

'It's important to give back to the community,' she'd said as calmly as she could, 'so I'm not giving that up. Nonna won't get in the way. If anything, she'll be a help to us.'

He'd snorted. 'And you'll have even less time for me.'

She didn't know what he meant – he never asked to spend time with her. He went to work, came home and went to the shed. But there was no point trying to bargain further. 'Please,' was all she'd said.

He'd agreed – after a few days.

Now he seems to like having Nonna there, because she's happy to talk about the cricket and she's an excellent cook. Andrew prefers Nonna's lasagna to anything Theresa makes. But at the time he'd whinged his way through each day of painting the walls and putting in a shower and toilet for her. He'd done it all himself, which surprised Theresa – she hadn't known he had those kinds of skills – but he'd brushed aside her thanks. She knows she's never able to say things in the way he wants her to, but she doesn't know how else to say them.

The air feels humid as she makes her way to Nonna's door. She thought there might be a storm tonight but it seems to have passed them by and left only its heavy promise behind.

She knocks softly. 'Nonna?' Her grandmother is usually still awake at this time of night but she never likes to presume.

'*Si*, Theresa,' comes the rich voice that has deepened with the years and Nonna's fondness for menthol cigarettes and afternoon aperitifs.

Theresa opens the door and finds Nonna with a ciggie in one hand and *La Fiamma* in the other.

'Can I get you anything?' she asks.

'No, thank you, darling.' Nonna wafts the ciggie in the air. 'I have everything I need.' She smiles and her face turns into a concertina, folds enveloping her eyes.

Theresa doesn't remember what her nonna looked like before she wrinkled, and can't help wondering if that's what she's going to look like herself one day. The only difference between them is that Theresa only smoked for a few years and quit before she got pregnant the first time. Nonna smoked through all her pregnancies and the breastfeeding too.

'Are you playing cards tomorrow?' Theresa asks, leaning in the doorway.

There's a regular game of poker at the house of one of her grandmother's friends; it has proved to be a source of funding of presents for Ollie and Sasha.

Nonna exhales smoke and nods. 'Yes. I need to have a victory.'

'Don't you have one every week?' Theresa raises an eyebrow. 'You're bleeding those old coots dry.'

Nonna smiles mysteriously. 'They deserve it.'

Theresa laughs. 'I bet they don't. I think you just like to win.'

'Don't you?'

Theresa hears the front door slam and winces. Andrew should know the kids are asleep by now. The noise could wake them.

She looks at her grandmother and wiggles her eyebrows.

Nonna shrugs in response. 'He's your husband,' she says and takes another drag on her cigarette.

Theresa makes a face and steps out of the doorway. '*Ciao*,' she says as Nonna waves her off.

Inside, she can smell Andrew before she sees him: hops mixed with the smoke cloud that hangs in every pub. As she walks into the living room he's already slumped on the couch and turning up the volume on the television.

'You'll wake the kids,' she says, and can hear the irritation in her voice. She shouldn't have to talk to him like he's a kid himself, yet that's all she seems to do, especially when he isn't sober.

'Hello to you too,' he says and she feels the rebuke in it. She knows she forgets to say hello and goodbye to him most days, but he doesn't say anything to her either.

'Andrew – the volume.'

'They'll live,' he says.

Theresa's shoulders hunch and she feels her jaw tense. She doesn't want to be like this around her own husband – she wants to welcome him with open arms and a big kiss, but he makes that impossible.

Not once has he arrived home and said he's happy to see her. In the early days she used to say she'd missed him and he'd wink and slap her bum, although he'd never say he missed her too. It took her a while – perhaps too long – to realise that he never says anything much that could be construed as affectionate or appreciative. He doesn't even tell the children he loves them.

She'd asked him about it once and he said she was spoiling them by telling them all the time. 'You'll make them sooks,' he'd said.

She shouldn't have been surprised, because 'sook' is his father's favourite word. Andrew was a sook of a kid, apparently, until he learnt to harden up. Andrew's father believes that Oliver is heading the same way: too sooky because he always wants his mum, but 'he'll grow out of it, mark my words'.

Theresa has never marked any of her father-in-law's words but she knows Andrew does.

Looking at Andrew sitting on the couch, his face half in shadow because the bulb in the lamp is near the end of its life, Theresa thinks he looks like his father. He's getting the same jowls. She can't say she's ever found jowls sexy. Combined with the fact that she's exhausted all the time and seems to have three children instead of two, it's no wonder they haven't been naked together for so long she can barely remember what he looks like. Maybe it was New Year's Eve. Which makes it . . . almost a year. Cripes. According to *Cleo* it should be a lot more regular than that if she wants to 'keep her man'. Not that he's making the prospect appealing.

'Where have you been?' she says, because she still cares about what he does even if he doesn't care about her.

'Out.'

She counts to five so she doesn't come back with a retort that would only earn her an argument.

'The kids missed you.'

'Yeah?' He sinks a little further down but doesn't turn to look at her.

'I'd really like you to be here to have dinner with them.' She tries to sound assertive. She's read about that in *Cleo* too.

'They eat pretty early,' he says. 'I'm not hungry then.'

Another count to five.

'Fair enough. But they'd still like to see you before they go to bed.'

'And I'd like you to be here when they wake up,' he says.

Now his bleary eyes are turned her way, and she can't tell if he's angry with her or simply saying something true. They stare at each other as a movie plays on the TV. She thinks she can hear John Wayne talking.

'You get to do your swimming,' Andrew says, 'and I get to go out with the boys. Fair's fair.'

There's a certain logic to it, she has to admit. But if she starts to do the maths on what she does versus what he does and who comes out in front, they'll get stuck in the same muck they've been in for a long time – too long. Their marriage is a push-and-pull of who wants what and who doesn't get what they want. Each of them feels hard done by. She feels like if she's awake she's working to look after this house and their children; and he says he has all the financial burden and that should count for a lot.

She can't escape the conclusion that the only way out of it is for her to give up the fight. To stop asking for things. To stay quiet. To be the obedient little wife and maybe then Andrew will start coming home early enough to see the kids. He's never going to change, so she has to be the one to do it. It would be less stressful, that's for sure.

Except she's not giving up the swimming. She has come to need it. When she does that swim she achieves something, and Theresa doesn't feel like she achieves anything else in her life apart from just getting by. Maybe when her children reach adulthood in one piece she'll feel like she's accomplished something, but that's a long way off.

'I'm going to bed,' she says, as she does every time.

'Right,' he says, his head already swivelled back to the TV.

Slowly, Theresa makes her way to their bedroom and undresses. Andrew will probably sleep on the couch tonight, like he's been doing lately. She doesn't miss him thrashing around in the night but she's not rapt about the development. It doesn't feel like a temporary situation.

Once upon a time she thought the sun shone out of Andrew, and believed he thought the same of her. Each night now, as she's waiting to fall asleep, she tries to figure out how they can get back to that, because it would be a more peaceful way to live.

There's an obstacle, though, that she just can't shift: for her, the sun now shines out of Oliver and Sasha. If she'd once thought her love for Andrew was endless, she found its limits – but she knows, with each cell of her body, that her love for her children is as big as the universe. She can only hope, for Andrew's sake, that he feels the same.

CHAPTER 9

While swimming each morning might have seemed like a good idea in theory, Elaine isn't convinced that it's one in practice. Not when she's spent the night before drinking gin and tonics while waiting for James to get home from work – which he did, late, kissing her once and falling asleep sprawled across her torso. Luckily he was too tired to notice that she was drunk, or there would have been words. Each time he sees her with a drink he counsels her to 'slow down', but it's all right for him with his twelve hours a day at work while she's at home, missing her children and the business she used to run and the friends she used to see, and the parents she used to pop round to visit and do the crossword with and take to the doctor.

Elaine's sister has to look after their parents now. All Elaine has to do is try to adjust to this new country that is not new to her husband, who has picked up again with all his school and university friends, and whose mother is delighted to have her only son back home. Precisely no one is delighted to see Elaine. Except James, when he's conscious. She supposes she should feel grateful for that – she knows more than a few women whose husbands are boors, and bores, and neither party is delighted to see the other, ever.

Not that it's stopped her drinking too much. She knows it's too much, but what started as a way to pass the time, and distract herself from the fact that the housework does not at all fill her day, has become a habit she can't seem to break. Which is *ridiculous* because it's not as if she doesn't have willpower. She has exercised it almost every day of her life since she was a teenager, including throughout her pregnancies. Her food intake is monitored in what one might call an ascetic fashion. Booze, on the other hand, is proving harder to control.

This morning, that lack of control has left her with a pounding headache to match the pounding waves that she's trying to avoid thumping into her as she swims back to shore. She must be foolhardy to attempt to swim at all in this surf. She grew up swimming in nice local lidos and on beaches in Norfolk. James tried to warn her about Australian surf, but she breezily informed him that she had several blue ribbons in all sorts of swimming strokes and she would be *fine, thank you, darling, just fine.*

Today's definition of *fine* includes wanting to vomit – because of her hangover and the panic resulting from the tug at her feet that is a rip or sweep or whatever Australians call it that carries people out to sea. She's fighting it to get back to the beach. She's stronger than this. *Fitter* than this. She shouldn't be having so much trouble.

'Oi! Marie!' she hears a man call as her feet find purchase on the sand and she uses her hands to pull herself through the water. 'Bloody tourists!'

Elaine looks to her left, where an older gent stands with arms folded over a hairy suntanned chest and tight swimming costume.

'They all think they can swim,' he goes on. 'Getting into trouble all the bloody time.'

'Shut up, Trev,' says a woman with grey hair who, Elaine can see now, is hauling a teenage girl out of the water. 'You could give me a hand, you know.'

'You're doin' all right,' he says. 'Besides, I've done me back in.' He winces in an exaggerated fashion and puts a hand to his hip.

Elaine can see that the girl's eyes are closed and her body is limp, so that Marie – she presumes it is Marie carrying the girl – is struggling with her. Finding some speed, Elaine steps onto the sand and hurries over.

'Can I help?' she says, picking up the girl's legs and seeing the relief in Marie's eyes.

'I'm coming, Marie!' Elaine hears from behind, and glances over her shoulder to see a younger woman having the same trouble she did getting out of the surf.

'Watch behind you,' Elaine says as Marie starts to stumble up the sharp incline of sand carved out by hard-crashing waves.

'Thanks,' Marie grunts, adjusting her grip under the girl's armpits as Elaine tightens her own on the ankles. Above the water's reach, she adds, 'Let's put her down. Easy.'

Once the girl is on the sand, the other woman appears. 'Sorry – so hard to get in,' she says breathlessly. She kneels down and puts her cheek next to the girl's mouth. 'She's breathing, but let's get her on her side.'

Elaine can only watch as Marie puts her hands under the base of the girl's head while the other woman looks as if she's about to wrestle with her, her arms wrapping around, then she rolls the girl onto her side. Much to Elaine's shock, the next thing she does is put her finger in the girl's mouth.

'Clearing the airway,' Marie says, catching Elaine's eye. 'In case there's sea water or anything in her mouth. We don't want her to *stop* breathing.'

Elaine nods, struck mute by the choreography of this unlikely scenario: two rescuing women, an unconscious girl, a man standing by and doing nothing. And her, also doing nothing because there's nothing she knows to do. These women seem to have some intrinsic knowledge about how to save a life. Perhaps that's something else that comes with living in Australia.

The girl coughs and moans, her eyelids fluttering.

'Hello?' says the woman. 'Can you hear me? What's your name?'

The girl coughs again. 'Kathy,' she says croakily.

'Kathy, you got into some trouble in the water,' Marie says, stroking the girl's forehead. 'How are you feeling?'

'Um . . . a bit strange.' Kathy attempts to move.

'Stay there,' says the woman. 'Don't rush anything. You've had a bit of a shock.'

She and Marie look at each other.

'Theresa, you go,' says Marie. 'I know you have to get the kids to school.'

Theresa's forehead crinkles. 'I don't want to leave her.'

'I'll stay with her,' Marie says.

'I can stay too,' Elaine says. It's the least she can offer.

The woman – Theresa – smiles at Elaine. 'Thanks for your help before.'

Elaine makes a noise of disbelief. 'I hardly did anything.'

'It helps just to know someone else cares.' She stands up. 'I'm Theresa. This is my friend, Marie.'

'I'm Elaine,' she mutters in the shy way of a new girl in the school playground.

'Thanks again. But I have to get going. Maybe I'll see you tomorrow?' Theresa doesn't wait for an answer as she bustles over to a nearby towel folded on the sand, picking it up as she wrests her swimming cap off her head. 'Bye, Marie!' she calls as she almost skips over the sand towards the stairs.

Marie waves and turns her attention back to the girl, who is now pushing herself up onto one hand. Trev, Elaine realises, has disappeared.

'Here,' she says, offering her hands to Kathy, who is slowly getting to her feet.

Marie takes the girl's elbows. 'How are you feeling?' she says.

Kathy blushes. 'A bit embarrassed. I thought I was okay.'

'We all think that, love,' Marie says kindly, 'until we're not. Just take your time. See how you feel standing up. There's no hurry.' Her eyes catch Elaine's and she nods her head to the side. 'Let's give her a second,' she says softly.

Elaine steps away and Marie follows, both of them keeping watch on the girl.

'You swim often?' Marie asks.

'Hm?'

'I saw you here the other day.'

'Oh – yes. I've started coming down in the mornings.'

'You may prefer to swim on your own, but if you don't Theresa and I are here at sunrise each day. You're welcome to join us. We swim to Little Beach and back.' Marie smiles. 'I don't know how Theresa fits it in. She has a lot to juggle. Kids at primary school. She volunteers at the hospital. I know she skedaddled this morning, but she's usually very friendly.'

Elaine feels something like shame. Theresa has a life full of obligation and she still managed to take care of a stranger in distress. Elaine has a life full of emptiness and can't manage her way out of her own distress.

'And I think I know her well enough to say she'd welcome another swimmer,' Marie adds, looking at Elaine as she smiles.

'Thank you,' Elaine says quickly, not sure whether to believe Marie. What if Theresa wouldn't want her to join them? Elaine doesn't want to be tossed out of yet another group.

Kathy stands up a bit straighter and turns to look at them.

'Are you all right to walk?' Elaine calls and moves towards her.

Kathy nods. 'Yes. Thanks.'

'Can I walk you somewhere?' Elaine asks, happy to have a potential task.

Kathy nods again. 'Yes, please. My bag is at the surf club.'

Marie smiles approvingly. 'Thanks, Elaine.'

'It's nothing. Honestly.' She puts her arm through the girl's.

'See you,' Marie says, and Elaine isn't sure if it's meant for her or Kathy.

Elaine only glances back once as she carefully escorts Kathy to the club. She sees Marie walking slowly, deliberately, her head bowed as if she's examining each footstep. Perhaps she's someone Elaine could get to know; someone who might like to get to know Elaine. But if Elaine doesn't turn up to swim with Marie, neither of them will ever find out.

SUMMER 1982-1983

CHAPTER 10

'Morning, Theresa.' Marie's smile is just visible in the dawn light but Theresa would recognise those broad shoulders anywhere.

'Good morning, Marie!'

Theresa feels almost as happy to see Marie as she does to see her children every day after school: it's the warmth of knowing you like someone enough to miss them and then enjoy their company again.

At least, Marie gives the impression that she likes Theresa. Each morning whoever is there first waits for the other, then they swim together, striking out for Little Beach. Sometimes they stop offshore and tread water for a while. Marie says it's good for the legs. Theresa's legs already feel like they're getting enough exercise with the swimming, but Marie looks athletic for an old duck so who is Theresa to doubt her word?

And she really shouldn't think that Marie is old. She's just *older*. Theresa knows that Marie is in her sixties, because once she said something about being in her twenties during World War II. Theresa's idea of people in their sixties used to be that they were glued to their favourite armchairs, doing the crosswords and reading the death notices in the *Herald*. That's because her father's parents used to do that, and Andrew's parents still do.

Nonna doesn't, though, so Theresa should remember not to make assumptions about people before she knows them. It's a bad habit and she's always done it. She could blame her mother for telling her over and over that girls whose skirts were a certain height above the knee were 'cheap' and if their hair was dyed a certain way they were 'common'. It's not that her mother is mean, either; it's what she and all her friends think. Theresa has no idea where they get it from but it infected her for a while. She's making herself stop. You have to take people as you find them. That's what Marie did to her, and she's doing it to Marie. No judgements. The way friends should always be with each other.

Theresa snaps back to attention when she realises that Marie is sighing as she looks at the water.

'What was that for?' she asks as she tucks her hair into her cap.

'Hm?' Marie turns to look at her.

'That sigh.'

'What sigh?'

'You *sighed*. It was loud. You didn't notice?'

Marie frowns briefly and Theresa worries that she's put her foot in something she didn't even know was there.

'It's . . .' Marie sighs again and shakes her head. 'It's a day.'

'What do you mean?'

Marie's lips part and close, and her shoulders slump a little. 'I had a boy.' She keeps looking at the ocean but Theresa wishes she'd look at her, because she sounds so sad. 'He was stillborn. Today. Thirty-three years ago.'

Now she gives Theresa a smile, except Theresa feels like crying for her instead.

'He'd be thirty-three. Obviously.' Another sigh. 'I don't think of him all the time, but on this day I do.'

Theresa puts her hand on Marie's arm. They may be friends now, but she doesn't think she knows her well enough to hug her. 'I'm so sorry,' she says, and it sounds hollow. Meaningless. Especially when Marie told her once before not to say sorry about her husband. 'It's not the right thing to say but I never know what the right thing is.'

'There is no right thing.' Marie looks at her kindly. 'And there's no wrong thing, either. It's nice for me to be able to talk about him to someone. Norm and I . . .' She pauses. 'Well, we didn't talk about it. And Nicole can't remember it – she was only two. So I don't like to talk about it with her. My friend Gwen was a godsend at the time, but we haven't spoken about it in years.'

Theresa nods because she's not sure what to do apart from acknowledge what she has heard.

'Time's a funny thing, isn't it?' Marie goes on. 'It seems like yesterday that he was here. And it seems like another lifetime. In my head I'm still that young.' She shrugs. 'Yet most days I feel old.'

Theresa takes her hand; *that* feels like the right thing to do. 'What was his name?' she says softly.

'Duncan.' Marie squeezes her palm. 'Thank you for asking.'

They stand there for a minute, maybe two, maybe three, as the sky turns their faces orange. Normally Theresa is keen to get in the water because she knows how much is waiting for her at home. Get in, get out, choof off, plough into the day. Today, though, she's happy to be still for a while.

'Er . . . hello?'

Theresa turns to see the lady from last week – the one who helped with the half-drowned girl. She looks nervous.

'Elaine, isn't it?' says Marie, and Elaine's face relaxes.

'Yes. Hello . . . Marie. And Theresa.'

'You can come closer – we're not that scary,' Marie says.

Theresa wants to laugh at that. Marie can seem imposing sometimes – she looks like a warrior walking out of the water, and she doesn't smile that readily.

Theresa knows she gives her own smiles away perhaps too much, although that's what she was told to do when she was a little girl. *Smile, Theresa, no one likes to see a pretty girl with a scowl* – her mother's broken record. It didn't matter who they were with, Theresa had to smile while her brothers could just be themselves. She can feel the unfairness of it still – but she's used to stuffing those kinds of feelings down.

'Do you mind if I join you?' Elaine asks, and Theresa can't help the instant pang of – what? Jealousy? No. It's . . . disappointment. She won't have Marie to herself, and she's become used to that.

Ah well, life is nothing if not change. Nonna likes to say that, and she's lived through two world wars so Theresa thinks she should believe her.

'I told Elaine we wouldn't mind a third,' Marie says, and her eyes look like they're pleading a little bit.

'It's fine!' Theresa says. 'You look like you're fitter than me – you can probably keep up with Marie.' She rolls her eyes. 'I can't. She's *so* much better.'

'No, I'm not,' Marie says with what sounds like a *tsk-tsk*. 'I'm just more experienced. I'm guessing from your accent that you probably didn't grow up swimming in the ocean, Elaine?'

'No, I didn't. And I haven't been in Australia long enough to get much practice.'

'What brought you here?' Theresa asks.

'My husband is Australian. We met in England – we've

always lived in England.' Elaine's face clouds momentarily. 'But he wanted to come home.'

Marie's eyes narrow a little. 'That can't be easy for you. Do you have kids?'

'Two sons. They're grown-up so . . .' There's the cloud again. 'They stayed in the UK.'

'Oh no! You must be so sad,' Theresa says, unable to imagine not having her children nearby – in fact, she's not even going to try to imagine it. But maybe she's making it worse for Elaine by reacting so strongly? She should have thought before she opened her mouth.

Elaine looks almost relieved, however. 'I am,' she says, with a small smile. 'I miss them all the time. But they have their own lives now. We couldn't expect them to rearrange everything just because their father quite rightly wanted to be near his family and friends for a change.'

'I think a daily swim is just the thing for you then,' says Marie. 'It's a good discipline. A good . . . distraction. I'm speaking from experience.'

The look on Elaine's face shows that she understands. 'I've been enjoying the swimming so far,' she says. 'Although I had a shock the other morning – it was harder to manage than I'd expected.'

Her eyes flit from Marie to Theresa, almost as if she's seeking approval.

'A word of caution, then,' says Marie. 'Always respect the ocean, and never turn your back on a wave.'

Elaine frowns. 'But how do you—'

'Get out?' Marie smiles. 'Keep checking over your shoulder. Even when the surf is small, there can be one that surprises you. Like today – they're mostly small but each seventh wave has a kick to it.'

'Seventh wave?'

'Seven waves in a set. The last one is usually the biggest.' Marie winks. 'Stick with me, you'll be right.'

Elaine nods. 'I will.'

'And I'll be watching from far, far behind,' Theresa says as she removes her sarong and folds it up, putting it under her towel. Elaine hurriedly puts her own cap on.

'Ready?' Marie says.

'Ready,' Elaine says emphatically.

'Lead on, Macduff!' Theresa says, giggling.

She walks slowly so that Elaine can accompany Marie into the surf, her earlier disappointment put aside. It's been lovely – a privilege – having Marie to herself but she's really too special to hoard. Besides, Theresa likes Elaine already, in the way that you just know you like some people even if you can't say exactly why. *Kismet*, you might call it. She read that word in a book once. It was kismet that she met Marie, and now it might have happened again, and she's not going to argue with that.

CHAPTER 11

Today is the day. After her lessons, and Matt's reassurances that her freestyle is 'coming along nicely', Leanne is ready to swim in the ocean. With Theresa and her friends.

She hasn't arrived at this decision lightly; she could even say she's capitulated to it. To Theresa's bouncy campaign to persuade her to swim in the ocean instead of the pool. 'Beautiful morning,' she might say as she passes Leanne in the corridor. 'The water is so warm now – almost like a bath!' Then she'll keep walking, as if she's doing nothing more than giving Leanne a weather report. But the next day there'll be something else: 'I can't believe how good I feel swimming every day.' Or: 'It's so much fun swimming with other people. I don't have time to think about whether or not I'm getting tired.'

Leanne has been nodding along to these statements as if she's a bystander, not their intended audience. She's impressed by Theresa's willingness to persevere. It makes her think that she really wants her to come swimming.

The only clue Leanne has as to why Theresa might be doing all of this came a couple of weeks ago, when Theresa asked if Leanne was seeing her friends on the weekend. Leanne was looking through a file at the time and only half listening, which is why she didn't have time to obfuscate as she normally would.

Because there aren't any friends. Instead she has a small garden to tend; on Saturday mornings she goes to the local library to stock up on books for the week, and on Sunday afternoons she attends the local cinema.

'No,' she replied.

'Why not?' said Theresa, and that's when Leanne realised her mistake.

'Because, um . . .' She'd turned away and hoped that Theresa wouldn't press the issue – which was completely irrational, because Theresa is the last person who would let that kind of thing go.

'Leanne?'

'Hm?' She kept her back turned, which was rude, of course, but she didn't want to engage.

'You never talk about your friends,' Theresa says, and it's not an accusation. She sounds curious, and maybe a little sorrowful, as if Leanne should be pitied.

'Because that's nothing to do with work,' she'd said as strongly as she could, thankful that Theresa couldn't see the lie written across her face.

'Okay,' Theresa said meekly, and left, and Leanne felt bad.

After that Theresa started asking her the occasional question: What would she be doing on the weekend? Had she seen such-and-such movie? It didn't sound like concern so much as nosiness, yet Leanne knows that Theresa isn't so pointed.

Or maybe Leanne just doesn't want to believe that the campaign to persuade her to come swimming is born out of pity – but she can hardly ask, and she won't let it stop her. In order to get herself here today, she's had to trust that Theresa means well, and no more than that. Whether or not Leanne joins her little group, it's clear she has friends to swim with and doesn't need Leanne. So it's altruism that's motivating her. Or maybe she likes to have a lot of friends. Leanne can't imagine why Theresa would want to be her friend, given how difficult she can be, yet she's persisted.

She didn't tell Theresa that she would be joining her today. Or any day. She didn't want to feel locked in – and if she'd made a promise, that's how she'd feel. But a couple of days ago Theresa mentioned that she and Marie now had another person with them, Elaine, and that Elaine had only just started swimming in the ocean. Leanne felt reassured: she wouldn't be the only novice. That's when she realised she was truly ready – or as ready as she could be. Leanne has learnt to love the liberation – the disembodiment – of being in the water, and she wonders how much greater it might be out there with only the horizon to limit her.

Except now she's holding her breath as she stands on the sand and waits for Theresa. She's bought a new swimming costume for the occasion: a plain black one-piece. And a cap – also black. She bought it at the pool, along with the goggles that don't fit perfectly, but they'll do.

It's a Sunday, which Leanne chose because if she's slow – if she takes twice as long as the others, which she suspects she will – she doesn't have to rush off to work. She's going to say something like: 'You go on without me.' It sounds almost noble. Not that she is noble. Or generous. She's had to preserve all of her energy for herself these last few years so she's hardly been offering it to others. But it won't cost her anything to tell them to go ahead – indeed, it will free her to paddle around behind them.

When she got out of bed before sunrise she felt almost excited to be testing her new abilities. Except now, looking at the water that is still dark in the pre-dawn light, she can't help thinking about what it can hold: mysteries, obviously, and also terror. Once she was walking on the beach and saw the lifesavers rush to pull someone from the water. A girl whose family were shrieking on the sand. What's the line between having a lovely morning swim and being carried from the surf?

'Leanne!'

She turns and sees Theresa waving from a few metres away, a sarong tied around her waist and a towel over her shoulder. Theresa often talks about how she's 'let herself go', but Leanne doesn't see that. She thinks Theresa looks strong as well as voluptuous.

'You didn't tell me you were coming!' It might have been an admonishment, but Theresa is beaming and Leanne feels pleased – satisfied, even. 'Marie will be happy.'

'Will she?'

'Oh look, there she is – yoohoo, Marie!'

In the growing light Leanne can see the older woman walking slowly but confidently over the soft sand, her bare feet sinking into it.

'Hello, Leanne,' Marie says, her voice throaty. 'Theresa's told me about you. I'm glad you decided to join us.'

'I'm – ah, so am I.' Leanne feels nervous even though she knows it's ridiculous. Just because there's no black line to follow doesn't mean she won't be able to swim just the way she does in the pool. Matt told her it would probably be easier because salt water is more buoyant. 'I'll be going slowly,' she adds quickly. 'I haven't been swimming for as long as you have.'

'That's quite all right,' Marie says. 'We won't make you go fast. And I'm sure you're better than you think.'

'I'm sooo slow,' Theresa says, making a face. 'Poor Marie! She must get sick of it.'

'Not at all,' Marie says and her voice sounds firm and calm. 'I can go as slow as anyone wants.'

Leanne senses someone near her shoulder and turns to see a tall, lean, middle-aged woman dropping her towel next to them.

'Ladies,' she says.

'Hi, Elaine.' Theresa grins. 'I'd like you to meet Leanne. She's going to join us today. Maybe every day!'

Theresa looks at her hopefully and Leanne feels her resolve weaken. She hasn't made plans beyond today, and she's not at all sure she wants to turn up *every* day. That would involve a commitment to people she hardly knows.

'We'll see,' she says.

'How do you know Theresa?' Elaine asks, and now Leanne can hear an accent. English.

'I work at the hospital. Theresa volunteers on my ward.'

'Leanne's a nurse,' says Theresa with a note of pride. 'The children *love* her.'

'I don't think that's true,' Leanne says, feeling self-conscious.

'It is! You're their favourite. But I don't tell the others or they might get jealous.'

'Sun's coming up,' says Marie.

Leanne looks towards the horizon and half closes her eyes against the intense golden light that looks as if it's opening up the whole world. The bay seems enormous: the pool is a contained space and she realises she's built her confidence within those constraints. But now, with an ocean that reaches the horizon and beyond, she's not feeling so sure. Then there are the waves, which aren't as big as she's seen them, but as she's used to the flat pool, they seem like an obstacle.

'How, um, how far do we swim?' she says, swallowing.

Marie points towards Little Beach, where Leanne has run many times along the path. 'Over there and back. It's not as far as it looks once you're used to it.'

'If I can do it, *anyone* can do it,' Theresa says, giving Leanne's arm a reassuring nudge. 'Honestly. I'm so unfit.'

'Not any more,' says Elaine, smiling. 'You keep a very good pace.'

'Don't worry – I'll swim alongside you,' says Theresa. 'These two tear away pretty quickly.'

'We always come back though,' Marie says with half a smile.

'As you're passing me in the other direction!' Theresa sounds indignant but she's grinning.

Leanne glances from her to Marie to Elaine and sees them all smiling at each other, their body language indicating their ease. Meanwhile she feels like a spinning top wound tightly and about to be released. She's not sure if that's a good or a bad thing.

'Anyway, not much of a rush today – I don't have to get the kids to school.' Theresa sighs and gazes at the sea. 'It's a luxury.'

'Do you have children, Leanne?' Elaine asks.

Leanne almost rears at the question, although it's a reasonable one: she's the right age to have children. She just hasn't put herself in the position to be asked about it for a long time. She avoids social gatherings when she can, and doesn't say much if she does have to go along. If someone persists, she knows that the easiest deflection is to ask questions about them: most people will cheerfully talk about themselves for hours. Theresa, she knows, isn't like that – she likes to ask questions – but at the hospital her questions are easier to contain. Now Leanne has three people staring at her, waiting for an answer to a question that is, no doubt, kindly meant, but that doesn't mean she wants to respond to it.

'No,' she says, looking down, hoping that will end the conversation.

Elaine tries again. 'A husband?'

'No.'

'Nor do I,' says Marie. 'He died. Very thoughtless of him.'

Leanne meets her eyes and sees understanding in them. She's been let off the hook, and she appreciates it.

'Come on, into the water!' Theresa says, sounding as though it's the most inviting place in the world.

Leanne presses her hair into her cap, picks up her goggles and follows the others as they wade in. The water is surprisingly cold against her skin. She's used to the pool, which catches the sun's rays during the day and holds the warmth for her post-work swims.

A small wave crashes against her belly and she gasps with the impact, which is harder than she'd expected.

There are larger waves rolling towards them, and she sees Marie dive under one, then Elaine, so naturally that they look like porpoises. Leanne can't do that. She can't dive under a wave. She has no experience in the ocean and was stupid to think she could manage this.

She doesn't want to panic, but her mouth opens and she starts to breathe so quickly it's like panting. She stops and wonders how badly Theresa will think of her if she turns around and goes back. The pool is safer. Contained. While she likes gazing at the ocean, the reality of being in it is too overwhelming. This is wilderness. This is not something she can control.

'Leanne?' Theresa has stopped and turned around.

'I . . .' She swallows.

'It's normal to be afraid,' Theresa says, wading towards her. A wave unfurls against her back but she doesn't move even a millimetre and Leanne wonders how long it takes to become so used to the surf. 'I was.'

'I'm not afraid,' Leanne snaps, but doesn't know why she said it. Why is she worried about what Theresa thinks?

Theresa pushes her goggles up onto her head so Leanne is looking into those deep, sympathetic pools she sees at the hospital.

'It's not like anything I've done before,' Theresa says. 'But I did go to the beach as a child. You didn't do that, did you?'

'No,' she says, scrunching her toes into the sand to try to stay calm.

'You don't have to do anything, of course,' says Theresa. 'You can wait for us on the beach. Or go home.' She looks out to sea. 'Like I said, I was scared too. But it's the best thing I've ever done, Leanne. When you're out there, all your troubles disappear.' As she turns back to Leanne there's kindness in her smile. 'We all have troubles, don't we?'

Leanne can't imagine what troubles Theresa has; she always seems carefree. Yet she's aware that nothing about her own behaviour tells the story of her past. She is diffident with adults, and more so with men than women. She knows – because Matron has told her – that her more lively behaviour with the children is noticed, but no one has ever asked her why. She doesn't know what she'd tell them if they did.

'I guess,' she says.

'The ocean may not be the right thing for you, Leanne. And that's okay. But if you do want to go in, I promise I won't leave you.'

The water is still running past her thighs and Leanne feels how her body has adjusted to the temperature. It didn't take long. Other adjustments may not take long either.

'All right,' she says, trying for a smile.

'Really?' Theresa looks like she's been told that Santa Claus is real.

Leanne nods and hears a strange sound rising from her chest: a laugh. 'Let's go!'

Theresa pushes her goggles back down, takes Leanne's hand and leads her towards deeper water. As the next wave rolls in, Theresa grins at her then dives underneath it.

Leanne follows her and feels how this world is familiar yet strange: not the warm cocoon of the pool but not unlike it either. She opens her eyes and sees the wave rolling over her, the curve of its action making a shape so perfect she can't believe it's real. She sees gradations of light and sand being churned. She feels suspended inside a story that has no beginning or end.

Then she sees Theresa, pushing up towards the surface. Putting her feet down, Leanne erupts into the air, gulps a breath and dives under again straightaway.

CHAPTER 12

The room is almost oppressively hot. Elaine clutches a glass of tepid riesling with one hand and tugs at her dress with the other. Why on earth she chose to wear something *lined* she cannot imagine. It's summer, it's humid, and she's in a small room with no air conditioning in a cocktail dress with lining – she has clearly lost her senses. If she perspires any more, her make-up will slide off. She's given up on her hair, which is clinging to her neck and feels like it's plastered to her scalp. So much for hairspray. Before she left England she had it cut short, in the style of the Princess of Wales, because she thought that would be more manageable in a subtropical climate. As it turns out, thick hair at any length isn't comfortable in the subtropics.

'Hello, darling,' says James as he reappears beside her. 'Are you enjoying yourself?'

She feels her eyes form a shape that is en route to a glare and stops herself. She's at this wretched function to support her husband and that's what she's going to do. He doesn't need to know that she's been standing on her own since he left her to chat to some urologist and another fellow with a job title she can't remember. Precisely no one attempted to talk to her in that time, and it only took her about a minute to feel mortified enough to render her incapable of approaching strangers to say hello.

Elaine was brought up to be more socially adept than this – she knows how to talk to people. She can even be charming when she wants to be. However, it seems that all those skills work only in an environment in which she's comfortable. Here, thousands of miles away from it, she's starting to suspect she's a failure.

She isn't even making much headway with her swimming group. Granted, there isn't a lot of conversing to be done when they're all in the water, but she hasn't had much of a chance before or after the swim either. Clearly, she put her foot in it *colossally* when she asked Leanne if she had children. The poor girl looked as if she'd been shot. There must be a reason why, but Elaine may never have the chance to find out if she can't work out how to be less gauche.

'Somewhat,' she says, her voice thin. 'You?'

He looks bemused. 'Only with certain people. Those orthopods are like rugby players with hacksaws – I wouldn't want them coming anywhere near my bones.'

Elaine smiles as if she understands what he's talking about but she's never really known all the different medical disciplines. James does hearts – that's the only thing she's sure of.

'Mr Schaeffer, good to see you,' says a tall, bullocky man as he grasps James's hand and almost wrenches his arm out of its socket.

'Neville, good to see *you*.' James smiles broadly and Elaine marvels at his ability to tolerate certain people. She knows who this Neville is – a colleague of James's who hasn't been very kind to him – yet here is her husband acting as if he's delighted to see him.

'And this is the little woman, eh?' Neville turns his half-lidded gaze and ruby nose her way.

Elaine glances at James and sees him widen his eyes, and knows why: he doesn't want her to make a fuss. So she won't; she'll find a compromise.

'I'm quite tall actually,' she says, smiling as sweetly as she can and throwing in a flutter of her eyelashes for good measure. Over the years she's learnt what that combination, added to her good posture and shapely bosom, can do to a man.

'So you are.' Neville looks her up and down quickly. 'Now, what's this James tells me about you being an *interior decorator*?'

He says it slowly, as if he's talking to a toddler. Accordingly, Elaine wants to kick him in the shins. She stretches her face into a smile so forced she feels her eyes almost disappearing inside it.

'I was. At home. I had a business. I sold it when we were planning to move here but I'm still interested in interiors.'

'A *business*!' Neville's laugh rumbles up from his substantial belly. 'How on earth do you have time for that with James doing what he's doing? My wife certainly doesn't have time for a *business*. I need her to be at home.'

James squeezes her elbow and while she knows it's partly to encourage her to be civil to this uncivilised man, she also knows it's a reassurance. He's reminding her that he's on her side. So she does the only thing she can to keep herself quiet while buying some time to formulate a response: she drinks her glass of wine in one gulp, grimacing at the taste. At room temperature and no doubt out of a cask, it's not her preferred drop.

'Elaine is a woman of many talents,' James says, smiling and wrapping his arm around her waist. 'I could never have managed my working life without her, but it's important that her life isn't all about me.' He peers at Neville over the top of his glasses, one of his grey curls falling onto his forehead. 'I'm sure you'll agree that as much as we like to think we're the centre of the universe, it's not actually true.'

Neville's laugh is louder than before and he claps James on the shoulder so hard that James staggers. 'I like to think it is,' he says, and his face shifts into another, nastier gear. 'And you'd do well to remind your wife who pays the bills.'

Elaine weighs up whether or not to mention that *she* was the one paying the bills while James studied in his specialty, then did all his years of training without much of an income while they had two small children. This is a battle she knows she can never win, however. James's world is full of Nevilles, all convinced of their own importance and blind to the assistance they've had along the way.

For all Elaine knows, James is a Neville himself when she isn't around. But she's never seen it; and before he told her that he wanted to move home to Australia he had never directly asked her to sacrifice anything for him. The sacrifices, such as they were – she knows she was lucky to have the business and to have her parents helping her with the children – were made by her willingly.

'I need another drink,' she says to the air. 'James, would you like one?'

He frowns at her and she remembers the conversation they had in the car: he asked if she'd already had a G&T today, and she lied and said she hadn't. Of course she had – she'd no intention of facing a room full of strangers without some kind of assistance.

'No, I'm fine,' he says with a meaningful look.

She knows he won't tell her not to drink any more – not in front of Neville. So she's in the clear, for now.

'I'll leave you to it. Neville – *enchantée*.' She smiles her sickliest smile, then strides towards the drinks table.

There is the offending cask, but she doesn't care. She wants to anaesthetise herself against this room, so she pours one glass, drinks it quickly and pours another. There's no one to see her – everyone is caught up in their conversations.

She takes her glass and pushes her way through the throng until she finds a doorway. Outside there's the cool breeze she's come to expect of this city in the evenings. She sees a step, and sits on it, and this time drinks her wine slowly, closing her eyes and thinking of her sons.

Henry is tall like her but he looks like James; Marcus isn't quite as tall and resembles no one so much as her grandfather. She did a good job, she thinks, with them. They are kind men. Rational. Patient. Actually, now she thinks about it, those are James's qualities.

She's never had so much time to contemplate her children as she does now, in her absence from them. It wasn't until she and James had been in Australia for a few days that she felt the pain – the intense, jagged pain – of leaving them behind. It feels more acute than any grief she's known. No wonder she wants to dull her senses each afternoon.

Her eyes shoot open as she feels a warm hand on her wrist.

'I've been looking for you, darling,' James says as he slides his hand up her arm and down her side, sitting next to her as he does so.

'Sorry.' She grimaces. 'I'm just not the party girl I used to be.'

'I've noticed,' he says, putting his hand on her thigh and kissing her neck, his way of making sure she knows he's not being critical. 'But I blame Neville. He's a dickhead.'

She gasps out a laugh – James is usually so polite. 'It's not just Neville,' she says.

James's nostrils flare as he inhales. 'I know. Australia is full of dickheads.'

She laughs again, despite a minor flash of irritation that he's deliberately moving her away from the truth.

'I'm sorry,' he says. 'I'm making light of something that's not light.'

Ah, so her irritation has shown on her face. She's never been quite as practised at hiding her feelings as her mother would like her to be.

'It's not your fault,' she says. 'I'm still adjusting to . . . being Australian.'

'Oh darling,' he says, squeezing her thigh, 'I hope you never are. I love you being you, English and all. And I am grateful – in case I haven't said it before – that you're here with me. It was a lot to ask.'

'You stayed in England for me,' she says, smiling as warmly as she can. 'So I'd say we're even.'

She takes a sip from her glass, but the wine is beyond tepid and she makes a face.

'Let's go,' James says. 'I'd rather be home with my beautiful wife than here with Neville.'

He stands and offers her a hand. She takes it, and wishes that her next thought isn't one of regret that she's leaving the wine behind and won't be able to have a drink when she gets home, because James will be watching. And she wants him to watch; she wants him to notice what she does. Mostly, though, she wants distraction. A temporary oblivion. The absence of longing for her sons, for her home, for the person she was when she was there.

But it's not coming tonight, so she holds her husband's hand, and smiles and waves as they exit the party, then rests her head against the car window as he drives them home, past jacarandas in bloom and bushes full of white stars of jasmine, along streets that look like nothing she knows and nowhere she's been, and tries not to wish that everything was different.

CHAPTER 13

When this sandstone cottage was built it was probably the only house within cooee, surrounded by trees and rocks and wildness. Certainly, there aren't a lot of sandstone places in Shelly Bay and their distinctive blond colour marks them as residences from a much earlier time. The sandstone was hewed out in the local area and used to make houses and larger buildings. A century or more later it has proved its durability, the only sign of possible weakness the metal brackets on each side of the cottage that prevent the stone from bulging. Marie has long thought that the potential to bulge suggests that the house is alive, or still part of the earth it came from.

She loves this house, even if it has witnessed her sadnesses over the years: the loss of her baby boy; Nicole's struggles at school when she couldn't make friends and couldn't get good enough marks to satisfy her teachers, and Marie was helpless in the face of her distress. Norm's death. The years since. Not so many sadnesses in the context of a long life – not compared with those of other people she has known – but enough to make the house sometimes feel like it is full of shadows.

She doesn't give in to them, though. One whistle to Charlie Brown so he will hop up on her lap and she knows she can distract herself long enough to prevent her mind going down a dark path.

There's another reason too: Theresa. She has a habit of enlivening every day – not that Marie knows how she can fit in a swim given how much running around she does. The addition of Elaine and Leanne to their little group hasn't diminished her appreciation for Theresa and the light she brings. It's made everything seem more manageable.

Not that Marie would tell Theresa that because it sounds like it's an expectation, that Theresa is responsible for her happiness. Marie knows she's responsible for her own happiness; it's just that Theresa makes it easier to think that each day brings possibilities instead of drudgery.

One morning not long after they started swimming together, as they were drying off afterwards, Theresa talked about going home to the children and Marie said she was only going home to Charlie Brown. It was an offhand remark – or so she thought.

'You've said that before,' Theresa murmured.

'What?'

Theresa's eyes were shiny, as if she was upset. 'You say it almost every day. That there's only Charlie Brown at home.'

Marie shrugged. 'Because it's the truth.'

'I hope . . .' Theresa hesitated, then smiled wistfully. 'I hope you know you're not alone. That you don't have to be alone.'

'But I am,' Marie said quickly.

'You're not!' Theresa's tone was one of defiance. 'You have me!'

In Theresa's eyes Marie saw not a neediness so much as a fervent wish: that Marie would be her friend perhaps. At the time, she wasn't sure what to do with it.

'That's kind,' she said, and Theresa's face crumpled a little. 'I mean,' Marie added quickly, 'you don't have to say that.'

'I know I don't,' Theresa said, then she smiled, and there was such kindness in it that Marie felt as if she was being blessed. 'I just wanted you to know that I like you. That's all.'

It was so simply expressed – the way one child might say it to another – that Marie couldn't believe it was that easy to make a new friend. But it was, because Theresa had made it so.

And Theresa is the reason that Marie has been delaying having the conversation she needs to have with Nicole, about what's to happen with this house. Because of Theresa and their swimming together, Marie has been lulled into thinking that her life might hum along again and she won't have to deal with the problems she knows are there. Rather, the one big problem: money.

She can't wait any longer, however, because it's not going away. Her cupboard is bare, sometimes literally. That's why she's invited Nicole over today, to have a chat about the plan she's formulated. She even said that: 'Let's have a chat.' It's not a phrase she's used before, so Nicole is probably thinking Marie wants to talk about Christmas presents or whether they have hard sauce with the pudding this year. 'Having a chat' sounds benign. What Marie wants to say won't sound benign, though, and it's something Nicole has to manage on her own. If her brother had lived, she wouldn't have to. That was a big reason why Marie had wanted another child: so Nicole would have a friend in childhood; and, in adulthood, someone to work with to manage all the decisions that come with having ageing parents.

After Duncan, Marie and Norm talked about having a third child, although Marie never told him that she wasn't sure if she could bear it. She feared that she'd spend the whole pregnancy worrying about what would happen; she fretted that she'd always think of the new child only as a replacement.

Then the doctors found a growth in Marie's uterus and out it all came. No more babies. Just comments from supposedly well-meaning people who'd ask her when she was going to have another child, or say, 'You only ever wanted the one?' And the guilt – oh, the guilt that still visits her sometimes. She thought the hysterectomy was punishment for losing her son, although his death wasn't anyone's fault. She just couldn't shake the idea that she should have been able to save him.

Now, Marie's one child is watching her own child playing in the garden. Marie's often thought that Nicole is a blessing, and she's never taken her for granted. Which is why she wishes she didn't have to create a burden of decision for her.

'Jessie, darling, don't do that,' Nicole says as she waves a finger at her six-year-old daughter, who is attempting to pin down a little skink.

'But he wriggles!' Jessie looks delighted as she keeps trying to grab the lizard.

'That's because he doesn't want to be caught.' Nicole gives Jessie a warning look.

Marie smiles, a little sadly, to hear her own firm parenting tone coming out of Nicole's mouth. Was she really so strict? She knows she was a cautious parent. She'd thought that caution came with parenting, or you weren't really doing a proper job.

'Tea ready, Mum?' Nicole asks, smiling at Marie.

'Should be.' Marie lifts the lid on the pot and glances in. 'It's had a few minutes to steep.'

'Jessie, do *not* pull up that plant.' Nicole is waving a finger again.

'It's all right, love,' Marie says. She knows how hard it is for little people to keep their hands to themselves.

'I'm trying to teach her to be careful, Mum. Since it seems to be too late for Toby.'

Nicole smiles at Marie, and a lifetime of their own exchanges is in her eyes: all the times Marie told her to be careful because she wanted to protect her. Because she didn't want to lose her.

'What are Toby and his father up to?' Marie asks.

'Playing cricket at the local park. If we're lucky Toby won't break anything this time.'

Nicole makes a *what am I going to do with him?* face. Toby has always been an active child, and there's nothing malicious about his propensity to damage property and himself – it just seems to happen.

'He's a good kid,' Marie says.

'Most of the time.' Nicole reaches over to pour the tea. 'So you wanted to have a chat?'

'Mm-hm.' Marie takes her cup, which has just the right amount of milk in it. Nicole has always been precise. She thinks about how to start the conversation, as if she hasn't been thinking about it for weeks now.

Nicole suddenly looks stricken. 'Are you sick?' she says, her voice tight.

'No,' Marie says quickly, feeling foolish for not thinking her daughter might leap to that conclusion. 'It's not that.'

'Oh.' Nicole's face relaxes.

'It's the house.'

'Has that bloke from up the road been pressuring you to sell again?' Nicole looks amused.

Dimitri, the man's name is, and for the last couple of years he's stopped by every now and again to see if Marie is interested in selling. His wife loves the house, he says, and he'd like to buy it for her. Marie's always said it's not for sale, which has been the truth. Although in her current predicament it's starting to look like an easy, if distressing, solution.

'Not lately,' she says, attempting a smile. 'But I . . .' She swallows. Last night she tried to convince herself that something that scares you is less scary when you actually do it. In practice, this is not proving to be the case. 'I think I need to sell anyway,' she says in a rush.

Nicole stares at her, only stopping when Jessie lets out a cry. 'I got him!' she says, holding up the skink.

'Jessie, put him down,' Nicole instructs, met by a pout from her daughter. Then she turns back to Marie. 'Why, Mum?'

'It's too expensive to run. The work . . .' Marie throws her hands in the air and is surprised to feel tears in her eyes.

This discussion was meant to be calm and considered. She doesn't want to get emotional in front of Nicole, because that will set off a loop of concern: she'll be upset that Nicole is upset, and Nicole will be upset because Marie's upset, and so on. It's a loop she's been caught in before, and she has to be the one to break it because she's the parent, even if the roles are reversed sometimes. That seems to happen with mothers and daughters. Gwen's daughter took to mothering her as soon as the first grandchild arrived. It's as if once their daughters have children they find it easier to mother everyone instead of differentiating between age groups.

'Mum,' Nicole says, her voice warm with concern, 'it's okay. Don't get upset. I'm sure you don't need to do something as drastic as sell.'

'The front path is cracked. That needs fixing,' Marie says, embarking on the list she's been keeping in her head. 'The roof leaks over the bedroom whenever it rains. That shed,' she points to the contraption Norm built when Nicole was a child, 'is about to fall over so I either need to tear it down or fix it. But I can't . . .' Her voice catches. 'I can't afford to do that. So I've got a ramshackle old thing in my garden and it's ugly.'

'It was always ugly,' Nicole says wryly.

'I know! But . . .' Marie swallows her emotion. 'My point is that this house will continue to fall apart if I can't afford to stop it. And the pension doesn't cover home repairs. I can barely afford to buy new underwear.'

'That can't be true!' Nicole says, looking incredulous.

'There are council rates,' Marie goes on, 'quite apart from the other bills. It adds up. I don't have any savings.'

She stops, believing she's made her point, and from the look on Nicole's face, she's right.

'I had no idea,' Nicole says, looking to the garden. 'Jessie! Do *not* pull up Granny's plants!'

Marie sees her granddaughter with a primula clutched in one hand and wants to tell Nicole, again, to go easy. But she won't be able to buy plants to replace anything Jessie pulls up, so perhaps she should be a little more firm.

'Just put it there, Jessie,' she calls. 'I'll plant it again later.'

'Sorry,' Nicole mutters. 'She's never like this at home.'

'The garden will survive,' Marie says reassuringly.

'Don't sell.' Nicole sounds fervent now. 'Please. I know you love this house. *I* love this house. And it's your home.' She pauses and looks thoughtful. 'Let me talk to Pete and see if we can't help you out with the rates and the jobs that need doing. I also think you could use a hand taking care of the garden.' She raises her eyebrows.

'It's a bit messy, isn't it?' Marie says. Nicole's own garden looks like a mini Chelsea Flower Show, with topiary and all sorts of plants that are improbable in a subtropical Australian suburb.

Nicole looks sheepish. 'A bit.'

'I don't want you to pay for so much, though,' Marie says, and she means it. That's a lot of money for her son-in-law to come up with.

'Mum, just let us help. You took care of me – isn't it time I took care of you?'

Marie sighs. 'I didn't realise I'm so old I need taking care of.'

'Oh *gawd*.' Nicole looks momentarily exasperated. 'Stop being pathetic. We're not putting you out to pasture. Just paying some bills.'

Marie feels gratitude, and also embarrassment that it's come to this, yet she's in no position to refuse – unless she wants to leave the place that has been her home since she was born.

'Thank you,' she says, and relief melts the tension in her neck and shoulders, down her torso and all the way to her toes.

'I just wish you'd told me sooner,' Nicole chastises, 'instead of getting your knickers in a knot about it. If anything like this comes up again, *please*,' she grabs Marie's hand, 'say something.'

Marie nods and leans over to kiss her daughter on the cheek. Then they sit back, hands still connected, and watch Jessie rub dirt on her face.

CHAPTER 14

laine has grown to love Shelly Bay's tough little trees, kept small and made hardy by the buffeting coastal winds. She's even grown used to their leaves, which have a strange hue of emeralds that have been left too long in the sun. The native bushes and their almost aggressive-looking flowers are charming in their way, although she misses the abundance to be found in English gardens. All that rain – she had no idea how much of a difference it made until she moved to Australia and learnt that torrential downpours every now and again don't have the same effect on plant life as the steady drizzle of home. Despite that, there are gardeners in Shelly Bay who make the most of the conditions and produce lovely, ordered plots that offer some relief from the tangled mysteries of the bush at the water's edge.

However, Elaine hasn't ventured much past Shelly Bay; she hasn't really had reason to. James's parents live in a country town to the south-west, but they always come to the city to see him because James isn't able to take enough time off work to make a visit worthwhile. Three hours in the car means you want to stay overnight before driving home, and he's had so many commitments that it hasn't been feasible.

Yet as Christmas is approaching and his parents are planning to spend the day with James's sister and her family on a property even further west, James decided that this weekend they should make the effort.

Elaine relished her swim this morning, knowing there wouldn't be another until Monday. She'll miss it; she's started to look forward to seeing the other women almost as much as she anticipates the thrill of diving under the first wave of the day. As someone who has never experienced the surf before, she's surprised by how much she likes it.

'Penny for your thoughts?' James's voice brings her mind back to the car.

'They're worth considerably more than that!'

'I'm sure they are,' he says. 'But I'd still like to know what you're thinking about.'

'If I said I was wondering if turkey takes less time to cook in a warm climate, would you believe me?'

It's not too far from the realm of probability: this year will be the first time Elaine has been responsible for a Christmas feast, ever. Her mother has always been the cook, with more time to spend planning and shopping and creating. Elaine would work up until Christmas Eve and arrive at her parents' house on Christmas morning limp and exhausted, with two excited children and a similarly exhausted, overworked husband. She thought that would never change, so never learnt how to do all the things her mother makes look effortless.

'No, darling, I would not,' James says. 'But I would like to note, for the record, that I don't expect you to cook a turkey. We don't need to replicate your parents' lunch. The boys won't be with us, so . . .'

As he stops, Elaine bites her lip and looks out the window. They are passing land that is yellow and brown and khaki.

In the distance there's a brighter green rectangle, but it looks like a misplaced patch on a sad quilt. It doesn't belong. And neither does she. Her children are in another hemisphere and James is right: without them, there's no need to have an elaborate Christmas. Except that's the main reason she wants to do it – she will feel closer to them if she has the same kind of experience they'll be having with her parents. Or maybe it's because she feels guilty she won't be there with them.

'We should have gone back,' James says gently.

'We decided it was impossible.'

'*You* decided it was impossible,' he replies, his voice still mild. 'I would have found the time.'

But she'd known when they spoke of it, when she thought about it, that going home would mean she would never want to leave again. To travel all that way for a week – and that's all it would have been – then return to this alien place with its humidity and flies and hailstorms, with its vast distances that mean that in the time it takes them to reach James's parents, she could drive from her own parents' home to Scotland . . . She couldn't do it. They had to stay put.

'It's done now,' she murmurs.

She loses track of the kilometres as they pass caravans and horse floats, and signs that display names of places she's never heard of, and some she has because they're replicas of place names she grew up with: the transplantation of Britishness to this decidedly un-British place.

It's only when the car comes to a halt that she realises she either dozed off or was in a trance, for she's jolted back to the present as James hops out of the car and opens a gate.

'Not much further now,' he says with a grin as he gets back into the car, puts a hand to her cheek and kisses her strongly, lingeringly. 'I know this isn't your ideal way to spend a weekend. Thank you for coming with me. Mum and Dad are really pleased you'll be here.'

He looks into her eyes and she realises something that hasn't occurred to her before: she made a choice to be with her husband, to leave her children to the lives they had already established, because she made a commitment to him many years ago, as he did to her. These past few months she's been thinking about what she's lost – wallowing in it, actually – without stopping to consider what she still has. She is still married. She is still loved. And she loves in return.

'My ideal way to spend a weekend,' she says softly, 'is to be with you.'

He looks surprised for a second, then he kisses the tip of her nose and puts the car into first gear.

As his parents' house appears at the end of a driveway so long that it's almost a road, Elaine is taken aback as she sees that it's not as big as the surrounding land suggests. All those hectares yet their home is about the size of her own cottage in Shelly Bay. Rather, James's cottage. Having grown up on the land, when he moved to the city as an adult to study and work he fell in love with Shelly Bay and the water all around. He bought the white weatherboard-and-brick cottage not long before he moved to England, thinking he'd be gone for only a year or two. As his life took root overseas he put tenants in, and luckily they took care of the place, keeping its gardens neat and its neighbours onside. There is space enough for two of them now, Elaine thinks, but it's just as well they didn't try to raise children in it: the boys would have outgrown it before they reached their teens. Still, it's large enough to feel empty when she's home alone for hours.

'Hello, love,' James's mother calls as she opens the front door onto the verandah.

'Hi, Mum,' he says, enfolding her in a hug and raising one hand to greet his father as he appears around the side of the house.

'Elaine, love.' His mother offers a twinkly smile and a kiss on the cheek. 'Come in. Good to see you. How was the drive?'

'It was fine, thank you, Amy – interesting. There's so much land between here and the city.'

'Too right,' James's father, Tom, says, kissing her hello. 'How else do you think we keep you city slickers at a distance?' He winks. 'Here – let me.' He opens his hand towards James, who gives him one of their bags.

'I know it's probably early for a drink,' says Amy, 'but I know you like a G&T, Elaine, so we're all set up. It's after midday, so we're in the clear, I reckon!'

Elaine meets James's eyes and sees the suggestion of concern. She hasn't thought about having a drink once today, and that's an achievement – even though it's entirely due to the fact that she's been distracted thinking about all the people and places she's missing. That's not a long-term solution, though: she can't make herself miserable in order to stop drinking.

'Thank you, Amy,' she says. 'I can wait a while.'

James is still looking at her and now she can't read his expression. She doesn't want to worry him; she doesn't want to worry herself. Yet if his mother has noticed how much she drinks, they're probably past the point of worry and tipping over into a problem.

'Suit yourself,' says Amy. 'Anyway, let's get you inside and unpacked, then we can have a nice chat.'

Elaine follows them towards the house, through dirt that clings to the white sandals she's foolishly worn. It infiltrates the spaces between her toes and under the soles of her feet, and she knows that her carefully chosen outfit is going to wilt in the heat of this place. For a second or two she lets herself feel wretched. This country is not hers, and she doesn't understand it. She's not sure she ever will.

'Darling?' James calls, and that's how she knows she's been dragging her feet, probably literally.

'Yes,' she says wearily, and lets him take her hand to lead her up the stairs and into the house.

CHAPTER 15

'Andrew, can you get the phone, please?'

Theresa has her hands in a rissole mixture as she hears the *tring-tring* continue.

'*Andrew!*'

With no response, she uses her least-sticky hand to pick up the receiver in the living room and hears her father on the end of the line.

'Hi, Dad,' she says and tries to keep her voice light even though her parents know this is the worst time of day to call: Theresa is making dinner, the children are always running amok because she can't watch them at the same time and Andrew can never seem to manage it either, while Nonna observes the whole thing. Theresa just knows her grandmother thinks it should all be better managed. That in her day the children wouldn't be unsupervised while Mamma worked in the kitchen. Well, in Nonna's day there were grandparents around to help – all those generations living in the one house – but Theresa's parents decided to move away when Oliver was born, so she has no help. Not from them, not from Andrew, and not from Nonna either for that matter, although she doesn't expect that. An elderly woman should be allowed to be elderly, even if she wants to use her time to drink Italian aperitifs and smoke the strongest cigarettes she can find.

'Are you busy?' her father says, sounding tense, and again Theresa has to restrain herself, because when is she not busy?

'No, it's fine,' is what she says instead.

'I need you to come here for a few days,' he says, and that's when Theresa realises the trap she's walked into. The question about her being busy didn't refer to *right now*. It was a bigger question about life. So her answer should have been 'yes'.

'What for, Dad?'

'Your mother's hurt her back.'

Theresa pauses. Her mother's back has been a problem off and on for years. Normally she goes to the doctor for some painkillers, then takes to her bed for a day or so and that tends to set her right for a while. Theresa isn't sure why that means she has to go to their place.

'I'm sorry to hear that,' she says. 'But I can't fix it for her.'

'Not that,' her father says with irritation. 'You need to come and do the housework and cooking. I can't manage it.'

'Dad, you've been fine in the past. And you know it will only be for a day or two.' She's trying to keep her voice even as she thinks of the mince going brown in the kitchen and the time elapsing before her ravenous children start complaining they want dinner.

'My knee's playing up,' he says. 'I can't do everything.'

Theresa takes a deep breath, her training to be a good daughter warring with her instinct to tell him to grow up and take care of himself. He's almost seventy years old and he's acting as if he's Oliver's age. But she has to take that back, because Ollie knows how to switch on a vacuum cleaner and use the washing machine. She's shown him because he's interested.

'Dad, your knee won't stop you cooking,' she says slowly.

'What about the rest of it?' he sputters.

'Mario lives five kilometres away from you – ask him!'

Her oldest brother followed her parents up the coast, and she knows he has the time to help them because he doesn't lift a finger to help his own wife with the kids and the house, and he's always boasting about how little time he has to spend at his business because he has staff to run the place for him.

Her father makes a sound that could be disgust, but it's hard to tell over the phone. 'He has enough to do. I can't bother him.'

'Dad!' Theresa says, exasperated. '*I* have enough to do!'

'It's your duty to help your parents,' he counters.

'And it's not Mario's?'

'He has his own family to worry about.'

'What about *my* family, Dad? Who's going to look after my house and kids?'

'Theresa, it is your duty. You must come.'

The buzz in her ear tells her that he's hung up on her. The other sound she can hear is rage bubbling inside her. She knows her mother will have listened to the whole conversation and likely condoned it, because she would rather have her daughter turn up to run everything than her husband attempting to do it. Theresa was always the one to take over when her mother needed help, and not just when she had a bad back. When Nonno was still alive, and Nonna asked for a hand with something, her mother would go and it was simply assumed that Theresa would do whatever was needed at home. Well, now she has Nonna and her own children, *and* she lives two hours' drive away, so she doesn't see how it's reasonable that she's the one who has to drop everything.

That won't get her out of it, though, so she's at least going to have to go through the motions of telling Andrew.

She puts the receiver back in the cradle and closes her eyes, remembering how happy she was, oh, only twelve hours ago. She was catching up to Elaine as they rounded the point on the way back to Main Beach. Finally, Theresa is getting faster. Even though she didn't quite catch Elaine, she wasn't far behind by the time they reached the beach, and the others were happy for her. There was laughter, and Marie pinched her cheek and told her she was a 'little champion'. Theresa achieved something, and she has a goal to work towards. Not like here, at home, where everything runs on an eternal loop and she never gets ahead but it certainly feels like she could fall behind.

'What's goin' on?'

She opens her eyes to see Andrew standing in front of her wearing a clean shirt and his newest jeans. Half an hour ago he arrived home in his dirty work clothes and headed out to the garden to see the kids.

'Why are you wearing that?' she asks.

'I'm goin' out.'

Theresa holds back the heavy sigh that wants to escape from her chest. 'Where to?'

'Just out.'

She looks at his shirt again. 'Who are you going out with?'

'Why don't you stop askin' me so many questions?' he snarls.

'Because I'm making dinner for us all and you're going out. Again.' This time the sigh can't be held in, and brings with it tears that hover inside her lower lids. 'Don't you want to spend time with your children?'

'I've already spent time with them,' he says dismissively. 'Besides, they've got you.' His lips press together and his eyes go dark. 'And that's who they really want, isn't it?'

'Don't be silly,' she says, trying to keep her voice light although she knows what he says is true. But it's only true because he's never here any more, so the children are getting used to him not being around.

'They love you,' she adds.

He looks sceptical and turns away.

'I need to talk to you about something,' she says quickly.

'What?' He sounds irritated.

'Dad needs me to stay with him and Mum for a few days.'

'Why?'

'Mum's hurt her back. He wants some help around the house.'

'Why does he need you? He can bloody do it himself!'

Theresa almost smiles at this. Andrew, who has never done a skerrick of housework in his life, is judging her father for being the same.

'Well, he can't,' she says. 'He's insisting.'

'And who's meant to look after *this* house? What about the kids?'

'School's almost over for the year – I could take them out early and we could stay up there for a few days.'

'And what am I meant to do?' He sounds pathetic but Theresa's sure he doesn't realise it.

'You're never here anyway,' she says slowly. Deliberately. She wants him to appreciate the impact of what he's been doing lately.

His eyes flicker and she can tell he's trying to come up with a different argument.

'So you're goin' to leave me here with your nonna?' he says.

'She can manage. Although I'll need you to take her to her poker games.'

'Fucked if I'm goin' to do that.' Andrew squares his shoulders, as if he's ready for a fight.

Theresa pauses. She doesn't really want to go to her parents' house but feels the obligation to do so. There's also a part of her that wants to make Andrew take care of himself for a few days. And another part that knows she'll have several days without a swim, without seeing the others. The one part of her day that gives her space, the part she needs to cope with all the rest, will be taken away.

A noise at the back door makes them both turn their heads.

'I can *hear you*,' Nonna says as she steps inside the kitchen, her eyes narrowing.

'Sorry, Nonna,' Theresa says, embarrassed.

Nonna turns a steely gaze on Andrew. 'And the children can hear you.'

Theresa wants to melt into the floor. She thought the children were down the bottom of the garden, where they usually play.

'You're not goin',' Andrew says. 'I'm not goin' to live in a dump just because your mother can't be bothered lookin' after her own house. Sort it out with your father.'

Without giving either of them a chance to respond he picks up his car keys and slams the front door behind him.

Theresa and Nonna stand looking at each other. Outside, Sasha and Oliver have gone back to their noisy playing.

'The men always want control, *mia* Theresa,' Nonna says, putting one hand on the kitchen bench. 'You cannot let them have it. You have to be smarter. You have to control first.'

'That's just not me, Nonna,' Theresa says sadly. Besides, she thinks, the time for controlling Andrew is long past.

'That's because my daughter did not show you how.' Nonna throws her other hand in the air. 'That father of yours, she lets him be in charge. *Stupido!* I did not bring her up like this.'

'I'm sorry,' Theresa says. 'I didn't mean for you to hear that. I don't know what to do with him any more.'

Nonna grabs both of Theresa's arms with the same strong

hands that used to play piano for hours when they were all younger. Much, much younger.

'You *take control*, Theresa,' she says hoarsely, then lets her go. 'That is all I am going to say.'

As she turns to leave she gives what looks like a dismissive wave – the same wave she'd use when Theresa was a child and had done something naughty.

Back then, the punishment was scales on the piano for half an hour. It took Theresa a few years to realise that the punishment was actually an education and it made her a better pianist. She hasn't played for years though. Andrew wouldn't let her have a piano. It took up too much space, he said, and he wanted a big couch.

'Dinner's in half an hour,' she calls limply.

Theresa hears the strike of a match.

The smell of cigarette smoke wafts in the back door as she wets her hands and goes back to making rissoles.

CHAPTER 16

Marie tries to keep her face in a neutral expression as she removes her T-shirt, but Theresa spots the truth straightaway.

'What's wrong?' she asks, her eyes wide.

'Nothing,' Marie says, hiding her wince behind the garment as she struggles to get it over her head.

'*Marie.*'

'I've hurt my shoulder,' she confesses, huffing as she drops the T-shirt on the sand. 'I was pulling out weeds. I was . . . a little too enthusiastic.'

She remembers the exact moment the muscle in her shoulder told her that she'd done the wrong thing. Charlie Brown was the only one there to hear her cry out, but she still felt like a fool as she fell out of her crouch and onto the garden bed.

'I thought Nicole was organising someone to help with that?' Theresa says as she waves to Elaine further up the beach.

'He can't start until the new year,' Marie says, frowning. 'Who knew that gardeners are so in demand?'

'I can help,' Leanne pipes up, and Marie swivels to face her. The girl is so quiet a person can almost forget she's around.

'If you need some weeding done,' Leanne adds quickly, then turns away to pick up her cap and goggles. 'I live near you.'

'Do you?' Marie can't recall them ever discussing where they live – and she would, because she hasn't had many conversations with Leanne at all.

'You're in the sandstone cottage near Livingstone Road?'

'Yes.' Marie can't remember mentioning it, but she must have. Or perhaps Theresa told Leanne.

'I'm at the other end – the harbour side. Just around the corner on Elliott.' Leanne gives a quick smile then looks away again.

Honestly, it's harder to hold that girl's attention than it is to get a cat to like you. Which is why Marie's never had cats: they're too standoffish. She glances at Theresa, who looks fascinated by the exchange. As she would be, because it's the most Leanne has ever said in a morning.

'Well, it's kind of you to offer,' Marie says, 'but I think I'll wait for the gardener now.'

Leanne looks briefly crestfallen and Marie wonders if there was another motive for her willingness to weed.

'Good morning, ladies,' says Elaine, striding towards them.

Marie envies those long legs: Elaine makes walking on soft sand look no more difficult than a ship sailing on a calm sea.

'Marie's hurt her shoulder,' Theresa announces.

'I see.' Elaine's eyebrows lift. 'So this is my chance to lead the pack. At last.' She smiles mischievously.

To date Marie hasn't had an ego about the swimming, but now she feels a ping of umbrage that tells her that's only because she's always been in the lead. She's not keen on the idea of being slow. It reminds her too much of getting old. If she's out in front she's still not old – or that's her rationale, at least. And, just maybe, she likes to win. Small victories are the only ones she's ever had.

'Indeed,' she says. 'But don't get too used to it.'

'Actually . . .' Elaine says, drawing it out in that cut-glass accent: *Acc-tuu-a-llyyy.* 'I think we should all swim breaststroke. That's fair.' She smiles at Marie. 'It's easier on shoulders than freestyle.'

'Oh no,' Marie says, wishing she'd been better at hiding her impediment from Theresa. 'I'll just go slowly.'

'I like breaststroke!' Theresa says brightly.

Leanne looks almost relieved. 'I like it too.'

'So we'll swim together, then?' Elaine says. 'How convivial.'

'Morning, ladies. Long time no see.'

Marie sighs as she sees Trevor King on the approach. 'We've been here, Trev. You must have been slacking off.'

'Did me back, didn't I?' he says, putting a hand to his side.

'Oh, that's right,' Marie says drily. 'I remember you being in pain the day we pulled that girl out of the water.'

Trev shakes his head. 'Geez, it's been bad. Couldn't get out of bed. Couldn't even get a beer!' He laughs as if this is the funniest sentence imaginable, then turns his gaze Leanne's way. 'Hel-lo. You've got a new one.'

'This is Leanne,' Theresa says. 'She's a nurse at the hospital.'

'Where you from?' Trev asks.

'I live on the other side of the hill,' Leanne replies, her voice even.

The look on his face suggests that he thinks she's an idiot. '*No,*' he says, shaking his head. 'Are you one of those boat people or something?'

Leanne's face doesn't move, and Marie wonders how many times she's heard this over the years. None of them has asked Leanne about her background – Australia has people from all over, and Leanne's accent is as Australian as they come, so as far as Marie's concerned she's Australian.

Heat erupts on the younger woman's cheeks and Marie

can't stand the fact that stupid old Trev King has made Leanne feel embarrassed.

'What on earth do you think you're talking about, Trevor?' she snaps.

'You know,' he says, gesturing towards Leanne.

'No, I don't know. Do you know, Theresa?'

'No.' There's a fierce look on Theresa's face that Marie has never seen before.

'How about you, Elaine?'

Elaine's chin goes up and her shoulders back. 'Not a clue,' she says.

Marie turns a dazzling smile on Trevor. 'Sorry, we have no idea what you mean, and we're sure Leanne doesn't either.'

Trevor's frowning as he looks from one to the other, but not at Leanne. 'Oh,' he says and seems to shrink a little.

Marie keeps smiling. 'Off you go. We're late for our swim.'

He again looks at each of them, but this time he glances at Leanne too, with confusion. 'Right,' he says, then turns and shuffles away.

'Dickhead,' mutters Marie.

'Sorry about that,' says Theresa.

Leanne shakes her head. 'It's not your fault. And it's not as if I haven't heard it before.'

'I'm still sorry,' Theresa says.

Marie nods ahead of them. 'Come on, let's leave him behind and get in the water.'

'This will be fun!' Theresa says in Leanne's direction, a little too eagerly.

Marie has to admit to herself that breaststroke will be a lot easier. Her shoulder isn't ruined, just sore. By tomorrow she should be back to normal and back to freestyle, but it will do her good to make an adjustment today.

The water has lost some of its bite, she notices as she submerges up to her shoulders. Not only is it warmer than it was yesterday but the swell is almost non-existent, meaning they can breaststroke their way out.

'Thank you, Elaine,' she says as she draws alongside. 'This was a good idea.'

'I have them occasionally,' Elaine says, but she doesn't sound convincing.

'I didn't ask you how your trip to the bush went,' Marie adds, keeping pace with Elaine's graceful strokes.

Elaine sniffs. 'It was all right.'

'Oh?' In Marie's book, 'all right' doesn't mean 'good'. But because she can't see Elaine's eyes behind the goggles she has no idea what she's really thinking.

'James's parents are lovely,' Elaine goes on, her voice firmer. 'But I . . . the countryside – it's so . . . drab.'

Marie wants to disagree – to say that Australia is beautiful all over – yet to an Englishwoman she knows it wouldn't be. No point being patriotic if it's only going to make someone else feel bad.

'Sorry,' Elaine adds. 'That sounds mean.'

'It's brown,' Marie says. 'There's no getting away from that.'

'And there's a lot of it!' says Theresa. She's drawn level with Elaine's other side, while Leanne is next to Marie. 'The first time my parents took us to that part of the state there was so much brown I thought there'd been a fire.'

'There probably had been,' Marie says. 'Or a drought.' Her shoulder pinches a little and she reduces the amount she extends her arm when she strokes. She glances at Elaine. 'It must make you homesick. Not at all what you're used to, eh?'

Elaine shakes her head and appears to swallow some water, coughing before she answers. 'I kept thinking about my parents' place in Kent. Of course, that led me to think about them. And my sons, spending time with them while I'm here, not spending time with any of them.' She exhales loudly through her mouth, as if in distress.

'It's hard when you miss people,' Marie says. 'How about we stop here and tread water for a bit? It's a beautiful morning. Let's take it in.'

Elaine frowns, as if Marie is suggesting a punishment, but Marie's motives are pure: she thinks Elaine may become even more upset and swallow more water, which won't improve her morning. They form a little circle off the point, in the spot where the water is shallowest near the rocks. Without waves this morning, they're not likely to be swept against those rocks. Usually they have to be careful not to get so near.

'There's a few people I miss,' Marie says. 'My husband, obviously, and I can't do anything about that. But my friend Gwen – she moved a few suburbs away and I miss her, but I just haven't gone to visit her. I can't work out why.'

'Maybe you're having so much fun with us you don't miss her like you used to,' Theresa says.

It's a good point. Marie thinks of Gwen but she doesn't miss her as much as she did a few weeks ago. There's now a new emotion: guilt.

'Perhaps,' she says. 'You *are* very entertaining.'

Theresa looks pleased.

'But that's no excuse for me to let the relationship go,' Marie continues. 'I've been slack. So I'm going to visit her soon.'

'You're good,' Theresa says. 'I was meant to go and visit my parents – well, Dad asked me to go there for a few days and help. I said no.'

'As you should have,' says Marie. 'You have a lot of responsibilities here. Too many, I'm prone to think.'

Now Theresa is the one to show guilt. 'I'm a bad daughter,' she says.

'You!' Elaine bursts out. '*I'm* the daughter who lives half a world away from her parents.'

'But you'd visit if you could,' Theresa says, sounding miserable. Or perhaps self-pitying, although Marie doesn't think that's her style.

'If they lived nearby, probably not,' Elaine says. 'I'd be wrapped up in my own life, as I used to be.'

'What about you, Leanne?' Marie asks. 'Are your parents close by?'

Out of the corner of her eye she sees Theresa shaking her head vigorously.

'Um . . .' Leanne says, and her mouth disappears under the water. She bobs up. 'Yes.'

Marie glances at Theresa, whose eyes are now wide with what looks like alarm. She presumes that Theresa – being Theresa – has already tried to get information out of Leanne about her family and perhaps been unfruitful. That's no reason, however, for Marie not to try.

'Do you see them often?' she asks.

'No,' Leanne says, swimming a little more towards Elaine and away from Marie. Perhaps, Marie thinks, so she doesn't have to look at her.

There's clearly a story there. Leanne strikes her as a fairly solitary person and she wants to know why, because she's too young to be alone for the reasons Marie is.

'May I ask why not?' she says.

Leanne treads water, looking up at the sky. 'They don't want to see me,' she says, still gazing up.

'That can't be right,' Marie says quickly. 'You're a lovely girl.'

Leanne drops her head, but with the goggles hiding her eyes Marie doesn't know what's going on. 'Maybe I'm not as lovely as you think,' she says, her voice tight.

'Of course you are!' Theresa says. 'You're wonderful with the children.'

Leanne says nothing.

Elaine's head swivels from Leanne to Marie and back again. 'I think I need to keep swimming,' she says. 'Shall we move on?'

And Marie notes that her lovely manners have probably salvaged an awkward situation.

Leanne moves away and kicks herself into a freestyle action, leaving them behind.

'Oh,' Theresa says, 'she's going on ahead. Marie, you can't . . .' Her forehead wrinkles.

'Let her go,' Marie says. 'I pushed too much. I've upset her.'

'Don't worry, I've done it too,' Theresa says. 'It can be hard to know when you're past the point of just being friendly.'

'I'd say she has burdens we can only guess at,' Elaine says, moving slightly ahead of them. 'But I'll keep her company, if you don't mind?'

Marie nods. Her legs make their frog kick, and she and Theresa carry on in silence.

CHAPTER 17

'Good morning, Leanne.'

'Good morning, Dr Jacobs.' Leanne nods at the paediatrician as he strides past her station. She watches as he disappears inside Matron's office, then lets her shoulders drop. Whenever there's a doctor around she feels like she's on guard – like she'll be told she's doing the wrong thing.

She's had a lifelong fear of doing the wrong thing, which can't be traced back to her upbringing because her brothers did plenty of wrong things before she came along, and afterwards, so she knew it was possible to do the wrong thing and survive. There was no incident that made her this way; her parents never imposed the belief on her directly. Yet she has screeds of memories of desperately wanting to be the best-behaved student, of wishing her brothers wouldn't misbehave, of trying to teach her younger sister to be good.

It hasn't escaped her attention that what brought her life undone was a monumental exercise in someone else not doing the right thing, to her, and she took the only course of action she thought could set it right. She knew she might pay for it forever. But it was what she had to do. Years of hearing her mother issue judgements about 'bad girls' – girls who had found themselves in similar situations to her – told her what was necessary.

Now it's easier to be alert to other possible missteps and never put herself in a position for them to happen.

'Sister?' Matron calls from the hallway.

Leanne scurries towards her.

'We have a new patient arriving today,' Matron says. 'Dr Jacobs has just told me she's to be transferred from the Children's Hospital.'

Leanne frowns: it's unusual for a child to come *from* that hospital, the only dedicated hospital for children in the city.

'She's from this area,' Matron explains, 'and her parents want her to be closer to home. She has kidney disease. They're keeping her in while they work out the best course of treatment.'

'Okay,' is all Leanne can say. She isn't sure why she's being given a briefing now when everything she needs to know will arrive with the patient.

'She needs to be specialled,' Matron says impatiently, as if Leanne is being deliberately dense. 'We'll be looking after her as normal during the day, but the parents want someone with her at night. I'd rather it be someone already on staff.'

The request is unusual – most parents don't even know they can hire a nurse to look after their child alone within a public institution. Leanne has never done it before; she's never been asked. She's not even sure she's being asked now.

'So do you . . . want me to organise someone?' she says.

'No, Leanne, I want you to do it. If you have time. The parents have asked for you.'

Leanne is taken aback – how would anyone know to request her specifically? Children come in and out of here with regularity but no pattern; some of them leave alive and some of them don't. She is professional at all times, but would be hard-pressed to remember the names of the children's parents. Although she always remembers the children.

'How could they – I mean, why?'

'You nursed the eldest child two years ago. Brain tumour.' Matron looks at the file in her hands. 'Daphne Sullivan.'

Leanne recalls a pale child with green eyes and mousey-brown hair and a smile that transformed her face, although they saw it rarely. She never made it home. Leanne also remembers a younger sister, Imogen, and the pang that came when the little girl told her – with the pride children have when they announce their age – that she was born in July 1976. She was the same age as Leanne's baby. The baby who is the reason Leanne is isolated from the people she loves, the family she grew up in, the brothers and sister who were her best friends and who she's left behind. She has spent the last seven years constructing battlements, and for good reason: to keep out the memories that could destroy her.

Except that on the nights when she has trouble sleeping it is always because of the one memory that resists all her attempts to keep it out.

'How could you let him do this to you?' her mother says to her in this memory, over and over. 'How could you let him touch you? Put his filthy hands on you? Who else have you allowed to do this?'

It's a question Leanne won't answer because she knows that any number she gives – even one – is wrong, and 'no one' will not be believed.

In this memory she feels her father's palm hitting her cheek. The sensation is a different pain to twisting an ankle or grazing your shin. Those pains tell you that something is going wrong and it needs to stop. But the pain in her cheek is the pain of letting down the people she loves, even though she hasn't done anything wrong – not in her own eyes. She didn't want that man – her oldest brother's friend, someone she trusted – to put those filthy hands on her. She didn't want anyone to find out.

'I didn't allow anything,' she says softly, hoping her parents believe her.

Her mother's eyes show flint and outrage. 'And how are we meant to believe that?'

'Because I'm telling you.'

But Leanne knows that the truth – her truth – isn't going to be enough of a defence and she can feel her life not so much shattering as disintegrating. The structure that has held it together since her birth has become dust, and she will never be able to rebuild what she has always known.

'That's not what we heard,' her father says, so angry that his face has become ugly, and he has never been ugly.

'But I'm the one involved, and I'm the one telling you,' Leanne says as firmly as she can muster. She may be alone in this confrontation with her parents, but years of having older brothers have taught her how to stand up for herself. 'No one else knows.'

'Apart from *him*,' says her mother, and Leanne can see her lip trembling.

Each time, in that memory, she sees her mother's lip trembling – except Leanne doesn't know if it's because her mother is worried for her or disgusted by her.

She and her mother have never been close the way some mothers and daughters are, but their relationship has been harmonious. Leanne would like to think that her mother has only concern for her, but she knows she's also concerned about what other people think, and will be worrying about that now. Because they found out from someone else that Leanne is pregnant. Because Leanne trusted one of her brothers with the information and he betrayed her. And Leanne knows that as much as her mother is horrified about the pregnancy, she's also aware that her son didn't keep this most private of secrets. So he'll probably have told other people. Told them a portion of the story but not the full story, because only Leanne knows that. Only Leanne and the man who did it to her.

When she replays the memory, Leanne tries not to go further. She tries not to remember the calculations she ran through that day. The decision she made, in the middle of all that upset, to leave and never go back. No – it's easier to cut off the memory at the point at which she opens the door and walks out.

She realised long ago that she replays it mostly because it's the last time she saw her parents' faces. The last time she heard their voices. The decision to leave them behind was hers; she didn't ask them what they wanted. Perhaps they have been relieved, all these years, to not have to deal with her. They probably think she has a child, on her own: a living symbol of her bad behaviour.

Except that baby never became hers. Leanne felt so trapped that she freed herself the only way she could, like an animal gnawing off its own foot. So she could survive. But she knew there would be a price to pay. What she did tipped the scales somehow, and there had to be something to balance them. So she decided on the price: to never let anyone get close to her. If there is a God, or some being who decides the way things work, she hopes it's paying attention to what she's done. Because she's alone now. She doesn't have friends; she has acquaintances.

Theresa has tried to be her friend, over and over. Now Marie and Elaine are trying too. Leanne has never let anyone get that far, though, because friendship requires reciprocity and while she is interested in other people and their lives, she doesn't want to share hers. There are stories that she wants to keep to herself. Histories that she doesn't want to repeat.

Except it's hopelessly naïve to think you can evade the past. Even her attempts at remaining alone have failed, because something in her wants that connection with other people – why else would she have joined Theresa and her friends? There are days when Leanne is a mystery to herself; many days, in fact. Perhaps she should stop trying to work herself out and just give in to being human.

And here is a child the age her own child would be now.

'Yes, I remember Daphne,' she says to Matron. 'And Imogen is her sister.'

Matron looks pleased. 'She is. Coming here this afternoon. I don't expect you to special her every night – you'll wear yourself out if you do that, and I need you in tip-top shape. Why don't you work it out with the parents, then let me know what you've decided?'

'All right. Thank you.' Leanne nods deferentially and walks back to her station.

She hears Matron talking to Dr Jacobs again, and takes the opportunity to slip away to the kitchen so she has a minute to herself. She could refuse the extra work, come up with an excuse – although she knows there isn't one. Her life isn't so full of commitments or hobbies that she can't spare the time. The extra income would be useful – her rent won't stay where it is forever and she doesn't have many savings. Perhaps she could even have a holiday somewhere.

Yet she wonders what it will be like to sit with a sick child – *that* sick child – each night and not be able to do anything other than make sure she is comfortable and not afraid.

She doesn't know what Imogen will be like, but it's clear her parents are already concerned. Leanne has seen it before:

a run of bad luck that can seem like a family curse. She can't remember if there were any other siblings; as she saw only Imogen, she suspects not. Imogen's parents will be blaming themselves, as so many of the parents here do. But there's no blame, and no responsibility either; only that trite but true phrase – the luck of the draw. Leanne has four brothers and a sister and none of them had a serious childhood illness. But here is Imogen, already without her one sister and now sick herself. If Leanne were religious she might believe it was God's will, or God's work. As she isn't, she can see only random chance in any of this.

It's a comfort, and also not, to think that the same principle applies to her own life.

So Leanne will special this child, and try to improve her odds of getting better, of going home well, of simply sleeping through the night. Just as she has tried to improve her own odds, each day of her life, by getting up and working hard, by doing all the right things and staying away from the wrong, so maybe, one day, she will believe that her slate is clean.

CHAPTER 18

This Australian tradition of having a hot Christmas lunch in summertime is something Elaine will never understand. Hot food is for cold climates, and as she feels sweat trickling down the back of her neck and running towards her bra strap she wants to kick the oven door.

'Let's have a few friends over,' James had suggested. 'People who can't be with their own families on Christmas Day.'

As Elaine doesn't have any friends in Australia – at least, not people she knows well enough to consider asking to her house for Christmas – he obviously meant his friends. She had presumed that anyone who couldn't get to their families for Christmas must be from overseas – maybe there would be a European or two with whom she could chat about northern-hemisphere things. But, no, they were Western Australians and Queenslanders with not enough leave over Christmas to make it home.

She can hear them now, laughing in that loud way a lot of Australians do, especially the men. When they first arrived here she found herself flinching whenever she was around a group of them. Then she heard cockatoos for the first time and understood: Australians are loud because they're competing with those parrots. Cockatoos, kookaburras, random other native birds – they're so noisy that sometimes she can't hear herself think. Between the birds and the sharks, and the possums in their back garden, she has become convinced that Australia is a giant free-range zoo.

Their Christmas guests started arriving at eleven o'clock and immediately opened cans of beer and bottles of wine. James never drinks beer – not that she's seen before – yet there he was, pulling the ring on a 'tinny', as he called it, and knocking it back as if he was the Sahara and it was a downpour. He was even slapping men on the back and calling them 'mate'. Over the past few months Elaine has seen her husband in the company of colleagues and a couple of friends at a time, but has never seen this version of him. It's at odds with the man she's known for twenty-five years in England. It's possible he's putting on an act, trying to be a proper Aussie bloke for his *mates*, yet it happened so naturally, and quickly, that she's secretly convinced that he's been pretending to be someone else for the entire time she's known him. It's not a comfortable idea.

'You're dreaming!' she hears one man yell, then there's laughter, something that sounds like a chair falling over, and high-pitched giggling. That would be Joanne, the new second wife of one of the mates.

Elaine didn't ask for a background briefing on today's guests, and so feels foolish as she tries to navigate the possibility of children who are absent because they're with first wives, and attendant sensitivities. She shouldn't have presumed that she knew who James's friends would be – and he shouldn't have presumed she knew either. They're here now, though, expecting turkey, ham, roast vegetables, plum pudding and who knows what else.

'I hope there's a pav!' one of them had declared as soon as he'd stepped in the door.

James had looked at Elaine apologetically and said nothing. She has since deduced – after numerous hints from Wayne, as she thinks his name is – that *pav* means pavlova: a meringue-based concoction that is best not made in the sort of humid weather they're having today. She's going to have to let Wayne down by revealing that there'll be no pav because her husband told her that plum pudding would be fine.

More laughter, another thud.

Elaine reaches for the glass of Champagne that has grown warm in the kitchen and gulps it down. If she has to be in here doing all the work, she may as well entertain herself, and she's certainly not sharing the Bollinger with the guests.

Another glass, and this one she drinks faster so it doesn't have time to get tepid. Right, what should she be doing? Stuffing. Gravy.

She hiccups and tastes some of the Champagne again. Whoops – too quickly consumed. She turns on the tap and fills a water glass, drinking slowly this time.

'Are you all right in here, darling?' James is standing in the doorway, looking bleary eyed.

'What if I said no?' she responds, feeling bolshie.

'Oh.' Uncharacteristically he pouts, then walks over and plants a sloppy kiss on her cheek. 'Does that make it better?'

'Not really.' She sniffs. 'But if you give me a hand, that might.'

James looks around the kitchen and she appreciates, as she often does, his lovely face. She knows it was shallow to marry a man partly because of his face but she rationalised it to herself – still does – by saying that it's not a classically handsome face. It's a nicely arranged face: he has a good nose, and eyes that are closely set but not so much that he looks odd instead of intense, which is the usual impression they give. He has surprisingly delicate cheekbones and strong brows. Skin that tans easily, and he does like to be in the sun – an ongoing issue when they lived in a country that rarely saw it. Mainly, it's a *kind* face. That's what first attracted her to him when they met.

A friend of her parents' had asked if they could 'take care' of a young Australian doctor who was doing some training in London. He didn't know anyone. Might they show him around? Her parents had deputised Elaine, satisfied that James was a friend of a friend so no chaperone would be needed. They'd been comfortable with each other straightaway, talking easily, sharing their memories of wartime and how their countries had changed since. He said he'd resented having to leave Australia to further his career – and that should have been her first clue that he would want to return eventually. But he'd slipped into London life so easily that she didn't think he belonged anywhere else.

Today, seeing him with his friends, she considers the possibility that he may be able to slip into many circumstances with ease – not in a disingenuous way, because that's not his style, but with a fluidity that she lacks. That is, no doubt, why it was so easy to get on with him when they met, and a central component of their success as a couple since. He's the charm, she's the follow-up. After he made new contacts, she was the one to organise lunches, dinners, picnics, outings. It looked like she was the friendly one but it was all him. Besides, she had her own friends and parents, and her children to worry about. And now that they're here, in a place where he's laden with friends, she's deficient.

'So what can I do?' James says, hands on slender hips, looking from one side of the kitchen to the other. He points to what remains of the Champagne. 'Have you drunk that *whole* bottle?'

'Not the whole bottle,' she says, because it's the truth. She's drunk most of it. That's all.

He frowns. 'Darling, it's barely afternoon. Shouldn't you slow down?'

'Shouldn't you?' she snaps. 'I think you've been indulging too.'

'I haven't drunk as much as you,' he says, in that infuriatingly rational way he has.

'Well, I'm in here *alone* while you're out there with your *friends*.' She sounds drunk even to herself. Perhaps she has gone too far, but he shouldn't have abandoned her.

'They're your friends too.'

'No, they are *not*.' She's being snotty but she can't seem to help it. '*My* friends would talk to me.'

She's aware she's waving a carving knife in the air, and puts it down.

He walks over and puts a hand on hers. 'It's fine to indulge on Christmas Day. We all do. But I'm worried about how much you're indulging at other times.'

Her shoulders hunch around her ears – her only form of defence against the ugly truth. Because he's right – of course he's right. James would never say anything like this just to make a point or to hurt her. He's better than she is, clearly, because she's just said things to hurt him.

'Don't get upset, darling,' he says softly. 'I care about you. That's all.'

'I'm not indulging too much at other times,' she says brusquely. 'I'm having just the right amount.'

She hears him inhale and he takes his hand off hers. 'All right,' he says. 'I don't want to push.'

'Good.' She yanks open the oven door and, without thinking, puts her bare hand on the roasting dish. '*Shit!*' she cries as her skin registers the heat.

As she pulls her hand back her mind goes blank. What is she meant to do now?

'Here,' James says, coming to her swiftly and taking her wrist as he turns on the cold tap in the sink. He holds her hand under the water and tears spring to her eyes.

'God,' she says, feeling foolish. She's never burnt her hand cooking in her life. Once on an iron, and she felt just as foolish then.

'It's all right,' James says, although he's not looking at her and she can tell it's because he thinks she burnt her hand because she's drunk. He's wrong: she's not drunk, just stupid. 'Keep your hand under the water.'

She yelps as the pain resurges.

'I need to get the turkey out,' she says, wincing. 'It will be dry if I don't.'

He lets go of her and picks up two tea towels, using them to grab the roasting dish. 'There.' His smile looks forced as he puts the dish on the stovetop.

'Thank you,' she says.

'Let's have a look.' He takes her wrist again. 'I'll get you something to cover it. Put it back under the water.'

She nods and tries to look contrite, although now the Champagne is really going to her head so she thinks she looks loopy instead.

From the sitting room she hears him telling their guests there will be a slight delay with lunch. She sighs, wondering what they're all thinking of her, and wishing she didn't. She'll get the lunch on the table, and then she'll clean up later. She wants to keep being a good wife to James, even if she is drinking too much. Or so he says. Right now, she thinks the Champagne is helping to dull the pain so it's actually proved to be very useful.

When she inspects her hand and sees the big, angry red welt, she decides she deserves another glass for her trouble, and there's just enough left in the bottle. Before James returns it is poured and consumed, and she feels better about how the rest of the day will run.

CHAPTER 19

Theresa is sure she broke the speed limit driving down the hill to the beach. She just couldn't wait to get here and have some time to herself. Her parents and brother and his family have taken over the house and she's been desperate to get away from them. Christmas Day – no chance, even though Marie said she'd be swimming that morning. Boxing Day – forget it, they all had to go to church, and the only bright spot was seeing Marie in the congregation. Although Theresa decided just to wave and not inflict her family on her friend, because then her mother would get nosy and ask questions, such as why was Marie there on her own? Did she not have a husband? Where were her children? Her mother *is* nosy sometimes, and, yes, Theresa is aware that she's nosy herself but she doesn't do it to be rude. Her mother does it to judge. If she had met Marie, and Marie had said she was a widow and her daughter was with her husband's family, as soon as she walked away Mum would have said something like, 'What kind of daughter leaves her mother alone at Christmas time? Clearly she wasn't a good mother.' Then her father would have an opinion, and so would Mario, all of them conveniently forgetting that Theresa's other brother, Angelo, moved to Canberra a decade ago and has never once come north for Christmas. He keeps saying Canberra is beautiful in summer. *As if.* Still, he gets away with it.

The beach, by comparison with life with her family, is paradise. Mostly empty. And she's early, so she has time to sit in the half light and watch the waves. There are surfers out there already. What did Andrew say once? Surfers on dawn patrol are shark bait.

Andrew used to surf once upon a time. He'd been surfing the day they met around a bonfire on Killarney Beach, not far from Shelly Bay, where he and his mates had gathered, and her friend Sheryl had basically ordered Theresa to accompany her because she was going out with Andrew's friend Bonza. Andrew told Theresa that the 'hot chicks' never went for him but here he was talking to her, so maybe his luck had changed. She was twenty-two then but still unsophisticated enough not to question whether he was lying about there being no other 'hot chicks'. She was a good girl – she'd never gone anywhere near a boy, because her father and brothers would have killed her. So when Andrew said she was hot that's all she needed to hear. Later she thought he was a spunk and a good catch because he had his own business – car repairs, in his own garage – and he pulled out the chair for her in restaurants and said he wanted two kids, just like she did. She's wondered, many days since then, how she could have thought that was enough to build a marriage on. Because it wasn't.

'Oh – I thought I'd be the first one here.'

Theresa's view of the ocean is blocked by the tall figure of Elaine who, even in the kind light of dawn, looks a wreck. Her face is blotchy, her shoulders slumped and her hair is standing half up on her head. Usually she glides onto the beach looking like she's the teacher of a deportment class.

'Good morning!' Theresa says. 'We're both early birds.'

'Yes. So it seems.'

Elaine looks almost as if she's scowling, but that's a really un-Elaine thing to do. Looking stern is as far as she goes. So Theresa decides there's something wrong.

'Aren't you feeling well?'

'Why would you say that?' Elaine asks, a little too quickly. Now Theresa is *sure* something is going on.

'You just look a bit . . . off. Sorry. I shouldn't have said anything. I just worry too much.' She busies herself playing with the edge of her sarong.

Elaine says something that sounds like 'hmph', but she drops onto the sand next to Theresa and wraps her arms around her legs.

'How was your Christmas?' Theresa asks, trying a different tack.

'Interesting.' Elaine is looking at the surf. 'How was yours?'

'Full of noisy people I didn't particularly want to see.'

'Ah.' Elaine smiles her way, but it looks like it hurts. 'It sounds like we had the same Christmas.'

'Oh, right.' Theresa tries laughing as a way to move on from her awkward inquisition. She really doesn't want to upset Elaine, who intimidates her just a little bit. Elaine is elegant and graceful and sophisticated in that way only non-Australians can be.

'You're right,' Elaine says, 'I am a bit off. I, uh . . .' She squints, then relaxes her face. 'I drank slightly too much over Christmas and now I'm paying the price.'

'I don't blame you! I wish *I* could have drunk too much. It would have helped!'

'I was feeling sorry for myself,' Elaine says. She shrugs. 'Moping, I guess. I'm homesick. I miss my children. I miss having work to do each day.'

Theresa's surprised at how readily the confession tumbles out: Elaine doesn't seem like the confessional type. Not like Marie, or Theresa herself. That's what a lifetime of being marched into an actual confessional once a week will do; they spill their guts without much prodding.

'You don't like having a rest?' Theresa asks. 'I know I can't *wait* for my kids to grow up and not need everything done for them any more. Of course, Andrew will still want to be taken care of.'

She sighs, thinking of the chores waiting at home. Truthfully, being with her children isn't amongst them. That's a pleasure, most of the time, even if she does sometimes get annoyed by the fact that motherhood is a seven-day-a-week job. Why doesn't anyone warn you before you give birth? She hasn't had a day off in eight years.

'I was lucky – I had help with the children. Because I had my business. Now . . .' Elaine's eyes close briefly. 'It all seems somewhat empty.'

'Can I send my husband to you for a while, then?' Theresa says, nudging her gently. 'Because he's one child too many.'

Elaine laughs, and Theresa is glad she's been able to shift her mood.

'Oh, look,' she says, 'Marie and Leanne are here.'

Elaine turns to look in the same direction. 'Leanne's quiet, isn't she?'

'Only around adults. She's great with kids, but she doesn't like adults.'

Elaine looks surprised. 'She's here, isn't she?'

'Yes, but I think that's because she wants people to swim with. So we're . . . what's the word? Convenient.' Theresa frowns. 'No, that sounds mean. She just doesn't want to be friends. And that's okay.'

'Is it?' Elaine is looking at her with amusement. 'I suspect you like to be friends with people.'

Theresa laughs, although she wishes she wasn't so easily found out. It's always been that way though: her mother told her she should learn to control her emotions better because everyone could see them on her face. Theresa tried for a while but it was too exhausting trying to not be herself.

'You've been very friendly to me,' Elaine goes on. 'And I appreciate it.'

Theresa feels warmly pleased, like she did when a teacher at school gave her a good mark. 'I like you,' she says, and is surprised when Elaine looks as if she's going to cry.

'Do you?' she says.

Theresa puts a hand on her arm because there's no time to say anything more: Leanne and Marie are upon them.

'Well – look what the cat dragged in,' Marie says to Elaine, who appears confused. 'Did you have a big night?' Marie goes on, her eyes narrowing.

Elaine swallows. 'What do you mean?'

Marie looks at her askance. 'I think you know.'

'Not big. Just . . . long,' Elaine says, her voice light.

'Right,' Marie says slowly.

'Hi, Leanne,' Theresa says. 'How was your Christmas?'

Leanne's smile is brief. 'Quiet.'

Theresa knows that's as much as she'll get out of her for the moment. She wants to find out more, though; she worries that Leanne is lonely. Even if she doesn't really like talking to adults that much, she's so different with the patients that Theresa can tell she has a warm heart. Which means she likes connecting with people. Which means she might be lonely if she doesn't have anyone in her life.

'Shall we go in?' Elaine says, getting to her feet. 'I'm keen to start.'

'Good idea,' Marie says. 'Let's wash off the residue of Christmas.'

Elaine's eyes go round but she says nothing.

'Last one in is a rotten egg!' Theresa cries, then remembers that because she has the longest hair it's going to take her the most time to put her cap on properly. Which makes her the rotten egg.

She doesn't mind, though, and she's not long behind the others as they make their way through the waves, striking out for Little Beach and the day ahead.

CHAPTER 20

When Gwen had first said she and Fred were moving to a retirement village she'd sounded so pleased, as if she was going on a lovely vacation. But Marie shudders each time she thinks of a retirement village. She can't bear the idea of being surrounded by old people, even if to the untrained eye she looks like an old person herself. She doesn't want to look old, think old or feel old, even if the walk up the hill from the beach each morning causes her knees to complain and she puffs a bit more than she used to. She's fit from the swimming – as she's always been and intends to stay – and likes to think it's helping her not need to move to a place where she'd have to meet a bunch of new people and learn new routines. The routines she has still serve her well.

But she misses Gwen after so many years of knowing each other, even though she's not sure that Gwen misses her. They speak on the phone, but the easy rhythms of the past are no longer there. What did they have to say to each other all the time? The more they saw each other, the more they seemed to have to talk about, yet now they're stuck in conversations about their grandchildren and the government. Marie doesn't talk about what's happening in Shelly Bay because it won't interest Gwen any more, and she doesn't know what to ask about the retirement village because she hasn't been there yet.

So she's decided to remedy that today with a visit. It's a long bus ride and a train trip, then a kilometre's walk downhill from the station, causing her once again to rue the fact she never learnt to drive. It was so easy to have Norm drive her everywhere, and for some reason it never occurred to her that he might drop off the perch first and leave her without a ready means of transportation.

The streets on the way to Gwen's new home are quiet, populated mostly by trees that crowd into the front gardens of the heavy-bricked homes. This is the same city but a world away from Shelly Bay. Here, there's a sense of being hemmed in; there, a sense of unending sky and ocean. It amazes Marie that her friend could grow up in Shelly Bay, live there as an adult, raise a family there, then want to leave. Marie is so attached to the place that she's convinced her blood is really sea water, and feels personally acquainted with every grain of sand on the beach.

The retirement village is all new buildings in a tortoiseshell brick and immature bushes in neat garden beds. Gwen told her that she has a little duplex. Marie finds the number she's been given and presses the doorbell.

She hears slow steps inside, then the door opens and there is Gwen, smiling toothily the way she always has.

'Oh, Marie,' she says, opening the door and hugging her. 'I've missed you.'

Marie holds the hug for longer than she ever would have before. It feels like she's clutching on to the past, as if letting go of Gwen will mean they really have to move on into this new phase where Gwen lives here and she lives there. When Gwen moved, Marie never imagined they wouldn't see each other for this long, but she's been forced to realise that her life is narrow. She wears out the same track around the bay, and it is Gwen who has been the adventurer.

'I'm so sorry I haven't visited earlier,' Marie says, embarrassed now that she knows the trip, while long, wasn't difficult. 'It's not as if I don't have time to come here, I've just . . . been slack.'

Gwen smiles kindly. 'We've known each other a long time, Marie, and I'm not going to stop being your friend just because we don't see each other every day.' She scrutinises her. 'You're looking well. Still swimming?'

'Of course,' Marie says, not without pride. She doesn't know many people who exercise regularly – though she's met a few who talk about how they'd like to. 'And I have some people to swim with now,' she continues.

'Really?' Gwen looks uncertain.

'New friends!' Marie says brightly and sees Gwen's uncertainty grow. 'I'm sure you've made some friends here too?' she adds.

How silly, she realises, not to think that Gwen might be as worried as she is about their friendship not surviving the move.

'Some.' Gwen's smile is brief. 'No one like you.'

Marie puts a hand on her arm. 'And I haven't met anyone like you.'

That's almost a lie, she thinks: her affection for Theresa is deep, and she's fond of Elaine and Leanne. But Gwen doesn't need to know that; and none of them will ever be her friend for as long as Gwen has been.

'Is one of them a man?' Gwen says hopefully.

'No!' Marie splutters. 'Thank goodness. I can't be bothered with that any more.'

'Oh?'

Marie waves a hand. 'Imagine having to train someone new. No, thank you – I'm too old. Speaking of men: am I seeing Fred today too?'

'No,' Gwen says, looking guilty. 'He's playing canasta with some people at the club. He said to say hello.'

Marie isn't surprised: Fred has never really taken to her. She thinks it's because she has known Gwen far longer than he has, and he's jealous. Or perhaps he simply doesn't like her.

'That's all right,' Marie says. 'I'm here to see you anyway. Now, why don't you show me around?'

Gwen gives her the tour: bedroom, sitting room, kitchen, bathroom, small courtyard out the back.

'Quiet neighbours,' she says, gesturing over the back fence. 'I'm starting to think they're all dead!'

Marie smiles then stops herself, because for all she knows it could be true soon enough.

They sit, and Gwen bustles around filling the kettle and bringing the tray.

'How's the house?' she says as she makes Marie's tea just the way she likes it, with a splash of milk and a dollop of sugar.

'Still there, and still costing me money. I need to get some new braces for the sandstone or the walls are going to bulge to a point beyond decency.'

Marie smiles to make light of it, even though the subject is serious. The house was built in 1878 and, like any centenarian, needs regular, expensive upkeep.

'You should sell it,' Gwen says, pushing the cup and saucer towards Marie.

This is a subject Gwen has been fond of for a while, dating almost to the time of Norm's death. She told Marie then that it would be hard to afford the upkeep. Marie hadn't wanted to listen. She could be obstinate when it suited her – as Gwen knew – but in this case her resistance was because the subject upset her.

'I'm not quite there yet,' she says now.

'Marie, you know you should.' Gwen sighs, picking up her own teacup and sitting back in her chair. 'It's causing you stress. It's mucking up your aura.'

Ah yes, her aura. About five years ago Gwen's eldest child, Bronwyn, had decided she was psychic and started telling Gwen – and anyone else who would stand still for five minutes – about her aura. Gwen was wholeheartedly persuaded that her daughter's new beliefs were right, did her own exploration of mysticism and other things, and now declared her religion to be 'New Age'. Which Marie found curious when Gwen decided to move to a Uniting Church–run retirement village. That isn't to say that Marie dismisses Gwen's beliefs. Her friend is good at diagnosing when Marie's out of sorts just by looking at her, although Marie doesn't know whether that's because of her aura or the fact that she looks haggard and worried.

'Well, I don't want to muck up my aura,' she says, sipping her tea and only half trying to be sarcastic.

'*Marie.*' Gwen frowns at her.

'I'm not making fun of you,' Marie says. 'But I don't know how to fix my aura.'

'I'll ask Bron to give you a call. Or we can talk about selling that house. That'll do the trick.'

'Nicole would never let me.'

'She doesn't get a say.'

'It's her inheritance!' Marie protests. 'Besides, I don't want to move if I can avoid it. And Nicole and Pete are very kindly helping me out with some bills for a while.'

'You can't live there for the rest of your life,' Gwen says. 'On your own,' she adds pointedly.

Marie looks away, at Gwen's collection of family photos. At her life, crammed into one sitting room, one bedroom, half a kitchen and a small bathroom. She thinks of her own cottage, which isn't huge but it's her home.

'I'm doing all right,' she says quietly.

'Really?' Gwen emits something like a snort.

'I have Charlie Brown.'

'Marie! You're going to trip over that dog one day and you'll break something and lie there for who knows how long until someone finds you.' Gwen huffs. 'It's not *safe* being there on your own.'

She knows Gwen has a point, because this same point has occurred to her. Each time she gets on a stepladder to change a light bulb she considers the possibility that she'll fall and not be able to reach the phone to call for help. If she lived each day worrying about it, though, she'd never do anything.

'It's safe enough,' she says, although she could have made herself sound a little more convincing.

They sit in silence for a minute or so, drinking tea and eating biscuits.

'It's only because I worry about you,' Gwen says, and when Marie looks at her she can see it's true.

She laughs. 'I worry about me, too, but not about tripping over the dog.'

'What's your biggest concern?'

Marie has a list of concerns, but she doesn't want to burden Gwen with them. Gwen has simplified her life by moving here; she doesn't need it cluttered with Marie's petty problems.

'Nothing I can't handle,' she says.

'Don't be like that.' Gwen reaches over to pat her knee. 'A problem shared is a problem halved.'

If only that were true. Marie doesn't think she'll miss Norm less if she talks about him; she doesn't think the cost of living will decrease if she tells people that staying alive is expensive. But she knows the sentiment behind it – and Gwen is just trying to help. If she stops telling her friend what's really going on in her life, they won't be friends for much longer. Since Gwen's move Marie has learnt that the intimacy of friendship requires careful tending, and it's always vulnerable. You can't take anyone for granted – especially the very people you think are rusted on to your life. As the last few years have shown, even they can be removed suddenly and soon the whole structure of your existence is starting to wobble.

'The money is a problem,' she admits. 'There's too much going out and not enough coming in.'

'You have paintings you could sell,' Gwen says, looking pleased at coming up with the suggestion. 'Those ones your mother left you.'

Marie's mother had friends who were artists working nearby around the turn of the century, some of whom became quite famous. Her mother would never say much about them, although Marie suspected she painted herself. When she was younger she used to think that some of the paintings were really her mother's, signed with another name, but she had no proof. The paintings bear mostly the names of those famous men and Marie's aware she could get a few dollars for them, but they're all she has left of her mother. Besides, if she sells them she'll have nothing on the walls.

'I'll think about it,' she says to Gwen, because she appreciates that her friend is trying to help.

'If you moved in here you wouldn't have to worry about anything!'

'I don't know if my place would be worth enough to get me in here.'

Gwen shrugs and sips from her cup. Marie has no doubt she'll try that line again before the visit is over.

'Tell me about the kids,' she says, feeling that the topic of her house has been exhausted for now.

Gwen's face transforms with a beaming smile. 'They're wonderful. They were just here yesterday.'

Marie sits back into the couch and relaxes a little. As Gwen talks she remembers what it's like to spend time talking of subjects that seem small but say so much: grandchildren, family, shared experiences and laughter. It's a reminder that she shouldn't leave it too long before she visits again.

CHAPTER 21

The balcony doors on the surf club's expansive first floor are open but the air inside is still hot, and heavy with cigarette smoke. Theresa tries breathing through her mouth, which achieves precisely nothing because she can still smell the smoke. Once upon a time she wouldn't have noticed – she might even have enjoyed it – because she would have been amongst the smokers. Everyone she knew smoked. She only gave it up when she became pregnant for the first time, because she decided her baby should have a choice about whether he or she would be a smoker. The withdrawal was worse than the morning sickness, and now the sensations of both are intertwined so the smoke inside the club is making her feel like she's going to be sick.

'Here,' Andrew says, pushing a plastic cup filled with pale liquid into her hands before walking away.

Theresa was surprised when he was so keen to come to the party – they never usually do anything on New Year's Eve apart from pass out with tiredness; that same tiredness every parent she knows seems to have.

She wishes she was already asleep tonight – she's been more tired than usual lately – but Trev trapped her into coming to this party, the other day when she was waiting for the others to arrive for their swim.

When she mentioned it to Andrew she hoped he'd kick up his usual stink – as happens any time they have to go to an event at school, for instance – but he said, 'Oh yeah, I heard about that. Should be good.'

'How did you hear?' she asked, risking his irritation with her questioning.

'Chook, down at the garage. He's a member.'

It's Chook who Andrew rejoins after presenting her with this unidentifiable beverage, and now Trev is approaching and she's going to be stuck. She's also busting to do a wee and she just knows that Trev is going to keep her from getting to the ladies.

She looks towards Andrew and his friend, but they're play-shoving each other and cackling about something. The only other person she knew at the party – Brian, from across the road – has disappeared. What she really wants to do is go home, but she doubts she'll prise Andrew away.

'G'day, Tess,' Trev says, standing a little too close.

'Hi, Trev,' she says weakly.

'Nice evening for it.' He looks her up and down and gives her what can only be described as a leer. 'You look nice too.'

'Thanks,' she says.

She doesn't want to sound too grateful for the praise, because that might encourage Trev to step even closer. But Andrew hasn't said a word about how she looks, even though she's pleased that her dress is hanging a little looser than the last time she wore it. The swimming is paying off, in lots of ways. In the water she feels carefree, graceful, strong and brave. Out of the water she's sometimes tired and sore, but that's part of the deal, and in exchange she's in better shape than she has been in years.

'Is your wife here?' she asks Trev, drinking quickly from the cup and making a face, because whatever's in it doesn't taste like something she wants to drink.

'Yep.' Trev nods towards a woman standing near a potted palm. She has a close-set perm and a polyester dress that doesn't belong inside a stinking-hot surf club. Then he hikes up his pants just the way he does with his swimming costume. 'That's the little lady. Nance.'

Theresa's mind whirrs with conversational options: the cricket, the surf club, the brawl that broke out inside the pub last night. But before she can land on one she notices Andrew and Chook walking away, out of sight. Typical of Andrew to leave her stranded. He does it every time they go somewhere.

'So where's your husband, Tess?' Trev asks, with a return of that leer.

'Um, he . . . he just went somewhere. I should go and find him.'

She starts to walk away but Trev grabs her arm. 'Hang on – come and meet Nance.'

Theresa tries to look happy about it, but she doesn't want to be friends with Trev, nor does she want to meet Nance. Yet here Nance is, smiling and taking her hand with that lady's half-handshake that Theresa has always found weird – why can't they just shake hands like men? – and asking her about her children, not noticing that her husband is still leering.

Maybe five minutes go by but they feel like fifteen, and now her bladder really is protesting. 'Sorry,' she bursts out with what she hopes is an apologetic expression on her face. 'I really have to go to the loo.'

'Oh.' Nance looks offended – but Theresa is telling the truth.

'Sorry,' she says again. 'Two kids – you know how it is! I can't keep it in.'

Trev goes red and mumbles something inaudible. Theresa knew that suggesting she has a weak pelvic floor would be a get-out-of-jail-free card. She puts her drink down on a trestle table and sets off in search of the loo, which she's pretty sure is downstairs.

As Chook passes her, going in the other direction and on his own, Theresa stops. 'Where's Andrew?' she asks.

Chook shrugs and avoids her eyes. 'Dunno.'

Theresa resists the temptation to get cross at him, because it's not Chook's fault that her husband has, in all probability, left her there and either gone to the pub or gone home.

She trots down the stairs and goes to turn right to the toilets when she sees him. Him and someone else. A female someone else. A girl. Or young, at least. Younger than Theresa. She's blonde. Her hair is straight. She's slender. She's nothing like Theresa. Of course.

It's the perkiness of her boobs that makes Theresa think she's younger – and it's hard to avoid noticing them because Andrew has his hands on them.

There are people going past her, up the stairs, and all she can think is thank god her neighbour Brian has gone home, and that Trev and Nance are still upstairs, so there's no one to witness this.

No one apart from her.

Now one of Andrew's hands has slipped between the girl's legs.

He must be drunk. She hasn't seen him drink much tonight, but it makes sense, right? At a New Year's Eve party people get drunk and do stupid things. Which doesn't mean she isn't mad but it's an explanation. She might have flirted with a bloke at a Christmas party one year after one glass of spumante too many, so she's in no position to throw stones in this particular glass house.

Except she's stuck here, gripping the banister and realising she can't go to the loo because her husband is kissing another woman in front of her, and she can't confront him because that would draw attention to the scene, and she sees how they're looking at each other. Staring into each other's eyes as he gropes her and she slides her hands down his back.

They know each other already.

It's there in the way the woman is stroking his cheek. More than that, it's in the way Andrew looks at her: the way he used to look at Theresa several years and two children ago. His face is soft. His smile is sweet. He looks like a teenager in love.

Theresa thinks about the past few months – all the nights he's been out with his mates. The Brut 33 that he doesn't have in the bathroom cabinet, but which is on his skin when he comes home. She wants to laugh – out loud, and at herself. She's been ticked off that he's prepared to doll himself up for nights out with his mates but not for her. How stupid – *how stupid* – could she be to not realise that it isn't his mates he's interested in impressing? To *believe him* when he told her he was drinking with the boys at the pub? He knew she'd never check. She can't leave the kids at home alone to trot down to the pub and find out where he is.

The front door is right in front of her. The night air is so much cooler than the shame that is heating her cheeks and making her want to throw up. She flees outside – to the bushes next to the club – and up come the sausage roll and party pie and whatever the cheese on the Jatz cracker was. She hasn't thrown up like this since . . . since she was pregnant with Sasha.

As she thinks of her babies, at home with Nonna watching over them, she wants to scream. How could Andrew choose that girl over them? How could he prefer to spend time with her when his children love him unquestioningly?

As Theresa straightens up she's vaguely aware of people walking nearby, talking – perhaps about her – but they leave her alone. She's grateful. She needs some time to think about what to do next. She doesn't want to confront Andrew. Not here.

Then something else clicks: he was making no effort to hide himself. So maybe other people know. Maybe everyone knows.

If she had anything left to throw up, she would. Shame is an emotion that her religious upbringing encouraged, but Theresa can't remember feeling this way before. Shame about sinful thoughts is one thing; shame because your husband is making no secret of his affair, in front of people you know, is another.

What is she meant to do, though? Leave and go home on her own? Then what – have it out with him later, while her children are asleep, and risk them waking up and hearing her accuse their father of cheating on her?

No. She's not going to do that. She needs to work this out. Because it's not as straightforward as telling him what she saw. If she accuses him of cheating on her, he'll fire back with his usual complaint about how he's had to work so hard for years to 'support my family'.

Theresa wishes she could give him an invoice for everything she does around the house. If he had to pay for someone to cook, clean and wash his clothes, let alone raise his children, he wouldn't be able to afford it.

And to think she almost had a teaching degree to qualify herself for all of this. She wanted to finish the degree, but Andrew asked her to marry him and that was that. Andrew hadn't wanted her to work – like what she does every day of her life in their house isn't work! And her mum told her it was her 'duty' to make a home for her husband. Theresa had wanted to ask about her duty to herself, but life didn't go like that, did it?

She didn't completely listen to her mother: she worked in the bakery down the street until she fell pregnant with Ollie. Then she had to leave – Andrew had insisted.

Now she can see how she's trapped herself inside a world of his creation. All this time she's been telling herself that despite the fact she earns no money of her own, the house, at least, is her domain. But it's not, because he's brought whatever he's been doing into their house, their marriage and their family. It can't be her domain when someone else can infiltrate it so easily.

She sits on the low brick wall outside the club and closes her eyes. The night air is like a balm, and the sound of the waves just a few metres away reassures her. They're her constant, those waves. Tomorrow morning she'll be in them again. Tomorrow morning she will have time to think. Maybe time to talk. Because she needs advice from someone wiser. Like Marie. She's seen more of life than Theresa and she's a sensible woman.

Theresa doesn't feel she can tell Marie about it yet, though; it seems too soon. Or maybe it's that telling Marie would make it absolutely real.

After a while she walks back upstairs and sees Andrew standing with Chook by the drinks table. Chook must know what's going on; that's why he couldn't look her in the eye. She feels sick again, but she's not going to run. That's not the solution – not tonight.

'We've had a record number signing up for bronze medallion training,' she hears Trev say as she walks up to him and Nance.

'Sorry for running off,' she tells them.

'No worries,' Trev says, looking at his feet.

Andrew appears at her side. 'Ready to go?' he says.

From deep within her, Theresa summons the best acting performance of her life – better than when she played one of the seven dwarves in a school play. 'Yes,' she says, smiling at him. 'I am.'

The whole way home she lets him talk about Chook and the garage and how he should maybe join the surf club because there are 'good blokes' there. It's proof that he didn't see her standing at the bottom of the staircase, watching him. If he had, she doubts he'd be so talkative.

When they arrive home she checks on the children, then goes to the bathroom to have a shower and scrub off the cigarette smoke and the shame and the stink of vomit that Andrew didn't notice.

Afterwards she finds him sprawled on their bed, taking up all the space, so she turns on the TV in the lounge room and doesn't notice the time passing until the dawn light appears through the windows.

CHAPTER 22

As the morning light spreads over the water like a cheerful blanket, Elaine keeps her head up and breaststrokes for a while. It's too beautiful not to look – and this way she can keep an eye out for bluebottles. They had blighted the first few days of January, in what Marie called an 'unseasonal infestation', and Elaine's first experience of them came one morning when Marie bent over to examine the wet sand where it met the dry and made a 'hmph' sound.

'What is it?' asked Theresa.

'Bluebottles,' Marie said, straightening. She sighed and looked at the water. 'The tide's going out so they may all be on the beach.'

Elaine glanced at Theresa, who looked startled. 'Um,' she said, her eyes moving from Marie to Elaine to Leanne before landing back on Marie.

'Is there a problem with bluebottles?' Elaine asked, noticing brilliant blue flecks on the sand near Marie's feet. 'What do they do?'

'They sting. I usually go in when they're about, but this one,' Marie jerked a thumb towards Theresa, 'may not feel the same.'

'I got stung when I was ten,' Theresa said, grimacing with what looks like a memory of pain. 'It was not good.'

'What are the chances of getting stung?' Leanne said quietly as she bent to examine the specimen.

Marie shrugged. 'Who knows. It's not pleasant when it happens, but in all my years I've only been stung twice. So . . .' She looked meaningfully at Theresa. 'Our odds are pretty good.'

'Then I'll go in,' said Elaine.

'That's the spirit,' said Marie, pulling her T-shirt over her head.

Elaine had noticed she wears the same one every day; it bears the legend *Life. Be in it.* Given that Marie's husband is dead, she wondered at the meaning behind it.

'I will too,' Leanne said. 'I'm so slow that I'll see them.'

'What about you, Theresa?' Marie said as she kicked off her shorts.

'Well, I don't want to stay here on my own,' Theresa said uncertainly.

'I'm sure Trev would keep you company.'

'I'm coming.' Theresa whipped off her sarong and tied her hair back.

'Just a little tip,' Marie told them all, 'keep an eye out for them. Most of them are on the beach, I'd say, but it can't hurt to be wary, especially as we're heading out through the waves.'

Elaine took heed and swam through the waves instead of going under them.

This morning they saw only two bluebottles on the sand but Elaine is still swimming with caution, even now that they're past the breakers, and with the sunlight on the water it's easier to see what's about. She thinks they're in the clear but it's no hardship to keep her head above water for a while. She rolls over a bit and sidestrokes, something she hasn't done for many years. It takes her a few metres before she swaps sides.

She hears splashing water and Theresa pulls up beside her. 'You're sidestroking!' Theresa says, breathless. 'I didn't think anyone remembered how any more.'

'Sometimes I like to try different things,' Elaine says with a smile as she rolls back into a breaststroke.

She feels her hips expand with the frog kick, and her chest open as she pushes her hands out and around. It's a lovely stroke – she's always enjoyed it – just not as efficient for the purposes of exercise. Freestyle – the Australian crawl, as she first learnt it – is more vigorous and challenging, and you can swim further faster. If she were to breaststroke every day all the way she'd be out here for hours.

Up ahead, Little Beach beckons. It's their regular destination, but Elaine usually has her head in the water so she's never had a chance to see what's around it. The small beach is guarded by a ridge of rock on one side, covered by houses, and another curve of rock on the ocean side, giving it protection from the wind. There are no waves here either.

Behind the beach there's a grassy area with picnic tables that are unoccupied at this time of day, but when Elaine has walked around here on the occasional weekend she's found the place packed. To her right she can see the kiosk with its advertisements for Paddle Pops and Schweppes soft drinks. It's closed now; she's not sure it opens on weekdays anyway.

On the ocean side, the rock leads to scrubby bush: the light green, low, hardy plants that are typical of the coastline here, able to withstand salt and wind. Somewhere back there are spots for cars, she knows – all those visitors have to park somewhere.

With the rest of Shelly Bay at her back, it's possible to pretend that Little Beach is part of a village far from the city. Although some of the appeal of this whole place for Elaine is that it *can* feel like this yet still be part of Australia's largest city.

Marie has already turned at the beach to head back. Usually Elaine isn't far behind her but today she doesn't mind being the one to lag. Rather, she doesn't mind too much: there's a little competitive streak in her that she has never encouraged but which likes to remind her it's there. Consciously, rationally, she doesn't care if Marie beats her back to Main Beach; subconsciously, that competitiveness tells her she will always care. She likes to think it keeps her sharp, and stops her from doing nothing but lying around at home dreaming of gin. If she didn't feel that niggle to be better and do more, she couldn't imagine who she'd become.

'I'm going to freestyle back,' she announces to Theresa as they near Little Beach.

'Okay! I will too.' Theresa sounds cheerful but looks more strained than usual.

Elaine has heard of the demands on Theresa's time, and as much as she misses her sons she's pleased that she's past the stage of having to get children fed, bathed, clothed and out the door each day, let alone checking on a grandmother who sounds as though she thinks smoking is the secret to eternal youth.

By the time they're back at Main Beach and emerging, bluebottle free, onto the sand, Elaine feels invigorated – but Theresa looks even more weary.

'Are you all right?' Elaine asks as they walk slowly to their towels – just as a dripping Trev passes them at a clip.

'Feeling better, love?' he calls.

It's not clear who he's addressing but Theresa turns her head away.

'Who are you talking to?' says Marie.

'Tess.' He winks at Marie. 'Think she had a few too many sherbets at the New Year's Eve party.'

'Oh yes?' Marie looks barely interested.

Theresa, on the other hand, looks like she hopes quicksand will suddenly form and swallow her whole.

'She was vomiting in the bushes, wasn't she? That's the rumour,' Trev says a little too gleefully, and Elaine is horrified that he's been so indiscreet.

'Who hasn't done that?' she says, wanting to deflect attention from Theresa. 'I've been known to not even make it to the bushes.'

She glances at Marie, who is frowning at her, then at Theresa, who looks like she wants to cry.

'Like to get on the turps, do ya?' says Trev, hoisting the back of his Speedos so they hug his groin a little more tightly.

Elaine smiles and makes sure it doesn't reach her eyes.

'Off you go, Trev,' Marie says.

He chuckles as he toddles up the beach, swimming costume wedged up his backside.

Marie turns to Elaine. '*Do* you like the turps?' she says, and Elaine colours.

'Sometimes. Anyway, I should get home to see James before he leaves for work.'

'Thank you,' says Theresa limply.

'No need to thank me,' says Elaine, wrapping her towel around her waist.

'And what happened to you, Theresa?' Marie asks. 'That sounds completely out of character.'

Of course – Elaine should have asked that. Instead she was self-centredly trying to escape scrutiny of her own behaviour. She glances towards Theresa and sees Leanne looking at her with a slight frown, as if she's disappointed.

'Oh – ah – just ate a bad prawn!' Theresa says with a high-pitched laugh, and it's clear she's lying.

'But we saw you the next day,' Marie says slowly, 'and you didn't look like someone who was recovering from food poisoning. Or someone who'd had too much to drink the night before.'

'Food poisoning sounds so dramatic!' Theresa says as she ties up her sarong in record time and picks up her flip-flops. 'Anyway, must run! School holidays, you know. The kids are probably already tearing the house apart.'

'The-*reeee*-sa,' Marie says.

'Cheerio!' Theresa moves faster over the sand than they've ever seen her.

Marie glances at Leanne, then towards Elaine. 'Something's wrong,' she says. 'Leanne, any chance you can get it out of her at the hospital?'

Leanne shakes her head quickly. 'She's not rostered on this week. Or next. Because of the holidays. And I, uh . . .'

'Wouldn't ask?' Marie makes a face. 'We're all too bloody polite, aren't we? Not a criticism. Just a comment,' she adds as Leanne's face falls.

'I imagine she'll tell us in her own good time,' Elaine says, 'if she wants to.'

Marie turns completely towards her. 'Yes,' she says. 'I imagine she will.' Her gaze is piercing and Elaine feels completely exposed. 'I imagine we could all do that if we want to. Since we're friends here now, aren't we?'

Elaine knows exactly what point Marie is trying to make, but if she thinks Elaine is going to declare anything right here, on the sand, she's wrong. Declarations are not part of her genetic make-up. But she doesn't want to ignore the hand of understanding that Marie has extended.

'We are,' she says after a few moments have passed.

Marie nods as if satisfied. 'Right.'

'I have to go,' Leanne says. 'Early shift.' She nods to each of them and slips away in her quiet Leanne fashion.

'I'm going too.' Marie wraps her towel around her neck. 'And you should get home to that husband. I'll see you tomorrow.'

'Goodbye.'

Elaine watches as Marie walks in a plodding, determined way over the soft sand and up onto the promenade. It takes her a few seconds more to realise what was acknowledged between them this morning: that they are friends. That they are all friends.

While Elaine revealed more of herself than she intended, she can't chastise herself for it. She has made friends in this place where she was, not so long ago, friendless. It's a moment for being gloriously, ineffably pleased with life.

CHAPTER 23

The staff roster has been all over the place since the new year arrived, and some of her colleagues appear to have forgotten what time their shifts start, so Leanne feels like she almost has the hospital to herself today.

After placing her handbag in her locker she rolls her shoulders back and forth, feeling the effects of the swimming. After the first couple of days in a row she was sore in muscles she didn't know she had; but it's been weeks now and she's still discovering new parts of her body that ache. It's good to put her lessons into practice, though, even if she hasn't actually been for a lesson for a while.

She's going to head to the pool after work today, because there was no ocean swim this morning, or yesterday. Heavy rain two days ago means a risk of pollution, and Marie has always been clear that they need to wait two days, at least, until they swim again – 'unless you want to inhale a poo', she said. The warning was effective enough for Leanne to stay away. Although she suspects that Marie doesn't take her own advice, because she's been in the habit of daily swimming for so many years it's hard to imagine her not doing it.

Marie is the sort of swimmer Leanne dreams of being, instead of the uncoordinated mess she feels like. She was never this uncoordinated as a child. Some days during a swim she'll wish she'd stuck to dry land, but then she'll have a day when it all clicks and she'll feel capable and accomplished. The others are so much faster, though, and more at ease – even Theresa, who says she's hopeless but clearly isn't. Leanne wonders if she'll ever swim like that.

Walking towards the station desk all she can hear on the paediatrics floor is quiet. Several patients were sent home for Christmas and New Year – either returned for good, or taking an authorised break from their treatment – and the influx that is surely coming hasn't yet started. That means she can give more attention than usual to the children who are here. And there's at least one person she wants to see: the same person she has spent nights sitting beside, watching her sleep, listening to her breathe. When Matron asked her to special Imogen she knew the job wouldn't be hard so much as long, because mainly she's providing reassurance for Imogen's parents – and she knows the form that reassurance takes: they want to know that their child is still alive. So Leanne sits and listens to that breathing throughout the night; she sacrifices her own sleep because she, too, wants to know that Imogen is alive. She cares for all her patients, of course, but she can't help feeling just a little more attached to this one.

'Hello, Imogen,' she says as she approaches the wan child. She's in a room on her own, with three empty beds.

'Hello, Sister!' Imogen smiles, and Leanne marvels, as she has before, at the girl's ability to stay cheerful throughout harrowing treatment.

She smiles back. 'You can call me Leanne. We know each other well enough now, don't we?'

Imogen nods and hugs her doll closer. The doll belonged to

her sister – Leanne remembers it because it has one eye missing and its hair chopped diagonally.

'What's your doll's name?' she says as she picks up Imogen's wrist to measure her pulse and covertly observe her breathing.

'Bunny.'

'Bunny!' Leanne counts the beats in her head. 'She doesn't look like a bunny.'

'No!' Imogen's nose wrinkles and she scrunches her mouth into a smile as her eyes roam over Leanne's face. 'Your hair is very black.'

Leanne places Imogen's hand on the covers. 'It is.'

'And very straight.'

'True.' She fills Imogen's water glass.

'My hair is curly.'

Leanne smiles. 'Yes, it is.'

'At my school my friend has hair like yours. She's from Japan.' Imogen looks as if she's delivering serious news. 'Are you from Japan?'

Leanne shakes her head quickly. 'No. I'm from Australia. Don't I sound Australian?'

'She sounds Australian too! But she says her parents are from Japan.' Imogen puts her head to one side like she's thinking about something.

'Did you eat all your breakfast?' Leanne asks, trying to appear as if she's in charge even as her young patient steers the conversation in a direction she's not sure she wants it to go. She doesn't talk about herself to the children or their parents, even though a lot of them ask. It's better to maintain a barrier.

Imogen makes a face. 'I don't like porridge.'

'So you didn't eat it?'

Imogen drops her head as Leanne shakes out a thermometer and puts it in her armpit. 'Hold still for me.'

Imogen's eyes go to the top of Leanne's head. 'Are you sure you're not from Ja-paa-aan?' she singsongs, and Leanne knows she'll need to say something or Imogen will keep asking. She's as curious as most children her age, and sometimes a little more so.

Yesterday she asked Leanne why her sister died because her parents wouldn't tell her. In the end Leanne had to make up a line about how we don't always know why things happen the way they do. It was too vague to satisfy anyone, let alone a bright six-year-old, but she could hardly tell Imogen the truth when her parents clearly don't want her to know.

'I'm not from Japan,' Leanne says, keeping her voice light. 'My mum is from Korea. That's why I have this hair.'

'And your eyes are funny. Not like mine!'

Leanne thinks of the teasing she endured at school about her eyes. Back then the taunts were all variations on her being from China, not Japan, not Korea. She figured then, and still does, that for all the sarcasm Australians like to indulge in, they're lazy with their insults.

'That's true. They're not like yours,' she says, removing the thermometer. Thirty-eight degrees. So she wasn't imagining that Imogen looks paler than usual. She reaches into her pocket for some paracetamol. 'They're like my mum's.'

'Do you have any brothers and sisters?'

Imogen has already asked this question, several times, and Leanne has told her yes, but demurred when it came to giving a number. Not only because she wants to keep it private, but because she thinks it's unkind when dealing with a child whose only sibling has died.

'You know I do,' she says. 'Now, I have some medicine for you. I'm just going to find some orange juice for you to take it with. Will you keep Bunny company while I'm gone?'

Imogen wrinkles her nose again and nods quickly. 'Mm-hm.'

Leanne reaches out and pats the side of her head. 'Good girl.'

She walks quickly towards the kitchen, her heart beating a little faster. If Imogen's temperature is up, something is going wrong. They've just stabilised her and now she's going backwards. It's what Leanne has worried about some nights as she's sat beside Imogen's bed, then she's chastised herself for being too attached. Imogen is one patient out of many. If Leanne worries about her more than she does the others, she's not doing her job.

After she's administered the paracetamol she calls the registrar and asks him to come and check on Imogen, then continues her rounds. At the end of them she finds Imogen asleep, and a note on her chart indicating that paracetamol was given. Now all she can do is wait and hope that Imogen improves.

The day passes quickly – they all do when she's here, in constant motion – and once her shift is over she walks briskly home to pick up her swimming gear and head for the pool.

It's one of the advantages of living in Shelly Bay that everything is in walking distance, yet it doesn't seem like a small place. There are so many different people coming and going from the hospital, and tourists ebbing and flowing on the weekends, that there are always new faces. Shelly Bay expands and contracts to fit the people who need it. Like her. Without her realising, this place took her into its care and has kept her there.

As Leanne reaches the turnstiles at the pool she feels a fat drop of rain on the back of her neck. If it becomes heavy she can add another day onto her forced exile from the ocean. The pool is an acceptable alternative, although she prefers to come after work when there are fewer agitated men in the fast lanes trying to get in their twenty laps before the day starts. She made the mistake of turning up in the morning yesterday, and even the 'moderate' lane was full of hazards. It wasn't pride so much as practicality that kept her out of the slow lane: that's the domain of breaststrokers, who are lucky to do fifty metres in under ten minutes. She knows she's faster than that. She's come a long way in just a few weeks and she deserves to be in that moderate lane – at a time when there are fewer rivals for it. So she sighs with relief as she sees that there are two moderate lanes this afternoon and only one person in each.

She has no idea how many metres she swims between Main Beach and Little Beach each day, so she's trying to match the time: forty-five minutes or thereabouts. Swimming in chlorine is harder because there's no salt to buoy her, so it's a more tiring forty-five minutes, but it still proves to her that she's achieved something – even if she sometimes does the last few laps as breaststroke. A fast breaststroke.

She ducks into the change room and peels off her uniform. She always tries to be quick even if there's no one else around. Her parents didn't encourage their children to walk around the house nude so she learnt to scurry from bath to bedroom. She's never seen any of her family naked, not even her siblings.

When she swims at the beach she never feels as exposed as she does at the pool. Perhaps it's because the other women are so relaxed about their bodies. Theresa makes cracks about hers, but she's still out there in a swimming costume. Marie may be in her sixties but she's proud, Leanne can tell, of the achievement of making it that far in life and of her years of swimming. Elaine is so lissom that Leanne doesn't believe she could have had a self-conscious moment in her life.

As she emerges from the change room, spitting rain gets in her eyes and she looks around for a place to put her bag and towel. There's one table with an umbrella up and she almost sprints towards it before anyone else can have the same idea. With her eyes half closed against the rain, she doesn't see the person she collides with.

'Whoops!' says a man's voice, and Leanne is mortified to find that it's Matt. The same Matt she hasn't seen for lessons for a while.

'Leanne,' he says, his face transforming into a smile. 'I didn't realise you missed me so much.'

Leanne has no idea how to respond. She hasn't missed Matt – although she sometimes wishes he was in the water with her, giving her tips on improving her stroke – but she doesn't want to say that. If she was Theresa she could come up with something light-hearted. Instead she emits half words, then tries smiling, although she's sure she looks weird.

'Sorry,' she says. 'I was hoping to get these things under shelter before it starts to really rain.'

'Oh.' He looks at the belongings in her hands. 'I'll put them in the office for you.'

He beckons her to follow him before she has a chance to protest.

'You're looking well,' he says over his shoulder, then a shy expression crosses his face. 'I mean, you look in good shape. Have you been swimming a lot?'

'Yes. Every day.'

He nods in a way that suggests it's an answer he expected.

When they reach the office he takes her things and puts them behind the door. 'We don't lock it, so just come and get them when you're ready.' He grins.

'Thanks,' she says, starting to shove her cap over her hair and wondering if it's rude to turn around and walk away from him.

'So how have you been?' he asks, and the matter is decided for her.

'Fine. The swimming I'm doing – it's in the ocean. So it's toughened me up a bit, I think.'

Matt nods vigorously. 'I thought I hadn't seen you here lately.'

'Oh, I was here yesterday.' Leanne tucks in the last of her hair.

'Right.' He nods again, looking crestfallen. 'So . . . no more lessons?'

'I'm good for now. Thanks.' She half smiles.

'Right.' He has a funny look on his face but she has no idea what it means.

She has to think of something to say to end this conversation or she may never get in the pool. 'You were such a great teacher that I'm swimming really well. And I can keep up with the ladies I swim with. They're really good. Experienced.'

Something crosses his face then and she thinks it's genuine pleasure. If only she'd thought to tell him this earlier – she feels almost cruel not letting him know that he's helped her so much. She has been grateful, but mainly only aware of it when she's in the sea, far from being able to tell him.

'That's really terrific,' he says softly. 'Good on you.'

She smiles as fully as she can. 'Thank you.'

'There's, um . . . something else I'd like to ask you.' He fidgets with the handle on the office door as she looks at him expectantly. 'It may sound a bit strange, because of how we met, but, um . . .' He looks flustered. 'Would you like to go out for dinner one night?' he says, then seems relieved, as if he's finished a three-hour exam.

Leanne is too surprised to know how to respond. She had no inkling that he thought of her as anything other than a student – although she supposes that means he did his job professionally. Should she be upset that all the while he had other designs on her? No, probably not, because she doesn't know if he did, and it's not as if he called her home number – which he could have, because it's in the office records. So he's not a creep. And she doesn't want to think he's a creep. She's just not sure if she wants to think he's anything else either. He hasn't been someone she might consider going on a date with.

Not that she's thought of anyone else that way. That hasn't been part of her life. Until right now, she thought it never would be again. Men don't ask her out – that's what she's always told busybodies at work when they've asked why she 'doesn't have a fella', and it's easy to say it because it's mostly the truth.

'Leanne?' Matt says gently. 'Sorry – did I say the wrong thing?' He looks worried.

'No, you didn't,' she says. She takes a breath, because she feels, all of a sudden, the past seven years running up to meet her.

Seven years of not sitting across the table from a man, making conversation. Seven years of thinking that she would be a spinster forever and it would be all right. Seven years of sometimes longing to feel the touch of someone else's skin, then remembering what the cost of that has been in the past. She has, for those years, believed that men can't be trusted because they want to hurt women. They want to hurt *her*. Even her father and brothers, in the end, hurt her.

It's not feminism that's made her like this. She isn't inclined to read *The Female Eunuch*, even though Marie has encouraged her to, and she put aside Simone de Beauvoir's *The Second Sex* on her sole attempt at reading it. Leanne doesn't think she needs books to tell her that women deserve the same rights as men. She knows they do. And she also knows that in life it seems impossible to achieve.

Yet here is Matt, with warmth in his voice and kindness on his face. He is happy for her that she's swimming regularly and he helped her achieve that.

There has to be a point, Leanne knows, at which she decides how much she wants to keep hold of the ideas she has; how much they are worth to her stacked up next to the life that's still ahead of her. And she needs to be brave if she is going to mark the end of those seven years. She needs to believe that her future can be better than her past. And she does believe it, because she has already made it so.

Matt may not be the man of her dreams; then again, she's never had one of those. She hasn't let herself wonder or daydream about a man she might form a life with. Matt may not turn out to be the man of her immediate future either, but she won't know if she doesn't start.

'That would be lovely,' she says, and gives him her best smile, the one she's been trying to use more often. Inspired by Theresa, who smiles so readily.

'Really?' Now he looks as excited as a child who's won a prize at the fair.

She nods. 'Really.'

'Great. Great. That's really great. Can I – um, you need to swim. Can I call you later?'

'Sure.' She smiles again.

'Well, uh . . . have a good swim then.' His smile is broad and she feels pleased.

'I intend to,' she says, and turns to walk towards the pool, out into the warm rain that is now falling steadily. She barely notices the change as she slips into the pool, under the surface and pushes off the end.

CHAPTER 24

'Jesus, Andrew, don't let him do that!' Theresa feels like stomping the way her children sometimes do, and not just because she's annoyed that Andrew's not stopping their son from decorating the kitchen with the mayonnaise she's trying to put into the potato salad.

She still hasn't said anything about what she saw at the party and the compulsion to do so is reaching a high-tide mark inside her. She worries that it will flow out of her mouth in front of the children if she doesn't say something soon. Yet they're at her parents' home for a few days, and before that they were in the car driving here, and before that the only times she was alone with him were the seconds when they passed each other in the hall. She's been asleep each evening when he's arrived home.

Theresa's been falling asleep earlier and earlier each night, and she's not sure if it's because she feels exhausted – which is the case, but she's been exhausted for years – or because she's been subconsciously avoiding the very conversation she needs to have.

She glares at her husband but he doesn't even register her request.

'Andrew – *please* help me,' she says. She pushes her hair back from her sweaty forehead and realises she's smeared herself with mayo.

'That's a good look,' Andrew says, picking up his tinny and taking a long swig.

'I swear to God—'

'God, Jesus – you're havin' a good run of it.' He takes another swig of his beer, which makes her want to scream.

But Sasha is standing by her legs, looking up at her with those gorgeous brown eyes, and her lips are quivering the way they always do when her parents fight.

Oliver is high on the rapture that comes with being in his grandparents' home, from the bowls of jelly and ice cream her mother always gives him. And Theresa knows Andrew won't do anything to stop him misbehaving, because he never does.

Andrew never used to be like this. When it was just the two of them he'd tell her to forget about the ironing and the washing up and come to bed. As soon as Oliver was born he changed, and she slipped into chains she's never managed to break.

'Mamma,' Sasha whimpers.

Theresa wipes her hands on her apron and bends down to pick up her daughter, wincing as Sasha presses against her breast. That breast has been so sensitive lately, and Theresa's tried to work out if she's using one arm differently when she swims. But she's no expert, and the effort of trying to analyse her freestyle stroke while actually swimming freestyle has been taking a lot of fun out of the whole experience.

'It's all right, darling,' she whispers, kissing Sasha's temple twice before putting her down again. 'Why don't you go and see what Nana is up to?' The atmosphere in the kitchen isn't likely to become less tense and Sasha will be better off in another room.

'What's going on?' Her father is in the kitchen now, carrying his own tinny.

Theresa sighs and forces a smile. 'I'm trying to get Ollie to calm down. He's throwing food everywhere.'

She offered to make lunch so her mother could have a break from Nonna, who has been demanding games of backgammon because she's missing out on poker by visiting her daughter – but didn't count on having to wrangle her children while she did it.

'Oliver,' her father says, putting his shoulders back the way he's always done when he wants to command authority, 'how about some cricket, eh? Your nana put the bat and ball somewhere in the garden. Once we find it, we can have a hit.'

Oliver grins.

'Ollie, put the jar on the bench, please,' Theresa says, only to see her son drop it on the floor as he runs towards the back garden. Mayonnaise spatters across the kitchen cupboards.

She lets out a shriek. 'OLIVER!'

'Leave him alone,' Andrew says, drinking more beer, burping. Charming. 'It's his school holidays. Only a few days left.'

'That doesn't mean he's allowed to do whatever he wants,' Theresa says, picking up the Chux from the kitchen sink and wiping down the cupboards. 'And it's not you cleaning up the mess.'

'Because that's your job,' he says, not even looking at her. 'I do enough as it is.'

Of course: he does so much; he does it all. He pays for everything. She does nothing. The housework is easy. Looking after the kids is easy – until he has to do it and then it's all too hard. She's sick of it.

She's not going to get upset, though. It doesn't get her anywhere. So she stuffs the anger back down, throws the Chux into the sink and turns on the tap, dousing and wringing the cloth.

'Dad,' she says, hanging the cloth over the tap, 'aren't you going to play cricket with Ollie?'

'Oh. Yeah.' Her father nods to Andrew and leaves the kitchen.

Theresa turns to face her husband, who is gazing at her with what might be called indifference if Theresa was being kind to herself, but is more likely to be something stronger.

'Are you having an affair?' she blurts.

Andrew stares at her. 'Don't be bloody ridiculous,' he says, but she hears a quavering in his voice.

'I saw you,' she says, feeling bolder.

He glances away then back to her. 'I don't know what you're talkin' about.'

Because she knows he's lying, somehow it allows her to feel calmer. She's the one speaking the truth. Why didn't she do it earlier?

'At the surf club party,' she says. 'By the toilets. You were . . .' How can she describe the spectacle she saw? 'You were groping a woman.'

'Was not.'

He sounds like Oliver when he's denying something that he's definitely done. Trying to get her son to admit the truth never works, so Theresa doesn't like her chances with his father.

She didn't think about what she'd do if Andrew denied her accusation – she just wanted to get it out of the way. But if he insists there's no affair when she knows there likely is, or something close to it . . . what will she do next? How is she meant to keep living with her husband knowing he prefers another woman, and he knows that she knows?

'Fine,' she says, because it's all she can come up with.

Andrew looks stunned. 'Fine?'

'Why don't you join Dad and Ollie outside?'

She picks up the Chux and drapes it again. Picks it up. Drapes it. If he doesn't leave, she worries that she'll say something else – scream it, maybe – and she doesn't want to fight any more than they have. She wants her children to enjoy their time here – the garden is twice the size of the one at home, there's a swing on one of the trees, and her father has limitless patience with his grandchildren. It is, as Andrew reminded her, their holidays. She has happy memories of summer holidays, and Ollie and Sasha should have the same.

She stays facing the sink but feels him close behind her.

'It didn't mean anything,' he says.

She can smell the hops on his breath and her stomach turns, but not because of the smell. 'So you're not denying it now?'

She doesn't want to look at him so she's going to stay here, where she can see her father and son through the kitchen window.

He sniffs. 'What's the point?' he says wearily. 'But that was the only time.'

'You knew her,' Theresa says. 'I could tell.'

'She's Chook's sister.'

Of course. Which means Chook is a party to her humiliation as well, just as she suspected.

'I didn't know she'd be at the party.' He sniffs again. 'I just . . .' His exhalation is ragged. 'She's had a thing for me for a while.'

As if that explains it. Except it's the excuse he's allowed himself, so clearly it does.

'And that meant you should do what you did?' she half whispers.

'I just . . .' He sighs. 'Gave in.'

In all the scripts Theresa's run in her head about this situation, she never once had Andrew saying he'd given in. He was meant to tell her that he's in love with this woman, at least. In one of the scripts he's going to leave her because the other woman is pregnant. Or there's already another child and that's why he's been gone so often. Theresa wanted a drama to match her reaction that night. Something big. Now she feels something very much like disappointment mixed in with the churn of embarrassment and betrayal.

She turns to face him. Wants to see how he reacts as she says, 'You were right there in front of everyone. Didn't you care who saw? Didn't you care if *I* saw?'

There are clouds in Andrew's eyes, and she notices that he's unkempt. He hasn't shaved in a while. His hair is in need of a cut. The skin on his forehead is peeling because he never wears a hat when he's working outside and she stopped, long ago, trying to make him. He looks uncared for, and she hasn't seen it because she hasn't looked at him closely for a long time. Maybe she looks the same; she doesn't really take the time to check each day.

'Of course I care,' he mutters. 'Why do you think I did it?'

Theresa feels like a hot wind has blown into her eyes, so she half shuts them against the world. 'You wanted me to see?' she says hoarsely.

'I wanted you to *react*,' he says, an edge to his voice. 'But you didn't. Not until now. And now is . . .' He looks like he's sneering, then he shakes his head and it's gone. 'You used to think I was hot shit. You could never get enough.'

She has a memory – an image that flashes in and out of her mind – of Andrew telling her she was the most beautiful girl on the beaches. 'I could say the same about you,' she says quietly, although she knows she's not that girl any more. Besides, she doesn't believe that he still wants her. If he did he wouldn't have looked elsewhere for company. He'd have stayed loyal to her. But she doubts he'd buy that argument.

'You stopped wanting me first,' he says, swallowing. 'I never stopped.'

His eyes are red-rimmed but she doesn't think he's about to cry. She's never seen him cry. Truth be told, she's never wanted to. She's never liked to see men cry because she wants to believe they can be stronger than she is; strong for her when she needs them to be. Crying is weak, isn't it? That's what the magazines say.

'Andrew,' she says, 'most of the time I'm so tired I don't know what I want.'

'Yeah, well . . .' He picks at the ring-pull on his tinny. 'A man's got needs.'

And a woman doesn't? She can't say that, though, because she knows the answer, and it's *no*. Her needs are secondary to everyone else's.

'I'm sorry you're feeling that way,' she says, because keeping the peace is another of her jobs. 'I'll try to make more time for you.'

'You could stop swimming,' he says quickly, as if he's practised saying it. As if he's been waiting for the chance to say it again.

'What?'

'Instead of rushing out every morning, you could spend a bit longer in bed.' He looks at her suggestively.

Once upon a time she'd have taken up his invitation, but now her immediate reaction is to want to tell him to get lost. Swimming is the one thing she has for herself, to herself. In the water she's free. Accomplished. Capable. All the things she doesn't feel on dry land.

Yet if she refuses his request, he can say he's tried to fix things and it's her not making the effort.

'Mu-um!' Sasha's voice rescues her from Andrew's checkmate.

'I'd better go,' she says.

'What a surprise.'

'I'll – I'll think about it,' she says, although she's lying. She just needs time to come up with a compromise.

'Sure.'

'Mu-uuuum!'

She and Andrew stare at each other for a few seconds, then Theresa rushes from the room.

CHAPTER 25

When Marie arrives home from her swim there's a message on her answering machine. She knows it will be Nicole, because Nicole is the only one who leaves messages.

Hi Mum – I forgot to tell you that your new gardener is starting today. His name's Gus. I don't know what time he'll be there. I said you'd be home. You will be, won't you? Love you. Bye.

Marie looks outside and sighs. The arrival of the gardener is sorely needed: her garden is on the verge of being ramshackle and she knows Norm would hate it. This Gus will probably think she's lazy or useless, but she can't be worried about that because he's probably young and will barely notice she's there. That's what happens when you start to go grey and your posture's not as straight as it used to be: you become invisible. As far as most people are concerned Marie's an old lady; and she may as well be a ghost as she passes them on the street, so intangible does she feel. Luckily she wasn't invisible to Theresa when they met.

Marie smiles as she thinks about this morning's escapades, with Theresa swimming underwater for as long as she was able before popping up next to Elaine, who yelped.

'You could have been a shark!' Elaine cried, as Leanne looked on with amusement.

'But I'm not,' Theresa said, gasping as she trod water. 'I'm not as good at that underwater thing as I'd like to be, though.' She started to float on her back.

'You'll go out to sea if you try that,' Marie said as she swam back towards them, for once not so interested in getting to her destination.

'I need a rest,' Theresa said weakly.

'You should have come up for air earlier, you fool,' Marie chastised. 'People can blow valves or something if they hold their breath too long.'

Around them the water was rolling slowly with the motion of the waves that would break on Main Beach but never manifest right where they were. They were about fifty metres from the walking path; there were people jogging and strolling along it, some with dogs. It was one of those perfect mornings when the sky is cloudless and the light is golden, turning the leaves on the nearby trees a more lustrous green and the sand a richer hue. Marie has been looking at this place her entire life yet she doesn't always see it. Too much time has passed since she's stopped to appreciate it.

She's still thinking about it as she showers and makes her breakfast. The whole day seems suffused with the glow of the morning and she feels like it's seeped into her marrow.

The click-clack of claws on her kitchen floor snaps her back to the present. 'What is it, Charlie Brown? Have you finished your breakfast already?' She bends down to scratch behind his ears.

'Knock knock,' she hears, and straightens up to see standing on her verandah, by the back door, a man with a full head of salt-and-pepper hair and a slight stoop to his tall frame. He has grey-green eyes set in a complexion that's either olive-skinned or browned by the sun, and he's looking at her with curiosity.

'Hello?' she says, her heart beating fast at the sight of a stranger in her home, even if she's sure this is the new gardener.

'Are you Marie?' he says, smiling – and, she notices, still standing outside. At least he has the manners to wait for an invitation.

'I am,' she says.

'I'm Gus. Nicole sent me. Sorry for surprising you – she said to take the side gate.' His crow's feet crinkle in a way that suggests he smiles a lot.

He's older than she was expecting and looks nothing like a man who's spent his life doing manual labour. For one thing, he's wearing a linen shirt with the sleeves rolled up, tucked into moleskins that are secured with a new-looking belt. He's wearing boots, though, so that's workmanlike. Around these parts a lot of the tradesmen wear thongs. She once had a man cleaning gutters while wearing thongs and spent the whole day expecting him to fall off the ladder.

'Please – come in,' she says.

As he steps inside, Charlie Brown starts to dance around his feet. 'Who's this?' says Gus, bending down to bring his face closer to the dog's.

'Charlie Brown. He runs the place.'

She watches as Gus holds the back of his hand towards Charlie Brown, the way someone used to dogs would.

'Do you have a dog?' she asks.

'I did, a long time ago.' He stands up. 'An Alsatian. Lovely fellow.'

He extends his hand towards her and she shakes it, feeling the dry warmth of his skin, conscious that hers will feel cold to him. *Cold hands, warm heart*, Norm used to say.

'Lovely to meet you, Marie.'

There are those crinkles again and he's looking at her more intensely than any man has since Norm died. She doesn't quite know what to do with it, especially as he must be at least a decade younger than her, so she's sure he doesn't mean it in the way Norm did.

'I suppose you saw the garden on your way in,' she says, nodding towards the back, reminding herself why he's here.

'I had a glance. But I'd love you to show me properly.' He has the modulated tones of someone with training in received pronunciation.

Marie smiles quickly and steps around Charlie Brown, who then hangs off her heels as she walks onto the verandah.

'How did Nicole find you?' she asks over her shoulder.

'My son knows her husband,' Gus says as he follows her down the stairs to the garden path. 'And he mentioned I've been doing some gardening work around the place. Nothing too fancy.' He flashes her a smile as he stops beside her. 'I should warn you that I'm self-taught, but I haven't managed to butcher a garden yet.'

She looks up at him. 'Well, I've almost managed to butcher this one, so you can't make it worse.'

He puts his hands on his hips and looks around. 'I think you're being hard on yourself. Everything's in the right place – it just needs a bit of attention.'

Their eyes meet.

'Don't we all?' he adds smoothly, and she doesn't know whether to be shocked or pleased that he seems to be if not flirting with her then allowing her to believe he is.

Marie breaks his gaze and gestures towards the shed. 'I'll show you where the tools are. My husband kept them in there.'

She doesn't know why she's mentioned Norm – there's no need to tell Gus that the tools were his.

'Nicole told me that he died several years ago. I'm sorry,' Gus says, and he sounds genuinely concerned.

'It's not your fault.'

He laughs. 'That's what I say when people say that about my wife.'

Marie feels a pinprick of jealousy – something else she hasn't experienced in a very long time.

'You're widowed too?' she asks.

Gus nods. 'Around the same time you were. That's when I started this.' He opens his arms to the garden. 'I spent years in the law and I lost my taste for it. It's satisfying when you have a victory, but the rest of the time you don't feel like you're doing much good. However, it did give me enough of an income that I could step back and do what I pleased.'

He looks abashed. 'I ran on a bit there – I apologise.' He looks at her with that intensity again – the same look as when he arrived. 'I suppose I feel like I know you because I've heard about you from Peter. Forgive me.'

Marie raises her eyebrows. 'There you go again, saying sorry.'

She hears a noise and follows it to where Charlie Brown is digging up a flower bed.

'Charlie Brown!' she says crossly. 'Stop that.'

Gus strides over and picks up the dog in one easy movement. Charlie Brown looks too surprised to protest and Marie is much the same.

'Let's see these tools,' Gus says, walking towards the shed with the terrier tucked under his arm. 'Then we can talk about the amount of work involved.'

Marie fights the impulse to want to be tucked under his other arm and follows him into the shed.

AUTUMN 1983

CHAPTER 26

This morning's swim was sublime. Almost effortless, right up until the point Elaine decided she'd attempt to catch up to Marie – who still has the advantage most days – only to feel her shoulders protest, reminding her that while she may think of herself as being athletic, she hasn't been swimming for as long as Marie.

Nor can she really call herself athletic with the amount she's drinking. It's become more than a bad habit now. For so long she has kidded herself that gin has been keeping her company in the late afternoons while she waits for James to come home from work, and after he falls into bed exhausted.

Occasionally he wants to make love and she never minds that – she welcomes it, in fact, because it gives her a chance to forget herself. On those nights she doesn't drink nearly as much and she doesn't miss it. On those nights she tells herself that she doesn't need to drink as often as she does; she can do without it.

Then the next afternoon arrives and she thinks, *Just one.* Then, *Just another one.* Her body is so used to it now that it takes more and more to achieve the same small oblivion she's always looking for.

And now that James has noticed she's drinking a lot, she's become sneaky. Starting to drink earlier in the day so she can sober up a bit before he arrives home, then creeping out of bed to have a tipple or two late at night.

She's hiding a huge part of her life from her husband and part of her relishes it, because it makes her feel like she has some control again. Not of him, but of her circumstances. It also makes her homesickness disappear. Most of her, though, detests what she does yet feels completely out of control. She wants to stop, but can't. She doesn't want to stop, and doesn't.

She tops up her tonic to dilute the gin, and turns down the radio in the kitchen. The hour of music has turned into talkback and she flinches at the sound of some of the flatter Australian accents of the callers. They say inscrutable things such as 'I dint come down in the last shower' and 'He was all over the place like a dog's breakfast'. They talk about the 'gummint', which, after some study, she believes to be the *government*.

The male callers – and they're mostly men – use the term 'mate' a lot, especially when they're being hostile. She has realised that Australians use this term as a friendly greeting and as a warning. Deciphering its intention is all in the tone. When it's friendly, the speaker tends to use a rising inflection, as if there's an exclamation point: 'Mate!' If it's a warning, the tone is usually lower and the word spoken more sharply, almost like it's 'met': 'Listen, *met*.'

Clearly Elaine has too much time on her hands if she's trying to decode local speech, but she knows it's useful. For example, when she met James's colleagues she noticed that they didn't use the term 'mate'. They addressed each other by name. That's led her to a theory: that for Australians who aren't any good at remembering people's names, 'mate' serves as a useful substitute. If everyone uses it, who's to notice that you're forgetful? Although, more likely, it's deployed as a weapon of faux egalitarianism: everyone's a 'mate'. Except they're clearly not.

She's heard Australians railing against the English class system yet she only has to look at the social pages in the Sunday newspapers to see there's at least the pretence of such a system here. There are Ladies who are wives of Sirs rather than being born with any blue blood. For example, Lady Sonia McMahon, who's a regular in those newspapers and given prime position in the layout. Elaine is quite sure she's not the daughter of an earl, like the former Lady Diana Spencer, yet she's fawned over like minor royalty.

Elaine's tennis ladies had their own idea of a class system. Someone's daughter was being given a better start in life because she was going to a private school rather than a public school. Yet another's son was in a selective public high school, which was better than the other public high schools yet not as prestigious as the private school. Humans strive to sort themselves into strata wherever they find themselves – even, or perhaps especially, in a former penal colony.

The only group where she hasn't found that is in her little swimming circle. Marie, Leanne and Theresa don't seem to mind where she's from or what she did before they met. They're all equals in the water: each of them wanting to be out there, feeling the embrace of the ocean, the power of achievement, the sun on their faces as they dry off afterwards.

Elaine takes another long sip of her drink as she thinks about her new friends. Theresa: so vivacious yet Elaine can see a vulnerability behind her bright smile and determination to be happy every day. Leanne: giving the appearance of being closed off to the world yet she keeps turning up to swim with them each day, so perhaps she doesn't really know what she wants, or she's telling herself a story about it. As for Marie – Elaine knows she's a widow and there's a layer of sadness there, yet she's a sturdy type, and not just because she's so fit.

Elaine looks at the clock on the kitchen wall. It's almost five and James said he'd definitely be home for dinner tonight, so she needs to start thinking about what she's going to cook. She puts her drink down and yanks open the fridge door. She has some spinach and tomatoes. No meat. And James does like his lamb chops. *Why* didn't she check this before?

There's a butcher at the bottom of the hill who sometimes stays open past five. If she hurries, she can make it. Her keys and handbag are by the front door. She almost runs to the car, turns on the engine and pulls out of her parking spot.

Her head feels a bit light and she probably shouldn't be driving given how much she's had to drink, but if she walks to the butcher she's never going to make it in time. And she can't give her husband spinach and tomatoes for dinner, because then he'll know she's slipping up and wonder why she's not as attentive to home duties as she should be, given she has no other duties. If he doesn't already suspect why.

Not that Elaine has ever pretended to be in love with home-making. In their former life she had a housekeeper to keep things running while she took care of her business and of being a mother. She always felt that mothering needed to take up all the time her work didn't, and cooking and cleaning shouldn't distract from it. That excuse doesn't exist any more with her two grown sons still in the northern hemisphere. So she really should be better at homemaking. She should have noticed she didn't already have chops.

Suddenly she feels an impact and hears a scraping sound, but she's not sure if it's real. It seems like it's happening somewhere else, to someone else. Except her head is ricocheting on her neck, and when it stops she can see she's driven into the old Mercedes-Benz that's always parked at the end of their street, just before the T-intersection. It's the car that's stopped her, not her foot on the brake, because she didn't get around to that.

There's a *thud* now. Fainter than the first sound. Faster. Her heart. She can't get her breath. She's gulping in air but it's not going anywhere.

Her car is poking out into the street and she can see in the rear-vision mirror that another car is coming. She's sure it won't be able to get past her. This is a mess. She's caused a huge mess. And her head feels funny.

The other car manages to squeak past, and she recognises Colin from up the street, frowning at her. Wonderful – now she has an audience.

Colin stops his car and gets out. Now his car is also blocking the road and it's all her fault. She would be mortified if she weren't feeling so appalled.

As Colin approaches her side of the car she rolls down the window and summons the smile she's been trained to give since childhood: the everything-is-lovely smile common to her people; a cousin of the stiff upper lip.

'You all right?' Colin says, bending down and looking around her car's interior.

'I'm so *silly*,' Elaine says slowly, controlling her words, conscious that she may slur them otherwise. 'I wore heels to drive the car and I slipped on the brake.'

She hopes he doesn't look too deeply into the footwell to see that, in fact, her heels are sensibly low.

'You hit your head?' he asks.

'Oh no – no!' she trills. 'Nothing like that! Sorry to disturb.'

He narrows his eyes and nods slowly. 'Need a hand moving it?'

'It will be *fine*. Honestly. Please, you go. I'm holding you up.'

Mea culpa always works as a social strategy, especially when it's the truth. Besides, she has to fix this. Right now. Before James gets home. He can't see what's happened, otherwise he'll want to know why.

As Colin gets back in his car and drives off, thoughts are moving around inside her head like a murmuration of starlings. So much for alcohol dulling her senses: she is vibrating with alertness.

What can she do? Who can help her? Who is nearby?

Theresa. The name pierces the fluttering in her brain.

She pushes open the door, dragging her handbag and the keys with her. Her neck is telling her she shouldn't move so quickly but she needs to get help. Shoving the door closed, she walks as fast as she can back to the house, drops the keys twice trying to get them in the door, and flings her handbag onto the floor as she moves towards the sitting room to make the call.

'Hello?' says Theresa's voice on the other end of the phone.

'Theresa – it's – it's me,' Elaine says, simultaneously thinking that's a ridiculous thing to announce: *me* could be anyone.

'Elaine?' There's concern there.

'I – I need help.'

'Give me your address,' Theresa says and after she has it she hangs up.

She didn't ask why, or what sort of help. Elaine feels tears stinging her eyes at the idea that someone could be so generous.

Theresa arrives with an apron over a cotton dress and a smile that is lower in wattage than her usual.

'I'm drunk,' Elaine says, figuring that Theresa will smell it on her breath.

Theresa's face doesn't change. 'Okay.'

'I crashed the car.'

Now there's a small wrinkle on her forehead. 'Are you hurt?'

'I . . .' Elaine exhales through her mouth. 'I don't think so. Maybe a bit of whiplash.' She swallows. 'The car – it's up the street. And James will be home soon and I don't have his chops.' Her face crumples.

'Don't worry about the chops,' Theresa says as she puts her arm around Elaine's shoulders.

'I have to!' Elaine says, sniffing back the sob that's in her throat. 'If I don't have his dinner right he'll know I've been doing nothing except drinking!'

Theresa squeezes her closer. 'I'll call Marie. She'll have chops.'

'No! Please. I don't want her to know.'

Elaine can't bear the idea of Marie judging her for being drunk in daylight. She saw the look on her face the other day at the beach when Elaine only hinted at drinking too much from time to time.

'Elaine,' Theresa says in a tone of voice that Elaine presumes she uses on her children, 'there are a few things that need to happen and we're going to need more help. I'm going to call Leanne to come over and check that you're not hurt. And Marie can help with the car. And the chops.' She smiles that sweet, reassuring smile that always makes Elaine think everything will be fine.

'Okay,' she says.

'Good. Now – where's the phone?'

Elaine lifts her chin in the direction of the sideboard. While Theresa makes calls she slumps onto the couch.

'What am I going to tell James?' she moans when Theresa hangs up.

Theresa comes over and sits next to her, taking her hand. 'How about the truth?'

Elaine starts to shake her head but the pain in her neck stops her. 'I can't. He already thinks I drink too much and now ... well, there's proof, isn't there?'

She closes her eyes, trying to picture what it would be like to have that conversation with James, and the thought is more alarming than the memory of the crash.

'Then ... maybe you need to think about what you can do?' Theresa says. 'You're my friend and I don't like to see you in this much distress.'

'You're so kind,' Elaine whispers. 'If I were you I'd judge me fairly harshly.'

'It's not my place to judge,' Theresa says. 'But it is my place to help. What can I do?'

'You've helped already.' Elaine rests her head against Theresa's briefly.

'What about AA? It's meant to be really good.'

'I'm not an alcoholic,' Elaine says sharply, and regrets it instantly because Theresa looks hurt. 'I mean – I drink too much but I haven't been doing it for long enough to be an *alcoholic*.'

It's the label she's been resisting all this time because she can't bear the idea of it being applied to her. Alcoholics are old men in falling-down trousers with straggly beards as thick as forests. They're sad women who sit alone after a lifetime of no husband and no children. They're people who *can't cope*. That isn't her. It simply cannot be her.

'It could still be good,' Theresa says. 'You might get some tips that could help you. Or you might realise you're not as bad as you think.'

Elaine looks sceptical. 'Maybe. But I don't know that I'm good in groups.'

'You're good in our group,' Theresa says gently, 'and I guess it can't hurt to try.'

Elaine emits a sharp laugh. 'I wouldn't know where to begin.'

'I'll find out! I think I saw a sign when I walked past that church on the plaza.' Theresa puts her arm around Elaine again. 'You're not alone,' she says.

As Elaine looks into Theresa's eyes, she knows it's the truth. What she doesn't know is how to stop feeling so alone that she wants to drink the day away. Or maybe the wanting is the key. And if it is, perhaps she is an alcoholic after all.

'Thank you,' she says. 'If you could find out some information I would appreciate it.'

Theresa nods once then stands up. 'Come on. Let's go and look at this car.'

As much as Elaine wants to crawl into a hole and let the others deal with the problem she's created, she knows she has to face it. And keep facing it. Each and every day until she feels as though she has a handle on this problem that's overtaking her life.

If only it were that simple.

CHAPTER 27

The pleasant morning temperatures can't last much longer now they're halfway through March and almost at the equinox. Australia marks its seasons by months but autumn doesn't really start until the equinox. So there's no chill in the air yet, but there will be in another fortnight or so, most likely, and then they'll start to sniff Easter, and then it will be winter. Leanne imagines they won't keep swimming as a group once the weather turns, although Marie has made it clear that she swims all year round. What Leanne can't work out is if Marie disapproves of people who don't – and she finds herself caring if Marie disapproves of her or not.

Leanne's the first one here this morning, so she closes her eyes and feels the breeze on her skin. After she moved to Shelly Bay she learnt that living by the water means living with the elements – earth, water, air, ether. No fire, not yet. She hopes never. There are bushfires on the outskirts of the city each summer but none has erupted in this little peninsula. Instead there is wind, each afternoon, so regular she could set her watch by it. In fact, she's been by the water and felt the wind come up and assessed that it's likely one o'clock. The mornings are rarely still, either, but they have a breeze instead of wind.

She opens her eyes to take in the earth element: the plentiful trees that line the beachfront and the path around to Little Beach. They're not all native to this place, or to this country, but they're thriving.

And the water is there, beckoning her. Since that first day in the ocean she has craved it. If only she'd known there was so much joy to be had by diving under a wave, by swimming out so far from the shore that you feel like the world has unlimited bounty, she would have done it sooner. She's tempted to blame her parents for not introducing her to the ocean, but she doesn't think they knew either: they didn't grow up near the beach.

Perhaps she's fibbing to herself, though, because it was at the pool that she first came to trust herself in the water – to believe that she could move in it, keep herself safe in it. That was thanks to Matt and his encouragement, as well as the way he taught her. He never let her feel that she wasn't learning at just the right pace. He would smile at her with such reassurance.

She flushes as she thinks of that smile, and the one he gave her the other day at the pool when she saw him again. He smiled at her like she made his day, but she doesn't know if she deserved it, because she hasn't arranged to see him since, although he's been calling. Despite her determination that day to be open to what he was offering her, once she was out of his sight she lost her nerve. And it's only because of him, really, that she's standing here, taking in this view she loves so much, craving that salt water on her skin.

She knows she is made of mostly water; all humans are. But that was just an idea – a fact – until she found out what it really means to her. The ocean calls her, and she wants to respond.

It's a point of commonality with Marie that binds them, even if they don't know each other well enough yet to talk about it.

She can see it in Marie's eyes each morning – the recognition of home – and she hopes that Marie sees it in hers too.

'Magic, isn't it?'

That's Marie's voice, and for a second Leanne wonders if she's daydreaming. But Marie herself steps next to her, real as the day.

'Yes,' Leanne murmurs. 'It's . . .'

She tries, every day, to think of the best words to describe what these mornings are like. She can't. Perhaps those words haven't been invented. Perhaps no one in charge of words has stood on a beach at dawn in early autumn and tried to conjure just the right combination of vowels and consonants to describe what it feels like. There are words for the sights: sunlight, water, waves, foam, sand, ocean. And for the sounds: seagulls calling, waves crashing, the hissing of water on sand, the susurration of other humans nearby. But she has searched her mind and her memory for a word to describe this feeling and found nothing appropriate.

Maybe she's being unfair. The word she's searching for could be particular to her experience of being here on this exact beach each day, with women she is learning to appreciate more and more for their friendship offered so unquestioningly and the gifts they've given her of company and comradeship. Also for their personalities, their histories, and how all of them understand that this time in the water together is a capsule of belonging that is just for them. They part each day knowing that they can take the morning with them, and tomorrow they'll be here again to repeat the actions but have a different experience. Each day is precious, new. Each morning is alive with vigour and a certain rapture.

For the first time since she was eighteen Leanne feels like she belongs in her body again. It is not a territory invaded by an enemy; it is not a hollowed-out ground for something she could not bear to nurture. She loves her job yet she knows she's been play-acting: there's a version of herself that's great with the kids, and another that deals with the adults, and neither has been really her. The real her – the essence of her – has been trapped in a reservoir. She doesn't know if she did this to herself, or circumstance forced it, yet now she feels it bubbling up towards the surface. Her hard-baked surface that she's taken so much care to guard against cracking. She should feel scared of it splitting and exposing her after all this time hidden away. But she doesn't. She feels brave. What was trapped in that reservoir were all the things she was as a child: the fearless girl who climbed trees and hit cricket balls and rode bikes and ran with her brothers for hours, tired and exhilarated. She was in her body then, and she didn't even question it. Now, as she returns to herself, she's not questioning it either. This is where she belongs: in this shell called Leanne. That's what these days have taught her; this is what the ocean has given her.

'Hello! What a beautiful morning.' Theresa is pushing herself through the soft sand, her sarong flapping open.

'I'm here too,' says Elaine as she arrives from the other direction. 'I know I'm a bit late.'

'We're not sticking strictly to the clock,' Marie says, smiling.

'I know. But still . . .' Elaine sighs as she drops her towel on the sand.

'Are you all right?' Marie asks.

'I'm fine.'

Marie looks dubious and Leanne knows why: they didn't see Elaine yesterday, or the day before. They haven't seen her since Theresa asked them to help her out of that mess with the car. Leanne's job has inured her to surprises – she's shocked sometimes, but rarely surprised, simply because she sees so many different things in that hospital. But she was surprised that day.

She'd always thought of Elaine as being somewhat untouchable: tall and glamorous, with lovely elocution. The woman she saw that day seemed small and lost and rumpled. Vulnerable.

'Honestly,' Elaine says, although she looks tired.

'What did James say?' Marie asks, and Leanne is glad someone did, because she imagines they're all wondering.

'He was cross,' Elaine says. 'But he sorted it out with the owner of the other car, and he's taken mine in for repair.'

'What did you tell him?' Theresa joins in.

Elaine's eyelids flutter. 'Not the whole truth.'

Theresa looks disappointed but Marie seems unsurprised. 'He'll have guessed,' she says. 'He's just not saying anything.'

Elaine's smile is tight-lipped. 'Perhaps. Shall we swim?'

Marie half rolls her eyes. 'Sure.'

She and Elaine look as though they're having a race to be first in the water, but Leanne hangs back and is glad that Theresa does too. She wants to talk to her.

'Theresa?' she says tentatively, and is rewarded with an expression on Theresa's face that looks like shock. Which Leanne supposes is reasonable: she's never initiated a conversation with any of the three women.

'Yes?'

Leanne gestures to the water. 'Let's, uh ... I'll talk while we walk.'

Now Theresa looks as if Leanne has given her a present.

'I – I need some advice,' Leanne says as they walk slowly.

Marie and Elaine are already a few metres offshore with arms and legs working hard.

'Oh? Yes?'

'I got asked out to dinner.' Leanne has wondered how to start talking about this subject and this seemed the least inflammatory way.

'You mean, on a date?' Theresa says, her voice going up an octave.

'Maybe.' Leanne stops. Perhaps she doesn't want to talk about this after all. Theresa is an understanding person, but private things should stay private. Shouldn't they?

'Who is it?'

Leanne starts walking again. 'His name's, uh, Matt. He works at the pool.'

'I know him!' Theresa says, and Leanne feels instantly the cold sweat of embarrassment. She didn't think she'd be asking advice about someone Theresa knows – and there's no way to back out of this conversation now that Theresa has a stake in it.

'He taught the kids to swim,' Theresa goes on. 'He's *lovely*. Handsome! How do you know him?'

'I . . . took some lessons from him.'

'He did a good job with you too, then – you're swimming so well.' Her smile is encouraging.

'Thank you,' Leanne says.

Now they're in the water and she has no idea if it's cold or not because she's focused on controlling this conversation.

'So when's the dinner?' Theresa asks as they breaststroke through the small waves.

'That's just it – I've been putting it off.' Matt has called her three times to ask when she is free for dinner and she kept saying she'd check her diary; by the third call he sounded confused. No doubt he would be, as she hasn't returned to the pool either.

'Why?'

'I don't think I should go on a date with anyone.'

'Why not?'

'I don't . . . I don't have a lot of luck in that department.' Leanne dives under a wave so she has no idea if Theresa says anything right away.

As soon as she pops up she hears, 'How would you know if you never go on a date?'

'Well, I did,' Leanne says quickly, because this is the point she wanted to reach yet she's also scared about saying anything out loud. 'Once. When I was eighteen. He, uh . . . wasn't nice.' She can hear her voice faltering.

'Stop!'

Leanne obeys.

'Take those goggles off and look at me,' Theresa orders, and lifts her own.

Leanne hesitates to remove hers because she's mortified to realise that she's crying. She never cries. Crying is for people who are emotional and that's something she's trained herself not to be. If she got emotional about her patients, for example, she'd never make it through the day.

'Lee-*anne*.'

She dunks her head under the water, hoping it will stop her crying, but it doesn't and she can't stay under here forever.

'Whatever you're avoiding telling me is obviously bad,' Theresa says, but she doesn't sound bossy any more, just concerned.

'Sorry,' Leanne says. 'I didn't mean to get upset.'

'No one ever *means* to get upset,' Theresa says. 'But I'm not fit enough to tread water for a long time, so you need to talk.'

Leanne gulps a breath. Of course this was going to be hard to talk about when she's been avoiding it for such a long time. She should have realised that.

'I went on a date once,' she says. 'He was – he was a friend of my oldest brother's.'

'Mm-hm,' Theresa says, her face uncharacteristically devoid of expression.

'I never had a boyfriend in high school,' she continues. 'I was . . . too busy. Playing sport. You know. I wasn't really interested.'

Theresa says nothing, but what is there to say, really?

'So this was my first date. And he . . .'

She stops, her mouth open, feeling her breath catching in her chest. She's trying to gulp in air but it's getting stuck. Now she's sinking, and her arms start to flail.

Then she feels Theresa pulling her over onto her back and placing her hand underneath her, making her spine arch. Leanne remembers this: it's what Matt did when he taught her how to float.

'Breathe,' Theresa whispers in her ear.

She feels more hands beneath her and hears Marie and Elaine muttering to Theresa. Or maybe they're not muttering – maybe her hearing is distorted, because it sounds as if she's inside a speaker and looking out through a fishbowl. She's panting and still Theresa is whispering, 'Breathe. Slowly. That's it.'

'She's panicking,' she hears Marie say. 'What happened?'

'She was telling me a story. She just . . .'

'Let's take her back to shore.'

That's Elaine, Leanne thinks, and feels the thud of a decision within her.

'No,' she says, moving herself so she's upright once more. She sees three faces that look as worried as those of most parents she deals with. 'I need to keep swimming,' she sputters.

The others are silent, and she knows their legs are moving like egg beaters underwater. She's delaying them. She's delaying herself.

'Please,' she says.

'All right.' Marie turns and kicks herself into a breaststroke for a few metres, then a freestyle. Elaine follows. Only Theresa is left.

'I think I know what you were going to say,' she says, floating on her belly now, her goggles still on the top of her head. 'And that's awful. Terrible. *Terrible.*' She shakes her head. 'No one should have to go through that.'

Leanne hiccups with the surprise of acknowledgement after all this time. And no judgement – but what did she expect? Theresa was the one she wanted to tell because Theresa is the one she knew wouldn't judge. All this time watching her at work has taught Leanne that.

'So I think you're brave if you go out to dinner with Matt,' Theresa goes on. 'But I also *know* you're brave, Leanne. You could barely swim when you started with us! And now . . .' She gestures to the horizon in front of them. 'Look where you are. No one else did this for you. You did it for yourself.' She laughs. 'I did it for myself too. We're all brave! Except Marie. Swimming is her habit.' She wrinkles her nose. 'But I think she's brave too, sometimes.'

Theresa rolls onto her back and makes a shape like she's sitting on a lumpy banana lounge, her knees out of the water while her arms drape just under it.

'You don't have to go,' she says. 'But I will tell you this: Matt is a good person. He's not going to hurt you, I'm sure of it. And if you're really worried, I can be your chaperone.' She winks.

She and Leanne look at each other for a few seconds. Out of the corner of her eye Leanne can see Marie and Elaine receding and she wants to start after them. She wants the water to carry her along and wash the past away.

'Thank you,' she says.

'No worries.'

Theresa yanks her goggles down and rolls over once more before she puts her head down and starts to kick. A second later her arms pull through the water and she's off.

Two seconds later Leanne joins her.

CHAPTER 28

It's weird, sitting here in the dark. Theresa has only just realised that in her thirty-eight years on earth – thirty-nine in a few days, on May the fifth – she's never sat in the dark. Although it's not completely dark: the television is on. She thinks it's showing a re-run of *Quincy, ME*, but she's not really paying attention. The sound is off. That's another weird thing. She's never sat in front of the telly with the sound off. Because there's no point in that. Is there?

She licks her lips. Can't remember when she last drank some water. Or had a cup of tea. Or coffee. Maybe this morning? It must have been this morning, after she dropped the kids at school and Brian from across the road came over, looking nervous as he found her in the back garden hanging out the washing.

'Theresa,' he said, and smiled in that way people have when they don't really want to smile.

'Brian!' She put the washing basket down. He'd never come past her front fence before. Usually they chat about his roses and his porcelain collection, and he asks about the children. Once he gave her a recipe for his favourite lemon syrup cake and asked her not to share it with Muriel down the road. He said Muriel had been after it for years but he only gave it to special people. Theresa felt like she'd been inducted into a club she hadn't known existed. Even then, though, he hadn't left the footpath.

'How are you?' he said nervously as she tucked the pegs into her apron.

'I'm well,' she said, because that's what she always says when someone asks her that. It's the polite thing to do.

'Good.' There was that strangled smile again. 'Look, I, ah . . .'

'Are you okay, Brian? You've gone pale.'

'Oh – well – ha! Ha! I am okay, thank you. But, I, uh—'

'Theresa, who is it?' Nonna said, appearing from her granny flat.

'It's Brian,' she called over her shoulder. 'From across the road.'

'Ah.' Nonna waved. 'Thank you for the tip, Brian. You were right about that horse.'

She waved again then retreated into her flat, leaving a mystery behind. Since when had Nonna and Brian ever spoken? Truly, her grandmother could be running a small country from that flat and she'd never know.

'So, Brian, can I . . . help with something? Is my grand-mother being a pest?'

'Oh – no.' He shook his head. 'Nothing like that. I just . . .' He sighed. 'I was in the hotel last night.'

'The Ox?' That was the pub all the locals went to.

'Yes.' He looked at her as if she was meant to guess something, but her mind was still trying to grasp why he was telling her about his evening.

'Okay,' she said, hoping he'd take it as a prompt.

'I saw your husband.' His eyebrows formed an upside-down V.

'Yes, he likes it there. I can never go . . .' She gestured towards the house. 'The kids.'

'Yes. Well . . .' The eyebrows were now in a pincer movement. 'He was with a woman.'

And now the eyebrows were almost at his hairline. That's what Theresa noticed, or made herself notice, so she could ignore the fact that her heart felt like it was wedged between her collarbones and beating at a mile a minute.

'Was she . . .' She swallowed. 'Blonde?'

His face fell. 'Yes.'

That was all she needed to know. She can't remember what she said after that, or what Brian said to her, but she remembers feeling alternately grateful that he told her and humiliated that he saw her husband being so obviously not with her.

She ignored Nonna's questions as she went back inside; it was only later that she remembered the washing and saw that it was all pegged up. Nonna must have done it.

Nonna would be the perfect person to consult about all of this: she's lived through two world wars and narrowly missed Mussolini's rule, so she knows things. She's seen things. Probably all of the things. But Theresa also knows what Nonna will say: *Get rid of him*. Nonna can be ruthless, and she's never been that fond of Andrew. She thinks he's lazy and selfish, and Theresa can't say she's wrong. She's not ready to be so ruthless, though. Not yet. She has to consider her children. She has to consider herself and how she – they – can afford to live if he's not around.

Except perhaps he's a step ahead of her. He might be planning to come home and tell her that he's leaving. Or that she has to.

Andrew is out. As usual. Drinking with the boys, he said, but he must realise that Theresa knows that's a lie. Or maybe he thinks she's gullible. Or stupid. Actually, yes, he must think that, to carry on with his girlfriend in front of other people in a place where her neighbour could see them. Did see them. Who knows how many other places they carry on in.

Maybe he'll try to force her out of the house to move his blonde in. Theresa's pretty sure he won't want the kids – they're too much work for him, and she knows his mother won't help him look after them – so she's going to put her foot down to stay if it comes to that.

Thinking all that through has been easier with the lights off and Jack Klugman on.

Theresa jumps as she hears Andrew's key in the door. There was no sound of a car. Not that he'd be driving, because he's probably drunk, but she would have thought he'd take a taxi home.

'Hello?' she says as the door opens, so he knows she's there. She may be plotting the next phase of her life without him but that doesn't mean she wants to scare him when he walks inside.

'Oh – hi.' He steps inside and flicks on the light. 'Why are the lights off?'

Theresa shrugs. 'I felt like it.'

He drops his keys on the coffee table.

'How's the blonde?' she says, as breezily as possible.

'Wh-what?' He staggers a little as he steps towards her.

'Chook's sister,' she says, flatly this time. 'Your girlfriend.'

'What the fuck are you talking about?'

Despite his language, he sounds more wounded than angry. As if she's accused him of something unfairly. Theresa sighs. He's clearly going to make this hard.

'The woman you were with in the pub last night.'

Now he looks indignant. 'I don't know who you're talking about.'

Theresa sighs again. He's definitely going to make this hard. Draw it out. Why would a man cheat on his wife and then try to deny it when she raises the subject, thereby making the whole thing more difficult than it already is? Does he want to cheat and keep cheating and just never get caught? She supposes so. That means the denial is selfish, in the service of wanting to continue cheating. In other words, just what she'd expect of him. And she's sick of it.

'Andrew,' she says, walking over to the television to switch it off because she's getting distracted, 'a friend saw you with a blonde woman at the pub last night. And I saw you with a blonde woman at the New Year's Eve party. Remember? I asked you about her.'

His right eyelid twitches and he looks away. When he looks back she sees defiance in his eyes. Ollie gets that look too, except he's usually defending his right to have Froot Loops for breakfast.

'Yeah,' Andrew says slowly. 'Okay.'

'Okay?' Theresa's laugh is hollow. 'You told me it was a one-off at that party. Now it's clear that you've had a girlfriend for however long and it's meant to be *okay*?'

'So what? You still haven't gone anywhere near me. What am I supposed to do?' His words are nonchalant but the sound of his voice suggests that he's scared. It makes her feel like she has some power here, but that's a trick, because she has none. She probably never had it. That other woman has the power in her marriage now. Part of her wants to give in to it. Or give up. But there's still the part of her that sees their marriage as a long-term project – that's what they promised each other on their wedding day, that they'd be together through good times and bad. These years of the children being young, of her being too tired to be a full-service wife, won't last forever, then they could have more time together. Maybe she should have told him that. Yet, once more, she feels the utter exhaustion of the responsibility of making their marriage work being entirely on her. And she realises that it will always be. She can't make him do his share.

'I'm sorry I can't take care of everything you need,' she says at last, 'but you could have given me more time.'

'I did,' he says, his chin jerking a little. 'You didn't bloody change. And Susie was still keen, so . . .' He shrugs one shoulder. 'She takes care of me.'

So she has a name, Chook's sister.

Theresa thinks of all the things she'd really like to say to Andrew now – about how obviously Susie can take care of him because she's barely out of puberty and therefore doesn't have children; about how that would change if she and Andrew did have children and then he'd find himself in the same cycle – but she knows it would be fruitless. He doesn't care about her any more. She doesn't know when he stopped, and she doesn't want to try to figure it out. Her earlier indecision has fallen away and her world has come into focus. The children are what's most important to her, just as she told him, and she needs to concentrate on them right now.

'Then you should be with Susie,' she says softly.

She can see from the look on Andrew's face that he wasn't expecting this response.

'I imagine you won't mind if the kids and I stay here,' she goes on. 'At least while we work out what to do next.'

Andrew's mouth opens. Then he shakes his head. 'I didn't say good night to them.'

'I'll tell them you've had to go and see a friend.' She smiles sadly. 'That's kind of the truth, isn't it?'

'I didn't, um . . .' Andrew squints and scratches his head. 'I just wanted a bit of attention, you know?'

So do I, Theresa feels like saying to him. Screaming at him. But he'd no doubt say she has attention, from the kids.

'I understand,' she says instead. She nods towards their bedroom. 'Why don't you pack enough to last a few days and we'll work out when you can pick up the rest?'

He nods, and now he can't meet her eyes. She doubts he's ashamed. Maybe he's just feeling stupid for getting caught before he was ready.

He used to be handsome, her husband. Now he looks like a washed-up fool trying to relive his glory days by clinging on to someone who's too young to remember them.

She turns the TV on again, and the volume up. A different show is on. It could be a movie. Maybe with Jane Fonda in it.

Theresa leaves the lights on, and doesn't hear Andrew when he leaves.

CHAPTER 29

'Can I give you a lift home?' Theresa says.

Her face looks pinched as she stands before Marie in her tracksuit, her arms folded tightly across her chest. Marie is still getting used to seeing the others in clothing rather than swimming costumes.

The colder weather has led to a group decision to walk up and down the beach for the same amount of time they'd swim, although Marie was happy to keep going once it turned cool. As soon as the water temperature hit seventeen degrees, though, she had trouble convincing the others. So this is the first May for many decades that she hasn't spent in the water. She can't say she's missing it. In fact, the walking has reintroduced her to her calf muscles and she is surprised they complain so much.

It's possible Theresa's body is complaining too. She's been looking tired the past few days – or perhaps not tired so much as worn out. Marie is trying not to worry about her because it feels almost like an intrusion, but Theresa has become a good friend in a short period of time and it's hard not to wonder what's causing such a marked change.

Marie thinks about the offer of a lift. She always walks home from the beach. Theresa knows this and has never before offered to drive her. Usually she's sprinting off to get the kids ready for school, although today is Saturday so Marie supposes she can afford to take more time. Still, the only conclusion she can reach is that Theresa wants to talk to her about something – and she's not going to deny her.

'Sure,' she says.

'Oh.' Theresa looks relieved. 'Good.'

They say their goodbyes to Elaine and Leanne, then get into Theresa's car. The drive up the hill won't take long, so if Theresa has something to say she's unlikely to get it out in those two minutes.

'Maybe you could even come in for a cuppa,' Marie says as they head away from the beach.

She glances at Theresa, whose face looks like it's about to dissolve.

'That would be . . .' Theresa swallows. 'That would be lovely.'

Marie nods. She doesn't want to press Theresa to say anything now. Time and care and attention are no doubt required, and if she doesn't afford her that, Theresa may keep her mouth shut, to her own detriment.

Once out of the car, they walk through Marie's front gate and the small garden with its camellias in bloom and azaleas starting to show buds.

'Oh! This is your house?' Theresa stops before they step onto the verandah. 'I've always loved it. Not that I . . . I mean, I haven't been staring at it. I've just noticed it whenever I've been up this way.'

'Theresa, it's fine,' says Marie, turning the key in the lock. 'This house stands out. Sandstone, on a corner, across the road from the milk bar – people notice it. Every time I go over there for the paper someone asks me about the history.' She arches an eyebrow. 'I usually tell them it was the first gaol in Shelly Bay – and they believe me.'

The hallway is cool and dark; Marie gestures for Theresa to walk down it and through to the living room.

'I think we'll sit in here,' she says. 'Not as hot as the back garden. Even in autumn it can be like a cauldron back there.'

Theresa nods and sits on the couch. That pinched look is back on her face.

Marie sits next to her and pats her hand. 'I don't think we really need that cuppa, do we? You want to talk.'

Theresa's breath catches and her eyes blink rapidly, the irises shining. She looks like a naughty child at the headmistress's office.

'Yes,' she says, nodding quickly.

Marie takes her hand properly. 'Whatever's the matter?'

Theresa squeezes her fingers. 'Andrew's having an affair.' She blinks again. 'I think . . . I think our marriage is over.'

'All right,' Marie says carefully.

She's been in situations before where women have said things about their husbands – things that make the husbands sound like very unsympathetic characters indeed – and Marie has learnt not to express an opinion, let alone a judgement, because those women rarely leave those husbands, and Marie will end up seeing the men at a social function, knowing what they've done and having to watch her friends acting as if the husband is the best thing since Cary Grant.

'I've been wanting to tell you. Since I saw him with – with her.' Theresa's breath catches again and Marie pats her hand. 'I've been trying to work out what to do. What to say . . .' She shakes her head. 'I feel like such an idiot.'

'Why on earth would you feel like that?'

Theresa looks up, surprise on her face. 'Because I should have known. Because I should have been brave enough to say something to him the first time. Because it took my neighbour – *my neighbour* – seeing them together *at the pub*. Because I . . .' She stops, something that looks like embarrassment taking her over.

'Caused it? Is that what you think?' Marie hopes that her expression strikes the balance of showing Theresa that she thinks she's being ridiculous and wanting to be supportive.

Theresa looks to the ceiling and blinks several times, but the tears roll down her cheeks anyway. 'I haven't had time for him,' she says, shaking her head again.

'Bullshit.'

Theresa makes the small noise of someone unused to hearing a woman swear.

'You've been raising those kids and running that house,' Marie goes on. 'All he has to do is fix cars and drink beer with his mates. *You* don't have time for *him*?' She huffs. '*He* doesn't make time for *you*. And if he chooses to run off with someone else because he's feeling neglected at home, that's not on you. Has he ever tried to make you feel wanted?'

Theresa shakes her head.

'Does he tell you you're beautiful? That he loves you?'

More shakes, now accompanied by sniffles.

'But I . . .' Theresa stops, and sighs. 'I don't tell him that he's handsome. So maybe someone else did.'

'Or maybe he's an idiot.'

Theresa opens and closes her mouth, and it reminds Marie so much of the goldfish Nicole used to have that she starts to laugh.

'What?' Theresa says, looking hurt.

'Oh, love.' Marie pats her cheek. 'I'm not being mean, I promise.'

They sit side by side while Theresa sniffles and Marie tries to think of what to say next. How much of her own experience to share – because everyone's life is their own, and things she knows may not apply to what Theresa is going through. Or they may, in which case she has a duty to say something. To make sure Theresa knows she's not alone.

'Marriage is hard, isn't it?' Marie says eventually. 'Living with anyone is hard, but at least with your kids you love them unconditionally.' She makes a face. 'We're *meant* to love our husbands unconditionally but I don't know who came up with that rule. It's ridiculous. You have to choose to love them, every single day of your life, and you know they have to do the same thing. For two people to keep choosing to love each other, three hundred and sixty-five days a year, for decades – well, that's a bloody miracle. And miracles aren't that regular.' She smiles ruefully. 'I should know,' she says, picking up Theresa's hand again and holding it in hers. 'Norm had an affair.'

'*What?*' Theresa clutches on to her.

Marie nods slowly. 'We were at about the same stage you and Andrew are. Nicole was young, and I was tired all the time – and that was with one child, so I don't know how you do it with two, especially with your own mother not close by.'

Theresa's eyes are round and she pushes her hair out of them. 'It's been tough at times,' she says softly.

'Too right.' Marie sighs. 'Anyway, it was messy because she was married to one of his mates. Their marriage broke up. Ours didn't.'

'Why not?'

Theresa leans towards her, and Marie can see that she genuinely wants to know the answer. She wants to find a way out of the situation, but Marie isn't sure she can give her one, because not everyone is prepared to do what she did.

'I forgave him,' she says. 'And I also told him that if he did it again he'd be out of the house, out of the marriage, and I'd tell Nicole all about it.'

Theresa looks impressed, and slightly scandalised. *'Really?'* she says, almost whispering, as if Norm is still around to hear her.

'It wasn't easy,' Marie admits. 'And it wouldn't work for everyone. But he never strayed again – as far as I know.' She laughs. 'Maybe he did and he just got better at keeping it a secret. At any rate, he seemed to respect me more after that. Like he'd been waiting for me to lay down the law. Like he wanted it.' She considers something for the first time. 'Maybe he had the affair to test me. Push me.'

She and Theresa look at each other; she can tell that Theresa doesn't approve of her late husband and Marie understands: at the time, neither did she.

'If that's the case, it worked,' Marie continues. 'But I don't know what your Andrew's reasons are. And you may not want to know.' Theresa's tears have returned and Marie wipes them from one cheek. 'As I said, marriage is hard. And you need to do what's right for *you*.'

Marie is only slightly surprised when Theresa grabs her in a hug.

'I wish I knew what that is,' Theresa says into her ear. 'I wish I knew what to do next.'

Marie hugs her tighter, then lets her go. 'Keep swimming. That's how I worked things out.'

She remembers the days she spent churning up and down the beach, telling herself that she had to come up with a solution for what to do about Norm, eventually emerging with her decision.

'Of course, we're not going in the sea at the moment but sometimes I find that just looking at it does the trick. The ocean is more vast than our problems, my girl,' Marie adds. 'Trust it to help you.'

Theresa is regarding her with something that resembles hope.

'He hasn't been home for a few days,' she whispers. 'I kind of told him to get out.'

Marie wants to offer more advice, but she never reached this point with Norm. She's not sure what to tell Theresa now without it sounding like she's giving her instructions.

'Time's a funny thing,' she says at last. 'A few days – a few minutes: when you're hurting they can feel about the same. Don't think anything is over until it's over.'

Theresa blinks and nods.

'Now,' Marie says, 'it's the right time for that cuppa.'

WINTER 1983

CHAPTER 30

The piece of paper says that Alcoholics Anonymous meetings are held every Tuesday at 7 p.m. at St Vestey's Church on the plaza. It is Tuesday today, and it's six-thirty. Elaine feels a clutch at her throat. The first time at anything new is hard, she tells herself, but it's only the first time once. It sounds trite, but she has no licence to be snobbish about motivational phrases.

It seems incongruous that a bunch of drunks would meet in the house of the Lord. Or perhaps it's poetic. They're meant to offer themselves up to a higher power, after all. That's what she's heard.

Not that she's heard much. She hasn't paid attention to any details about AA before now, and if Theresa hadn't suggested it she's not entirely sure she would have found her way to a meeting – even if it has taken her several false starts to get here. Nor does she know what she would have done otherwise. Because she's a coward – that's what she's realised about herself. She's been drinking to run away from reality, and she was too ashamed to tell James the truth about why the car was dented. It wasn't even brave going to Theresa, because she knew Theresa was the one person who would be kind to her. Theresa wasn't the only person who could help her, though: James could have done that. Except she didn't tell him.

And now she has to, because he's home unexpectedly early and she isn't going to use that as an excuse to miss the meeting. On top of the excuses she has already made, that is. Just as she became an expert at lying to herself about how much of a drunk she was, she grew adept at telling Theresa she was 'definitely planning' to attend a meeting. Until yesterday, when Theresa was uncharacteristically firm and told Elaine that she had to go and she wouldn't accept another excuse. She also asked for a report tomorrow morning.

'Short day, darling?' she says after he kisses her hello – always on the lips. 'Relatively speaking, that is.' She hopes she sounds light, carefree, blasé, but is sure she doesn't.

'There was a meeting but it's been moved. What's that?' He points to the piece of paper in her hand.

'It's, ah . . .' She gives him the fake smile she's used on his colleagues in the past, to suggest, in what she hopes is a playful manner, that she's about to say something awkward. 'It's the details of an Alcoholics Anonymous meeting that's on tonight. Shortly, actually.'

She drops the fake smile and swallows her nerves. James may make the occasional comment about how much she drinks but he's never called her a drunk. And in front of him she's never claimed the label either.

He puts his keys on the sideboard. 'Oh?' He looks like he's about to laugh. 'Who's that for?'

She blinks. 'For me,' she says, trying for a real smile this time. 'I . . . thought I should go.'

He perches on the sideboard and folds his arms. 'I see,' he says softly.

Moments pass as he inhales and exhales, his gaze on the ground.

'I'm not an alcoholic,' she says in what she hopes is a convincing tone. 'But I don't want to *become* one. That would be . . . inconvenient.'

James sighs. 'I knew it was going too far,' he says, his voice still low. 'I should have said something earlier. But I . . .' He glances at her, then out the window that reveals their back garden. 'I felt bad. I made you move here. It hasn't been easy, I know. If you needed a drink here and there, well . . .' His eyes are dark as they meet hers. 'Who hasn't, from time to time? But if you're doing this . . .' He sighs again and shakes his head. 'I've let you down.'

While she loves this man, Elaine can't help feeling a tingle of anger towards him. *It's not about you*, she wants to yell. *It's about me!* Except she's lived with him long enough to know that he sees her problems through the prism of his experience. Most people are the same. It's another reason to feel grateful for the friendships she's forming with Theresa and Marie: not once has either of them tried to interpret anyone else's life by looking at their own. In Theresa, it seems to be the result of a surfeit of compassion; in Marie, of a long life and what Elaine suspects to be some hard times. Even Leanne, in her self-contained way, is supportive.

So she can't blame James for looking at her problem and taking it on as his own. Perhaps she should be grateful that he wants to bear that much responsibility, even if what she needs – what will help, she thinks – is to claim that responsibility for herself.

She remembers that old joke: *How many psychiatrists does it take to change a light bulb? One, but the light bulb has to want to change.* She wants to change. Thus far she's lacked the tools to do so, but she thinks that going to this meeting may give her what she needs.

'You haven't let me down,' she says firmly. 'And I haven't let myself down either. I've just gone off the rails.' She walks over to him and puts her hand on his shoulder. 'It's time to get myself back on.'

He puts his hand over hers and pulls her towards him with the other, narrowing his eyes. 'What's changed?' he asks.

'What do you mean?'

'You've been moping around.'

She opens her mouth to say that 'moping' is too strong a descriptor, then he kisses her nose.

'Don't disagree with me,' he says. 'I've seen it. You know it's true. I should have said something about that too.'

'I'll accept "moping",' she says. 'I think it's normal for a mother who's away from her children to mope.'

'Especially a mother who is half a world away from them.' He hugs her to his side. 'I'm sorry I've done that to you.'

She goes to say, *It's all right*, but that would be a lie that serves neither of them. Instead, she chooses to answer his question.

'You asked what's changed. I have friends now. I think.'

He pulls back and looks at her, almost with confusion. 'Who?'

'You know I've been swimming each morning. Now walking because it's cold.'

'Mmm.' He pats her bottom. 'It suits you.'

'Thank you,' she says. 'I think it suits me too. And it's so nice being with the others.'

'Theresa and . . .' He stops. Frowns.

Elaine's mentioned their names several times but she doesn't expect him to remember them. He has so much on his mind. He couldn't remember her parents' names for several months

218

after he first met them. But he always remembers his patients' names. Once she told him it's because he relies on her to remember the details of their domestic life so he can focus on his work. He hadn't disagreed.

'Leanne and Marie,' she supplies for him now.

He smiles. 'That's right. So you all get along?'

'Yes,' she says emphatically. 'It's not like the tennis debacle—'

'It wasn't a debacle,' he cuts in. 'Those women just weren't right for you.'

She smiles, appreciating his kindness in the face of the facts. 'Perhaps. Anyway, they're lovely. We don't spend a lot of time talking each day but all those little bits add up. I've become . . .'

She was about to say that she's become close with them. To admit that she went to Theresa for support about her drinking before telling James. But no matter how much he loves her she's not sure what he'll think about that.

'Yes?' he prompts.

'They're very kind. And open. So I think we're friends now.'

The memory of a late-summer swim pops into her mind. In the midst of a rough surf, there was Marie pulling a jelly-fish out of her swimming costume and brandishing it before flinging it into the ocean, and Theresa fishing seaweed out from the back of her costume and asking if she should use it to make a bikini, while Leanne hid her smile by putting her mouth underwater. If Elaine existed just in those moments – if all of them did – life would be easy. Together they have created a bubble of light, and that is what illuminates her path now.

'I'm so glad.' James kisses her again. 'People deserve to know you. Even if I do want to keep you to myself sometimes.'

He hugs her and she feels the relief of not carrying a secret, and of knowing that for all her missteps she is loved. That can be hard to remember when she's feeling out of control of behaviour that's damaging her; she will have to keep reminding herself, she is sure, over the weeks ahead. Because even now, as James holds her and she sees on her watch that she needs to leave for the meeting right away, she is thinking about having a drink. Rationally, she doesn't need one, but her habit is pounding beneath her skin and that is what she needs to conquer.

'May I drive you to the meeting?' James says.

'That would be lovely.'

Still holding the piece of paper, she takes his hand as they walk to the front door.

CHAPTER 31

Marie is sure that Gus hasn't needed to be here two days in a row. Very sure, because she told him so. In the time he's been doing work at her place he's made every single garden bed tidy. He's pruned the bushes that need pruning. Yesterday he said he wanted to clear the gutters now, before spring arrives, so he would come again this week, but she told him they've been full of dead leaves for five years so they could wait until next week.

Not that she wanted to wait until next week to see him again. She's been enjoying having him around. They converse easily – banter even. Norm wasn't much for talking, and while that didn't stop them being close she sometimes thought it stopped them really knowing each other. He loved her, she was sure of that. Just not that intrigued by her. She never stopped wanting to know about him but eventually she stopped asking, and as much as she loved him she did sometimes wonder if she had imagined him to be a more complex man than he really was. Perhaps there were no depths there to explore. Not that Norm ever said there were.

Once she'd mentioned to Gwen that she thought Norm's lack of curiosity about her meant he didn't really care.

'That's just how some men are,' Gwen had said. '*Most* men, don't you think? Do you know any who like to chat? I don't.'

Marie could think of one: Bradley, a sweet young man she knew at church – he was the sort who never had a girlfriend and her mother would have described as 'precious'. Even Father Paul, for whom talking was part of his job, never seemed quite as at ease with it as Bradley. The last she'd heard of Bradley he'd moved to a country town to take up a teaching position. She missed his conversation.

It's conversation Marie needs to feel the connection of close friendship, and because Gus loves to talk she's aware that she may have a false idea of how friendly they've become. Except he does seem to be genuinely interested in her life. He's made it clear that he wants to know about her because he asks her questions. Sometimes she finds herself rambling on and stops, self-conscious that she's doing all the talking, as she's been doing today.

Despite Marie's protests, Gus turned up this morning saying that her gutters absolutely need to be cleared: she lives in a bushfire zone and her house will be a 'tinderbox' if she has leaf litter.

She told him that she can't recall there being a bushfire in Shelly Bay in her entire lifetime, but he insisted.

So now he's up and down a ladder, clad in long work shorts and an open-necked shirt with its sleeves rolled up, and she's doing everything she can to not watch him as he stretches and reaches. Because it feels rude to stare, for one thing, and because she shouldn't be observing him so closely. He's her gardener. She hardly knows him.

Yet she's caught him looking at her too. Right from the first day.

The second time he came, she made an effort to wear clothes that weren't shapeless from too many turns round a washing machine, and was rewarded with an admiring glance.

'You're pretty fit, aren't you?' he said, and she could have sworn he looked her over like he was a judge at the Royal Easter Show assessing a cow. She could also have sworn that she enjoyed it.

'What do you mean?' she said, because she was a little flustered and really wasn't sure what he meant.

'You're . . . fit.' He smiled, and the skin at the corners of his grey-green eyes crinkled, and she felt a little flutter in her belly. 'You look like you play sport or something. Do you?'

'Oh, well, I . . . I've spent most of my life swimming every day.' She felt ridiculous – she never stumbled over words like this. 'Most of the year, that is. In the ocean.'

'Really?' he said with an admiring tone. 'Down at Main Beach?'

'Yes.'

'I've probably seen you. I kayak there sometimes. What time of day do you go?'

'Sunrise,' she said, so breathlessly it sounded like she was issuing him an invitation.

'Yeah,' he drew out as he bent over to pick up sticks, 'I would have seen you.'

He gave her a look that suggested he already knew her and liked what he knew, although she can't recall being aware of a kayaker, and she's sure if she saw him on the beach she'd have noticed.

Or maybe not. Marie stopped looking at men *like that* a long time ago. Not when she married – it's one thing to pledge your life to someone but that doesn't mean you turn off the tap. Eyes can see and hearts can race; that's all part of being human and alive. For her, being married meant choosing not to let it go further than that; you've made a commitment to someone. So she'd noticed attractive men over the years, but noticing was as far as it ever went.

Norm didn't make the same choice on at least one occasion, but she understood it. He was human too, and as wounded as she felt at the time she didn't condemn him for not doing what she did. Her faith, her upbringing, taught her that adultery was a sin, but in her heart she couldn't write off a man she loved simply for making a different choice to her. And according to her religion, she should never have looked at another man either, even if it was impossible to switch off those human impulses. So she'd made a deal with herself: she would keep her faith but adjust it for the realities of life. Norm wasn't a priest and she wasn't a nun.

Once she reached her fifties, though, her hormones slowed their merry dance, and if she saw a handsome man she noted he was handsome and nothing more. She and Norm were still physical – she enjoyed that – but it lost its urgency. After Norm died she thought about whether or not she should seek out a new companion, but it was an intellectual exercise, not a yearning, so she left it alone. Besides, she still felt married to Norm because she didn't choose to end the marriage. Death was another state of being, not a divorce.

It's been five years, though, and she has felt him slipping further from her. She doesn't think about him multiple times a day any more. But that doesn't mean she was looking for anyone else, so it's a shock to find herself paying attention to Gus in a way that conjures memories in her body.

Marie's conscious that her desire may look obvious to him, which is part of the reason why she keeps talking and talking – to deflect from it. Just now, for example, she's telling him about how Charlie Brown came to be her dog, and Gus is smiling and nodding as she recounts how he wouldn't leave her alone for the first few weeks and she thought she'd never get out of the house.

'He seems settled now,' Gus says as he stuffs dead leaves into a garbage bag. 'He's quite a happy little fellow.'

Charlie Brown stands up from the spot in the garden bed where he's been sitting.

'Yes, mate, I'm talking about you,' Gus says with a laugh.

He's even easy with the dog. Marie wonders if there's anyone Gus *can't* talk to.

'Just let me know if he gets in your way,' she says.

Gus gives her that wondrous smile. 'I doubt he will.'

'I hope you don't have much more to do. So you can get on with your day,' she says in a rush.

'This is my day.' He puts his hands on his hips and gives her a funny look. 'It's not a hardship to be here.'

'This garden can't be . . .' She looks around. 'The prettiest you've been in.'

'That's why I'm here – to make it pretty. That's what I do.'

He takes off the gloves he was wearing to gather the leaves and places them on the edge of the verandah. As he bends over she admires the length of his back, and isn't quick enough to hide it as he straightens and catches her looking.

'Th-thank you for coming back so soon,' she says, flustered, glancing towards the roof. 'The gutters are grateful.'

He laughs. She likes the way he laughs: his head tilts back and his laughter seems to come from deep in his chest, almost like a wave rising.

'I am too,' he says. 'It gives me another opportunity to see you.'

He smiles and Marie wonders if she's heard him right.

'To see *me*?' she says, determined to make sure.

Gus laughs again. 'Well, I'm fond of your azaleas, Marie, but not half as fond of them as I am of you.'

Her mouth hangs open, and she shuts it before he thinks there's something wrong with her.

'I enjoy your company,' he says. 'It's become . . .' He pauses. 'Addictive. I think that's the word. It's been a long time since I've found someone so easy to talk to. And so easy on the eye, if you don't mind me saying so.'

They stand looking at each other, and Marie is aware that he's offered her something and she needs to decide if she's going to accept it or reject it. If she reacts in a way that isn't true to what she feels and thinks, she may never have another opportunity.

'I think the same of you,' she says, feeling bold. 'About being easy on the eye, I mean. You're a shocking conversationalist.'

His eyes widen, then there's that laugh again.

'I'll try harder,' he says. 'Maybe if we have dinner this Saturday I can get in some practice?'

He looks at her with confidence and expectation, and Marie appreciates how much this is smoothing the way for her. He is making it clear that he's interested in her and this frees her to express interest in him. They are, as others might term them, senior citizens. There's no place for false coquettishness on her part, trying to hide what she really wants because that's what nice girls do. How marvellous to have left that stage of life behind. How extraordinary to meet someone else who has arrived at this new stage.

'I'd love that,' she says.

'Wonderful. May I pick you up at seven?'

'You may,' she says, wanting to turn away so she can smile as widely as she wants to. 'For now, though, how about a cup of tea?'

'Yes, please.' Gus's smile makes her feel warm all the way to her toes. 'I'll just take these leaves to the bin.'

She nods, breathing faster to match her heart beating, and turns to walk inside. As she approaches the back door, she permits herself a little jig.

CHAPTER 32

The nerves are to be expected, Leanne supposes, because of her past, but she tries not to go too far down that memory rabbit hole as she dresses for her date with Matt. Her dinner. It doesn't have to be a date, although she's sure he doesn't want to be just her friend.

She spends half an hour trying to work out if she even has the right clothes to go out to dinner. Her life is so circumscribed that she has clothes to take her to the beach and the shops, and for the occasional walk, but nothing that could be described as remotely fancy. In the end she chooses one of her two A-line skirts, a shirt that she rolls up at the sleeves and pairs with the only necklace she owns, and flat shoes she once wore to a work function. They do have functions occasionally – usually when a ward is being opened by a local politician. Leanne always thinks it would be more appropriate for the nurses to wear their uniforms to those things, but apparently it isn't. She obviously doesn't know what is appropriate, hence her lack of suitable clothes for dinner.

Matt seems to appreciate them, though. 'You look lovely,' he says when he picks her up at exactly the time he said he would.

She doesn't think she's meant to say he looks lovely too, except he does. He's wearing a crisp shirt open at the neck, underneath a blazer, with slacks and lace-up shoes that don't quite go together but are the sort of thing a man used to living in shorts and thongs might wear to dinner. He's made an effort, that is clear; he's made the effort for her. And, she realises, she's made an effort for him.

He drives her to a small French restaurant in the next suburb, hesitantly chatting about the weather and the dramatic change of leadership of the Labor Party from Bill Hayden to Bob Hawke just before the March election, and Hawke's subsequent elevation to the prime ministership. Matt likes 'Hawkey', thinks he's a good bloke, but still says he voted for the Liberals, because the local seat has been Liberal since Moses was a boy, and why change it if you don't need to?

Leanne listens but doesn't comment, because she's never paid much attention to politics. She reads the newspapers and listens to the radio, sometimes even watches the news on television, but most nights she's reading Georgette Heyer and the occasional crime novel. These past few years she's preferred escapism to reality.

Now, with their first course in front of them, Leanne knows she has to initiate some conversation. Matt has been doing all the work, just as Theresa, Marie and Elaine do all the work at the beach.

'I'm glad you're doing lots of swimming,' he says, picking up his knife and fork. 'Most people who come for lessons just have a couple then don't do anything.'

'Really?' Leanne thinks that's a waste of everyone's time – and she should say that, because that's how you have a conversation, but she's so used to keeping her opinions to herself that it feels like this one is stuck in her vocal cords, waiting for something to propel it out.

'Yeah.' He puts a small piece of chicken in his mouth and chews with his mouth closed. For some reason that makes her feel relieved. 'They think they're going to keep swimming,' he says after he's swallowed. 'Or maybe I should say they *want* to think that. But they don't stick to it. You stuck to it, though.'

He grins and his face changes – his eyes seem full of light, and he has too many crinkles around his eyes for a man so young but it's a sign that he smiles a lot, and she likes that.

'I love it,' she says, and his grin grows bigger still. 'It's, um . . .' She searches for the right word. 'Liberating. But I think those people who have lessons with you and don't keep going are wasting your time.'

There, she's said it.

He shrugs. 'I guess so. But I'm used to it now. And I can usually pick 'em. You looked like you were taking it seriously and paying attention. Some of 'em – even some of the little kids – think they know more than me.'

'Even kids?'

'I think they get it from the parents – they're usually around. I tell them that the kids can goof off if they want, but it won't be funny if they think they know more than they do and drown because of it.' He winks. 'That usually gets them good and unhappy.'

Leanne gasps and it turns into a laugh. She didn't realise he's audacious. He has only ever been respectful to her.

'So how come you never learnt to swim as a kid?' he asks.

'My parents didn't push us to and I didn't really think about it.'

'Us? You have brothers and sisters?'

He's leaning towards her so she can tell he's genuinely interested, but she genuinely doesn't want to discuss this and shouldn't have slipped up like that, even if it's normal to talk about your family. Or so she supposes.

'I do,' she says. 'Do you?'

'One brother,' he says, his expression changing. 'But we don't get on.'

'Oh?'

She hopes he'll let her keep prompting him to keep talking, because then she won't have to. Despite her resolve to make conversation, it's hard work.

Matt sits back in his chair and glances to the side before picking up his cutlery again. 'He's a bit older than me. Bigger, you know what I mean?' His eyes are bright as they meet hers. 'When he hit his late teens he, ah . . . he got a bit *angry*. With our parents. With the world. But he took it out on me.' He bends over his plate so Leanne can't see his face properly. 'I was so careful not to do anything to set him off, y'know? Never worked. Anyway,' he says, his head still down, 'he's not like that now, but I haven't forgotten. Or forgiven.'

Now he's looking at her again and he's no longer happy-go-lucky Matt, but she thinks she likes this Matt more. This Matt is someone whose life isn't as one-dimensional as she assumed. And she shouldn't have assumed, because she's met enough people through her work to know that there's never just one dimension.

'Do you talk to him at all?' she ventures.

'Only at Christmas.' He spears a green bean and pops it in his mouth. 'I keep the peace, for my parents' sake. They want us to be happy families. But that puts all the pressure on me and none on him. So I can only do it for one day.' He sighs. 'But you don't want to hear about that. It's boring.'

'No, it's not.'

She wants to tell him that she understands about family relationships going wrong, but to do that she'd have to tell him why hers did and she doesn't want him to know the story. Not yet.

'I'm surprised you don't have a boyfriend,' he says, smiling at her again. 'You sure you don't?'

'I'm sure,' she says, and feels her cheeks colouring.

'You're so pretty,' he says.

She knows that's her currency – it's all women's currency – but she can't help feeling a little disappointed that it's the reason he's asked her out.

'That came out wrong,' he continues. 'I mean, of course you're pretty. It's hard not to notice. But I liked the fact you always paid attention in the lesson. You're serious.' He nods slowly. 'I like serious. It means you won't laugh at me if I tell you I play chess.'

He looks a little nervous and she finds it charming.

'Do you?' she says, slightly incredulous because he keeps dismantling her preconceptions.

'Yeah. My brother taught me before he turned aggro. I'm always looking for people to play with. You play?'

She shakes her head. 'Never.'

'Want to learn?' He's looking at her with eagerness mixed with a trace of those nerves.

This is a point, she thinks. A significant point. If she says yes, she'll see him again and that may lead to seeing him after that too. If she says no, that's probably the end of it. She doesn't think he's doing it to trap her, though – he seems to actually want to play chess with her – so she'll respond accordingly.

'I haven't thought about it before,' she says slowly. 'But . . . okay.'

'Really?' His grin returns.

She nods.

'I reckon you're going to love it,' he says.

As they continue with their meal they talk about hobbies and games. She tells him about being athletic as a teenager, and they compare notes on childhood broken bones earned from adventures up trees and in dry creek beds. Two hours pass and she realises he hasn't tried to get her to talk about anything she doesn't want to talk about. He's let her guide the conversation without doing it obviously. And when he drives her home and walks her to her door, after they've arranged a date to play chess, she is disarmed when he kisses her hand.

He may be the first man she's had anything to do with in years, but she's prepared to believe that Theresa was right. He is a good person.

CHAPTER 33

'So then me wife left me. Said it was her or the dogs.'
The man scratches his beard. 'I've been bettin' on the
dogs all me life.' He shrugs, and Elaine realises with a
small shock that this man in her AA meeting chose betting
on greyhounds over his marriage.

It was a surprise to her when she arrived at her first meeting
and discovered she was expected to stand up in front of strangers
and say her name and also say that she's an alcoholic. Because
that's not a word she wants to apply to herself in front of
strangers. It's the word for a long-term problem, whereas she has
a short-term problem, and the better noun for that is 'drunk'.

When she hesitated to say it, that first time, the man
running the meeting – Gerard, who runs every meeting, as
she's realised – smiled at her condescendingly and said, 'All in
good time, Elaine.' She wanted to hurl her cup of weak tea at his
head, followed by her milk arrowroot biscuit. He doesn't know
her, so how can he know what will happen in her good time?

She doesn't even know herself, as it's turned out. The Elaine
she thought she knew would never have crashed into someone
else's car because she had too much to drink. That Elaine
wouldn't have foisted herself onto a friend she doesn't know
well to ask for help. She's grateful that Theresa lent her a
sympathetic ear but Elaine had no right to do that to her. The

only explanation is that she was desperate to talk to someone, which doesn't excuse it. Talking about herself that much – it's not something that comes easily to her.

It comes even less easily in a room full of strangers, so Elaine hasn't yet stood up in front of these people. But there's no shortage of others willing to share their stories, like this fellow before them now.

'That's when I started drinkin',' he says, scratching the other side of his beard. He laughs, a deep rasp. 'I gave up the dogs not long after.' He makes a face that seems to say: *What can you do?* 'Should've kept the missus instead but . . .' Another shrug. 'She didn't want a bar of me. 'Specially once she found out about me twelve beers a day. I tried to tell her it was cheaper than the dogs.'

He laughs again and Elaine almost joins him, because somewhere inside that man's paradox she can see the humour.

'Anyway, she took the kids and moved to South-A-bloody-'stralia. Got a job workin' for Holden.' He rolls his eyes. '*South Australia.* They only just got rid of that Don Dunstan. I told her if she likes a man who wears pink shorts, I can see why we didn't get on.' Another rasping laugh, and this time he grips the sides of the lectern. 'Point is, if I don't stop drinkin' I don't get to see me kids. She'll let them come and visit if I'm off the beers. So I'm givin' it a try. That's all.'

He glances at Gerard, who nods slowly. 'Thank you, Walter. Very insightful. We're all here to support you.'

There's a smattering of applause; Elaine perfunctorily joins in. She's yet to fully embrace these meetings – partly because she feels like a fraud. Afterwards she goes home and all she thinks about is having a drink. Still. She hoped that going to the meetings would be enough to stop the impulse, but it's as powerful as ever.

Derek – the one person she's chatted to in the group – told her that's normal and she should prepare to feel that way for the rest of her life. Elaine's opinion is that she should be strong enough to *not* think about drinking every day. Derek told her she will, at some stage, come to accept that she's an alcoholic and then she'll understand.

But Elaine doesn't want AA to be a lengthy commitment. It's not as if she's been drinking for years. She was just drinking a lot for a short while. And, yes, drinking a regular moderate amount before that, but that wasn't a *problem*.

The length of time doesn't matter, Derek said, it's more to do with her behaviour around alcohol. So she can never drink again.

Elaine's been able to honestly tell him that she's stayed away from gin since she started coming to meetings, but she hasn't told him that her abstinence has been made easier because she's started some projects. She suspects that keeping busy may be a better solution to her drinking problem than coming to AA, but she hasn't seen that anywhere in the twelve steps.

'Who else would like to speak?' Gerard says, looking around the room.

Elaine ducks her head because she doesn't want him to call on her.

'Claire?' he says to a mousey-haired woman at the end of Elaine's row who shakes her head vigorously. Claire is newer than Elaine is, so she can get away with 'no', for now.

'Elaine?'

'What?'

Elaine realises her mistake: because she was thinking about Claire she didn't say 'no' straightaway like she usually does, and now she's opened a conversational opportunity for Gerard.

'Would you like to share anything with us?' He's looking at her with a combination of superciliousness and insistence.

Elaine has, on occasion, wondered if Gerard's not really an alcoholic but rather an actor paid to run these meetings. He seems to know just which expressions to use to get the outcome he wants – and today his expression suggests that he's not going to accept her 'no' any longer.

'Not particularly,' she says, almost swallowing it. She likes to kid herself that she can stand up to people, but she does have a tendency to wilt in front of authoritative individuals.

'That's an advance on your usual position.' Gerard smiles, showing his teeth – a rare sighting.

'Is it?' Elaine looks around the room, catches Derek's eye.

He's grinning at her, the bastard, because he's been waiting for this day. He spoke at his first ever meeting and thinks her reluctance is partly snobbery – she thinks she's too good for this crowd. That may be correct, but it's also because she wasn't brought up to share sob stories with strangers.

Derek nods his head towards the lectern.

'Elaine?' says Gerard.

For all her resolve to not speak, she's battling with another part of her nature: the library monitor, the school prefect, the vice-captain of the hockey team. That girl did what was expected of her. That girl didn't let people down. Perhaps Elaine's problem started as a way of rebelling against that girl, because *she* would never dream of drinking gin at two o'clock in the afternoon. *She* wouldn't have sulked about moving to Australia; she would have just got on with things.

But at this point in her life, Elaine realises, it's irrelevant whether she was trained to be that girl – as her mother and grandmother were before her – or whether that girl is who she really is. She can't tell the difference any more. What she knows is that if she accepts her nature, life may be easier. She's had her little rebellion against what's nice and normal for a girl – a woman – like her, and it hasn't worked.

The thought is enough to lift her to her feet, along with the knowledge that if she doesn't get this over with, Derek and Gerard will keep hectoring her.

She clears her throat and stands as straight as she can. Shoulders back, stomach in, sternum lifted, just as she was taught in ballet classes. She almost turns her feet into first position just to feel more at home.

'My name is Elaine,' she says.

'Hello, Elaine,' comes the chorus back.

'And I'm . . .'

She falters. For all her resolve of mere seconds ago, she doesn't want to say these words. She is not this person. She is not weak. She is not out of control. She is not a *failure*, and that's what these words would announce.

Except she is. Or she feels like it. She's let her life turn into a mess because she's failed to control it. She couldn't get on top of her misery when they moved here. Up until a year ago she'd led a charmed life, really – by anyone else's account, and often her own. And there was one hiccup. *One.* She couldn't even handle that.

Elaine knows that people have suffered far worse than she has. She was a child during World War II, and read the newspaper stories about the Blitz while she was tucked up in her grandparents' home in Devon, far from danger. Yet she's allowed herself to wallow. To *indulge.* She has been miserable because she wanted to be, not because misery was imposed on her. She drank because she wanted to. So she can stop if she wants to.

'I'm an alcoholic,' she says.

SPRING 1983

CHAPTER 34

'**C**ome on, put your back into it!' Marie yells from behind, and Theresa is tempted to turn around and poke out her tongue.

It was Marie's idea that they try a bushwalk today instead of walking on Main Beach or around the path to Little Beach, as they've been doing over winter. It'll be easy, she said. Up and around the headland. So pretty. So wild. You'll love it.

She failed to mention that it involves several steep parts and some clambering over rocks, as well as some dodging of scrubby trees and spiky native bushes. Theresa has never been agile – she tried ballet for a year but the teacher told her mother that Theresa would be better off playing Dumbo in a school production – so she is lumbering from rock to rock and feeling cross.

Leanne and Elaine are athletic – you can tell that by looking at them. Theresa, on the other hand, is fit and trying to keep the kilos off. It's a different proposition altogether. The others don't even look bothered by what Theresa would define as climbing, not walking. Look at them! They're laughing, joking. *Talking.* Either the swimming didn't make her as fit as she hoped or she's lost a bit of stamina over winter.

Two hands attach themselves to her bum and she yelps. 'Marie! What are you *doing*?'

'Giving you a shove. You look like you're reluctant to get up those rocks.'

'That's because I *am*.' She makes a noise of exasperation but lets Marie push her along.

'Are you keeping up?' Marie asks, more seriously, and Theresa knows she's not just talking about the walk.

'I don't know,' she says honestly, looking ahead to where Leanne and Elaine have stopped at a level spot, their hands on their hips, looking across the sea.

'Isn't it glorious?' Elaine says, grinning at Theresa once she arrives.

'Yep,' Theresa says, trying to get her breath back. 'Lovely. Wonderful.'

Elaine gives her a funny look.

'The perspective sure is different up here,' Marie says. 'When you're in the water the horizon doesn't seem so far away.'

'I've never been here before,' Leanne says. 'And I live just over there.' She turns to indicate behind her, and looks sheepish. 'I should come here more often.'

'It's a great spot,' Marie says. 'I'd walk up here with Nicole after school. Thought I was giving her an appreciation of the natural world.' She shrugs. 'Now she lives in a terrace house in a cramped suburb and has one geranium to her name.'

'I'm sure she does appreciate it,' Theresa says. 'She'll come back one day, I'll bet.'

Marie sighs. 'I'd like that. I'd get to see her more often.'

Theresa's face clouds. 'I guess that means once Ollie and Sasha grow up I'll hardly see them, either.'

'You're not getting enough of them now?' Marie says pointedly.

Theresa knows what that point is: they've discussed her telling the others about what's going on in her life. Marie says they deserve to know, and she's right, they do, because they hear all the boring details about the books Sasha is reading with her teacher and the footy team Ollie likes, and how Nonna has made enemies out of every aged pensioner with a gambling streak within a two-kilometre radius because she keeps beating them at cards – yet she's been keeping the most fundamental detail of her life from them. Because telling them is going to make it real. She hasn't even told her parents. Only Nonna, Marie and the kids know, and she's kept it that way for months now.

She glances behind her and sees a natural seat formed of rocks. 'Can we sit for a couple of minutes?' she says, looking at Marie.

'Sure,' Marie replies, and the others smile mildly as they stretch out their legs and keep their eyes on the horizon.

'Not too long! We don't want to get cold!' Elaine says cheerily.

She's been gradually more cheery since she started going to AA and sometimes Theresa misses her occasional moroseness, because the cheeriness has the gleam of a cult about it. She's proud of her, though, for making the commitment and sticking with it.

The only other person Theresa has known to have a drinking problem – apart from Andrew and his mates, although they always say it's 'just blokes being blokes' – was her Uncle Mario, and the way the family handled it was to never mention it. They'd just hide the alcohol at family gatherings and hope he wouldn't realise it was to stop him drinking it all. Except once her grandfather had called him an *ubriacone*. Only the once. Theresa had pretended not to know what it meant because she was sure Nonno hadn't meant to say it out loud. Uncle Mario is the reason Theresa is glad she was able to help Elaine, as modest as the help was. If only someone had helped Uncle Mario instead of judging him, if only they'd talked about the problem, maybe he wouldn't have fallen out with his children and ended up dying slowly as his liver packed up on him. They were all afraid to say anything, but not saying anything meant he thought no one noticed. Or that no one cared.

Elaine can be in no doubt that they all care about her. And Theresa should be in no doubt that it's reciprocated.

'What I have to say won't take too long,' she says.

Leanne bites her bottom lip. 'That sounds . . . ominous.'

Theresa releases a nervous little sound that's halfway to a laugh, although a laugh would be inappropriate. Unless it's gallows humour. A requiem for the end of her marriage.

'It kind of is,' she says, her voice small.

She exhales loudly and looks at the ocean. A year ago, she never would have imagined she would voluntarily swim in that. It is terrifyingly large – yet to her it seems like home. She has made friends because of that ocean. She's had the chance to make friends with herself too. The Theresa who first yanked a cap over her springy hair would never, she thinks, have stood up for herself the way she has over the past months. That's what Marie said too.

That Theresa owes a lot of her new self to the three people who've been showing up for her and with her day after day. In the past she's never had a reason to contemplate the idea that families aren't necessarily made from blood. The relatives she has are enough of a handful. Now she knows that the family you create, voluntarily, can bring joy instead of pain, and support and love and strength. They're who she chooses to be with.

'Andrew left a few weeks ago,' she says, looking from Elaine to Leanne. 'Months, actually. He's not coming back.'

'No!' Elaine gasps, and Leanne draws back, her eyes hooded.

'I haven't told you because . . .' Here Theresa falters. How to describe shame? Or the concern that you've failed at one of the two roles society has assigned to you: wife and mother? Even when you believe your friends love you, that doesn't stop you worrying about their reactions.

'Because the dickhead got himself a girlfriend and you shouldn't have to explain that to anyone,' Marie says decisively. 'It's not your fault. And I *know*, Theresa, that even though you're in a better place now there's a little part of you that's taking the blame. It's called Catholic guilt, and listen: I'm a good Catholic but I don't think the guilt is reasonable.'

Theresa presses her lips together, trying to control the emotions she's been keeping a lid on while she's helped the children adjust to their new life.

She remembers how Nonna reacted when she told her that Andrew had gone to be with someone else.

'Stupid boy,' she muttered, taking a drag on her cigarette. 'He thinks he should be the centre of the universe.'

When Theresa had protested, still trying to defend him for no reason other than habit, Nonna had added, 'They all think that. Some are just better at hiding it than others.'

She needs to keep remembering that, because it's the answer to sloughing off the guilt: Andrew's behaviour is all about Andrew; Theresa's is mainly about others. So he's responsible for everything he's done, and she owns none of it.

'I'm sorry,' Leanne says.

'It's not your fault,' Theresa says, then looks at Marie and laughs. 'I'm stealing your lines.'

'You're welcome to them.' Marie smiles at her the way Theresa wishes her mother did. Then says to Elaine and Leanne, 'She's been a brave girl.'

'You know I'll support you,' Elaine says, reaching over to place a hand on Theresa's wrist. 'Whatever help you need with the children. I have time, after all. I'd welcome the job.'

Theresa's nose twitches – her usual sign that she wants to cry and is trying not to. 'You're very kind. But I've been doing it all on my own for years anyway.'

'It doesn't mean you have to continue,' Elaine says, smiling reassuringly. 'Honestly, let's make a time to talk about it.'

Theresa nods. 'Shall we keep walking?' she says, sniffing and wiping a finger under each eye.

'Sure,' Marie murmurs and they all stand.

Elaine leads them off, and Marie follows, so they don't see Leanne wrap her arms around Theresa and squeeze her before letting go. Theresa doesn't think she's been more surprised in her life.

'I really am sorry,' Leanne whispers. 'You're so kind to other people. This shouldn't happen.'

'No, it shouldn't,' Theresa says, and Leanne looks so young and vulnerable that she feels a big-sisterly urge to take her hand as they start to walk along the path. Although she doesn't do it, because Leanne is a grown-up and she may not appreciate being treated like a child. 'And don't let it put you off men,' she continues. 'Not that I presume it would.' She shakes her head. 'That was a strange thing to say.'

Leanne flashes a smile. 'No, it's not.'

'Anyway!' Theresa straightens, feeling her shoulders begin to release some of the burden they've been holding. 'They're not all like Andrew. And I have no idea if you're seeing Matt, because I don't want to pry and you haven't said anything, but I can't imagine him ever behaving the way my husband has. Ex-husband. Or can I not say that yet? We're not divorced.

Oh!' She throws her hands in the air. 'Who cares. Ex. Now, let's catch up to the others.'

Theresa and Leanne increase their walk to a trot. The wind from the ocean hits them and Theresa giggles at the surprise of it. Up here, out there, the world keeps doing what it's doing, and her life is just one of billions moving in and out of the planet. She knows she's going to be fine. Eventually.

And if she never has another relationship with a man again, she won't care. She has three friends who are very good company.

CHAPTER 35

Leanne has to admit it to herself: the paediatric ward has been a lot quieter without Theresa, and also not as pleasant a workplace. It's not that work has to be fun – Leanne has never expected that – but having been the beneficiary of Theresa's sunniness, the place is gloomy without it. But Leanne understands that her friend needs to reduce her responsibilities for a while: Theresa doesn't know if she can stay in the house, for one thing, and she is trying to work out where she can go with two children and a nonna. Sometimes Leanne worries that Theresa will have to leave Shelly Bay – it's not the cheapest suburb in the city and without Andrew's income Theresa may have to move further away. Which would make swimming – or walking – difficult, if not impossible, and may also mean she doesn't come back to the hospital, as she plans to eventually.

'But it's possible,' she said that morning as they finished their walk, 'that Nonna is sitting on bags of money. She seems to win a lot at poker. Perhaps I should ask her.' She winked, her voice sounding light, but Leanne doesn't think this phase of her life can be light. She thinks it's probably very hard.

It's selfish of her to wish that Theresa was still at the hospital when there's so much else she needs to do, but Leanne can't help it. Theresa used to wave if they saw each other from afar.

If they passed in the corridor she'd give Leanne a wink and a hello, or she'd make a remark about that morning's swim.

'Like a millpond, wasn't it!' she'd say if the sea was calm.

'That was better than a ride at Luna Park!' she'd reserve for days when the waves were bigger than usual.

The phrases weren't necessary, nor were they always original. But they were thoughtful. They let Leanne know that Theresa *saw* her. Acknowledged her. In return, Leanne is trying to learn how to do that for others.

Leanne is good with the children; she always makes sure they know they're important. Some, like Imogen, turn out to be more important than others. They're the ones she misses when they go home. Or never go home. If they die she tries not to think about them too often; she wouldn't be able to function if she did. It was one of the great reliefs of her life that Imogen actually did go home. She will be in and out of hospitals for years, and Leanne may never see her again, but she can allow herself to think of her, knowing that the thought causes no pain.

The adults she has to deal with, on the other hand, have for so long been – not a cause of pain, really, but a source of vexation. They want to talk to her, and ask questions about her life, which, as far as she's concerned, is none of their business. Children can be nosy but they also respect 'no'. Adults, in her experience, do not. What she didn't allow for, though, is that she's likely been seeing only what she wants to see. She hasn't given many adults a chance to be kind to her – men, for her own very good reasons, but also women.

Yet three women in particular have been very kind to her, each in their own way. Leanne doesn't know what she has done to deserve it, because she's hardly been as kind to them. She saw a chance, though, when Theresa needed help, and has been taking Oliver and Sasha to the park each Saturday morning so Theresa can have some time to herself. It's something practical she can do, to show Theresa that she cares.

Leanne's not good at words – she can't say 'I care about you'. She's confident she will never be able to say 'I love you' to anyone. That's not her. But she can show someone she cares, so that's what she's doing. Theresa understands, Leanne is sure. She doesn't make a fuss about the fact that Leanne has offered to help; she just accepts it and says thank you.

In the past Leanne thought she couldn't accept help from people because there would be a price: she'd have to offer something in return. Watching Theresa, though, and observing her own behaviour has been instructive, if not enlightening, because it occurs to her that people usually only offer to help if they want to – as she has offered help to Theresa – and there is no price other than saying 'thank you'. Not that Leanne wants to rush off and get help from people, but she could be a little less staunch in her independence. Even at work – if she's struggling to carry something, for example, and someone offers to help her carry it, she doesn't have to say no.

When Leanne leaves the hospital today, it's not quite as dark as it was yesterday. They're turning towards summer and she can't wait to get back into the water. She makes an effort to say goodbye to people, where before she would scurry off. Her colleagues showed surprise the first few times she did it, but now everyone's used to it. As is she.

Not that she's confessing details about her life to anyone yet – and she hasn't mentioned that she has a boyfriend. It's hard to say the word even to herself; it was Matt who said it first.

'So . . . we've seen each other a lot,' he said the other night as he was dropping her home.

At first she felt tense, worried he was going to try to rush her into doing something that she isn't unwilling to do – surprisingly – but that she wants to be prepared for. She's attracted to him: her whole body tells her that each time she sees him. He's made it clear he thinks she's 'gorgeous', although she's sure that's an exaggeration. She's never been gorgeous. But she appreciates that he says it without seeming to expect anything in return for saying it. She has come to trust him, not because of what he says but how he acts: respectfully, slowly. It's enabled her to start thinking about what it would be like to take things further. To kiss him somewhere other than in the front seat of his car. But when he made his statement she was still at the stage of thinking about it, not taking steps to make it happen.

'We have,' she said.

He smiled and took her hand. 'Does that mean . . .' He raised an eyebrow and she still felt tense. 'That I can call myself your boyfriend?'

Her mouth gaped and she felt the tension release. 'Oh,' was all she could manage at first. 'Yes.'

'You sure?' He looked worried.

'Yes. Yes!' She smiled reassuringly.

'I know you, um . . . haven't had a boyfriend before.' He squeezed her hand. 'So I didn't want to rush into saying it.'

No, she hasn't had a boyfriend before and she knew what he'd interpret that to mean – that she hasn't *been* with a boy before. That's one of the things she has to work out how to negotiate once they move beyond the front seat of his car.

'It's fine,' she said, squeezing him back.

He kissed her, or she kissed him. These days there is no routine to it. At the start he would always kiss her first because she was still clinging to the ideas of what a 'nice girl' should be – then she remembered that being a nice girl hadn't kept her out of harm's way, so she should do what she feels. And what she feels, often, is that she wants to kiss him first.

Remembering last night's kiss, she smiles to herself as she walks out the hospital's main entrance and starts around the semicircular driveway that allows for patient drop-offs and pick-ups. If she follows the road to the left it'll take her to Casualty; instead she leaves the path and starts to walk through the car park.

'Leanne?'

Her head cracks to the right at the sound. The ancient sound of her name spoken in her mother's voice.

Leanne's heard of people saying 'I just froze' when they're in a bank robbery or something like that, and always thought it a strange reaction. But she's doing it right now, as she sees her mother standing a few metres away, an imploring look on her face.

Her mother has barely changed in eight years, which would seem impossible were it not for something Leanne remembers her saying once: that her own mother always looked the same until she reached sixty, and then looked immediately eighty. 'Her mother too,' she'd said with a knowing nod. Leanne hadn't believed it, but now she thinks she should have.

'Leanne?' her mother says again, taking a tentative step closer. She's clutching a boxy handbag that Leanne remembers.

'M-Mum,' she says, still frozen. 'How did you find me?'

She's never had her number listed in the phone book; she's never been in the newspaper. A clean break is what she wanted and she had it.

'My friend.' Her mother gestures towards the building. 'She works with you.'

'Which friend?' Leanne mentally scans the staff for anyone who might be a candidate. But she knows so little about them – on purpose, of course. She doesn't know where any of them live. For all she knows, one of them is her parents' neighbour.

'Your matron,' her mother says, nodding once, decisively, as if she expects Leanne to argue.

'Matron?' Leanne calculates quickly. Matron is younger than her mother, she's sure of it; not that that rules her out, as Leanne knows: Elaine, Theresa and Marie are older than her.

'She's married to a friend of your father's. She said she has a lovely young nurse here – Leanne. She said Leanne looks like me.'

Her mother seems scared now, as if Leanne is about to get angry at her. She doesn't feel angry. She feels surprised. Startled. Perhaps slightly scared herself, given what happened the last time they saw each other.

They're standing, looking at each other, when a car horn toots and Leanne realises she's in the way. She moves quickly out of its path and towards her mother.

'Leanne,' her mother says again, pleadingly. 'Where have you been?'

Her mother's face crumples, and Leanne feels a pain she hasn't felt in years. The pain of disappointing the person she loves the most. No, not just disappointing her – causing her extreme distress, even as Leanne was in distress herself.

What happened to her, how it happened, the result of what happened – it was all of a piece. A horrible ball of mess from which there could be no good outcome. Leanne chose to do what she thought would reduce the pain the most: she would remove herself and take care of the pregnancy. But the shame never left her. It just trickled into her marrow, where it will stay forever.

'I've been here,' she says, almost choking on the words.

Her mother is right in front of her now, reaching out a hand, taking hers. 'What happened . . . to you?' she says, gasping.

'I gave up the baby, Mum.' Leanne tries to keep her voice steady and fails. She swallows. 'She has her own family now. You don't have to worry about it.'

She knows that's the equivalent of sticking a dagger into her mother's side: implying that the only thing she would be worried about is what became of Leanne and her supposed bad behaviour. So that could be why her mother starts crying. She's holding Leanne with both hands now, shaking her head from side to side, tears dripping off her chin.

Leanne tries not to let her heart break as she sees that, yet again, she is causing her mother distress. She thought she had tied it up neatly back then, made it so her parents could get on with their lives, and she, eventually, would get on with hers. Never did she imagine she'd have to reckon with all that pain again.

'We looked for you,' her mother says, putting a hand to Leanne's cheek. 'We looked and we couldn't find you.'

'You have now,' Leanne says.

Suddenly the noise of the car park fills her ears. They're here in public, making a scene. In front of her workplace. She feels like she's going to be sick.

'I have to go,' she says, breaking free of her mother's grip. She kisses her on the cheek and wipes the tears from her chin. 'I love you, Mum,' she says, then pulls away from her.

'Leanne!'

She hears her mother calling as she runs through the car park and down the long driveway to the street, trying to think of the safest place she can go. It's not something she wants to burden Matt with; Marie is closest and would welcome her but she may not be alone. Theresa's and Elaine's houses seem too far away when what she needs is a shelter, right now.

She runs past the falling-down weatherboard houses; past the sturdier Federation houses; past the frangipanis in front gardens and the dogs yapping at gates and the milk bottles left out for collection. She arrives on the flat ground and smells the salt in the breeze.

The noise of the waves reaches her before she can see them, a ceaseless reassurance that the world keeps turning and this ocean will be here for her for as long as she needs it.

Throwing her bag onto the sand, she rushes to the water's edge, drops to her knees, puts her hands into the white foam, and sobs.

CHAPTER 36

Marie can feel spring in the air as she steps out of the church ahead of the other congregants, but she's glad of her light cardigan as a cool breeze wafts past her neck. They'll be back in the water soon – she announced that to the others this morning. The water is warming, and while it's far from balmy she knows from experience that the temperature will be less of a shock.

She was surprised that Leanne seemed the most enthusiastic about it, considering she's been swimming at the pool over winter. The *heated* pool. Marie isn't sure she approves of that, although Theresa assures her that Leanne is only doing it because her boyfriend works there. Boyfriend! Leanne is certainly a dark horse. Marie had no idea from the very little she says that she has a beau in her life.

Perhaps she is being ungenerous about the swimming, though: Leanne is the one who has been most serious about their endeavours. She would stand on the beach looking as if she was just about to take an exam – a small frown of concentration, a setting of her mouth – before meticulously tucking her hair into her cap. Such lovely, straight, long hair: Marie dreamt about having hair like that most of her life. Instead she has hair that does nothing remarkable.

The breeze finds her again and this time she shivers.

'Are you cold?' Gus says as he touches her elbow, and she feels instantly warm.

She smiles. 'No. Just wishing it was warmer. So how was that?' she asks, standing as close to him as she can without scandalising the church regulars.

They aren't at a stage of being demonstrative in public – although she was never at that stage with Norm, because that's just not what they did – yet she finds that she always wants to be close to him.

'You mean, how does a former altar boy feel about going to mass after decades in the wilderness?' He smiles down at her and she feels his hand lightly touch her back then move away. She marvels that at her age a simple gesture can make her feel so enlivened.

'Something like that.'

Gus is here because, despite his reservations about religion, he said he knows that church is important to her.

'It was all very familiar,' he says, looking over her head to where others are slowly exiting.

Marie moves to a spot where Father Paul will see them. She wants Father Paul to meet Gus. She's mentioned Gus to him in a light, I-have-a-new-friend way, which of course he saw through.

'Do you mean you have a *boyfriend*, Marie?' he said, almost salaciously.

Marie considered being shocked, but reckoned that Father Paul probably knew more gossip than anyone, what with the confessional, so he wouldn't really be that outraged by her news.

Busybody Dulcie looks over and Marie knows she has mere seconds before Gus becomes the subject of an inquisition. Except just as Dulcie steps towards them, Father Paul intervenes and takes her hand. Marie is sure it's to help her – she's never known Father Paul to willingly spend time with Dulcie.

'I like your Father Paul,' Gus says. 'He seems sensible.'

'He is. And he's very kind. He's been . . .'

She stops, not wanting to tell Gus that the Marie he knows now was on dim wattage not that long ago. Their friendship – their relationship – is new enough that she still wants to present the best of herself to him. She's worried that if he knows the sludgier parts of her life he may not like her.

It's not entirely to do with him, either. Marie isn't that honest with Nicole. Although she confessed some of her money worries, she didn't tell her daughter that it took her so long to emerge from Norm's death.

To Nicole, it wouldn't have looked as though her parents had a great romance – and they hadn't, not in an Elizabeth Taylor and Richard Burton way. Tempestuousness isn't Marie's style, and it certainly wasn't Norm's. But in their own way it was a very good marriage: they enjoyed their life together, and she never thought there should be fireworks every day. She loved him for him, and he loved her for her.

When he died, her body and brain seemed to take forever to adjust to her new reality. She was still engaged in the same rituals of life with Norm – she'd start to make him breakfast, for example; and if she heard something interesting on the radio she'd go to tell him. Each of those little slips added up each day and she was exhausted from the adjustments she had to make as she remembered.

And once her brain did catch up to the news, about two years after he died, she felt as though she was unmoored from time and space. Nicole would ask why Marie looked so tired, and she didn't say she was waking up at one o'clock each morning, panicking, unable to go back to sleep. She didn't want Nicole to worry. It hadn't occurred to her that by not being honest with Nicole, she wasn't inviting Nicole to be honest with her. And now that she's feeling more like herself, she realises there may have been unintended consequences of that over the past few years.

'What has he been?' Gus says lightly, and for a second Marie thinks he's talking about Norm. But it's Father Paul he's looking at, and she has to remember, again, that she's in this place now, in this time, with Gus.

She isn't ready yet to tell him the whole truth about the last few years, but she can open the door to it.

'I wasn't doing so well for a while there. It was hard, without Norm.'

'I understand,' Gus says.

'I know you do.' Marie presses his hand quickly. 'Father Paul noticed, although he was subtle about it. I'll always be grateful to him for caring.'

Gus glances over her head once more. 'And he's heading this way.'

The breeze ruffles Father Paul's hair as he approaches.

'Hello, Marie,' he says, taking her hand in both of his. 'It's good to see you, as always.' He turns to Gus. 'I'm Paul,' he says as they shake hands.

'Gus.'

'Marie has told me very little about you,' Father Paul says with mischief in his eyes.

'Maybe because there's not much to say,' Gus replies laconically.

'I can't imagine Marie keeping company with anyone who isn't interesting.' Father Paul tilts his head slightly as he looks at her. 'She's certainly one of the most interesting people I know.'

'That can't be true, Father!' Marie is genuinely surprised. Her quiet suburban seaside life is hardly anyone's definition of interesting.

'Marie, you forget how much I know about you.' Father Paul's eyes twinkle, causing Marie to wonder exactly what Dulcie and some of the other church gossips have been saying. Not that she thinks Father Paul would share anything untoward with Gus.

'Did Marie tell you that she speaks two other languages?' Father Paul went on.

Gus gives her an admiring look. 'No, she didn't.'

'You can't *speak* Latin, Father,' Marie says quickly, not wanting anyone to make a fuss.

'*I* can,' he replies, winking. 'And I wasn't thinking of Latin. Don't you occasionally read novels in French and German for fun?'

'Not for a while,' Marie mutters.

Gus's expression is quizzical. 'You told me those books belonged to Nicole.'

Marie purses her lips. She didn't intend to be the subject of conversation today. This is meant to be the Gus-and-Paul show. Just because she decided to learn some foreign languages while Nicole took them at school, and just because she decided to keep up her studies long after Nicole stopped, doesn't mean everyone needs to know. Men don't like smart women – her mother used to say that.

'Father, I don't think Gus needs to know all of this.'

'I think I do,' Gus says, grinning conspiratorially at the priest.

'There's more to know, Gus,' Father Paul says as he puts a hand on Marie's arm, 'but I think Marie will show you in good time.'

'I look forward to finding out.'

As Gus smiles at her, Marie feels herself relax. She doesn't know why she's so comfortable with him. No, that's not the right word, because he makes her heart beat faster and that's not comfort. Comfort is more anodyne. There is an *ease* between them and the edge of attraction with it. Desire, she would call it if she were allowed, but she's not sure women her age are.

Perhaps the word she is looking for is *trust*. She trusts him – improbably, because they haven't known each other long enough. It's the way he looks at her, though, with such care and regard. She hopes she expresses the same to him, but she can't see her own eyes.

'I should move on,' Father Paul says. 'Marie, I'll see you next Sunday. Gus – until we meet again.'

'Goodbye, Father.' Marie nods once – her own gesture of respect.

Gus offers her the crook of his elbow. 'Shall we stroll? The temperature should be just right by the water.'

'All right, Goldilocks,' she says, taking his arm.

As they walk in the direction of the promenade by the beach, chatting easily, she feels light and carefree, the future full of delicious mystery.

CHAPTER 37

When Marie suggested it was time to return to the water, Elaine was surprised at how excited she was. The temperature will hardly be warm: eighteen degrees, if they're lucky. But she doesn't care. Walking is pleasant, and she's seen more of Shelly Bay than she did during a whole year of living here, but it's plodding and graceless compared with swimming. She's enjoyed keeping fit, and being with the others, but she'll enjoy it more in the water.

She hasn't had a drink for several weeks now and while she resents – at times bitterly – the abstinence, she's sleeping better and feeling far less sad and sorry for herself. It seems that her initial attempts to ameliorate her homesickness by drinking it away had at some point started to exacerbate it. If only she'd been able to identify that point, she wouldn't have ended up having to call herself an alcoholic, which she's been doing with regularity at the meetings.

She once expressed to Derek her dismay that she has to announce this status each time she wants to say something – or, rather, when Gerard expects her to say something. Derek looked at her as if she was growing peonies out of her scalp.

'*Elaine*,' he said, 'do you not *get it* yet?' Then he sighed and shook his head. 'You will be an alcoholic *forever*.'

She opened her mouth to protest – how ridiculous, surely one stops being an alcoholic when one stops drinking all the time – but his facial expression told her not to. Apparently she missed the part where joining AA means the first A appends to you for life.

Afterwards she thought about the fact that she will always have to call herself an alcoholic, and decided she finds it freeing. It means she won't have to make choices: will she drink today or won't she? The answer will always be 'no'; and she can cope with missing the taste of gin, if that's what it takes. What is truly ridiculous is that she once thought she couldn't function without it. The last weeks have clearly proved that she can.

Returning to the water will also help. Each morning in the ocean she can experience the sensation of things being washed off her: the barnacles of bad habit. She might call it a ritual cleansing if that didn't sound so dramatic.

'Hi, Elaine,' says Theresa as she arrives, her smile not as bright as it used to be. She hasn't been herself for a while now.

'Hello!' Elaine feels like wrapping her in a hug to celebrate this auspicious day, but that would be strange: who gives hugs just because they're going for a swim?

'How was your meeting with the lawyer?' she says instead, and Theresa's face gives her the answer.

'Not that good.' She presses her lips together. 'Andrew's saying that he doesn't make an income from the business, and he's living with a friend who's claiming that he doesn't pay rent because he's so broke. So he's not going to pay anything to help me with the children.' She sighs. 'And I haven't worked for years – because he didn't want me to – so it's not as if I can go and get a job.'

'Well, you *do* work,' Elaine says. 'You raise children and run a household. That's work.'

Theresa laughs in a way Elaine has never heard from her: laced with bitterness. 'Except the value of that work is determined by my husband, isn't it? And he's saying that because I volunteer at the hospital and see my friends every morning to exercise, I'm not that committed to my children.'

'Oh, Theresa.'

Elaine decides a hug is now appropriate, and she's glad that Theresa accepts it, her head almost falling onto Elaine's shoulder.

'Do you need some money?' Elaine asks as she draws back. 'Because when I sold the business I just put it all into an account and it's still there – in sterling, which is worth considerably more here!'

She laughs to make light of the fact that she has never faced the financial situation Theresa is now in. She feels slightly guilty about it. Even without her own money, James makes more than enough for both of them.

Theresa looks startled, then her face relaxes. 'That is so lovely, but I couldn't – and it's fine. It's really fine.' She half smiles. 'It turns out Nonna's been stashing her poker winnings under her bed and there are several thousand tax-free dollars there. Don't tell anyone!' Her giggle brings back the old Theresa. 'We can get by. I don't know what will happen with the house but—'

'Good morning, you two,' Marie says.

'Good morning,' says Elaine. 'You look like the cat who ate the cream. What on *earth* is going on?'

Marie's smile becomes bigger. 'Nothing!' she says breezily. 'Or something. Gus and I had a lovely dinner. I'm just in a good mood.'

'He didn't . . . stay *overnight*, did he?' says Theresa, grinning.

'Not in the way you're suggesting, Theresa.' Marie smiles again.

'What!'

'Hi,' Leanne says, walking into the middle of their conversation.

'Hi,' Theresa and Elaine chorus.

'Are you all ready to swim?' Theresa adds. 'Because I am *busting* to get out there. Never thought I'd be so keen on exercise. I guess you're never too old to be surprised.'

Marie snorts. 'As if you're old.'

'As if *you* are!' Theresa says, and laughs, and sighs. 'That feels better. I thought I'd lost my sense of humour when I woke up this morning.'

'I don't blame you,' Elaine murmurs.

'Leanne, you have a face longer than a wet week,' says Marie. 'Whatever is the matter?'

Elaine's eyes widen in alarm. She loves Marie but she can be too direct sometimes, and Leanne has always reminded her of a cat: best not approached directly, allowed to approach on her own terms and in her own time. They've barely coaxed her into drinking milk from the bowl and now Marie's gone and stepped in it.

'Um . . . nothing.' Leanne offers her trademark tight smile and her glance away.

Yes, she's a cat, looking for a ledge to jump onto so she can run away.

'Leanne,' Marie huffs, putting her hands on her hips, 'that worked once upon a time but *not now*.' She wags a finger. 'Thank goodness you don't play poker with Theresa's nonna – you have a lot of tells.'

'Marie!' Theresa says. 'That's not very nice.'

'But it's true. Come on – out with it.'

'Really,' Leanne says, her breathing becoming more rapid, 'I can handle it.'

'So there *is* something,' Marie says more gently, stepping closer. 'Well, you're not taking it into the sea with you. You'll get distracted, you'll swallow water, and the next thing you know I'll be dragging you up the beach so Theresa can give you mouth to mouth.'

'And I'm sure you don't want that!' Theresa says breezily, but she doesn't look as though she's joking.

Leanne bows her head and puts it in her hands. 'I don't know what to do,' she says, her voice muffled.

Elaine is stunned, and she can tell the others are too. Leanne has never expressed a firm opinion, let alone an emotion, and they don't recognise it.

'What's happened?' Theresa asks. 'Is it something to do with Matt?'

Leanne shakes her head, then lifts it. Her face is blank, almost like she's not there any more.

'I'm so sorry I didn't notice you were upset before this,' Theresa says, looking as though she wants to cry. 'I haven't been at the hospital for so long.'

How could she have noticed, Elaine thinks – Leanne keeps everything to herself. For a while she thought it was because Leanne wasn't interested in being friends; she was swimming with them because it was safer than swimming alone. After a while she realised that Leanne is just very self-contained. Elaine's sometimes thought of her as being ascetic, keeping everything minimal, including conversation, so she can serve a higher purpose, such as her work.

'My mother turned up,' Leanne mumbles.

'What?' says Marie, leaning closer.

'My mother,' Leanne says more clearly. 'She turned up at work. A couple of weeks ago. I've been . . .' She stops and blinks slowly. 'It was hard.'

Her head tilts forwards again as Elaine, Theresa and Marie exchange looks of confusion.

'I know . . .' Theresa starts, stops, and bites her lip. 'You don't talk about your family. I didn't realise there was a problem.'

'I haven't seen them for eight years,' Leanne explains, and Elaine thinks this is the most she's ever told them about herself on one day.

'Right,' says Marie calmly. 'Do you want to tell us why?'

Leanne looks at each of them, almost defiantly, as if she's challenging them to accept what she's about to tell them. 'When I was eighteen, I . . . was raped.' She sucks in a breath and doesn't seem to let it out.

Elaine has the strange sensation of her spine going cold and bile rising in her oesophagus. It's shock – it must be – at learning that this tough, quiet girl who has been swimming with them for months has endured something so awful.

'By my brother's friend.' Leanne swallows.

'That's what you were trying to tell me that time,' Theresa says, her voice soft.

Leanne nods. 'I . . .' She gulps air and Theresa puts a hand on her arm.

'You don't have to tell us,' she whispers.

'I want to,' Leanne says quickly, and there's that defiance again.

Elaine admires it. Covets it, almost.

'I got pregnant,' Leanne continues, her eyes blinking rapidly.

Elaine risks a glance at the others and can see them trying to hide their surprise, as is she. Theresa looks as though she wants to ask questions, but they need to let Leanne be in charge here.

'It was too late . . . by the time I found out, it was too late to do anything,' Leanne says quietly, evenly. 'And I wouldn't have known where to go anyway. When I told my parents they said I'd brought shame on them. My father . . .' She closes her eyes. 'He was furious,' she whispers. 'My mother couldn't even look at me. They weren't going to forgive me.'

'But it wasn't your fault!' Theresa interjects.

Leanne smiles sadly. 'It's always our fault, isn't it?'

Elaine feels that shot of cold again as she remembers the two girls at her school who mysteriously vanished and were never seen again. Everyone knew they were pregnant and everyone thought badly of them – including her. Not a single person said anything about the men who made them pregnant. Elaine had judged those girls as much as anyone and she's ashamed of herself. As her cheeks burn she wants to turn her head away, but she knows that will look like she's turning away from Leanne – and she's not going to do that.

'So I left,' Leanne says, and her eyes glint with something that looks like pride. 'Found a job as a cleaner. Saved money. Did what I had to do so I could go to uni. I haven't spoken to them since.'

Simple phrases that describe a journey of pain and strength. Elaine marvels at the achievements of this woman she is only now beginning to know.

'What happened to the baby?' Marie asks.

Such a practical, logical question, and such a heartbreaking one too.

'I gave her up,' Leanne says, and Elaine hears Theresa sniff.

They are all silent for several moments. There's really nothing any of them can say that won't sound ineffectual. And won't be too late.

'I'm fine with it.' Leanne looks at each of them again. 'I couldn't have looked after her. I actually . . .' She grimaces, so briefly it's hard to catch. 'I didn't want to keep her. Because of what happened. Every time I looked at her I'd think about it.' She shakes her head. 'I couldn't.'

She releases a long sigh, then gives them a smile Elaine has never seen before: relaxed, natural.

'So your mother . . .' Marie prompts.

'She wants to see me again,' Leanne says. 'She wants me to see them all. She says they're sorry.'

'Maybe they are?' Elaine says. She doesn't know the details, of course, but if Leanne is distressed enough to tell them the story, her mother must be playing on her mind.

'Maybe.' Leanne's tiny say-nothing smile is back.

Marie pats her shoulder. 'You need to do what's right for you,' she says. 'If you want to see them, see them. If you don't, don't – but don't be hard on yourself if that's your decision.' She glances at Theresa and Elaine. 'You know we'll support you whatever.'

Leanne's eyes widen, then half close. She nods quickly and ducks her head.

'Come here, little one,' Marie says, putting her arms around the smaller, slighter woman and rubbing her back the way Elaine used to rub her sons' backs as they fell asleep. Perhaps all mothers know how to do this; perhaps Leanne's mother used to do it, too, years before her children grew up and there was no chance to do it any more. No way to express her love so simply.

Elaine remembers how painful it was when her sons crossed the threshold into the time when they no longer wanted her to hug them. They were boys becoming men, and her hands felt empty for years when she couldn't use them to convey her love and protection any more. She had to find other ways to do it. Ways to say it. She's not sure she's succeeded and she wishes she could just rub their backs again.

'Can we go swimming now?' says Leanne, muffled against Marie's chest.

'What a good idea,' Marie says, letting her go.

'It's going to be cold.' Theresa makes a face.

'I'm ready,' says Elaine with a smile at Leanne.

'Me too.' Leanne pulls her cap on.

'Last one in's a rotten egg!' cries Theresa as she takes off at a trot, and within a minute they are a mass of arms and legs pushing and kicking and diving, four unlikely mermaids swimming for the distant shore.

CHAPTER 38

Theresa tries to tie her towel like a sarong around her waist after her swim, except it's too thick and now it's falling to her ankles as she arrives home and wrenches open the front door. She really should do something about that handle or she'll end up not being able to get into the house. Andrew kept saying he'd fix it but he never did, and he's not here to fix it any more. Maybe Gus does odd jobs. She'd pay him, of course. Or Nonna would.

They wouldn't be getting by without Nonna's ill-gotten gains, and Theresa tells her that she's grateful every day. Nonna just waves a ciggie in her face and tells her it's better than keeping it under the bed.

Theresa also wouldn't be able to go swimming if Nonna didn't mind watching the children. She suspects Nonna enjoys bossing them around, and if that's the price they're paying for an ordered life, Theresa doesn't mind. It just means her children are growing up the way she did, because Nonna tended to impose discipline where Theresa's mother did not.

Nonna can't fix that door handle, though – or maybe she could, but Theresa isn't going to ask her to. So she tells herself to remember to write it on her to-do list, even if the most likely outcome is that as soon as she steps inside a million other things will happen and she'll forget.

The towel falls off completely as she shuts the door behind her and she almost trips over it just as Oliver runs into the room.

'You're WET!' he says, giggling.

He's always been a happy child, unlike his more solemn sister. No judgements, though – not of her own kids. The happy child isn't worth more than the sad one, even if Sasha gives Theresa more to worry about. Especially lately. Ollie has almost breezed through his father's departure whereas Sasha has been moping. Theresa understands: she wants to mope too some days, for different reasons, but she doesn't have the luxury.

'It's just my hair that's wet, Ollie.' She quite likes the drips on her shoulders – they're reminders that only minutes ago she was in the sea. 'Anyway, you're *nude*.'

He's always loved doing a nude run around the house. Andrew used to think it was naughty, but Theresa doesn't care. In her experience kids like to be nude, and she wouldn't mind walking around the house like that herself sometimes. It must feel like freedom. Except in her case it would also feel slightly uncomfortable because her boobs would be flapping in the breeze. That's what breastfeeding does for you.

Oliver giggles again and runs towards his bedroom, where she knows he'll put on his school uniform. He can be quite conscientious. She supposes eldest children usually are – although Angelo isn't and Theresa's always felt like she's the most responsible child in her family.

'Sasha!' she calls. They should both be dressed for school by now but Sasha is always reluctant.

'Where's Nonna?' she asks Oliver as he comes back into the living room, his school shirt wrongly buttoned.

'She's in the show-ahhhh,' he says.

Theresa peels off her swimming costume. She was hoping to have a shower herself straightaway so she can get the rest of the day going, but she's back a bit later than usual so she's thrown out the timing. If only Andrew had put a shower in the granny flat when Theresa had asked – Nonna is too old to get in and out of her bathtub now.

'Aw, Mum, ew! I don't wanna see you in the nuddy.' Oliver pretends to shield his eyes but she can see him grinning.

She grins back. 'Ollie, you have been seeing me in the nuddy all your life!'

Theresa's always tried to be relaxed about her body around the kids. She doesn't want to hide it from them, especially after they were both breastfed. How confusing would that be? Here, you can see my breasts all the time, put your mouth on them, pat them with your hands, and now I'm going to lock them away like there's something wrong with them.

'Sasha!' she calls again, louder this time. 'Ollie, your shirt isn't done up properly.'

'She's sick,' Oliver says, rebuttoning his shirt.

'What?' Theresa can't have a sick child today. She has so much to do, including taking Nonna to her poker game and to the doctor early in the afternoon. Plus she promised Sarah, another school mum, that she'd take her kids home after school because Sarah's working and her babysitter's away.

'What's that?' Oliver says as Theresa wraps her towel around her torso.

'What?'

He sighs. 'It's gone.'

'Ollie, what are you talking about?'

'That funny thing.' He points to her chest.

'The towel?' She frowns at him, confused.

He points again. 'That thing on your booby.'

'You mean my mole? That's always been there.'

'No!' He shakes his head as if she's the silliest person he's ever met. 'Underneath.'

She doesn't know what he's talking about and has no time to look. Right now she has to check on her daughter, get into the shower and take these kids to school.

'Good morning, *bella*,' Nonna says as she enters the room swaddled in her favourite terry-towelling dressing gown, which bears the strong aroma of the several cigarettes she's already smoked this morning.

'Hi, Nonna, did you have a good sleep?' Theresa tucks the top of her towel in more snugly.

'Why are you naked in front of the boy?' Nonna says crossly.

'I'm not naked! I have a towel on. I'm waiting to have a shower.'

'I've seen Mummy naked heaps, Nonna,' Oliver says seriously.

Nonna's disapproval is evident but Theresa doesn't think she has any right to judge – she's hardly a paragon of virtue. That's one of the reasons Theresa loves her so much.

'I haven't had time to put the coffee on,' she says as she heads towards Sasha's bedroom.

'I'll do it,' Nonna says.

Theresa walks into Sasha's bedroom to find a wan-looking child, her hair still tousled from sleep, bravely trying to pull on her uniform.

'Hi, Mum,' Sasha almost whispers and Theresa's heart contracts. Her baby girl looks like she's trying so hard not to be unwell.

'Hello, darling.' Theresa picks her up and sits on the bed. She kisses the side of Sasha's head and feels the softness of her curls against her face.

Despite that long to-do list she would stay like this all day if she could. She loves being around her children, and always wishes she had more time to simply be with them, without them all flinging themselves around the way life seems to demand they must. School, playing with their friends, ballet lessons for Sasha, tennis lessons for Oliver, reading to them as much as she can, cooking, cleaning, mending clothes, tending to the garden, and maybe, sometimes, getting a few minutes to herself.

She smiles at her daughter and strokes the hair that's sticking up on top of her head. 'You're not well, darling?' she says softly and Sasha shakes her head.

Theresa tries not to sigh. She doesn't want Sasha to see how this complicates her day. Almost everything on her list involves her being elsewhere, rather than home with a sick child. She also can't not turn up to take Sarah's children home from school, never mind Oliver. And Theresa can't put Nonna in a taxi to poker because Nonna thinks all the drivers are stupid and usually ends up yelling at them.

So Theresa needs to be resourceful today; she needs a solution to look after Sasha and manage all the other things. It won't come from within her own family: Andrew has never been her back-up childcare option, especially now; and it also won't come from his parents, who have a regime of VIEW Club meetings, bridge games and beers at the sailing club to uphold. Her own parents are too far away to get here in time. It's a two-hour drive, and that's on a good day.

She thinks about the school mums, most of whom have their own kids or jobs to worry about. Then she remembers something Marie said to her once, when Theresa was moaning about all the things she had to juggle that day.

'If you ever need a hand with the kids, let me know. I'm not far away.' She had a funny expression on her face, almost like she was hopeful that Theresa would take her up on the offer.

Theresa had thanked Marie but never thought she'd actually ask her to help, not because she wouldn't trust her with the kids – Marie is definitely the responsible type – but because she doesn't want to take advantage of her.

She doesn't have another option, though. Not today.

'It's okay, darling,' she says, kissing Sasha again, 'I just have to make a phone call.'

'Of course I can be there,' Marie says, and Theresa feels herself relax.

'Thank you. What would I do without you?'

'And what would I do without *you*?'

Theresa can hear the smile in Marie's voice and hopes Marie can't hear her sniffling. Some days are hard, and some aren't, but because she sees Marie and the others every day they always start with laughter.

'What time do you need me?' Marie asks.

'I'll run Ollie to school and come back. So . . . nine-thirty?'

'Works for me.'

'Thanks again.' Arrangements made, Theresa heads for the shower. 'Nonna, can you get Ollie's breakfast?' she calls.

'*Si, si*,' comes the slightly grumpy reply and Theresa smiles.

As the water hits her she remembers what Ollie said about seeing something on her breast, so she has a bit of a feel. There, on the bottom side of her right breast, there's a funny little thing. A shape. That's how she thinks of it. Not a lump.

She knows what breast lumps look like because her Aunt Gloria was always keen to show hers, to make sure the rest of the family knew what she was going through. Those lumps were so far gone by the time Gloria did anything about them that she was dead within a few months. This one is little. But visible to her son, so Theresa can't believe she didn't notice it before.

Not that she has time to think about groping her boobs looking for lumps, and it's not as if anyone else has been groping her either. Even before he left it had been a long time since Andrew went anywhere near her 'fun bags', as he used to call them. After she breastfed two babies he started saying that her boobs didn't belong to him any more. She could never tell if he was sad or angry about that.

It's not as if they belonged to *her*, either. It wasn't until breastfeeding that she really understood that her breasts had a purpose other than keeping Andrew happy and sometimes being the cause of remarks as she passed strange men on the street. She thinks they're still remark-worthy. Remarkable, even. Two kids later they haven't lost their shape completely, even if they do hang a bit lower than before.

The knock on the bathroom door startles her.

'Mu-um! I need to do a wee!'

'Okay, Ollie. Come in.'

By the time her son has finished his wee, Theresa has almost pushed the lump to the back of her mind. She'll write it on her to-do list, along with everything else. That's the only way she'll remember to talk to someone about it.

CHAPTER 39

The house is as Leanne remembers it, and not. It looks more aged, and it looks the same. Her memories are a veil over the reality in front of her, telling her that this is her childhood home and also the place she vowed never to see again. If it's possible to feel like you are in two places at once – to be two people at once – then she is.

'You're really, really sure about this?' Elaine says, taking her hands from the steering wheel and swivelling towards her.

'No.' Leanne gives her a weak smile. 'I'm not sure of anything.'

After she told the others her story, after she knew that they wouldn't question her decisions, she felt free. A bad thing had happened to her; she'd accepted the consequences. She'd taken charge of things as much as she could.

There have been days, though, when she wished she could take it all back: she would still have her parents and her siblings; she might even have that baby. It had seemed logical at the time: to divest herself of shame by staying away from its witnesses and removing its cause. After her mother appeared at the hospital that day, though, Leanne hasn't been sure she made the right decision. Except she's created a whole life around that decision, and she doesn't know who she would be otherwise.

'Do you not want to talk to your mother at all?' Marie had asked the other morning after their swim.

'I . . . don't know.'

Leanne had looked out to sea. Her life was so simple when she was out there. Arms and legs moving. Opening her mouth, breathing. The sun starting to rise. The occasional seagull hovering. Her only preoccupations to get to Little Beach and back, and keep track of the others. Not because she's competitive with them but because she likes knowing they're around. Her little tribe.

Tears had come to her eyes unbidden. She never meant to involve other people in her mess. In any part of her life. Yet now she has three friends, and a boyfriend, and while that makes her existence more complicated than it was before, it's also richer. Fuller than she can believe. Which is why she accepted Elaine's offer to accompany her today; she has come to realise that she's allowed to have help. It's too hard, and too exhausting, to do everything on her own.

'I'll sit in the car,' Elaine said when she suggested it. 'I'll be waiting when you're ready to leave.'

Something else Leanne told the others that morning was how she'd regretted running away from her mother at the hospital. She wasn't ready to talk then, but she is now, if her mother is.

'She'll be ready,' Marie said firmly. 'If she's found you after all these years, I'd say talking to you is what she wants most and she's not going to be so easily put off.'

Leanne felt her doubt muddled up with her guilt. 'It wasn't the right thing to do,' she said.

'It was the right thing for you to do at the time.' Marie could be so practical and blunt, and that day Leanne was glad of it.

Now, with the house in front of her, she feels more doubt: what if this still isn't the right thing for her?

'I can come in with you,' Elaine says. 'I don't mind.'

Leanne presses her lips together to stop her chin trembling. 'No,' she says in a half whisper. 'I need to do it. But I really appreciate you being here.'

Elaine smiles kindly.

'I'll go now.' Leanne pulls the handle on the car door without waiting for Elaine to respond.

She closes the door behind her, and takes swift steps towards the gate, up the path, to the familiar wooden door with a new-looking brass knocker on it.

Three firm knocks, and she hears noise behind the door.

It opens, and her mother is there, looking tinier than she did at the hospital.

'Leanne?' she whispers, as if she can't believe what she's seeing.

'Hi, Mum,' Leanne says, trying to smile but her chin wobbles again.

Her mother nods at her and steps closer. 'You came.'

'I shouldn't have left you the other day. I'm sorry.'

Her mother puts her hand on Leanne's hair and strokes it once. 'It's okay,' she says. 'You got a shock.'

Leanne feels something thick, like packed sand and salt water, in her throat. She pushes it down. She's not here to get upset. She's here to make amends. Not to ask for forgiveness or even for them to understand her. They may never understand each other. That's what happens in families, and sometimes amongst friends. You love each other anyway. She hadn't known that when she was eighteen. All she could think about was her own pain.

That's what she kept going over in the car while Elaine drove her here, leaving her alone with her thoughts, not trying even once to intrude. It's what they're used to, after all: being alone together in the water, each woman inside her own head. The comfort of wordless company that understands you implicitly. *We're all here, engaged in the same activity, and you don't have to explain a thing to me.* 'Sisters in swimming', one of them called it once. Probably Theresa. Leanne can't imagine that phrase coming from anyone else, and it's certainly not the sort of sentimental thing she'd come up with herself.

'I missed you,' Leanne says raggedly, although she's never admitted this to herself before, let alone said it out loud.

She couldn't allow herself to miss them. That would lead to regrets and she's been determined to not have those. A whole life can be wasted wishing you'd never done something, but the past can't be changed. The only thing that changes is how you deal with what's happened.

'We've been so sad, Leanne.' Her mother closes her eyes. 'We didn't know what to do. Your brothers. Your sister . . .' She sighs. 'They haven't been the same.'

I haven't been the same, Leanne wants to say, but it seems too obvious.

'I'm sorry, Mum.'

'You're here now.'

Her mother smiles that hopeful, childlike smile Leanne always loved. When she was young it made her think her mother was a co-conspirator: that she saw whimsy in the world the way Leanne did. Once she was a teenager she wished her mother would grow up too. Now she knows that smile is not a relic of her mother's youth but a declaration of optimism: her mother sees every day as an opportunity to start anew. Right now, Leanne sees in it her own fresh start.

'I am.' She reaches for her mother's hand. 'Will you show me the garden?'

Her mother's eyes widen. 'Do you want to see your cumquat trees?'

Leanne smiles. She planted those trees when she was eight or ten or some age like that. They bore fruit that the neighbours made into jam. After a while Leanne ignored them and they flourished in spite of that.

'Yes, please.'

'Your father has been looking after them,' her mother says, opening the sliding door. She stops and turns. 'He misses you too.'

The garden looks as neat as it always has, but the cumquats are definitely taller. At the base of the largest tree Leanne sees a small shrine with stones and trinkets and incense. And a photo of her, covered in plastic. She remembers other shrines her mother made, for relatives in a distant land. They were always in her mother's thoughts and in her murmured pleas for their health and safety.

'I've been praying for you to come home,' her mother says.

Leanne closes her eyes against the memories of the last time she was in this house. The stories she has told herself about what needed to happen. She may not have regrets, but if she could change one thing it would be that she believed her parents' love for her was greater than their shame and their anger. And greater than hers. All this time, there has been love here. All these years, she has denied herself that.

No more. The heart she closed eight years ago is cracking open to let in those who come to her with their own hearts ready to give to her, and to receive. She is loved. She loves. For all the shadows of the past she has kept at bay there is now light. Just like the light of day she sees each morning as salt water washes her clean. Each day new.

'Let's burn some incense, Mum,' she says, kneeling down.

They sit together and light a flame, and Leanne quietly says prayers of thanks that she has found her way home.

SUMMER 1983-1984

CHAPTER 40

Marie isn't given to having butterflies, but she has them right now as she speeds around her kitchen, peeling potatoes for Nicole's favourite potato salad, checking on the turkey, thinking about when to make the gravy. She's been in a frenzy since she woke up but it only seems to make her slower.

'You're working too hard,' Gus says as he walks in carrying the plum pudding she's had hanging in the shed for weeks.

'Not hard enough,' Marie mutters. 'I'm not getting anything done.'

She feels his hand on her arm. 'Stop for a second, love.'

The butterflies' wings beat harder now that he's touching her.

Marie's never been interested in romantic stories, unless they're movies starring Katharine Hepburn or Grace Kelly, so she's been surprised at how swept up in her own romance she's become. She thought she was too mature to think about things being romantic, but that's not the truth, because Gus has reintroduced romance to her life, and her to his. It's not in big gestures like bunches of flowers and elaborate dinners, but in small gestures and close attention. It's listening carefully to each other and remembering what you hear. It's thinking of him first thing each day and last thing at night, especially when he's not there. It's allowing him to suffuse her world, and embracing the fact that she does his.

For all her love for Norm, Marie never felt swept away like this – not because they didn't love each other, but because she felt so responsible, so caught up with concerns. She had a household to run and a daughter to raise. She was always conscious of doing the right thing, her mother's admonishments in her head: *You shouldn't let Nicole do that, she'll develop bad habits. Aren't you going to iron those sheets?* They were lines that her mother would have heard from her own mother, and so on back to who knows which generation started thinking their worth to society, and their self-worth, was tied up with ironed sheets. That's what you get for living in the same house as your parents when you're a parent yourself. Now Marie's in the house alone she can't believe they all lived here without killing each other.

At this stage of her life, she has a lot of care – for Nicole, Pete and the children, for Charlie Brown, for Theresa and Elaine and Leanne, for Gwen, for Father Paul – but very little responsibility. Not that long ago she thought her life was becoming tighter, narrower. Now it feels more open than ever and she wants to explore it. She feels curious about what's to be seen and done in this world – and that's something else that's been dormant for a long time. Strange, how you can start to disappear a little and not realise. Now she feels like a flower unfurling in the sunshine: one petal at a time but gloriously colourful.

Gus has shown her how to be free, and given her a reason to embrace the fullness of each day. Before this she was good at appreciating parts of it, such as her morning swim, but she wasn't alive to the possibility of each moment. He is, and she has learnt from him. Her only sadness about it is that Norm never lived long enough to be this free.

She knows it's weird to be thinking about her dead husband when she's with her new . . . friend? What is she meant to call him? 'Boyfriend' sounds absurd for someone her age. 'Lover' sounds slightly tawdry and not for use in front of children. Besides, they're taking that part slowly. So, yes, she probably shouldn't be thinking about Norm now she has Gus, but she can't exactly make herself stop. How can you prevent a memory or a thought popping into your mind? However long she lives, it's unlikely Gus will be in her life for longer than Norm was. Norm's part of the fabric of her, and he's Nicole's father.

And that's another reason why she's nervous about today.

She starts peeling again.

'Marie – *stop*,' Gus orders. 'It's Christmas lunch, not manoeuvres on the Western Front.'

'I just want it to be *right*,' she says, annoyed at this nasty little streak of perfectionism that she's only recently developed. As in, only over the past few days since she started planning and preparing for Christmas lunch.

'Have you ever worried about it this much?' Gus asks.

She thinks for a second. 'No.'

'So what's the problem today?'

He looks amused, and she wants to say that it's all very well for him but it's not his cooking that will be judged.

'Ahh . . .' She looks around the kitchen as if there's an answer hidden in the fruit bowl or the cutlery drawer. Then she looks into his eyes. 'You,' she says.

'Me?'

'Yes. You're the problem.'

His facial expression suggests that he doesn't know whether to laugh or be upset.

'May I ask why?' he says cautiously.

Marie takes a breath to think about how to phrase it. It's something she's been wanting to say for a while, and she knows she doesn't lack for courage. Or perhaps someone who wilfully ignores the existence of sharks on a daily basis is merely foolhardy.

She starts with the simplest truth. 'Because this is a big day.'

He nods but says nothing.

'Christmas is a time for family. And you're . . .'

'Not?' He frowns.

'No, that's not it.' She swallows, feeling those butterflies again. 'I love you, Gus.'

Now she's said it and she can't take it back. She can only hope that the surprise she can see in his eyes also means he's pleased.

'I wouldn't have asked you to be here if I didn't,' she continues. 'It's a big day because I want it to be right. I want you and Nicole and Pete and the children to all like each other and get along. Nicole and Pete will be fine. You know Pete, of course. You've spoken to Nicole. But Toby remembers Norm a little. Jessie doesn't at all and she's never seen me with anyone. And today's a big day.' She swallows again. 'Maybe I shouldn't have done it. It's too much pressure.'

'Why?' Gus says with a quizzical expression. 'It's just Christmas.'

Marie sighs heavily. 'But . . .' Her heart starts to hammer even though she knows she is the one who has raised the stakes of today because she's told him that she loves him. 'I hope it's not the only Christmas lunch we have together.'

Gus is gazing down at her and she sees the corners of his eyes crinkle. He takes her hands and lifts them to his lips, and for a second she worries it's the prelude to him bidding her adieu.

'I love you too,' he says. 'Which is why *you're* having Christmas dinner with *my* children.' He pinches her cheek lightly. 'I think I forgot to explain that to you, though. In my head, you've always known that I love you. I just wasn't sure how you felt about me.'

Marie's laugh is short and incredulous. 'You love me?'

'Of course.' His smile is confident and wide. 'You're very lovable, you know.'

'Sometimes I wonder,' she mutters, but he stops her saying anything more by kissing her. That kiss is familiar to her now but that doesn't make it any less thrilling.

As he breaks the kiss he hugs her to his side and kisses the top of her head. 'I'll finish here. You have a break.'

'I need to get changed.' She unties her apron and hands it to him. 'Thank you.'

In her bedroom she fluffs around with dresses, pulling them on and off in succession, going back to an earlier choice, deciding against it, choosing another. The whole process manages to muss up her hair so she has to start again with that too, carefully brushing it into its usual unfussy shape. She takes a good, hard look at herself in the mirror and decides that she needs lipstick, she really does, if only she could remember where she put the one lipstick she owns. That Revlon one she bought at the chemist the Christmas before last . . .

In the middle of looking for it she hears the knock at the front door and almost jumps out of her skin. She'll just have to go bare-lipped, as usual.

When the door opens there's her daughter's lovely face and big smile.

Nicole glances curiously at Gus as he walks up behind Marie. 'Hi Mum – Merry Christmas.' She kisses Marie on the cheek then hesitates.

'Darling, I'd like you to meet Gus – at last.' Marie looks from one to the other. 'Although you've spoken on the phone enough that you're almost old friends.'

'Yes, he always seems to be answering the phone. Makes me think he never leaves the place.' Nicole gives Gus a wink while Marie has a moment of startled realisation that the relationship she thought was developing slowly has, to her daughter, seemed like something altogether more permanent.

'Merry Christmas, Nicole,' Gus says heartily before pecking her cheek and stepping back so she can walk past.

'Hello, Pete,' Marie says as her grandchildren mob her legs, hugging tightly and stopping her walking anywhere.

Weeks may elapse between seeing them but Marie knows they'll always be this excited about her – it is one of the unexpected blessings of her life, to have the chance to be joyful with her grandchildren the way she couldn't be with Nicole. When you're directly responsible for a child's wellbeing, education, shelter and care, there are endless opportunities for concern and precious few moments for joy.

'Marie.' Pete kisses her on the cheek and extends his hand to Gus, nodding once as they shake hands.

Her son-in-law is a man of few words but he's also one of magnanimous gestures and kind-heartedness, and Marie is fond of him, even if it's harder to get to know someone when they don't say much.

'Who are you?' says Jessie, looking up at Gus as she lets go of Marie's legs. While Toby, already starting to explore his independence, stands to the side and regards Gus with frank curiosity.

Marie starts to answer Jessie but stops. Gus can handle himself around a six-year-old, she's sure of it.

'I'm Gus.'

He crouches so he's more at Jessie's height, and Marie marvels at his flexibility, as she does whenever he's working in the garden. She may be fit, but everything seems to get stiffer with age. She wonders what he'll be like when he catches up to her and knows, with a certainty in her heart, that she will see that. They will still know each other then. She's completely sure of it, and that makes her calm.

'I'm a friend of your grandmother's,' Gus says, holding out his hand for Jessie to shake it, 'and I love her very much, just as I'm sure you do.'

Marie's breath catches at his admission, and as she looks at Nicole she could swear hers does too. Then Nicole smiles at her – in fact, she beams – and Marie feels any last skerrick of concern evaporate.

'I do,' Jessie says matter-of-factly, then holds out her other hand to Gus. 'Can you take me to the garden so I can visit my fairies?'

Gus glances up at Marie and she feels their exquisite complicity in this moment, in this life and in her family. Her heart felt like bursting once before, when she gave birth to Nicole; and it felt like it would shatter when she lost her son. So she knows the extremes of love; she knows the risks and the rewards and the difficulties and the triumphs of it. And as Gus takes Jessie's hand and straightens up, she feels her heart fit to burst once more.

'Charlie Brown!' Toby cries as the dog trots into view, his tail wagging furiously, and in a flash boy and dog are heading out the back.

'The garden's looking wonderful,' Nicole says as they wander down the hallway, through the living room and out through the kitchen to the back verandah. 'Thank you for taking care of it.'

'I should be thanking you,' Gus says over his shoulder. 'You're the reason I met your mother. Thank you for engaging me to work on the garden.'

Nicole looks pleased with herself. 'You're welcome.'

As Gus and Jessie walk into the garden, a lopsided pair, Nicole puts her arm around Marie.

'I like him,' she says.

After that, Marie knows, everything will be perfect.

CHAPTER 41

'Mummy?' Marcus says.

'Darling!' There's silence for a few seconds as Elaine's reply is carried across the world.

'How are you?' he says.

Hearing her son's voice makes Elaine immediately, painfully homesick, but she's not going to dwell on it. Instead she pictures her handsome son with his thick brown hair and nuggetty physique. It feels like an age since she's seen him, because it is, but in her mind's eye and her heart he is right there with her, always.

'It's so lovely to hear you,' she says.

'And you. Are you well?'

Elaine thinks of her day thus far: the morning swim, and some teasing of Marie about her relationship with Gus – Theresa called them 'lovey-dovey' and Marie blushed. Blushed! Elaine didn't think Marie knew how. She had lunch with Leanne at the hospital – they've become closer since she drove her to see her parents. Leanne is still reserved but she laughs more now. She just won't tell Elaine much about Matt. Then she went to an AA meeting, came home and cleaned and made plans for dinner, and read a novel in between gazing at her garden and wondering how she could improve it. Improving things used to be how she made money: doing up houses and making people happy. She misses it. Now she's waiting for James to arrive home. In fact, he's late. He said he'd be home at seven and it's seven-thirty.

'Yes, darling, I am well,' she says truthfully. 'And you?'

'Very.'

There's a pause and Elaine isn't sure whether or not she's meant to speak again. These long-distance phone calls can be confusing.

'I have news, Mummy.'

'Oh?' Her heart seems to pause as her immediate reaction is to think it's bad news. Her eternal worry as a mother is that there will be bad news.

'I've asked Caroline to marry me and she's said yes.' He sounds so pleased, and proud.

Elaine quickly calculates how long he's known Caroline – they hadn't started seeing each other when James and Elaine moved to Australia, although they'd known each other for a while, as friends. Elaine has never seen them together; she has no idea what they're like as a couple. Her son is so grown-up now that he's to be a husband and, probably soon, a father. He'll have his own family. His life is separate to hers and they will never intersect the way they used to. If she felt far away from her children before this, now she feels as though she's on Jupiter while they're happily ensconced on Earth. She doesn't think she has ever felt this lonely before in all her life – yet she can't show it. Mustn't show it. This is happy news.

'Darling, that is wonderful – absolutely wonderful,' she says, her voice as joyous as she can make it. 'You must be thrilled. *She* must be thrilled. Lucky girl.'

'Is Papa there? I'd love to speak to him.'

'Not yet,' she says. 'He's late. Shall I ask him to call you?'

More seconds of silence.

'It's fine,' Marcus says, although she can hear that he's disappointed. She can recognise every variant of every emotion in her sons' voices. 'Would you tell him for me?'

'Of course, and I know he'll be delighted. Have you set a date? We'll come home for the wedding. That's if you want us there,' she adds uncertainly.

'Oh, Mummy! We wouldn't let you *not* come!'

'Lovely.' She smiles, putting on a brave face even if he can't see it. 'I'm so happy for you.'

He chortles. 'I'm pretty happy for myself, I must say. Look, I'd best go. I have to get to work.'

'Love you, darling. I'll give Papa your good news.'

'Love you, Mummy. Bye.'

Then he's gone, and she puts down the receiver and her house has never seemed so empty, her life never so pointless. Her son is engaged – he is making a whole new life without her or James – and she's not there. What is she doing? Why are they *here*? They should be there, with Marcus, with Henry. She doesn't want to be the mother who turns up just for the wedding. She wants to be there for the weeks beforehand. The months afterwards.

She wishes she didn't love her husband; she would never have followed him here. This country is absurd – in a different hemisphere, thousands of miles from another continent, with ridiculous weather and strange animals. The people couldn't round a vowel if their lives depended on it, and they think it's funny to have a prime minister who holds the world record for drinking beer quickly. Yes, she's made friends. Lovely people. And she enjoys the swimming. But is that it? Is that all Australia can offer her?

She has to go home. She doesn't care if she has to leave James to do it. They can love each other and live apart. It might even be romantic. She can't stay here.

But she has to stay here.

What would she be going back to?

She sold her business, so she won't have an income. Henry is at university, and Marcus has his work and soon will have his wife. Her sons' lives have moved on. And the worst part is that they seem completely content. They don't appear to miss her at all. Now she thinks of it, when she and James announced they were moving to Australia the boys seemed to be *happy* for them.

If she returns, all she'll be doing is meddling in their lives. She'll be a pathetic, grasping mother who can't leave her grown-up children alone because she doesn't have enough interests of her own.

Elaine is not that person. But she doesn't want to be the person who is stuck in Australia, either, far from the people she loves.

This is a conundrum. And she knows what she needs to help her with a conundrum: she needs to not think about it. To not think at all.

There's only one way to do that.

Flinging open the French doors, she rushes into the garden. At the time she started going to AA meetings she hid a bottle of gin under the camellia. She liked the idea of testing herself, and she knew that if she disturbed the earth there was a chance James would notice. So she'll just have to be careful, won't she?

She uses her hands to dig into the soil, not caring that there will be dirt under her fingernails. She can wash her hands. Nor does she care about the dirt on the knees of her pale pink trousers. She can wash those too. They don't matter. There's only one thing that matters.

Yanking the bottle out of its grave, she twists the lid and pours it straight into her mouth. She doesn't have any tonic – another part of the test. She believed that if she didn't have tonic she wouldn't drink gin. Ha!

She screws up her face as she tastes juniper, then lets the liquid slide down the back of her throat. It's been months since she had a drink so she really shouldn't have much. Just enough to stop her brain from thinking. Then she'll put the bottle back.

Another slug. Another swallow.

She waits to see if it's taken effect. Not yet.

The bottle is to her lips again when she hears a noise at the doors.

'Elaine!'

The bottle is still at her mouth as she turns. She wants to see James looking disgusted. Disappointed. She's broken her promise to herself, to him, that she won't drink any more. Instead he looks upset.

So now they're both upset, because she's still not drunk and her brain is still working so she's having thoughts about how lovely it is that Marcus is engaged and how awful it is that she can't be with him, and what about when something significant happens to Henry and she's not there for that either? What about her parents? They're old. They could die and she won't be there.

This is all a mistake. She's a mistake. Her life is a mistake. The gin is a mistake.

That's what she's thinking as James pulls the bottle out of her hand and flings it into a garden bed, as he holds her tightly and puts his nose against her neck, as she starts to sob about how she misses her babies, until she lets him carry her inside and lay her on the lounge.

'I'm sorry,' she whispers hoarsely and he strokes her forehead. 'You have nothing to be sorry for.'

'I do.' She gazes out to the garden.

'You'll have to start it all again,' he says softly.

'I know.'

And she does know. Because her life has to be here now. She told James she'd come with him and she won't leave him. That would make her sad too. So she's stuck, torn between her loves, between her loyalty to her husband and the care she owes her children. And while the solution to it all would be to love less, she's not prepared to do that.

'I'll get you some water,' he murmurs.

'Thank you,' she whispers, and while she hears the tap running she closes her eyes and thinks of where she was last happiest: this morning, in the water, with the sand below her and the sky above, and all the time in the world.

That is where she needs to start over again.

CHAPTER 42

Kicking helps. Kicking hard. Kicking as if she's kicking Andrew. That's what Theresa's thinking as she heads for Little Beach. But she's so tired. Tired from staying up late worrying about the future, and the present: the fact that her husband isn't overly interested in seeing his children; the bills she needs to pay that she has to ask Nonna to help with; the question of where they're going to live if she has to sell the house.

Still, she keeps kicking, and moving her arms. Stroke, stroke, kick kick kick, breathe. Repeat. Keeping herself going is the only thing keeping her going.

As she nears Little Beach she almost swims straight into Marie, who is standing in the shallows.

'Sorry!' Theresa says as she pulls up just short.

'Right,' Marie says, and she has her hands on her hips the way she does when she wants to make a point. 'What is going on?'

'Hm?' Theresa gets to her feet.

Elaine is sitting in the shallows with her goggles pushed up onto her head. Leanne is only a few metres offshore now. Nearby there's a man walking his black Labrador, and a couple of joggers are drinking from the bubbler. Theresa likes it over here: it's quiet at this time of day, and she can pretend it's an island, separate from the rest of Shelly Bay and an oasis away from care. Unless Marie is asking her probing questions.

'I've never seen you kick like that – you looked like a deranged whisk.' Marie raises her eyebrows.

'I did not! That was me sprinting!' Theresa looks at Elaine for back-up, but she just shakes her head a little and starts to laugh.

'Don't try it again,' Marie says. 'You're not made to be a sprinter. You're a long-distance swimmer.'

Although Theresa knows she should feel mildly insulted by part of what Marie said, she's quite pleased about the last bit. She smiles. 'Am I?'

'You're getting there.'

Leanne walks towards them. 'Why are we stopped?' she asks.

'Theresa was doing something funny,' says Marie.

'I was not!'

Marie looks at her askance. 'There's something going on. Better you tell us what it is. You know we give good advice.'

Theresa purses her lips. 'I don't know if advice can help me.'

The other three look at her expectantly.

'It's just . . . stuff.' She flaps her hands but doesn't really want to wave this off. Trying to manage it all herself – to work things out, even if there are no solutions – is exhausting.

'Tell us,' Elaine says. 'Please.'

Theresa nods slowly and pulls off her goggles. 'Andrew's still saying he has no money, plus he hardly sees the kids. He keeps saying he's busy, and the kids were fine with not seeing him at first but now they miss him. I don't have an income and I can't keep asking Nonna to help pay for the bills and the mortgage. My parents are pressuring me to move in with them and sell the house, because I'll have to when we divorce anyway. And . . .' She sighs. 'I saw Andrew and his girlfriend going into the pub the other day.'

'How do you know it was his girlfriend?' asks Marie.

'Because he had his hand on her bum,' Theresa says, sighing again.

'Are you sure you're going to divorce?' Elaine asks.

Theresa can't help laughing. 'Um – yes. I am. He has a girlfriend.'

She glances at Marie, who smiles sympathetically.

'Don't rush anything,' says Elaine. 'Marriages have survived worse. This may be a phase.'

'I don't want him back! He'd have to spend a week sitting in a vat of Domestos before I'd touch him again and that's not going to happen!' Theresa blinks. She didn't actually know she felt that strongly until now.

'I'd say you're a woman who knows what she wants, then,' says Marie. 'And we can work with that. We'd better get back, though, because we all have places to be.'

'Oh,' says Theresa. She hadn't been sure what would result from her spilling her guts but didn't think they'd all just listen and keep swimming.

'Don't fret, pet,' says Marie, patting her shoulder. 'I've got my thinking cap on.' She taps the side of her head. 'Working on some ideas.'

Theresa has no idea what they could be, but she allows herself to be led into the water. This time she can't kick hard even if she wants to: it's as if confessing to her friends has made her floppy, because she's practically dragging herself through the water. Leanne passes her, and Marie and Elaine are already ahead.

The swell has changed since they set out and the water gets choppy as she nears Main Beach. She gets tangled up in a wave and a pain in her side causes her to gasp. It's not a stitch – she's had those before – but it feels like her ribs are protesting. She doesn't want the others to know, though, because she's already imposed on them enough, so she rearranges her face as she gets out of the water and tries to keep her breathing slow and even.

'Guess I'm lucky last!' she says as she approaches the others but can't help wincing.

'It became a bit messy out there,' Elaine says.

Theresa smiles at her. 'I think you're just trying to make me feel better.'

'No way,' says Marie. 'It was so rough on the way back I swallowed half the Tasman Sea. Was starting to think I'd need a snorkel.'

Theresa wraps a towel around her shoulders and huddles into herself. 'I just need to get a bit fitter.' She smiles. 'And here I was thinking I was already doing that.'

'Don't be too hard on yourself.' Marie steps towards Theresa and gives her a peck on the cheek. 'Anyway, I have to run.'

'I'll walk with you,' Leanne says, and she smiles briefly at Theresa and Elaine.

'*Ciao*,' Theresa replies. She rubs her back before dropping the towel on the sand. Her next sigh is heavier, longer. 'I must be getting old. That stint on the way over wore me out.'

'You're not old,' Elaine says. 'But you are wincing. Is something hurting?'

Now Theresa's ribcage feels like it's spasming. 'I'm just . . . worn out. And . . .' She blinks rapidly and sniffs, wiping her nose with the back of her hand.

Elaine steps closer and puts a hand on her arm. 'Whatever it is, you can tell me.'

Her face is open and Theresa can tell she's being sincere. She's come to know that Elaine is always sincere, even if her accent and her manner can sometimes make her seem like a snob. She's not, really. She's a friend. A mate. And Theresa didn't tell the others everything she's worried about – but she wants someone to know. She wants to share the burden of it so she can stop carrying the worry on her own.

'There's something . . .' She takes a breath. 'On my breast. I – I found it the other day, then I forgot about it, then I remembered.'

She laughs, then stops herself. Why is she trying to make light of this? Is she trying to tell Elaine that it isn't serious? Or tell herself?

They all do that, don't they? All the time. Try to make the world happier, brighter, less troublesome. It's what good girls do. Theresa should know, because she was raised to be one. To be upset but not show anyone; be worried but don't tell anyone. Everything's fine, it's fine, I'm fine.

'Theresa, you don't have to pretend to be okay.'

Theresa nods quickly.

'You need to see a doctor,' Elaine says.

'Do I?'

'You know you do.'

Yes, she does. She's known it ever since she found that lump, but there just hasn't been time. How is she meant to fit in going to a GP, who's invariably running late, when it means she might not be there to pick up the kids from school or take Nonna to poker, or do the shopping or the washing?

'Let me help you,' Elaine says in a softer tone. 'I'll call and make the appointment.'

'You don't have to do that,' Theresa says, glancing away.

'I know I don't,' Elaine says firmly. 'I want to.'

Theresa feels her breath catching. Her worry is shared, but now it's also more real.

'You're not alone,' Elaine says quietly.

'My aunt died of breast cancer,' Theresa chokes out, and Elaine pulls her into a hug.

'This may not be breast cancer. Try not to worry until you've seen the doctor.'

Theresa wipes her eyes with a finger. 'Can I drive you home?'

'Yes, please,' says Elaine, slinging her towel around her neck.

As they walk their feet sink into the soft sand, and Theresa wonders what it would be like to keep sinking down, down, down into the centre of the earth. Her problems could be left on the surface – along with all the people she loves.

No, she would hate that. She doesn't want to be alone, and Elaine is right: she isn't alone. So Theresa will let her help, and she will try to take things one day at a time and not worry too much. She can't know what the doctor will say, and it's a fool's errand to try to predict the future.

CHAPTER 43

Daylight saving will be over soon and they won't have this light in the early evening – the gentle fading of the day that is a hallmark of summer. Leanne will miss it; although once they turn the clocks back she'll be happy to have more light at the start of the day for a while. They've almost been swimming in the dark, trying to fit it in at a reasonable hour, which means not necessarily waiting for the sun to be over the horizon before they start. That pre-dawn light is pretty, but the water is almost grey, and certainly more mysterious, if not a little intimidating.

It's the light she's looking at when she realises Matt is saying something to her.

'Queen to king's knight five,' he says with raised eyebrows and a tone that suggests he's repeating it.

'Sorry,' she says. 'I'm away with the pixies.'

Matt gives her a funny look and laughs. 'I've never heard you use that phrase before.'

'Theresa says it.' She glances down at the chessboard and can tell that after his last move she's not in a winning position. 'I don't know what to do here.'

'Take your time. You should always take your time. And while you do, I'll go to the bar. Would you like something?'

She shakes her head and he picks up his empty glass.

Leanne looks out the window again. The pub is across the road from the beach, and she can see the spot where she and the other women congregate each morning. Loud laughter brings her attention back to the pub and she sees a woman with her hand on Matt's arm, and the two of them laughing. They look like they know each other, their body language suggesting ease.

Her chest and head feel tight, and nausea starts to swirl in her gut. It comes on so suddenly that her first thought is that there was something wrong with the chicken she ate for dinner. She hadn't wanted to eat at the pub but Matt thought it would be nice to stay in one spot: have dinner then play chess.

No, it's not food poisoning. The edges of the sensations aren't sharp enough for that. This is . . . an ache. And with each laugh from Matt it pulses.

Her father used to say, 'Jealousy tells you what you want' – and she thinks that's what this is. She didn't recognise it straightaway because she's never felt it before.

So, she wants Matt. That's what her body is telling her and it's a revelation.

Intellectually, she's interested in him. They've spent considerable amounts of time together over the past few months and he has many qualities she likes. Despite the fact she enjoys kissing him, however, there just hasn't been the pull she was expecting – to the point where she's been wondering if she's attracted to men at all. She hasn't met any women she's attracted to, either, so hasn't had proof one way or the other. But now here it is: a physical manifestation of . . . what? Desire? Yes.

She shouldn't be surprised, she supposes: over the past few months she has reconnected with her body after years of separation. It used to be easier to think of it as a necessary companion rather than as part of her. That way she could believe that everything that had happened to it hadn't really happened to *her*. Except it did, and she's accepted that – with help. Help from Elaine, Theresa and Marie. Help from Matt. He was the first person to tell her that her body could achieve things: she could swim. He's been encouraging her ever since, often asking about her times to Little Beach and back, encouraging her to try harder, change her breathing. She's had a built-in coach.

More laughter, and now Matt glances over at her. There must be something written on her face because his own drops and he nods to the woman and returns to their table with his empty glass still in hand.

'That was an old school friend,' he says, looking nervous. 'Haven't seen her in years.'

'Oh,' is Leanne's only response, because she's still not reassured.

'She's here with her husband,' he says.

'Oh.' Now she gives him a quick smile.

Matt puts the glass on the table and tilts his head to the side. 'Are you jealous?'

Leanne stares at him. 'No,' she says. It's her first instinct, because she's sure Matt doesn't want a jealous girlfriend. She doesn't want to be a jealous girlfriend either.

'You are,' he says, a grin starting to form.

'I'm not,' she says, but doesn't sound as convincing this time.

He bends down, putting one hand on the table, his lips not far from hers. 'You don't have to admit it,' he says quietly, 'but I know it's true.'

They stare into each other's eyes and she can see him clearly. He has never tried to lie to her. If he thinks something, he tells her. If he wants to say something, he says it. The Matt he presents to the world is the Matt he is. If not, he's a terrific actor – but she's seen him fail to sugarcoat things too often to believe that. If one of his students isn't doing something right, he tells them. If a kid wants to win a blue ribbon at the school carnival but they're too slow to even come in third, he'll tell them.

She is the one not telling him the truth. But, then, she's had practice. For most of her adult life she's successfully concealed herself from everyone. Literally everyone. It took the ocean and three women who offered her unquestioning friendship for her to stop hiding. They've all embraced her.

'Yes, it is true,' she says after the staring has gone on for long enough.

'Ha!' he says, looking incredibly pleased. 'Well.' He puts his hands on his hips. 'And I was starting to think you were going off me.'

'Why?' She quickly searches her memory for an instance of this.

He frowns briefly. 'You, uh . . . you never let me get further than your front door, for one thing.' He holds up his hands. 'I have no interest in pressuring you for anything. But I would like to see where you live. You don't give me many clues, you know – about who you are.'

Leanne can see a bit of skin peeling off his nose where he's been burnt again. Always forgetting to wear his hat. She knows things about him like that. She knows he likes chocolate and golden Labradors but thinks the black ones are insane, and is no fan of small dogs of any variety. He loves his parents and doesn't see them enough, by his own reckoning. His grandma taught him to knit, and while he doesn't usually wear socks in winter he has knitted himself some to wear around the house to keep warm. He tried out for the national swimming team once but wasn't good enough, and seems cheerful about it. He likes to read the *Daily Mirror*. He listens to FM radio.

He doesn't know equivalent details about her, because revealing the small details might lead to revealing the big story, and she's been wanting to keep that from him. In case *he* goes off *her*. Wouldn't it be better, though, to find that out sooner rather than later?

'Do you really want to know who I am?' she says nervously, scared of the answer.

'Of course,' he says, sitting down.

'There's a reason why . . .' She inhales and closes her eyes for a second. 'Why you haven't been past my door. It's not because I'm messy.'

She's trying for levity, but knows she can't pull it off. She's not a light person.

He reaches across and takes her hands; she feels calmer.

'I didn't think that was the reason,' he says. 'Leanne, I – I kind of guessed there's something. You're . . . guarded. With men.'

She is surprised he's noticed that. 'I'm guarded with most adults,' she says, then smiles shyly. 'Somehow you slipped through.'

'It's because I'm charming,' he says, not smiling but squeezing her hands.

'You are,' she says, 'in your own way.'

His smile is small and kind. She breathes in and out. In and out.

'I've only had one experience with a – a man.'

As she holds his gaze she's proud of herself for pressing on. Of course, she's been practising: pressing on to Little Beach, not giving up on the others. On herself. She's trained for this moment.

'It went further than I wanted. Much, much further.'

She hopes she is conveying the truth to him with her eyes, because she doesn't want to say it all. She doesn't want to give it life by describing it exactly.

'I understand,' he says, his voice deeper. His hands still hold hers, and she's glad of that.

'There's more.' She sniffs and notices his irises growing slightly larger, then contracting. 'I got pregnant.'

Matt's mouth opens slightly and she knows she has to continue quickly, otherwise he's likely to think she has a child stashed away somewhere.

'I went through with it. I gave her up for adoption.'

He closes his mouth and bows his head, then lifts it. His thumbs are pressing into her as he leans across the table – knocking the chess pieces over – and kisses her on the lips.

'I knew you were brave,' he says when he sits back. 'I could tell that by the way you went about your swimming.' He nods slowly. 'Now I think you're the bravest person I know. To give me a chance.' He tilts his head again. 'Thank you.'

Leanne feels something that she'd call light-headedness if she didn't also feel anchored in the room, by his hands. It could be that she wants to laugh from relief. Or float away with happiness that Matt hasn't reacted in any number of other ways he could react. She's not sure what the feeling is, but hopes it lasts.

Releasing her left hand so he can restore the chess pieces, he winks and says, 'Now – queen to king's knight five. What are you going to do about it?'

She grins. 'I'm going to take you on,' she says, and giggles as he leans over for another kiss.

CHAPTER 44

'Thanks so much for looking after them,' Theresa says after Oliver and Sasha have disappeared into the back garden.

Elaine is sitting on the couch, perched forwards, waiting for news. Theresa knows this because she's the keeper of the news, but she's in no hurry to share it.

'And for organising the appointment,' she goes on. 'I don't know how you managed to find someone who does house calls on a Saturday.'

'James knew someone,' Elaine says lightly, as if it was the easiest thing in the world to organise and she didn't have to invite the doctor and his wife and children over for lunch. James hadn't extracted the price – she'd offered it. It seemed the polite thing to do. And, in the wash-up, not onerous. She would have done much more to ensure that Theresa saw a doctor.

'I really do appreciate you taking the kids. I couldn't ask Nonna to watch them while the doctor was here. It was her daughter who . . .' Theresa falters. 'Who, um . . . who died of breast cancer. Gloria. Besides, Nonna went to visit a friend. Who knew she has friends? I thought everyone hated her because she keeps winning their money.'

She can hear herself babbling, delaying the inevitable. As Elaine has probably guessed.

'You don't have to explain,' Elaine says. 'I was happy to have them. They're delightful.'

Theresa looks sceptical. 'That may be going too far.'

'Not at all. Is your grandmother back now?'

Theresa thinks of the moment when Nonna walked in the back door and could see that she'd been crying half the afternoon.

'Theresa,' she said as she waddled into the kitchen, her eyes narrowing, 'what is going on, hmm? You crying.'

Theresa shook her head quickly. 'It's nothing.'

'It's *something*.'

'It's not.'

'It *is*.'

She'd turned away, wishing her face wasn't the open book her mother always said it was.

Count to three, she told herself, *count to three or you'll start crying again*.

It was too late, though, because Nonna's hands were on her shoulders and Theresa's head was resting against her neck, and even though she's taller than Nonna now she felt like the little girl she used to be, crying because some kid at school had called her stupid or smelly or whatever the insult had been.

'*Bella mia*,' Nonna would croon, 'they just don't know you like I do.'

It always made her feel better. Safe.

But Nonna couldn't fix what was happening to her now, so Theresa stiffened her back.

'Theresa, do not hide from me,' Nonna said, her voice low.

'I'm not,' Theresa said softly, except of course she was hiding.

'Okay.' The expression on Nonna's face left no doubt that she didn't believe Theresa for one second. 'You come see me when you ready.'

After that Theresa had calmed down. And she's still feeling calm – relatively speaking.

'Yes, she's home.' Her smile is tight. 'Can't you smell the smoke?'

'Ah.' Elaine nods. 'I can.'

At that moment Oliver runs in, squirting a water pistol. Sasha follows him, squealing.

'*Ollie!*' Theresa cries, getting to her feet.

He stops and gives Theresa that 'who – me?' face all kids perfect at an early age.

'Who said you could use the water pistol in the house?'

She's mortified that her children have chosen *right now* to show how undisciplined they can be – and even more mortified to think they might have been like this with Elaine today. Elaine's children are probably perfectly behaved English gentlemen.

'Nonna asked me to use it to put out her cigarette,' Oliver says innocently, and Theresa can almost hear her grandmother cackling from the back garden.

'Is her cigarette in here?' she says, putting her hands on her hips.

He pouts. 'No.'

'Then I suggest you take the water pistol, and your sister, outside.'

'Mu-um, it's not faaa-irrrr!'

Theresa gives him a stern look. 'Life isn't fair, and the sooner you get used to it, the better.' It's exactly what her mother used to say to her in the same kind of situation.

She nods in the direction of the garden, and is only slightly mollified when he takes his sister's hand to lead her out of the room.

'Sorry about that,' she says as she sits down on the couch near Elaine.

'No need to apologise. And there was nothing like that while we were at the zoo.' Elaine winks. 'Just to reassure you.'

'Thanks.' Theresa smooths her dress.

'So?' Elaine says, and she makes it last. *Soooooo?*

'So!' Theresa replies, as if they're playing a game. It's no game, though. No game and no fun.

'Theresa.' Elaine frowns.

Theresa takes a moment to admire her lovely English skin that is completely unmarked because she didn't grow up in the sun.

'*Theresa.*'

'Oh.' She knows she's stalling. She just doesn't want to say a particular thing out loud. 'Yeah, I, um, have to go to a specialist.'

Elaine nods. 'Yes, that's to be expected.'

Theresa makes a face. 'The GP was a bit noncommittal about what it could be but, um . . . he doesn't think it's good. The lump's quite big.' She forces a smile. 'I don't think it's a pimple.'

Elaine doesn't look worried, which makes Theresa relax a little. 'All right, so when's your specialist appointment?' she asks.

'Next week. The doctor made a call and got me in. Said it's his friend from uni or something.'

Theresa remembers how pleased the doctor seemed that he could organise this for her. Like he was doing her a favour. She supposes he was, but she still feels like it's a sentence.

'Great,' Elaine says brightly. 'That's great. I'll take the kids again if you like.'

The fear that's been sitting in Theresa's belly releases a little. If Elaine is being this chirpy, maybe she has nothing to worry about.

'Are you going to tell Marie and Leanne?' Elaine asks.

'Um . . . not yet. No. Nothing to tell, is there?'

Elaine gives her a look. A somewhat scolding look. '*Theresa*.'

'What?'

'Wouldn't you want to know if it were them?'

Theresa's sigh is intentionally one of exasperation. 'I suppose.'

'I know they'll want to know,' Elaine says quietly.

The sound of more shrieking floats in from outside.

'*OLIVER!*' Theresa yells.

The shrieking stops.

'He's not a bad kid,' she says to Elaine. 'He's just . . .' She shrugs. 'Spirited.'

'He's a boy,' Elaine says, smiling wistfully. 'I remember when mine were young – they spent so much time running around that I thought there was something wrong with them. I told my mother. She said, "Little girls sit in the corner and scheme. Little boys let it all out physically. Which would you prefer?"' She arches an eyebrow. 'I won't tell you what I said.'

'Sasha doesn't scheme,' Theresa says with her own wistful smile. Her daughter may still be moping a little but has never been troublesome – not unless she's indulging her brother in one of his activities. Theresa should be grateful they're both healthy. The thought makes her inhale sharply.

'What about Andrew?' Elaine says, breaking into her thoughts.

'Hm?'

'Andrew.' Now both of Elaine's eyebrows are up. 'Are you going to tell him?'

Theresa shakes her head, but not too hard. She wants Elaine to think she's considered it, because that would be the reasonable thing to do: she should tell the man who's still her husband that she has a potentially serious health problem. Except he wouldn't be interested.

'I don't think he's ever once asked me how I am. So I don't think he'll care.'

'I'm sure he would,' Elaine says in a vaguely chastising tone.

Theresa laughs in that harsh way she knows she's developed over the past few months. 'Then you don't know my husband. And before you suggest I tell my parents: no. Mum will just say we're cursed, because of Aunt Gloria. She thinks she has a bad back because the family's cursed – Nonna's brother had a back injury once and Mum keeps saying she's inherited it. An injury!'

She throws up her hands, but it's to hide the fact that she would dearly love to tell her mother. After the GP left today Theresa wanted nothing more than to have her mother hold her and tell her that everything will be all right. Except her mother can't know that, and neither can she.

'Well, I'm not going to push,' Elaine says. 'And I think you probably want to get on with your evening.' She stands, and Theresa joins her.

'I'm sorry,' Theresa says. She tucks her hair behind one ear; it's what she used to do when her parents were cross with her.

'What for?'

'For being difficult.'

'Oh, silly.' Elaine hugs her. 'You are the least difficult person imaginable. I just want to help. And I'm not sure how to go about it, so that's my solution.'

'You *are* helping,' Theresa says. 'Thank you. So much.'

'Mu-um, we're hungry,' Oliver singsongs as he skips into the room.

'That's my cue,' says Elaine. She puts her mouth near Theresa's ear. 'And let me know when that specialist appointment is – I can take the children again if you need.'

Theresa nods quickly and mouths her thanks, then Elaine hops into her Renault and drives home, leaving Theresa to wrangle two children now covered in dirt and grass into a bath, through dinner and bedtime. She is glad of the activity, to have her mind filled with the minutiae of running a household and caring for others, instead of the yawning uncertainty that will take her over as soon as the house is quiet.

CHAPTER 45

Marie would recognise Theresa's figure anywhere: she has seen it so many times now, in dim light, walking towards her across the sand. But soon she'll have to make adjustments to the familiar image that's stored in her memory, because as Theresa said when she called the other day to tell her about the surgery: 'I'm going to be lopsided!' She was so chirpy, as if she was talking about a pair of socks that aren't both the same length. Not the kind of lopsided where they take off a breast.

Theresa tried to make light of it. 'It's not that big a lump – well, it's not a golf ball or anything. Still, big or small, they take off the boob. That's what the doctor said. They take it off then find out what the problem is.' She made a sound too much like a laugh to be appropriate. 'Which seems like a lot of fuss, really, but he's not giving me a choice. Guess it's just as well I've finished breastfeeding.'

Despite the forced jollity, Marie felt numb. Her Theresa – *their* Theresa – with cancer? Not confirmed yet, of course – they won't know until they do the pathology – but that's what it seems like. Theresa said her aunt had it. Died of it.

Marie's family was big on arthritis and bad hearts, which is part of her reason for keeping up the swimming; cancer has never darkened her door. Not up close. Not like this.

As Theresa draws nearer, Marie puts on her biggest smile then realises that Theresa will recognise it's fake. She doesn't need fake now. She needs friends.

'My last swim and the sky can't even be bothered smiling,' Theresa says, gesturing at the low cloud. 'How dare it!'

Now Marie's smile is real. 'How are you, love?' she says, throwing one arm around her and planting a kiss on her cheek.

'That's new,' says Theresa. 'You've never greeted me with a kiss for a swim. You must think I'm not coming back.'

'Don't be ridiculous,' Marie says, although she had the fleeting thought earlier today. And banished it, in case it was bad luck. She's not superstitious, but she said a quick prayer to ask forgiveness for her thoughts.

Theresa exhales loudly. 'I haven't told Leanne yet.'

'Oh.'

'I haven't had the chance. I haven't been at the hospital in ages, and I didn't want to tell her before a swim. And when I've called her place she hasn't been home.' Theresa makes the face of a child who hopes she's not in trouble. 'But I'm going to have to tell her today.'

'Yes, you are. Morning, Elaine.'

'Hello.' Elaine kisses Theresa too, and now Theresa looks upset.

'You *both* think I'm not coming back!' she says.

'Not true!' Elaine says with assurance. 'I'd kiss you every morning if I thought I could get away with it, but that would make Trevor far too happy.'

Marie glances towards the clubhouse, where Trev is animatedly discussing something with a younger man. He's been keeping his distance lately – ever since Leanne beat him one morning after he decided he'd race her to the point. She didn't know she was racing him but was faster regardless.

'Here's Leanne now,' Marie says under her breath.

'Have you told her yet?' asks Elaine, a little more loudly. 'Oh,' she adds, as Theresa looks at her with alarm.

'Good morning,' Leanne says happily.

She's now in the habit of smiling each morning and Marie barely recognises the girl who didn't say boo a few months ago. She's crediting the boyfriend for the change, although Leanne doesn't say much about him.

They busy themselves folding towels and clothing, picking up goggles and caps.

'So this is my last swim for a while,' Theresa says as she pulls her cap over her head.

Leanne stares at her. 'What are you talking about?'

'Sorry, Leanne,' Theresa says. 'I tried calling you but you haven't been home.'

'I've been at Matt's,' Leanne says quickly. 'What do you mean – your last swim?' She looks at Marie then Elaine.

Marie tries to keep her face in neutral because this is Theresa's story to tell, but what she really wants to do is say that she's worried for her friend, that she wishes Theresa didn't have to go through something this brutal, and that she would take it all away from her if she could.

'I'm having a bit of surgery at the hospital in a couple of days.' Theresa takes a breath. 'I need to have a mastectomy.'

'What?' Leanne says. '*What?*'

Theresa shrugs casually, like she's just said she's going to trade in her car. Marie doesn't know if she's playing it down as a way of managing her own worries, and can't begrudge her that if she is.

'I have this lump,' Theresa is saying. 'I . . . let it go too long.'

'When did you find out?' Leanne says sharply.

'I've had the lump for a while,' Theresa explains. 'I just didn't do anything about it. The specialist told me a couple of days ago about the surgery. I'm lucky he can fit me in so soon.'

Leanne stares at Theresa.

'I'm still me,' Theresa says, her mouth puckering and a vertical crease appearing on her forehead. 'I'm not different. I'm not going to be different. Leanne?'

Leanne lets out her breath in a rush. 'Yes,' she says. 'Sorry.'

'Are you all right?' Elaine asks, putting a hand on Leanne's shoulder, startling her.

'Yes!' Leanne says shrilly.

'It's okay, Lee,' Marie says, squeezing her other shoulder. 'She's not dying.'

'Not yet!' Theresa says, too brightly.

Marie can see it now: Theresa's bravado is indeed covering her fear. It's there in the slight twitch of her eye and the way she's twisting her mouth. She never used to do that.

'I'm sorry,' Leanne says, dabbing at her eyes with her towel.

'Don't be,' says Theresa and smiles awkwardly. Then she looks down at the sand and wipes her eyes. 'I'm flattered I can get that kind of reaction out of you! You're usually as cool as a cucumber.' She tries to laugh but tears now spill onto her cheeks. 'Christ, this is inconvenient,' she mutters, putting her hands on her hips and turning towards the ocean. 'Sorry, Marie.'

'That's quite all right. I'm sure He'd understand.'

Theresa sniffs. 'I always saw myself going into old age with two boobs, you know?'

'You can get a falsie,' says Marie. 'No one'll know the difference.'

'They bloody well will!' Theresa isn't looking at them now. Marie can see her shoulders shaking. 'Anyway, *I'll* know,' she says, so softly they almost can't hear it.

Marie steps in front of Theresa and takes hold of both her shoulders. 'You'll always be the complete package to me. I don't care if you have one breast, three or none. You're our girl.'

Theresa starts hiccup-crying.

Elaine turns half away, one hand against the side of her head to hide her tears.

'Come on, you lot,' says Marie. 'We need to wash off this salt water with some salt water.'

'I'm certainly ready for a swim,' Leanne says loudly, surprising Marie. 'Theresa, how about you?'

Theresa turns towards her. 'Yes,' she replies. 'I'm ready.'

'Let's go,' Leanne says. 'Elaine, I'll race you.'

'Race me?' Elaine pulls off her T-shirt and shorts and throws them to the sand. 'You'll need a head start if you have any chance of winning.'

Elaine scoops up her cap and goggles and is halfway to the water's edge before Marie even thinks to get ready.

'You go,' she calls to Theresa, who is looking at her enquiringly.

Theresa shakes her head. 'I'll wait. I'm in no hurry.'

Within seconds Marie is by her side and they walk together into the water, the foam hitting their shins at the same time. Pulling their goggles over their heads, they dive under a wave and strike out in the same direction as Leanne and Elaine, keeping pace on their way to Little Beach. Marie lets the others go ahead of her, watching three forms that are now so familiar, and which will not be in this formation again for quite some time. But she will not let herself become maudlin. This is not an ending, just a change. She has become used to change, and she'll become used to this one – but she will look forward to the day when the four of them will swim to Little Beach once more.

AUTUMN 1984

CHAPTER 46

Theresa remembers counting backwards from ten and making it as far as eight. Right before that, she heard the surgeon say hello to her. A little while before that, she had an injection to relax her before the anaesthetic. The anaesthetist had gentle hands and hard eyes. Theresa didn't know if that was the right combination, but obviously he knew what he was doing because here she is, waking up.

'Theresa,' a woman's voice is saying. She doesn't recognise it. Should she? Where is she?

'Theresa, you're in Recovery. The operation is over. Mr Phillips said it went well.'

Mr Phillips – that's her surgeon. She was calling him Dr Phillips until one of the nurses corrected her and said that surgeons are called 'Mr'. Although she never found out why.

'How are you feeling?' The nurse is bending over her now, not smiling, but not looking worried. That must be a good thing.

'A bit . . . um, woozy.' Theresa tries to swallow and it feels like her mouth is sticking together. 'Am I going to be sick?'

'Not likely.' The nurse pats her hand. 'Although it can feel like that. You'll be here for a little while, then we'll move you to the ward.'

And after that? What am I meant to do with one boob?

That's the question she really wants to ask but she doesn't think anyone has an answer.

Her bravado in front of Marie and Elaine and Leanne – talking about how she's going to use a falsie and it will all be fine – never took root in her. She can be a good actress when she needs to be and she thinks she had them all believing she's okay with all of this. Except she's not.

She swallows again as her head seems to swirl, and wishes her mother were here. In the end she decided to tell her parents and grandmother that she was having 'a procedure', because the stress of keeping it secret was worse than any reaction they could come up with. They don't know everything, though – she didn't give details, just said she would be in hospital for a couple of days or so.

Although now she's wondering why she insisted this surgery would be 'nothing, Mum, just a little op'. It was to spare her parents the worry, except she's set herself up to feel like the loneliest person in the world right now, with no one to sit by her bed and hold her hand and tell her everything's going to be all right, the way her mum used to do when she was a child and sick in bed, with lemonade and a straw, and a cool hand on her forehead and a lullaby to help her go to sleep.

It's horrible, this business of being alone after they've cut off a part of you. Nurses bustle around to other patients who all seem to be more important, although everyone probably gets the same amount of attention. Everyone's coming around from being out of it. There's probably someone worse off than her. Maybe they had a leg off. Now *that* would be bad. You can get by with one boob, but one leg would be a lot harder. She's lucky, and she needs to remember that when they come back and tell her it's cancer. Because she knows it will be, just like Aunt Gloria.

Then what? That's the bit she doesn't want to think about.

Aunt Gloria withered away and died within a few months. Her kids were grown-up though. Oliver and Sasha are only in primary school.

Theresa has no interest in dying just yet. She feels pretty good too – well, not right now, because of the anaesthetic, but with the swimming she's been feeling fit. It's bloody inconvenient, this lump business, and not least because she'll have to miss swimming for who knows how long.

That's all ahead of her. Right now she needs to get through the aftermath of this surgery, get back to the kids and keep going with the business of being a single mum. She's been putting that off, given this other pressing matter, but she can't do it forever.

'We're ready to take you up now, Theresa.'

It's the same nurse. Theresa must have been daydreaming for longer than she realised if it's time to go to the ward.

She closes her eyes as they wheel her into a lift and up to another floor. She doesn't want to see the rest of the hospital because she's going to try to focus just on herself and her recovery. That's what Elaine suggested she do.

'Here we are,' says a different nurse – she must have appeared while Theresa was in transit. 'Let's get you settled. How's your pain?'

'Fine. I mean – I don't have any.'

Which strikes Theresa as strange: she's had a breast removed and she feels . . . nothing. Except misshapen, sure, because she has dressings and whatnot over her chest, but there's no pain. There should be. She should have the sensation of having lost something she was quite fond of, really, if she thinks about it. Her boobs have seen better days, but they fed her babies and looked all right in a tight dress, with the right bra. Thankfully tight dresses have been in her past for a while, because she's not likely to wear anything form-fitting for the rest of her life. No matter how good the falsie is, it's hardly going to match her remaining boob.

'Now, you have a visitor,' says the nurse, smiling brightly.

'Do I?'

Maybe Elaine is here – although she said she wouldn't visit today because no patient wants anyone to see them straight out of surgery. 'Not even the people who love you the most,' she'd said, 'because you feel horrendous and it's just too much work to be polite.' So it's probably not Elaine.

'Your husband's here,' the nurse says, and before Theresa can protest she's out the door and returning with Andrew.

'I'll leave you to it!'

The nurse is gone but Theresa wishes she wasn't, because Andrew is glaring at her and if she thought she didn't have the energy to deal with people who care about her, she really doesn't have anything in the tank to deal with him.

'When were you going to tell me, hey?'

Andrew's arms are crossed and his feet are planted wide apart. She's seen him use that stance when he's arguing with someone who thinks they're being charged too much for a new muffler.

'Andrew, I'm not feeling great,' she says, leaning back against the pillow. 'I've just had surgery.'

And I haven't seen you in weeks, so why would I tell you? That's what she really wants to say, but she certainly doesn't want to have an argument right now.

'Which you *didn't tell me about.*'

'I *did* tell you,' she says, trying not to waste any energy getting upset.

'You just said surgery. You didn't say what for.'

'And you didn't ask!' Her voice is shrill and she clenches and unclenches her hands, telling herself to stay calm.

She hadn't wanted to give him the details of the operation because she was sure he'd use it as an excuse to say she isn't looking after 'his house' properly. That's what he's been calling it since he moved out. His house. Not their home.

'I shouldn't have to!'

He steps closer and she flinches. Which makes him stop and drop his arms. And a look crosses his face – Theresa could swear it was concern, if she didn't know better.

'Theresa, look,' he says, his voice calmer, 'I just wanted to see how you are.'

'How did you find out?'

'One of the nurses here is married to one of my boys. She told him you were admitted this morning. He asked me how I felt about you having a breast off.' He's glaring again. 'I had to pretend I knew.'

Theresa feels the white heat of shame that her private business is known by Andrew's employees. 'Nurses aren't meant to talk about patients like that.'

He keeps glaring.

'Why is he asking you about it anyway? Don't they know you're not at home any more?' she says, not able to resist making that point. Why should she cop his frustration because she didn't tell him something that, as far as she's concerned, he no longer has a right to know?

He looks down and shakes his head slowly. 'Nuh. I told Chook to keep it quiet.'

Because, of course, Chook's sister knows exactly why Andrew isn't at home. But it's not the time to say that. It's never going to be the time. She's not going to focus on the past when she has to concentrate on getting out of here and back home to the people who really love her.

'Well, sorry if I made things difficult for you,' she says. Appeasing him is the fastest way to ensure he leaves. 'I didn't want to bother you.'

'Where are the kids?'

'With Marie.'

'Who's Marie?'

'I swim with her. I've told you about her.' She winces as she shifts so she can sit up straighter. She may not be in pain but she is restricted by whatever it is the doctor has done to sew her back together.

'You let someone else take our kids so you could come in here and have your boob cut off?'

'You've been a bit *busy*,' Theresa snaps.

She can see he's surprised, because she's not given to losing her temper, but all she can perceive is a man who is thinking only of himself and not caring one iota about her. It's the story of their marriage, and of the end of their marriage, and now he's even making the removal of her breast about him and what she hasn't told him. If she wasn't already starting to feel relieved that Susie's taken him off her hands, she would be now.

'So?' he says. 'You still could have told me.'

'So you could do *what*, *exactly*, Andrew? You wouldn't have given up work to look after the kids. I would still have had to make arrangements. And you have *not once* asked me how I am.'

'Is everything all right in here?' It's the nurse, poking her head into the room.

Theresa wants to tell her that it's not all right, but you're not meant to air your dirty laundry, are you? Even if it's managed to drag itself into your hospital room.

She stares at the nurse, then at Andrew. Then says, 'I'm feeling tired. I wasn't expecting to see anyone so soon after surgery.'

The nurse steps all the way into the room. 'Best leave her to rest now,' she tells Andrew. 'You can come back later.'

'Or tomorrow,' Theresa says.

Andrew glances from the nurse to Theresa. 'Fine,' he says, before shoving his hands in the pockets of his work shorts and stalking from the room.

'Or come back never,' Theresa mutters.

'Get some rest,' the nurse says pointedly, drawing the curtains around Theresa's bed.

For the first time Theresa is alone with her solitary breast, and her wound and her dressings and the drip that is attached to her arm. She's alone with thoughts of her children and how much she wants to see them. Alone with her fears of what comes next, of the unknown.

But she knows one thing for sure: she doesn't want to be married to Andrew any more, and as soon as she can she's going to get that divorce, even if it means she no longer has the house.

As hard as it is to get comfortable so she can sleep, Theresa closes her eyes and thinks of her last swim with the others. She goes over each stroke, each kick, each wave – and each laugh, each smile, each kind word. The memories comfort her until she drifts off.

CHAPTER 47

'Look at you, all gussied up in bandages,' Marie says at Theresa's bedside.

On her walk up the hill to the hospital she decided she'd be cheerful, and now she's seen how forlorn Theresa is looking she's glad she did.

'I'd rather be gussied up in a nice dress and going out for cocktails,' Theresa says. She lifts her arm. 'Of course, my friend the intravenous drip would have to come too.'

'We all need a dance partner, love.' Marie bends down and kisses Theresa's cheek. 'We missed you this morning.'

'You went swimming without me?' Theresa's mouth drops open. 'How dare you!'

'We dared. It wasn't the same, of course.'

'You have to say that.'

'I think you know me well enough to know that just because I have to do something, it doesn't mean I will.' Marie puts two books on the bedside table. 'Here you go – some Barbara Cartlands. Quick, easy, and you can leave them behind.'

Theresa makes a face. 'Maybe I'll get some tips about how to pick a better husband next time.' Her expression softens. 'Thank you, that's very thoughtful.'

'The kids are with Gus,' Marie says, gesturing to the sole chair. Theresa nods and she sits down. 'In case you're wondering. And he was with them this morning while we were swimming. He took them for a run along the sand.'

'They were up that early?' Theresa looks sceptical.

'We didn't give them a choice. Besides, he promised them an ice cream.' Marie winks. 'We figure a few days of bribery won't hurt, then you can have them back.'

'Gee, thanks.' Theresa's smile is tight. 'Are they okay?'

Marie waves a hand. 'They're fine. They're tormenting Charlie Brown and helping me make cakes. They've barely noticed you're not around.'

It was mostly true. Last night both children insisted that they had to see their mother before going to sleep and Marie ended up singing lullabies and rubbing their backs until they calmed down. Sasha is too young to think of what specifically is happening to her mother but Marie is sure that Oliver has worked out something is wrong – he may be rambunctious but he's sharp, and she saw the worried look on his face when he asked about Theresa.

Theresa shifts position and looks uncomfortable doing it. 'They've always wanted a dog.'

'Well, they have one now,' Marie says brightly. 'For a few days.'

She sits back and looks at Theresa, who looks at her. A thousand small emotions flit across her friend's face.

'There aren't many things as difficult as this,' Marie says after a time. 'You're being very calm about it, but I know it's hard to cope with.'

'I don't feel calm,' Theresa says, strangling the last word. 'I feel like I don't know what I'm going to do next and how I'm going to manage.'

Marie wants to be reassuring but she also doesn't want to lie. 'That's because you *can't* know what you're going to do next. You just have to get through this day. And the next. Then the next. There's no other option.'

She looks away from Theresa. When she looks back, she can tell she is being scrutinised.

'Norm's death must have been hard,' Theresa says quietly.

'It was.'

The look they exchange is frank: one wounded bird to another, both of them flapping their remaining wing and hoping they can still fly away.

The patient in the next bed is listening to the radio. Marie didn't realise this is a shared ward, although the curtain drawn around the next bed should have tipped her off. She looks towards the window, which gives her a glimpse of harbour but no encouragement. Despite her deepening friendship with Theresa, she hasn't revealed that much of herself yet, and they don't have the shorthand that Marie has with Gwen.

'Mainly because it made me remember a lot of things I'd forgotten,' she says. 'Or tried to forget. When I lost my boy.'

Marie immediately thinks it's selfish to say this to Theresa now. Then she thinks it's a distraction, so maybe a good thing. When she sees Theresa crying, she knows it's neither.

'Oh, Marie,' Theresa says, her chin puckering and her forehead collapsing. 'I forgot.'

'Don't you cry, or I will,' Marie says. She tries to blink back her own tears, because she's been brave about this for a long time, so she should keep it going now.

'We haven't spoken about it really, have we?' Theresa sighs heavily. 'I didn't want to pry at the time. And then there was no other time, was there? It's so sad, Marie. That you lost him.'

Marie nods. 'It is. But my life is how it's been. You know what I mean? There is no other life in which he lives.'

Theresa looks down and pulls at the sheet that covers her abdomen. 'I'm wondering . . .' she starts, then lifts her eyes to meet Marie's, and there is anguish in them. 'I'm wondering if there's another life in which I live.'

Although Marie saw Theresa's fear before this operation, it still strikes her as discordant: Theresa, who attacks waves and open water with laughter and brio, hasn't seemed like a candidate for fear. But of course she's afraid. Of course a woman who's had a breast cut off is worried about what it means. If Marie had thought for half a second about her friend and not about herself, she'd have realised that.

'Don't be ridiculous, my girl,' she says with as much authority as she can muster. If Theresa is scared, Marie needs to be the bossy boots who makes her feel as though there's nothing to be worried about. 'We'll get you sorted. You're going to be out of here in no time, and then we'll tackle the next steps. You're not alone in this. I won't allow it.'

'But my aunt died of breast cancer,' Theresa says softly.

'You don't even know if it's cancer yet!' Marie says.

Theresa stares at her. '*Marie.*'

'All right.' Marie sighs. 'It probably is. But you're not your aunt. You're my friend and we're getting you through this. And by "we" I mean Elaine and Leanne too. If we can see each other half naked every morning, we can certainly help you with one breast missing.'

Theresa looks surprised, then she starts to laugh. 'How did this happen?' she says.

'What? The breast cancer?'

'No!' She keeps laughing. 'How did we get here – you and me? Elaine and Leanne? I didn't even know you two years ago.'

Marie looks at this woman she has come to hold so dear and it feels like she's known her for aeons. Perhaps she has, and it has just taken them until now to recognise it.

'Bluebottles have a way of bonding people,' is what she offers instead.

'Nasty buggers,' Theresa says knowingly.

'Just like your husband, right?' Marie says.

She is rewarded with Theresa's shrieking laugh, and the nurse checking in to see if everything is fine.

Then the lunch trolley arrives and Marie makes a retort about the parlous state of the jelly on the tray, before she is told that visiting hours are over. She leaves Theresa trying to negotiate a chicken sandwich she doesn't want to eat.

She's about to walk out of the hospital and home when she decides to make a detour.

The hospital's chapel is non-denominational and Marie believes – hopes – the Lord will forgive her for that, and also for the fact that she's been so happy lately she hasn't felt as though she's needed Him as much. She's been feeling some guilt about that happiness while Theresa has her travails, yet knows Theresa would be the first to tell her not to do that.

Still, there it is, and here she is, crossing herself and kneeling in a pew.

Her prayer is the same one she's been making every day since Theresa told her about the surgery. Usually she says it to herself while she swims, but today she feels the need for rein-forcements. In this quiet space she can be more direct. More demanding, maybe. Because she wants her God to pull Theresa through this victoriously.

After she's made her request, Marie leaves the hospital and walks down the hill. The day is cool, verging on cold. Autumn is becoming entrenched and soon they may take up walking again. Or maybe not. Elaine and Leanne are veterans now. Like her, they may find it harder to give up the winter sea than to embrace it.

Before long she sees Gus at the side gate, holding Oliver's and Sasha's hands, and she gives thanks for the bounty that is in her life even as she continues to pray to God to take care of Theresa, one of the greatest bounties of all. Because Marie is firmly of the belief that everything that has come into her life over the past year – almost two years – is because of that woman. Theresa, her big heart, and a stretch of water that has drawn in companions Marie never dared to dream she would find; companions who've opened her heart to a possibility she never thought existed: a new love, with all its strangeness and familiarity.

'Hello, darling,' Gus says, kissing her on the lips as she reaches them. 'We've missed you.'

'And I've missed you,' she says, as the children rush to tell her about their day, and Charlie Brown sits by the door, waiting for her, and the smell of whatever Gus is making for dinner wafts down the hall.

CHAPTER 48

Leanne dips a toe in the water then steps back. It seems to be colder than yesterday. However, she won't be deterred. She's already decided to keep going as long as she can stand it, and perhaps beyond, because as nice as walking is, it's just not the same. There's no sense of achievement at the end of a walk the way there is each day she swims. Even though they're still swimming the same distance, she can experiment with going faster and changing strokes. Matt has been encouraging her to try backstroke. She feels like she's going to drown half the time but she's improving. She may even practise this morning and surprise him when he's back.

For the Easter long weekend he's gone to his family's beach house a couple of hours away. He called her yesterday to say his brother had turned up unexpectedly and he didn't know if he wanted to stay.

'I'm not sure if I can give you advice about that,' Leanne said. 'I'm not the best at family relationships.'

'But you're talking to them,' Matt said, and she could almost see the look of pride on his face. He'd told her he was proud of her for staying in contact with her mother and, slowly, her father. Her father's is the anger she's found the hardest to forget.

She puts her whole foot in the water and smiles as she thinks of Matt's warm hand taking hers as they walked back to her place after dinner on Thursday night. He felt strong, and safe. Each time she sees him she feels less on guard. Hardly at all now.

'Good morning, Lee,' says Marie. She puts a hand on Leanne's back and kisses her on the cheek.

They're all kissing each other hello now. It's not a sporting group any more; it's a meeting of friends.

'Hello, ladies,' Elaine says as she strides over the last of the soft sand and meets them on the hard. 'How was your Good Friday lunch, Marie?'

'Wonderful. We went for a barbecue in that park on the headland. Gus did the cooking.' She smiles.

'Fish, I presume?' Elaine says, taking off her long-sleeved top.

'Of course. Morning mass, fish for lunch – I like the rituals.' She winks. 'What about you, Lee? A bit of time to yourself with Matt gone?'

Leanne nods. 'And I'm working today. I thought I'd take the long weekend so some of the others could go away.' She shrugs. 'I don't mind it over Easter. It's quiet. Like Christmas.'

They stand there looking at each other.

'It's funny,' says Marie. 'I still keep waiting for Theresa to arrive.'

Elaine laughs with relief. 'Me too. I spoke to her last night and she said she wished she could join us.'

'I called her in the afternoon,' says Leanne.

'So did I,' says Marie. 'She probably felt bombarded.'

They all know, though, that it's better to bombard her than not. They all call every day, and visit when they can. No one wants to overload her with visits, because even though she says she enjoys them she's still recovering, and simply being with the children takes energy, let alone having conversations. Besides, Theresa's nonna has turned into a bodyguard and none of them thinks she'll let them in if they turn up more regularly.

'How are you going, Lee?' Marie says. 'You keep so quiet I forget to ask sometimes.'

'You don't have to ask,' Leanne says, because she's content to not be the focus of enquiry.

'I wouldn't find out otherwise, would I?' Marie says drily. 'You are what is known in the business as a closed shop. Which I understand,' she adds quickly. 'But that doesn't mean I'm not going to ask questions.'

Leanne accepts her fate. 'I'm well,' she says as a seagull hops by. Then she notices something different. 'Is that . . . a pelican?' she says, gasping.

'Sure is,' says Marie. 'I haven't seen those here for years.' She looks around. 'There have to be others. They're rarely alone.' Her head swivels to the left. 'There – two more.'

Elaine looks delighted as she takes a step closer to the water.

'I loved *Storm Boy* when I was little,' Leanne says dreamily.

'Nicole loved it too.' Marie's eyes follow the majestic birds. 'I preferred *Sun on the Stubble* when I was reading to her. It's a riot.'

'I've never seen a pelican before,' Elaine says, watching as one of them takes flight. 'They're magnificent.'

'The other two will go now – watch,' Marie says, and within seconds they do.

'Maybe they're parents following their young.' Elaine's neck is craned to watch them as they fly towards Little Beach.

'Speaking of which . . .' Leanne can feel Marie staring at her. 'It's been a while since we've had an update, Lee.'

That's true. Theresa's medical condition has engrossed them all; and Leanne's also been talking to Matt about her family, so she hasn't felt the need to talk to Marie and Elaine. But that doesn't mean she shouldn't. It occurs to her that they might be interested in her life without expecting her to need them for anything.

'Mum wants us all to have lunch together at home,' she starts. 'But I'm not sure. There are . . .' She considers how to phrase it. 'There are some things that are hard to forget.'

She closes her eyes and sees her father's furious face, hears the things he said to her, feels the sensation of him slapping her. Being there with him, with them all, would seem too much like a re-enactment of the last time they were all there.

Matt has suggested she invite them to Shelly Bay and she's thinking about it. 'I could be there,' he'd said, looking hopeful. 'For back-up.'

'Has your mother said if your father is sorry for what happened?' Elaine prods gently.

'Yes. But maybe she's just saying that because she wants it all to stay in the past.'

Leanne isn't sure whether she believes that or just wants to, because it's easier to not reconcile with them all. There's work ahead if she walks down that path, just when her life feels carefree for the first time.

'I guess you won't know unless you talk to him,' Marie says. 'You'll hear it in his voice. Were you close before?'

Leanne thinks of the man who built her a cubby house – just for her, so she had a space away from her brothers, even though they'd always try to get into it. She thinks of him patiently drawing illustrations for her school projects because she was hopeless at drawing.

'Yes,' she says.

'Then that's not gone, love,' Marie says. 'Now, let's get in the water. It's colder out here than it will be in there.'

They've been talking so long the sun is further above the horizon than usual and its light turns the bay into a pool of gold. Near them the first surfer of the day is paddling out.

They quickly discard their clothes and wade in. After a few seconds underwater, the cold disappears and the water becomes the balm it always is.

CHAPTER 49

Elaine parks her old Renault in front of Marie's charming home. She's noticed this house before on her many long walks around Shelly Bay and wondered at its age. Sometimes even wished she were living there.

As she gets out of the car she glances across the street to a building that has the name *Therese* over its doorway and smiles at the coincidence. Not exactly the same, but close enough.

Theresa is the reason Elaine's here today: to help Marie with Oliver and Sasha. Gus is working and when Marie mentioned this morning, after the swim, that she'd be alone with the children after she picks them up from school, Elaine asked if she could join her. She has grown fond of Theresa's pigeon pair.

Theresa has been insisting that she's 'all right, really' and doesn't need any more help, but Marie's been insisting that she rests as much as she can. If she takes the children for a few hours, Theresa can sleep or read or watch television – whatever she likes.

'*Bonjour*,' Marie says as she opens the door and kisses Elaine on the cheek.

'You speak French?'

Marie colours. 'A little.'

'*On peut parler en français si tu veux*,' Elaine offers, although her French skills have grown rusty since she left the northern hemisphere.

'Maybe. One day. I'm, uh . . . not that fluent.'

Elaine gets the message and steps inside. As they walk down the hall she hears the sound of chattering children.

'How are they?' she asks.

'They're kids,' Marie says, smiling. 'They're focused on what's going on right now. Which happens to be making mud pies.'

She leads the way out the back, to where Sasha and Oliver are sitting in a garden bed, dirt on their faces and hands and feet, talking about who has the bigger clump of dirt and what they're going to do with it.

'I told them I'd hose them off at the end,' Marie says, folding her arms and looking down at the children with something resembling pride. 'I think they like the idea of that more than anything, so they're getting as dirty as possible.'

Elaine smiles to see the children unworried about their mother, or anything other than what they're doing right now. She wishes she could be like that, but she left it behind as soon as adolescence arrived.

'Hello, Ollie, hi, Sasha,' she calls.

'Hi, Lainey!' Sasha waves.

Oliver looks up and gives a nonchalant little-boy nod.

'That's new,' Elaine says. 'He used to be very happy to see me.'

'He's too cool sometimes, that kid,' Marie says, laughing. 'Come on, let's get a cuppa. We'll hear if they get into strife.'

The children burble away to each other as Elaine follows Marie into the house, noticing the shift from the warmth of the garden to the cool interior. Autumn is vacillating between cool and heat, throwing up the occasional day that recalls summer not long past. Elaine's own house doesn't give the same relief from this city's high temperatures, although she has started to adjust to the climate. She doesn't find herself resenting it any more; she doesn't grumble to herself about how lovely and mild English summers are. It would be ungrateful to do so when she has an ocean at the bottom of the hill and can stay in it all day if she wishes.

'So how are things?' Marie says as she turns on the kettle. 'I see you every day but we don't really chat much, do we?'

It's true: they don't. Elaine has found that the language created by swimming together – the way she has come to recognise the other women's facial expressions and signs of fatigue or joy or fear sometimes – obviates the need for much discussion. On many subjects, at least.

'Things are . . .' she starts, before realising that she doesn't have a neat answer. And Marie has enough to think about at the moment – she doesn't need Elaine whingeing about her transgressions. 'Fine,' she says with a tight-lipped smile.

'Love, I didn't come down in the last shower. I know you far too well to believe that little performance.' Marie cocks her head as if she's issuing a challenge.

Elaine inhales sharply through her nostrils. 'Yes. Perhaps you do.' Another tight smile.

'So?'

Elaine folds her arms. 'It's been easier to not say anything. Easier to hide.'

Marie's expression softens. 'You don't have to say, love. I didn't think it was anything serious.'

'Oh, it's not,' Elaine says breezily. 'Not really, in the scheme of things. I'm just a failure, that's all.'

'AA,' Marie states.

'Still going,' Elaine says, her chin lifting slightly, 'but I had to start again.'

Marie looks relieved. 'So you had a slip?'

'Yes.'

'That's all?'

Elaine frowns. 'Yes.'

'Well . . .' Marie starts laughing. 'If you thought it was going to stick the first time . . .'

'Shouldn't it?'

'No!' Marie chuckles. 'I'm sure you think that just because you're disciplined enough to turn up for a swim every morning, you should be able to stay off the grog. So now you're wondering what on earth happened, because you had a drink, and clearly if you'd just applied yourself the way you do to swimming, you'd be fine.'

'Yes,' Elaine mumbles.

'Elaine, my dear, that is not how it works.' Marie sighs. 'I wish it were. Alcohol is not sea water. Drinking is not good for you.'

'But giving it up is! Like swimming is good for me.' Elaine can hear that she sounds like she wants a gold star.

'True. But it's not the same thing. Slipping up just means you're human.' She gives Elaine a piercing look. 'Or maybe that's the part you don't like.'

Elaine stares at her, because she knows there's truth in that. She would like to think herself preternaturally able to cope, to rise above life's challenges. To glide, dare she say it, like a swan over troubles. Her behaviour over the past few months has been more like that of a fish caught in a net, flapping away, futilely searching for escape. She's been kidding herself about who she really is and Marie has seen right through it.

'You may be right,' she murmurs.

'I usually am.' Marie smiles and lifts the tea tray. 'Shall we sit on the verandah?'

'Sure.'

'And why don't you tell me more about your sons,' she adds, 'because we don't talk about them on the beach.' As she smiles, her eyes almost disappear inside her crow's feet.

'Only if you tell me about Gus,' Elaine says. 'I have a feeling Theresa knows more than I do.'

Marie shrugs. 'Maybe.' She winks and gestures to a chair that overlooks the garden where Sasha and Oliver are still busy getting themselves dirty.

'Is Theresa going to be all right?' Elaine asks as she sits.

'That's only for God to know,' Marie responds, pouring the tea for them both.

'So you believe in God?' Elaine asks, genuinely interested.

Her religious upbringing was unobservant Anglican and she can hardly say she has a spiritual life. And religion hasn't been a subject during their swims. Elaine was brought up to never discuss religion or politics and she's found Australians in concordance on the first point, but not the second. They're all very keen to discuss politics and politicians and why they think they're a 'pack of mongrels', as Derek said once.

'Of course,' Marie replies. 'Do you?'

'I don't know.'

'Hm.' Marie smiles mysteriously as she sips her tea. 'Don't they make you submit to a higher power in AA?'

God has never been a consideration for Elaine. The world has always turned, the grass has grown and the sun has shone. After she left childhood, her curiosity about it all faded. But she looks at the children squealing with laughter as they play, at Charlie Brown as he decides where he's going to sit, at the flowers in the garden and the flower pattern on her china teacup. She is aware of Marie sitting next to her and how two years ago they didn't know each other. She thinks of the mornings spent in each other's company and the friendship each of the women has given her. If it's not God doing all of this, then who? What? How is it possible that two years ago she was miserable and friendless, and then the kindness of Theresa and Marie and even Leanne, in her quiet way, changed that for her? She was heading for a serious drinking problem, then she was offered support without judgement. All that came from the ether, not from her. Someone – something – has given her these riches.

'Yes, they do,' she says at last. 'So I'm thinking about it.'

Marie nods approvingly, then they sit and sip their tea – Elaine wincing because it's stewed just a little too long for her taste – and talk of men and marriages, of bad decisions and recovering from them, as the breeze comes up, chasing the heat away, and the late afternoon brings the children to the verandah. Marie washes off the evidence of the garden on their skin, before Elaine drives them home to their mother.

CHAPTER 50

It's taken Theresa several pep talks to herself and from Marie to get to the beach this morning. Not because she doesn't want to be here – she's missed her morning outings – but because she knows it won't be the same. While the others swim, she will have to stay on the beach. Her surgical wound – the thing that's holding her together to cover the place where her breast used to be – is still healing; and even if it wasn't she doesn't know how she'd go about presenting herself in a swimming costume. The falsie might be fine for lying around on the sand, but what is she meant to do if she wants to swim like she used to? That's been one of the pep talks: how to get back into swimming with a false breast.

The house is silent as she prepares to leave. Marie suggested that Ollie and Sasha stay with her last night so Gus could watch them this morning, because Nonna's been doing more than her fair share of childminding. Theresa forgets that Nonna is in her eighties, and sometimes a woman that age doesn't want to be bothered with children, even if she's been preserved in nicotine and chianti.

It was so kind of Marie and Gus to offer to have them – although it did make Theresa wonder how often Gus stays the night at Marie's place. That's as far as she lets her imagination wander, though, because while she's curious she really doesn't want to think about Marie having a more active love life than she has. Theresa can only hope that if she makes it to Marie's age she'll find herself a nice bloke who's handy around the house and doesn't mind looking after other people's children. He's a bit dishy, too, Gus is. Not that Theresa's ever been interested in older men, but she certainly understands what Marie sees in him.

She's not allowed to drive yet so she's going to walk down to the beach and Elaine will drive her home. It's a decent walk but she has time: she'll arrive after they've all started swimming and wait for them to get out of the water. No sense sitting there while they do the full swim. She might get upset at what she's missing out on. There's been a bit of that going on lately.

The light is dim as she walks down the road to meet the beach. At this end there are surfers already in the water and not many waves to keep them busy. But she knows that likely doesn't bother them: surfers seem to enjoy the peaceful times sitting out there on the board. Theresa never really understood it until she spent more time in the water – until she got deeper, that is.

Her childhood weekends were spent playing in the shallows, then venturing out further as she grew older, but never too far. Even when she was in Nippers she was reluctant to go too far out. Her mother wasn't a keen swimmer – although she loved living by the beach – and thought that dangers lurked beyond the waves. Perhaps they did. Theresa never found out, because she obeyed her mother and kept within a few metres of the shore.

Swimming to Little Beach, however, has given her a different understanding of the water. The world of that swim is so different to the one she knew growing up. While she was scared the first few times, once she realised she was going to be fine she opened her eyes and saw what was there. Not just fish – although there are some of those – but a place that's strange yet so much like home. She was free there. She was graceful. She was able. Sometimes she even felt fierce.

She was never a fan of mermaid stories when she was younger, but once she started ocean swimming she wanted nothing more than to grow gills and a tail and be able to stay underwater for hours. Out there, in the open water, she wasn't Theresa, she wasn't Mum, she wasn't anyone's wife or daughter or friend. She was part of something huge. Part of the planet. The rhythms of the water felt like they belonged to her and she belonged to them. The swell felt like the undulations of her own blood. It was bliss, being there. Then she'd have to leave and go home.

She once told Marie about what she felt; she figured that if anyone was going to understand it would be the person who's been swimming every day for decades.

Marie had nodded, a serious look on her face. 'That's it, yes. We're part of something much bigger than ourselves. I find it a relief.' Her face had clouded briefly. 'A salvation, sometimes. We're nothing in the ocean, and we're everything. Every drop of water is us. Every grain of sand.' She turned to Theresa. 'Which means we're not so different, you and me. So don't go thinking I won't understand things that are going on in your life, and I won't think that about you in respect of my life either.'

It took Theresa a while to appreciate what Marie was offering her right then, but she did eventually. Which is how she's found herself accepting help from the three women while she recovers. She honestly doesn't know how she would have managed the children and the cooking and cleaning and washing if she hadn't had them. It was hard enough managing before.

As she continues walking she sees fewer surfers in the middle stretch of the beach. She looks ahead to the southern end: somewhere up there Marie, Elaine and Leanne are already in the water. Her longing to join them is physical, and closely followed by a pain in her chest where her breast used to be.

'Yeah, yeah, I hear you,' she mutters, glad that the only other people around are jogging too fast to notice what she says.

Maybe she's overdoing it, walking this far, but she can't stay on the couch forever. Before the surgery she was fitter than she'd been in years, and she doesn't want to lose more of that than she needs to. She also needed to get out of the house – it's been quiet without the kids there. Without Andrew around.

Theresa's had plenty of time to think about their marriage, especially during the night when she can't fall asleep, or when she wakes in the wee hours and can't get back to sleep. Perhaps she should have been a different wife. A better wife. She could have been a little less loud and a little more subservient. Andrew would have liked that. Every man she knows would like that. She just doesn't know a lot of women who like doing that.

That's the conundrum, isn't it: the way men want the world to run isn't the way that women want it to run, but men are bigger and stronger so women do what men want. For all time, that's how it's gone.

Thank god for friends or you'd go spare.

She can see them now: Elaine in the lead as they leave the water, then Marie. Leanne is . . . Theresa can see her, trying to catch a wave. That's an achievement in itself, because Leanne has never been keen on body surfing.

They look fine without her. They look like a group of friends having a laugh. Enjoying their swimming. Maybe they don't need her after all.

'Theresa!'

Elaine is waving so vigorously Theresa thinks her arm may fall out of its socket.

And that's all it takes for her insecurity to be gone: a wave, a call, a big smile, and Marie and Leanne and Elaine walking towards her as she descends the stairs to the sand.

'Let me give you a hug,' says Marie, 'even though I'm all wet.'

'Hi,' says Leanne, and Theresa could swear she sees a smile.

'Hello, hello.' Elaine kisses her on both cheeks and leaves sea water behind.

'Did you have a good swim?' Theresa asks.

'We did,' Marie says slowly. 'But it was definitely not as much fun without you. It hasn't been as much fun any day.'

'Oh, sure,' says Theresa, although she's quietly thrilled.

'It's true,' says Elaine with a kind smile. 'Without you I'm far less entertained than I was.'

'I'm still really slow,' says Leanne, pulling a face. 'So you're definitely going to swim faster than me. When you're back.'

'Yes . . . when I'm back.'

Theresa feels her breath catch in her chest. She didn't think she'd feel sad coming here – she thought she'd be happy to see them, and invigorated at the idea of getting into the ocean again. Instead, she feels like she's lost something before it had time to really start. Although that's a ridiculous idea, and she's being overly dramatic. Her mother always called her 'my little Sarah Bernhardt'.

'It'll take a while, love,' Marie says. 'It's cold now, so you may want to wait until winter's over.'

'Really?' says Elaine with a mischievous look on her face. 'Does that mean we get to take a break?'

'No such luck,' says Marie. 'I'm used to having you around. So you'll just have to buy a wetsuit or something.'

Theresa smiles, although she doesn't like the idea of waiting until after winter to swim again. She'll have to ask the doctor about it when she goes for her appointment tomorrow. That's when they're going to talk about what happens next. She hasn't let herself worry about it because she can't control the outcome. Very mature of herself, she thinks.

'How about you all come back to my place for a while?' says Marie. 'The children will be up.'

'That sounds lovely,' says Theresa. 'Thank you.'

'All right, well, let's get dry and get our clothes on, then off we go.'

Theresa relaxes as Marie takes charge and lets herself be led first to Elaine's car, then into Marie's house, where even Leanne participates in the conversation. She feels warm and loved, and for a little while her mind is quiet and focused.

She tries to make the feeling last as long as she can, knowing that tonight she'll be lying awake again, her thoughts racing, trying not to worry about her present and her future.

WINTER 1984

CHAPTER 51

The days are so short now that on an afternoon walk there is barely time to enjoy the last light of the day from the headland looking west, with the Tasman Sea behind them and the city in front of them. The city Marie barely visits, despite her fears that her world is too small, because she's been content to stay close to Shelly Bay. She's also found that keeping herself confined physically has not stopped her world breaking its bounds in other ways.

Meeting Gus, falling in love with him, has made her grow. If her heart has expanded to accommodate Elaine, Leanne and Theresa, it has ballooned to take in this wondrous man who goes for walks with her and calls her just to say hello. The man who is sitting here with her now as they hold hands, share kisses and dream of a future together.

'Theresa's been in the wars, hasn't she?' Gus says, rubbing the back of Marie's neck with one hand while he leans on his other.

'She has,' Marie mumbles, 'but if you keep doing that I'm not going to know what you're talking about.'

'Enjoying it, are you?'

'Mm-hm.'

'I'm glad.'

She feels his lips on her cheek and smiles, then the smile vanishes. 'I think she's worrying a lot but she's not telling us, so it's hard to know how to help. She doesn't want us to go round there to do the housework any more, but I don't think her grandmother can do as much as she says she can.'

'How do you know?'

Marie feels guilty and it probably shows on her face. 'Because the kids told me.'

'Marie!' Gus laughs. 'You weren't extracting information from minors?'

'Maybe.'

'I'm outraged.' He starts rubbing her neck again. 'But it's a good tactic. I doubt Theresa would tell you herself.'

'I wish she would, because the three of us would be in there like a shot. We had a roster going. We can start it up again.' She sighs. 'I don't think it's that she's too proud. I think she just doesn't want us to know what it's really like. As if she's failed or something.'

Gus stops again and moves so she can see him better. Marie aches for the feeling of his hand on her skin.

'Tell me,' he says, 'after Norm died did you let anyone help you?'

'I didn't have a choice. Gwen kept barging in with casseroles and baked goods.'

Marie remembers a fridge overflowing with Gwen's generosity, and not a moment to herself to think for quite a while. At the time she'd found herself getting irritated, holding back from being short with Gwen. It wasn't until the activity had stopped that she appreciated it.

She remembers another time, too, many decades before, when Gwen didn't bring food but her presence, sitting with Marie while she wept for the child who didn't come home from hospital. Did she thank Gwen on either occasion? She thinks not, and Gwen wouldn't have expected it. Tomorrow Marie's going to visit her old friend and put that right.

'But Gwen was trying to help me through grief,' she says. 'With Theresa—'

She stops because she sees it now: Theresa, too, is grieving. Perhaps for the loss of her breast, but more likely for the end of the life she once knew. Her marriage is over and although she expresses no regrets, it's still a fundamental change. Combined with the illness, she'll never be the same person again. She may not even realise it yet but that won't stop her feeling a sorrow she can't name.

'I think you need to go back there,' Gus says gently. 'Don't take no for an answer, just help her.'

'I can't barge in! She has her grandmother there.'

'She *needs* a friend.' He rubs her back. 'And you're a good friend.'

There's a deepening orange in the western sky. Soon it will be night and they'll have trouble seeing their way down the path.

'Am I?' Marie says quietly.

'You're a good friend to me.' Gus kisses her temple. 'The best.'

She leans into his chest. 'And you are to me.'

They sit in silence that is broken only by the calls of birds flying home for the night. Kookaburras busy themselves in nearby trees, chattering about who knows what. A magpie calls as it flies overhead.

'It's busy up there,' Gus says.

'It is. We should think about getting home to the nest too.'

'Another minute or so, eh?'

He squeezes her shoulder and she's glad of the warmth of him as a guard against the cooling of the evening. And for other reasons: it's a reminder that he's real and he's here; that he's properly in her life no matter how unlikely and unexpected that is.

'You make me very happy, Marie Kathleen Veronica,' he murmurs, and she smiles. He recently discovered her confirmation name when he read it in her Bible and he's been using it liberally ever since.

'You make me very happy too, Angus George.'

'I know we haven't been acquainted very long,' he says, 'but I hope you don't mind me asking if you've ever considered getting married again? Not that I'm proposing. Yet. Don't want to scare you off.'

At that moment Marie feels the purest sensation of joy she's had in ages. Uncensored and unbridled. She is a long way from being scared.

Then she pulls away from him because she wants to see his face, to work out if he's joking. He's not the kind to joke about something like this, but she has to check. It's too dark to see him properly, though, so she'll have to ask instead.

'Are you being serious?' she says.

'Of course I am. So what's your answer?'

She takes a breath. 'I would consider it,' she says. 'And aren't you full of surprises?'

'A lifetime's worth,' he says, and she can hear the smile in his voice. His hand finds hers in the gloom. 'Come on. Time to get back and start dinner.'

'That's it?' She gets to her feet as he does. 'You're not going to say anything else?'

'That was a reccy,' he says. This time when he kisses her it's on the lips.

He produces a torch from inside his windcheater and switches it on so they can see the footpath.

'I didn't know you brought that,' she says.

'As I said, a lifetime of surprises.'

He shines the light ahead, and beyond it she can see the lights of the first line of houses starting to be switched on.

His hand is strong on hers as they walk and she likes to imagine hers is strong in his. But she's prepared to let him take the lead and help her get home. Tonight, and every night.

CHAPTER 52

'So tell me again,' James says as he leans against the kitchen table, his eyes dancing.

'Why?' Elaine says, although she's giddy enough to do it.

'Because I want to see how happy you look when you say it.' He gives her that smile she still falls for, over and over.

'Henry's coming to visit!' she declares, laughing. 'Before Marcus's wedding!'

'And?'

'And I've booked our flights so we can go back together for the wedding!'

Now James is laughing. 'Come here,' he says, opening his arms and closing them around her as she giggles into his neck.

'You know something?' he says into her hair.

'What?'

'That's the first time you've said "go back" instead of "go home".'

She's so surprised she loosens her grip on him a little. 'I think you're right. Although it sounds as if you've been keeping track.'

He shakes his head. 'Not at all. I've only noticed because you used to wince a little each time you said it.'

No doubt he's right, although she's never been conscious of doing that. Taking his hands, she kisses him gently. 'I'm sorry.'

He stares into her eyes. 'For what?'

'That was hurtful of me, to do that.' She kisses him again. 'My home is with you.'

'Darling, I understand. I've always understood.' His smile has a tinge of sadness to it. 'Even if sometimes you've seemed very far away.'

She nods. 'I have been. But I'm here now.'

The kitchen clock chimes seven.

'We have to leave!' she says. 'We need to be at your friends' place at half past.'

'I would hope they're your friends too,' he says, starting to undo his tie so he can change his shirt for the one she's put out on the bed.

'That's a lovely hope, darling, but I have my friends.' She winks, such an uncharacteristic action for her that James looks taken aback.

'Don't you think I should meet these mysterious swimmers?' he says as he walks down the hall towards their bedroom and she follows.

She's been dressed for an hour but that doesn't mean she won't want to watch him undress and dress again. It's one of her favourite pastimes.

'Honestly, it is *so* hard to corral them at night. Leanne has a boyfriend. Marie has a . . . a Gus. Theresa has the children.' She has a thought. 'Perhaps we could all go there for dinner. That would save her needing to make arrangements. In a little while, I mean. When she's up to it.'

'I really would like to meet them,' he says as he pulls his shirt over his head and drops it on the floor. She frowns. 'Oh, right – washing basket,' he says, grinning, and picks it up.

In the few seconds it takes him to walk to the basket in the corner by the door, Elaine lets her mind flit to the other news of her day. Although not news, really, so much as a thought, or a thought process.

'What are you worrying about?' James says as he puts on the clean shirt and starts to button.

'Nothing!' she says brightly. 'I'm not worrying. Just pondering.'

'About . . . ?'

She gazes at him and considers how much to say. It's a new plan and it may come to nothing. Or something. When she first started considering it she panicked. In England she had friends who supported her business initially, and she was forever grateful for that. She didn't have any such contacts here. She would hardly ask James to see if any of the other doctors' wives want their homes decorated. She didn't even know if Australians liked decorating their homes. From what she was able to tell, they spend most of their time outside. Perhaps she should become a horticulturist instead, then she could decorate gardens. And without any clue of how to find clients, there seemed little point going to the trouble of sourcing suppliers and finding a shopfront or other space. Their house was charming but not big enough for what she needed.

All that talking herself out of the job made her loathe herself, briefly. She was being lazy. Or scared. She spent a few days wearing herself out with ruminations, then decided to look at what was really bothering her.

Her hesitations mainly stemmed from the fact that, despite her robust friendships with the ladies in her swimming circle, she is, truly, shy. It was masked when she was in her home environment and her friends were women she'd known since school. It didn't manifest in her business either because she was playing a role. It took a move to the other side of the world for that veneer to fall away and leave her exposed as someone who doesn't make friends as easily as she thought. Her boat had never been rocked until it came ashore here in Shelly Bay, and for quite a while she didn't have the resources to handle it.

She had to be brave, in the end. Brave enough to believe that Marie, Theresa and Leanne would like her. Brave enough to believe that she'd like them. That was the realisation that spurred her on: if she can swim to Little Beach and back every day with three people who were strangers when she arrived here, she can certainly create a business in a place where she has to make new connections.

It would be good not to have to rely on James financially any more too. She still hasn't grown used to that – for years she had her own income and loved not being dependent on anyone. James doesn't seem to mind; indeed, he appears to relish the fact that she needs him. Which is a pity, as he'll have to give that up.

'I'm going to start a new business,' she says. 'Much like the old one. I've been doing some research about what's needed.'

James's face lights up. 'That is *sensational*!' he says, and she almost believes he's going to do a jig on the spot. 'Interior decorating?' he prompts.

'Yes. Or . . . perhaps a shop.' She smiles mysteriously. 'I might have looked at a couple of properties for rent.'

The idea of the shop came to her when she conceded she wouldn't have the appropriate space at home. She could run the design business from a shop, and that would give her room for storage and display and a space separate from home all at once.

James loops his tie around his neck. 'Can we drive past them on the way?'

'It's dark! You won't be able to see anything,' she says, although she can't help smiling at his enthusiasm.

'I don't care. Show me.'

'Oh, all right.'

She picks up her evening bag and lets him take her by the hand as he almost trots down the hall, collecting his keys and jacket from the chair by the front door, then out into the street.

As he closes the passenger door and jogs around to the driver's side, she laughs at his boyishness, and marvels that she can be married to someone who cares about her so much. Theresa has a husband who seemed to have only disdain for her. For some reason Elaine has ended up with a man who has nothing but regard for her.

There is so much luck in this world, she thinks, and very little design. Although she is closer to believing in that higher power – whatever it is – that Marie asked her about. For now, though, she will be grateful for her luck.

It's taken her a long time to realise that moving to Australia was luck, not tragedy, but now she is going to grab that luck with both hands and see where it takes her.

CHAPTER 53

If Matt squeezes her hand any more tightly Leanne is sure her circulation will never be restored. He is probably thinking the same thing, because she is squeezing him back. The plan – to meet her parents next to the beach, so they could take a walk in full public view, thereby reducing the chances of her father becoming angry with her – seemed sound, until now. Standing here, surrounded by tourists and seagulls stealing their hot chips, she thinks that all she's done is create an audience for what may turn out to be a failed meeting.

Her mother reassured her that it would all go well. She and Leanne's father are so happy she wants to see them, she said. Of course they will come to Shelly Bay, even if they've never been before. In Shelly Bay Leanne knew she'd feel most at ease, if not safe.

Matt is the other piece of the insurance plan. He appeared genuinely pleased to be asked.

'Are you sure?' he said. 'It's a big deal.'

Which she knows, of course. Such a big deal that she's felt queasy about it for weeks.

'It would be a bigger deal without you there,' she told him, because it's true, then realised it sounded strange. 'I mean, it would be harder. To deal with.'

'Lee,' he kissed her forehead, 'I know it's scary but they really do want to see you. You just need to create some new memories with them. That last memory is the main one you have so it feels like it's the only one. It's kind of . . .' He paused and his eyes flickered away. 'When I was a kid, I got dumped by a wave. Full washing machine. Thought I was going to drown. Worst experience of my *life*. And it was a wave my dad told me to catch. He was gutted, obviously, but I blamed him – and I *never* wanted to catch another wave. But Dad told me I had to. Right away, that day. He said I needed to catch a better wave so I didn't think that being dumped was all there was.' He grinned. 'So I did. And I went on to be a bloody good swimmer, as you know.'

She understood the analogy but wanted to tell him that in her memory her family aren't so much washing machine as terrifying carnival ride. That wouldn't have been kind, though – he was trying to be understanding. And he was. He is. Which is why he's here now.

'There they are,' she whispers urgently, seeing a man who is smaller and more bent over than she remembers, with her mother holding his arm tightly.

'Leanne,' her mother's mellifluous voice calls. 'Leanne!'

She's waving, so Leanne waves back. As they approach she lets go of Matt's hand.

'Mum,' she says, kissing her hello. 'Dad.'

His eyes are still blue, although their colour has faded. He looks like a little old man instead of the fit, tough father of her youth.

'Leanne,' he rasps, holding out his hand to clasp hers.

'Mum, Dad, I'd like you to meet Matt, my boyfriend.' She feels Matt's hand squeeze her shoulder. 'Matt, I'd like you to meet my mother, Ji-woo, and my father, Pádraic.'

'Good to meet you both.' Matt extends his hand to each of them. 'Pádraic – are you Irish?' he asks as the handshake ends.

'My mother was. It's a family name,' her father says, his eyes coming to rest on Leanne.

'Shall we walk for a while?' she says, smiling as hard as she can, feeling the forced nature of it.

'Leanne.' Her father puts a hand on her arm. 'Please. It's been so long.'

She stiffens and draws in a breath. Is he going to cause a scene? She really doesn't want a scene.

'New wave,' Matt whispers in her ear and she relaxes.

As she turns towards her father she sees pain in his eyes, and in her mother's. The difference between who she is now, though, and who she was then is that this time she doesn't blame herself for it.

Her father takes one of her hands in both of his. 'Can you forgive me?'

Leanne looks from him to her mother and back again. Perhaps forgiveness is what they came for. It's not something she has ever thought to ask of them. She has asked it of herself, and given it. Withholding it from them would be cruel, and she may be many things but she is not that.

What is that saying? To err is human; to forgive, divine. She doesn't need to be divine to grant them something that is so intrinsically a part of being human.

'Leanne!' calls a familiar voice, and her father's face falls.

Turning towards the sound, Leanne sees Marie walking in their direction from the Little Beach end of the promenade.

'Lee!' she calls again, and Leanne waves. If she thought she needed a benediction to grant forgiveness to her parents, she could not have asked for a better person to appear. If Elaine and Theresa also turned up she wouldn't be surprised.

'Hello, love,' Marie says, kissing Leanne's cheek. 'Can you believe we see each other down here every morning and we've never bumped into each other at any other time of day?' She laughs, then registers the presence of three other people. 'Oops,' she says. 'Sorry – I'm interrupting.'

Leanne hesitates over who to introduce first, and decides to go with the order in which Marie knew of their existence.

'Marie, this is Matt,' she says, beaming for a second because she's conscious that at this point in her life Marie knows her better than her parents do, and knows more about Matt than they do too.

'The famous Matt,' Marie says, shaking his hand vigorously. 'You're right, Lee – he *is* ugly.'

Matt's momentary surprise is replaced by a good-natured shake of the head. 'Don't worry, I've heard things about you too,' he says as Leanne's eyes flicker sideways to watch her parents' reactions.

She has told her mother about her morning swims, and mentioned the women's names, but she's never said enough for her mother to know how close she has become to them.

'And these are . . .' Leanne takes a breath. 'My parents.'

Marie stops and stares at her, then gives her a tiny nod and a wink.

'Hello, Mrs Leanne and Mr Leanne.' She smiles, and adds, 'I think I'd best keep walking. Gus is waiting for me somewhere. Oh, there he is.' She raises an arm and waves. 'We're heading off to visit his sister. It's a day for meeting the family.' A reassuring smile for Leanne as she starts to move away. 'Lovely to meet you all. See you tomorrow, Lee.'

Leanne watches her go. Although she doesn't believe in angels or kismet or anything mystical, she is tempted to believe that Marie was sent to her at just that moment, by something or someone, to remind her of how far she's come. Her lonely life – the one she chose, after she felt she didn't have a choice – is no more. It's time to catch that new wave.

'Yes, Dad,' she says, turning back to face her father, 'I forgive you.'

His eyes tremble and he bows his head.

Leanne steps beside him and offers her his arm, while Matt takes her other hand. Four astride, they stroll along the promenade, taking their time.

SPRING 1984

CHAPTER 54

The cancer wasn't content with taking Theresa's breast – it came for her lymph nodes too. The doctor said taking them out was a 'precautionary measure'. She wanted to ask him what he thought he was precautioning against, but she's not a doctor – not an expert in anything – so she has to trust him.

'We need to go back in,' was the way he phrased it.

Back in where? That was the first thing that came into her mind. She didn't want to sound stupid, though, so she played along. 'Oh, yes. Right,' she said, nodding, as if that was a helpful thing to do.

'We took a sample of one of your lymph nodes and the pathology suggests the cancer might have spread. So we'd like to take them all out.'

He had this flat tone of voice, like he was discussing whether a lamb roast should be in the oven at two hundred degrees or one eighty. To him she probably was just a piece of meat, so that explained it. Just one of his patients. After she left he'd probably talk to some other poor woman about her lymph nodes. Or worse.

That's what Theresa has to keep reminding herself: it could be worse. She could be living in a place without a doctor or a hospital. She could be in a country town and have to leave her children behind to come to the city for treatment.

She met someone like that when she was still volunteering in the hospital: a young woman who needed an operation on something she wasn't prepared to discuss. Theresa learnt that she had three kids who had to go back to the far west of the state – several hundred kilometres away – with their dad while she stayed. They were on holiday in Shelly Bay when whatever the problem was came up. That was tough, Theresa thought – to be so far from home when something so serious was happening. She had her friends to help her, and Ollie and Sasha and Nonna to make her smile, and that poor woman had no one. So it could be worse. For sure.

But it could also be better, and this time she took Marie's advice and told her parents the full story and asked them if they could come and help. Theresa doesn't want to burden Marie, Leanne and Elaine with helping out with the kids and the house because it just isn't fair.

'It has nothing to do with fair!' Marie protested, but Theresa doesn't agree. How can she ever even up this ledger?

Marie also asked – as she did the last time – if Theresa was going to tell Andrew about the second round of surgery.

'No way,' was her response.

'Theresa, this is more serious now,' Marie said.

'And so am I. If I tell him he might try to take the kids away.'

'Love, he hardly sees them – wasn't the last visit a fortnight ago and all he did was take them to McDonald's? Don't you think it's unlikely he'll want them all the time?'

'He'd make his parents look after them,' she said, starting to panic as she imagined a scenario where her in-laws left Ollie and Sasha behind at the sailing club after they had too much to drink one day and the children weren't found until morning.

'Theresa, whatever you're thinking, stop it,' Marie said. 'You look like you're going to explode.'

'I'll tell him I'm having more surgery but I'm not going to tell him why,' she said defiantly.

That was when Marie pointed out that in that case there was only one solution, and it was to ask Theresa's parents to move in for a while.

Her parents fairly flew down from the Central Coast and arrived on the doorstep only a few hours after Theresa called them.

'You should have told me sooner!' her mother admonished the minute she was in the door.

Theresa wanted to point out that this really wasn't the time for her mum to be telling her off, except she guessed some things would never change and it didn't matter if you had cancer. She'd like to think she wouldn't say that to Sasha in the same circumstances.

She hates the idea that this could happen to Sasha. She hates the idea of anything bad happening to her children. So she'll give her mum the benefit of the doubt and presume that she's covering her fear by switching into strict-parent mode. Or a different sort of strict-parent mode.

Theresa's always felt that her mother has been tough on her, and for no reason other than that she seems to think daughters are to be treated differently to sons. Theresa's brothers never had to apologise for wrongdoings as kids; never had to explain where they were or why they wanted to do something.

Her mother once hinted that Nonna had been tough on her, too, but Theresa has no proof of that. All she knows is that Nonna was never harder on her granddaughter than on her grandsons. If anything, she treated Theresa like a friend and her brothers like irritants. 'Silly little boys,' she would say, shaking her head each time Theresa's mother indulged them.

Once her mother knew that Theresa was having this surgery, though, something seemed to shift. 'You need us,' she said, and in that simple statement was a clue Theresa had waited a lifetime to find: perhaps her mother had simply wanted her daughter to need her. Or perhaps she'd been waiting for an excuse to show her daughter that she cares.

Before recent events, Theresa had pretty much mimicked her mother's life. When she gave birth, that was no different to anything her mother had done. But now their paths have diverged. And there her mother was, wishing Theresa had told her sooner.

'I didn't want to worry you,' was Theresa's excuse, and her mum looked at her the way she used to when Theresa was little and tried to 'help' make cakes by throwing flour all around the kitchen.

Now her parents are set up in the spare room and saying nothing about Andrew not being in the house. They've been invaluable, giving Theresa time to be convalescent; but at the same time she hasn't been left alone long enough to dwell on things. Marie and the others were so helpful last time, but what they couldn't do was be there every minute, filling up her time so she didn't sit around worrying.

The kids have had enough red frogs 'as a treat' to keep them bouncing off the walls until Christmas. And Theresa has time to see 'her ladies', as her mother once referred to them. Her swimming circle.

Elaine had called them that once, in her posh accent: 'the Shelly Bay ladies swimming circle'. Theresa thought that meant they may need to learn synchronised swimming, because otherwise where was the circle going to come from? She said as much and Elaine laughed.

'It's just a turn of phrase,' she said, 'and perhaps not a good one.'

But afterwards Theresa thought it sounded right. They feel like a circle – not a square, not a rectangle, not a straight line. They are a group. They are a collective hug, and what could that be but a circle?

She may not have been swimming with them for months now, and she isn't always there to meet them at the end of a swim, but they call, they visit, they chat to her parents so she can have time to herself. They have helped her cope.

She said that to Marie once, and was surprised to see Marie get teary.

'Don't you know,' she said, 'what *you* have done for *us*?'

No, Theresa doesn't know. She's just herself, muddling through each day and trying to make it the best it can be. Life is hard enough without everyone being grumpy. If she can bring a smile to someone's face, that's a good day's work. If she still went to church, she might think what she does is religiously motivated: she's doing the work of the Lord. Instead she likes to think she's doing the work of being human. What's that phrase she heard the other day? Good karma. She's spreading good karma. Or something.

Besides, she has to be an example to her children. If Ollie and Sasha see her smiling each day, if they remember their mum being happy even when she's really not, that has to be a good thing.

Theresa's started to think like that since the news about the lymph nodes: thinking about the kids remembering her. It's so bloody morbid, she knows that, but she has to be practical too. What if this gets worse? What if they keep chopping bits off her until there's nothing left? She has to prepare the kids.

It's probably bad to think like this. She needs to *be positive*. That's what Elaine said.

Theresa said it sounded like AA was having an effect. The Elaine she first met would never have popped out with a phrase like that.

'I agree,' Elaine said, looking surprised. 'I'm still not sure I said it.'

'You did,' Theresa said. 'But I can pretend I never heard it if you like.'

Elaine snorted. 'No, it's fine. It's a good thing. I'm *changing*. And didn't I need to?'

Theresa isn't sure she did. She likes Elaine just as she is.

Last night Theresa's mum came in and sat on her bed, taking her hand. 'How's my girl?' she said, in a tone Theresa had never heard her use.

'I'm . . .' Theresa tried to be brave but it didn't work. Besides, her mum can read her like a book. 'I'm afraid,' she said and her mum nodded.

'Of course you are. I would be too. But they're on top of things – your doctors. It must be so hard to go through all this, but it's good they acted quickly.'

Theresa nodded. 'I know. I just wish they could tell me what happens next.'

Her mother had smiled that smile mothers give when they want to be reassuring.

'We'd all like to know that,' she said. 'Or maybe we wouldn't. Sometimes it's better to think that nothing is decided. It's too much worry otherwise.'

That had worked – as her mother probably knew it would – and Theresa slept for more hours than usual.

Today she's moved to a chair in the garden, and is watching the kids running through the hose their grandfather is holding for them, even though they've been wet for so long they're turning blue.

Theresa remembers him doing it for her too. He was hard on her a lot of the time, but not always.

Simple pleasures – she's never lost sight of them. Swimming is that for her now. Was that. She feels that longing in her bones again, growing more intense with each day she can't be in the water. As her body becomes more of a battleground she wishes more fervently that the water could take her away from it.

'Here you go,' her mum says, handing her a lemonade.

'Thanks, Mum.'

Theresa tries to get comfortable in the flimsy outdoor chair she's had for years, and watches her mother attempt to do the same in the folding chair she brought with her from home. They're like two little old ladies sitting in the garden, except even Mum isn't particularly old.

'How's your pain?' she asks in a light tone.

'It's fine,' Theresa replies, trying to match it. 'The painkillers are pretty good. Even if I need to take a nap every now and again.'

Her mother nods.

'Does Andrew know about all of this?' she says, in that same tone. Like it's a bog-standard question.

Mind you, Theresa should have expected it. They could hardly not talk about Andrew all this time.

'No.' She takes a sip of lemonade.

'Don't you think he should?' Her mother is watching the kids but Theresa hears the scold meant for her.

'No.'

'Theresa.' Her mother looks at her, but Theresa can't see her eyes behind the cat's-eye sunglasses she always wears. 'That's not reasonable.'

'*He's* not reasonable!' She wants to storm off but she can't move quickly enough.

'Theresa.' Now her mother has that you're-not-in-trouble-but-you-might-be-soon tone of voice that she's never quite lost even though Theresa has been an adult for, oh, twenty-odd years.

'What?' She attempts to huff, but it makes her stitches pull and she ends up saying 'ow' instead.

'He's Oliver and Sasha's father, and their mother is sick. And not able to look after them all the time. He needs to do his share.'

'He wouldn't know what his share is.'

'Then it's time he learnt. He has an easy life, swanning around Shelly Bay like it's his personal kingdom. His job's here, his house is here. He probably has palpitations each time he has to go further than City Road.'

Theresa can't hide her surprise.

'Well,' her mother says primly, 'I've never been a fan.'

Theresa giggles. 'Really?'

'He was never good enough for you. But it was your choice.' Her mother holds up a hand. 'Not my place to interfere. And he's given me two beautiful grandchildren, so I have to tolerate him. He has time, though, that's my point. Time to help you with the kids.'

'I don't want him to know,' Theresa says firmly.

'You don't want *him* to know,' her mother's head swivels towards her again, 'or you don't want the *girlfriend* to know?'

'What's the difference?' Now she *really* wants to huff but she accepts her limitations.

Her mother keeps watching her and Theresa wishes she could see her eyes, to know what she's thinking. She's always been hard to read, whereas Theresa couldn't hide an emotion if her life depended on it.

'Your dad and I won't be staying forever,' her mother says. 'We'll drive you mad if we do. And I know you have friends, but it's not fair to them either. Andrew has to pull his weight. He won't do everything the way you would do it – you're just going to have to let that go.'

Theresa knows her mother is right. The children will likely say something to him anyway, and he might try to use her secrecy against her. Not that she thinks he'll want to have the kids full time – that would cramp his style, and his lifestyle. He might do it to be mean, though, because all bets are off when your marriage breaks down and you're the guilty party. You'll do what you can to save face.

'I don't want to talk to him,' Theresa mumbles.

'You don't have to,' her mother says, so cheerily that Theresa knows she expected her to fold. 'I'll do it.'

'Ollie, doooon't!' Sasha wails, and Theresa looks up in time to see Oliver turning the hose directly on his sister.

'Oliver, put that down,' she says with as much force as she can muster.

'Wouldn't it be good,' her mother says, 'if you didn't have to do this all the time?'

Theresa nods resignedly.

'Close your eyes, love,' her mother instructs, as Sasha's cries turn to laughter once more. 'Have a snooze. I'll go and make the call.'

CHAPTER 55

Elaine pulls into Theresa's driveway and turns off the engine. The street runs along the ridge between Main Beach and Sunrise Beach, so there are ocean views wherever you look. Theresa told her that she and Andrew have lived here, on Royalist Road, since they married. Andrew's childhood home is one street away and he didn't want to move far, although his parents were already on their way to a new place half an hour's drive away by then.

'Early retirement,' Theresa had said, 'which means they're usually too busy to look after the kids.' She sighed. 'So my parents are on the coast and his parents are on acreage, and they all love their grandchildren but don't want to see them very often. Did your parents help you out?'

'They did,' Elaine said, feeling slightly guilty. 'I was very lucky. They lived close by and they were happy to help. It meant I could run my business.'

Whenever Theresa asks questions about the business – as she does from time to time – she makes Elaine feel as if running a business while having children is a superhuman achievement. Perhaps it is. At the time it was simply her life and she didn't think it extraordinary. Now she wonders if she should have given herself more credit.

Since that conversation Elaine's been determined to do for Theresa what her parents did for her – especially as Andrew's involvement with the children seems to be short on the responsible side and long on the side that's all about fun. The meagre times he spends with them he takes them to the mall for donuts or to the beach for fish and chips, and they're only gone an hour at best.

It's made Elaine cast James differently. She never thought him a bad father, although his work always kept him away from the children each weeknight and sometimes on weekends. But she never fussed about it, because she hadn't minded, which meant the children didn't mind either. What she hadn't appreciated was that during the times James was with the boys he didn't try to make up for those absences by being 'fun dad'. When he was there, family life carried on as normal. He always praised Elaine in front of the boys, and told them how lucky they were to have such a wonderful mother – to which they'd either groan or not respond at all – and told her that he was lucky to have such a wonderful wife. In other words: he didn't use fatherhood to boost his ego.

As she approaches Theresa's front door, Elaine can hear Oliver and Sasha playing in the back garden so she knows that Theresa is home. Theresa's parents have gone to Canberra to stay with one of her brothers for a couple of days – 'to give me a break from always getting in trouble', as Theresa explained it.

'Mum keeps saying I need to do this and I need to do that,' she said when Elaine called a couple of days ago. 'She even rang Andrew to tell him that he should be looking after the kids a bit. I didn't hear the call, but she told me she said he's the laziest father she's ever met and if he doesn't get his act together she and my father are going to give me money to sue for full custody. It didn't work. He says he's too busy,' Theresa went on.

Elaine could hear the false levity in her voice, the sign that she was making an effort to not be disappointed. But she must be – Elaine would be. Anyone would be upset that their children's father can't be bothered to fulfil basic parenting duties.

'I'm not too busy,' Elaine had said, knowing it would be no hardship for her to continue to assist Theresa, nor to take the children to school.

'Theresa?' she calls through the screen door into the living room beyond. Seconds pass and all she can hear is the children.

'Theresa?' She calls a little more loudly now.

'It's open,' a faint voice responds.

As Elaine opens the screen door and steps inside she can barely see Theresa on the couch because the blinds are closed. She's never seen the blinds closed – Theresa is a fan of letting in the light, even if it means her neighbours from across the street can look into her sitting room.

'Theresa?' she says, almost whispering, because the darkness suggests it.

'Yes. Hi.' The shape on the couch shifts. 'Elaine.' Theresa's voice sounds off – weak and thin.

'Can I turn on the light?' Elaine says.

'Um . . . okay.'

Theresa moves slowly to sit upright. With the light on Elaine can see that she's not a good colour – in fact, she looks almost yellow.

Elaine last saw her four days ago when she popped over briefly; they've been talking on the phone since and Theresa hasn't mentioned feeling unwell. Marie and Leanne haven't seen her for a few days either. They've all been calling, though – they talk about it each morning before the swim.

'Theresa, what's wrong?' Elaine says, moving quickly to sit next to her.

'Oh, I'm . . .' Theresa trails off and looks towards the window. 'Why are the blinds down?'

'I don't know.' Elaine puts a hand to Theresa's forehead – years of raising children have made this action an instinct. If her children looked the wrong colour, it was the first thing she'd do. 'You're hot,' she says. 'How long have you been feeling unwell?'

Theresa looks confused. 'A couple of days.' She frowns. 'Where are the children?'

'In the back garden.'

Elaine tries to stay calm but she can't help feeling a flicker of panic. Theresa isn't careless with her children, even if she's appeared carefree. She always knows where they are.

'Oh.' Theresa licks her lips.

'Do you need some water?'

Elaine goes to the kitchen without waiting for a response. She fills a glass and brings it to Theresa, who sips a little and puts it down.

'I feel a bit sick,' she says.

'I'd say you *are* a bit sick.' Elaine keeps her voice as light as possible. 'Where's your nonna?'

Theresa frowns. 'I think she's here,' she says slowly.

'I'll check,' Elaine says with false brightness.

She doesn't want to believe that the other adult in the house hasn't noticed that Theresa is clearly unwell, so there must be something wrong with Nonna too. Through the screen door of the granny flat Elaine can hear a radio and smell cigarette smoke.

'Nonna?' she calls.

'Who is it?'

'It's Elaine, Theresa's friend. We've met before.'

'Lainey!' Oliver cries as he rushes up to her. 'What are you doing here?'

'I've come to see your mum,' she says.

The screen door opens and Nonna stands there, looking a little more wizened than the last time Elaine saw her.

'Yes?' she draws out.

'Oliver, how about you and Sasha put all that dirt you've dug up back into the garden?' Elaine says, patting his shoulder.

'Okay.' He grins before racing off. 'Saaa-shhhha, Lainey says we need to put it all baack!'

Elaine turns to Nonna and folds her arms, wanting to contain her rising tide of worry. 'Theresa's not well,' she says.

Nonna stares at her and Elaine sees a glimpse of the tyrannical poker player Theresa has described. 'I know. She has the cancer.'

'No, I mean she's not well *today*. She's listless, she has a temperature – she's not herself.'

'What is *listless*?' Nonna sniffs.

'She's . . . she's . . .' Elaine didn't reckon on being a dictionary. 'She's not focusing, she can't remember where the children are – where you are.'

'I thought she just tired. She don't make breakfast so I make it.' Nonna shrugged. 'I don't mind.'

'She didn't get like this quickly,' Elaine says. 'How long has she been so unlike herself?'

It's the best indication Elaine can think of that something is profoundly wrong. She's seen infections develop before – and she suspects that's what this is. She saw it in Henry, when he had an ear infection that raged too far and ended with him in hospital. While an infection can escalate at speed, the infected person usually shows some symptoms before that point. Elaine has still never forgiven herself for missing the signs in Henry so she knows she should be more gentle with Nonna, except she doesn't feel gentle.

'Maybe one day. Maybe two.' Nonna's eyebrow twitches. 'I noticed. I did not want to . . . what is it? Make a big fuss.'

Elaine wants to laugh from dismay, because she understands too well: it's the story of her life, to not make a big fuss. She is sure Theresa doesn't make big fusses either, nor Marie or Leanne. They're all so well trained. They're women. Nothing that happens to them is a big fuss, the subtext being that they're not important enough to have big fusses. They exist to take care of other people's big fusses. And what's most mortifying is that this lifetime of what amounts to submission to others' needs before their own has, Elaine is sure, led to Theresa being in this situation today. Theresa has likely been feeling ghastly for a while, but when it began she would have told herself she couldn't make a fuss about it – not even to her or Marie or Leanne. Now Theresa is past the point of worrying about that, but if she'd only said something sooner she wouldn't be so sick.

At what point, Elaine thinks, does the relentless rampage of an illness become so great that you're prepared to overthrow years of believing you're not important enough to worry about your health? It was the same story with the lump: Theresa noticed it weeks before she told Elaine, but was too busy looking after the children and everyone else to make herself a priority.

Today, however, Elaine is going to make her the priority.

'I think she needs to see a doctor,' she says to Nonna. 'Can you please watch the children?'

'As long as they are not naughty.' Nonna glares in their direction.

'I'm afraid you'll have to regardless of how naughty they are.' Elaine smiles as politely as she can but she has no time for nonsense.

Nonna's glare falters. 'Is she really sick?'

This time Elaine tries a reassuring smile instead. No sense causing unproductive amounts of worry. 'I think she's sick enough to see a doctor.'

She isn't going to say that the first doctor she plans to consult is James, but that's only because the main person she doesn't want to worry is Theresa. No sense packing her off to the hospital without checking first.

Elaine walks back into the sitting room and dials the number for James's rooms while Theresa lies unmoving on the couch.

'Mr Schaeffer's office,' says a voice Elaine knows well.

'Hello, Barbara, it's Elaine.'

'Elaine, hello.'

'Is he in?'

'He's with a patient,' Barbara says, as Elaine expected.

'I really need to speak with him. It's fairly urgent.'

As that's not a word Elaine is prone to using, she hopes it has the intended effect.

'Putting you through,' Barbara says, then there are seconds of silence in which Elaine glances over to see that Theresa still has her eyes closed.

'Darling,' James says and Elaine feels the relief of knowing someone else is going to help her make decisions.

'Hello. I'm sorry to bother you but I'm at my friend Theresa's house.' She takes a quick breath, aware that she's starting to panic and trying not to. 'She's not a good colour. Remember I told you she had surgery recently – a mastectomy? Then some lymph nodes removed a week or so ago. She's been fine – getting back to normal, I thought. I saw her four days ago. Spoke to her two days ago. Now she's hot to the touch and seems to just want to sleep.'

There is silence for a few seconds and Elaine knows James

will be formulating the right answer. He is careful, bordering on cautious, when it comes to giving advice.

'Have you checked the wound site?' he says.

'No. Shall I?'

'Actually, don't. Just take her to Casualty, right away.'

He sounds calm and she wishes she could match it, but that's not the instruction she was expecting.

'What do you think it is?' she says.

'I'd rather not say. Can you get her to the hospital?'

'Yes. We'll go now.'

'Call me when you get there. I'll come and meet you if I can.'

'All right. Thank you.'

The line goes dead and Elaine knows that James will be back with his patient. Which isn't to say he doesn't care, but she's the one here, in this moment, with a responsibility to her friend.

Her next call is to Marie, who says she will meet Elaine at the house and help her put Theresa into the car.

Then Elaine sits by Theresa, taking her hot hand and stroking it. 'Theresa?' she says softly.

'Mm.' Theresa moves her mouth as if she's trying to swallow.

'We need to go to the hospital.'

Elaine feels the sting of new tears as she watches the lack of reaction from Theresa. How sick she must be – how far from herself – to not even register what Elaine has said. But Elaine's tears are useless; she has to take charge, and be competent, and steadfast. All the things she once believed herself to be. All the things she can be.

She can hear the children in the back garden while she waits for Marie to arrive. It's only then that she wonders if she should try to find Andrew. As little regard as Elaine has for him, Theresa is going to be in hospital for a while and he should know.

But Elaine doesn't have time for him now, just as he hasn't had time for his wife and children. If only he'd been paying attention – if only they all had – Theresa wouldn't be in this situation.

CHAPTER 56

When Leanne pokes her head into Theresa's hospital room she expects to see her friend sitting up, bright-eyed, the way she always looks. Instead she finds her lying down with an IV in each arm, her skin a strange greyish-white colour and her hair matted. Theresa's eyes are closed and for that Leanne is grateful, because it gives her time to rearrange her face so she doesn't look so shocked.

Leanne feels guilty for not knowing her friend was in trouble. They all rely on Theresa to jolly them along, and when she couldn't they didn't stop to wonder why. *She* didn't wonder why. She hasn't been to visit Theresa since before her last operation because Theresa's parents were staying with her and Leanne didn't want to intrude. That's the excuse she's been giving herself, but the truth is that she didn't want to have to make small talk with strangers. She let her own neuroses prevent her from checking on her friend and for that she can't quite forgive herself.

Elaine told her it was bad. She missed yesterday's swim and turned up this morning, explaining that she's helping Nonna look after Oliver and Sasha so that's why she missed the day before. Explaining that Theresa is very sick and in hospital again.

'She's septic,' Elaine said simply, and Leanne knew what that meant.

Leanne caught the expression on Marie's face as she looked back at Elaine: fear.

'How did she get it?' Leanne asked.

Anything can happen with wounds, she knows, but Theresa hasn't seemed more unwell than she should have been after the surgery.

'Her surgical wound became infected and she mustn't have noticed that it was spreading,' Elaine explained. 'She's been on painkillers. They might have masked the symptoms. That's what James . . .' Elaine stopped and glanced away, looking stricken.

'I should have checked on her earlier,' Marie said.

'We've all been talking to her,' Elaine said. 'She didn't say anything. She didn't sound any different – I mean, she hasn't been sounding like herself anyway.'

'What happens now?' Leanne said.

'Ideally they cut out the infected flesh, but because it's so close to her mastectomy site they're . . .' Elaine's exhalation was ragged. 'They're not doing it. Yet. They have her on antibiotics.'

'Is she improving?' Marie asked.

'I don't know. I've been focused on the children.'

'Isn't – isn't Andrew taking care of them?' Leanne said, feeling like it was the least contribution she could make to this conversation. She knew why Elaine and Marie didn't tell her yesterday: she was at work, unable to help them with anything. For the first time, she resented her job.

Marie turned towards her with an expression of slight amusement. 'Well, he might if he seemed to think it was important. But either he doesn't want to believe Theresa is that sick or he doesn't think he can take the time off, because he seems to think her grandmother can do it all.'

'I think Theresa's parents will take over, though,' Elaine continued. 'I spoke to her mother last night and they're coming back today.'

After they swam – slower than usual, and slower to leave the beach too – Leanne decided she'd visit Theresa after work. At lunchtime she took a jar to the beach and scooped up some sea water. It was the only thing she could think of to give Theresa that might mean something more than flowers would.

If it's guilt that brought Leanne here, it's concern that takes her to Theresa's bedside, holding the jar of water with both hands as if it's the most precious thing she owns.

Theresa's eyelids flutter open.

'Hi,' Leanne says softly.

Theresa half smiles. 'Leanne,' she says croakily.

'Hi,' Leanne repeats, finding it hard to think of the right words.

There is an intimacy in visiting someone in hospital – implicit in the visit is the acknowledgement that the person is weak and vulnerable. There is no pretending that everything is fine. Trite phrases, expressions that are familiar yet mean nothing, are emptier than usual. 'How are you?' has no purpose here. For Leanne, who has taken refuge behind social niceties, who has ducked and weaved out of intimacy's way for most of her adult life by replying 'Very well, thank you' each time she is asked how she is, who uses 'please' and 'thank you' like protection spells so that no one looks any closer, being here with Theresa is a test – and one she has no right to be worried about. She's here because Theresa created their friendship by inviting Leanne to come closer. Theresa wasn't afraid of knowing her better; she has never minded if someone's answer is not 'Very well, thank you'. So Leanne cannot mind now.

'I brought you some water,' she says, putting the jar on the bedside table, 'from our end of the beach. I thought . . .' She looks at the jar and feels slightly foolish for imagining this could be any kind of gift. But it's here now and she needs to explain it. 'I thought if you can't get to the beach, I could bring it to you.' She shrugs casually. 'It's a bit silly,' she says, feeling silly herself.

'No,' Theresa says, pushing herself up a little. 'It's lovely.' Her words are slow, deliberate. 'So thoughtful.'

They sit looking at each other, and Leanne searches for the light that is usually in Theresa's eyes. She can't find it.

'How long do you have to be here?' she asks.

Theresa smiles, and it looks like it takes an effort. 'As long as they decide it's necessary.'

'Are you in pain?'

'No. I'm just . . . whacked.' Theresa's eyelids half close. 'I never knew I could feel this tired.'

'I won't stay long,' Leanne says. She should have considered that Theresa might not want visitors.

Theresa shakes her head. 'No, you're fine. It's really nice for me to have a visitor. I'm so bored of my own company.' She closes her eyes again for a few seconds, then half opens them. 'Marie told me . . .' She licks her lips. 'That she saw you. With your parents.' A smile appears and disappears. 'And Matt.'

'She did, but we don't need to talk about that. You have other things to think about.'

'What if I want to talk about it?' The smile stays this time. 'I'm missing out on the gossip.'

Leanne nods. 'Not so much gossip, really.'

'So . . .' Theresa swallows slowly. 'How was it?'

'It was strange, but good. Comforting, in a way.'

Theresa looks at her encouragingly.

'We talked about the hospital,' Leanne goes on. 'My parents asked lots of questions. That was the strange bit. They don't know . . .' She stops, trying to recall all the details of that day, wanting to tell Theresa a good story. 'There's a lot they didn't know because we haven't seen each other. They asked Matt a lot of questions too.'

'And what happens next?' Theresa prompts.

There's a noise at the door and they both look towards it.

'Sorry, I'm, um, I'm interrupting.'

It's a man Leanne has never seen before. He's tall and slightly overweight. His hair is shaggy, his skin is half sunburnt and his eyes are bloodshot.

Leanne turns to Theresa for guidance and sees her tense.

'Andrew,' Theresa says flatly. She catches Leanne's eye but it's impossible to tell if she wants her husband there or not.

'I should go,' Leanne says, because she can see Andrew is irritated by her presence.

'No, you shouldn't,' Theresa says with more force than Leanne has heard from her so far. Her face is hard now; Leanne has never seen it like this.

'The, uh, the kids want to see you,' Andrew says.

Theresa looks furious. 'Why are they with you?'

'Your mum told me . . .' He scratches behind his ear. 'She said I couldn't leave them with Nonna or your friends.'

A flash of something resembling anger comes Leanne's way.

Theresa's eyelids flutter closed for a few seconds. 'They do need their father. Despite what you think.'

Leanne wishes there was another exit to the room, because she thinks if Theresa was in her right mind she wouldn't want anyone to witness this.

'Look, do ya want to see them or not?' Andrew says.

'You didn't bring them here?' Theresa says, glowering.

'They're in the car.'

'Jesus, Andrew.' Theresa slumps back against the pillows.

'I'll go to them,' Leanne says. She turns to Andrew, who is frowning at her. 'I'm Leanne. I swim with Theresa. Sasha and Oliver know me.'

'Right,' he says, still frowning.

'What does the car look like?'

'It's a Falcon. Station wagon. Red.' His face relaxes.

Leanne turns back to Theresa. 'I'll take them for a walk while you two talk.'

It sounds like a directive, and she means it to. She's not going to bring them to Theresa's bed, because no children should see their mother with drips in her arms. They wouldn't understand it and the scene would, no doubt, upset them. She will do the only thing that makes sense and keep them away.

'You've got twenty minutes,' she says to Andrew before giving Theresa a quick kiss on the cheek. She's never kissed her before so it's no wonder Theresa looks surprised.

'I'll be back,' Leanne says, and almost runs from the room, leaving the complication of Theresa's marriage behind, heading for the much more straightforward business of looking after her children.

CHAPTER 57

'So you're managing to stay off the booze?' Marie asks as Elaine puts on her indicator. Left up this street, then right, right again and they'll be at Theresa's house.

'Mm,' Elaine says, not really wanting to have the conversation but appreciative that Marie is prepared to talk about the subject. Not everyone wants to address the hard things.

'That doesn't sound confident.'

'I haven't had a drink since that relapse I told you about.'

'But . . . you've been thinking about it.'

'Yes. I have,' Elaine says grimly. 'I know I shouldn't.'

'Of course you should,' Marie says. 'That's why it's so hard giving it up – as previously discussed. I'm not an alcoholic, but my understanding is that you're going to be thinking about it for a long time. Maybe for the rest of your life.'

'That can't be true!' Elaine says, aghast even though she knows it is.

She doesn't want to have these thoughts forever. She needs to free her mind to contemplate other things. Better things. Which is proving impossible with Theresa so sick, and it's occurred to her more than once that thinking about gin is a reflexive distraction, the way actually drinking it used to be. So maybe the thoughts are useful: she doesn't need to drink because simply thinking about it is having a similar effect. Or maybe that, too, is a self-deception and she's stuck in a pattern that will, as Marie suggests, go on for the rest of her life.

'Well, you'll find out,' Marie says, not unkindly.

There's silence as Elaine makes the last turn.

'How about Leanne?' Marie adds. 'They say still waters run deep – she's the living example.'

'Yes,' Elaine says. 'It's wonderful that her life is coming together. At last. She's had a difficult time.'

She turns the engine off and looks to the house.

'Yes, she has,' Marie murmurs. 'She's been brave, our little Leanne. She has more courage than I do.'

'I don't believe that,' Elaine says as she opens the screen door.

Three sharp raps of the knocker bring a man to the front door. Andrew, they presume, because it was Andrew who answered the phone when Elaine rang to see if Nonna needed anything. He said he'd moved back in. For now.

'Oh,' Elaine had said. 'May I ask why?'

'Mum told me I had to. She said Nonna's too old to look after the kids.'

Elaine couldn't help feeling irritated that it took his mother's admonishment to get him to do anything. But she kept it to herself. It's good for the children to have their father around. No matter how indifferent he might be to them – or seem to be – he's their only other parent.

'G'day,' Andrew says now, holding the door open to let them in. 'Thanks for comin'.'

His eyes are bleary – whether from lack of sleep or over-consumption of beer, Elaine doesn't know.

'Where are the children?' asks Marie.

Andrew scratches his head. 'Nonna's taken them to the park.'

'Is she up to that?' Elaine has never seen Nonna walk a longer distance than the path from her granny flat to the kitchen.

He shrugs. 'She suggested it. Can I get you anything?'

'No, thank you,' says Marie. 'We're just here to see how you are.'

'Shithouse,' he says. 'How do ya reckon?'

Elaine flinches. She's not used to men swearing in front of her; it's another characteristic of this country she has to learn to accommodate.

'Have you been to the hospital today?' Marie asks him.

'Nuh.' He folds his arms across his chest. 'The kids want to come with me and Theresa doesn't want to see them.'

'That can't be true,' Elaine says, then realises it sounds as if she doubts him, and that's not what she came here to express.

Andrew looks momentarily upset. 'She, uh . . . she doesn't want *them* to see her. Yeah. That's what I meant. With all the tubes and everythin'.'

Elaine thinks of the way Theresa looked yesterday: like she was fading to the point of disappearing into the white hospital sheets. The light that has always been so bright in her seems to have dimmed to the point of being extinguished, and Elaine didn't mind admitting to Marie that she's scared of what that means.

James has spoken of how the difference between someone living and dying can so often be an element that doctors can't see or describe. 'It's the will to live,' he said. 'You can have two patients with the same life-threatening problem and all the factors that you think will influence the outcome – weight, age, general health, whether or not they smoke – don't have as much of an impact as the will to live.'

When Elaine met Theresa she thought she had the biggest life force of anyone; now she wonders if there has been a cost. If being so bright and capacious for everyone else has diminished

Theresa so greatly that she doesn't have the reserves to draw on to come back from a shock to the system like this. Or that she may not want to. Theresa adores her children, she loves her parents and her grandmother. But all that love goes out, and Elaine isn't sure it comes back in sufficient quantities to make up for the deficit.

It's the first time she's thought that being a little reserved, the way she is, the way Leanne is – even the way Marie can be – might have benefits she hadn't reckoned on. She worries that if the mastectomy didn't get it all, if Theresa still has cancer and all that follows that diagnosis, she may not have the strength to make it through if she doesn't learn to pull back from being herself.

There is pure selfishness in this concern, because Elaine loves Theresa as she is. She wants her to always be the same, just as she wants Marie and Leanne to be – and she knows that, in return, they feel that way about her. To be accepted like this, to know that there are three other people who have arrived at the same place, who have decided to be her friend just as she has decided to be theirs, has been perhaps the greatest act of grace in her life. So unexpected, so beautiful, and so rare.

'Andrew, what have you told the children?' Marie says with a softness to her voice that Elaine hasn't heard before.

His forehead wrinkles. 'Not much. Just that their mum's sick but she'll get better again.'

As Marie glances her way, Elaine can see the same fear she has, and she feels as if her guts are turning themselves inside out. If Marie, who has seen more of life than she has, is worried about Theresa, that means they can't tell themselves lies about what happens next, and they can't encourage Andrew to stay in the dark either.

'You know,' Marie starts, 'that this infection has weakened her. A lot.'

Andrew looks as if he has no idea what she's saying. 'So?' he replies, almost resentfully. 'She'll be all right.'

'They haven't said what's in her lymph nodes yet, have they?' Elaine asks.

He shakes his head slowly. 'They want to wait until she's better. To talk about treatment.'

Another glance from Marie, and Elaine knows she understands what that means: there is something sinister inside their friend, and a long road ahead. And because Andrew is still her husband, he is her next of kin and will be in the position to make decisions about it if she can't.

'Andrew, everything has to change,' Marie says evenly. 'Your business, the way this household runs . . . it can't go on the way it was. Not for the foreseeable future. Theresa is going to need care.'

'Someone has to pay the mortgage!' he says with an edge, but it's weak. 'It's still my house too.'

'We understand that. But someone also has to get these children to school and wash their clothes and make their dinner. Theresa is not going to be capable for a long time. Nonna can't do it.'

'So what are you saying? That I give up the garage and go on the dole just so I can pick the kids up from school? I'm not gonna do that.' His eyes flash.

'No, Andrew,' Elaine says as calmly as she can. She and Marie are there to help but they can't if he keeps fighting them. 'Marie and I are prepared to do a lot of that work for you. Leanne wants to but she has a full-time job.' She looks at Marie, who nods encouragingly. 'We have the time and we want to do it. What we don't want to do is force ourselves on you. But we don't think you can manage on your own.'

He juts out his chin then looks at his feet. 'I'm not a charity case,' he mutters.

'For goodness' sake, stop being so pig-headed,' Marie remonstrates. 'Your wife's in trouble. No one's offering *charity*, Andrew, we're offering *housework*. There's a difference.'

Elaine wants to smile, because she quite likes seeing Marie riled up.

Andrew sniffs a couple of times then shoves his hands in his pockets as he looks up. Elaine sees the outline of the face he used to have and understands how he might have appealed to Theresa. He was good-looking once; perhaps he was good too. She'll never know.

'What does she tell you about me?' he says, still defiant.

'Not much,' says Marie. 'Because from what I understand you're not here very often, so there's not much to tell.'

'That's because she doesn't want me here,' he says. 'Does she tell you that too?'

Marie sighs and Elaine knows why: neither of them wants to get involved in Theresa's marriage more than they need to. However, they have to defend their friend.

'That's not true, Andrew,' Elaine says. 'But we're not going into it now.'

'None of this had to happen if she just loved me like she used to,' he says, quick as a flash and hard.

Marie raises her eyebrows. 'I didn't love my husband the way I used to, either, after we had our daughter and all the other concerns that come with being a family. That's how marriage works.'

'Yeah, well, I still love her the way I used to,' he says, so softly it's almost inaudible.

They stand in silence, and Elaine feels the impossibility of responding to what he's said. He still loves his wife but he chooses to protest the way their lives have changed by not being around her, which leads her to think he doesn't love her, and she responds accordingly.

It is a miracle, Elaine thinks – a large one, not a small, domestic one – that she and James have never arrived at this point. Perhaps there's nothing either of them has done to achieve it, or deserve it.

'Will you let us help you, Andrew?' Marie says after a time. 'We want to.'

He sniffs again and pushes his hands deeper into his jeans pockets. 'Yeah, okay.'

Elaine wishes she could feel more relieved, but the reason they're here isn't one they ever wanted. They'll make the best of it, though. She and Marie will work out their days between them and ensure the children are looked after. And when Theresa comes home they'll figure that out too.

'Thank you,' Marie says. 'We'll be in touch.'

As they leave she gives Andrew a quick kiss on the cheek, so Elaine does the same. He looks surprised, but says nothing as they go.

CHAPTER 58

It took Theresa a while to ask to be moved to the bed nearest the window. She wanted to see trees and sky and a glimpse of the harbour. It's not the ocean side of Shelly Bay, where she swam all those mornings; where she found so much happiness, even if it only lasted while she was in the water. Happiness, and tired muscles. That was the story of her swimming.

She still has these drips attached to her, but from the little she can hear of the nurses' conversations, what's in the drips isn't helping her as much as it should. Not that they will tell her that. Apparently the deal with medical treatment is that the patient is kept in the dark up to, during and after procedures. She's been jabbed at by random people taking blood samples; other people have stuck warfarin needles in her abdomen so she doesn't develop blood clots, leaving a colourful bruise display; nurses check the chart at the end of her bed and disinterestedly measure her blood pressure. Not a single one of these strangers asks her how she is. If they did, she'd tell them she's bewildered, and overwhelmed, and scared. She feels like her insides have melted, her wound is still throbbing, and they haven't told her if they're going to take her back into surgery to fix it.

Leanne came to visit last night. That was a bright spot. And Marie and Elaine have called. She hasn't seen Andrew for a while.

She hasn't seen the children in days. It was her decision, because she doesn't want to scare them, but she regrets it now. She misses them. She misses Sasha's fluffy hair and Oliver's eyes full of sparkle. Sometimes she closes her eyes so she can daydream about them. Her precious babies.

She tries to take a breath. Breathing has been getting harder, but she can't seem to convince the nurses of that. They tell her that she's tired. And that's true, she is. Although tiredness is too meagre a description for what feels like nothing she has ever known. She carried two humans inside her and that didn't feel as alien as what is happening to her now.

None of the nurses has mentioned something that's been bothering her for a day or so: she feels like she's swelling. Her skin is tight. If she pushes a finger into her forearm – which takes some effort, but she does it – the dent stays for a while. That's not normal. But she has a lot of time to think, and worry. Maybe she's making this worse than it is. All of these signs could be normal for what she has.

It feels hard though. To stay alive. She's been here for days now – she's lost track of how many. Visitors come and go, but she already sees how they leave her and slip back into their lives. She's a blip; an errand to run.

It's not that she doesn't think she's loved – she knows she is. She can see it in the eyes of her parents, of her friends.

There is something else she knows, though: they would be all right without her. Even Sasha and Oliver would be all right. She is more important to them than to anyone else, but they would continue to grow and learn. They would be loved too.

So she's been thinking it may not be so bad. In fact, it may be easier. If she were to simply step off this planet and go into the universe, that would be the easiest thing of all. For all that time she spent in church as a child, she doesn't believe it's God waiting for her. But she's pretty sure this big, beautiful universe with all its stars and planets and moons and rocks is going to look after her. Sometimes she feels its pull. Like now, when it's so hard to take a breath.

Her next breath might be the hardest. She just doesn't know.

'Theresa?'

There's a feeling on her shoulder . . . someone's hand, perhaps. Whoever it is, they're pushing her. But she can't see because the light outside the window is bright and she's closed her eyes against it.

'Theresa? Theresa, it's Leanne.'

She thinks of that first day she met Marie. From that point on, swimming didn't seem like a chore, something she was suffering through in order to get in shape. It became the highlight of each day.

She smiles to herself, even though it hurts. Everything hurts her now.

Better to think of more pleasant times. If she concentrates she can conjure the feeling of the foam against her legs. That first shock of cold, because the ocean in Shelly Bay is never as warm as you want it to be. She's dreamt of going to Queensland for a holiday because the water is warmer there. To the tropics, where it's like a bath. Or so she's heard.

Now there's a hand on her wrist. It feels cool. Or maybe she's warm. The nurses were talking about her temperature this morning. She didn't catch whether it was good or bad.

'Theresa, can you open your eyes?'

When she waded in at Main Beach she would make it quick. Some people like a slow adjustment to the temperature but that was never her style. Rip off that band-aid, she liked to say. Head under, full immersion, and gasp if you have to. It never took long to adjust. Especially once she started moving.

She tries to remember the fish she would see swimming off Little Beach. What colour were they?

'I need some help in here! Sister! *Sister! Now!*'

There's Marie, ahead of her. Always ahead of her. So fit and fast.

Elaine's passing her. She really does like Elaine. It took a while to get to know her but it was worth it.

And Leanne, close behind. She's worked so hard to keep up with them. To achieve something. It's admirable.

They're all women she loves, and she knows they love her in return. It's been enough to get her through some days, and she knows what Marie would say: it never ends. Love is eternal, just like the good book says.

Theresa believes it.

CHAPTER 59

'Oliver, take your sister's hand, please.' Marie watches as Oliver and Sasha walk slowly down the steps onto the sand, Sasha a step behind her impatient brother. 'Stop there, please, while we wait for the others.'

She turns around to see Elaine and Leanne carrying towels and bottles of soft drink: Leanne with her efficient walk and precise steps, and Elaine with her more loping stride. They are talking to each other but they're still too far away for her to hear what they're discussing.

Gus will walk down the hill from Marie's home in a little while. 'Let them have some time with the three of you first,' he said.

The sun is behind them in the western sky, still an hour or so from setting. Marie loves the waning light. These last few evenings she's been making a point of watching it. Delaying the time when she goes inside and sits with her thoughts. Then goes to bed with those same thoughts and barely sleeps. The last few nights she's had an hour, maybe, or two.

Gus has been staying with her and she's envied his heavy slumber. He's been caring of her in the mornings, bringing her breakfast in bed. She doesn't know if Elaine and Leanne have anyone doing that for them, but she knows they, too, are having sleepless nights. She can see it on their faces each morning. Leanne, especially, looks haunted.

It was such a scare for Leanne when she found Theresa like that. She's tried to tell them what she felt – they've encouraged her to – but she loses her words each time. She gets as far as, 'I just went down to see her on my lunch break.' Then the story skips to where Theresa is in intensive care.

For a few days they didn't know if they'd get to keep her. If they could hold her here on earth and never let her go. They weren't able to see her. One visitor at a time, they were told, and her parents had priority. So they called to check. And Leanne used her connections to find out what she could.

It was only two days ago that they allowed Theresa back on the ward. It's been many more days than that since her children have seen her. Marie doesn't mind, not for a second, taking care of them as often as she can.

She and Elaine and Leanne are still swimming; of course they are. They're all awake in the early hours anyway. And swimming gives them purpose now in a way it never has before. In the past it was for fitness, and the fun of seeing each other. Now it's a chance to be together and understand each other so well that they don't have to speak, while knowing that if they do speak they're safe among friends. True friends. Because they're still shocked. On some level they may always be. Their friend, their beloved friend, almost slipped away from them while they were watching. Nothing feels safe now. Everything is unstable. Yet never has it all been so sure. Nothing matters, and everything does. In almost losing their friend they have all found their purpose, and it is to let love guide them. To say 'I love you' to those they love; to receive it joyfully. If they thought Theresa was a gift before, they are convinced of it now. If only they could tell her in person.

In good time.

Meanwhile, they are focusing on her children. Initially Andrew resisted but a few days ago he was more agreeable.

'I'm not trying to be their grandmother,' Marie said when he consented to her taking them that day. 'I know they have two of those. But I've spent a bit of time with them and I miss them.'

'Right. Okay,' he said.

'I'll pick them up at nine,' she said, before he could change his mind. 'I presume you're in the house?'

'Yeah.'

'You're welcome to come too, Andrew. You and Nonna.'

'Nah, it's all right,' he said. There was silence for a few moments. 'Reckon I should have some time alone with Nonna. She's a bit cut up about the whole thing.'

We all are, Marie wanted to say. Instead she told him that was a good idea.

This afternoon when she picked up the children, with Elaine driving, she promised Andrew she'd give them dinner and have them home by seven. He nodded, then kissed each child goodbye on the top of their heads. Marie was pleased to see the children didn't seem too different to their normal selves as they fought over who got to sit on which side of the car.

As Elaine and Leanne reach her, Marie takes a towel and a bottle of drink from them.

'Shall we set up over there?' She nods towards the boat ramp next to the surf club. 'Or more out here in the middle?'

'I like the middle,' Leanne says. 'We get a better view of the ocean.'

They find a spot amongst the people still soaking up the last hours of Sunday. No matter the season, there are always people on this beach.

'Kids, over here,' Elaine calls as Sasha and Oliver reach the water's edge.

They run squealing as a wave comes in and froths around their ankles.

'They're going to get wet,' Marie says, smiling.

'They should,' says Elaine. 'They're kids.'

'Your mum does that sometimes,' Marie tells Oliver and Sasha as they approach. 'If the water's cold, she'll make a face and laugh.'

Oliver squints into the setting sun as he turns to her. 'But she likes swimming?' he asks.

'She does.' Marie pats a spot next to her on the towel. 'Come and sit here and I'll tell you all about it. Sasha, you take my other side.'

'I'll go and get the fish and chips,' Leanne offers.

'I'll come with you.' Elaine smiles but Marie can see the strain in it. She's seen that strain in her own mirror.

'Ollie likes lots of salt on his chips, don't you?' Marie says. 'Lots and lots.'

Oliver looks aghast. 'No, I don't!'

'Oh, it must be Sasha who likes it.'

'Noooo!' Sasha shakes her head so hard her hair flies around.

'Guess it's no one then.' Marie shrugs. 'Just normal chips for us.'

Leanne and Elaine walk slowly in the direction of the shops, their heads turned to look at the water. They probably don't even realise they're doing it, Marie thinks. It happens, though, after you've been swimming for a while – you unconsciously check the waves and see how big they are, how constant. You start to chart your path out the back. Theresa once told her that she wishes she had gills, and Marie understands completely. She has the same desire herself. To be able to swim indefinitely, to see more of the world underwater – that would be worth more than riches.

'Did you know that your mum's got caught in dumpers a few times?' she says to the children.

'What are dumpers?' Oliver asks.

'They're waves that pick you up and toss you all around. Not like normal waves that you can bodysurf on. See, like that man is doing.'

They watch as the man's head bobs out of the white wash, then he gets to his feet in the shallows.

'How do you know which one is a dumper?' Oliver looks serious.

'They curl over at the top. So if you're looking at a wave as it's coming towards you, watch the top and see what it does.'

'Huh?' He frowns.

'How about I show you one day?' Marie says. 'We'll have a bodysurfing lesson.'

'Okay,' he says in the way children do: agreeing without really understanding what they're agreeing to.

'Now, why don't you tell me about school,' she says to Sasha. 'Is your teacher being nice?'

Marie listens as the children fill her in about their teachers, about the new boy in third class who is taller than all the other boys and meaner too. About the books they were allowed to take home from the library, and how Dad forgot to dress them in their sports uniform on Wednesday.

Leanne and Elaine come walking across the sand, each carrying fish and chips in one hand and their shoes in the other. Marie checks her watch: Gus should be here soon.

The light is softening further and the seagulls are getting louder, competing for the last scraps of the day. On the other side of Shelly Bay the tourists will be boarding the ferry that will take them back to the city. Patrons will be sipping beer in the pub as the shops nearby start to close for the day. Everything is the same as it ever was, Marie thinks, even when it's not.

Another wave rolls in. And another. As they always will, for eternity. No two the same. Her whole life, she has seen God's design in the waves, and the sky, and the earth. Through her greatest sadnesses, she has always trusted in God's will.

She's been tested these last few days, though, and has been mad at herself. She should hold her friend closer. She should tell her that she is loved more than she knows. Gestures are all well and good, but there is no substitute for saying the words that every single human being longs to hear: *You are loved, Theresa. I love you. Elaine loves you. Leanne loves you.*

She will say it soon, though; as soon as she can, as soon as Theresa is allowed visitors. For now, though, she will offer it to the water and let it roll back in with each wave, over and over, here on the beach that has come to mean so much to them all.

'Whoa! Look at that wave, Marie!' Oliver says as a dumper crashes to the shore.

'That was a big one,' she says.

As the children continue to chatter away she puts her hands on their shoulders and looks out to sea. To the place she loves, where she'll be tomorrow morning, with her friends. They will swim to Little Beach and back, and they'll do it every day. She doesn't know how long this time will last. She doesn't know what her life holds. It is profoundly clear now that none of them can rely on anything. She is, however, sure about this: once summer arrives, Theresa will be strong again. Marie will make her be.

The four of them will get in the water, even if all Theresa can do is float on her back. Marie will float with her. So will Elaine. So will Leanne. Then the next day they'll get her to float a bit further. The day after, maybe dog paddle. Bit by bit. That's how she'll get better. That's how they all will.

SUMMER 1984

CHAPTER 60

'Y ou ready?' Marie holds out her hand.

'Can you tell?' Theresa says, looking down at her chest as she takes Marie's hand. 'That it's fake?'

Leanne and Elaine watch with amusement. Leanne is tempted to rub her eyes to check that it really is Theresa standing there in a swimming costume, whole if not entirely hearty.

Marie rolls her eyes. 'Only if I'm really staring at your chest. And you're an attractive woman, Theresa, but I have no interest in looking at your breasts.'

Theresa grimaces. 'I don't feel too attractive. I look like a stringy hag. But I guess Andrew got what he wanted.'

'How do you mean?' Marie frowns.

'He said I was fat. Needed to lose some weight. Ta-da!' She giggles.

Theresa lost a lot of weight during those nightmare days in hospital and hasn't put it back on. So she doesn't look like herself, especially as she also lost some of her hair because of the trauma. Those bouncy brown locks will come back, though; Leanne has seen it before.

'He's left, by the way,' Theresa says, and Leanne can see how hard she's gripping Marie's hand.

'What?' says Elaine. 'After everything?'

'All that "everything" is why I'm happy he's gone,' Theresa says, taking a step into the water. 'Nonna was annoyed all the time and he was shirty with her. Whenever Mum and Dad stayed they got on each other's nerves. It was making the kids upset.'

'I'm sorry that happened,' Elaine says with an expression of regret.

Theresa throws up her free hand. 'It was never going to be a fairytale ending. Seeing me sick wasn't going to make him behave better. He saw me cut in half to get Sasha out and it barely bothered him.' Her face clouds. 'I should have left then.'

'So he's . . . ?' Elaine prompts.

'Back with his parents. Or with his girlfriend.'

'Don't tell me she's still around!' Marie cries.

'I honestly don't know and I don't care.' Theresa takes another tentative step. 'I have other things to care about.'

She doesn't look at any of them and they know why: she's out of the woods, but not the forest. There was no cancer in the other lymph nodes that were taken months ago, but her doctors gave her no assurances that there wouldn't be at some stage. She needs to be vigilant.

They will be vigilant with her, Leanne thinks, even if they drive her mad.

'Elaine, could you take her other hand?' Marie asks.

'Sure.' Elaine reaches out.

'Lee, why don't you take Elaine's hand. Safety in numbers.'

Leanne complies, although she knows it's nothing to do with numbers. Marie just doesn't want her to feel left out.

'Right, ladies, heads up. Take a good look at that amazing sunrise.' Marie gestures with her chin.

Theresa sighs contentedly. 'I can't believe I'm back here.'

'We can,' says Elaine. 'We weren't giving up on you.'

For a second Theresa looks as though she's going to falter. 'No, you didn't give up on me,' she says. 'I'll never forget it.'

'As I've said before, it was a team effort,' Elaine says briskly. 'I just happened to be there at a critical point.' She pauses. 'No pun intended.'

Theresa smiles.

'Besides, I was just the start of the chain.' Elaine nods towards Leanne. 'This one was the end. The lucky end.'

That moment – that luck – visits Leanne at odd times of the day. She sees Theresa lying in the bed. She feels time slowing down. She remembers telling herself to not panic. To think of Theresa as a patient, not as her friend. To make decisions as she would for a patient.

'Why were you even there?' Theresa asked her the first time they were able to speak alone, once she was past the worst. 'You'd just visited me the night before.'

Leanne didn't have a good answer. The truth is, she had a feeling. A hunch. An intuition. She was on her way to the canteen for lunch when something made her deviate towards Theresa's room. The thought popped into her head, that she had to go to Theresa immediately, and she obeyed it. She hasn't always obeyed those sorts of thoughts, and has always regretted it when she hasn't. That day, she wasn't going to take the risk.

She hasn't told Theresa that, though, because she's superstitious about it. If Leanne says what really happened it might all unravel. There's no proof that it won't, only her sense that everything is too fragile to be taken for granted. So the answer she gave Theresa was an element of the truth, if not the whole: 'I wanted to see you,' she said.

Now she is able to see Theresa again every morning, because while Theresa isn't ready to swim yet, she's pledged to be there at the beach every day.

'Do you want to go all the way in?' Marie asks. 'Or are you worried the falsie will escape?'

Theresa blows air out of her mouth. 'Only one way to find out!'

They hold steady as they walk in, all keeping an eye on the waves that are strong, if small, and breaking close to shore.

'Let's go a bit further,' Theresa instructs, and soon they're up to their waists, then chests, then they let go of each other's hands and push off the bottom so their legs rise into a float.

'Ah, this is the life,' Theresa says.

'Sure is,' Marie responds.

Leanne giggles as Elaine bumps into her.

'Sorry!' says Elaine as she rights herself. 'It's hard to float when there's a swell.'

Leanne, too, stops floating, and she and Elaine watch as a wave breaks on top of Theresa, who shrieks and disappears.

She emerges with her hair plastered across her face, laughing.

'All right, sunshine, that's enough for you for today,' Marie says.

Still laughing, Theresa nods her agreement. 'Okay. But it was fun.'

As they walk back towards the sand, Theresa stops. 'Wait a second! We can't go!'

'Why not?' says Elaine.

'I've lost my falsie!'

Marie's incredulous expression says it all. 'On your *first swim*?'

'Quick!' Theresa says, looking around her, patting the water. 'We have to find it before it floats away!'

The women turn in circles but there's too much movement in the water to see anything.

'Oh, love,' says Marie. 'I think it's gone.'

Theresa grins and pulls out something from the side of her costume. 'Got you!' she says, brandishing the falsie aloft before sticking it back into place.

Marie and Elaine roll their eyes.

'Good Lord,' says Elaine. 'Please do *not* try that again.'

'How did you manage that?' Leanne asks.

'I took my chance under that wave.' Theresa sashays through the shallows and swings her arms from side to side. 'Ladies,' she says, turning around to face them, 'it is bloody amazing to be alive.' Her face lights up. 'And I like it even better with you three along for the ride.'

'So do we, love,' says Marie, taking the hand Theresa offers as they climb up the steep portion of the hard sand.

They are slow to reach for their towels as they watch the day break over the surf.

Marie's head jerks in the direction of the surf club. 'Oh no – Trev incoming.'

'Shall we adjourn to the promenade?' says Elaine.

'Even better – to my place,' says Marie. 'Gus made some Anzac biscuits. He's taken over my recipe.'

'Sounds good,' says Theresa, and the friends hustle their way towards the steps and onto the footpath, chattering away.

At the top of the steps Leanne turns to look back at the beach. She sees Trev gazing after them longingly, and a jogger going past him on the sand, and a father and son heading for the water hand in hand. She knows she'll be back tomorrow, but she wants to take it all in today.

Today is all she has; and tomorrow will be another today, as will the day after, and she will cherish them all.

QUESTIONS FOR DISCUSSION

1. The Shelly Bay ladies are brought together by a sporting activity. Has sport or exercise been a way for you to meet friends? Is it the best way to unite people who are of different ages and stages in life?

2. What are the difficulties of making new friends when you're an adult? What most tends to stop you from becoming friends with someone you'd like to befriend? Perhaps it's the fear of rejection, or even the difficulty of arranging to meet someone in amongst all the demands of life.

3. Have you ever gone on a 'health kick' like Theresa and had it change your life, for good or bad?

4. Elaine has left behind her life in England, and her grown-up children, because her husband wanted to move home to Australia. Although this might not be something women in 2019 are prepared to do, in the 1980s it would have been scandalous if she hadn't. Have you ever had to give up something you love for someone you love? Would you move countries for someone you love?

5. Not unlike Elaine, Theresa is putting up with things she doesn't like for someone she loves – in her case, she has a husband who treats her badly but she has her children

and her grandmother to think of, so she wants to keep the household intact. Do you think she puts up with too much?

6. Leanne is estranged from her parents. Do you think there's ever a good reason to not talk to your parents, or should children always forgive their parents?

7. Marie finds love again later in life. Would you – or have you – done this or do you think it's all too much hassle?

8. Theresa's nonna is an important part of her life – have you ever had an older relative living with you? If so, was it a positive or negative experience?

9. Marie's life is carried out mostly within the boundaries of Shelly Bay. If the place where you live provides you with almost everything you need, do you think there's a reason to leave it?

10. Elaine didn't want to admit to herself that she was an alcoholic. Do you think she was wrong to wait so long to start asking for help and going to meetings?

11. Leanne closed herself off from other people as a way of protecting herself. Do you believe that is a valid thing to do, or does it only create more problems?

12. Women can spend large parts of their lives at what feels like the mercy of their bodies, through menstrual cycles, pregnancies and menopause; there are also many ways in which women's bodies start to feel as if they are the property of others, whether it's children or partners or society in general. Sport, exercise or movement can be a way to re-engage with the body, and to find out what it's capable of in a way that does not involve others. Have you ever found a physical activity that has helped you connect with your body after a period of disconnection?

ACKNOWLEDGEMENTS

Thank you to Rebecca Saunders and Fiona Hazard, the publishers of this book, for taking such good care of it.

Thank you to my literary agent, Melanie Ostell, for being a kind listener and a great reader.

Thank you to Sarah Brooks for carrying the ladies of Shelly Bay beyond Australian waters; to Abby Parsons and Cath Burke at Sphere, and to Andy Hine and the Little, Brown UK rights team.

At Hachette Australia, thanks to Vanessa Radnidge, Louise Sherwin-Stark, Justin Ractliffe, Daniel Pilkington, Anna Egelstaff, Ella Chapman and, actually, everyone else!

I have been so fortunate to work with Karen Ward as the editor of this book and of *Fairvale*. Oceans of gratitude to Celine Kelly for her editorial eye, and to Nicola O'Shea and to Fiona Daniels for theirs.

Books have been a central part of my life because my parents, Robbie and David, ensured they would be. Eternal love and gratitude to them and to my brother, Nicholas.

Love and thanks to Jen Bradley, Isabelle Benton, Chris Kunz, Ashleigh Barton, Amelia Rowe, Neralyn and Col Porter, Richard and Robbie Hille, Kate Farquharson, Katie and Brian Sampson, Jill Wunderlich and Marg Cruikshank for their interest and support.

The inspiration and teaching provided by Shiva Rea keep my creative fire alight.

This book has a long lineage that includes *Home and Away* and *All Saints* – two masterclasses in Australian storytelling. It also includes Australian country music artists such as Fanny Lumsden, Harmony James, Brad Butcher, Beccy Cole, The McClymonts, Lachlan Bryan, Lyn Bowtell, Felicity Urquhart and Kasey Chambers, who open their hearts and shape their songs to bring joy and meaning to their audiences.

And to all the readers, including readers of *Fairvale* who sent me tweets and messages, or who spoke to me at events – thank you so much for spending time with my stories.

Ring 12/10/20

The Lost Letters of William Woolf

Praise for *The Lost Letters of William Woolf*

'A quirky, enjoyable novel about communication, relationships and love' *Woman & Home*

'The Must-Read' *Irish Tatler*

'A strong debut. Cullen's great strength is the way she writes so movingly about how day-to-day life can chip away at a once-solid relationship until it crumbles' *Belfast Telegraph*

'An effortlessly assured debut about how finding a lost letter and a twist of fate can make you question whether the love of your life is really meant for you after all . . .' Rick O'Shea, *RTE Broadcaster*

'What a brilliant book. I couldn't put it down' Larry Gogan, *RTE Broadcaster*

'Once in a while a book comes along that captures your heart, and this one charmed me from the first page . . . An enchanting and bittersweet exploration of what love really means' Maria Dickenson, Managing Director, Dubray Books

'*The Lost Letters of William Woolf* is an entertaining and enriching novel that is capable of inducing in the reader acute apprehensions of the complexities of our inner lives, and of the inner lives of others. Entertaining and enriching' *The National*

'A strong debut . . . Helen Cullen writes movingly about how day-to-day life can chip away at a solid relationship' *The Herald*

ABOUT THE AUTHOR

Helen Cullen is an Irish writer living in London. *The Lost Letters of William Woolf* is her debut novel.

The Lost Letters of
William Woolf

HELEN CULLEN

PENGUIN BOOKS

PENGUIN BOOKS

UK | USA | Canada | Ireland | Australia
India | New Zealand | South Africa

...nies

Set in 12.5/14.5 pt Bembo Book MT Std
Typeset by Jouve (UK), Milton Keynes
Printed and bound in Great Britain by Clays Ltd, Elcograf S.p.A.

A CIP catalogue record for this book is available from the British Library

ISBN: 978-1-405-93495-4

www.greenpenguin.co.uk

MIX
Paper from
responsible sources
FSC® C018179

Penguin Random House is committed to a
sustainable future for our business, our readers
and our planet. This book is made from Forest
Stewardship Council® certified paper.

Dedicated to Demian Wieland

'More than kisses, letters mingle souls'
                                    – John Donne

I.

Lost letters have only one hope for survival. If they are caught between two worlds, with an unclear destination and no address of sender, the lucky ones are redirected to the Dead Letters Depot in East London for a final chance of redemption. Inside the damp-rising walls of a converted tea factory, letter detectives spend their days solving mysteries. Missing postcodes, illegible handwriting, rain-smudged ink, lost address labels, torn packages, forgotten street names: they are all culprits in the occurrence of missed birthdays, unknown test results, bruised hearts, unaccepted invitations, silenced confessions, unpaid bills and unanswered prayers. Instead of longed-for missives, disappointment floods post boxes from Land's End to Dunnet Head. Hope fades a little more every day, when doorbells don't chime and doormats don't thud.

William Woolf had worked as a letter detective for eleven years. He was one of an army of thirty, having inherited his position from his beloved uncle, Archie. Almost every Friday throughout William's childhood, Archie, clad in a lime-green leather jacket, rode his yellow Honda Dream 305 over for tea, eager to share fish and chips doused in salt and vinegar served with a garlic dip, and tales of the treasures rescued that day. Listening to Archie opened William's mind to the myriad extraordinary stories that were unfolding every day in the lives of ordinary people. In a blue-lined copybook, he wrote his favourites and unwittingly began what would become a lifelong obsession with storytelling, domestic mysteries and the secrets strangers nurse. What surprised William most when he started working there himself was how little Archie had exaggerated. People send the strangest paraphernalia through the post: incomprehensible and indefensible, sentimental and valuable, erotic and bizarre, alive and expired. In fact, it was the dead animals that so frequently found their way to this inner sanctum of the postal system that had inspired the Dead Letters Depot's name. A photo taken in 1937, the year it had opened, showed the original postmaster, Mr Frank Oliphant, holding a pheasant and hare aloft, with three rabbits stretched out on the table before him. By the time William joined in 1979, it was a much more irregular occurrence, of course, but the name still endured. He still felt Archie's presence amid the exposed red-brick walls of the depot, and some of the older detectives sometimes called William by his uncle's name. Their physical similarities were striking: muddy brown curls, chestnut beards flecked with rust, the almond-shaped hazel eyes that flickered between shades of emerald green and cocoa, the bump in the nose of all Woolf men.

In a vault of football-field proportions hidden below Shoreditch High Street, row upon row of the peculiar flotsam and jetsam of life awaited salvation: pre-war toy soldiers, vinyl records, military memorabilia, astrology charts, paintings, pounds and pennies, wigs, musical instruments, fireworks, soap, cough mixture, uniforms, fur coats, boxes of buttons, chocolates, photo albums, porcelain teacups and saucers, teddy bears, medical samples, seedlings, weapons, lingerie, fossils, dentures, feathers, gardening tools, books, books, books. Copious myths and legends passed from one colleague to another; stories of the once lost but now found.

Each detective cultivated their own private collection of the most remarkable discoveries they had made. For William, there was a suit of armour dismantled in a tarnished silver sea-chest, an ebony-and-glass case housing two red admiral butterflies, each wing secured by a tiny pearl pin, and a miniature grandfather clock only three feet tall. 'More of a grandson clock, really,' he always joked.

There were still some deeply unpleasant discoveries to be made. The detectives harboured daily fears of strange stenches, soggy parcels and departed creatures; mostly, white mice, cockroaches and bugs originally destined to feed pet lizards, snakes and rats. At least William hoped that's what they had originally been intended for, before they met another, equally unpleasant end in 'The Furnace', the final destination for contaminated goods, the unrecyclable and unsalvageable. It sat shoulder to shoulder with the gnashing, monster shredder where lost letters became dead letters and all hope was vanquished.

Every day, the detectives opened letter after letter, parcel after parcel, searching for clues. The satisfaction of solving a mystery never faded. The joy of knowing that something so anticipated could find its way after a lengthy

3

diversion remained exquisite. It was the thousands of unsolvable conundrums that wearied bones and wasted skin on paper cuts. Sometimes, there just wasn't enough evidence to trace, no clue to worry over until the blessed eureka moment. Over the years, William had learned not to fret over the truly lost, to let them go and to invest his time instead in those that presented greater hope of a solution. Every week, hundreds of new puzzles arrived, so the mountain of mail in the depot seemed self-replenishing. A pessimist could find much to confirm a bleak worldview in this museum of missed messages. Only a quarter of the post that passed through the depot ever found its way home, but just one very special victory could sustain a detective for weeks in their endeavours.

William had recently reunited a battered Milk Tray chocolate box brimful of wedding photos from 1944 with the bride, Delilah Broccoli. The son of her maid of honour had found them when executing his mother's estate and tried to post the box back to the last known address, but the street, never mind the individual house, no longer existed. When items discovered lost in the post held considerable monetary or sentimental value, or had been missing in action for an exceptionally long time, the letter detectives would courier them to their rightful home rather than send them off into the cavernous postal system once again. A still-breathing tortoise, a crystal chandelier and a silver pendant hanging from a garland of rubies were among some of the undeliverables William had elevated to his personal care. In some very exceptional cases, the letter detectives went one step further and delivered items in person, out of fear that something so precious may become lost once again. On this most recent occasion, William had successfully traced Delilah to the nursing home in East Anglia where she now lived and decided this should be one of those exceptions.

When William entered Delilah's bedroom, she looked confused as she tried to place him. 'We haven't met before, Mrs Broccoli,' he reassured her. 'I work for the post office, and wanted to deliver a parcel to you that went astray.'

He moved a pink plastic cup of water from the table-top tray that lay on her lap and placed the world-weary chocolate box before her. It was the same shade of purple as her dressing gown; velvet with a white lace collar. Delilah's eyes flitted from William's to the box and back again. She tried to speak, but the words caught in a raspy net in her throat. Her silver curls were flattened on the right side of her head from where they were crushed against the pillow. He moved closer and laid his hand gently on her arm.

'It's all right, nothing to be frightened of. Here, let me help you.'

He prised the lid from the chocolate box and placed the crinkled photographs before her one by one. Delilah traced a finger beneath the row of sepia and a look of recognition spread across her face. She picked up one with a trembling hand and held it close to her nose. William watched as a shy smile illuminated her expression and her eyes grew misty.

'I'll leave you in peace now, Mrs Broccoli,' he said.

She reached out and grabbed his sleeve with her

papery grip and held on tight for a second. It was days like those that kept his faith alive.

Lately, William had retreated more and more into the soft silence of the post delivery room, away from the chatter and bustle of the shared office space where the letter detectives worked. He had never been very good at rising above his moods and found it increasingly hard to shake off the melancholia he brought from home in order to join in the collegiate banter. In the solitude of the delivery room, he rummaged deep into postbags, a shirtsleeve rolled up to his pointy elbow, to extract what he hoped would be something special. Each time, he closed his eyes and forced his breath to grow slow and deep. His ribcage expanded like the bellows of old, his lungs paused at their fullest expansion, before he slowly exhaled, with a gentle whoosh. He hunched over the slate-grey canvas bag, with his left hand supporting the small of his back, and wriggled the fingers of his right hand inside. His thirty-seven years didn't command this posture; it was more an affectation that had evolved as part of his hunting regime. With great concentration, he would linger over the folds of the envelopes, squeeze parcels tentatively between forefinger and thumb, until, instinctively, he would clasp one, tugging it gently free and drawing it to the surface. He imagined he was like the mechanical arm of a teddy-bear machine, retrieving a soft toy. These rescue missions were different from the piles of post left indiscriminately on his desk every morning at six by the night-owl team who accepted the midnight deliveries. The letters that he found this way, he believed were destined for him. Over ten years of flirting with coincidence, defying the odds and witnessing serendipity had left him superstitious and more inclined to believe in a divine intervention he would have mocked in his days before the depot. He now was convinced that some letters found him because only he, with his particular personal collection of experiences and insights, could crack their code. Other letters depended upon different detectives, of that he was sure, but some were searching specifically for him.

Last Tuesday, Marjorie, the longest-standing member of his team, had crept up behind him as he indulged in this ritual. He turned and saw her standing there, in her coral-pink mohair polo-neck, multiple gold chains dangling, her hand on her hip. The twinkle of a tease glinted in her eyes. The shock caused him to drop the letter he had retrieved and he felt a blush spread from under his collar and burn through his beard. With no explanation of his furtive activity to offer, he just nudged his black, square-rimmed spectacles further on to the bridge of his nose, mumbled a noise somewhere between a hello, a throat clear and a cough, and brushed past. Her satisfied laugh followed him to the cloakroom, where he rested his forehead against the cool dampness of the mirror and willed his cherry cheeks to fade. His bowel twisted and churned. Why had her see-ing his routine bothered him so much? How deeply embarrassed he felt that his secret-self behaviour had been witnessed; actions he performed for himself that had never been intended for an audience. His mortification slowly gave way to irritation. Why had she been creeping about, anyway? No decent person wears shoes that whisper.

William risked a long look in the mirror. His curls looked tangled and his beard needed trimming. Something about his eyes made him nervous. They seemed, well, less brown. Like faded chocolate. It was probably just the fluorescent light bulbs. Eyes don't fade, do they? Was he vanishing? A man diluted? He shrugged his navy-blue pullover into position and braved the sorting office. Stifled giggles followed him as he took his seat at the end of the old boardroom table. He liked to sit with his back to the wall with the window overlooking the street to the right, mysteries lined up in rows to his left. His seat was the furthest away from the furnace trolleys, too. He hated the cremations. Failure in every spoonful of ash.

The faint strains of an old jazz number floated up from the street. It swirled out from one of the heaving hot spots that left William so cold. He could almost place the song, but it danced just beyond his consciousness as he tried to ignore the taunt. Was it 'Old Devil Moon'? He drifted away from the cardboard box of blue fountain pens he had opened, soon to be returned to a warehouse in Leeds as per the enclosed invoice, and tuned into the melody. He closed his eyes and followed his wife, Clare, down the spiral staircase to the jazz club of their first date, the Blue Rooms, on Montgomery Row in Notting Hill. He remembered how his hand had been slippery on the rail, his corduroy blazer too restrictive, his throat dry and knees shaky as he watched her stamp down the stone steps in her white fur boots. Her blonde hair was tied up messily in a yellow silk scarf that looked to be tickling the back of her neck. His fingers itched to do the same. He ached to pull that silky knot loose and watch her hair tumble about her shoulders.

All during the evening, he couldn't quite believe that he was there with Clare in a romantic capacity. Was she just filling in time with him while awaiting a more deserving suitor to woo her? Could she possibly also harbour hopes of something more than friendship?

They had met in very platonic circumstances, when William attempted to organize a book club on their university campus to tackle some of the great literary tomes. Week one: *War and Peace*. No one came. Week two: *The Divine Comedy*. Once again, he was a lonely soul in the Daffodil Room of the library, which he had so enthusiastically reserved; he had even asked the librarian to bring in some extra chairs. *Ulysses* was to be his third and final attempt, and he waited with dwindling hope for some like-minded folk to help him fill that echoing room. When the door creaked open, he was flustered by the vision that floated towards him. Clare, bundled up in a crimson duffel coat and white denim dungarees, looked more modern-day fairy tale than first-year student. Blonde tendrils escaped from an untidy bun held in place on top of her head with green chopsticks. Her left shoulder sagged under the strain of a canary-yellow canvas bag crammed full of books. When she dropped it on the mahogany desk, the contents spilled across the polished surface: *The Female Eunuch*, *Mother Courage and Her Children*, *Persuasion*, sunflower seeds, colouring pencils, a battered and bruised burgundy leather address book and a sepia postcard of James Joyce completely covered in tiny

9

cursive handwriting. For ever after, William would always feel a certain gratitude to Joyce, not just for writing the books he loved so much but for bringing this woman into his life. Her words tumbled out in accompaniment to her belongings as she scanned the empty room.

'Are you William? Am I in the right place? Where is everyone else?'

'Eh, yes, I am, and I've been asking myself that for a few weeks now, but it's just me, I'm afraid. And you – you are?'

'Clare. Clare Carpenter.' She pulled a ratty, striped mitten off her hand and reached out to shake his. 'Do two people make a group?'

'A very exclusive one, perhaps. Or, at the very least, a conversation. That is, if you'd still like to stay?'

Clare slid into the seat opposite him, the legs of her chair screeching violently on the marble floor. His nose twitched at a faint smell of cinnamon.

'Why not?' she answered. 'At least we won't have to compete to get a word in.'

William steeled his nerve to hold her gaze.

'Gosh, your eyes are two different colours. Like David Bowie. How bizarre!' He hesitated for a moment. 'How lovely.'

Clare looked away as she gathered together the contents of her bag. 'It's not as uncommon as you might think. Let's begin, shall we?'

Discussion of *Ulysses* evolved to talk of books in general and favourites in particular. Over the following weeks, Clare introduced William to Iris Murdoch, Edna

O'Brien and Jane Austen; he shared his passion for Albert Camus and Samuel Beckett. Dissecting the worldview of the characters allowed them to delve into subjects that otherwise would have been too emotive for a casual acquaintance.

'Would Virginia Woolf have surrendered her writing for a peaceful mind? I don't know if I would smooth out all my edges at the expense of what she found in those corners.'

'The reason women love Mr Darcy so much is that he changed for the love of a good woman. How many lives have been wasted in the hope of that very outcome to a futile situation?'

'What Jack Kerouac gives me is a licence to be discriminatory about how I spend my time, who I spend it with, not surrendering to small talk and sycophants who need us to reflect and reinforce each other so that we can all feel we're okay. It sounds harsh, but it's true: I'd rather be alone than pretend.'

The sanctuary of the Daffodil Room was soon replaced by cluttered coffee shops and the little alehouse off campus which their professors monopolized. They baked cheese scones and experimented with cooking Indian food, making pizza and mixing mojitos at home. They cheered along the drama society's faltering theatre programme and volunteered at a homeless shelter, dishing out hot soup and self-conscious smiles on the last Thursday of every month. Sometimes, William saw Clare linking arms with other men as they crossed campus between lectures or sat clinking glasses in The Lighthouse pub. He tried to curb his jealousy by reassuring himself that their friendship was different, closer, but he didn't know if that was true. He craved to know her passionate self – whether she dabbed perfume behind her ears or smudged on red lipstick when she heard him at the door – but that part of her eluded him. In the beginning, they left notes in each other's lockers to confirm dates and times to meet, but soon their deposits had expanded to include little jokes, mix-tapes or snippets from newspapers, and William became prone to copying out passages from his favourite poems for her. What he had not yet discovered was how Clare secreted away each one, pressing and smoothing them carefully under the plastic sheaths of an army-green-cloth-covered photo album embroidered with yellow roses. It became a written record of their courtship as it delicately evolved. She gave it to him as his wedding present: the story of them so far, with blank pages left over for them to continue.

William cast his mind back to the afternoon when they had taken their first tentative steps to what would become a shared life. It was autumn. A westerly wind scattered crisping leaves around their feet and stirred a profound change within William. He could not endure one more minute of this constant low-level anxiety about their friendship, nor bear to sustain his neutrality for another second. As he sat on the floor of his bedsit, helping Clare to sand down a rocking chair she had dragged home from a flea market with the intention of painting it duck-egg blue, the urge to speak bubbled up inside him with increasing force. They had been working in silence for twenty minutes when he abruptly stood up and started folding his sandpaper into an awkward square.

'Clare, there's something I have to ask you.'

She looked up from where she sat; her legs stretched on either side of the rocker in a perfect triangle, black-and-white striped socks peeking out from inside the hem of her tartan flares.

'Uh-oh. This sounds ominous. Should I be worried?'

'I hope not.' William's eyes danced across her face, lingering on her own before they darted away at the critical moment. 'I was just wondering, could I, perhaps, take you out on Saturday night?'

Clare coiled her hair into a braid that curled around her throat and watched him fidget in his too-shiny brown leather brogues. Earlier, she had teased him that they looked like they were fashioned out of conkers. She pushed a bruise on her forearm.

'What are you talking about? We go out all the time. We've spent every Saturday night together for the last six weeks.'

William sighed. 'Not on our own we haven't.'

He cursed himself for not considering in advance what to say, but the words had just burst from him like air from an over-inflated balloon. Clare jumped up and punched him playfully on the arm, a huge grin on her face.

'William Woolf, are you asking me out on a date?'

He stood tall, shoulders back, with his hands clasped behind him as if he were appealing to a jury in court.

'Yes, indeed! That's exactly what I am doing and, if you don't want to, well, I guess I'll live down the mortification in about eight to ten years, but I would be grateful if you saved me the pain of having to avoid you for that length of time. I really don't want to have to drop out of uni, or move to Alaska, or start wearing disguises to avoid you. All in all, I think it would be much easier for us both if you just agreed.'

He made a little bow at the end of his speech and a flop of brown curls tumbled across his forehead. She reached forward to brush them back behind his ear and said, 'Well, when you put it like that, it does rather appear so. Hypothetically speaking, if I were to say yes, where would we go?'

'I haven't quite worked that out yet, but does that mean you're coming? Stop smirking – you're torturing me.'

'Well, I'll think about it and –'

'Oh, I see. Well, I appear to have misinterpreted things here,' he interrupted, his face crestfallen. 'I'll carry this home for you so you can be on your way.'

He struggled to pick up the rocking chair in a bear hug and began wrestling it towards the door. Clare's guffaw followed him and intercepted his flustered flee. He turned towards her and she helped him lower the chair to the floor.

'Of course I'll come, you fool. You wait four months to raise the question and then expect an immediate acceptance! You're not very good at this, are you?' She sighed and sat back down on the floor with fresh sandpaper in her hand. 'Maybe that's a good thing,' she said.

And so William had followed a yellow silk scarf down the wrought-iron staircase of a smoky jazz club, wondering if a kiss waited in the air between them. They sat in the smallest booth, tucked away in an alcove. Clare drew circles in the threadbare blue velvet of the banquette with her finger and tucked one bare leg beneath her. William reshaped the melting wax of the candle into odd little figurines and nudged closer to her. Over rum cocktails they could not afford, and bowls of olives they stole from other tables, stories saved for night-time were told. They shared confessions in the shadowy candlelight: tales of childhood, secret dreams of the future, the little worries they carried like pebbles in their pockets.

'I don't need to know where you came from to know you had a happy childhood, William. I have a sixth sense now for children of my ilk; I can see it in their eyes, but yours have no shadows at all.'

'In all honesty, I'm terrified that I'll end up a mediocre man who never had the nerve to turn his dreams into something real. I don't want to become an English teacher bashing teenagers over the head with books they don't care about. I want to write my own, one that will set their brains and hearts on fire!'

'I've never wanted to get married and I hate the thought of a wedding; parading my dysfunctional family in front of my friends while I waddle along in a big white dress. I really can't imagine anything worse. Could you see yourself doing it?'

Not long after midnight, they ascended the stairs from the basement back out into the city night. This time, Clare led William by the hand. It had started to snow. He spun her in a circle, a light, white dust sprinkling down on them. Clare wrenched a red-and-white polka-dot umbrella from her denim rucksack and released it above their heads.

'There are,' she said, 'few things more romantic than a shared umbrella.'

He kissed the top of her head and whispered, 'I can think of one.'

Their first kiss chased away any lingering doubts he had about her feelings for him. When they arrived back at William's, he unpacked a Super-8 camera from a compact charcoal leather suitcase under his single bed. They stood on the front steps of the Georgian house where he rented the basement flat and filmed the snowflakes dancing in the moonlight. Clare lay in the garden in her crimson duffel coat and fanned her legs and arms to make an angel. William captured it all on film; it was a silent movie he often returned to in the years to come as he settled down to sleep. He remembered drying her legs in his only good towel, the orange one with a giraffe in the centre, which had been airing on the radiator. He rubbed life back into them as she hummed along with David Bowie singing 'Wild as the Wind' on the radio. It was much too early to tell Clare how much he loved her, but Bowie sang the words for him. It was easy to believe they were the only two people listening to John Peel that evening and that he had chosen the song just for them.

William sat in the depot and ran that film through his mind once more but, these days, the actors felt like strangers. His wife's hair was brown now, rather than blonde. And much shorter. She had stopped dying it when she started her work experience at the solicitor's. Nobody takes a pretty blonde barrister seriously, apparently, and definitely not one with silk scarves in her hair. It wasn't just their physical selves that had changed, though, that part was easily understood; what confused him was trying to identify when their feelings had altered. Was it a million little incremental changes over a long period of time? Or something obvious he had missed? If their essential selves were still the same, couldn't they find each other again? Or had they travelled too far down separate roads to reconnect in a different but happier place? The music swarmed over him like a misty fog rolling in from the Atlantic Ocean, and he luxuriated in it. The past felt more friend to him, now, than the present.

Marjorie snapped William to attention for the second time that day; she clinked a silver spoon with a peach-coloured plastic handle against the side of his Charlie Chaplin mug. 'Yoo-hoo, William! Time for elevenses! It's your turn to do the honours.' He touched his lips with his fingers. Were these the same ones Clare had kissed? Had he really pulled that sliver of silk free? He rose and carried his mug to the kitchen, where he guiltily stirred two spoonfuls of sugar into a fresh cup. Sugar was banned in his home and William had made a ludicrous promise to stop taking it in tea altogether. Now, the refuge of a milky, sugary mugful was tainted by Clare's cross voice, but he couldn't resist the sweetness. When had he lost the will to argue over sugar? The right to surrender to tooth decay, false highs or type-two diabetes of his own free will had been robbed from him. Why admit defeat on this point when they had slammed doors over so many other things: moving the driver's seat in the car back and forth; whose turn it was to wash up; what the answering-machine message would say; where to spend Christmas; whether to go on holiday and, if so, where; temperature control; volume control; affection control?

So many power struggles, but the sugar ban could not be contested. Each grain was a thread Clare longed to pull. One pinch led to his self-indulgence, another to his alleged Peter Pan syndrome, a third to his lack of ambition. It would leave him open to questions concerning his lack of responsibility and her unhappiness with their lot. William had become acutely aware of the triggers. He walked blindly into so many kitchen catastrophes that their early life together had not prepared him for: finishing the leftovers, not finishing the leftovers, buying a rose for her from a market stall, not posting her mother's birthday present, admitting he was thinking about re-forming his old band, the Bleeding Hearts, with Stevie.

The very thought of William cavorting about the country with Stevie and his misfit collective caused a muscle in Clare's temple to throb visibly. At university, she had possessed a greater level of tolerance for their antics and peculiar brand of glam-folk, but her enthusiasm waned when advancing years did nothing to deter Stevie from his flamboyant misadventures in self-destruction. William looked back on their 'Toilet Tour' triumphs with a bittersweet nostalgia that sometimes overwhelmed him. He missed the swagger by association of playing keyboards for Stevie; the confidence and confidants; the potential for calamity and hilarity erupting at any moment. He pined for the nights when Clare had swayed in front of the stage, arms bedecked in dozens of silver bangles that twinkled in the light, purple leg-warmers sliding towards her ankles as she danced. Whenever he looked out at the audience, she always caught his eye, and he felt himself grow taller by her witness.

These days, the only moments of unpredictability in

his life came within the walls of the depot. At home, he felt like a frightened rabbit, constantly sniffing the air for an ill wind. Clare was a queen of entrapment, but some traps the rabbit saw glinting miles away. The sugar was a dare he would not challenge. He wasn't trained for this heart-to-heart combat and was desperate to avoid any more injury. William nursed his contraband and tuned back into the conversation that was circling around him.

'I just think,' said Marjorie, 'that valentines only matter if they arrive by the fourteenth. A couple of weeks could be the difference between 'appily ever after and takin' out a personal ad. There'll be a lot of soggy pillows an' sulky silences if some of this lot don't make it.' Her left hand, stained with orange fake tan, nails painted metallic pink, formed a right angle with her hip.

Mr Ned Flanagan, the Dead Letters Depot director, opened and closed the kitchen cupboards with increasing speed.

'That's all well and good, Miss Clarke, but there are just as many other undeliverables we need to get through that are far more important than Sarah in the sixth form telling some pimply *footie* player that she is *up for it*, or what have you. We cannot simply ignore everything else and prioritize love affairs over all the other, more important, business of the world. There could be –'

Marjorie cut him off as he removed his glasses to polish them in a peach linen handkerchief.

'Well, with all due respect, sir, it's clear you ain't ever been in love. Nothin'll slow down the business of the world like broken 'earts. We 'ave to help Cupid do his job. That's *our* part to play.'

'More like we must help Stupid! I'll have you know, Mrs Flanagan and I have enjoyed a love-filled marriage for over thirty-five years now. If you don't love someone enough to remember their post code, it doesn't look too good, from where I'm standing. Billy, what do you think?'

Mr Flanagan rapped his knuckles on the counter-top to get William's attention. He was the only person who called him Billy.

'William, sir. It's William.'

'Yes, Yes, William, Billy, Willy – it's all the same. Now, what do you think about this idea to move everyone on to valentines duty?'

William scratched his fingers through his beard. 'As much as I share Marjorie's soft spot for a love story,' he said, 'I think everything should be dealt with by normal procedure, and the valentines just have to join the back of the queue. Otherwise, it's not fair on the others.'

In truth, however, William was not sure he was in the right frame of mind to be facilitating love's young dream, not when his own great love story was being stretched so thin. A thought struck him: if he and Clare completely dissolved, did that mean she wasn't his great love, after all? He shook the question away as he watched Ned's back retreat.

'There you are, Miss Clarke,' he called over his shoulder. 'The voice of reason. Good man, Billy. Now, go team!'

Mr Flanagan had recently attended a seminar on Staff

Motivation and Morale, with, at best, mixed results. He thrust a self-conscious fist into the air in lacklustre victory and skipped out of the room, away from Marjorie's look of blatant contempt. William splashed the dregs of his drink into the sink and ran after him, catching him on the stairs.

'Mr Flanagan, I was just wondering if you've had a chance yet to read my presentation on the Supernaturals? If you think it's worth developing, I'd love to get started.'

'Yes, Billy, I gave it a glance. First of all, I don't think God can really be considered a supernatural being.'

William shuffled a little on the step, pausing before he spoke again. 'I see. Well, I just meant it as a collective term for those addressees that don't exist in reality. We could try something else. Maybe "Mythical Creatures" or "The Others"?'

Mr Flanagan raised his eyebrows and leaned in a little closer. 'So you think God is a *mythical* creature, Billy?'

'I don't really think anything at all about him, sir. What we name them isn't really the point. It's more what we do with them.'

Of all the fascinating worlds opened to William by the Dead Letters Depot, the Supernatural Division (as he thought of it) intrigued him the most. On the fourth floor, rows of mail sacks were lined up in metal-framed structures like flip-top bins. At the front of each row, a laminated sign in bold moss-green capitals was taped to the floor to identify each category: GOD, SANTA, SCIENCE FICTION, SAINTS & PROPHETS,

TV/FILM CHARACTERS, LITERARY FIGURES, STARS and OTHER. It was true that much of the mail in the depot was intended for flesh-and-blood people who walked the earth. It was the degree of magic that people must believe in for *the other* types of mail to be delivered, however, that forced the fourth floor to adopt a supernatural element for William. An uncanny number of people all over the country took pen to paper and wrote to idols, icons and ideas: Elvis, the Tooth Fairy, Yoda, St Anthony. These messages in a bottle, trails of bread left in the forest, obsessed William. Who were these true believers and how long did they wait for a reply? Was the writing more important than the response? Did the writers tell anyone that they had written these letters? Were they relieved or saddened that their unanswered prayers had fallen on deaf ears?

For some time, William had wanted to create a volume of these missives for public record. He felt there was a cast of thousands currently speaking into the void but who deserved to be heard. Other letter detectives had their own obsessions: Trevor had sought his job purely to fuel his philately; Morgana had a collection of questionably private photographs that everyone pretended didn't exist; Roger diligently worked on translations from foreign languages; Dolores was determined to reunite manuscripts, books of poetry or short stories with their scribes; and for Marjorie, it was, of course, love letters and, in particular, valentines. The Supernatural Division was William's great obsession and what inspired the stories of his imagination.

There was already a Seasonal Santa Unit, commissioned every December to answer all the children who wrote to Father Christmas and helpfully included their addresses. The staff tried to personalize the letters a little so as not to dispel belief, should the children compare with each other. Fan mail to stars of stage and screen was sent to production companies or agents. Missives to deceased celebrities were despatched to next of kin, their fan club or the manager of the estate. It was the letters to God, to mythics and mystics, to the *other*, that haunted William and formed the basis of his work. He had started collecting his favourites in the filing cabinets that lined the echoing Supernatural Division. He painstakingly typed out those he wanted to include in the volume and took photographs of the original documents. In his mind's eye, he saw the two laid side by side on glossy, ivory pages within hard covers, the book entitled 'A Volume of Lost Letters'.

Mr Flanagan peered over his spectacles at William. 'The truth of it is, Billy, we shouldn't really be opening those letters. You know very well it is illegal to open any mail unless we believe that there is some chance we can forward it on to its ultimate destination. If a letter is addressed to God, what do you think you are going to learn from the contents about the intended address? It seems a bit dubious to me, if I'm truthful.'

'Some of the letters we have here are over fifty years old,' replied William. 'Nobody is going to lodge a complaint, and I think people would get a lot out of being able to read them. They're cultural artefacts, really.' William stopped his left foot tapping on the marble step when he saw Mr Flanagan peering at his mustard polka-dot socks.

'I admire your enthusiasm, Billy, but I just think it's terribly unfair on those people who believe they really *are* writing to God. If they discover in your book a whole edition of other people's letters and understand that the only recipient was one of us, what will that do to their morale?'

'Maybe they'll just be pleased to know that someone is listening?'

'Dear boy, with all due respect, I doubt they were hoping for *you*. I'm afraid we'll never get it past the board. Not at the moment, anyway. I agree that the archiving you are doing is worthwhile – a time capsule, if you will – but making these letters public is just not feasible. Also, it has been noticed that you have been spending too much time on the fourth floor. It's time to get back to the business we hired you to do. God can take care of the others.'

Mr Flanagan gave William's shoulder an awkward squeeze before hastening downstairs to hide in his office until Mrs Flanagan collected him at five o'clock in their turquoise Ford Fiesta.

William gulped back disappointment, ran his fingers through his hair, pulling the frustration from his scalp, through the messy curls. The tugging released some tension and he indulged in a long, deep breath that made his woollen jumper swell and collapse. In an act of self-satisfied defiance, he continued up the stairs to the fourth

25

floor, despite Mr Flanagan's warning. A new trolley of fantastical endeavours awaited him, and he dived straight in. The first letter he pulled out had just one word on the envelope: 'God'. It looked like the handwriting of an old lady: curvy and elegant, letters practised first in chalk, then pencil and, eventually, ink. The 'G' started strong, the nib tearing a tiny scratch in the manila envelope. The 'o' and the 'd' were frailer, as if the writer had grown tired even before finishing the word. William read slowly.

Dear God,

It has been a long time since I went to confession. The last time I went, Fr Fitzpatrick told me a woman with six children could have no sins, so I never went back. It's not right, though, because, as you well know, I am a sinner. Every morning, I wake up and curse the light meeting my eyes. I wish that you had let me go in my sleep – to be with Joe. I know that's a terrible sin. I should be grateful for the new dawn, more time with my children and the grandkiddies. But I'm a burden on them now, and Joe's the one who needs me. I'm sure you're looking after him, but he has his own way of going on, and I'm not sure he'd make a fuss if he was worried. He's never been very good at speaking his mind to strangers. He'll just draw in on himself, like he did during his spell in the hospital. After all those years, I think he'll miss having me to talk to, and the way I helped him into his overcoat, and out of his boots, made sure none of the different types of food touched each other on his plate. Unless you have more work for me here, will you let me go to him? I had a dream last night that I was in Heaven. Joe was sitting beside me on a promenade by the finest-looking sea – bluer and greener than I've ever seen in Blackpool, that's for sure. An orchestra was playing on the bandstand and Joe asked me to dance, and we could. His old hip was like new, his hands steady, back straight, and no touch of arthritis in my legs. We danced like we were sixteen again. And when I woke up, I cried like I was a silly sixteen-year-old, too.

Dear God, forgive me and please let me come to you. Help me find my Joe.

Your faithful servant,

Mrs Vera Flynn, Number 16

William folded the pale-blue page back along the crease and slipped it carefully inside its envelope. He couldn't imagine Clare pining for him like that now, worrying about him after he'd gone, wanting to join him. He mourned for *her*, though, so much already, even though he saw her every day. Each time he heard her laughing on the telephone, or saw her hands waving animatedly at a party, he wished the joke were his, the banter with him. He missed her teasing him about what she called his 'grandad chic', how she had persisted in coaxing him on to dance floors, where his two clumsy feet could be only an embarrassment, missed the way she picked all the raisins out of her scones and made a little pile on his plate for him to finish for her. So many little moments, inconsequential on their own, but the cumulative effect was staggering. He stopped himself unravelling before the pang sank in too deeply, placed Vera's letter in the GOD bin, and returned to his desk, where he scooped up a bundle of new letters from the top of a postbag. He opened them one by one. The first was in an A4 brown envelope with sticky residue where once an address label must have lived.

Mr Papadopoulos,

I hope this letter makes its way to you before your wife gets a chance to intercept it. Why must she always stand between us? It won't be long now until we can be together – I am sure of it. Keep saving, as will I, and our time will come. In the meantime, I will blow you a kiss every day as I wait for my bus across from your shop. If the light is right, I can catch a glimpse of your white coat as you work. How I long to lay my head against that starched cotton once again and breathe in the smell of flour and dough from your skin.

Until then, I remain your impatient love,

J.

A baker named Papadopoulos in London? He was hopeful that the letter could be delivered, if not for the outcome of that delivery. Did the man know that J was watching him? It was not his place to judge; just to mediate, where he could.

The second envelope barely housed its contents, so ragged had it become from having, clearly, been submerged in water. The typed letter inside, though streaked, was just about legible.

Dear Ms Joyce,

Thank you for your recent submission to our *Human Bodies* periodical. Unfortunately, we are unable to include it on this occasion, but we do appreciate the time you evidently spent preparing it. Your accompanying cartoons were particularly illuminating.

Yours in writerly felicity,

Elizabeth Tartt

William was sorry that Elizabeth Tartt hadn't returned the cartoons so he could see them; how bizarre! Perhaps some things were best left unseen.

The third envelope had no address at all; 'Desmond Downe' was all that was written on the front. Had someone forgotten to write the address before they mailed it, or had it been posted in error?

Dear Desmond,

I know that I owe you an explanation, and a better one than this letter can offer. I know, too, that I am a coward to run without speaking to you in person, but I was afraid that, if I tried to, you would talk me round. There is no easy answer as to why I can't marry you. You have only been loving and good. I know that any woman would be blessed to have a man such as you to take care of her, but I think that's the problem – I don't want to be taken care of. I feel so safe with you, but so much so that I end up feeling like I'm smothered in cotton wool. I need to see more of the world, to try some more things that scare me and find out what I'm capable of. I know that you will find that hard to understand, but please know you haven't done anything wrong. And I promise there is no one else, at least no one that I've met yet. I'm just chasing the dream of another sort of life that's full of sights and sounds and smells that are unfamiliar and mysterious, shocking and soothing. Someone else will come along who will take so much pleasure in your lovely life amidst all your fine things in Herne Hill, a life that would have been wasted on me. Until she comes along, take good care of yourself, and please, try not to think too poorly of me.

Yours in friendship,

Melanie

William left Desmond's letter to one side to see if he could track him down in Herne Hill. He would surely know by now that Melanie wasn't returning, but at least if the letter found him he might have a better understanding of why she had left. He couldn't imagine anything worse than arriving home one day and discovering Clare had gone without a word. How long would you wait before accepting that your partner wasn't coming home? Could you forgive them if they did? The fourth envelope had nothing at all written on it.

Mr Piot,

I return these leather gloves to you in addition to the pot of lilies, the oyster truffles and the silk scarf that I have already sent back. Please stop sending me these presents; it is entirely inappropriate and my husband is becoming increasingly furious. The connection you believe we share is entirely fictional and I have

given you no encouragement. The next letter I write
will be to the police.

Sincerely,
Mrs Assumpta Llewellyn

Marjorie was right: they were overwhelmed by valentines. William took a perfunctory look to see if the parcel
containing leather gloves could have come undone in
transit, but there was no trace. He wished Mr Piot, Mrs
Llewellyn and Ms Joyce well as he dropped them into the
shredder receptacle; there was nothing more he could do
for them. He decided to launch one more search mission
before he returned to his desk. He assumed position and
rummaged around in the overflowing trolley. This time,
he dug deep. His fingers brushed against an unusual
texture, thick and soft with grooves, like old wallpaper. It
was just as he imagined paper might have felt in days long
ago, when men on horseback carried letters through the
night. When he manoeuvred the envelope out into the
light, its colour surprised him. He had expected it to be
ivory, or brilliant white, a very elegant wedding invitation, perhaps, but it was midnight blue. The colour just
before blue becomes navy; the darkest, most mysterious
shade on the spectrum. And his favourite.

The handwriting on the front consisted of curls and
spirals, dramatic capitals, carefully crafted lower-case
letters, all in a dripping silver ink. There were just three
words: 'My Great Love'. William held the envelope close
to examine the grooves in the darkness of the pages, and
smelled the faintest trace of vanilla. Something stirred

inside him. He ached to open this envelope. Not here, though. He slipped it inside his shirt pocket and felt it radiate hot light through the cotton and on to his bare skin. He had never taken a letter home before. He longed to read it but wanted to save it for somewhere else, a private moment on his own. He couldn't risk Marjorie seeing it and whisking it away to be part of her lonely-hearts collection; somewhere deep inside him, he knew this one was different.

The afternoon crawled along, a dying man clawing for the border. Eventually, William and his little mystery could wrap themselves in the cherry-red wool scarf knitted by his mother and vanish into the city. He hoped he would be able to exit the building without bumping into Marjorie, who would insist they walk together up the Bethnal Green Road. She was always 'just ready to run', but still managed to delay for a further fifteen minutes, changing her black patent court shoes for old runners, popping to the *little girls' room*, collecting her Wonder Woman lunch box from the fridge and, most maddeningly of all, turning the coffee-shop sign she hung over her desk from OPEN to CLOSED. Infuriating. As if any work happened when she was 'open', or anyone ever came looking for her. Everyone was far too busy pretending to be on the telephone, rushing to a meeting, or hiding under their desks whenever Marjorie did her rounds. With alarming regularity, she patrolled each floor, resting her ample buttocks on any desk where she sniffed out a welcome. Her 'Auntie of the Year' cup often left a tea-stain ring in her wake.

On the pained evenings when William was subjected

to walking with Marjorie, he cursed his misfortune all the way to the bus stop. She always linked her arm in his, and he worried, with a deep sense of shame, that despite their obvious age difference, passers-by might think they were a couple. He always felt compelled to wait with her until the bus came, holding her plastic bag containing the lunch box and a copy of *Woman's Way* for her while she smoked a cigarette, trying not to stare at the line on her jaw where the orange make-up stopped and the pale, blue-veined skin of her neck began. Clare always stuck up for Marjorie, said she was lonely and he shouldn't be so heartless, that Marjorie could be her Ghost of Christmas Future, for all they knew. William thought it was easy to be compassionate about people who exist to you only as an abstract idea, as opposed to the physical beings who leave tea stains on your files and choke you with Poison perfume. He couldn't bear to see Marjorie again today, to bat away her incessant valentines campaigning, so he broke Rule Eleven of the 'DLD Charter for Good Professional Practice' and slipped out through the fire escape.

Clare would be home late that evening; Tuesday nights were reserved for her pole-dancing class, of all things. She was constantly starting courses that she seldom finished and was often away attending conferences. In the last eighteen months, Clare had lost fourteen pounds of fat she couldn't afford training for a marathon she didn't run; half made a summer dress that hung forlornly without sleeves in their wardrobe; joined a photography group and devoted a whole weekend to making a stop-motion film of the pages of a book slowly turning. She studied

Vietnamese cooking without ever preparing them a meal, and learned Italian with no immediate plans to set foot on the Boot. They talked about her classes, but she never invited him to come along to any final-night drinks or sign up for one with her. He worried it was all a ruse to avoid coming home, but he was too afraid to ask. The pole dancing had unnerved him the most. Clare insisted it was just a high-energy fitness class, a more interesting method of calorie burning and muscle toning than working out at a gym. It had nothing to do with erotica, apparently. And yet, when she packed her bag before work, with a pair of white stilettos, black shorts and a slinky silver vest, he felt jealous to be excluded. When he mentioned the class to Trevor in work, the look he received was one of sympathy. 'If it were my wife,' he'd suggested, 'I'd be asking myself some serious questions.' His reaction did little to ease William's discomfort, but he was determined to believe the classes were less about him and more about Clare's relationship with herself.

There was a time when she used to dress up for him; every occasion, a different ensemble, always when he least expected it. Before he met her, he thought antics like that existed only in films but, somehow, he found himself dressing up as Indiana Jones, eating mango as he perched on the stair handrail. His wife, who was always so sophisticated, elegant, refined. To think she had turned their bedroom into a bordello for his birthday weekend and collected him from work wearing nothing but a black silk ribbon under her winter coat. He sighed at the memory, but truly what he missed most was Clare at her most natural; perhaps stretched out on the couch in her awful lilac terrycloth dressing gown as she negotiated swapping a fried-egg sandwich for a hot-water bottle. Now, the stilettos peeking out of her bag, the flush on her cheeks when she came home after class, were cruel reminders of the fun they had once had. He longed to see her dance, tortured himself imagining how she looked as she span in time to the music, watching herself in the mirror. That part of her was slipping further and further out of his reach now, and he didn't know if he could ever have it back. It reminded him of when they had first met, before their first date, when he could only dream of knowing her so intimately – except, this time, he felt anxiety rather than excitement, because he had so much less hope. Less hope, he admitted, but not none. All was not lost.

William slammed the door of the fire escape and hastened up the street. He and Clare had lived in a flat in Tower Hamlets for five years. Clare had transformed it from a dingy two-bedroom disaster over an unpopular curry house into a home. All the furniture had been collected piece by piece from antiques markets, auctions and fairs. The mismatch of colours, history and texture should have clashed, but each element complemented something else, just as her good eye had intended. She had almost studied art at university before committing to law, and William wished she had, although Clare was pragmatic about it now. Only very occasionally would he hear the drag of her old portfolio across the wooden floor of their bedroom. Once, he watched her from the doorway as she held her paintings up to the light, running her fingers gently over the lines, smelling the paint. He had crept back down the hallway before she noticed him.

Although they loved their flat, had built it together, Clare had wanted to move for a long time. As the years wore on, she became more frustrated that they remained in a starter home, while their friends' houses, families and status grew. William refused, insisting they could only live somewhere if they could split the mortgage equally, and he was already at the limit of what he could afford. With every promotion Clare won at work, her dissatisfaction with their nest seemed to intensify. She thought it archaic that he wouldn't countenance them moving somewhere more expensive when she could afford to pay the mortgage on her own. He wouldn't back down, though, and Clare knew, on this point, she would never be able to change his mind.

William's route had defaulted towards home but instinct told him he should not take the letter there to read. Every so often, he ran his fingers over the pocket of his shirt to reassure himself he hadn't lost it. He thought about stopping in the Carpenter's Arms for a glass of red wine but couldn't face talking to Aggie, the landlady. If anyone was going to ask him about the letter, it would be Aggie, her silver locket tickling the top of the bar as she leaned across it to speak to him in her croaking voice, so he navigated towards Broadway Market. William crossed the bridge and walked along the riverbank to a bench beneath a streetlight. The envelope glowed in the yellow haze of the lamp. He tried to reason with himself for a moment. Where had this rush of anticipation come from? What had possessed him to sneak a letter out from the depot? He exhaled a deep breath and turned the envelope over. He broke the seal, running his finger under the fold, and creaked it open. Eased the letter from its home. Three pages, creased evenly in thirds, writing on one side only. He twisted on the bench to tilt the paper towards the light and started to read.

My Great Love,

Maybe this is the year you will find me. I hope so. I have been saving up so many stories to tell you, and I'm worried that if you stay away much longer they will all have slipped from my memory. I've forgotten so much already. Are you hiding somewhere? Are you lost? Do you not feel ready? I wish you would hurry.

I remember, when I first moved to this city, I loved how everyone was a stranger, but I also remember believing that my solitary state was a temporary situation. You are taking much longer to find me than I'd hoped. This morning, while waiting for the bus, I watched a dapper man's suitcase snap open and a pile of papers dance down Old Street. He was laughing, despite the calamity and the wind poking icy fingers between buttons, down collars and up trouser legs. London was grey and howling and his laugh carried in the wind like a tangerine lasso, pulling everyone in. A gaggle of girls in wine-coloured school uniforms rushed to help him. If he felt foolish, he was a happy fool. I wondered if it could be you. I ask myself that all the time as I walk about the city, when a certain sort of someone catches my eye. I find myself waiting for you to look up and notice me noticing you.

It will soon be Valentine's Day – what a perfect time to write to you, when lovers everywhere are wrapping, writing or worrying. I am in good spirits, although my hands are cold as I grip this silver pen. I've just arrived home from New York and the radiators have forsaken me now that the first spot of snow has fallen. I do love long-haul flights: the suspended reality, the anonymity, the disconnection from everything and everyone. Every passenger, an island. It's the most captivating waiting room in the world: sad eyes from leaving-behinds, excited hearts for going-tos, nervous bellies for the unknown, eager longings for the familiar. High up in the skies, we are free from decisions, action, responsibility, identity – reduced to being toddlers pushed in a pram by a stranger. Landing came almost too soon because, every time I fly, I dread the Arrivals lounge. It is so bittersweet to walk out past Security and see all the expectant faces of people waiting impatiently for someone who isn't me. In times gone by, my father would always be there, watching the Arrivals board for any changes, in position too early, just in case he missed me.

I wish you had been waiting for me when I came in this morning, an unread newspaper twisted under your arm, hair still ruffled from sleep. I wouldn't expect you to bring me flowers, but a fresh carton of milk waiting at home in the fridge would be lovely. I know you would take my suitcase and sweep me off my feet in one swift movement – I would well up, even though I hadn't been away for very long at all. But you weren't there. Instead, I dragged my case along by myself and waited in the rain for a taxi back to the city. When I eventually dripped into my flat, it was freezing. The milk in the fridge had turned sour and the bed was still messy, as I had left it. I'm not trying to make you feel guilty, I promise, but I have to tell you all the ways I miss you. The gaps you could fill are widening and I worry they will soon become too big for one person to satisfy. How can anyone be all the things that another needs? Answer all questions?

I wonder now if the choices that brought me to this city were clever ones. Since Christmas, I feel as if I am slipping further and further away from all that is familiar, all those that I love. I furiously write long letters on my lunch break and crackle down phone lines to try to connect with people at home, but it's not enough. My life is synopsized now into anecdotes and reflections after the fact. News is old before it is told, feelings forgotten before they are cried or laughed over, questions answered before they are asked. My old friends have no window into my life now. They can no longer picture me eating breakfast in Donnybrook, in the little flat over the cake shop that they knew so well. There are no faces for new names as we talk on the telephone. I try to paint some wordy pictures, but it gets harder.

I miss my friends and family so much, and that has made me miss you even more. It's true. I hope you miss me, too. Do you? Are you wandering around London, feeling that you've left your umbrella behind? (I do think you're the sort to carry an umbrella.) Do you have dreams of somewhere you've never been but wish you could go? Is your head full of thoughts that no one has quite the right ears for? Do you read about exhibitions, concerts, tours, plays, trips to the seaside, and wish you knew someone who would want to go along with you? Is your hand lonely in your pocket? It's me, I tell you! I'm your forgotten umbrella!

Oh dear, it just dawned on me that you mightn't be in London. Oh, I hope you are. It's hard enough filtering all those millions of people down to one as it is. Or worse still – you could be back in Ireland! No. I won't believe it. If you're not in London, you must come to find me here.

I'm not sure what I will do with this letter now, although I feel better for writing it. Forgive me for counting all the ways that I am lonely; it is not something I can do out loud.

I hope, somehow, that it finds you, and finds you well.

Yours,

Winter

3.

Clare couldn't force herself to look in the mirror, did not want to recognize herself as the creature before her. She resented her pale, pear-shaped body. Like a turkey hanging in the butcher's window at Christmas. With every year that passed, her bottom half widened but her upper body stayed the same and, in her mind, the disproportion had taken on gigantic importance. Having been effortlessly slender in her twenties, it shocked her how quickly her body had changed in the five years since she became thirty. She signed up for pole dancing, thinking it would make her feel better about her now more curvaceous shape, boost her confidence and help her remember how she used to move. In times past, she had felt graceful, conscious of the heat of men's eyes on her as she strode along the marble corridors between court rooms or danced until dawn at the jazz clubs she and William used to frequent. After she graduated, she bought her first pair of stilettos and practised walking up and down the aisles of the supermarket, pushing the trolley for balance and support. It paid off. Before long, she struggled to walk in anything flat; the arches of her feet were now unaccustomed to being horizontal and she loved the added height, even though William was a good two inches shorter than her. It never seemed to bother him either.

Of late, though, she had felt uncomfortably conspicuous, being so tall; an advantage wasted if you couldn't hold your spine straight, your shoulders back, your head high. Her grace felt balled up in her belly. She constantly resisted the urge to bend over and nurse it. The advertisement on the noticeboard at work for pole-dancing classes seduced her with the promise of sculpting her body back to its 'former glory' and 'rejuvenating her va-va-voom' with this new, vaguely taboo, craze. She knew that her self-esteem should not be determined by her physical appearance, but this wasn't about looking good for other people – this was about her own self-control, what made her feel strong and proud. Feeling like she had lost her fitness, her physique, made her worry that she was in a state of decline, but she wasn't ready to surrender just yet. The advertisement failed to mention, however, two elements crucial for the transformation: loving (or at least tolerating) your scantily clad reflection under fluorescent light and at least some natural capacity for gymnastics. Clare struggled through each class with mounting embarrassment. She could hold her position on the pole but, when the time came to slide down, she just couldn't let go. Instead of elegantly gliding to the base with her back arched, Clare descended inch by inch in stops and starts, burning the palms of her hands and leaving friction marks on her thighs. When all her classmates were ready to mount again, she was still clawing her way to the bottom, trying to ignore the looks of pity and the stifled laughter. She was sorely tempted to quit after the first week, to scuttle away with a feather boa between her legs, but she knew the failure would lower her spirits even further and so she persisted. Every week, Clare was optimistic that she would have a breakthrough moment. Each time, the other girls looked more and more accomplished and she remained clinging midway up the pole, praying for an end to come soon.

When Clare arrived home after class, she then had to suffer William's feigned nonchalance as he asked how it had been, if she had enjoyed herself. She couldn't tell him how awful it was, that it was the least erotic experience she had ever had the misfortune to undergo. In the past, they would have been in hysterical fits as she regaled him with her humiliation at the hand of Miss Fortuna. Not any more. His poorly disguised curiosity was probably the only bit of satisfaction she gleaned from going. After the first class, William had asked her if he would ever have the pleasure of a private performance. Clare was taken aback; she couldn't tell if he was genuinely excited at the prospect, saying what he thought he was supposed to, or mocking her. She walked to the bathroom without meeting his eye. 'Seeing as it took you eight months to install the towel rack,' she said, 'I won't hold my breath waiting for a pole.' William didn't reply. Before the door had fully closed, the tears she had been swallowing squeezed out in streams of salty sadness down her hot cheeks. She buried her face in William's dressing gown, the one he said made him feel like a Siberian prince, and inhaled the lingering peppermint smell of his soap. If she opened the door and showed him how upset she was, wouldn't he comfort her? Couldn't he still find ways and words to pull her out of this molasses? She missed him despite being no longer sure that the man she missed still existed.

On the evening of the day that William discovered Winter's letter, Clare was feeling particularly low. There was an option to sign up for an end-of-course performance and she was the only woman in the class who didn't want to do it. No one was surprised. Nor did they try to talk her into it. She sat in the car outside their flat holding her red-raw palms over her eyes, breathing through the bout of anxiety that crawled over her body like an army of ants. She could see the light on in the kitchen and knew William would be sitting there, reading yesterday's paper, unaware that he had grown cold until he stood up and stretched. A cup housing an Earl Grey teabag would sit on the counter, waiting for him to remember he had boiled the kettle. She knew him so well: the light and shade of his moods; when his eyes strained to see; the spot where his muscles always knotted in his left shoulder blade. Clare had always collected stories from her day which she thought would fascinate him, or jokes that would tickle him. She made a note of films, gigs or exhibitions he would be excited about, and stored them in her 'William' vault. She still mined all those observations, conditioned as she was to the practice, but she didn't share them with him any more. They were just filed away and forgotten. Any affectionate words stuck in her throat; she felt that any act of kindness would be taken as a reward for his disappointing behaviour. At times, she felt the fact that she was still with him at all was more than he deserved. She had done everything she could: keeping them financially afloat, humouring him when he spent the first summer after they were married on tour with Stevie, expecting patiently his great novel that never came. All these years, she had waited for him to fulfil the promise he held when they met. How could he be satisfied with working in that godforsaken depot? When people met them for the first time now, she knew what an unlikely pairing they must seem. If they themselves could meet anew as strangers, she thought it questionable they would even be friends – and a romance would be completely inconceivable. And yet, she couldn't turn her back completely on the memory of how much they once were the perfect pair. When her granny met William, she hugged Clare and said, 'When God made ye, he matched ye. For every sock, there's a shoe.' And she had known it was true.

She had started dating much too young: older boys who somehow tricked her into thinking they were the ones who needed impressing; insecure men who had tried to control her in order to feel more powerful. When she met William, she was shocked at how utterly effortless it was to be with him. And not because she didn't care enough, but because they both cared, and in equal amounts. William knew the punchline to her every joke; in his company, she was wittier, more outspoken, fearless in a way that she had never even considered being before. And in her attention, he bloomed. Before she met him, in her romantic entanglements, she had felt like she was trying desperately hard to recreate an idea of love she had drawn from black-and-white films shot on Parisian boulevards. After him, life was vivid; in full Technicolor.

When she walked into the flat, an aroma of soup wafted from the kitchen. Hearty, thick; real vegetables from the ground, stewing hot in a pot. Warming. Loving. Calling. She followed the trail and was amazed to find the kitchen gleaming in godly cleanliness. Normally, William's cooking involved ingredients exploding into every crevice of the kitchen and a mountain of encrusted saucepans balanced precariously in the sink. He turned down their crackling old record player, softening Bob Dylan's crooning of 'Don't Think Twice, It's All Right', and crossed the kitchen floor to peck her on the cheek. He was clearly very pleased with himself but trying to behave as if this little miracle of domesticity was an everyday occurrence. Clare was immediately suspicious; she hoped he didn't want to have a 'talk' or give her an ill-considered surprise. The last time he had made this big an effort was to announce that he had impulsively adopted a puppy. That was not a happy weekend. William had sulked like a child for a week after she made him take the mongrel back to Morgana in the depot. Why could he not have considered the practicalities of housing a growing dog in their already cramped living space without making her be the spoilsport again? She edged her way to the kitchen table, murmured something about the nice smell and waited for the bomb to drop while he ladled some soup into her favourite sea-green ceramic bowl. They had bought a set of four from a local potter on their honeymoon in Sorrento, but this was the only one that still survived. William had often said that he planned to order more for her, but had never quite managed it.

'So, what's all this in aid of, then?' she asked, while rifling through her briefcase. 'Have you broken something? Or invited a homeless person to come and live with us? Oh God, you haven't bought a motorbike, have you?'

William chose not to dwell on the worrying assumptions his wife made when confronted with his good deeds and swallowed the sting. 'No. Nothing in particular,' he answered, stirring the soup. 'I just know you've been working hard and, well, sometimes I feel I could do more here to –'

'I've been working hard for ten years, William. Don't start feeling guilty now. We'll never get all the worms picked up from the floor.'

Clare felt a pang of remorse when she saw his face but couldn't bring herself to take it back. It was as if the only way she could cope with the weight of her worries was to release a little bit of pressure with a series of tiny blows. She couldn't explain how she really felt to him, not until she could accept the idea that the end of the conversation could herald the end of them, too. Instead, she pulled a copy of *Marie Claire* from her bag and smoothed it open on the table. She scanned an interview with an American opera singer, Carletta da Carlo, who had retired to Rome and was growing ever plumper from a heady mix of sunshine, pasta and a new romance. Her eyes wandered over black-and-white photographs of Carletta posing on the

Spanish Steps in an ivory satin evening gown, and her mind travelled back to her own, more painful, excursion to the city, when she had still been in the throes of her last, angsty affair before she met William.

She could see herself now, perched on the rim of a dried-up old fountain, the sleeves of her jumper stretched over her hands, past their give, the stitches strained at the shoulders. She could still feel the scratchy black wool on her face as it soaked up the angry tears and runny mascara that stung the corners of her eyes. She crouched, her back a half-moon, head upon hands upon knees. A hot little cave of rage, sounds of her hiccupy sobs booming in her ribcage. She could feel the eyes of strangers upon her and was relieved when no one offered any help. Eventually, as she felt the grip of panic loosening, Jamie's shadow fell across her, blocking the relentless Roman sun. She refused to look up and just stared at his oxblood military boots with the ridiculous black-and-white chequered laces and buckles flapping open. Although she desperately wanted some kind of resolution, she wouldn't ask for it. He grasped her shoulders and pulled her to her feet. She didn't struggle but kept her head lolled forward like a puppet with its strings cut until he let her go. With her eyes squeezed tightly closed, she held her breath. A moment passed as she listened to his breathing, fast, hot and impatient, but he didn't say anything. She looked up at him through her frizzy fringe. He was pointing a camera straight at her. The shock stopped her crying. The flash blinded her for a second then he instantly turned on his heel and strutted off across the square.

'What are you doing? What's wrong with you?' she shouted after him.

He turned, cold, and with a smirk of satisfaction stretched across his face. 'Just a little memento of our romantic trip to Rome, Clare, in case I ever need reminding why we broke up here.' Her fury rendered her speechless as she watched him cut through the tourists and vanish from sight.

That night, the humid air hung heavy about them as they held hands across a candlelit table in the courtyard of a quiet *osteria*. Little white lights hung from the veranda as the waiter *prego*-ed back and forth, smiling at these strange young lovers who clutched at each other but looked so unhappy. Her stomach was churning, doubling and dancing with the shame of his disrespect and her inability to walk away, but now he was smiling and she was too relieved to jeopardize the fragile peace that had settled between them. She hoped they would make love that evening but dreaded the thought of it. Had not yet learned how much she could expect from love. And so it continued: the Jamie period of her life. Before their relationship had reached its ultimate crisis point, after so many near-misses. Before Clare's little sister, Flora, was called to come and collect her in the middle of the night. Jamie had pushed her out of the door of his flat, tossing her clothes, books, a mini bonzai and her handbag down the stairs in her wake. When she tried to gather her belongings up in her arms, she lost her balance and tumbled down, down, so far down. She cracked a rib on the bottom step and scraped her hands and knees on the gravel. Jamie just closed the front door and left her lying there. Later, he said he knew she was okay when he heard her crying. A passing neighbour helped her to her feet and telephoned Flora while Clare sat in his parlour, drinking sugary tea.

When Clare eventually tried to talk about Jamie to a counsellor, it felt like someone else's story. As she struggled to understand why she had stayed with him for as long as she had, her account was always interrupted by memories from her childhood invading the narrative. The sessions never caught up to recent events. It was meeting William that eventually gave her the peace to leave Jamie and the emotional fallout of their relationship behind her. He helped her to understand that she deserved kindness and how a relationship could strengthen you instead of stealing your power. The difference between intensity and intimacy. It was an epiphany for her: unconditional love that was so far removed from that of her childhood home or the toxic men she was consistently drawn to throughout college and her first year at university. She hadn't understood that you could find creativity, passion and adventure living inside a dependable, trustworthy man. It was an irresistible combination, with which William had completely seduced her; the memory of it sustained her even now, when the light in him had dimmed so. If they did separate, was that the end of love for her, or could she find it again with someone new? Perhaps it was time to stop resenting William for having grown into someone different and just let them both move on? Maybe some other woman would accept him the way he was and not hold old promises against him.

Over the years, William had sometimes suggested she see a counsellor again, usually when he was campaigning for them to have a baby. It was an easier way for her to show willing than to try to explain to him directly the disappointment she felt in their married life, but she had never really felt that it helped her to resolve anything. On the day of her last appointment, a year before, she left sobbing and swore she would never return. In the therapist's office, she remembered her first day at a drama summer school when she was seven.

Clare had worried herself into a tight little knot beforehand about strange faces, lisping out loud or if she would need to be able to do cartwheels (which she couldn't), but it had never crossed her mind that the shame of unwashed feet would be her downfall. It wasn't that her family was dirty or that her mother wouldn't have been appalled if she saw the black between her toes. It was more that her mother just couldn't see it. She was as oblivious to the grubby soles of Clare's feet or Flora's unwashed hair as she was to the runs in her own sagging tights or the egg stains on her blouse. Her mother, Teresa, felt invisible and so believed that she was, and her slovenly condition too. Somewhere over the years, her mother had transformed from a militant housekeeper who scrubbed kitchen tiles, cloth nappies and scruffs of necks with equal vigour, into a half-person who had abandoned herself to apathy. Clare understood now that her mother had been suffering from a severe depression but, as a child, it just confused her and she tried to cover for her as best she could and to protect Flora from the worst of her episodes.

At the summer school, while the rest of her classmates pulled off their shoes and socks with excitement, Clare retreated into the corner and surreptitiously peeled back her left sock to assess the condition of her feet. The sight of her heel was enough to stop her and she yanked the sock straight back up again. How she wished she had filled the red plastic basin with sudsy water the night before and given her feet a scrub. She always loved the feeling of submerging her feet in the soapy water before wrapping them in a towel and drying away the wrinkly sensation. It just wasn't something she made a habit of. Cleanliness had become political in her house, and being too keen to tidy up or be clean yourself seemed almost a direct assault on her mother, who resented the insinuation, however true, that she wasn't capable of doing these things herself. Of course, there was a certain element of laziness, too. She hadn't learned to care for her own sake yet. Not at that point. Clare slipped around the perimeter of the room and sidled over to Miss Mimi's side, where she tugged on her sleeve and whispered, 'I can't take off my socks, Miss, because I have an infection on one of my feet, Miss, and the bandage might come off.' She watched as Miss Mimi looked down at her twisting feet, where no contour of a bandage was visible through the thin cotton socks.

'A bandage on both feet, Clare?' she asked, bending closer to whisper. Clare smelled roses from her skin.

'No, Miss, just the left one, but I think I'd feel strange with one sock on and one sock off. Uneven.'

Miss Mimi gave her a long look, then turned Clare to face the room, her hands on her shoulders.

'Very well, then,' she said. 'Leave them on for now, but try not to slip. Hopefully, you'll be footloose and fancy free next week.'

Clare couldn't meet her eyes but said a little prayer of thanks for the reprieve. Next week, her toes would squeak. She had learned a lesson: to take responsibility for herself. She longed for the day when she would be a grown-up lady. Not like her own mama but like the other children's mothers, with toenails painted red or pink peeping out of white, high-heeled summer sandals. Smelling of soap and roses.

As she sat at her shining kitchen table now, it crossed her mind that she had perhaps taken that lesson too much to heart. Was she so self-sufficient that it rendered William's role in her life redundant? She wanted them to be equals but strived so hard for perfection and control in her life that maybe she'd made the gap too wide. If she let her grip on things loosen just a little, would he tighten his?

William was one of the few people who understood what her childhood experience had been. When she had nightmares, as she sometimes did, he would brush her eyelids closed with the palm of his hands, over and over again, slow and steady, until her breathing calmed and her forehead cooled, just like her father had done when she was a little girl to calm her down after another vicious row between her parents. It had taken a long time for her to feel ready to explain where those dark dreams came from; to share with William the memories of the alcohol-fuelled rows and psychological violence on the part of her mother. Despite the public façade of respectability they all maintained, she and Flora had suffered. It pained her to explain that when, eventually, plates stopped smashing and shouting gave way to sobbing, her father would escape the aftermath in the kitchen and wearily climb the stairs to see if she was sleeping. She always waited for him on the top step, hugging herself, her nightdress pulled down over her knees. She worried about how tired he would be when the alarm called him for work, dreaded the silence she knew would smother the house at tea-time the next day. She sat on the stairs, shivering, but she would not fetch herself a blanket. Little Clare had believed that, if she suffered, maybe her daddy would have to suffer less. She knew the people she described were at odds with the family William met when Clare finally invited him home to meet them. He found it hard to reconcile them with the stories he had heard, but never doubted her, nonetheless.

'What are you thinking about?' William's voice cut through her thoughts and Clare realized she sat holding a spoonful of soup in mid-air. She was too tired to try to explain to him what was running through her mind.

'Nothing. Just a case I'm working on.' She turned the pages of the magazine, scanning the headlines, and allowed herself a moment to take pride in how far that little girl had come.

After Clare left home for university, she worked hard

to recreate herself in the image and likeness of those other mothers, the career women, not her own mama, who had stayed at home with the curtains drawn. The decision to study law and not go for an art degree was made easily in her head. Her heart struggled to follow suit, but she would not allow herself to be emotional when confronted with the choice between struggle and poverty and success and security. Perhaps that was partly what had attracted her to William, as he floated through his creative-writing degree. She could flirt with his life-style, walk with him as he talked about the challenge of this plot twist or that character's arc; it was light relief from laboriously reading tome after tome, writing essay after essay, until she rose to the top of her class. Sometimes, she allowed herself to daydream of an alternative life where she spent hours choosing the exact shade of green to paint a particular leaf or sketching spectators in the Natural History Museum. The day she discovered William's book club, she had arrived exhausted by yet another battle to prove her position among the public-school boys who fell just short of pulling her pigtails in class. They loved to remind her how recently it was that girls had been allowed to attend the university, as if it were a privilege that could be revoked. Clare was search-ing for a different tone of conversation, something dove grey, where she could feel her way through a conversa-tion, instead of marching to a black-and-white beat she never felt quite in step with.

William looked like he had been caught eating stolen cookies when she walked in; guilty he had no one else to offer her, worried that he was wasting her time. His thumb curled through a hole in the sleeve of his jumper, his spectacles were lopsided on the bridge of his nose. The glossy brown curls erupted from his head at all angles and fell over his eyes in a fringe that tried hard to disguise how handsome he was. This jumble sale of a man thawed something inside her. While they sat together, he flicked through the yellowed pages of a notebook with a cracking, navy-blue leather cover. She put her hand on his to make him pause. 'What are all these notes?' she asked. A flush sneaked from behind his ears. She soon learned that these blushes seemed always to be lying in wait for any opportunity to creep out and expose him.

'Oh, just some silly stories. Sometimes, I'll notice a stranger on the street and make up a little life for them, imagine where they are going, what they care about, who they are.'

It blew her heart wide open. Perhaps he would become a hugely successful novelist one day and she could forget about the law and spend her days painting in a little studio. How wrong she was. She could never have anticipated that William would surrender his dream so easily for what she saw as the drudgery of the depot; that was never his long-term plan. All that time he spent typing out those supernatural letters on that battered Imperial typewriter. Why couldn't he write stories of his own any more? Even if he had focused on his ill-fated band with Stevie, that might have fulfilled him more. Much as she had loathed the influence Stevie exerted on William and the trouble they always managed to get themselves into, perhaps William would have been happier. It would have been very hard for her to endure Stevie's constant presence in their lives; they were fundamentally allergic to each other. He, with his fantastical dress sense and eccentric lifestyle, thought she was far too pedestrian, despite what she considered to be creative styling of her own; she thought he was a self-indulgent poser who had never done a day's work in his life. She remembered him staggering up to William's bedsit one day with a dozen flattened washing-machine boxes; he was going to put their demo tape inside them and deliver each one to the radio stations wrapped up as a giant present. He had considered getting in himself before jumping out and presenting the cassettes in person, until she convinced him his scheme would most likely end in either suffocation or arrest. This, of course, he had interpreted as Clare spoiling their fun, as usual.

In fairness, though, at the time, she had believed that William really was going to have great success with his writing; otherwise, she might not have been so quick to encourage him to leave the band to take up the depot position. It was supposed to be temporary. In the beginning, he worked only three days, leaving two days to write in the British Library but, over time, he admitted that he wasn't really getting as much writing done as he had hoped and that he might as well do some real work until he felt inspired again. She wondered now if it wasn't inspiration he lacked but courage. It was hard to respect that.

The thought pulled her focus back to the kitchen

table, where William sat looking at her with searching eyes. She avoided looking back into them. The William she first met would never have settled. If she had told him then, flushed with the confidence of too much wine, that one day in the future they would sit in awkward silence at their kitchen table, he would never have believed her. She would have struggled to believe it herself. What chased that man away? Was it her? Was she ready to accept that they had lost the war? That William was missing in action? The questions circled in her mind like sharks. To lay the blame at his door neatly and begin again, somewhere else, would at least allow her to move on from living within this stagnant cloud. Was that what she wanted? She wasn't sure, not yet. Instead, she buttered some bread, her shoulders hunched. At least the vegetable soup was warming. At least there was that.

William was keenly aware of the physical proximity of his colleagues. Every sigh, fidget and sneeze rattled his emotional infrastructure. The scrape of chair legs felt like claws down his back. The atmosphere stifled him. The heating was still on its winter cycle, even though white sunlight speared through the dusty venetian blinds. The cleaners who arrived every evening at seven seemed to make little headway in their eternal battle against the dust; the white-washed frames on the floor-to-ceiling windows were no barrier against the dirty air percolating from the traffic below. The Victorian floorboards offered endless chinks and grooves to hide away the daily debris that gathered with the post. Despite it all, however, the depot always felt illuminated by the streams of sunlight flowing in from the south and alive with the coloured patchwork cushions that lay scattered on the chesterfield sofas and the prints on the walls: Klimt's *Apple Tree*, Kandinsky's *Yellow-Red-Blue*, Monet's water lilies, a black-and-white photograph of Johnny Cash and June Carter looking over their shoulders at a fairground, a pen-and-ink drawing of two penguins, wings touching as if they were holding hands, staring out from the perimeter of an iceberg. The depot colleagues had clubbed together to buy them as an office Christmas present two years before, each detective choosing one, and it made all the difference to their working habitat. Each detective's desk was unique, also, infused with their individual characters: William's old mahogany polished to a shine, Trevor's leather and chrome, Marjorie's wicker and pine. The lack of uniformity complemented the higgledy-piggledy nature of their work.

'Marjorie, could you open the window a crack? It's really stuffy in here,' William asked, as he wriggled in his chair.

'The window? When I'm sitting in the direct path of the draught? I don't think so. If you didn't go around dressed like it's Christmas every day, you wouldn't feel so 'ot and bothered. It's a shame to see a young man dressing like he should be drawing his pension. Why don't you get yourself some nice new jeans, eh?'

William regretted the corduroy shirt and cardigan combination chosen in haste that morning. The grey cashmere, normally such a soft comfort, had a newly acquired texture of Brillo pad. It scratched the skin of his neck unmercifully, but the damp patches forming under his arms prevented him shedding the suffocating layer; he would rather endure feverish discomfort than the embarrassment of being exposed as a man not in control of his bodily functions.

At the Dead Letters Depot, time defied the laws of physics, speeding faster than light one day, dripping along like a tired old tap another. That day wound down like a bucket descending slowly into the driest of wells. Every second a minute; every hour a day. Work did not expand to fill the time allowed for it, despite the volume requiring attention; William's fingers were clumsy figs. His trolley of undeliverables overflowed and parcels and letters formed untidy piles at his feet. Envelopes haemorrhaged out of postbags all around his desk. His reputation for clearing his allocation every week had always been considered an example to all. Usually, by Friday lunchtime, every one of his letters and parcels had been attended to. It wasn't entirely selfless; clearing his allocation allowed him time to focus on the Supernatural Division, bought him some hours of peace to click-clack away, typing up letters to add to his collection. Rather than popping out for a tipple to toast the end of the working week, this ritual was his reward. On Mondays, when a new tide of post flooded into his domain, he was generally excited to start the process all over again. And yet, for over a month now, he had barely been meeting his quota. His typewriter lay sulking under its red leather cover, neglected. He avoided Mr Flanagan, skipped staff meetings when he could and ate lunch at his desk, alone. William struggled to find his usual inspiration in the stories from strangers that passed before him or to get excited by his role in their delivery. He was drowning in lethargy. Lethargy and letters. How could he care about the plight of others when he feared his own personal life was accelerating towards a moment of crisis?

He picked up a parcel wrapped in brown paper and tied tightly in string and turned it over in his hands, grimacing to hear it rattle. No address anywhere. He untangled the knot and peeled back the paper to reveal a shoe box that had once held soccer boots, size five. Inside, a large egg shape was cocooned in bubble wrap; it felt heavy in his hands as he laid it to one side and picked up the sheet of dotted paper that accompanied it. The precision of the neat, joined-up handwriting gave the distinct impression of being a newly acquired skill.

Dear Sirs and Madams of the Royal Geological Society,

My name is Penelope Bernardine Foxcroft and I am a keen amateur geologist. I have built an impressive collection of rocks and fossils, as I am lucky to live in Aberlemno in the north-east of Scotland, where I can hunt for them in the mountains and along the shore by the sea. I have enclosed a photo of me with my display, holding the Cairngorm granite I found last spring. The reason I am writing to you is I think I may have found a lump of fossilized whale vomit, or ambergris, to use its proper name. I know that this could be quite valuable and so would appreciate it if you could authenticate it for me.

Yours truly,

Penelope Bernardine Foxcroft

William found the photograph of Penelope in the shoe box. He smiled at her earnest expression as she stood in front of shelves weighed down by Kilner jars and rocks on little mounts. She was wearing a grass-green-coloured T-shirt with GEOLOGY ROCKS emblazoned across the front. He toyed with the idea of unwrapping the offering but wasn't sure he really wanted to get further acquainted with whale vomit. Instead, he called the Royal Geological Society and made an appointment to meet Dr Rosamund

O'Reilly, who was very excited indeed to hear about Penelope and her discovery – it could be worth thousands of pounds, it seemed, and Dr O'Reilly was shocked that someone had just popped it in the post. He called over Sally, their disinterested but charming work-experience student, and showed her what he had discovered.

'That is the most disgusting thing I have ever heard,' she said, and poked the parcel with one pointy scarlet fingernail.

'Well, be that as it may, it's a victory for us!' he replied. 'Would you like to bring it over to the Society with me? Get away from here for an hour or two this afternoon?'

Sally tried to perch nonchalantly on the edge of his desk but couldn't find a comfortable resting position; she tossed her head and swung her ebony ponytail over her shoulder as she slinked up to standing.

'Absolutely. Shall we go out for lunch and carry on from there? I'll swing by your desk again at one, but this time it's definitely on me.'

William felt the judgemental eyes of Morgana and Trevor boring into him. Sally's father was Chairman of the Board at the depot, and they never missed an opportunity to accuse him of designs of advancement by charming her. That was never his intention, however. If anything, he revelled in the newness of her, her lack of cynicism and her spirit.

William felt the familiar sense of satisfaction on completing a successful mission, but it didn't excite him now as much as it would have once. Lately, his interests had evolved from a general fascination with other-world idolatry to a very specific one. He groped about in the mail sacks, imagining little eyes in his fingertips, searching for a familiar groove, hoping for an instinctive path to another letter from Winter. He tried to accept that there would probably not be any others, just that one message in a bottle tossed into the sea by a lonely woman, but still he searched. Instinct powered him forward; his heart needed this, despite the inability of his head to rationalize why. Every time he reached inside a postbag, hope poured from his shoulder blades down his arms, a waterfall flowing over every bone, nerve and sinew to become streams in his fingers, pulsing and pushing.

Winter's letter lay flattened in the L section of the *Oxford English Dictionary* on his desk, between a page that began with 'lady' and one that ended with 'lamb'. For days, he had agonized over whether or not it might be safer to hide it at home after all, but everywhere he considered, he imagined a beacon of light suddenly calling Clare to it: the manila folder of old bills, a hat box filled with their collection of super-8 films, under the tower of her university texts, which never budged. He couldn't risk Clare ever finding it. The thread of trust between them, already so frayed, would surely snap with any further strain. How could he explain why he wanted to keep that letter? Especially when, for so many years, he had refused to bring any letters home, despite her consistent pestering of him to do so. In the beginning, she had been so curious about his working world and wanted to be complicit in his detective work but, over time, as her resentment about his salary and his preoccupation with the job grew, her interest in discussing these mysteries had waned in direct proportion. He couldn't even begin to explain why Winter's letter had stayed with him without unravelling miles of words unspoken between them about where the romance in their own marriage had disappeared to. He didn't know what the simple explanation was for his attraction to Winter's words, or if one even existed. If they walked even two steps down that road of exploration, he worried they would never come back.

The letter had completely unsettled him. Winter's words swam around in his head, exotic fish in an aquarium: *Are you hiding somewhere?*, *Are you lost?*, *your forgotten umbrella*, *wordy pictures*; bobbing around the everyday, goldfish lexicon he shared with his wife: *What's for dinner?*, *The electricity bill came*, *I'll go and put the bins out*. He thought again of the letters that he and Clare used to write to each other, even though they saw each other almost every day, letters full of yearning and dreaming, a way of sharing their inner selves that found expression on paper but which they sometimes struggled with in person. What would he say if he wrote to Clare now? Had those letters been more honest for the element of anonymity paper brings, or less? Had they allowed them to present an idealistic image of themselves they both wanted to believe in or helped them to become even more real to each other? He wasn't sure any more.

He slipped away to his fourth-floor domain and visualized a midnight-blue envelope waiting for him. He ached for it, calling it into being, beseeching the universe, foolish though it felt, that a good wind would blow through and offer him this reprieve. There were two new trolleys awaiting him, and he spilled the contents of the first on to the floor, a tide of white, browns and greys across the mustard tiles. An occasional splash of colour mingled amid the monotony of everyday stationery: an indigo envelope, a polka-dot parcel, a brown-paper package covered in drawings of Christmas trees. And there! There it was! Brazen and bold, buried two letters deep; a midnight-blue envelope with curling silver writing. William pressed his hot forehead to the cold tiles and offered up a prayer of thanks. Why did he care so much that the first letter had not been the only one? How could he dare hope for more? He knelt among the lost letters, his feet tucked beneath him, and opened the envelope.

My Great Love,

How are you? I just saw a very fetching man walking across the courtyard under my window. He was crunching an apple with admirable enthusiasm and a great sense of purpose while a very excited electric-blue scarf struggled to be released into the skies. Maybe it wanted to be sky blue instead. Oh, that it was you arriving home from work with a Tunnocks tea cake hidden in your satchel for me! I will toast the day.

I'm writing to you from the kitchen table as I spy on my neighbours coming and going below. How I envy the couples as they struggle to carry in their shopping and bicker about much of nothing – they are oblivious to the extraordinary beauty of the ordinariness of their lives. If one or the other were suddenly gone, I wonder how much they would mourn these unexceptional days they take for granted? Or would any of them be relieved? Are any of them trapped in a marriage they haven't the heart or nerve to try to escape from? It must be even worse to feel lonely inside a couple than when you're alone. At least my loneliness offers the hope of someone coming along – and I am free to run into their arms if they do.

My window is a glass door that opens out on to a tiny balcony where regular successions of plants arrive, blossom, then die under my neglectful eye. There is a lovely occasional waft of jasmine on the breeze from the vase on the windowsill. I walked down to Columbia Road Flower Market this morning and staggered home under the weight of my finds. My favourite stall is at the very end of the street and run by a man who is blind in one eye; he wears a patch and a pirate hat! As you bob along the avenue, brushing against the human traffic, traders heckle on every side. I listen and look, greedily drinking in the cacophony of colour, but push through to the very end to my pirate. He hates to see any flower left behind at the end of the day so, as time draws closer to Sunday lunch, he paces beside his stall and combines bunches together, bouquets of wild combinations of everything from chrysanthemums to orchids and wisteria to lily of the valley. It's almost impossible to resist reaching out your arms for them to be filled. Ladies line his parade, waving five-pound notes at him, desperate to catch the flowers of the day. He wrapped up twenty white roses with a clutch of yellow tulips and a woman beside me squealed out, 'Ooh la la!' as if she had seen a living miracle. He plucked five pounds from her creamy, perfectly manicured hand and placed the prize in her arms as if it were a baby. She dashed off, jealously guarding her flora, lest someone bump them from her hands or crush them against her chest.

On impulse, I brought him a coffee today, from the cart that also sells helium balloons; I always think it will float away one day, and secretly hope it will. When my turn came to be given my flowers, the bouquet was a triumph. White paper hugged pink roses, white lilies, my jasmine and the sweetest bunch of daffodils. I have such a weakness for those noble stems. If ever we have a garden, will you plant a whole bed of daffodils where I can see them from the kitchen window? My mother grew them in the garden, and they're the first flowers I ever remember picking. Today on the market, a dilapidated yellow Volkswagen Beetle had been converted into a giant flowerpot filled with those very beauties and dozens of daisies and sunflowers. I used half of my camera film taking photographs of it – I hope when I develop them there is something special to send to my mam. You'll meet her one day, I'm sure.

I keep fantasizing about bringing you home to Ireland with me. I sense that my friends and family are anticipating your arrival also. First, we can visit the little village where I grew up and then we'll abscond to the city when it starts to feel too claustrophobic. We might even take the Dart out to Bray and walk along the promenade. I want to take you on a historical tour of the places that mean the most to me in Dublin: the Italian restaurant where I waitressed for years when I was a poor student; the hat shop where I hosted a student radio show in the attic for a few years, until the Gardaí shut us down. Maybe I can finally buy myself a hat there, after so many years gazing at them in the window. We can go dancing in Whelan's, where all the best bands play – I even saw The Cure there once! It was one of the most spiritual experiences of my life. When Robert Smith sang 'Pictures of You', I was shattered into smithereens. When he sings about gazing at pictures of someone for so long he begins to believe that they are real, I understand.

I want to huddle in the window of the Long Hall pub and drink hot whiskies as we watch the Dubliners dash by. I spent every Friday evening there, and sometimes Saturdays, too, before I moved. It's always overflowing with writers and journalists fishing for stories and drowning their writer's block with potions that are either the cause or the cure of their ailments. When you are squashed into that old Victorian magic spot, it could be any decade in Dublin; the characters there feel timeless, too. Shall we meet there? I can think of no better place to find you. I'll be the girl with the long red hair wrapped in a white rabbit-fur coat. Green eyes, Granny-Smith-apple green. Keep a look out for the most Irish-looking girl you can imagine, and that will be me. I always loved to quietly photograph the patrons in their oblivion, and some of those black-and-white portraits hang on the wall there now. I can point out which ones in the gallery are mine when we finally find ourselves there.

Some of my best work was born in those smoke-filled rooms. Those pictures gave me my first tentative inklings that I wanted to make photography my life's work. It's why I ultimately ended up here in this city, chasing that dream. One thing is for certain, however, this city is an endless runway of incredible portraits to capture; I love to walk the streets at night and spy creatures who come out only under the cover of darkness; to walk with protestors and paint their pain on film; to make invisible people visible. Have I photographed you in my travels? Would I know you if I saw you? I have so many happy memories of Dublin, and I hope I'll feel the same about this city one day. My camera allows me to participate in the life of the town, even though I'm alone; I can hide in broad daylight. No one notices you when your face is hiding behind a lens. Could we turn London into a home together? Write a new history here?

I think I can face the day now. I'm going for a walk along the South Bank to fill my wicker basket with paperbacks from the book stall. What are you doing today? Are you reading the Sunday papers? Cooking a roast? Driving in the country? Maybe you have something more adventurous planned. I'm jealous of whoever gets to spend the day with you.

I hope this letter finds you, and finds you well.

The small of my back misses your hand.

Yours,

Winter

William read the letter a second time, savouring now the words he had first raced through. London was his geographical time machine, as Dublin was for Winter; the ghosts of he and Clare lingered throughout the town, their entire adult lives so far played out on those streets. Were they a couple who didn't appreciate the wonder in their ordinary lives, like the couples Winter watched? Or was he one of the men who did not have the backbone to set them free? Maybe courage was what was needed to save them, too. He conjured up an image of Winter in his mind's eye: apple-green eyes, long, red hair vibrant against white rabbit fur. How he would love to walk with her down Columbia Road and choose a flower to tuck behind her ear. He remembered the excitement of those early dates with Clare, when she answered the door with only hope in her eyes. No doubts. To see that look in her eyes again would take a miracle. Had he any left inside him? How the idea of experiencing that feeling again seduced him; an open heart, a hopeful one. A heart like Winter's.

When he came home that evening, he found himself alone once again. Forgoing foraging in the fridge for fortification, he instead walked straight to the record player and placed The Cure's *Disintegration* album on the turntable. He lay on their cream corduroy sofa, the music swimming among his senses for 71 minutes and 47 seconds, and allowed himself to dream until the fatal click and whirr of the vinyl ending. Instead of waiting up for Clare, he went upstairs to bed, but not to sleep. By the light on his bedside locker, he scribbled pages of his chicken-scratching handwriting along lines and lines of an old refill pad that had hitherto lain dormant beneath a stack of patient books. He had been released.

Clare tried her utmost not to think about what had happened, but the knowledge stalked her like a hungry animal; the memory lingered like the smell of spilt milk on carpet. She knew now that moments of great reckoning happen on days that appear to be as ordinary as any other. They don't involve thunderstorms, premonitions or shivers down your spine.

They feel exactly the same as any other day, until the something happens. The sound of the telephone ringing had penetrated Clare's ears, past the defence of her shampoo. She was luxuriating in the feeling of frothy foam bubbling down her arched back, breathing in the aroma of coconut as she tangled and untangled her tresses. It was probably her mother, or a sales call – no one worth clambering from the shower for with sudsy hair and slippery feet. Blistering-hot water cascaded over her, the strain of a sleepless night swirling down the drain. Last night's annual Dead Letters Depot Fancy Dress Fundraiser had presented a more intense blend of discomfort than usual. Normally, the extent of her suffering was enduring the nonversation of William's colleagues as she feigned interest in their politics, hobbies, careers, and their children, whose names she had forgotten.

'So, when are you and Billy going to grace us with a

little Woolf? I'm sure he'd love a son to kick an encyclo-paedia around with.'

'We didn't see you at the sports day. I suppose it's just for those of us with kiddies, really, but you're still very welcome, you know. We had karaoke for the grown-ups. Would that appeal to you at all?'

'I was reading an article the other day about how the number of youths going through the courts every year keeps rising. What's the answer, Clare? Where did it all go wrong?'

This year's event had presented a further layer of stress. Clare's case had been adjourned to the evening session and so she knew she was going to be late even before the event began. A man was on trial for battery; he had defended his sister when her husband attacked her, and his brother-in-law pressed charges. The sister and brother were depending on Clare to win him his freedom. It was one of only three cases she had ever lost. Afterwards, there wasn't a moment to wipe the prosecutor's clammy handshake from her skin, to drown out the woman's quiet keening as her brother was led away. She couldn't flood her mind with Nina Simone songs or distract her-self with a recording of *Desert Island Discs* as she lay in the tub. Instead of indulging in a little cry before washing her face and painting a new one back on, she was forced to go straight to the party so as not to risk missing it entirely. There certainly wasn't time to don the Georgian-lady ensemble William had collected from the costume-hire emporium for her.

Her heels click-clacked down the marble hall towards

the function room, an echo of her courtroom walk. There, she was respected, powerful, in control. In the Prince Regent ballroom of the Highbury Hotel, she was a misfit among the fairy-tale characters, movie icons and monsters. Mr Flanagan appeared before her in a monk's habit. He looked far too convincing.

'Clare, you made it! Wonderful!' He leaned in with a kiss for her cheek, but it landed awkwardly on her ear instead. 'We called you up during the speeches to acknowledge the most generous donation made by your firm but, alas, you missed it. Your husband was very gracious about it, said you wouldn't want a fuss. Not to worry.'

'I'm sorry I wasn't here, Ned,' she answered, surreptitiously wiping her ear. 'I did hope to arrive earlier, but I was held up in court, unfortunately.'

He gestured her to walk with him and linked her arm in his. 'Don't concern yourself. We all know how busy you career girls are. Shame you couldn't dress up, though. Your Billy looks quite the picture in his tights.'

Clare smarted at being called a 'career girl' and turned away from him to face the dance floor. Mr Flanagan looked confused by her giving him the cold shoulder and, embarrassed by his confusion, scanned the room for William, who could relieve him. Clare's eyes found him first, although it took her a second to register that the bundle of energy spinning a Juliet figure swaddled in lemon chiffon was actually her husband.

'Ah-ha! There he is, with young Sally. Billy has been such a mentor to her over the last six months. I'd say he'll miss her when she's gone.'

So this was the infamous Sally. William had been suffering an extreme case of mentionitis since she had started working there: 'Sally came up with a terrific new catalogue system today – really quite remarkable in its efficiency'; 'Sally brought in home-made brown bread today, you really could taste the difference'; 'Sally told me the funniest joke today about Christopher Columbus'; 'Sally went canoeing at the weekend. Maybe we should try to get out in the world a bit more, try some new things.'

Canoeing! This from a man who wore his pullover to the beach on the hottest weekend in July last year. In fact, the only thing he hadn't mentioned about Sally was how utterly gorgeous she was. Why had she never asked him what Sally looked like? She had pictured a sad creature who got her kicks from birdwatching and making her own soap. The hue of the past few months shifted as she watched Sally shimmying around her husband, bending her back towards him. William was certainly not moping in the corner watching the door, as history had taught her to expect. Clare stood on the periphery of the dance floor, waiting for William to notice her. And on she waited. When he eventually stopped for breath, he was just in time to see Clare's back manoeuvring towards the exit. He shuffled awkwardly across the room, weaving around two vampires kissing, a giant apple and a very sad-looking clown. He caught Clare by her coat-tail as she slipped into the cool hallway, where the party became a strange-sounding, muffled other-world. A dark blush was creeping up from the lace collar of William's costume and his breathing was heavy.

'Clare, hey, wait a minute! Where are you going? Why aren't you wearing your costume? I was worried about you.'

'Not half as worried as you seem to be now. Having fun, were you?'

William's flushed face and burgeoning stammer did little to placate her.

'I was just dancing. Where are you going? How come you're so late?'

Clare readjusted the strap of the charcoal suede satchel that was slipping off her shoulder; the weight of its briefs set her slightly off balance and she cursed herself for not leaving it in the car. She was always so anxious in case it got stolen, details of her cases made public. The fallout from her old habit compounded her irritation.

'Well, I rushed straight here so as not to let you down, but I clearly needn't have bothered. Do you know how long I've been standing, waiting for you to finish your dance of the seven veils? Is that part of the work-experience programme? How to make a fool of your manager? Or his wife, at least?'

Clare noticed Marjorie eyeballing them from the dance floor and nudged William out of her sightline. He tried to take her satchel from her, but she yanked it back and hoisted it once again on to her shoulder. Their words rushed at each other like foot soldiers, focused only on their own purpose: not to listen, just to be heard.

'Clare, what are you talking about? I'm glad you've made it.'

'Don't try to pacify me, I –'

'I've spent most of the evening just sitting on my own, waiting for you. Sally –'

'So, it's my fault? Because I have responsibilities?'

'Sally dragged me –'

'Stop saying her name. I don't want to hear –'

'She just felt sorry for me.'

'What? The neglected husband? It's me she should have sympathy for.'

'I'm sorry I didn't see you, but it's packed in there. You should've come over.'

Clare let her satchel slam on to the floor. The thud on the marble tiles echoed around the lofty walls, and more faces turned to look. She took a breath, smoothing down the lapels of her suit jacket, and her voice became an angry whisper.

'What? And spoil the fun? Besides, I wanted to watch you. Witness how you behave when I'm not there. Who you are. You reminded me of someone I used to know.'

The words lashed out of her before she had time to think about what she was saying. Had she gone too far? William fell silent. Afraid of the look in Clare's eyes. Fearful of the bag of snakes squirming in his belly, afraid that one might circle his heart, rise up his throat and speak.

'Woolfie, Woolfie! There you are! Where's my champagne?'

Sally was aglow with excitement as she skipped down

the hall, her shining ebony hair spiralling in electric curls about her shoulders. She turned towards Clare.

'Hello. They seem to have run out of champagne. Could you ask them to send some more through?'

William jumped in before Clare turned a whiter shade of rage.

'Sally, this is Clare. She doesn't work here, actually. She's my wife.'

'Oh! Oh, I see, it's just . . . the suit . . . Well, it's so nice to meet you.'

Sally offered her hand to Clare, a limp invitation, held closer to her own body than Clare's. William slowly exhaled when Clare extended her own strong hand to complete the exchange. She didn't say anything to Sally, though, but turned to face William once more.

'I'm leaving. Come, if you like. Or stay and play. I've certainly had enough.'

'Of course! Yes, let's go. I'll just grab my coat. Wait here?'

Clare sat stiffly down in a brocade velvet armchair and gripped the arm rest. William hurried down the hall, Sally scampering along beside him. Clare watched as Sally took his elbow and stood on tiptoe to whisper in his ear. It horrified her that William jumped away, like a man receiving a blow. He glanced back over his shoulder to see if she was watching. Clare shook her head at him before rising and stalking towards the front door alone.

The drive home was impossibly long. A new, unfamiliar silence to those they were accustomed to settled between them. They became like three uncomfortable strangers forced to share a bed: a husband, a wife and the row that loomed. Clare clenched the steering wheel, turning the windscreen wipers on against the drizzles of rain, forgetting to turn them off again when the rain stopped, despite their dry screeching over the glass. In the past, theirs had been a gentle love, not prone to arguments, accusations, recriminations. Now, this new world, where a battle seemed always to be in the post, had somehow robbed them of their easy talking and familiar affection. Clare nursed her wounds through red lights, roundabouts and stop signs until the sanctuary of their home gave her licence to let go.

There, she bent over the kitchen sink, scrubbing dried-on cornflakes from the breakfast bowls they had abandoned that morning, running late as usual, escaping from the house. He hovered around the kitchen door.

'I don't really understand what's going on here, Clare. I was only dancing with one of the women from work. I really think you're overreacting.'

Clare froze mid-scrub, and her shoulders closed together another inch.

'William, you don't think I'm overreacting or you wouldn't look like a child who has dropped an egg. If there is nothing going on between you and that teenager, why are you acting so guiltily?' She turned to face him and watched the question flicker across his face while he searched for an answer.

'Because I do feel guilty.' His answer was a slap in the face, and she felt a momentary panic grip her. What was he going to confess to? William registered her shock and rushed over to her, placing his hands on her shoulders. 'Not because I've done anything wrong,' he continued, 'just because I've upset you. I wanted tonight to be a chance for us to have some fun. I can't believe it's turned out like this.'

Clare turned away from him and watched his reflection in the kitchen window.

'So you're telling me that this girl who you've been going on about for months means nothing to you? And the fact that you never mentioned she looks like she's walked off the cover of *Teen Vogue* was an accidental oversight?'

He started wrestling the rubbish bag from the bin, frustrated when the jagged contents caught on the rim. 'Why would I comment on what she looked like? And anyway, I hadn't really noticed that she was anything special to look at, not really.'

Clare clattered two spoons on to the draining board.

'Oh, please don't patronize me. At least if you acknowledged that you fancied her –'

'*Fancied her?* Are we back in Year Ten now?'

'At least then I might be able to believe you. *Pretending* you've never noticed just convinces me even more that you've got something to cover up. Admit it. You find her attractive!'

William's eyes ran around the room, looking for inspiration in the washing on the clothes horse, the glasses winking at him on the dresser, the grout between their no longer quite so white floor tiles.

'Fine. So she's an attractive girl. So what? It doesn't mean anything. I'm sure you meet good-looking men at work all the time.'

She turned the hot tap on full and the water blasted the sink.

'Yes, William, I do. But I don't spend every second I can with them, regale you with tales of how fabulous they are or spend the evening in their arms at work dos.'

'I don't spend evenings with her! You're exaggerating!'

'And I certainly would never lie to your face about them. In fact, as far as I know, that's the first time you've lied to me about anything. As far as I know.'

'I wasn't lying to you! I was just trying to protect you from worrying about something that doesn't matter. And anyway, what about Max?'

She bent over and held her hair in fistfuls in her hands.

'Oh, you've got to be kidding me! What has Maxi got to do with anything? Don't try and turn this around on me!'

William walked towards Clare and reached behind her to turn off the tap.

'Ah, yes, of course, it's Max*ee*. As if it wasn't tedious enough, the way he follows you around like a puppy, he has to have a name like a child's pet, too. I'm surprised he hasn't caused an accident in the workplace, with all the drool he leaves behind him.'

'Don't be so childish. We're just friends, as you very well know.'

'Do I? Really, Clare? Is that what he thinks?'

'Is that why you've been carrying on with Sally? To get back at me for having friends of my own at work?'

'Carrying on? Nothing has happened with Sally, okay? Can we just drop this? I just enjoy the company of a beautiful young woman at work. So what?'

The rage Clare had been trying to control erupted, and she smashed the last of their honeymoon bowls on the floor. It was a second before she realized that the shocked howl which accompanied the sound of breaking china had come from her. The noise reverberated inside her head. She gripped the kitchen sink, her arms trembling. Slowly, she floated back down inside herself, empty now.

William took a step closer but hesitated before he reached for her.

'Clare, that sounded bad, I know, but I didn't mean anything by it. Honestly. Why don't you go into the living room and I'll clean up in here? I'll get us a drink. Clare?'

The fragments of china crunched underfoot as she brushed past him and walked stiffly to their bedroom. Upstairs, Clare turned the lock and rested her head against the powder-blue door frame she had so carefully painted without smudging the walls. William had installed the lock for her so she could barricade herself in if burglars ever came during the night. She had never thought she would use it against him. He wasn't the sort of man who would kick the door down to get to her, although a part of her wished he was. Instead, he shuffled quietly up and knocked softly. A barely audible whisper coaxed through the wood. He told her he would wait outside all night until she was ready to talk, but it wasn't long before his shadow disappeared and she could hear him riffling through the airing cupboard for something to sleep under on the couch. Clare's anger slowly turned inward. She despised herself for losing her temper and lashing out like her mother would have done. She had worked too hard to rid herself of those fingerprints and was furious that William had provoked that in her. There was a reason she had settled with a man like him and not one of the Jamies of this world: he was supposed to be stable, solid, trustworthy; not someone who would cause her to smash crockery.

That night, Clare put on one of her father's old shirts which she had salvaged from the charity-shop pile her mother made when he passed away. Her wet cheeks dirtied the sleeves with her smudged make-up as she roughly scrubbed it from her face. As the clenching in her bowel eased, the emptiness of their bed enveloped her. Was she losing her mind? Maybe she *had* overreacted. Had he really given her any reason to doubt him? Was she just looking for an easy answer to what was already happening between them? Attack as the best form of defence?

She got up and sat on the floor with her back resting against the bed. William's question about Maxi settled on her now. Her husband was no fool, not really. So far, she had held Maxi at arm's length, but it was becoming increasingly difficult to rationalize why she did so, when William offered her fewer and fewer reasons to stay. Maxi seemed to offer everything William couldn't: an equal partnership, ambition, success. He was the most accomplished partner in their firm but still found time to publish papers in the *Law Review*, train for triathlons and take ski-ing holidays every quarter. Just the sort of man who would have been out of her league once upon a time. It was enticing, but would he make up stories for her about a superhero named Clare and hide them in her briefcase? Or wake up early to get the papers for her every Sunday, and present them to her on a tray (having taken out the supplements she wasn't interested in) with a pot of tea and toast soldiers with the crusts cut off? Would she ever feel confident enough to sing along to the radio in front of him, even though she couldn't carry a tune? Probably not, but maybe there would be other things, though. New intimacies she hadn't discovered yet.

She shook her thoughts away from Maxi. Maybe she should go to William and try to salvage a night's sleep for both of them, but every time she circled closer to the idea of reconciliation, the image of that girl on her tiptoes whispering to him slammed back into the forefront of her mind and paralysed her. William had looked at that girl in a way she thought he reserved only for her. Some-thing about the way his arm reached out to her, the lean of his head, the familiarity, their closeness on the dance floor. She couldn't convince herself that it was all in her mind. In her bones, she knew something wasn't right. She just didn't know if something had already happened or whether it was brewing. Maybe it wasn't too late, but if, all this time, she had been standing by him while he had been having an affair, she thought she would never recover.

★

When dawn broke, the sunlight was a searchlight exposing the madness of her night. She looked in the mirror in despair at her blotchy face, tangled hair and damp shirt. The crumpled sheets were balled at the foot of the bed. She lay still as a stone at the bottom of a black lake, straining for sounds of William, until she heard the front door close softly behind him. She was momentarily surprised that he hadn't come to see her before he left but was relieved not to have to speak to him just yet. The great purge of feeling the night before had cleared her thoughts. Things could not continue as they were; otherwise, in twelve months from now, five years from now, a decade from now, they would still be stuck. She needed to escape. This flat was oppressing them, and they would never face their fears, their feelings and failures, while they were living here together. She needed to do something drastic to force them into action.

That was when she staggered to the shower, where she attempted to wash the terrible row down the drain and ignore the telephone ringing. The first time. And the second. On the third attempt, with her hair rinsed clean, she surrendered. Wrapped in William's dressing gown, she ran to the telephone, determined to rid herself of the persistent pest. Wet tendrils sent shivers down her spine as she impatiently snatched at the receiver. She was drying her legs with the ends of the gown as she prepared for a quick disconnection, but the voice at the other end surprised her. It was Maxi, and he was calling from the telephone box at the end of her street.

6.

On the morning after the fancy-dress fundraiser, productivity at the depot was particularly low. Mr Flanagan cancelled the morning meeting because of poor attendance, and even Marjorie's constant sound effects were reduced to a low, plaintive whine as she nursed her headache on the mustard leather love-seat in the kitchen. The remnants of last night's mascara remained smudged around her bleary eyes. Sally had not shown up for work at all and William was relieved not to see her, as Clare's accusations continued to crash about inside his head. Nothing had happened between them. To say, however, that the charms of Sally in all her flirtatious glory had been completely lost on him was untrue. The ability to pull the thread lay at his fingertips and, sometimes, they twitched to do it. Perhaps he should have told Clare the truth, but he couldn't imagine any version of that story where he could emerge from the conversation unscathed. He knew there were no bonus points for fidelity – surely that was the baseline for reasonable behaviour – and he was prepared to accept last night as a warning. When that bowl smashed, he felt the very foundations of their marriage shake. Where had Clare's rage come from? It frightened him to think how easily she had snapped; how long had that temper been building inside her? In their early days together, he worried about how completely self-controlled she was, so cold when they argued, but now, it was as if the feelings she had suppressed were exploding from within. How much had she been hiding from him? He couldn't risk any further cracks permeating their marriage; it was time to douse out this frisson with Sally before something happened that he couldn't undo.

The day Sally appeared in the dust-filled hallway of the depot, with her shiny youth and infectious optimism, it had felt akin to an alien invasion. It would have been easy to get carried away by the attention she lavished upon him, surprised though he was to receive it, but in reality, he knew he was just enjoying the distraction. He was more relieved now than ever that he had stayed on the right side of that war; he would put more distance between them.

If only it was as easy to close the door on Winter, he thought; images of her quietly invaded his mind each day. As he walked the streets of London, his eyes searched for her, convinced that he would recognize her if she appeared. What would he do if she did? He was looking for a sign that these letters were brought to him specifically by some higher power, an entity greater than his common sense could control, something that would force his hand in the crucial moment.

William sat at his desk and sorted through a new bundle destined for the Supernatural Division: a letter to Godot, one for 'The Fairy Godmother of Lucy Sparrow' and a tired old envelope addressed in blue colouring pencil to

'The Ringmaster of the Circus'. He sliced through the top of this last envelope with the bone-handled letter opener Clare had given him to commemorate his ten-year anniversary at the depot. It was inscribed 'A decade of lost letters, 1979–1989'. It always felt so heavy in his hand that he felt infused with a sense of great purpose and importance when he used it. He prised out a sheet of grey paper that was almost as fine as tissue and began to read.

Dear Ringmaster of the Circus,

My name is Harvey and I am 10 and ¾ years old. You might think I am younger than that because I am a bit small but I really am almost 11. I might already even be that age before you read my letter so maybe I should have just said that's how old I am but I didn't want to tell a fib.

I don't know how long letters take to get to the circus but I hope not too long. We only have four days left in school before we break up for the summer. Everyone in my class is really looking forward to us getting out and they're all showing off about going on aeroplanes and summer camps and having lessons in all sorts of things. My dad doesn't believe in lessons, not those kinds anyway – just what he can teach me himself. Which I'm beginning to think won't be much good for me.

I'm writing to you because I'm hoping you might have a job for me this summer (and I wouldn't mind not going back to school in September if you wanted to keep me on). I've made a list of things you might need to know and tried to think up all the questions you might ask if you were standing here in your top hat and stripy coat.

- I haven't ever been inside the circus but every year I watch you from the bridge bringing all the animals off the trailers and I know every one you've got. The elephant is my favourite but I would treat them all the same. I'm not even frightened of the lion but don't fancy feeding him being my first job if that would be ok with you.
- I'm stronger than other 10, nearly 11, year olds because one of my jobs at home is bringing in the firewood and it's made me tough so I'm good for lifting and carrying.
- I'm not a fussy eater and don't need much feeding. Spuds give me cramps but I'll eat them if that's all there is.
- I have my own tent and sleeping bag that I've hidden in my friend Polly's shed. I won it at the sports day but couldn't bring it home in case my dad needs money for his stuff and sells it. Polly's mam lets me put it up in their garden sometimes when I need to get out of our house.
- I'm not bothered about making much money but if you could give me enough for stamps to send a letter to my nan now and then it would be great cos I know she'll worry about me.
- I'd be happy to do any work that you have but if I could work with the animals I'd really like that

best. I've a way of talking to them that they like and I trained my nan's spaniel to do all sorts of tricks. I wouldn't like having to use the whip, though. I hope I could just coax them along instead.

I'll keep my bag packed in case you need me so I'm ready to run if you send a note to my nan's house. Please don't come to my house because my dad wouldn't like it. There's no mam to notice me gone though, so don't worry about that.

Thanks very much, Mr Ringmaster. I promise I'll do my best if you'll have me.

From,
Harvey Lawless

William rocked back in his chair, balancing it on two legs. What happens when a little boy whose only hope lies in running away with the circus doesn't get an answer? William looked at the postmark; the letter was two years old. He made a note of the boy's name, age and the sorting office that first processed it to share with Social Services. It wasn't a lot of information to go on, but maybe they could find him. There was a lady he had dealt with before when worrying letters such as these came his way; she was relentless in her efforts to track down a child in trouble. He couldn't know to what extent the boy was being neglected, but he wasn't prepared to presume the best. If Harvey was still hoping for an answer, she was the best person he could send his letter to, and the best chance he had for intervention. He put Harvey's letter to one side and opened his second envelope of the morning.

My darling Nora,

Where are you today as you turn twenty-one and take your first steps into the world as a young woman? I try to imagine how you might look if your hair had stayed as black as it was on the day you were born but grew into the curls I might have given you. I'm sure your eyes are still the cappuccino colour of your father's and your skin the colour of caramel, but I find it hard to picture you all grown up. You were such a tiny baby, just five pounds, so I would guess you are petite now, like me and your grandma before us, but maybe your legs and arms grew tall like your daddy's. It breaks my heart not to know and to think of you wondering which of your parents you took after, or worrying that we didn't want you.

I can't say how your daddy felt, because he never knew, or at least I never told him, but I wanted you more than anything. When my belly grew big and they sent me away to the convent in Wales, I thought it was so I could bring you up there without anyone knowing. I had a story all made up in my head about your father passing away and leaving me a widow, that I'd had to sell my wedding ring to put a deposit on the flat, but that wasn't what they had in mind.

After you were born, they only left you with me for a day before Sr Assumpta in the hospital came to me and said your new parents would be there to collect you in the morning. I tried to explain there was some terrible mistake, but my father had signed the adoption papers. I was only fifteen, you see, and she said it was too late. I stayed up all night holding you in my arms, crying like the rain. I must have eventually dozed off because the next morning Sr Assumpta woke me as she snatched you and turned on her heel out of the ward. I raced after her, tripping up in my bed sheets as I ran, and made it half-way down the corridor before one of the orderlies grabbed me and wrestled me on to the floor. I could hear you crying through the sound of my own howls but, no matter how much I struggled, I couldn't get free. I remember how cold the tiles on the floor felt as I crumpled into a pile at the feet of the orderly and lay my cheek on the ground. From where I fell, I could see his navy trousers were an inch too short for him and exposed his ankles in two odd socks, one dark grey with a black stripe and one just grey. He pulled me up on to my feet and half carried me back to the ward, where one of the nurses was stripping my bed. I stood at the window and watched a couple lifting a Moses basket into the back of a silver saloon car and knew it was you. He wore a dark-navy suit with a royal-blue tie and she had on a white dress with a pink bolero jacket, a white headkerchief holding back blonde curls from the wind. And that was all I knew of them, the people who took you from me, but I hoped they would give you a good life, a better life than you might have had with me.

Not a day has gone by since when I haven't thought

of you, imagined you going on holidays in their silver car, holding hands with that lady as you walked to school, clambering on to those navy suit legs for a story. And I've tracked every milestone – when you would be walking, talking, sitting exams, every birthday, Christmas and New Year, wondering if you have a boyfriend yet and hoping, if you do, that he's nice to you. I'd give anything to know what your plans are for the future, if you've gone to university, or have travelled to faraway places. And most of all, I just want to know that you are happy and that my great sadness resulted in great happiness for you. I wonder if sometimes you missed me, even if you didn't understand the feeling of loss you had. On my good days, I hope you didn't but, in my heart of hearts, I'm terrified that you didn't miss me at all, that you might never ask the questions that could lead you back to me.

I'll be waiting for ever, just in case.

All my heart and my hope,

Mam

William scanned the envelope again, desperately hoping he had missed the presence of a return address, but it was in vain. He would do some research later: try to identify the convent, see if there was still someone there who might be able to help – but he feared the worst. This was the hardest part of his job; when a letter that had the potential to change a life was irrevocably lost. He could only hope they found each other by some other means.

He swallowed the lump that formed in his throat.

Why did Clare not have any of those maternal feelings? Had she so little confidence in him that she believed they wouldn't be able to make it work? If a fifteen-year-old girl had wanted to try to raise a baby herself, like so many others, why couldn't they, together? He absent-mindedly stirred the mail in the postbag while he tried to imagine it, he and Clare as parents, raising a child. What sort of person would be borne of the collision of their gene pools? He hoped their child would look like Clare; the very thought of a miniature version of her made his heart swell. He would speak to her again; maybe their relationship was stagnating because it hadn't evolved and was stuck at this impasse. Perhaps if he finished *A Volume of Lost Letters*, or was able to write something new, she might have more faith in him. It still felt, after all these years, like she was waiting for him to prove himself. If she wasn't monitoring his behaviour constantly, would he try harder without the scrutiny or give up the ghost altogether? The domino effect was impossible to predict; he had been holding everything so still for so long.

He swooshed letters around in the half-empty trolley while questions joyrided through his mind. His fingers recognized the texture of the envelope before his brain fully understood what he had found: another letter from Winter. He edged it to the surface, heart racing, paranoia prickling his skin. He looked left and right to ensure he was alone, holding it lightly between his fingertips, hands trembling. He leaned on the windowsill, smoothed the midnight-blue pages out before him and allowed himself to nurse an idea that his heart always returned to. Maybe these letters really were destined for him. Why else was it he who found them? No. He would not surrender to the power of this letter. He could not allow some idealistic vision of a one, true love to sabotage the real-life love he had at home. He was going to see his wife and put a stop to this madness.

He cringed a little at the crease he inflicted upon the envelope by folding it into the deep pocket of the Aran cardigan he wore. He closed the wooden button with determination and strode on to the fourth-floor landing. Should he go to Clare's office? No, home first, to change into something more respectable, tame his hair; he wouldn't suffer Maxi looking down his nose at him if he turned up looking like a middle-aged arts student. William wrapped a long tweed scarf about him and tucked it inside his cardigan. He scribbled a note about a minor emergency and dropped it on Marjorie's desk before he left, grateful that she wasn't there.

The wind scattered London debris around his feet as he tried to tidy his mind. He clenched and released his hands against the cold February bite. Had he left his gloves at the party? No, he remembered pulling on a rogue strand of wool that dangled from the cuff on the drive home. He had teased it, daring it to unravel, but the knot just tightened and caused the stitches to wrinkle together. He paused on the pavement two doors away from their flat to watch as the postman leaned from his bicycle to deliver their mail; today was not the day for a lengthy tirade on the internal gremlins of Royal Mail. He waited for him to push on to number twelve, and the sight of a gleaming jet-black BMW parked at the end of the street caught his eye. They must be lost, he thought. No one around here drives a car like that. He walked the last few steps to their door at a funereal pace, beginning to question the wisdom of this impulse. His initial determination was replaced by a sinking sense of foreboding. He rested his forehead against their forest-green front door before opening it slowly. He pushed the letters that had just arrived across their welcome mat and stepped inside. Silence. No sound of life at all. No radio playing. No kettle boiling. No footsteps. And then he saw Clare. Sitting sideways, watching him from the top of the stairs, a pen in her hand poised over a pad balanced on her knee. Her hair, still damp, was bunched in a loose knot on the top of her head, although she was wearing her grey mac, as if ready to leave the house. Her eyes were dry but glass-like, on the verge of spilling over. Their questions collided.

'Clare, what are you still doing here?'

'William, why are you back?'

She stood up and tied the belt on her mac tightly around her as she came down the stairs. He saw she was wearing his old *Star Wars* T-shirt underneath and took a strange comfort in it.

'I was just leaving you a note,' she said.

'What on earth for? Where are you going? Clare, what's going on?'

She walked past him at the foot of the stairs without meeting his eye. He reached out his hand to grab her shoulder as she passed, but she shrugged him away. In the living room, she perched on the edge of the sofa. Her eyes didn't rise to meet his when he came and sat beside her.

'I know last night was awful, but please don't do anything drastic. Maybe we just needed to have a blow-out, clear the air, so to speak.'

She turned to look at him, took his hand between both of hers.

'William, listen to me. I'm going to go away for a few days so that we can both have some proper time to think. It doesn't work, this passive-aggressive way we have of living here. We just skirt around our problems but never confront anything. Not properly.'

He pulled his hand away and stood up to protest.

'No, Clare. This is wrong. We should work things out together.'

She stayed perfectly still, her voice level.

'Why are you so afraid of me having some time on my own to think?'

He was lost for a moment in her gaze: one green eye, one blue. Watching her now from across the room, William wondered when he had last really looked at her. He held such a fixed image of her in his mind from when they first met. He often nursed a memory from when they had just moved in together: Clare lying sleeping in their new bay window, wearing just her Blondie T-shirt, white cotton shorts and blue knee socks. Her nap interrupted them painting the living room a shade of moody plum. The paintbrush dangled from the tips of her long, delicate fingers but she had not let it go. The deep purple paint streaked down her arms, blobbed on her feet and slowly dried in her still-blonde hair. In the fading light, she had looked almost translucent. William stroked her hair; she brushed his hand away and her eyelashes batted open. The smile that spread across her startled face and the love in her eyes were photographed by his heart and filed for ever as an image he would often return to in his mind's eye. They were never happier than at that time, when they had only hope for the future and no idea yet of how disconnected they would become.

Now, he realized with a wave of remorse how much their faces had aged since they met aged twenty-one and twenty-two; the work of fourteen years looked like more. Their youth had fallen between the floorboards of their flat while they were looking elsewhere. Now, a few strands of grey were weaving from her temples, tracing a path through her mouse-brown bob, extending the lines that seemed to have appeared around her eyes over-night. The texture of his skin had taken on a strange pallor, a tint of yellow; only the sun could warm the bloom back into his face. The pink of her lips had become so pale; his muscles, softer. Her eyes remained unchanged, though. The face around them might crinkle, but she could never look old to him when he looked into those eyes. They didn't grow older, only colder. As everything around them shifted, it was Clare's eyes that reminded him she was the same girl he had fallen in love with. The eyes he had made sparkle, flash, soften, cry.

'I'm afraid you won't come home,' he replied, his voice catching.

She smiled at him.

'Isn't that all the more reason why we need this?' she asked.

In his heart of hearts, he knew it was true, but the panic mounting in him wouldn't let him stand down.

'No, Clare. This is madness. I swear nothing happened with that girl. You believe me, don't you?'

She stood up and walked towards him.

'This isn't about anyone else, William. We both know that, don't we?'

He nodded, but kept his eyes fixed firmly on her pointy blue shoes.

'How long will you be gone?'

'I don't know. I've told the office not to expect me for a few days, at least.'

'But what about all your cases?'

'After ten years with barely a holiday, they can't really object to me finally taking some time off. And they know where to find me if there's an emergency.'

'And what about me? What if I need to find you?'

'William, ask yourself this. If I didn't leave and everything continued on as before, do you really think, in one year from now, we'd be somehow happy? Would anything have changed? Or would we still be stuck in the same place?'

He looked at her, searched inside himself for an answer that wouldn't come. The hopeful silence hung between them; if he could just find the right words to make her stay, he knew they would survive, but the atmosphere burst and the moment passed.

Clare placed her hand on his arm and leaned forward to kiss him on the cheek. As she turned away, he noticed his volume of e e cummings' poetry sitting open on the coffee table, where he had left it the night before. At the beginning of their relationship, Clare would often rest her head in the little dip between his shoulder and chest while William read his favourite poems softly aloud as he stroked her hair; cummings, Keats, Yeats, Blake, Wordsworth. For his wedding vows, William had threaded different lines of cummings' poetry together to make his promises to Clare. As he worried the ivory wedding band over her freezing cold finger, his voice cracked as he recited, 'i carry your heart with me (i carry it in my heart)'. He picked the book up in his hands; a worry bead to give him strength.

She placed her hands on top of it and whispered, 'I'm exhausted, William. I don't sleep. You don't sleep. We stay up half the night not talking to each other. I'm too tired. "Tired of things that break, and – Just tired."'

William felt a frost settle over his skin, prickling, numbing, crackling at the familiar words. He paused before he spoke, yearning for his gut to show him the way.

'Clare, wait! "But I come with a dream in my" –'

She pushed him away. '*No, William! No!*' she shouted. 'It's too late for that.'

William fell to his knees and buried his face in the pleats of her dove-grey silk skirt. His sobs were wretched and he couldn't hear her crying over his own wet, thick, desperate sounds of protest. Clare stood with the palms of her hands over her eyes, quiet little tears squeezing through her trembling fingers. She tried to step backwards without touching William. He fell forward but didn't let go, so she awkwardly wrestled his arms from around her knees and stepped over him, a semicircle heap of a man. He watched her pick up a suitcase in the hallway that seemed to have appeared from nowhere. How could he not have seen it as he came in? She didn't look back as she rushed out of the front door and closed it gently behind her. William remained immobile on the floor.

7.

After Clare left, William sat staring at the closed front door until his limbs fell into a sleepy ache. Without anything useful to do, he rose to put the kettle on to boil and stood watching it. He listened to its dry squealing for a moment before he realized he hadn't filled it with water. Steam burned his hand as he held it under the tap. The water flowed over, dampening the sleeve of his cardigan so the wool became soggy against his wrist. He slapped his hand against the edge of the sink and cutlery scattered across the draining board. How could he have let her leave? His gaze wandered around the kitchen he had spent so many evenings in with Clare, talking, kissing, cooking, eating, cleaning, decorating, dancing, fighting. He heard a quiet crinkle of paper as he leaned into the sink and remembered Winter's letter in his pocket. He sighed. Would it make him feel better or worse to read it now? Anything was better than the silence of their empty flat. He abandoned the full kettle on the kitchen counter and climbed to the top of the stairs, sat where Clare had been perched writing to him. The discarded notebook lay open; only 'Dear William' written before he had interrupted her. The hallway looked different from there; so far below, like a theatre set waiting for a performance to begin. He groaned, rubbed his tired eyes, removed the letter from its envelope and balanced it on his knee as he read.

My Great Love,

It is such a comfort to me, being able to write to you like this. To talk in a safe place where I can acknowledge you and how much you mean to me. It's difficult to discuss you with anyone else, of course. It's important to me that others don't know how much it bothers me being without you. There can be something so tragic about anyone whose life revolves exclusively around their search for a perfect mate. I often think, if they just spent less time obsessing about their potential other half, they would find themselves a complete whole, nonetheless. So please don't misunderstand me; I have a very full and, oftentimes, lovely life. I don't need a man per se and know I could carve out a life of great adventure entirely on my own – if I had to. I would just rather not. I'm not ready yet to let go of the idea that there is one great love for me out there, that you are still searching for me, too. I can feel it in my bones. I want someone to travel with and share the experience of discovery. Someone to talk to when I come home in the evenings so we can bear witness to each other's lives and understand the importance of a million little things.

I want someone to see me, all the colours of my personality, and love me anyway. But I would rather be alone than pretend to have found the right someone. To sit here and write these letters and wait impatiently for you rather than to talk myself into loving another. I refuse to settle for anything less than a magnificent love. I want the sort of love people have fought wars over, walked thousands of miles for, made sacrifices, forsaken all others for. I'll never ask you to do any terrible things to prove your devotion, but I want to know that you would. I want poetry and passion, a particular love that is specific to you and me. No roses or champagne or candlelit dinners – no generic romantic expressions but rather ones that could be inspired only by the most intimate knowledge of the very heart of me.

I want to have children with someone I believe will inspire them to be the most brilliant of humans, a man that will love them unconditionally and give them the confidence to follow their dreams. My father always encouraged me to believe that I could do anything, be anyone. If not for him, I might never have left home for London with just my camera and the idea that I could be a proper photographer if this city was my studio. Many people question if I made the right decision, leaving what they considered to be the perfect job at home. I spent years working for a small independent record label, coaxing Ireland's DJs to play songs and to promote albums for the next big thing. It was definitely an adventure – concerts, festivals, tours – but I reached a point where I thought I couldn't imagine doing it for ever. It was time for me to stop facilitating the dreams of others and allow myself the chance to follow my own. So I left. I swapped my wishbone for a backbone, as they say, and committed myself to the realization of the dream that brought me here. Any of the men I have known in my life so far, I have struggled to imagine them as a father and a best friend as well as my lover. Someone who will encourage me to follow my heart, while he does the same. Those two things don't have to be mutually exclusive, do they? That's why I'm still waiting for you. I'm not asking for too much, am I? When the moment comes, please don't hesitate. Seize it. Seize this spectacular love for us.

Maybe you'll see me this evening when I catch the Northern Line to Camden Town. I'm meeting my good friend Peter for some Mexican food and mojitos in our favourite restaurant by the station – a hot remedy to spice life up after a grey week spent in Ireland with his parents. He finds it hard to reconcile London Peter with the Peter from the small town he left behind. I can relate. It's far from Mexican food he was reared. Isn't that the magic of this city? You can experiment with a thousand different lives, experience something new, and then continue or cast it aside. Sometimes, I worry the city makes us do that to people, too. There's always someone else to turn your head; potential lovers race by as frequently as the Tube. What if your great love just hadn't revealed their true self before you moved on?

I declare tonight to be my new New Year's Eve. Why wait until 31 December for new resolutions, new beginnings? I wish you were here to kiss me at midnight.

Happy New Year, My Great Love. Can we please start a new year together?

Yours,

Winter

William lay on his back on the carpet of the landing, his eyes focused on the cobwebs in the corners of the ceiling. *I would rather be alone than pretend.* He whispered the words like a mantra; wasn't that the belief Jack Kerouac had instilled in him all those years ago? Back then, it was still easy to believe in a great love; he hadn't yet been disappointed, worn down. Was Winter naïve? Or was she just less jaded than him? A *spectacular love*: the younger William had believed anything less was a travesty. Now, after being in a relationship with Clare for fourteen years, had his essential self changed? Was the real tragedy not allowing their spectacular love to grow into something perhaps less sparkling but more stable? Was real romance just persevering when times were hard, hidden in the daily domestic rituals of a life shared? He didn't think he would ever convince Winter of that. Could he convince himself?

Perhaps Winter was right, and maybe he was one of those who spent too long obsessing about who should complete him instead of thinking of what he could do to complete himself. He needed to make himself whole. The thought of two people independently pursuing their dreams without either making a sacrifice struck him. Had he held Clare back? Was it fair for her to lay that at his door? It made him shiver to think how well Winter seemed to know him. He was so vulnerable to her command to find her. To want more. If Winter were a flesh-and-blood person standing in front of him and presenting her case, would he be able to resist? Oh, how deceitful his heart was to the logic his head struggled to hold! He remembered the quote from Blaise Pascal that his English professor had carved over her door: 'The heart has its reasons which reason knows nothing of.' He knew now that it was true.

He had to escape the flat. Before he had time to consider the wisdom of his actions, he reached for the telephone and dialled Stevie's number. Clare wasn't there to object. He answered on the first ring.

'Well, as I live and breathe, look who's crawling out of the woodwork. If you're going to ask me to reunite the band, well, you'd better have a good –'

Stevie's voice sounded hoarse, as if he had just woken up, which was always highly probable, regardless of what time you called him.

'I'm not, tempting as it is. Although, if I did, it would be far less mad than what's actually been happening recently.'

William caught the panicked tone in his own voice and tried to swallow it away while Stevie asked, 'Oh? What's going on? Oh God! You're not having a baby, are you? Please don't say that.'

'Why do you say that like it's the worst news I could possibly have to tell you? What if I was terminally ill or something?'

He laughed, despite himself, before Stevie shot back, 'I know which problem I'd rather have.'

William creaked the drawers of the dilapidated sideboard on which the telephone rested open and closed. He seemed incapable of sitting still any longer. 'Look, a baby wouldn't have to be a . . . Forget it. Clare's not pregnant, and I'm not dying of anything, not that I know of.'

'So, what's going on then, stranger?'

A silence hung between them on the telephone line.

'Nothing. Not really. I just thought it might be time for us to catch up and maybe have a few drinks, grab some food or something?'

Stevie snorted. 'For no particular reason? I don't buy it, but I'll bite. I've started working in a cool record shop on the Market, Seven Deadly Spins! You could call in to see me tomorrow? Or I have a gig with Blue Lagoon at the Windmill in Brixton next week, if you fancy it?'

'I'd rather eat my own feet than stand watching those clowns. What about this evening? Are you still in that bedsit in Chalk Farm? I could meet you in Camden, maybe?'

'Tonight? Has Clare not got something scheduled already for you? I didn't think you were allowed out on your own.'

William could hear the smirk in Stevie's voice but knew it disguised a very real hurt that he saw so little of him. He shouldn't have left it so long to call.

'Don't be daft,' he replied, in a softer voice now. 'Anyway, Clare's away. At the moment. With work.'

'Oh, I see. So, while the cat's away, eh? Fiiiiiine, I am free tonight, as it happens. This girl I was meant to take to the cinema cancelled on me because she has scarlet fever. Thank Heavens – she wanted to go and see *Ghost*. Patrick Swayze is in it, which is a plus, but apparently it's all about pottery or –'

William cut him off. 'So, will I meet you at Camden Tube at eight? Do you know any Mexican restaurants around there?'

'Mexican?' Stevie sounded indignant. 'What do you want Mexican for? Let's get a curry, like we always do.'

Why did everything have to be a battle? 'I just fancy it, that's all. Maybe we can have a walk around and see if we find one. You're the one who says I need to try new things.'

Stevie emitted a little whine, but acquiesced.

'Oh, aaaaallll right, then. I think there's one on the way to Mornington Crescent. Sombrero Jim's, or something, it's called, but it looks kind of like a disco bar . . .'

William whooped. 'Yes! I bet that's the place. It's a date.'

'What do you mean, that's the place? What place?'

'Wear something normal, okay?'

'I refuse to be bound by your limited understanding of fashion and your lack of individuality.'

'Well, at least cover up, do you hear? Nothing with too much flesh showing!'

William hung up before Stevie could ask any more questions. He was already doubting the wisdom of re-introducing his old sidekick into the current turbulence of his life, but, for the first time in a long time, he was excited to be taking some action.

The 'S' and 'b' of Sombrero Jim's red neon sign had lost their illumination, and the giant sombrero covered in fairy lights filling the window had faded from years of sunbathing, but the aesthetic decline of the exterior did nothing to stop eager eaters filling the chipped red chairs. The waiting staff wore a strange combination of traditional Mexican clothing and the piercings and punk haircuts of Camden uniformity. Stevie and William made an unlikely coupling as they squeezed into a table for two near the bar. The accordion player touring the tables didn't bother serenading them and manoeuvred past. Stevie had shaved his naturally blond hair from the tops of his ears straight across the back of his head and wore his remaining hair in a ponytail on top with candyfloss-pink stripes. He was dressed in a striking ensemble of lady's purple velour smock, white Lycra leggings and petrol-blue biker boots but, in the dim light of the restaurant, he almost blended in.

'Can I ask you a question, Stevie? What do you wear when you go to visit your folks in the Lake District? I can't imagine your father has ever got used to the make-up or the high heels.'

'He hasn't. If the residents' committee cares, he sure as hell does.'

'So? Do you just calm it all down?'

'No. I just don't go home any more.'

'Never? When's the last time you saw your parents?'

Stevie looked up from the plastic menu he was holding tentatively between the black talons of his thumb and forefinger.

'Daddy dear? I don't know. A few years ago. Maybe. Ma sometimes comes to London and takes me to tea. She pretends for a while that she's cool with it – the band, the bedsit and the bankruptcy – but she always cracks and starts bombarding me with college brochures, job adverts or apprenticeship schemes. It usually ends in a row, and she goes home in tears while I go and get another tattoo or blow my dole on blow.'

He was so matter-of-fact. Always had been. William had long since stopped waiting for Stevie to grow out of his habits; he had realized, eventually, that his friend wasn't going through an extended-adolescence phase. This was just who he was, and William always respected him for having the courage of his convictions. He just sometimes wondered if Stevie had been so rigid in the construction of his identity that he had unwittingly painted himself into a corner he couldn't move on from. He wasn't alone in that predicament, if so. He gave his friend's hand a little nudge across the table.

'Do you never get tired of it all, eh? The struggle?'

Stevie swatted him away with the menu then flicked it towards William.

'Tired of what? Not giving up? Holding my nerve? Do *you* not get tired of it all?'

William rested his forehead on the yellow-and-white-checked plastic tablecloth.

'I do. I'm exhausted. I could curl up under this table and sleep for a decade.'

'Not under this table you couldn't. My shoes were sticking to the floor as I walked in. So, what's going on, then?'

'Maybe in about two drinks' time I can start telling you. I fancy one of those pink cocktails – something fruity, toxic and anonymous that'll work strange wonders on me. Do you know what you want to eat?'

William ordered *camarones borrachos* and *frijolas de la olla* with sautéed spinach and rice. Stevie, always a picky eater, grudgingly accepted that they didn't serve burgers or chips and poked at his *taco de pollo*, seeking out the pieces of meat and wiping off the sauce on the rim of his plate.

'You're lucky Clare isn't here,' William said. 'She really can't cope with fussy eaters. You should try her starters approach – always order something you've never had before as your starter so you get to experience new foods without risking your main meal being something you don't like.'

Stevie waved two sarcastic thumbs up across the table.

'Oh, Clare, she's such an inspiration to us all, with her experimental attitude to life. It really doesn't take much to freak her out, does it?'

'Be fair. When you stayed with us, you really pushed her quite far.'

'What? Just because I like to go out and enjoy myself and don't have OCD about housekeeping, the way she does? Just because not all of us want to work for the man?'

'You wet the bed. Twice.'

Stevie's mouth hung open, the forkful of chicken paused on its way to reach it.

'Did I? Well, it happens to everyone. It's not that big a deal. I cleaned it up.'

'Eh, you didn't actually, and, no, it doesn't happen to everyone. Certainly not anyone over the age of eight.

And you borrowed her grandmother's silk dressing gown that she'd left her in her will and lost it at a rave. And you brought home that girl who stole all her tights. And you woke her up playing the saxophone the night before her big –'

Stevie's perfectly manicured hands fluttered over his food, moving the salt and pepper shakers to one side, refilling their water glasses from a plastic lemon-shaped jug.

'Yeah, yeah, okay. So, there were a few minor clashes, but it was good for her. Loosen her up a bit. Where is she, anyway? Exciting yoga retreat up a mountain? Volunteering to save penguins somewhere, is she?'

William played with the food on his plate; his appetite had absconded with Clare.

'She's a lot more fun than you think, Stevie,' he said. 'You've just never seen that side of her, because when you're around she feels like she has to be the grown-up to stop everyone ending up in jail or the house getting burned down or taken over by squatters. She thinks you're a bad influence. Obviously.'

'So did your mum.'

'She was right.'

'How is the old dear? She never lost it, your mum. Still a cracker.'

William sucked the last of his cocktail into the fluorescent tangerine-orange straw.

'She's gone. I don't know where she is.'

'What? Your mum?'

'Huh? No, not my . . . It's Clare. Clare's gone.'

'As in, a missing person? Like, with police looking for her?'

For once, Stevie looked speechless; his mouth forming a perfect 'O' of pink lipstick.

'What is wrong with you? Of course not. Do you really think, if she'd been abducted, I'd be sitting here with you, drinking cocktails?'

William tried not to notice the faint look of disappointment that floated across Stevie's face as the drama subsided.

'I don't know. Maybe you were going to ask me to do a benefit concert or something.'

'Oh, for the love of . . . She's left me, Stevie. Of her own free will. Run away to God knows where for who knows how long!'

'What the? What did you do? Did she meet someone else? Some dapper gent in the law firm? That's it, isn't it? She was seduced by a nice suit with a yacht? She was always too much of a grown-up for you. How the mighty have fallen!'

William clenched his jaw and pushed his plate away from him.

'I'm already regretting telling you anything. No, it was me. It was my fault. Look, it's complicated. It's not really about anyone else.'

'Don't kid yourself, love. It always is.'

Stevie leaned back on his chair legs, rested his shoulders against the grease-stained walls and summoned the waiter with a toss of his ponytail.

'I think we should get a real drink.'

'Agreed. It's time for Mother's Ruin.'

William hadn't told anyone else about the troubles he and Clare were having; pretending everything was normal made them seem less real. As he tried to put into words how fractured their marriage had become, it felt like he was speaking of strangers in a film or a book; this couldn't be his story. Stevie remained surprisingly silent throughout, but his face registered reactions in waves of sympathy, incredulity and a particularly uncomfortable cringing. William couldn't bring himself to mention Winter. He wasn't sure the dream he nursed would survive the scrutiny of Stevie's particular brand of cynicism. He wasn't ready to defend something he struggled to understand or have faith in himself.

'So, what happens now? Are you going to try to find her?'

'I don't know. It's not as simple as that. I think she's probably right that we both need some space, and I can't force her to come home if she's not ready. What good will that do?'

This time, it was Stevie who reached for William's hand.

'That sounds like you're accepting she's not coming home, dear William. Because, if you are still hoping to resurrect your old life in a straitjacket, you'd better do something fast.'

'Is it really all down to me? She's the one who has run away, after all!'

'Well, far be it from me to defend Her Royal Highness,

but it sounds like not everything was perfect before that happened. Maybe she's doing you both a favour by shining a light on where you are, instead of trying to bury it.'

William drained the last of his gin and signalled to the waitress for another.

'I'm finding your moral superiority a little hard to stomach, I must say. It's not as if you've got the best relationship track record yourself.'

'Nope. I haven't, but I've never made promises I couldn't keep or pretended to be something I'm not. What you see is what you get.'

'Perhaps you should consider a career in relationship counselling.'

'Darling, my mother has had me in therapy since I was thirteen, when she caught me trying on all her lingerie. It's about time someone benefited from it.'

'Your poor mother, how she has suffered.'

'Haven't we all?' He rapped his knuckles on the table, as if calling order in court. 'Now, I think we should shake off all this doom and gloom and seek out some sparkle. Let's go dancing. Or, at least, you can hold my coat for me while I go dancing.'

'Tempting as that sounds, I think I'll just catch the last Tube home. Why don't you head off, and I'll get the bill?'

Stevie was already standing as he snaked a black feather boa around his throat and drained the last of his glass.

'Are you sure? If I run now, it's still free admission to Spiders. You sure you don't want to come?'

'No, you go. But Stevie, thanks. Thanks a lot, for listening to me. Let's not leave it as long next time, okay?'

Stevie leaned over and kissed him on the forehead.

'William, my dear, it was you who vanished, not I. Let me know how it goes.'

With a swish of his feathered coat, he sashayed out of the restaurant, casting a new darkness over the table. William called the elderly waiter over for the bill as he became aware that nearly all the tables were now empty. He left a generous tip and the waiter nodded his acknowledgement. As he began to clatter the plates together, William interrupted him.

'I'm sorry, but could I ask you a question?'

'Of course, sir. Is everything okay? You need a taxi?'

'No, no. I was just wondering if you've worked here a long time?'

'Six nights a week for fifteen years. My wife and I always go dancing on Sundays, and then Cracker's in charge. Why do you ask?'

'I just know someone who comes here a lot and I thought you might know them. A lady called Winter?'

'I'm afraid it doesn't ring a bell, sir, but there's always so many new faces around here, it's hard to remember everyone.' He smiled at William and shook his head as he balanced the dirty plates on his arm.

'She has very long red hair and green eyes. An Irish lady. Does that help?'

The waiter turned back to look at William again.

'Don't a lot of Irish girls look like that, sir? I can't

think of anyone in particular. I'm sorry, but perhaps you can come together another time and introduce me.'

'Perhaps. Thanks again. It was all delicious, really.'

William shuffled into his duffel coat and pulled the hood up. Finding Winter, if that was what he intended to do, was not going to be easy. As he stepped out into the crisp, frosty night, he thought about how much Clare would love this strange little restaurant. It occurred to him how much Winter and Clare had in common. It gave him a jolt: did Winter's letters remind him of the old Clare? The constant flipping in his mind from yin to yang was exhausting. He was trying to compare home with a foreign land he had never visited but had only read about in books. And he didn't know if the writers of the tale were telling the truth.

8.

Despite the late hour, and the circumstances which had led Clare to find herself alone in a hotel room in Wales, she felt surprisingly light and hopeful. As she lay in the middle of the bed, legs and arms stretched wide, her mind wandered back to that morning. It felt like days since she'd said goodbye to William, instead of just the mere hours that had passed since the telephone call that had set her on this path. Maxi had been concerned when Clare was absent from work. Things had become confused between them; he was worried that she was avoiding him, said he desperately wanted to see her and had driven to her street in pursuit. Those words from him on the telephone had rattled her; she was already so anxious to escape, even if it was just for a short while. Maxi told her he would take her anywhere she wanted to go. On impulse, she settled on Wales, where she'd spent summers as a child. Somewhere calm and safe, where she could be alone. Her feelings towards Maxi weren't clear in her mind. Had he become more than a friend? Or was she looking for a life raft to help her leave the lonely island of her marriage?

After they arrived at the hotel, he looked crestfallen when she asked him not to come in with her. They had driven there together mostly in silence; she presumed he thought the talking would come later. Instead, she stared out of the window while Kate Bush's *Hounds of Love* played on repeat. As she hugged herself in the car seat, her fingers found a hole in William's *Star Wars* T-shirt, just below her ribcage. She stroked her skin through it like a baby playing with the label on a blanket. Every so often, she discreetly pulled the neck of the T-shirt over her nose to breathe in the lingering smell of him: the gentle aroma of patchouli and cedarwood from the beard oil she loved.

Every so often, she stole a glance at Maxi out of the corner of her eye: his blond hair was cut short enough to kill the curl, his starched white shirt rolled to the elbows of his tanned arms. He drove like a man in control of a mission, staring straight ahead, weaving gracefully between lanes, accelerating rapidly when any stretch of road became clear. She liked him more for his silence; for not pushing her. After their awkward goodbye in the hotel car park, she was relieved to find a room ready for her and immediately called the office to see how her assistant, Nava, was coping in her absence. A little too well for comfort, it seemed, but Clare resigned herself to the knowledge that this time away was essential. Thinking of the pep talk the managing partner had given her when she had stopped at the office en route, she cringed. It was clear she hadn't been herself recently; it seemed she needed a break. So mortifying after all these years with a perfect record; how frustrating the glee he took in patting her on the shoulder and saying, 'You are only human, after all,' as if confirmation had been pending for years.

She unpacked her suitcase as slowly as possible, arranged her toiletries in descending height in the bathroom and perched on one side of the stiffly made bed, cradling the bedside telephone in her lap. She wanted to talk to someone but couldn't think of anyone she could bear to confide in. All her friends had become their friends. None of her relationships with colleagues had graduated past breezy platitudes or repetitive rants about parking, working hours or the sub-par coffee in the staff kitchen. Flora was the only option; the only person exclusively hers. As much as William had immediately adored Flora when she eventually brought him home, Clare had refused to cultivate the relationship between her husband and her little sister. Maybe she didn't want William ever to witness her through Flora's conflicted gaze. No matter how much you evolve as a person, the extent to which you change or improve, your family holds such a fixed notion of who you are; they won't allow you to leave your past behind you or become someone new. Clare had worked hard to grow out of the girl weighed down by their hefty familial baggage and she didn't want Flora dragging her back into that room. She hadn't really considered before why keeping their relationship separate was so important to her, but she was glad of it now. Maybe she would ask Flora to come and stay with her, after she'd had a day or two to think things through. First things first, though. She stood under the powerful hotel shower to cleanse the city of London from her hair and face. She polished her body with a scratchy flannel and appreciated the unfamiliar scent of the hotel's lemongrass soap. With her hair pulled into a messy bun, she dressed in the most comfortable cotton dress in her possession and was surprised to find she felt hungry. Usually, when she was upset her appetite failed her, but she craved something hot and savoury and so made her way to the restaurant in the hotel conservatory.

Over a dish of Welsh rarebit and a glass of Merlot, Clare watched the other hotel guests and indulged in a little eavesdropping. Her ears pricked up when she overheard dangerous words like 'divorce', or 'cancer', or 'pregnant' being whispered. She breathed a little more easily; the little titbits of other people's lives were a salve to the upsets of her own; a reconnection with a world outside the claustrophobic space she had started obsessively inhabiting in her mind.

'When we arrive at your mother's, please don't vanish off with your dad and leave me in the kitchen with her, Mike. Not again. Not after last time.'

'Can you believe Kay still thinks I'm a vegetarian? After all these years! If she ever catches me with a kebab, she'll keel over on the spot.'

'Valerie thinks I should try alternative therapies, but I'm not so sure. It just feels like I would be swimming against the river.'

'I just don't think I can love a man who doesn't appreciate the brilliance of Depeche Mode. It just shows such a fundamental lack of compatibility between us.'

Clare felt nostalgic for the time when the greatest problems she and William navigated involved not loving the same bands. She smiled, remembering the night he refused to go to the pub with her because she was wearing a Frankie Says Relax T-shirt. She left without him, of course, and he followed her half an hour later. Was it inevitable that two people who had met so young would eventually grow apart? If she was no longer with William, who would she become? Their relationship defined her; she was the responsible one, the careerist who gave them security. How had her identity become so wrapped up with her job? A job she honestly wasn't even sure that she loved. When was *her* time to follow her heart?

When she thought of herself as the little girl who loved painting, music and performing, she could never have imagined she would grow up to become this rigid lawyer with no artistic outlet at all. In her younger years, she was afraid of following an insecure path that could keep her stuck in poverty, but she didn't have to worry about that now. Her success to date would give her the freedom to do something different now, if she wanted. William refusing to allow them to take on a bigger mortgage had at least enabled her to save a significant sum. What was stopping her? She couldn't blame William, or their relationship, entirely. It was just so hard to imagine herself doing something else now. What if she no longer had it in her? She had harboured these comforting notions of her own untapped potential but without ever really confronting whether she had any talent at all. It was easier to believe in the theory while it remained untested. Often, adults have to balance a conflict between what they think they are compelled to do as a responsible person and what they desire to do. Why had that never applied to William? The imbalance of power between them was of little concern to him. He never questioned if she was truly happy to keep them afloat with her job while he pursued his flights of fancy, his writing and his endless fascination with the work of the depot. Would it be different if she was with someone like Maxi?

Perhaps if William had tried but failed, instead of just failing through what she considered an absence of effort, it would have been easier to accept things as they were. She remembered so clearly the day when his charade was exposed; the details were burned on her mind like a photograph kept permanently in her wallet. Sheets of rain collapsed from the skies as she drove her Mini home that day. The drops pounded on the tin roof; the windscreen wipers sploshed water back and forth without increasing her range of visibility at all. It made her nervous, driving through a storm so heavy, the sweltering air that fogged the windows from the condensation spreading, the blinking lights of other cars and traffic lights smearing before her eyes. When she finally splashed to a stop outside their house, she rested her head against the steering wheel in relief and released the tension she had been holding across her shoulders as she drove. Clutching a brown-paper bag of pastries, she doubled over against the onslaught as she dashed to the front door in the downpour. Just two houses away, but the rain soaked through her linen blazer, ran in rivulets down her back and clung to her eyelashes in the time it took her to reach home. The bag was disintegrating in her hands and puddles invaded her court shoes as she ran. She shrieked as she slammed the door behind her.

Wriggling out of her soggy jacket, she kicked off her shoes and wiped a blouse sleeve across her damp forehead as she scuttled through the hallway towards the welcoming fire she anticipated would be glowing in the living room. Shaking off the sudden shock of the storm, Clare became aware of a voice floating from the kitchen. Who on earth was visiting at this time of day? She tuned into the sharp tone of a woman's cut-crystal accent; it was familiar, but she couldn't quite place it.

'I suppose there's nothing else to say, but I hope you realize that this embarrassment is not exclusively yours. I have been covering for you for months, and you've made a fool out of me. I can't say this isn't a huge disappointment.'

The door yanked open before Clare could reach it. Olivia Longworth, William's literary agent, froze in surprise to see Clare standing there. She was flushed and agitated, unrecognizable as the elegant lady Clare had met previously, despite the uniform cream wool skirt and cardigan she always seemed to wear. For a moment, it looked as if she was going to speak, but instead she gave a curt nod as she brushed past Clare towards the front door. A curse exploded from her as she stepped out into the torrential rain. In the kitchen, William, pale and sickly-looking under the fluorescent light bulb, sat holding his head at the table.

'William? What's wrong with Olivia? Has something happened with the book? You look terrible. Tell me what's going on!'

Of all the possible explanations she may have expected, the one that he offered floored her.

'There is no book,' he offered quietly, without raising his head to look at her.

'What are you talking about? Dear God, she hasn't lost it, has she? I told you to keep making copies. Oh, no – they aren't pulling out of publishing it, are they? They can't do that – you have a contract . . .'

She dropped the soggy bag of pastries on the kitchen table as he slowly shook his head. Crouching beside him at the table, she asked again. 'William! You're scaring me. Please tell me. What's happened?'

And so the story unravelled. For eighteen months, no words had come to complete the novel he had promised to deliver. The short stories that had secured him the contract remained the only work completed. It wasn't that he hadn't finished the book; he had never even really begun. Before he had secured the publishing success he coveted, with its advances, opportunity and obligations, the blank page had held no fear for him. He had attacked it with vigour and Clare had marvelled at how effortlessly the streams of consciousness flowed from him. 'Like turning on a tap,' she used to say. 'More like rain running down a drainpipe,' he would joke in response. Now, though, the weight of expectation had flattened him, he explained. Squashed his inspiration. It was as if, by consciously trying, he could no longer access his subconscious. He had scared away his voice.

'Nonsense!' Clare shouted. 'You just need some discipline, hard graft, perseverance.'

She didn't understand, he insisted. 'It's not something I can force myself to do, it's not like building bricks or working in a factory. The harder I push, the further away it pulls.'

Clare dashed into the living room, grabbed the file she believed held his manuscript, the great novel she'd sworn not to read until it was ready, and shook its contents out across the kitchen table in impatient disbelief. Reams of white paper scattered; some had one or two lines typed, others haphazard diagrams, scribbles and crossed-out handwriting. Most were blank. He had been methodically filling the file every day with faux progression; it grew fatter with his lie and the mounting pressure.

'I kept hoping I would have a breakthrough, that I could salvage something,' he whispered. 'I couldn't admit to you what was happening, or to myself. I was sure I could claw it back.'

'And now?' she asked.

'The publishers won't wait any longer. I've missed the deadline for a first draft too many times. The editor demanded to see the work in progress. That's why Olivia was here. It's over. And they want their money back.'

Writing a cheque to repay his advance from their savings was the least painful part of the process. She tried to have some empathy for what he must have suffered while nursing his secret but was floored by the daily deceit. How could he lie to her day after day for all that time? She had learned to accept his explanation, but never to understand it. Who would throw away such a chance? And hide their failure from their wife? Why was he so scared to be vulnerable in her eyes? She remembered tossing the pastries the next evening, stale and conjoined now with the brown paper that had wrapped them. She hadn't brought William doughnuts home for afternoon tea since.

Clare drained the dregs of her wine and walked out of the hotel without a clear idea of where she was going. She followed the lane towards the village, enjoying how the drivers of passing cars waved in acknowledgement, regardless of not knowing her. St Gerard's consisted of just one square with a church, a pub and a school commandeering three of its sides. On the fourth, there was a tea room with striped deckchairs in clusters of twos and threes arranged around suitcases set as tables outside, and an antique shop selling furniture and bric-a-brac. Looking through the window at the paraphernalia, fixtures and fittings, it reminded her of the terraced house where she grew up and she felt a chill. Clare's mother had always told her she had an over-active imagination and threatened to ban her from the library if she didn't get her feet back on the ground. She looked at the heavy spiral wallpaper adorning the walls of the shop and remembered how, in her half-sleep, the ivory flock pattern on the rose-red wallpaper of her childhood bedroom had danced. She lay under pink ticklish blankets, fingers stroking the white silk ribbon around the edge, and tried to trick the dancers into staying until she called her papa, but as soon as she blinked, they were gone. The ghosts from the wall had haunted her nighttimes for years, until she turned twelve and paint became more fashionable than wallpaper and the paper with its dancers was stripped away. Her mother painted the walls oatmeal, a flat, dull non-colour that Clare later covered with the artefacts of her adolescence: black-and-white posters of John Lennon, a giant print of Bowie's *Ziggy Stardust* album cover and framed pictures of Greta Garbo, Ginger Rogers and Judy Garland. She missed the dancers sometimes after they were gone, when she no longer had to fear absorbing their strange, shadowy presence into her mind. They had been long forgotten by the time she found herself looking in that dusty window in the village square when they fluttered back into her consciousness.

The hem of her long-suffering sky-blue jumper snagged on a window box and a strand of wool unravelled. Clare released it, cursing another fray, for she could never part with it, no matter how mangled it became. She loved the white stars as big as her hands that her mother had clumsily knitted into the pattern. There weren't many happy memories from her childhood that she clung to, but the day she unwrapped that jumper was one of them and she didn't want to let it go. As she tied a knot in the loose strand, she watched through the window as little glass balloons bobbed from an oak bough perched on a mantelpiece: orange red and powder blue. Something about the light, how they danced in it, stirred an old feeling. She was eleven and her ghosts were dancing.

Clare shuddered, despite the brilliant white sunshine that illuminated the square, casting shadows and dispersing fragments of dust. She hurried next door, to a newsagent's that promised to sell 'all essentials and even some extras'. She decided to hunt for a novel to read in this newly acquired time for herself; the door jangled a dream-catcher constructed of seashells to announce her arrival. The back wall of the shop consisted of rows of paperbacks, and she made her way to it, past the ice-cream fridge, the carousel of postcards, the shelves of sweets in glass jars. As she crouched down to read the titles on the bottom shelf, a pile of clumsily stacked sketch pads in the corner caught her eye. She mooched closer and shuffled through them until she found an A5 version with thick ivory paper inside a soft mulberry leather cover. It surprised her to find something so exquisite in this little rural shop. Before she could change her mind, she grabbed it and marched to the counter, where she picked up a handful of pencils, an eraser and a sharpener. At the last moment, she threw a sherbet Dip-Dab and a Fry's Turkish Delight on top, too. She was on holiday, after all, of a fashion. She felt a rush of excitement as she tucked the striped lemon-and-white paper bag containing her treasure under her arm and clattered the shop door closed behind her.

Back in her hotel room, Clare opened the sketch pad on the first page and laid it carefully on her dressing table underneath a freshly pared pencil. She backed away from it for a moment, wary about discovering if she could still use these tools with any flair. She paced back and forth, poured herself a miniature gin and tonic from the mini-bar, and sat down; rolled the pencil between her fingers, feeling its weight, before making a few tentative, wispy strokes across the paper. Quickly, she tore the page from the spiral spine, scrunched it into a ball and tossed it on the floor. A memory of her art teacher in school came back to her. 'Leave everything on the page,' Miss Forde had said as she strode around in the room in black leather trousers. 'Be bold or be nothing.'

Clare swallowed the alcohol in two mouthfuls, wiped her mouth on a paper serviette and stared at herself in the mirror where she sat. She sketched out the long, oval shape of her face, drew a line from her forehead to where her chin would be, marked lines for the shape of her cheeks, nose and jaw and then began to define her eyes, mouth and ears. Her work was silent and steady until the natural light left the room, forcing her to turn on the lamp beside her.

She continued working as the drawing became more and more detailed, but her eyes grew weary. When she woke up a few hours later, she had fallen asleep at the dressing table, head slumped forward, pencil in hand. She held up her drawing and saw her own face staring back at her. Clare had to admit it was good. She closed the cover of the sketch pad, held it against her chest for a moment then crawled under the blankets of her bed. Reflecting on the day as she savoured the weight of the blankets engulfing her, she was surprised at how it was ending, despite its horrific beginning. It was a blessed relief to have no anticipation of human or alarm to wake her; to fall asleep with thoughts of herself alone and not the torment that had plagued her so. As she slipped away into a slumber, a small smile rested on her face.

9.

In the three days since Clare had left, William heard from her only once, via a message on their answering machine giving the number of her hotel in Wales. In case of emergency only. What was she doing there? Was she alone? William sat in the Dead Letters Depot, listening to Marjorie gossip about him through the partition walls: 'I'm just sayin', 'e looks desperate. I bet she's left 'im, she always thought she was too good for 'im.'

He leaned back in his creaking leather chair and contemplated escaping to the Supernatural Division as he scanned the postal debris strewn across his desk. A long cylinder wrapped in newspaper caught his eye, an irregular shape amid the pile of impatient homeless post awaiting him. He dragged it closer with a wooden ruler, bulldozing over the other parcels in its wake. The newspaper print was tattered and smudged, the name and address smeared into long streams of blue, a dirty mess conjuring up a damp smell of soggy paper that curled up William's nostrils. He gently tore the now tissue-like newspaper away, flinching as it caught under his fingernails. He edged carefully around the smudged address in case any of it could be deciphered. Ten sheets of newspaper peeled away. A final layer of protection – cardboard from a cornflakes cereal box – before a thin oak case with a copper clasp was revealed. William peeled a grey envelope from the cardboard where it had been secured carefully with Sellotape on all four edges. It was addressed to Mr Harry Prummel; the name was written in small, neat capital letters with a fine-tipped blue pen. William opened the case first. Inside lay a gleaming silver medal in the shape of a cross with an image of St George and the dragon at the centre; it hung from a navy-blue ribbon threaded through a silver ring. The inscription 'Francis Sillitoe', the date 26.07.42 and 'For Gallantry' were engraved around the centrepiece. William felt the cool weight in the palm of his hand, fingered the silk ribbon between his fingers. It reminded him of how Clare's skirt had felt against his face the morning she left, and he blushed. He laid the medal back in its case and opened the letter that accompanied it.

Dear Mr Prummel,

I call you Mister, although in my mind's eye you will always be the little chap of seven that I held in my arms. I don't know if you remember my name, or ever knew it at all, in fact, but I have no doubt you remember the day we met; some days are burned in our memories for ever, even those of a seven-year-old.

I was the man who climbed into your window and carried you from the fire on that last godforsaken night of bombings. We had been fighting the flames for fifty-seven days. I was exempt from active military service because I was a civil engineer but hated feeling like I was dodging my duty as my friends and brothers all did theirs. When the bombing began, I volunteered as an ARP and felt as though I was finally doing my bit, although my bit proved more than I ever could have imagined. When the first bombs started dropping, I coordinated a rescue team and, through the nights and days that followed, we did manage to save a great number of lives, including your own. I will always be proud of that. It was for these rescue missions that I was awarded the George Medal you find enclosed here. It was my greatest honour to receive it and I have held it dear all these years.

What you may or may not know is that on that last night of bombings, my own house was struck, and burned down. My wife, Dorothy, and my little boy, Charlie, didn't make it out. He was seven years old, too. I have regretted every day since that I was not there to save them, but I will never regret that I was there to save you.

I'm not long past my ninety-fifth birthday and I won't see another. I hope that I find Dorothy and Charlie in the next life, and that they've forgiven me for what happened. What worldly possessions I have will all go where they should, but my medal, I would like you to have. I will never forget your face when I picked you up; how your little hands gripped the back of my neck as though you would never let me go. I have never let the memory go.

You may be wondering how I have found you after all these years. Well, after the war, your mother and I stayed in touch. She was very distressed about Charlie and always sent me a letter on his birthday and filled me in on how well you were doing. It has been a joy to read of your successes all these years, and it has helped me to place what Charlie might have been doing if he was still with us. I was very saddened to hear of your mother's passing. She was a wonderful woman, as you know. Please accept this medal with my very best wishes for a long life, full of happiness.

If you do say some prayers, say one for me, if you think of me.

Yours sincerely,
Frank Sillitoe

William picked up the medal again and said a little prayer of his own for an old man who had lost his son while saving another. He gently spread the address label flat under the light of his desk lamp and scrutinized the diluted letters. The first two lines were completely illegible but he was sure the next read 'Clovelly' and, unless he was mistaken, there was only one Clovelly in the United Kingdom and this parcel had been destined for Devon. Without a doubt, this delivery qualified for special treatment. He reclined in his chair while an idea percolated; maybe he would take a road trip and deliver it himself. He dreaded his evenings alone in the flat and everywhere he went he was haunted by memories of Clare and apparitions of Winter. Every time a red-headed girl passed him, he wondered whether it could be Winter; convinced that she was close. Was that her walking ahead of him, reading a book on the opposite train platform, or looking out of the window as a bus whizzed past him? The city was shrinking around his shoulders. He needed some relief from the constant battle that raged inside him as he flitted from despair at the loss of Clare to hope at the thought of Winter. Thoughts of the two women pulled him back and forth. He still loved Clare, so why was he not impervious to thoughts of someone else? Even if it was something of a fantasy. Winter's appeal for folk to find strength in their own person lay heavily on his mind. He would travel to Clovelly, track down Harry Prummel and deliver the parcel himself. It would be good to focus on something tangible and real; he needed to accomplish something.

The following morning dawned crisp and clean. The sky looked as if it were painted by a child with only one blue in his paint box and no time for clouds. William donned the official postmaster blazer he was supposed to wear every day but seldom did and loaded up his beloved Ford Corsair. He willed it, first of all, to start, and then, ultimately, to survive the five-hour drive to North Devon. William had inherited this old motor from Uncle Archie and would never be able to let her go, even as 'Corina' grew more and more exhausted and begged for retirement. It was foolish to risk such a long journey in that jalopy, but William needed to feel the power of really driving, to breathe in the history of the leather seats, to surround himself with the safe cocoon of happier times. He was confident that Corina was on his side and would chug through. He packed chocolate peanuts, a bottle of apple juice and a Tupperware box of dried prunes into a Marks and Spencer plastic bag. In his overnight case, he crammed pyjamas, fresh clothing, a pair of binoculars for exploring and *The Woman in White*. *The War of the Worlds* on cassette would keep him company as the miles rolled under his wheels. He considered calling Clare's hotel to tell her where he was going but decided against it and left a note on the kitchen table instead.

Dear Clare,

I hope that you find this note, because that means you are home. I am sorry I was not there to see you walk through the door. Work has taken me to Clovelly. (Can you believe it!!?) I'll be home soon and I hope more than anything that you will be here waiting for me.

Love,

William

William felt the universe had granted him a little reprieve in placing Harry Prummel in Clovelly, of all places. He had wanted to visit ever since he was a little boy but, somehow, had never made it. As a child, he was obsessed with the legend of King Arthur and the great wizard, Merlin. He worked Merlin into every school project he could and, from as young as eight, had acquired quite an exhaustive knowledge of all the myths related to him. When people spoke about the Troubles in Northern Ireland, he loved to tell them that it was all Merlin's fault, really: 'You see, Merlin had advised King Ambrosius to build Stonehenge to honour the dead, but they didn't have enough stone to do it justice and so they invaded Ireland to gather the resources.' It was a theory that usually provoked some strong reactions.

Legend suggested that there was a waterfall in Clovelly where Merlin was born. William had always nursed a dream to hunt Merlin across the country, visiting all the places that he was associated with and retracing his steps. It felt a foolish pursuit for a grown man, however, and remained an inner-voice whimsy that was seldom vocalized when planning the annual fortnight's holiday with Clare. He was tickled to tick one destination off his list, though, and relished the idea of a night away from the loneliest bed in London.

It was almost six hours later that William proudly parked at the visitor centre on the edge of Clovelly. Corina had taken a little longer than he'd hoped but had not let him down; he felt vindicated. He hadn't realized that the fishing village was a private estate, but he imagined that was how such a famous idyll had managed to retain its old-world charm. He was pleased to see they had prevented the tumbling, four-hundred-feet-long cobbled high street from becoming festooned with tourist traps and souvenir shops. William stretched his arms over his head and shook away the driving cramps that had settled in his legs.

An elderly man with a white beard that twisted into a point at his knees sat watching him from a bench; he was methodically stringing multicoloured beads on to purple yarn to make long necklaces akin to the dozens he wore. William started when he caught his eye but the resemblance to Merlin felt like a good sign and he approached him to begin his hunt for Mr Prummel.

'Hello there. I hope I'm not disturbing you.'

'Not so far. I'm wonderin' if the disturbin' bit comes next.'

'Oh, I hope not. I'm just looking for someone. Maybe you know him, a chap by the name of Harry Prummel? Would you know where I might find him?'

'Is he hiding from you?'

'No, no. We've never even met. I just have to deliver something to him.'

'So you have his address, then? You look a bit long in the tooth for a delivery boy.'

'I work for the post office, actually, and his address was missing on a parcel. I just know he lives in Clovelly somewhere, and I wanted to make sure it gets to him safely, you see.'

'No, I don't see. In my experience, people who want to be found usually present themselves in the end.'

'But he doesn't know I'm looking for him in order for him to be able to present himself.'

'Well, you are in a pickle, then.'

'And even if he did, he wouldn't know where to find me.'

'In my experience, people who want to be found —'

'Yes, yes. They present themselves. I guess I'll just go and stand in the middle of the town, shall I? And wait for Harry to guess I'm looking for him?'

'You could. Or you could call into his office. Young Prummel is the only accountant in town. His rooms are at the foot of the hill, over Betty's tea shop.'

'Oh? Well, thank you, but you could have just said that.'

'Now, where's the fun in that? Enjoy your slow-down, Londoner.'

William walked to the turnstile and looked over his shoulder before he climbed through. His Merlin had vanished. He turned towards the village. His knees slowly adjusted to the bendy way of walking that kept him balanced as he began his descent of the steep cobbled hill. The city he had left that morning seemed to belong to another planet. The little whitewashed cottages, with their flower boxes and pretty patterned curtains, were straight from the lid of a biscuit tin. It looked as if only happiness could live there. Of course, he knew the opposite was probably true, as the inhabitants battled the elements and the private demons everyone faces. He was sorely tempted to stop halfway down for a cream tea in the shade. He longed to roll up his sleeves and drape his blazer over the back of a pastel-painted chair in one of the friendly-looking tea houses that lined the route but decided to complete his mission first. He found himself taking a surprising amount of pleasure at the unexpected sight of the donkeys passing by with their loads.

The entrance to Mr Prummel's office sat to the side of Devon Delights, a café William now understood to be owned by someone named Betty. He rang the doorbell but, receiving no reply, gave the red wooden door a little push. It swung wide for him, revealing a narrow, winding staircase. His knee creaked as he climbed up two flights of stairs before emerging abruptly into a tiny reception room.

A bespectacled woman sat behind an expansive mahogany desk that could not dwarf her formidable presence with its might. Her back was straight as a lamp post, her silver hair wound in a tight coil upon her head. A lilac paisley dress wrapped in a neat crease across her kitten-like frame. Her face was lined, but her eyes sparkled green as they darted from her typewriter to meet William's own. He wondered if Winter's eyes were the same shade of apple.

'Good afternoon. Can I help you?'

'Hello! I hope so. I was wondering if I could pop in to see Harry Prummel for a moment?'

'I should think not. People don't "pop" in to see Mr Prummel. He is a very busy man, you know. Did you not think to make an appointment?'

'No, unfortunately I didn't, but it's not for professional reasons I need to see him. I have a personal matter to discuss. Is he not free at all, just for a moment?'

She started busily squirting water from a spritzer on to a family of succulents on her desk.

'If it's a personal matter, I suggest you see him in his personal time. Otherwise, you'll have to make an appointment.'

'Fine. Could I just make one for later today, then, please?'

She continued squirting for a moment longer before flicking briskly through a desk calendar that could serve as a doorstop.

'The next available appointment would be three weeks on Thursday, 8.45 a.m.'

'But I'm only here until tomorrow. Could you not just pop in to him and tell him there is someone here to see him?'

'Are we back to the popping? As I've said, no one –'

'What time does the office close? I'll wait outside, if you don't mind.'

'Please yourself. Mr Prummel usually leaves at five o' clock, but he may leave earlier, maybe later. I'm not his keeper. I couldn't possibly say.'

William decided to treat himself to some fish and chips on the seafront and find a spot where he could sit and watch for Harry leaving the office. He walked along the waterfront, across the pebbly beach, and squirmed to feel grains of gravel invading his shoes. The vinegar soaked through the newspaper on to his hand and the salty smell intoxicated him as he perched on a low stone wall and relished in his indulgence. As Harry's finishing time drew closer, William began to worry that he had somehow missed him. Maybe he wasn't even working that day and his security guard had slipped out while he was buying his fish supper. Of course, it couldn't have turned out as easily as it had promised to; so little in his life ever did these days. He shuffled from one foot to the other, pulling up an unruly sock that slid under his heel. He rearranged the detritus in his pockets so left became items to keep (house keys, Polo mints, handkerchief) and right became things to throw away (stray button, toffee wrappers, pen lid). He tried for a moment to whistle a tune but lacked the puff and resorted instead to conjugating Latin verbs in his head. As the chapel bell chimed five, William became fixated on the red door. It hadn't opened once in all the time he had been waiting. He strained his ears at every suggestion of a creak, until, after ten more torturous minutes, it slowly opened inward. A jolly-looking man with a retreating hairline of fuzzy ginger hair casually strolled out, as if the most impatient man in England weren't feverishly awaiting him. William vaulted forward.

'Harry! Mr Prummel, excuse me! I was hoping to catch you.'

Harry Prummel turned, the tails of his jaunty red blazer spinning behind him.

'Oh, hello. I've actually finished for the day, but you can speak to Mrs Whisker about an appointment.'

William held up his hand in protest and shook his head.

'No, please. I've already met Mrs Whisker and explained that I'm only here for the day and wanted to speak to you about a personal matter. I've been waiting all afternoon. Could I just walk with you wherever you are going? I promise it won't take long.'

'I see. Perhaps we'd better go back upstairs?'

'That would be marvellous. Thank you. I'll explain everything.'

William followed Harry back inside and up the winding staircase, past a surprised and embarrassed Mrs Whisker, who was applying a little rouge when they appeared, and into an office even smaller than the reception area. There were potted plants everywhere and, as William caught his foot on a fern near his seat, Harry explained his partner, Liam, was 'going through a feng shui phase'. 'I'm not sure he totally understands what it's all about, but one unfortunate element he's latched on to is that plants foster prosperity, so now I'm working in a greenhouse. Anyway, how can I help you, Mr . . . ?'

'Woolf. William Woolf. I work as a letter detective in the Dead Letters Depot in London, and I have a parcel for you that was lost in the post before reaching us.'

'A letter detective? Well, that sounds fascinating. Does everyone get such a personal service, Mr Woolf?'

'No, but some things aren't worth risking losing twice, and I felt I should bring this to you myself, for my own peace of mind.'

'Well, this is all very intriguing. Hand it over, then.'

William placed a padded brown envelope on Harry's pristine emerald-green marble desktop and watched Harry survey it before nudging it closer to him.

'Would you rather I left you alone, Mr Prummel?'

Harry looked more confused than ever but shook his head.

'No, I think it's better if you stay until we see what this is all about.'

Harry slid the contents of the envelope out on to the table and touched the surface of the oak case with his fingertips.

'Can you tell me what's inside, Mr Woolf? I must admit, this is all making me a little nervous.'

'I think it's best if you just read the letter, Mr Prummel. Please. There's nothing to be afraid of.'

Harry swivelled his chair to the right to catch the last

fading light from the window. William stared at the brown spirals in the rug beneath his feet to afford him what privacy he could. A shocked, wet gasp burst from Harry, and William looked up to see him holding one hand across his mouth as he read. Tears were gathering in his eyes as he turned back to face William.

'Forgive me, Mr Woolf, for getting so emotional.'

He opened the oak case and laid the medal before him on the desk.

'William, please. I know this must come as something of a shock.'

'I owe you an enormous debt of gratitude, William. This letter releases me from a guilt that has clung to me my whole life.'

William sat up straighter in his chair, and asked, 'So you knew about Frank Sillitoe?'

'Yes, but I had no idea that he and my mother had communicated all these years. She's passed away now. I don't know why she didn't tell me about him. I've always been afraid that he regretted saving me, resented me for surviving when his son had not. To think I have always had his blessing. I feel a great weight has been lifted from me. Maybe I can go and see him and thank him myself.'

William smiled at him. 'I'm sure that he would be relieved to see you after all these years.'

'I don't know how to thank you. The work you do – you must witness so many people's stories, eavesdrop on their private lives, so to speak. It's a big responsibility.'

'Well, sometimes remarkable things happen, like today. Others, we have to let go because we can't find a way to help. That's always hard, but we try to remember that lives continue long after the last words of a letter are written and hope people find some other way. Maybe the letters who need us the most find us.' William blushed. 'I'm sorry, I'm sure that sounds silly to you.'

'Not at all. How could you believe anything else and do your job? I wish I could repay you somehow; you've come all this way. Will you at least join us for supper?'

William considered this for a moment. He was tempted, but wanted to spend some time alone, exploring the village, contemplating his next move. As he stood to leave, William leaned across the desk to shake Harry's hand, but he was instead pulled into a great bear hug.

His feet danced past Mrs Whisker's empty desk, skipped back down the stairs and into Clovelly at dusk. Once again, he was struck by the power of letters to change lives; the medium they offered those who couldn't or wouldn't communicate in person. How much would be left unsaid if people were devoid of the opportunity that pen and paper offered to speak from a safe distance? He would never underestimate it. This was the message he wanted to deliver in the *Volume of Lost Letters* he was compiling. It motivated him to keep working, despite the apathy he felt at home from Clare and in the depot from Ned. Wouldn't Harry's story be the perfect way to open the book? He was filled anew with the excitement of his project. People would want to hear these stories; he was sure of it.

He made his way to the Red Lion Hotel and was pleased to see that his room offered a panoramic view of the peninsula. He thought about how much Clare would love it here and decided to bring her home a postcard, if he could find one that did the little village justice. He had achieved his mission. Filled with renewed optimism, he set out to explore.

With a little map he picked up from the reception desk, William set off to climb the Look-out. The sun was setting in a blaze of blood orange. Dark clouds crept in from the west, charcoal snakes slithering across the sky and smearing it in blackness. He hurried to the waterfall that was hidden halfway up to the Look-out but, as he climbed through to the cave at the back of the crashing waters, the heavens opened. He huddled for cover from the downpour, cursing himself for not returning to the hotel when he first saw the gathering thunderclouds. The rain showed no signs of clearing, so he surrendered to the soaking and started pushing back towards the harbour, head bent against nature. A fork of lightning illuminated the sky; the world's greatest photographer turning on the flash of her camera to capture the dark, dripping village. William's eye was caught by a lone figure, dressed all in white, standing on the brink of the Look-out. A woman stood with her arms outstretched, staring down at the storm over the harbour. Her trailing dress was plastered wet against her body, blowing behind her like a forgotten sheet on a washing line. Her long red hair tangled in the sea spray, the tendrils dancing in the wind like serpents' tails, ribbons of fire against the electric black sky. He was frozen in time, spellbound. She melted back into the shadows and disappeared into the night.

William staggered back to his lodgings and dried his prickling skin with fluffy white towels that smoothed away some of the corners of his jarred state of mind. Hastening to pull the blinds in his bedroom, he kept his eyes lowered as he drew closer to the window frame. A childhood fear had resurfaced and caught him by the heart; he couldn't look directly at the glass or he would see someone looking in, or worse, another face reflected over his shoulder. 'Get a grip, you old fool', he mumbled. 'You're just winding yourself up.'

He decanted a hefty shot of Jameson's from the mini-bar into a crystal tumbler and breathed in the aroma before he drank his first hot sip. He held the whiskey up to the light: pure amber swirls, no particles or imperfections. When things with Clare had started to unravel, he had made a decision never to drink alone in the evenings, although he sometimes found the urge to resist difficult in mornings and afternoons, too. He didn't want to return to the months following his publishing failure, when most important occasions, and many inconsequential ones, were bookended by something to take the edge off in anticipation and something to savour in reflection.

He curled the liquor around in his mouth; a little ball of heat rolling over every tooth, dancing on his tongue. A slow swallow slid down his parched throat, along his spine, to tingle the tips of his toes. He turned on the radio and bristled at the screeching white noise of uncharted radio waves. The dial found him BBC Radio 3, and the comfort of the musical grace of Beethoven's 'Moonlight' piano sonata descended upon him. He rummaged in his satchel for a notebook and pen and sat straight-backed at the little pine desk in his room. The Prummel encounter had struck a nerve; he knew he had stories to tell. Down the drainpipe, rusty water flowed once again. On and on he wrote, and the words rang true. It was effortless. Just before midnight, he stopped. Ended on just the right sentence. This was the second time the words had come in as many weeks. He sat back in the stiff wooden chair and nodded. Maybe the drought was over.

The electric light from the skies crackled around the perimeter of the window blinds. Occasionally, the laughter and squeals of his neighbours next door reminded him he was not alone in this weather-racked hotel by the sea. If Clare had been with him, he was sure they would be sitting up in bed, excitedly watching the storm vent her fury, clutching each other under the covers with each crash. How he longed for Clare that night; missing her fostered tight pangs in his chest, fists beating the bones of his ribs, denting his heart-box. He desperately wanted to tell her about the writing; needed her acknowledgement. He unearthed the number of her hotel from his travelling bag and stretched to drag the telephone down from the locker on to the plush taupe carpet beside him.

After two short rings, a soft Welsh accent whispered into the phone.

'Good evening. Harvest House, how may I help you?'

'Hello, could you put me through to Clare Carpenter's room, please?'

'Are you sure you want to disturb her? It is after midnight.'

'Yes, this is her husband. It's fine.'

William counted the rings while he waited for Clare to answer. One. Two. She'll be stirring. Oh God, I hope she isn't too furious about me calling so late, or for calling at all. Three. It would be worse to hang up now. She's probably blinking into the dark, looking for the phone. Four. Five. Six. Is she wondering who it is? Why isn't she answering? Seven. Eight. Is she afraid to answer in case it's me?

Click.

'Oh, thank God. Clare, it's me. I'm sorry for calling so late. I just really need to talk to you –'

'Excuse me. I'm sorry. Mr Carpenter? You've come back through to reception.'

'Oh.' William paused, curling and releasing his toes in the carpet fibres. 'Can you try her room again, please? And it's Mr Woolf. My wife kept her maiden name.'

'I'm afraid I can see now that your wife's room is unoccupied at the moment. Her key is here in reception. Would you like me to give her a message upon her return?'

'But it's so late. Where could she be? Are you sure you have the right room?'

'I'm quite sure, and I couldn't hazard a guess. Shall I ask her to call you?'

'Yes. No. Please don't, it's fine. Thanks, anyway.'

William fumbled the handset back into position and

struggled to stand up; he could feel the effects of the whiskey in his knees now. The earlier euphoria drained from him. Where could Clare be? She didn't know anyone in Wales. Not that he knew of. Was it better if she did have friends that he had never heard of, or if she had met someone new and struck up an acquaintance? Surely she wouldn't just fall into conversation with a total stranger? That was really not like her, but she could hardly be out somewhere on her own? Maybe she'd had an accident. Oh God. If she were in trouble, no one would know for days that she was missing. Maybe he should call the hotel again and explain how out of character this was, see if the receptionist could check the hotel bar, enquire if anyone knew what time she had gone out, who she had left with. William paced the room, the storm raging once again inside him. The full force of Clare's distance from him hit him hard, a screw twisting in every one of his soft spots. And there was nothing he could do but wait.

The sooty night vanished into itself as a grey half-light swept in. William eventually fell asleep, muffled by the whiskey, a pillow squeezed tight against his naked chest. His dreams were wild visions of a woman with scarlet hair sitting on the distant rocks, calling him out to sea. Clare stood on the shore, growing smaller and smaller. The water around him turned blood red, thick and swampy, so his movements became slower and he struggled to wade waist-high through the tide. He looked over his shoulder at Clare. Her cries were keening in the wind around him, but she was static, a statue full of sounds who could not move. The sun seemed to shine straight through her, a blinding white light too harsh for him to stare at. William felt fingernails running through his damp hair, scratching down his spine, nibbling at his ears and neck, but there was no one there. He woke up at the wrong end of the bed, tangled in his sheets, a towel hot with sweat across his face. His eyes were glued closed by a salty crust and a little drummer boy pounded away in the darkest recesses of his mind. He staggered to the bathroom and sat in the shower, an ice-cold stream washing over him, shocking his body awake. He relished the cold tiles against his skin as he rested his forehead against the glass and waited for the dawn of a new day.

When Clare and Flora staggered into their hotel room in the early hours of Wednesday morning, several hours and too many drinks had passed since William's telephone call had rung into the silence. The alcohol bullied Clare's repressed feelings into reappearing, and she struggled to stay in control. It was harder than she had thought, asking for help, and it pained her to show Flora how much she was really hurting. Her first instinct was still to be the strong one; to protect her.

On Tuesday morning, Clare had been awoken by Housekeeping knocking on her bedroom door; the sudden disruption disorientated her as she recalibrated once again to the hotel room, her singular status and the mild throbbing in her temples. She staggered to the door, opened it a crack and asked them to come back later. The heavy brocade curtains were drawn tight, creating the illusion of night. When she pulled them wide, she was momentarily blinded by the sunlight that flooded into the room. For each day of her trip, Clare had slept late in the morning, and her body thanked her for it. After she had showered, dressed and coffee-ed, Clare called Flora and asked her to join her. If Flora was surprised to receive a summons from her big sister to come and stay with her in Wales, she hid it with aplomb.

In advance of her coming, Clare carefully packed away the sketch pad and pencils into her suitcase, evidence of the experiment she had continued to embrace in the last few days. They were the seeds of something very delicate; she didn't want to scare what she had discovered and risk it dissolving in the light.

It should have been a three-hour drive from Flora's garden flat in Clerkenwell to the hotel, but she arrived more quickly than Clare had expected. Upon her arrival, the sisters met in reception with an awkward hug that was all elbows and chins. Clare noticed that Flora's hair was longer now, and her own strawberry-blonde colour for once. She looked fresh in a white woollen dress with a butterfly brooch and wine cotton tights. Clare was surprised to see her little sister looking so put-together. They drank peppermint tea in the conservatory and shared little bits of small talk while they adjusted to being in each other's company again.

Flora rapped Clare's knuckles with a silver teaspoon.

'You're not listening to me. Come back.'

'What? Sorry. I'm here. You were talking about the china being like Nana's.'

Flora rolled her eyes. 'Yes, yes, I was. About fifteen minutes ago. Why don't you tell me what's going on, instead of having me sit here talking to myself?'

Clare poured more tea and gave her sister an exasperated sidelong glance.

'Oh, don't look so pained, Flora. You're making me feel worse, just looking at you.'

'I'm sorry, but I'm trying to keep my cool here, and

it's not easy. Can you please tell me what's happened? You're not sick, are you? Is William okay?'

Clare picked up the teaspoon and let it hover over the sugar bowl for a moment before placing it back on her saucer.

'We're both fine, but' – she hesitated – 'our marriage isn't. I haven't left him . . . but I am taking some time away.' She watched Flora's expression remain unchanged. 'You don't look very surprised. I thought you'd be shocked.'

'Well, things sound worse than I thought, but the last time I saw you both things seemed pretty tense. I guess I hoped I'd just caught you at a bad moment.'

Clare paused to sip her tea. 'It would have been hard to catch us at a good one recently,' she replied. 'I'm sorry. I didn't mean to panic you by dragging you down here. I just didn't want to be on my own. I feel a bit silly now. I hope you won't get in trouble at work?'

'No, you did the right thing. I'm glad you called.'

Flora's cheeks were flushed; it reminded Clare of the blush that had bloomed so easily from under the collar of her sister's ivory school blouse when she teased her at school. She had relentlessly tortured her as punishment for the easier life nature had bestowed upon her; the copper curls so often complimented, the solos in the church choir, her easy facility for spelling, maths and exams. It was a long time before Clare realized the impact her casual cruelty had had on Flora's development, the holes it had torn in her confidence. She had focused so much on protecting her from their mother's mood swings and alcoholic episodes that it had never occurred to her that she herself had caused Flora to suffer. The past was a moth endlessly fluttering at a hidden mohair jumper in her closet, undetected until the damage was done. She shrugged the thought away; this was not the time to revisit it. Their mother was confined to a hospice now; it was more difficult than ever to discuss what went before.

The teapot sat cold and abandoned on a tarnished brass tray; dirty tea stains ran in rings around the royal-blue-and white willow-patterned teacups. The crumbs of almond and raspberry slices stuck to a silver fork and clung to Flora's dress like mice on a life raft. It was all Clare could do not to reach across to brush them away. She watched her sister in silence for a few moments as Flora squeezed her bitten, unpainted fingernails between her legs. She resisted the urge to comment on them.

Flora jumped up. 'I think we need something stronger.'

Clare glanced at the porcelain clock hanging on the wall behind her and was surprised to see it was six in the evening already. She nodded her approval and followed her sister's lead as they ambled to their room. Flora paused on the stairs and smoothed her hand along the art deco wallpaper.

'Remember at Nana's, the way the pattern never lined up? She was so awful at putting it up but refused to get someone in. She would have cracked up, trying to match up all these little circles.'

They collected their coats from the bedroom and strolled up to the village inn, where they curled up beside each other on a rose-and-ivory brushed cotton couch in front of the stone fireplace. A large quantity of white wine spritzers operated as a conversational mid-wife. They spoke of Flora's trip to Thailand, of Thatcher, of Nelson Mandela's imprisonment and how soon they would start knocking down the Berlin Wall. Clare realized it had been a long time since her thoughts hadn't been completely consumed by either the status of a case or the state of her marriage. Sitting with Flora, she felt on holiday from herself, but she knew she couldn't avoid the headline news all evening. After a comfortable silence eventually settled between them, she braced herself to push the bruise.

'I know I haven't been very forthcoming, Flora, but I don't know how to explain. There's no one easy answer for what's happened.'

Flora waited a beat before she asked the question Clare had been expecting all evening.

'Is there' – she paused – 'anyone else involved?'

'No, not really,' Clare answered. 'I don't think so, anyway. He has definitely been flirting with a silly girl in the office, but I don't think anything really happened. That's never been something I worried about with William, I'll give him that.'

'And what about you? Have you –'

'*Of course not!*' Clare leaned further away from Flora and untucked her legs from beneath her. 'How could you even ... I'm sorry, I shouldn't have snapped, but no, there's no one else ... but I can't say that, some-times, I don't fantasize about the idea of someone new, or a different William, at least.'

Flora leaned forward, eager to keep pulling the thread.

'But why would you want anyone else? You guys gave me a template for a relationship I could believe in. You've no idea what that has meant to me, after the disaster of Mum and Dad. You always seemed so happy. I remember when you did that terrible karaoke on New Year's Eve, I sat there wishing *anyone* would look at me the way William looked at you.'

Clare felt an unwelcome sting behind her eyes as she remembered her and William's atonal Sonny and Cher duet. The moment held a crystallized beauty, from a time when their love and life was much less complicated. She glanced around the bar, distracting herself by surveying the two middle-aged women dancing with great abandon to Culture Club in the corner of the room.

'Things were different then,' she answered. 'Before the depot took on a life of its own and William basically gave up any hope of being a writer, of really making anything of himself.'

'He loves it there, though, doesn't he? And if it's enough for him, why can't it be enough for you? Are you ashamed of it or something?'

'Of course not. I just can't understand how it *could* be enough for him. It was only supposed to be temporary. I just feel like he gave up, and I think it's cowardly. It's really hard to respect that, especially when it means that I have to work twice as hard to support us and still can't reap the rewards of a nicer home or what have you. And don't forget, this *was* his dream, too. It's not like I've pushed it on him.'

Flora poured half of her almost full glass into Clare's; the effects of the alcohol were making her sister's features blur a little. She spilled some on the carpet as she rebalanced herself and rubbed it in with the sole of her shoe.

'Wasn't he putting a book together about the depot, though? He told me about it at Christmas and seemed really excited about it.'

'Allegedly,' Clare snorted. 'But we've been down that road before.'

Flora sat up straight. 'Okay, don't shout at me but . . . If you could let go of feeling disappointed and start imagining what a new future together could look like, you might feel better about everything and he might get his confidence back.'

Clare buried her face in the houndstooth throw that lay across the back of the couch.

'That's enough, please, Flora. My head is going to explode.'

Flora pulled the blanket away from her sister's face. 'Okay, I'll drop it,' she said, 'but all I'll say is, it can't be easy living with someone who assumes the worst of you all of the time and has such low expectations. I mean, you organized your own surprise thirtieth-birthday party because you didn't trust him to get it right.'

'Well, that's only because history has taught me what to expect from him.'

Flora started nibbling on her thumbnail but Clare pulled her hand away. 'Stop it! You look like a crazy person doing that.' Flora snapped her hand back and sat on it before speaking again.

'You still love him, don't you?'

Clare muffled a moan into the blanket.

'Of course I do, but as I get older, I realize that love is not enough on its own. It's the day-to-day reality of living with someone that really counts. What's love got to do with it?'

Flora's horrified face triggered Clare's funny bone and she collapsed forward in hysterical laughter. 'I have an amazing idea,' she whispered. 'Let's dance.' She pulled Flora behind her as she weaved her way around the tables to join the two women who were still dancing with gusto, this time to a Madonna medley. When Clare shimmied up towards them, they threw their arms around her like a long-lost friend and she felt emotion well inside her once again. She was all talked out and wanted to throw herself into the rhythm of the music, to climb out of her own head and feel the beat pulsate through her.

The hours slipped away as they danced to each and every song the DJ played. By the time they found themselves tiptoeing across the wooden floors of the hotel lobby, Flora looked exhausted. Clare had thought about booking a second room for her sister before she arrived but, in truth, she wanted the company during the night. They hadn't shared a bedroom, let alone a bed, since they were children, but it felt less strange than it could have. An unfamiliar shape in the bed was better than no shape at all. For the first time, Clare began to understand the appeal of one-night stands. The need for the physicality of someone else. To hear someone breathing and moving in the night. To know that, if someone touched your arm or leg, you wouldn't shatter into a million pieces. In the darkness of the room, Clare could sense that Flora was still awake. She sat up in bed and started furiously plumping the pillows.

'Why do I feel so guilty? I haven't done anything wrong, not really. I'm just trying to make a change, to get us out of this rut. If I thought there was a way back for us, I would take it. You believe me, don't you, Flo?'

Flora put her arms around her and held on tightly as she shook out angry little cries.

'I just feel like I need to do something drastic. To wake myself up. Before it's too late.'

'Let's try to get some sleep. Everything will be clearer in the morning.'

Clare lay back down, and Flora stroked her hair until her breathing steadied. The touch untangled the knotting threads in her mind. More tears were rising up inside her, but she didn't want to cry in front of her sister again. She rolled over and scrunched up her face against the pillow, wiping her nose on the silky rim of the pillow case. Where had all her self-control gone? She needed to button herself back up and make a plan. Tomorrow would be a new day.

II.

William's craving for coffee superseded the urge to collapse back into bed, so he made his way gingerly to the breakfast room of the Red Lion Hotel. His bones ached from walking, weariness and worrying. He sat out on the patio, where a whisper of wind could reach him and dance away shyly with some of the lingering thoughts that haunted him from the night before. He poured one strong brew after another. The weather gods had made peace and blessed Clovelly with a clear turquoise sky. William felt his mind clearing. The matronly waitress placed a full English breakfast in front of him and gave him a quizzical look.

'Are you all right there, mister? You look a little peaky.'

'I'm fine, thanks. Just didn't sleep very well. I think the storm unsettled me. Silly, really.'

'Not at all. There's plenty to be afear'd of in a storm like that one. Many that wasn't have met unfortunate ends around these parts.'

He nodded and nudged the sausage, bacon and eggs around his plate with a fork, his stomach churning at the thoughts of a runny egg mixing with the previous night's intake of alcohol. He forced himself to eat two slices of buttery toast and half a sausage before his delicate insides called a halt. He walked slowly back to his room and braced himself for another call to see if Clare had returned to her room.

'I'll put you through now, sir.'

One ring. Two rings. Three rings.

'Hello?' Her voice was cloudy with sleep and confusion when she answered.

'Clare! It's me. I just wanted to see if you were okay?'

'William? Of course I'm okay. Why wouldn't I be?'

'It's just, I tried to reach you last night, late, and you weren't in your room so . . . I was worried.'

'You want to know where I was, more like it.'

'No, honestly, Clare, I couldn't think . . . why are you whispering?'

He heard shuffling in the background and Clare's voice rose.

'You shouldn't have been calling in the first place. I asked you not to.'

'I'm sorry. It's just I'm down in Devon and there was a storm and I wanted to tell you that –'

'Devon? Why are you there? Look, actually, it doesn't matter. I'm hanging up now.'

'– that I missed you.'

Clare's voice softened.

'I'll be in touch soon, William. Okay?'

Her change in tone gave him confidence, her defences lowered for a moment.

'Clare, just wait a minute, before you go, *would* you tell me where you were last night?'

The phone call disconnected with a slam.

William cursed himself. Why had he pushed? Why couldn't he have just left well enough alone and ended the call nicely? Wherever Clare had been last night, he knew she wouldn't have been doing anything wrong, didn't he? He repacked his satchel and decided it was time to say goodbye to Clovelly and point Corina towards London.

In reception, a dozen American tourists were waiting to check in. He shuffled impatiently at the back of the queue; an elderly couple in matching salmon polo shirts, plaid shorts and white baseball caps were extracting every possible opportunity to bond with the hotel manager through their check-in experience; 'My parents stayed here on their honeymoon many years ago . . . I love how "vintage" the look is, it's so quaint . . . Are your family from Clovelly? Is the food you serve locally sourced produce? A real fountain pen, how lovely.'

William's patience couldn't stand it. He decided to take a final stroll through the village instead of waiting. In the morning sunlight, his jumper felt hot, scratchy and restrictive as he walked; he tied it in a loose knot around his shoulders and relished the fresh air settling on his bare arms. He stopped at the corner shop, bought a Lucozade energy drink, the *Guardian* and a white-paper twist of peppermints. On a low stone wall that hugged the harbour, he stretched out and inhaled the saltiness in the damp air as he gulped back the sticky orange elixir.

With every passing moment, as he flicked through the newspaper, he felt more revived. On page eleven, he was startled to see a familiar face peering out at him. Where did he know that little girl from? He scanned the article quickly for a name and laughed out loud. The Geology Rocks girl! Penelope Bernadine Foxcroft had made the news with her whale vomit.

Dr Rosamund O'Reilly cited Penelope's discovery and recognition of the value of the ambergris as a remarkable feat and commended her sound judgement. The young geologist has been handsomely rewarded for her achievement as the ambergris is valued at £10,000. When asked what she would do with her windfall, Penelope replied, 'I will invest it in my education, of course.'

William folded the newspaper in two and smiled at the photograph of Penelope and Dr O'Reilly holding the specimen somewhat awkwardly between them. He was a little disappointed that the article hadn't mentioned the depot, but it didn't take away from the huge satisfaction he felt at the outcome. What a victorious forty-eight hours in the life of a letter detective. He leaned back on the wall and turned his face towards the sun.

The good news carried him along the cobbled street, away from the harbour and towards the hotel. Should he bring something back for Clare? He paused outside Clovelly Fudge, admiring the towers of delectable treats covered in winking cellophane, like delicious chunks of edible Lego. Perhaps her sweet tooth would appreciate that. Across the street, a clapperboard sign advertised the Clovelly Gallery: ceramics and paintings inspired by the fishing village. Maybe he could find some new bowls to replace those that had been broken. He stepped into the whitewashed gallery and squinted as his eyes adjusted to the loss of sunlight. The room was cool and still, the stone walls hushed with secrets. He softened his tread to kill the echo of his footsteps pounding on the parquet flooring. As his eyes travelled over the walls, they rested for a second on each picture before skipping to the next. He was surprised to find not paintings of Clovelly but a series of photographs of flowers, indeed, a flower market. A strange sensation akin to déjà vu overcame him: had he seen these pictures before?

He picked up a photocopied leaflet that sat in a tidy pile on a tree-trunk table in the middle of the room.

Our visiting exhibition is a collection of works captured at Columbia Road Flower Market, East London, by the photographer W.W. The photographs will be on display until 1 May, when they will move to Shoreditch Town Hall, London. For sales enquiries, please contact Harry Prummel, Gallery Custodian, on 01237 422314.

Prummel! William found himself at the centre of some mysterious magic that he felt awaited his understanding before it revealed its intentions. Columbia Road Flower Market; he recognized it from the descriptions in Winter's letters. W.W. Those were his initials. And half, at least, of Winter's — assuming, of course, that Winter was her real name. A crawling awakening overcame him as he paced about the room; there was the Volkswagen Beetle filled with daffodils, sunflowers and daisies; the coffee trike with balloons floating high from the basket; the merchant in a pirate hat. He recalled the uneasy feeling that had soaked into him with the stormy rains: the woman on the cliff, the glow of wild scarlet, how the figure had tormented his dreams. Could this photographer truly be Winter? No. This was fanciful. He was letting himself get carried away. And yet, he had no explanation as to how Winter's letters had reached him. Were the same forces at play here? Was this why he had felt compelled to come, now, after procrastinating for so many years?

Once the thought had crystallized in his mind, he became more convinced of the need to trust his instincts, that his heart understood what his head could not. He dithered on the spot, walking two steps forward, pausing to look at a black-and-white print of a woman wearing a full-length leather jacket belted tightly around her waist clutching armfuls of white roses. Circling the room, he felt his life fast-forward to meet its destiny without the need for his permission. There was nothing else for it: he would have to find this photographer and confront them, however irrational and ridiculous that may seem.

William clenched the leaflet in his hand and called out for assistance. A teenager, a coil of dreadlocks wound about her head, slunk from the back room and watched him with sulky suspicion with her kohl-rimmed eyes, a half-eaten banana in one hand.

'Yeah? Do you need something?' she asked. 'I'm on my break.'

William strode towards her but tempered his tone when he saw her start and step back.

'Could I please use your telephone? I'd like to speak to Harry Prummel about this exhibition.' He waited. 'I promise I'll only be a moment.'

She sighed and beckoned for him to follow her with her banana peel through the heavy steel door she'd emerged from. The telephone was perched on an old wooden school desk with the seat still attached; a battered white leather-bound address book sat beside it, a string with a cracked biro taped to the outside. William attempted to wriggle into the seat but gave up in flustered shame when he heard the gallery assistant snort over his shoulder. He tried to ignore her inevitable eavesdropping and turned to face the wall as he listened to the ringing echoing down the line. Please pick up. Please pick up.

'Prummel residence. Harry speaking.'

William gave an involuntary squeal of relief to hear his voice.

'Harry! I'm so glad you're home. This is William Woolf, from yesterday. I hope you don't mind me calling but –'

'William, your ears must have been burning – I was just talking about you! We're still a bit overwhelmed here, but ever so pleased. Is there something I can do for you?'

The question threw him a little: what exactly was he hoping Harry could do for him?

'Well, this might seem a little strange, but I'm in Clovelly Gallery at the moment and I'm just wondering if you might be able to tell me a little bit more about the photographer who's currently exhibiting there?'

A second's silence hung on the line before Harry answered.

'Why, of course, she's a client of mine who I met through some business in London. Long story. Bit hush hush. Would you like to buy something? I'm sure I could help negotiate a great price for you.'

William's fingers traced the carvings in the lid of the desk – *FC heart PD* and a crooked star – while he considered this.

'I actually just think I recognized some of the pictures . . . I wondered if I knew her. Could you tell me her name?'

William gripped the desk as he waited for a reply.

'Alice-Ann Strout – why, do you know her?'

With those three little words, William was utterly deflated.

'Oh, no. I don't think I do, then, after all.'

He was about to close the call when a thought tugged him.

'Sorry, Harry, but why does it say "W.W." on all the photographs? Why not her real initials?'

'Oh, that's a pseudonym of sorts. I don't know what it stands for – her artistic nom de plume, I believe. You can ask her yourself, if you like. She's staying at Crazy Kate's old cottage. Very lovely woman. I'm sure she wouldn't mind you popping over. Tell her I sent you! But good luck getting away without buying something . . .'

William's mind was racing with the sudden onslaught of new information: there was still a chance. He refocused on Harry's chatter. 'Crazy Kate? Is that a real person?' he asked.

'It was once, God rest her. She was a poor woman who lived in what is now the oldest cottage in the village. She was driven demented by her husband drowning at sea and then, one day, she donned her wedding dress and followed him into his watery grave. Terribly sad. There but for the grace of God, as they say. You can't miss her cottage; it's the one overlooking the harbour with the long white balcony. If you call in, do send Alice-Ann my best.'

William retraced his steps back to the harbour; he could picture the cottage Harry had spoken of in his mind's eye. Euphoria about his epiphany soon gave way to the panicky realization of what might happen next. Could it really be *his* Winter? Or had he finally lost his mind? And if it was her, how would he explain who he was? *Hello, I'm your Great Love?* Was he? She had probably never anticipated anyone reading her letters. Yet, she must have hoped someone would. Would she be disappointed that it was him? Should he mention straight away that he was married? Reality slapped him. He stopped on the pathway for a moment. What would Clare say if she knew where he was going? Shouldn't he be chasing after her instead? She was the one who had left him, though; she was the one running away. If she hadn't left for Wales, he wouldn't even be in Clovelly. He tried to validate his behaviour by condemning hers, but it didn't sit right with him to blame her for him being here. He knew that this choice was his alone.

Having reached the cottage, William paused outside; a planet of uncertainty spinning out of orbit. There was no point searching for a voice of reason now. If Winter was this close, he had to go to her. What if this was all meant to be? If he was Winter's destiny and he was the only one who knew it? Maybe Clare leaving was all part of a grand design of which he knew nothing. Besides, it might amount to nothing at all, just an awkward conversation that ended with Winter fleeing back to London to throw her writing paper in the fire. If so, he could accept that, he presumed, but he knew he couldn't live without knowing. William was unravelling like an old wool jumper with every passing second; he needed to tie a knot in this.

He had never anticipated approaching Winter so impulsively; this pleasure trip was fast becoming one of the least relaxing experiences he had ever subjected himself to. William's resolution was fading rapidly as he climbed the wooden stairs to the front door of Crazy Kate's, but he held his nerve as he lifted the brass knocker and let it drop in one loud clang against the lilac wood. From inside, he heard a squeal and claws scampering across floorboards, then footsteps. As the door peeled inwards, a snow-white cat brushed past his legs and scarpered over the veranda. William's eyeline saw white tights first, inside black velvet ballet slippers, the ends of a purple-and-grey silk kimono, before looking up to find his question asked and answered in the same moment. Alice-Ann's long red hair framed a face William thought must have adventured through eighty years or more. Silver streaks snaked from her temples through the tresses he knew must once have been a spectacular fiery mass. In a lilting Scottish accent, she asked him his business.

'Your photos, Ms Strout,' he answered. 'I was hoping to buy the one of the Beetle, with the flowers.'

She gave him a long, hard look.

'Are you sure that's what you came here for?'

He found her gaze unnerving but held firm. 'Yes. Harry Prummel told me you were here.'

She stepped back into the hallway and handed him a pad of stiff cream parchment paper and a well-sharpened pencil.

'Here. Write down where we can contact you. Harry will organize something at the end of the exhibition. I'm not sure why he didn't take your details himself.'

William smiled at her sheepishly. 'I wanted to meet the artist,' he replied.

She tore off the sheet of paper he had scribbled on and glanced at it before folding it in two and slipping it into the loose pocket of her kimono.

'Did I see you last night, perhaps? On the Look-out?' he asked.

'Perhaps,' she answered, with a shy smile of her own that touched the dove-grey pools of her eyes.

He fought the urge to tell her why he had really come; he felt, but rejected, the impulse under the scrutiny of her gaze. As he walked away from Alice-Ann and tried to shake off the strange feeling of loss that settled upon him, she called after him, 'I hope you find what you're looking for, Mr Woolf.'

He turned and gave her a little wave.

'So do I, Ms Strout. So do I.'

12.

William sat on the edge of their marital bed, unmade, as he had left it when he departed for Clovelly. He pulled off his shoes and socks; grit escaped and vanished in the carpet fibres. It was a dispiriting memento of his excursion. He lay back on the crumpled duvet, turning his face to breathe in the familiar lavender smell that faded but never completely left their Egyptian cotton linen. He remembered arguing over buying such expensive sheets when they first married:

'I just don't think we should be spending money on luxuries when we are trying to save for our deposit.'

'A good night's sleep doesn't count as a luxury. Just imagine rolling around naked under this soft cotton every night. If we had sheets this soft, I might never wear pyjamas to bed again.'

It was an argument easily won by Clare. He envied now the problems he once lost sleep over: adopting a puppy; parental visits; spring cleaning; plans for Bank Holiday weekends. He missed the normality of bickering without subtext, sulks trumped by tickling; the everyday debates over which movie, cereal or newspaper to buy. Those were the days before everything became contentious and the flat littered with landmines that they awkwardly danced around. He knew they could not sustain a marriage through memories of better times alone. William groaned and rolled over, squashing his face into a pillow. It was a never-ending cycle. If they were going to stay together, this couldn't be the way they communicated – or failed to communicate – for much longer. Would Clare be throwing what he had done, or failed to do, back at him until he was eventually granted the sweet release of death? What a calamity his life had become. Clare had absconded to Wales and he was wasting time daydreaming about a woman he didn't even know existed. He fell asleep, still fully dressed, with his dusty toes dangling over the side of the bed.

On the walk to the depot the following morning, William tried to imagine a life with someone new. Being with Clare was truly the first proper relationship he had ever experienced. Could he start again and learn how to love someone else? Would it just happen naturally, if it was the right person? He had married his first real girl-friend. Were they wrong to be so hasty? To marry their future selves together when they didn't know who those people were yet? He knew so little when they met; he had acted purely on instinct and the lessons he had gleaned about love from music and books. Back then, there was no doubt in his mind that Clare was the one, and that such a person could exist.

At eighteen, he lost his virginity to one of his mother's friends; she propositioned him after hiring him to paint her house the summer he left school. Gloria gave him a basic education in how to please a woman, but she was not a challenging taskmaster. William sensed that any young body, far removed from her husband Ron's ageing bones and grey chest hair, was probably sufficient. In a moment of particular cruelty, Gloria once told him that sleeping with Ron was like hugging a big bag of yoghurt. Ron wasn't a hard act to follow. He convinced himself at the time that he loved Gloria, but it was more of a childish crush and it faded as soon as he arrived at university. He still thought of her fondly occasionally, of her leopard-print tracksuit, the smell of hairspray on her sticky perm, the lines on her ankles where the fake tan stopped, and wondered what had become of her, although he never dared ask his mother.

It took longer than he had hoped to meet someone new, and in the years before Clare burst into his life there were only two other girls. Oona was an owly creature, with a long brown ponytail that reached the base of her spine. She was studying anthropology and William dated her for nine months without ever sleeping over. They had passionate kisses that steamed up her glasses, but she held his hands firmly by his side and he didn't know how to either accelerate or terminate their relationship. She eventually broke it off with him after winning a scholarship to study in Bolivia.

Her successor, Leonora, was an entirely different species; she had inherited olive skin, jet-black eyes and wild ebony curls from her Greek mother and the long limbs and chiselled cheekbones of her Swedish father. She was the darling of the science department; men hovered around her, hoping for a secret smile or a soft word.

William became obsessed with her and worked very hard to win her attention, accompanying her to evening lectures he did not understand, learning to cook vegetarian meals, allowing her to sketch him while he posed half naked, scorching with embarrassment. She told him she liked how kind he was; how he didn't try to possess her like the other men on campus; how he bothered to listen to her properly when she talked – he wasn't just waiting for her to finish so he could speak again. When she at last led him to her bed, he felt completely unprepared for it. The night of unbridled passion he had fantasized about proved a quiet affair in reality; she politely offered a moan or two while he tried, with an increasing sense of despair, to understand how her exquisite, voluptuous body worked. He was paralysed with fear and moved without much delay from undressing her to finishing.

A lot of vegetables slowly rotted in his cupboard before he could accept that Leonora would not be visiting again. When they bumped into each other on campus, she always offered him a sympathetic smile, which only compounded his humiliation. He had been offered the forbidden fruit but, instead of taking a delicious bite, had dropped the apple in a puddle.

After the Leonora debacle, William's confidence ebbed away. He became a great friend to many interesting and attractive women, but never tried for anything more, until he met Clare; the fear of losing her far outweighed the fear of trying to win her. Clare patiently taught him how to make love to her; helped him understand how she wanted to be made love to. He began to understand that there was a delicate and powerful point where a woman didn't want to be asked for approval to continue but instead wants the man to proceed with confidence because he understands what she wants. What would it be like to sleep with someone else after all these years of knowing only one woman?

When he arrived at his desk, a note from Mr Flanagan awaited him; a summons to see him that morning. William was sure he was in trouble. The haphazard mound of post that now sat a foot high on his desk offered him little opportunity to convince Ned that all was well. He tore the sticky note impatiently from the cover of his diary, tossed it in the wastepaper basket and rubbed away with a resentful finger the faint trace of residue that remained. Had he come to the end of the road at the depot? Forced Ned's hand to let him go? Even if the time was close, he needed to be smart now. The last thing he needed was to have to tell Clare he had lost his job, even if it was a job she had come to loathe as a symbol of his great failure. If he was going to leave, it would have to be on his terms and not before he finished his *Volume of Lost Letters*.

He shuffled through the precarious pile of letters spread across his desk and tried to conjure up the old enthusiasm he once felt for his work. His life was in such a state of flux, restoring equilibrium to someone else's held little appeal, despite how much his recent successes with Harry and Little Miss Geology Rocks had buoyed him. He had no one to go home to and share the anecdotes with; no one to care if he succeeded in a particular mission or solved one of these puzzles. It reminded him of Stevie once saying that he didn't make as much effort at gigs if there wasn't a girl in the audience he was trying to impress. Maybe William's karmic balance was out of kilter and he could earn some redemption by engaging in professional good deeds. Would karma work in your favour if you deliberately chased it, though? Or was that in fact counterproductive? He decided it was best to do his job because it was his duty and not in the hope of heavenly reward.

He shook himself and decided that today he would seize control of the situation; make a serious dent in his backlog and show Ned that he had nothing to worry about. The great success he had achieved with Prummel and Penelope had to count for something, didn't it? He swept the pile of letters and parcels that had accumulated on his desk into an empty mail sack so that he could clear some space and tackle them one by one. Just tidying everything gave him some peace, and he felt confident as he started to work. He couldn't control what Clare was doing, he couldn't control whether any of Winter's letters came, but he could control what he did at his desk, and that is what he would do.

First, he withdrew a black-and-white postcard of a man walking on a tightrope across the Manhattan skyline. On the back, in a blue marker, the address offered only 'London-Irish Maria with the blue poodle perm, Clapham, England'. The note read:

Maria, my mystery woman with the bag of knitting and home-made cheese-and-pickle sandwiches. Why did you leave without saying goodbye? I looked for you everywhere, but you couldn't be found. Who knows if this will find you, but, if it's meant to be, it will! I'm playing the Astoria on 15 May. Come – I'll leave word at the stage door. Jimi. x

William thought of Jimi waiting on the night for a blue poodle perm to peep around the green room door. He felt for him but wondered why Maria had left him so unceremoniously. Maybe this was an unanswered prayer for the best. He pondered at the choice of postcard: what was Jimi trying to say? Have faith? The William of his younger years, when his faith in the idea of *the one* was so unshakeable, would have celebrated Jimi's perseverance. Nowadays, it was harder to hold on to that idealism. What happens when *the one* becomes a heartbreaking amount of work? As we change and grow older, does the one we need have to change also? Or was it possible he hadn't even met the one yet? Was the real one still out there, searching for him? Maybe even writing him letters? He stuck the postcard on the wall beside his desk with a red drawing pin.

The next, pale green, envelope was barely intact; it was water damaged and crumbling at the edges. A grey blur dragged across the page where the address had been and the stamp curled away at three corners. He pressed the stamp flat and smiled with surprise to see it was a half-cent one from New Zealand. Trevor had been hunting one for as long as William could remember; the orange-and-black butterfly against the powder-blue background was so distinctive. He carried the envelope over to Trevor's desk and placed it there for him to find. His denim jacket, the lapels covered in badges from metal bands, was hanging on the back of his chair and emitting a strong stench of smoke. William hoped he would be there to see his face when he noticed it and felt a thrill of excitement for him.

He was still enjoying thoughts of Trevor's discovery when, reaching into the postbag, his fingers felt the familiar groove of heavy parchment. He scanned the room for inquisitive eyes before allowing himself to pull out into the light what he knew would be a letter from Winter. He glanced down to confirm that it was really from her then quickly hid it inside his satchel under the desk. He knew he should be patient and wait until later, but he needed this today. Before Marjorie could ask him where he was going, he hastened for the corridor that led to the fire escape, where he could sit in peace. The steel steps were damp but he sat down regardless and leaned uncomfortably against the railing as he read. Marjorie's *Auntie of the Year* mug lay on its side in a puddle by his feet.

My Great Love,

I only have a few moments before I head out into the night, but I have to tell you something. I might be meeting you soon. In two hours, to be precise. At the Everyman Theatre in Notting Hill. There is a special showing tonight of the forties film *Hellzapoppin'* with a swing-dancing lesson on beforehand – it feels like just the sort of place I might meet you. There are few things

I love more than swing dancing; that music fills me with joy. In some ways, I feel a bit strange telling you that I may meet another man tonight, but you really have nothing to worry about. You see, the thing is, either it's you, in which case, tonight, a tuning fork will be struck upon the roof of the cinema and all the choirs of heaven will sing in tune, or else it won't be you, and the evening will fade into insignificance and whoever he is will slip away into the night with no damage done.

I'm wearing an emerald-green dress with an underskirt that makes it swish-swish as I walk. It was made for spinning about in. I bought it just before I left Dublin, in my favourite vintage clothes shop, on Dame Street. The owner of the shop told me the frock brings out the green in my eyes. I hope so. What colour are yours? I hope they are brown. Brown eyes are always warm. Blues can be so cold. I felt that the dress symbolized what I wanted my new life to embrace: adventure, colour and opportunities for dancing.

When you walk inside that store, it is like falling down a rabbit-hole to a Wonderland of possibility. You could not fill your wardrobe with such costumes and live a life of mediocrity. So often I have visited there and shyly tried things on but lost my nerve at the crucial moment. Not that time. I was dressing for London. I was dressing for the me I wanted to become. I had no idea then just how far those feathers and bows would take me. Here is a picture of my most extravagant purchase; see how they catch the light of the city and shimmer like a silvery moon? I wore them for the first time today. I'm getting braver. But I think I should save them up for a truly special occasion, don't you?

William peered into the envelope and found a Polaroid picture still waiting inside. It curved in his palm; a photograph of her two feet dressed in luminescent white cowboy boots. Were they covered in glitter? What made them sparkle so? Red woollen stockings peeked out from the tops. How bizarre to see even just this part of Winter's physical self. He returned to the letter.

I am slowly breathing in this city and breathing out a new me. I thought about changing my name permanently when I came here, but I'm not sure a girl by another name would feel as true. Sometimes, though, an adopted persona makes it easier to activate a new life plan. It's like buying a new coat that you can return if you change your mind. Whatever you call yourself, though, wherever you go, you take yourself with you. If you could start all over again tomorrow in a new city, what would you do? Would you choose the same life for yourself or try something new? What would you cast aside? I am grateful for this gift of a new beginning, and I won't waste it.

Oh, please, let it be you standing waiting for me tonight. Let the night take us dancing.

If all else fails, maybe I will at least meet some new people of my ilk. Do you find, as you get older, it becomes harder to make new friends? New people are exhausting: the flirtations with friendships and testing of old stories on new ears. One thing I do find very liberating, though, is the opportunity to reposition the past. Former protagonists are important to new people only if I present them that way. Perhaps this is why I like writing to you so much; on paper, I can be the version of myself I've always wanted to be. I am more truthful here, in a way that it takes such a long time to reach in person. I am determined that the me of my letters and the London me should become one and the same, and soon.

I feel quite nervous about maybe seeing you later. It's so much easier to talk to you like this. No pressure. No expectations. You can't let me down.

I must dash – I don't want to leave you waiting. Him waiting. You. Him. The night.

Yours, as always,
Winter

William picked up Marjorie's mug and walked back into the office. In the kitchen, he stood at the window overlooking Shoreditch High Street. He scanned the river of people flowing past on the pavement. Was Winter one of them? Would he start again, if he could? What *did* he most want? In truth, an end to the struggle and to be in the right frame of mind to write again. He wondered how Winter's evening had gone, if she was smitten now with some undeserving buffoon she had met. Surely she wouldn't have spoken to another man of the inner, secret life she wrote to William about, if that inner, secret person even really existed. It could just be a fantasy she spilled across those pages. Was he the one being fooled? He caught himself in that moment of realization; he really had come to believe that the letters were written for him, but why else would they keep appearing in his life, and at times when he was so open to receiving them? He flip-flopped back and forth as the traffic lights before him switched from green, to amber, to red and back again, but he could not convince himself otherwise: these letters were meant for him and he was meant to respond.

As he tidied up his desk before going home that evening, Marjorie sidled up to him, looking very self-satisfied.

'You had a visit from Mr Flanagan just now,' she said. 'He seemed very disappointed not to find you at your desk. Best go see him first thing in the morning, I should think.'

William sighed. He couldn't avoid Ned much longer.

When William returned to the flat, the bulb in the hallway blew as he turned on the light and made him jump. He fumbled his way upstairs in the dark and dragged the stool from Clare's dressing table to the wardrobe. Too tired to be dealing with this, he reluctantly climbed up to rustle about for a replacement bulb. As he tugged at a sleeping bag to wriggle the box they called 'Miscellaneous Madness' free, Clare's old briefcase tumbled down. Papers spilled out all across the floorboards. He cursed his clumsiness and knelt down to gather them together. His eyes traced over Clare's handwriting, so familiar to him, and he wished he could go back in time to whenever she had written this and start again from there. He tried to assemble the pages correctly but couldn't fathom an order.

An A4 envelope had slid under the bed and now peeked out at him. He stretched to reach it and dragged it across the wooden floor towards him. When he turned it over, he froze. His name was written on the front, in Clare's hand. What was this? Hardly a letter, when it was so official looking. Divorce papers? No! Seriously? Dear God. When would she have organized them? Why hadn't she given them to him? Maybe she hadn't decided yet for sure. If that's what was inside, should he open it? Oh, but then he would have to say he saw the papers and it might force things to a conclusion he wasn't ready for. And yet, he couldn't just ignore the envelope now; couldn't unknow that it was there, waiting for him, radiating a heat from inside the cupboard, burning through Clare's old brown leather briefcase, taunting him. The seal was weak and he reckoned he could open it without causing a tear. He understood that he should put it back but he also knew that he could not.

William tidied the rest of the papers into the case and perched upon Clare's little stool. He had watched her sit upon it so many mornings to put her make-up on, and again, every evening, to cleanse it back off. The strangeness of the things he missed hit him again. He closed his eyes as he slipped the pages from the crisp, white envelope; it was her firm's office stationery. When William looked down, he was surprised to see not a legal document but pages of yellow refill pad covered in Clare's handwriting. It was a letter, after all. He paused. No matter what this letter said, he would never be able to ask Clare about it. He could never pretend that he thought she meant for him to find it, not among her work things. He knew that he had to read it, nonetheless. It was too late to stop now.

William,

I couldn't decide whether to write 'dear', 'hello' or something else, so used no salutation at all. That seems to sum up what these last few months have been like. I don't know how to speak to you, how to address you, who you are to me, so I say nothing at all, or something mean.

When I was little, my mother used to say that emotional talks were always regretted; far better to write it all down and get it out of your system then throw it in the fire. I suppose she learned that the hard way. I don't know where this letter is destined – your hand or the flames – but I'm hoping talking to you like this will help me at least understand what I'm trying to say.

The truth is, I'm afraid to talk to you; afraid to tell you how I'm really feeling in case I push us down a road we can't travel back from. I'm afraid to tell you that I understand why you didn't tell me you weren't writing but that I still can't bring myself to give you absolution. I can't admit that I could feel how lonely you were sometimes and that I know I ignored it. I can't tell you that because I want you to take responsibility and seize control of your life. I've always felt, if I told you everything was okay, that would give you licence to just surrender completely, but I'm beginning to understand now that maybe I was partly responsible for your state of arrested development. We have both felt dissatisfied for so long, but I have held out for the answers inside us which I know could be there. I have never looked outside us for someone or something else, but I'm worried that I will.

In some ways, I feel like I have been teaching myself not to love you so that, when we finally break, I will already have moved on. But it has been hard. Harder than I thought. My stubborn heart won't let go of you. Even as I see you fading away, and moving further from me every day.

You were my best friend. Whenever anyone hurt me, you made me better. Whenever I was scared, it was into your arms I ran. Whenever I was lost, you found me. So what do you do when the person you count on most in the world is the person that's hurting you? Where do you go? To whom do you turn?

I know you think I'm angry all the time. Anger is the easiest place to go to. But mostly, I'm so disappointed at what we've become. I know you want to try and fix things; to go back to how things were. I believe you when you say you're sorry, but I don't know if we can find each other again. I just can't bear the idea that we held on for this long and didn't make it out the other side. Where is the return for all that emotional investment? I dread the thoughts of dividing up our stuff, of people feeling sorry for us, our friends choosing sides. But every day, I'm building my strength to do it.

Do I miss you? Every second.

Do I want to go? No.

Do I want you to stop me? Yes.

Do I think you can? I'm not sure any more.

This is an impossible letter to send. These are impossible words to say. Do you need to hear them? Probably. Will I ever have the courage? I don't know.

And I don't know how to sign off now, either.

Love/Yours – neither is a given any more,

Clare

William carefully eased the letter back into its envelope before shoving it inside Clare's briefcase as if it were the case's fault he had read those things. As if, by making the letter disappear, he could shake the words from his head, too. If only she had given this to him instead of running away, maybe everything would be different now, but he couldn't help but feel that her time away would pull them even further apart. He found the light bulb that had brought him to the wardrobe but, even so, he continued ransacking the deep shelves, without knowing what he was looking for. His fingers touched something warm and furry: the head from the wolf costume he wore on Halloween two years before.

He pulled it on and squinted through the eye slits to catch his reflection in the black wooden full-length mirror that stood propped in their landing. Six years on, and he had never attached it to the wall, as he had promised. He twisted his neck back and forth, up and down, straining for an angle, but he couldn't get a clear line through the shaggy brown wool. The headpiece felt tighter than he remembered. Hotter. Itchier. Disorientating. More ticklish. Less liberating. He remembered his grandfather telling him the ancient Native American proverb of the two wolves who lived inside each person, one representing evil and the darkness of the world and the other the light. 'They battle every day to control you, these two wolves, and you know which one will win?' he had asked William, as the boy sat on his knee. William shook his head. 'The one that you feed more,' his grandad answered. He hadn't thought about it in years but, today, he felt acutely aware of the battle raging inside him.

William wrestled the fur head from over his own, struggling like a little boy stuck in his pullover. There was no Clare to wriggle it free and toss it over her shoulder this time. He perched against the white wooden windowsill and smoothed the hairs on the wolf's face. The last time he had worn it, the mask brought out a mischievous streak in him that now lay dormant again. It had kindled a momentary internal fire which domesticity, doubt and drudgery usually squashed. Was it two years ago? Three? Clare had dressed up as Little Red Riding Hood, well, Little Dead Riding Hood, of course. They repeated the same jokes to every guest at the party, jokes that grew incrementally funnier – to them – each time: 'I'm normally a wolf in sheep's clothing, so tonight I'm finally living up to my name' and 'I'm Little Red after the wolf has had his way with her.'

For the party, Clare's red cloak was torn and covered in mud from the garden. Her tights showed long flashes of skin, her skirt was ripped in a diagonal across her thighs. A red corset burst out from under a shredded white blouse, black ribbons undone. Her hair was a tangled mess with twigs poking out at awkward angles. Red lipstick smeared across her bow lips; black make-up smudged around her eyes. Her feet were bare. With dirty hands, she led William through the party. A terrible guide, spinning him round and bumping him into doorways. It was the most fun they had shared in a very long time. When they staggered home to their flat that night, he fell on his knees and howled at the moon before Little Red dragged him to bed. Why had he not spent more nights like that, enjoying Clare, making her laugh?

He shoved the costume back into the wardrobe and resumed his search. What was he looking for? Clare's journals? The thought circled him like a cat of prey. No. That would not help him; there were quite enough of Clare's words swimming in his head from her letter. Now on a mission to clear out their wardrobe after so many years of neglect, he was completely committed to the task; he just hadn't fathomed what the purpose was. A hunt for this old typewriter with no ribbon? These old cassette tapes? That battered old biscuit tin filled with Christmas baubles? He spilled the contents of a padded envelope on to the carpet; a set of sepia photographs from Clare's parents' honeymoon: Teresa sitting on an inflatable beach ball, wearing a straw sun hat, eating an ice-cream cone; the couple posing outside their caravan, Teresa in a floral-print dress that blew sideways in the breeze, Eddie in blue swimming trunks, sun cream across his nose, his arm draped proudly around her shoulders. Such happiness as you might find only in a Saturday matinee movie from the fifties. He reached further into the shelves and his fingertips touched something squishy and soft. From the darkest recess, he eased the photo album Clare had filled for him as his wedding present.

Could his wounds bear another lick of salt from more nostalgia? He slowly turned the pages, and images from the past blasted him:

Clare holding her degree certificate in front of the university gates; she looked small against their might and her smile was shy.

William emerging from the water after a swim in the Lake District. He had taken his glasses off for the photo and squinted at the camera like a mole surfacing from the earth.

Clare dressed as a flapper on her hen night, wearing a little black wig and string after string of pearls.

William and Clare sitting awkwardly in a gondola in Venice, the gondolier hovering over them with a scowl on his face.

Clare and William sitting in deckchairs on Brighton beach, hands held across the space between them, faces sunburnt but happy, Clare's broken arm in a sling.

William closed the album, unable to look at any more pictures, and placed it safely back inside the wardrobe. As he stretched to reach the back of the top shelf, his elbow knocked a sports bag to the floor and a pair of old running shoes tumbled out. William rapped his knuckles on the wooden shelf. Eureka! His beloved white trainers with the navy stripes. He hadn't worn them in years, but now they had appeared just when he needed them. A run would clear his head, vanquish some cobwebs. He stretched each shoe out of the crippled, bent shape they had settled into. Dust scattered from their creases as he forced his feet into their old shells. The interior was hard and stiff. He sat on the floor and pointed each toe upwards in turn, then flexed each foot, rotated each ankle, wriggling his toes inside their rediscovered home. He stood and bounced on the balls of his feet, hopping from left to right, right to left, then ran on the spot as fast as he could. His lungs surrendered before his feet did but he was ready. He pulled on his brown hooded fleece, zipped the house keys into his pocket, jogged downstairs and out of the front door without a second thought. The abandoned contents of the wardrobe lay strewn behind him; bed-linen, a sewing machine, a red canvas bag full of odd socks and pieces of cloth, Volumes A, R and T of the *Encyclopaedia Britannica* and a retired Polaroid camera. How had they managed to squeeze it all in?

William's muscles scanned his body for memories of how to move. There were faint whispers of long runs in the woods during adolescence, occasional bursts about the streets of London, but nothing recent enough to train them for this sudden expedition. He refused to acknowledge the burning sensation on the soles of his feet, the tightness in his chest, or the slowness of his pace. The strain in his calves could not conquer him. His heart pounded in his ears and drowned out the Greek chorus in his mind. Glorious oblivion. He pushed past the rain spitting on his skin, shook his hair into the wind and clenched his fists. The streets stretched out before him like a call to arms; puddles splashed cheers around his ankles, the city watched him run. All along the Bethnal Green Road, he pad-a-thumped, his right leg stronger. When he reached Weavers Fields, he slowed down to do a lap of the lawns, before dropping on to a bench. He arched his spine over the backrest and let the sudden downpour of rain run down his cheeks, drip from his chin, along his throat and under the collar of his hood. Never had discomfort felt so luxuriant. He closed his eyes and called to mind two letter writers: one, his wife; one, a ghost. Whose call would he answer?

Indecision paralysed him. He must push his heart harder than he had his feet. He must take control, take action, take responsibility. It was time to make some decisions. First, though, he must find enough power in his legs to run home.

13.

William sat in the depot, lost in a daydream of letters; on his typewriter, he typed furiously for hours the stories he had been mindfully collecting. Clare had told him she was coming home tomorrow, and the prospect filled him with anxiety. He needed to escape his own thoughts and drown in other people's worries, their words and their worlds. Marjorie's voice cut through his concentration; she sounded even more excitable than usual, if that were possible. Poor Trevor was on the receiving end.

'This is my favourite bit,' she gushed. ' "I miss talking to you late into the night, but I'm saving my stories for you. Hurry up, now, dear man. The nights are drawing in." ' William watched her pause for dramatic effect and put her hand to her heart. ''e's 'er Great Love. Oh, I wonder what became of 'er, or if she ever found 'im.'

A sickening dread crawled over his skin as his eyes found the midnight-blue envelope tucked under the arm of Marjorie's fluorescent pink blouse. How had this happened? Those letters were meant for *him*. He tried to feign nonchalance as he strolled towards her.

'That sounds interesting. Can I take a look?' he asked, hoping his inner desperation was not showing on his face. Marjorie wagged her chubby forefinger at him. 'Oh, no, no, no, when I wanted to champion the valentines, you 'ad no interest. Why now, eh?' she asked. 'You've barely said a word to anyone in weeks. This is *my* discovery and I will take care of it, thank you very much.'

She perched on the edge of Trevor's desk, despite his wilful attempt to ignore them both, and read the letter again, mouthing the words to herself and emitting little sighs. William was flabbergasted; this could not be borne. Winter's letters were not a remedy for Marjorie's lonely heart, something to add to her private collection.

All morning, he surreptitiously watched her idling away her time, working as little as possible, and realized he was a victim of his own success. It was no wonder Ned was upset with his diminishing productivity if they were depending on Marjorie to actually carry her own weight. She had Winter's letter in the back pocket of her stonewashed jeans. The indignity of it! He watched and waited for his chance.

Eventually, she took the letter out to read it again at her desk. This was his moment. He slipped into the corridor, sidled along it with his back against the wall, head darting left and right for any colleagues passing by. Then, before he could change his mind, he triggered the fire alarm with gusto. The shrill screeching was shocking as he dashed back into the office, on the pretence of grabbing his blazer.

'Leave everything!' Marjorie commanded, thrilled to finally put her fire-marshal training into action.

William deliberately stalled to evacuate last, and swiped Winter's letter as he slipped past Marjorie's desk, tucking it into his interior breast pocket. Little beads of perspiration gathered at the nape of his neck with the intensity of the moment. His obsession had reached new heights.

After the commotion of the false alarm, the depot settled back into its usual routine, with the exception of Marjorie, who lamented her missing letter for the remainder of the day. Trevor joked about the irony of her losing a letter here, of all places, but she wasn't amused.

'You seemed very interested earlier,' she said to William. 'Are you sure you don't know anything about it?'

He stared her down. Indeed, he impressed himself with his coolness.

'Positively certain. I have far too much of my own work to be getting on with, thank you very much.'

The relief he felt, however, was palpable.

That evening, he was the last to leave. All Winter's letters were laid out across the top of his desk, the earliest ones now thin and a little grubby along the creases from too much folding, excessive holding and reluctant hiding. The one he had salvaged today, however, gleamed fresh and crisp before him, despite Marjorie's interference. Still unnerved by not having found it first, he questioned what this could mean. Had he taken too long to find it so the forces at play intervened and threw it in his path via Marjorie? Was it supposed to propel him into action? If he didn't act, would the opportunity be taken from him? Or was he simply the victim of Marjorie's meddling on the fourth floor, where she knew he didn't want her to interfere? There was no easy answer, but he settled down to read it for the second time.

My Great Love,

I wonder if I'll instantly recognize you when we meet? Even in some subconscious way? Will our great potential love be immediately obvious, or is the greatness something that will emerge over time? What if I mistake someone else for you and don't realize until it's too late? You could be sitting across from me on the Tube from Monday until Friday and never even look up from your newspaper to notice me, or the fact that I was reading your favourite book. You would look up, though, wouldn't you? And notice something in particular: that I have worn down the heel on my left shoe more than the right, that a real handkerchief was stuffed in my pocket, how my left eyelid droops a tiny bit more than the right? Anything? Any question it burned you to know the answer to. You would feel compelled to ask, even though good manners had taught you not to. Please, do ask.

I said a prayer for you today, lit a candle in the chapel in Hoxton Square. I don't believe in the church, not any more, but some traditions tug at my heart strings. Lighting candles is one; sitting in the peace of the pews stills fills me with a sense of calm like no other. I suppose it's just meditation, really, but I grew up learning to call it something else.

William paused. How do you know if someone is the one? You have to trust your instinct, he supposed. He remembered asking his father the same question once, and he'd answered, 'When you know, son, you know!', but he thought he had known about Clare, and look at them now. He turned his attention back to Winter.

Yesterday, I heard a mother drag the strangest promise from her teenage son on the Tube. She made him swear that, if he ever dropped anything on to the tracks, he wouldn't jump down to try and save it. He argued that he wouldn't do that unless he was sure he could reach it in time before the train came. His mother's eyes widened, and she squeezed his arm; 'That's exactly what scares me,' she said, 'You would always believe you could make it. Always. But you wouldn't. Promise me you'll just leave it there.'

It was as if his mother had already succumbed to a self-fulfilling prophecy that she would one day lose her son by his own hand, if not one way, then another. She could try and enforce her nurturing over his nature, in as many instances as she could think of, but one would eventually slip through. I could imagine her warning him about not running into traffic, not talking to strangers, not having unprotected sex, not taking drugs, not drinking too much alcohol, not climbing high walls, not skateboarding on busy streets, not giving cheek, not walking with too much swagger, not standing too close to the ledge, but his mammy's voice would soon get drowned out by more seductive ones; those of girls with long ponytails and short skirts, boys with long Saturdays and short attention spans. How often split-second decisions define us; how we expose ourselves when we don't have time to decide who we want to be. My mother always reminded me what Maya Angelou said: when someone shows you their true character, believe them the first time.

William looked up from the letter again. Was that why he procrastinated so much? Was he trying too hard to decide what was the right thing to do instead of just trusting his instincts?

There is a jukebox playing fifties songs in the corner of this bar, and any one of them could be a letter from me to you; it seems all the singers were just looking for love. I wish I knew what your favourite songs are. Maybe you'll make me a mix-tape one day. I love how they breathe new life into old songs, arming them with superpowers that allow them to creep in through the back door of your heart. The lyrics are a language you can borrow for all that you feel but cannot find the words to say. And so songs can become ghosts that haunt us. They are time machines to old flames, lost cities, melancholy summer days and nights danced away. We breathe them into our composition like a cold fog. When the songs surprise us, as they often do, by being played in the most unlikely of places, years fall off our faces and we are sixteen again, or twenty-one again, in Paris again, or holding your face again. Emotional arrest. I hope we have our own song one day.

I miss talking to you late into the night, but I'm saving my stories for you.

Hurry up, now, dear man. The nights are drawing in.
Yours,
Winter

William shuffled all the letters together with a new sense of purpose; he had stalled for long enough, and it was clear to him that the time had come for action, to take back control of his life. He could not resolve things with Clare one way or the other while the ghost of Winter haunted him. She must be banished. Or summoned. Secreting her away into a dark space inside him, a spot reserved exclusively for her, would not work. He knew her shadow would creep from her cubbyhole into any light he could use to search for Clare. In unguarded moments, it lingered overhead like a black star. What was he to do? He could not endure these two voices competing in his mind for attention. He listed his options on a clean new page.

Shred the letters and try to squash each memory of them as it arises with one of Clare. An act of active forgetting.
Try to find Winter and allow the reality of the woman to confront the fantasy.

He knew that there was no choice. Not really. Find Winter, he must. Or he'd be tortured for ever with the question of what if? Was he completely giving up on Clare if he pulled the thread of Winter? No. It wasn't that simple. He wasn't abandoning his marriage. He was just clearing up a mess he had stumbled into unwittingly.

Winter held so much power only because of her mystery. He would illuminate that room of speculation where his imagination so happily festered and expose the truth. It could just as easily save his relationship with Clare as destroy it, couldn't it?

William stood and stretched his calf muscles, still cramped and sore from yesterday's spontaneous sprint. What a fool he had been to force his body to such unexpected extremes. He kneaded the knot of tension at the back of his legs and remembered the last time they had seized up on him like this. Clare had cajoled him into going for a hike in the Coventry countryside for their anniversary. When they finally arrived at the inn after ten miles of tramping in the rain, they might have been celebrating their fiftieth instead of their fifth year together. They collapsed into bed, soggy and sore, almost too weary to make love. William ordered hot ports and roast-chicken sandwiches up to their room, and Clare ran a bath with lavender. Their shared suffering was a sweet one. Not like this teasing throbbing that taunted William and felt punitive and mean.

He walked twice around the office floor anticlockwise, lifted his leg on to the desk and felt the stretch burn through him, before turning back to survey the evidence before him. All those letters. They must hold dozens of clues. Would they be specific enough to help him find her? Wasn't that his job? Surely, now, he could put all that training and experience into good use for a personal mission. Was this why he had found the letters? Could it be that he was the only one who could use them to find her? He was facing what could be the most important letter mystery of his career.

He started with the postmarks, the first stage of any letter investigation. They reconfirmed what he already knew: all London – but the italic font told him that nearly all had been processed through the Bethnal Green sorting office, as close to his own front door as the grocery shop where he bought a pint of milk nearly every day. He could have passed her in the street so many times. It was no wonder he thought he saw her standing at every Tube stop, buying fruit at the market, waiting at the traffic lights to cross the street. He traced his finger over the pale-blue postmark and noticed that the collection time was the earliest possible on all but one of the envelopes. Was she a night owl prowling in the dark or an early sparrow flitting through the dawn? Did she slip them through the brass slit in the wall of the post office or feed them to the silent mouth of the red post box in the street? Maybe she held her ear close to hear the soft thud of paper landing on a blanket of envelopes. Maybe she kissed the seal before she let the envelope drop. Or did she toss it quickly in before dashing up the pavement, putting footsteps and seconds between real life and her foolishness as quickly as possible? Winter could never have imagined that her messages in a bottle would float to shore so near to her home. If it came to it, he could knock on every door in the borough. Could he? Wasn't that the sort of thing people did out of desperation when they were looking for a missing child? How could he ever explain what he was looking for? The letters pulled his attention back. Tug. Pull. Drag.

With renewed focus, he rearranged Winter's letters in the order he had received them and turned his pad sideways. Using a sharp pencil, he drew almost perfectly straight columns from top to bottom and wrote in capital letters along the top:

NEIGHBOURHOOD
WORK
NAMES MENTIONED
SOCIAL SPOTS
ROUTINE
PORTRAIT
DUBLIN

It was difficult at first to look past the language of the letters and seek out the reality of her life, the concrete world she lived in. It shouldn't have been so complicated for him, whose job it was to solve mysteries such as these, but he had never been so invested in his subject before. One thought haunted him like the brewing ache of a bad tooth: would the reality of Winter destroy the fantasy? When she wrote her letters, she had the power to be so selective about her life, about how she presented herself. Was it possible to get a true impression of someone, judging only by dispatches from their private self? How different would the public version be? What elements had she chosen to leave out? Webbed feet? Bad debts? Substance abuse? Did she lie in baths for hours at the weekend weeping as she listened to Barbra Streisand records until her skin grew wrinkled? Was her name even really Winter? Or did he have a secret portal to her truest self? One it could ordinarily take nights, months, years, of onion-peeling to get to.

In his mind's eye, the scant details of her appearance painted a portrait of a woman who could never have passed him unnoticed in the street: long, flame-coloured, waving hair, apple-green eyes, alabaster skin, a white rabbit-fur coat, those boots! Would she be recognizable from her description? Had he imagined her as being more beautiful than she was? How could a woman with that head and heart not be? Even if it was just something that glowed from inside her. Did it matter? He thought not. His imagination could conjure only so much; it was the words within her that had bewitched him.

He populated the columns with more debris from her life: the Mexican restaurant in Camden that had already proved futile, Columbia Road Flower Market, the Long Hall pub, former work in the music industry, a vintage clothes shop on Dame Street in Dublin, a bar with a jukebox of fifties records, a mention of photographing protestors. Where could he begin? Not knowing her full name made it difficult. The chapel in Hoxton? Why not start somewhere close? If he put himself out there, maybe the universe would somehow guide him. He carefully gathered the letters together, returned them to their hiding place and ducked out of the depot into the dusky light of a crisp London evening. He walked briskly up Redchurch Street, turned right on to Shoreditch High Street and followed the road left on to Old Street. Hoxton Street was just to the right, and the square one more left. William knew this area well; the band used to rehearse in the basement of the George and Dragon pub once upon a time. He paused outside the chapel gates; he couldn't remember the last time he'd been in a church and wasn't sure he'd ever stepped inside a Catholic one.

The golden light flooding through the windows made him feel more welcome as he tentatively pushed the great mahogany doors inwards. Rows of teak pews ran in parallel either side of a plush red carpet, great ivory beams curved overhead, the iridescent altar loomed before him under a circular stained-glass window that looked to William like a flower, but he supposed it held some greater symbolism. A few people were scattered among the pews; whispers echoed in the rafters from the vestibule, where two ladies were poring over a book of psalms. He hesitated before entering further, but the iron casement of flickering votive candles called him forward. To think Winter had sat here, maybe even just days before, and lit one for him. Well, not for him exactly, perhaps, but that's what it felt like.

He sat down in the second-to-last row and allowed the silence to settle upon him. The iconography unsettled him, but he understood why she found it meditative to sit here. He closed his eyes and wallowed in the peace. A hand gripped his shoulder and William yelped so loudly that all the faithful turned to stare. Slowly, he turned his head, to see Ned Flanagan beaming at him from the pew behind. 'You've been avoiding me, Billy!' he stage-whispered, louder than if he had just spoken normally.

William was confused.

'Mr Flanagan, did you – did you follow me here?'

Ned snorted.

'Don't be ridiculous. Just a splendid coinkydink. Come. Let's take a walk. We can't talk here.'

William had no choice but to shuffle along the bench and accompany his boss down the aisle and back into the symphonic onslaught of Hoxton Square. As they crunched across the gravel in the foreground of the chapel, William spoke first.

'Mr Flanagan, I know you think I've been distracted recently, but I can assure you I've been getting results. Did you see the article in the *Guardian* about the whale vomit? I've been meaning to . . .'

Ned looked perplexed.

'Whale vomit? That's not . . . never mind. The reason I wanted to speak to you is that your name came up at our board meeting.'

William sat down on a bench in the square.

'That sounds ominous,' he replied.

'Yes, I would have thought so, too,' Ned said. 'But it seems your little project has attracted the right sort of attention.'

William marvelled as Ned explained how Sally's father had heard all about his work from her, and that her enthusiasm had been infectious.

'They are keen to invest in that book of yours, produce it ourselves, it seems,' he said. 'And, of course, we both know I've always been behind you a hundred per cent.'

He held out his hand and William shook it vigorously.

'We'll iron out the particulars but, suffice to say – congratulations, William. You did it!'

As Ned shuffled away, William remained on the bench a moment longer, watching the lights inside the chapel as they were extinguished one by one. Would he soon hold in his hands the *Volume of Lost Letters*? He chuckled to himself at Ned's about-turn after his adamant opposition but, if this was divine intervention, he would take it. He had even managed to call him by his proper name. Miraculous, indeed.

14.

The following evening, William watched the street from their bedroom window, waiting for the familiar grumbling sounds of Clare's racing-green Mini slowing down outside. He arranged the books on the sill in alphabetical order, then by author, before finally returning them to their original positions in ascending height. He desperately wanted to tell her about his breakthrough with the Supernatural Division, but knew he had to tread softly, considering the role Sally had played in its development. He had spent the afternoon calmly working on the fourth floor, refining once again the letters he hoped to include, if he was going to expand the project to incorporate stories such as Prummel's. The anxious anticipation of seeking out a letter from Winter which usually affected him when he worked there was on hold; he had intercepted Marjorie's discovery only the day before. When he found another letter as the final dregs of the day were draining, he was shocked. Two on consecutive days? Were they accelerating in frequency, or had yesterday's been lying dormant while he was in Clovelly? Against his better judgement, he sneaked the letter out of the depot and read it as he walked along the Bethnal Green Road.

It was a blow to walk through his front door, a letter from Winter in his hand, and see Clare's coat back on its hook in the hallway. The heady mix of guilt and anxiety tarnished the relief he felt that she was back in London and would soon be standing in front of him in their home. He was aware how complicated his life had become and, predominantly, at his own hand. Whenever he was away from Clare, he found it so easy to believe in the possibility of Winter, but whenever they were together it seemed absurd to think that Winter was anything more than a ridiculous flight of fancy. Was his instinct for romanticism more powerful than the pragmatic logic he used to reason with himself? This must be how people felt when they had an affair. He had always scoffed when folk spoke of being in love with two people at the same time, but now he had a more empathetic perspective; it wasn't two different people they loved, necessarily, but the two different lives they offered, the two different versions of themselves that they could potentially become. Do we all need someone to see the potential in us for us to be able to fulfil it?

He was wearing a faded red tartan shirt with frayed cuffs and threadbare patches over the shoulder blades; it was Clare's favourite. The first night they spent together, a button had popped free from it while Clare was nervously undressing him. The next morning, he found her sitting cross-legged on the bedroom floor in her nightdress, concentrating fiercely as she sewed it back on. A little white wicker sewing basket was opened beside her. Her grandmother had bequeathed it to her, along with the silk dressing gown Stevie had lost, a set of bone-handled cutlery and an unfinished patchwork quilt. Every so often, she told him, she would pour a bag of materials on to the living-room floor in a fit of reverie and spend an afternoon quietly sewing hexagons together while being serenaded by Nina Simone. Ever since Clare had inherited the quilt, the order and logic of the pattern had gone awry; she had no patience for following the formula of yellows together, blues together, reds and pinks together. Her hexagons placed fuchsia stripes beside sunflower-yellow gingham, cornflower-blue floral connected to forest-green spirals, scarlet polka dots married to purple paisley. It was the disorder of multicoloured silks, cottons, corduroy and velvet that absorbed her, incompatibles forced together with unexpected but beautiful results. William remembered the first day he found her standing over the quilt, rearranging the newly sewn pieces into clusters of seven and placing them in rows underneath their ancestors.

'What do you think? I haven't attached them yet. This is the moment where I always lose my nerve, when they are joined for ever on to the whole.'

She held up the quilt by the top corners and was completely hidden behind it.

'Gosh. It's huge. How big do you want it to become?' he asked.

Clare turned to face him, a puzzled look on her face, as if the end result had never occurred to her before. 'It has become a bit of a monster, I suppose,' she said. 'I don't know if I'll ever be finished, if I'm honest. I guess I'd like it to be big enough to cover the whole bed and touch the floor all around it . . .'

She laid the quilt back down flat on the floor. William crouched over it and spread his fingers over the different fabrics.

'How long did your grandmother work on it?' he asked.

Clare knelt beside him, surveying the work.

'She started it when she first went into the nursing home, but she died six months later. Instead of people bringing her bunches of grapes or crossword puzzles, she asked for material – pieces from old clothes or curtains or whatever they had. These patches here are from my first baby blanket, and these were taken from my gran's old nursing uniform. She loved the stories being sewn into the fabric. My mother hated it. She thought it was creepy. "A blanket full of ghosts", she called it.'

William smoothed away creases in the cloth.

'Have you any more stories here?' he asked.

She leaned across the quilt to point as she explained.

'This peach one is the lining of a bridesmaid dress from my parents' wedding. My Aunt Polly brought that in . . . and this sea-green silk was an old cravat of Daddy's he used to wear on Sundays. I cut this red poppy material from the dress I wore on my graduation from secondary school. It was my favourite at the time, but I spilled blackcurrant juice all down the front of it that night and the stain would never lift. This section here came from Flora's christening dress, and these were cut from a nightgown with rainbows all over it that she loved. I've quite a few patches mixed in now. I was the one most interested in helping her. The rest of the family thought it was too sentimental, and I think they felt silly bringing in their old bits and pieces. Come on. Help me fold it.'

They held two corners each on opposite sides and joined them together. William kissed her forehead over the fabric that divided them and said, 'I'm sure that's why your gran wanted you to have it and would love the fact that you're going to finish it.'

'Maybe,' she answered. 'But she'd never understand why I wouldn't want to make it *nice*. Granny was black and white, rich and poor, good and evil, birds of a feather flock together, but me, I want the quilt to be as random and uncontrollable as the street out there is, as full of colour and contradictions and clashes as Brick Lane Market on a Sunday.'

He realized he hadn't seen Clare sewing in a long time; all her hours and minutes were absorbed by work, or sleeping to recover from work. He forced himself to stop twitching the curtains like an overzealous neighbourhood-watch man and walked downstairs to open a bottle of red wine. He hadn't eaten; the butterflies in his stomach weren't interested in food. Instead, he took down two goblets from the cupboard and placed them on the kitchen table, before changing his mind and returning one, not wanting Clare to think he was presuming anything.

A small wooden button dangled from a thread on the cuff of his shirt. He let it knock a delicate note against their pinewood kitchen table, twisting his wrist slowly left and right to make a rhythm. It reminded him of being a child and watching his grandfather taunt a small ginger kitten with a ball of purple wool. William thought it was cruel how the puppeteer allowed the hysterical creature to tangle its tiny paws in the wool before dragging it away with the kitten's little furry bottom bouncing along behind. He wanted to ask him to stop, but he was more worried about being called a cry baby than he was about the comfort of the entangled kitten. He snapped the button free, but it slipped through his butter fingers and rolled into obscurity beneath a cupboard. William ducked his head beneath the table to make a half-hearted scan across the floor. His eye was caught instead by a lump of green propped against the skirting board; it was the final remnant of Clare's last bowl from Sorrento. He crawled under the table and retrieved it, before bumping the back of his head on the table rim as he clambered back up to standing. The fragment of green sat in his open palm, winking at him in the light, a lost eye looking at him in a state of confusion. He squeezed his fist around it and dropped it into his shirt pocket.

He was debating whether he could pour himself a glass of wine, or whether he should wait, when he heard the front door slowly open. In his haste to hide away the bottle of wine, his foot caught on the leg of a stool and he crashed to a fall. Smithereens of glass scattered across the floor as the Rioja formed gloopy puddles on the white tiles. Clare chased the sound of the crash into the kitchen and screamed when she saw William lying there in a red, sticky mess. He staggered to his feet, his trainers sliding in the wine while he steadied himself and said, 'I'm sorry. It's just wine. I slipped. It's fine.'

William ran his hands under the cold tap at the kitchen sink to clean away the sticky wine. He peeled off his cowboy shirt, tossed it into the washing machine and began sweeping up the glass, smearing scarlet stains across the floor as he worked.

'The grout is the most important thing,' she said. 'Make sure you clean between the tiles.' She stepped into the kitchen and rooted around in the cupboard beneath the sink until she found a bottle of bleach. She mixed it with washing-up liquid and hot water in a Tupperware bowl and passed it to William, along with a scouring pad. 'Are you okay to do the rest? I'll walk around to Mr Patel's to get us another bottle. Do you want anything else?' she asked.

William shook his head as Clare gingerly stepped over the smeared tiles and escaped through the front door. As the power of his elbows fought the strength of the stains, he scrubbed as if the ability to wipe away the darkness in their marriage depended on the force of his will. Could he stem the flow of love that was trickling away, a slow but persistent stream, from what was once a deep, unfathomable lake?

It took Clare longer than it should have to walk to the corner shop, choose two bottles of wine from the range of four, dither over whether to buy some peanuts or crisps and make her way back to the flat. When she let herself in, the kitchen had been restored to order and William was waiting in the living room, now wearing a Beatles T-shirt and a striped woollen scarf. It seemed an odd combination, but she let it pass.

'Do we have to listen to Leonard Cohen right now? I think he might push me over the edge.' William walked to the record player, and turned the volume down before he lifted the needle.

'What will I put on instead?'

'Does there have to be anything playing? What could possibly be an appropriate soundtrack?'

William closed the lid on the turntable and stood against the fireplace.

'We always have music playing, that's all. It feels weird to have the flat totally silent.'

'It's not silent – we're talking, aren't we?'

Clare knew exactly what he meant, though; music was always playing in the background of their lives. She just didn't want to associate any songs, any band, with tonight, the night they might decide to finally call it a day. Was that what she wanted to happen? She remembered making a mix-tape to play if they came back to her flat after their first date so many years before, trying to choose artists who didn't remind her of any other boyfriends or evoke any memories, either happy or sad. She remembered the thrill of discovering a tape that William had made in her locker at university. Each and every song felt like a little piece of magic, a tiny planet of hope and discovery. She had been full of questions. Why did he choose that song? Are those lyrics about me? What do these songs make him think of? And to see his handwriting on the sleeve notes, the curves and strokes and shape of the letters. Clare didn't want a 'Night I left William for ever' soundtrack, songs that would haunt her afterwards, creeping up on her in the supermarket, or on the radio while she was driving to work. She sat in their overstuffed caramel-coloured armchair and pulled their crocheted Afghan blanket around her, as she always had. How much would she tell him of what had happened in Wales? Did everything have to come out now?

William interrupted her thoughts.

'I missed you so much, Clare. I hate this, us sitting here like strangers.'

She sighed and wriggled down further into the chair.

'How could you miss me when things have been so difficult between us?' she asked. 'It must have been a relief to get a break from the way things have been.'

He left his roost on the ridge of the mantelpiece and pulled up a footstool to sit close to her.

'I wasn't relieved that you left, but you're right, we couldn't continue in the way we have been. It's time we started being honest with each other, don't you think?'

Clare looked at the blanket on her knees and smoothed away a wrinkle in the fabric before she spoke.

'Okay, then. Let's hear it . . . the ugly truth, if we must.'

He topped up her wine glass, which was noticeably depleted after such a short space of time.

'You have to just give me a chance to speak, though, without shouting me down or getting defensive. Can you do that? Otherwise, it's pointless . . . and I promise I'll do the same for you when it's your turn. You're not in court now, remember?'

'What do you mean, shout you . . . Okay, okay, I'm listening. Tell me.'

She caught herself biting her thumbnail and quickly withdrew her hand.

He exhaled a deep breath before the words came tumbling out.

'My main worry is that you still seem to be punishing me for what happened with the book. I've apologized so many times, but it doesn't change anything. If I thought it was helping at all, I'd suffer it, but it *doesn't* help. You still seem to think I was some kind of fraud, deliberately making a fool of you, but it wasn't like that . . . No, stop, I can see you waiting to jump in, but hear me out. I hated lying to you, but I kept telling myself that all I needed was to find a way into the novel again, and then I could pull it back and you'd never need to know. It's not like I did nothing – I wrote the first twenty thousand words what feels like twenty thousand times, but I just couldn't move it on. I'm so sorry. I wish I could have. It completely broke my heart walking away from it, and disappointing you crushed me, but I can't change the fact that I failed.'

Clare threw her hands up in the air. A little wine sloshed on her legs, where she held the glass between her knees. She wiped it with her sleeve as she studied him.

'That's the bit you never seemed to get, William. I wasn't disappointed because you *failed*. It was the deception. You were lying to me for *years*, and I had no clue. How could I trust myself to ever know the difference again?'

He reached out to her.

'But you *do* know, Clare. You do know. Are you really telling me you didn't notice anything wrong during that time? That you couldn't see it wasn't working, that I wasn't myself?'

'So it was my fault? I should have somehow noticed and saved you from your own self? The neglectful wife who never bothered to notice that you had *changed*.'

William stood up and paced the floorboards as he tried to douse cold water on the heat in the room, which was escalating rapidly.

'Clare, please don't fight me. That's not what I'm saying at all. I'm just trying to make the point that you've watched me telling the truth a million times longer than you've watched me hide it, and I think, if I am telling you the truth now, you'll recognize it. That's all. I wasn't . . . the words, they just withered inside me . . . I was empty.'

Seeing him so upset, Clare's protests caught in her throat. She watched William's hands shaking as he spoke; his hands were the first thing she had noticed about him. Long, piano fingers. Deep creases in his palms. She wondered what a fortune-teller would say about those heavy lines and what they would mean for her. The wine softened her a little and gave her eyes something to focus on while William paced the room again. He paused in front of the mantelpiece and took another deep breath.

'I also just want to say I have never stopped loving you, but it is very hard to cope with how you blame me for everything imperfect in your life. Any disappointment you feel in your own lot, you trace back to me, and I don't think that's fair.'

He saw her bristle but continued speaking before she could interrupt.

'I completely accept that I've let you down and appreciate that you stayed loyal to us, even though you were disappointed in me . . . but if this is to work, Clare, we need to let go of what's happened and the idea of who we should be and just go into this accepting who we are right now.'

'You mean settle? What if I don't want to just give in and let go of who I think we could be? What if I think there could be more for us?'

He stopped pacing and stood in front of her where she sat. 'I don't mean "settle" at all,' he said. 'I mean letting go of the past to start fresh. You want more for yourself, and I do, too . . . I've had some breakthroughs with the writing recently, and great developments at work. I can't promise you roaring success, but what I do know is there is a much better chance of either of those things happening if I think you're behind me and haven't given up on me.'

She tugged on the end of his T-shirt. A small smile made a shy appearance.

'How many times have you rehearsed that little speech in your head?'

'Many. It's all I've been thinking about.'

William sat down on the sofa and focused his attention on her feet. That was mostly what he had been thinking about – except for the minutes stolen by Winter, of course. He quickly chased that thought away.

Clare swirled the dark red liquid around in her glass and watched William's reflection on the windowpane.

She had underestimated how relieved she would be to hear that he still wanted her. He was going to fight for her, for them, for the little world they had built in these four rooms. The question was, how hard? And was it too late? If they were going to try, she had to tell him the truth. After reprimanding him for so long about keeping secrets, she couldn't in good conscience live with the guilt of hiding her own bad behaviour. It was needling away at her constantly.

'Well, now it's my turn, and I'm afraid there's something you need to know that may change how you feel. Considerably.'

She avoided his eye as he watched her from across the room.

'This isn't easy for me to say, William, but I want to be honest with you, too, so please try to stay calm.'

He held his head in his hands and emitted a low groan. 'Those must be the least calming words ever spoken,' he said. 'What else has happened?'

'What else?' She looked confused, but carried on. 'Not much, I promise, but something. The day of the fundraising benefit at the depot.' She paused. 'I was stressed about the trial and dreading going to that stupid party, and everything just built up in me and I sat in my Mini at the courtroom and I just couldn't stop crying.'

He looked at her, aghast.

'Oh, Clare. Why didn't you tell me? Is that why you were so mad at —'

'Wait. I'm not finished. Maxi saw me there and got into the car to talk to me.'

'No, no, no. Not Maxi. Please don't tell me all of this has anything to do with him.'

'He just put his arms around me to comfort me and, well, we sort of, ended up kissing. That's it. Nothing more than that, but I know it was wrong, so I just had to tell you. It was stupid, I know, so stupid, and I'm sorry.'

She saw the colour in his face change to deep red; he was angry, but trying to control it. She felt tears welling and held her breath in anticipation of him blowing.

'And you had the nerve to accuse me of something happening with Sally? After you had already been with him? That's a staggering act of deflection, Clare. Are you *serious*? You let me stand here, beating myself up about what's happened between us, and all the time, you've been nursing that secret?'

She rushed over and crouched before him but was afraid to reach out and touch him in case he brushed her away.

'I swear, nothing else happened. It was just that one stupid kiss.'

The words swarmed between them like angry bees. A haze of you and me, he and she, why, how, where, when . . . Questions. Accusations. Positioning. Remembering. Pausing. Coaxing. Suggesting. Bargaining. Pleading. Threatening. Blaming. Surrendering. Offering. Rejecting. Shouting. Crying. Rage. Silence.

The curtains were drawn and lamps lit. William started the fire and Clare pulled the blanket from her knees up to her shoulders. The wine bottles were drained, the gin bottle followed and, eventually, the pot whistled for coffee. William stretched out on the couch, his feet resting on the arm of Clare's chair. It was the closest he had come to touching her since her confession. She nudged his feet into her lap, and he was too exhausted to resist. The glow from the streetlight outside crept in around the window frame and cast strange shadows over the tableau. Their conversation was disconnected now, as each of them drifted in and out of dozing, remembered a point from earlier that must be refuted, or was struck by something new. All thoughts soaked in liquor.

Clare's voice was drifting now.

'It's strange seeing the living room at this time, when, normally, we'd be sleeping. It reminds me of being a child; I always wondered what our house was like when me and Flora were at school. I couldn't imagine what my mother did all day when we weren't there.'

'I always tried to picture you at work – bustling about being busy and important, who you are when I'm not there. I used to worry about all the men who would try and sweep you off your feet.'

'None of them ever did, though, William. I swear. Not really. You know this was just a blip, a symptom of everything else that was going on. You believe me, don't you?'

Clare went to the bathroom and released her hair from a messy bun that had all but come undone. Her face was flushed and blotchy; she splashed it with cold water in an effort to cool down. She brushed her teeth and sat on the edge of the tub, enjoying the feel of the chilly tiles underneath her bare feet.

William remained downstairs, body and soul weak and tired. The thought of Clare in Maxi's arms nauseated him, but he knew that this was not the hill his marriage would die on. There was hope for them now, he could feel it, but he would need to dig deep and push past her stupid indiscretion, difficult though it was. He knew he was right to be furious at her about what had happened, but he also felt a blessed relief that things hadn't gone any further. He followed Clare into the bathroom and pulled her upright. She leaned against him, her head finding its old familiar spot in the groove beside his left shoulder as she breathed in the smell of him. He stroked the back of her neck, smoothing her hair up from her skin and letting it fall slowly between his fingers.

'Let's get some sleep,' she whispered.

'Okay. The bed is freshly made. I'll sleep on the couch.'

'Will you sleep in the bed with me? I know a lot has happened, but I just can't face being alone, thinking of you downstairs alone, too. Let's just be together.'

He hesitated but didn't want to argue any more. He led her into their bedroom, pulled back the duvet and turned on her bedside lamp. She stepped out of her dress and pulled on an old white cotton nightdress before slipping under the covers. William removed his clothes and awkwardly climbed in beside her; he felt more nervous than he had the first time she had invited him into her bed. He doused the light and lay flat on his back, afraid to touch her, although he longed to. He listened to her breathing, waiting for it to grow heavy and slow, but he could hear how awake she was, could imagine all the thoughts driving around the streets of her mind. It was a city he feared to tread through in the dark. She wriggled and turned to lay her head on his chest. He stroked her back, startled by how much weight she had lost. He could trace the lines of her ribs where, before, she had always been so soft. He held her as tightly as he could, afraid to wipe away the hot tears that ran down his face in case she noticed. Tried not to sniffle.

Clare heard his breath catching, slid on top of him and brushed the tears away with her hands. She leaned over him and kissed a line from the corner of his eye, over his cheek, past his ear and down his neck to where she had rested her head. It was such a comfort to lie on top of him and feel him respond beneath her as she moved over him in the darkness, swallowing the guilt of a story not fully told. She buried her full confession deep down, where it couldn't accidentally slip from her. So far, no one knew, and she hoped it could remain that way. That this was not the last night she would sleep in his arms.

William followed each movement of Clare's with his breath held. He was afraid a sudden move would scare her away. Was this the first thaw? Their first steps towards a new start?

When they eventually fell into a heavy sleep, mixed emotions crowded the air around them. William had been struggling to reconcile the horror of the thought of Clare in Maxi's arms with the odd absolution it gave him for the emotional infidelity he knew he was guilty of. He slipped out from under the covers and let the moonlight guide him from their bedroom. He tiptoed down the stairs and sat in the darkness of the living room, surveying in the ambient light from the street the detritus of the night they had spent together. He fumbled in the dark to remove Winter's letter from his satchel. He knew he had to let Winter and her letters go. He settled on the windowsill in the living room and strained to read her last letter again in the dim light. Where was she tonight while her words kept him company?

My Great Love, hola,

I write to you from under the Andalucían sun; your Winter is baking in an untimely heat, for I find myself on holiday. I have swapped the dreary, blank London skies so this hot light can drench me instead of showers. I came completely underprepared. My lightest dresses are too heavy here and my underexposed skin too white. My legs remind me of bottles of milk sitting on the doorstep, winking in the dawn light. A little child pointed at me in the street this morning, and I'm sure it was shock at my pallor. Maybe she thought I was a ghost.

At night, I lie under a rotating fan attached to the ceiling, the sheet clammy beneath me, air smothering above. I try to bargain with the gods for a breeze that will blow me to sleep, but I'm always disappointed. If you were here, I can't imagine two hot bodies could like squirming in these clammy sheets together. Maybe you would surrender and sleep downstairs in the hammock on the porch. Maybe we would just sit up and not struggle against it at all. I wish you were here to wade through the close night air with me. I'd suffer the extra heat of your heavy arm around me if you could tolerate my hot cheek against your chest. Instead, I sit on my own, listening to the songs of the sea, worrying that dark shadows moving across the horizon are sinister figures looking for me. I used to think I would be a fighter if someone attacked me. Here, on the rural coast, I am scared of the night without electric lights. Maybe I'm braver in the city. Here, I would surely flee, if my feet were not sinking in the sand.

This holiday wasn't planned, my love. It wasn't a date circled on the calendar for months. No new dresses or swimsuits were bought. Sadly, I came to recover from the passing of my grandfather – as if bereavement is so easily managed that I can allocate a period of time for it to do its worst to me and send me back to the living. I'm not sure that my head and heart have even fully signed up to try. They refuse to connect to the reality of it all and alter the reasons why am I here; make the funeral that of a stranger, change the identity of the old gentleman lying in the coffin. I've never known anyone who died before – not anyone close to me, anyway. I've witnessed grief, but not felt it beyond a vicarious sadness for other people's suffering. For a moment, you are acutely aware of their pain, maybe even feel the sting of tears, but then, you hug them goodbye and leave the house shrouded in black and your life is exactly the same as it was before you visited. Isn't that the bleakest part of all? The lover or sister or friend goes home after the burial to a coat hanging in the hall like a ghost, spectacles perched lop-sided on the bedside table. There is silence where their words should be. A plate, knife and fork left sitting in the drawer. And the rest of the world carries on regardless.

They laid him out in the parlour of his cottage. It was hard to fathom why his sons and daughters had to watch that beloved man be carried into his home in a wooden box. There was nothing poetic about it. His grandsons struggled to bear the weight. The coffin was too long to turn in the little hallway and they talked of pushing it through the living-room window or carrying it in through the back door. My Auntie May despaired that the back garden was too unkempt to take him in that way. My Uncle Jimmy surveyed the window to see how long it would take to remove. And all the while, neighbours gathered in twos and threes, and children cycled laps on bikes and trikes. His old neighbours hobbled closer on walking sticks if they could, or watched from behind net curtains if they couldn't.

My father stood with his hand resting on the side of the coffin. He is too old now himself to bear the weight on his shoulder, but he said he just wanted to be close to him. It almost broke my heart. I had never seen him cry before. An ice-cream van rollicked past, playing its regular, sunny Saturday siren, before spotting the hearse and dashing away. My sisters and I stood side by side in that little front garden. We didn't touch. Black daffodils standing still, no breeze. No one comforted the other, for we all felt the same. We were broken, watching our father breaking. How proud I was of him that he could show his grief. I saw my mother holding him up and felt so relieved for him that he had her there. How much harder it must be to bear these things alone. I don't want that to be me. I want you to meet my lovely father. Soon. I will miss my grandad terribly: my fiercest critic and my greatest advocate. I'm sorry he never saw me achieve something wonderful, but I know he was sure that I would. Maybe that's just as good. He was a man ahead of his time, encouraged my feminist grandma to pursue all her passions, to become a photographer too, shared the burden at home so she could work. He inspired his children to follow their dreams, and his grandchildren in turn. He gave me my first camera, and the very first picture I took was of my grandparents sitting on the wall outside their house. It sits beside my bedside, a daily reminder that I must not lose faith. 'Have heart, my dear,' my grandmother always tells me. 'Only dreamers find dreams come true.' I know how blessed I am to have had this family to love me; I know their love will be a buffer around me, no matter what this wretched world sends me.

I'm going to wait until I am back in London before I post this. For the rest of my time here, I will let the sun heat my pale skin. I hope my seventy-year-old self will forgive me the wrinkles, and I hope you will learn to love them. You should be here with me. Our time will come, won't it, my love?

Until you find me,
Winter

William lay on the couch and pulled Clare's Afghan blanket over him. The image of Winter as a black daffodil, mourning for her grandfather, her red hair harsh against the funeral clothes, caught him by the heart. He remembered the day of Clare's father's funeral; how distraught her mother and Flora had been, how frozen Clare was. It saddened him to think of Winter alone with her grief. It frightened him to imagine that for himself. Or for Clare.

He couldn't help but compare Winter's attitude about family to Clare's in a manner unfavourable to his wife. She never wanted to hear about his childhood and seemed almost to resent him for the happy family he was born into. He had never been able to explain to her how his middle-class suburban upbringing could be a burden on him, the passive-aggressive expectation that he would build on his parents' success with his own. The Woolfs had never wanted a writer for a son, although they weren't confrontational enough to stand in his way. Deep down, he knew that's what had triggered his writer's block: the knowledge that, if the work was a failure, he would have fulfilled their worst fears for him. The irony of him achieving that by doing nothing at all was not lost on him.

He had never been able to explain that pressure to

Clare; she couldn't tolerate any complaints on his part about his childhood when she had endured proper suffering. He knew it couldn't compare. In truth, he realized that his parents had always been a little too soft on him; they always solved any problem he presented as best they could. If he hadn't studied for an exam, they paid for private lessons, and they had financially supported all his whims without ever expecting him to get a job to support himself. Perhaps that was why he had found it so easy to let Clare take care of him. She had spoiled him, too, and he had revelled in it for too long. Allowing him to enjoy a lifestyle he couldn't afford, indulging him in expensive rare vinyl records and first editions of novels. It was time for him to take responsibility for his actions, late as he was to the realization.

He remembered a terrible row he once had with Clare when his mother went to hospital for an emergency appendectomy. Despite the relatively low-risk procedure, William's father was beside himself with nerves and had burst into tears when he saw William and Clare arriving at the hospital. He would never forget how small Clare looked when she turned and ran from the waiting room. Later that night, they were sitting in the attic at a friend's house party, drinking whiskey, when she tried to explain why it was so hard for her to witness that sort of unconditional love. She said it exposed to her so much that was lacking in her own understanding of what relationships could be, what she could expect from people.

Lying on the couch, agitated sleep washed over William with restless dreams of the sea lapping against the shore, black sails flapping on a boat on the horizon. He was shivering where he sat on the sand but could not move.

Upstairs, Clare had slept soundly, but she woke up to a sinking feeling. She reached out for William, but he was gone. Instead, guilt now filled the bed and smothered her where she lay. Images of her last day and night in Wales flashed in her mind: Maxi's car crunching up the driveway, their empty glasses in the bar, his knock on the door. She fought them away and resisted the impulse to go to William for comfort; she didn't trust herself to be silent. Instead, she lay diagonally across the bed as the light gathered momentum through the venetian blinds. The darkness she had felt before dawn slipped away in parallel increments until she felt calmer, stronger. Ready to start a new day. Relieved her secret was still safely tucked away, where it could do no more harm.

William bent over his desk, sneaked a segment of chocolate orange from the pedestal drawer, and placed the whole piece in his mouth before straightening in his seat. It wasn't greed that made him so secretive, or a reluctance to share the loot with his colleagues, but rather a desire to be left alone and avoid the jovial banter that shared confectionery always involved. With only the slightest excuse, Marjorie would circle him, like a bird of prey, desperate to indulge in the contraband. He cringed at the thought of the chocolate-orange mush swirling around in her mouth while she regaled him with snippets from the scandalous underbelly of community bingo. He couldn't endure it. Not today. Instead, he closed his mouth firmly around the half-moon slice of sin and swallowed surreptitiously as it melted and folded upon itself. Chocolate orange was Clare's favourite treat. Maybe that's why he chose it. A little taste of happier times, when he was lucky to scavenge the tiniest bite from her: 'I'll buy you one of your own, if you want, but I'm not sharing mine. Take my soul, but you'll never take my chocolate orange.'

She was always quite particular about having her own things, apart from everything they shared or bought together; her own bedside table with a little silver key to lock the drawer, a separate wardrobe for her clothes, shelves in the living room for her books alone, a chest in the attic for her keepsakes and childhood treasures. Once, in an argument about where they were going to spend New Year's Eve, he had accused her of being so independent because it meant she could pack more conveniently if ever she wanted to flee. Her response – silence – was frightening; he hadn't really thought it could be true until that moment. Maybe, in her heart of hearts, she had always carried a seed of doubt that they would stay together. Men had started wars over women they loved; women had moved mountains. Were those people suppressing little niggling doubts throughout? He doubted it.

In the weeks following Clare's homecoming, however, William was relieved to see how much things had improved at home. They were not suddenly reconciled but the atmosphere at home was at least conciliatory. He thought the shock of Clare being in the danger zone of an affair had forced them both to re-evaluate their priorities. When he thought of Maxi, William's jaw clenched, but really, in the scheme of things, it could have been worse. It would be too much to say that it had all been for the best, but he welcomed the sea change her indiscretion had heralded. Clare tried not to work so late in the evenings and they took it in turns to cook more at home: fresh salads and slow-roasted casseroles, Asian stir-fries and spicy curries. Less time was spent watching television and more was devoted to listening to each other. Clare cancelled a ceramics class she had been due to start and suggested they revive their old weekly cinema night instead. One evening, as they drained the dregs from a bottle of Riesling, she turned to him and said, 'It's a relief, isn't it? I feel like I was trying to carry a tray of plates that was too heavy for me up a flight of stairs. Letting them fall was a shock, but something of a relief, too.' William rinsed out the empty wine bottle and threw it in the recycling, flinched at the crash of glass on glass.

An ill wind had cleared the air, but there was still a ghost lingering in the corners of his mind. A question taunted him: if Clare had really left him for Maxi, if their marriage had truly been over, would he have tried to find Winter in earnest? And, if the idea was still tugging at his heart, was he right to be trying so hard to ignore it? He had made a conscious effort to banish Winter from his life but, sometimes, when he least expected it, her words whispered in his ear: *Our time will come, won't it, my love? . . . I'm saving my stories for you.* He was determined, however, to let her go. He and Clare had, just, pulled their marriage back from the brink. He couldn't be the one to run away now. How could he let Clare down like that, when she had always stood by him?

William spritzed furniture polish on to his desk and buffed the mahogany finish with a yellow duster. What a risk he had taken by allowing himself to be so seduced by Winter. All her letters were now sealed inside a brown padded envelope, buried beneath a telephone directory, an atlas and a heavy dictionary in his bottom desk drawer. He knew that he should send them to the shredder but couldn't quite bring himself to just yet. Would it be terrible to include one of Winter's letters in his *Volume of Lost*

Letters? He closed the door on that idea; he would be doing it only in the hope that she might present herself; he couldn't allow anything to jeopardize the progress he and Clare had made. The letters were a distraction, re-igniting the old belief in *the one* of his stubborn heart. He needed to let this foolish idea go: the letters weren't meant for him and he wasn't meant for Winter. Besides, it was weeks now since one had appeared, so perhaps she was done with him, too. The letters had stopped appearing after he had resigned himself to ignoring their call. That had to be a sign, hadn't it?

He picked up a collection of different-sized envelopes that dribbled across the paisley-patterned carpet by his feet and shuffled them into a neater, but still unyielding, pile. Each letter should receive his undivided attention; each deserved every possible chance of finding its way. A squidgy manila envelope, creased and battered, wilfully refused to fall into line and toppled the tower. William's superstitious mind had learned to trust his instincts and accept the letters as they fell. He stretched to reach for it; pulled it closer with his thumb and forefinger.

The address on the envelope had been written in blue colouring pencil, curling letters now bleeding across the page above the Isle of Man postmark. To Gordon? Gerard? Gregory, maybe? What was the surname? Davenport? That might help. The house number and street were smudged, but it seemed to be somewhere in Holland Park. William squeezed the parcel and gave it a little shake; lots of little pieces shuffled within. Was it a jigsaw? A puzzle? Something broken? He gently cracked the seal, and the contents scattered across the table, into his lap and on to the floor: hundreds of individual words cut from newspapers, magazines and goodness knew where else, each one glued to a piece of coloured card. He scooped the words up and gathered them into a little mound in the centre of the table.

Words jumped out at him in a kaleidoscope of so many different colours, typefaces and sizes: eleven, eucalyptus, lemon tree harvest, own goal, dirty washing, panda bear, summer drought, swarm of bees, Doc Marten boots, top hat, jealousy, silk, xylophone, blackbird, duke, nuclear attack, Mars, cellophane wrapping, letter box, penguin compound, snow, polka, paving stones, pumpkin pie, daffodils, anticipation, handwritten, chandelier, lost boys, library, cottage industry, racist attack, Juliet's balcony, protest march, entrepreneur, witchcraft, umbrellas, scarlet, star-struck, soup kitchen, forgiveness, fern, Laurel and Hardy, salt of the earth, Electric Ballroom, warts, shrinking violet, whistle-blower, calligraphy, cymbals, resonate, lamplight, rocking chair, myxomatosis, peaches, float.

William's fingers rifled through the randomness, separating, singling out and congregating the words together again. Why did some words disturb him? Crawl inside his mind and set up camp there? They flashed like neon against a jet-black night: blackbird, witchcraft, scarlet, lamplight, daffodils. He eased the remaining contents from the envelope, along with a sheet of squared paper from a mathematics copybook; it smelled of primary school. Doodles of flowers, butterflies and stars bordered the purple ink, and glitter clung to his fingers as he separated out the pages.

Hi Godfrey,

Thanks for your letter. It came on Tuesday and I managed to meet the postman on the corner, so no fear of my mam or stupid Tracy opening it first this time. Do you know it's actually against the law to open someone else's letters? I told my mam when I found that out, but she just said it was a bigger crime to give her cheek, so I'm not sure she's that bothered. I'll just try and get to the post first from now on, but maybe we can use some code words, just in case? Instead of saying you love me, maybe just say you love mashed potato or something, and I'll know what you mean. Maybe not potatoes, though, but something else that makes you think of me.

You're probably wondering what the bag of words is all about. Well, believe it or not, it's your birthday present. I'm sorry I couldn't get you a real present, but I'm not getting any shifts at the café now it's only open part-time for the winter, and I didn't want to ask Da; he'd only ask me too many questions. The thing is, I'm hoping you'll like this, even though I made it myself. It's to help you with your songs – I know you said that writing the words is the hardest part, and I heard David Bowie talking on the radio about how he writes his songs. He said he just cuts out loads of words and mixes them all together before picking different ones out like in a raffle to put together to make up sentences. It's called a VERBALIZER!! Isn't that the best idea ever?? So I made you one. And I know you said if I asked you to write a song about me you never would, but at least this way maybe I can inspire you, even if the song isn't about me. I hope you like it. It took ages to stick all the bits of cereal box on the back, but I wanted it to last you more than the one song if you liked it.

I have to run to get this in the last post. Good luck with the gig in the social. I wish I could come and see the Mad Frogs' debut gig. That's a much better name than the Slow Turtles, by the way.

Lots of mashed potato,

Tina . . . x

William wondered if Godfrey ever did know how much trouble Tina had gone to. Did he think she had simply not replied to his last letter? He pulled down the telephone directory from the shelf above his desk and flicked quickly through the pages until he reached the Davenports; there were just two in Holland Park. He gave a silent prayer of thanks that Tina's Godfrey wasn't a Smith or a Jones and dialled the first number. It rang and rang until a row of beeps disconnected him. His second call, to the next address, was answered on the first ring and a little girl sang down the phone with well-rehearsed importance, 'Hello, this is the Davenport residence. Who is speaking?'

'Hello, this is William Woolf calling from the Royal Mail. Could I speak to one of your parents, please?'

'We don't know any postmen.'

William struggled to suppress the impatience in his voice. He crossed through items on his to-do list, the receiver cradled under his ear, while he spoke.

'I'm not a postman. Could you call one of your parents for me?'

'They're not here. Daddy's golfing and Mummy is playing tennis.'

'Lovely. Well, who else is there?'

'I'm not supposed to talk to strangers and tell them things.'

'Quite right. So, can you call a grown-up for me?'

William heard muffled whispers as the receiver was intercepted.

'Arabella, who are you tormenting? You were told not to answer the telephone.'

'I think it might be Stranger Danger, Granny.'

'Oh, seriously. What nonsense!'

'Hello, Mrs Davenport speaking. Can I help you?'

William straightened up to answer. 'Yes, hello. My name is William Woolf and I work in a Royal Mail department that deals with undelivered mail. I was wondering if there is a Godfrey Davenport at this address?'

'Godfrey? He's my son, but he doesn't live here; this is his sister Camilla's house. Where did you get this number?'

'The telephone directory. The address on the parcel just told me the name and area so I thought I'd try my luck. Could you give me a forwarding address to redirect it to?'

There was a silence. William suspected she was considering his request.

'Do you know what this *parcel* contains?' she asked, her curiosity barely concealed.

'I'm afraid I'm not at liberty to say, but I do believe it is a personal item that he would want delivered.'

'How intriguing. Well, you can send it to me. Godfrey and his family will be visiting from the Isle of Man at the weekend.'

The Isle of Man! Was he living there with Tina, after all? William carefully collected the jumble of words into a clear plastic envelope and sealed the letter from Tina inside. Would Tina be standing beside Godfrey when he opened it? Or was he summoning a ghost from the past to haunt him? William dropped the parcel into the mailbag for next-day delivery with a short cover note which in no way justified the length of time between posting and receiving, and wished it well. He hoped Godfrey had married the right girl.

Later that evening, Clare laid her new peacock-blue cashmere coat across the bed, fastened the big pearl buttons and stepped back to admire it. She bit her lip, considering for a moment the eye-watering sum she had paid for it, but dismissed her buyer's remorse. It was a long time since she had indulged in something lovely for herself, and this was a special occasion, after all. Her oldest schoolfriend, Enid, was getting married in Dublin the following day, and she was looking forward to escaping London with William. It was almost five years since she had last seen Enid, and she had been relieved to find the wedding invitation on their doormat in the midst of their Christmas post. She was struck by how hurt she would have been not to be invited, despite the distance that had crept between them, which was far wider than geography necessitated. Clare carefully folded the layers of pale-pink tissue that had swaddled her coat and tucked them away in her dressing-table drawer. She caught her reflection in the mirror and smiled at the subtle blonde highlights her hairdresser had scattered through her hair that afternoon. 'Takes years off you,' he'd proclaimed, and she found herself inclined to agree. Baby steps.

Two cases lay open on the floor, Clare's filled with her clothing and belongings, William's still empty, despite the early-morning flight they would catch the next day.

'William, can you come and pack?' Clare called down the stairs, as she unwrapped the new pale-blue tie she had bought him to complement her outfit. She ran the silk through her fingers while she waited to hear some acknowledgment that he'd heard her; a mumble reverberated from the living room and she was content. She rustled through his sock drawer for the least exotic socks he owned, something sensible to peek out from the trouser hem of the navy-blue suit she'd collected from the dry cleaner's earlier. She lined up random trinkets that did not belong there on top of the chest: scissors (lethal, she thought), a used handkerchief, a pamphlet for Madame Tussauds (of all places), a box of plasters that belonged in the bathroom cabinet. She touched something faintly sticky and pulled it out into the light: a Polaroid picture of a pair of boots!

'What are you doing with all my stuff?' William brushed the paraphernalia of his untidiness back into the drawer with one sweep of his arm. 'Can a man have no privacy?'

'What's this picture?' she asked, not once tearing her eyes from it.

William only now noticed Winter's picture in the hands of his wife. He carefully rearranged the socks in an equally chaotic state of disorder as he cleared his throat.

'Oh, that?' he said, pretending to scrutinize it along with her. 'It's nothing. Just something I found in the depot. It ended up trapped in a book I was reading somehow, and I forgot to bring it back.' He saw Clare look at him quizzically.

'Are you sure that's all it is?' she asked. 'It seemed to have been hidden away back there.'

William turned away and shoved the drawer closed. 'Not hidden, just lost!' He plucked the photo from her fingers and tossed it in the waste-paper basket beside his bureau. 'Just some more of the random madness discovered in the daily mission.'

William pretended not to notice as Clare picked it back out of the bin to stare at it again, and focused on removing his suit from the plastic covers.

'Should I wear the jacket on the flight, do you think?' he asked. 'Save it getting creased in the case?'

Clare was still frozen in concentration over the image. 'I just feel like I've seen these boots somewhere before,' she said. 'But I can't place it. Don't worry, it will come back to me.' She smiled as she placed it down on top of the chest. 'Let's finish packing so we can have an early night.'

Later, William lay flat on his back, staring into the darkness. Why had he hidden that picture at home? So foolish! Why had he even kept it at all? He jolted as Clare grabbed his arm and gave him a little shake.

'William,' she whispered. 'Are you awake? I've got it!'

He rolled over on his side to face her, saw her silhouette sitting upright. She flicked on her bedside lamp; the sudden brightness dazzled him. 'I saw a girl wearing those boots a few days ago. I just remembered!'

William's heart pounded. He didn't trust himself to maintain a neutral expression and turned to drink from a tumbler of water on his bedside cabinet.

'Who?' he croaked. 'What do you mean? Where?'

Clare snuggled back down under the duvet. 'When I was waiting in the car for you outside the Indian restaurant the other night. She walked past and, honestly, it was like a scene from a film. That's why it stayed with me. She was wearing the boots, and this big white fur coat, and she had miles of red hair.' Her last thought trailed off into a question. 'It looked like maybe a costume of some sort?' She clicked off the light again. 'That's a relief. I *knew* I recognized them. Do you think they really could be the ones in the picture? Can't be too many glittery white cowboy boots walking around!'

'No,' William sighed. 'I would think not. Small world.'

He listened to Clare's breathing grow steady while he struggled to control his own. A white fur coat? It must be her. He felt the walls closing in around him. Would he never be free of this? He lay perfectly still under the duvet, eyes closed tight. Why was the universe so determined to throw this woman in his path? Had he fallen foul of some cruel trickery? For months, he had been scanning the streets for a sighting, and then, when Winter had finally appeared, he had been looking in another direction. What would he have done if he'd spotted her while Clare sat watching? He couldn't have just allowed her to walk past, could he? His restless legs started twitching under the covers. Worried that he would wake Clare, he tiptoed to the living room and lay on the couch watching *Fawlty Towers* with the sound turned off. It made for a confusing silent movie.

When Clare found him the next morning, he was contorted into an awkward shape under her blanket, cold toes stretched over the end of the sofa.

'I couldn't sleep, and I didn't want to disturb you.' he explained.

'Don't worry,' she answered, pulling the blanket away. 'But it's time to get up now. We are off on an adventure.'

16.

It was raining in Ireland, as it always seemed to be, but as they walked down Wexford Street, huddled together under an orange-canopied umbrella, William was thankful that the skies had opened. On the flight over, he had fought hard to squash the lingering anxiety he felt at Clare's unexpected encounter with Winter. Deeply engrossed in his novel, *The Haunted Bookshop*, he deflected Clare's chatting while the words swam before his eyes. Was Dublin really the best place for them to be visiting? The city was so firmly associated now in his thoughts with his secret lady of the letters. The invitation Winter had extended to explore her old haunts lingered in his mind, but he tried not to dwell on it. He linked arms with Clare and splashed through dirty puddles with enthusiasm. He was determined not to scan the streets for a redhead in a white rabbit-fur coat, but the habit was so instinctive to him now that it was almost impossible for him to resist. He stopped abruptly outside a narrow little pub with square glass windows running the full width of the exterior. A red-and-white-striped awning hung over the door, making the building look more like a barber's shop than a pub, but its name was painted in cursive scarlet script along a white banner: The Long Hall. Wasn't this the place Winter had spoken about in her letters?

Clare nudged him with her shoulder and asked, 'What is it? Are we lost? I think Temple Bar is just ahead.'

'It's nothing. Just this pub. I remember someone telling me about it once. I was just surprised to see it; you know the way you can never usually find places that people recommend.'

She stood on her toes to peer through a clearing in the condensation on the window.

'It's so tiny . . . but it looks like a nice old-man pub. Maybe we could come back later for a nightcap if the reception doesn't run too late.'

He gripped Clare's elbow and guided her to the pedestrian crossing. 'No, it's not important. We'd better hurry.'

He knew it was ridiculous, but the thought of taking Clare in there seemed somehow disloyal to Winter. Was he losing his mind? Surely the betrayal lay in thinking about another woman in the first place while he was away with his wife. And it wasn't as if Winter expected anything from him – she didn't even know he existed! As they waited for a break in the traffic so they could cross the street, he couldn't resist turning back to take one last look at the Long Hall. He felt sure someone was watching him. His skin prickled but, when he looked back over his shoulder, there was no one there.

The wedding ceremony of Enid and Seamus was held in the Smock Alley Theatre on Exchange Street. Their immediate families sat on long wooden benches in front of the black panelled stage, white ribbons running along each edge. Old milk bottles, painted in different shades of red and purple glowing from candles inside, made impromptu chandeliers that dangled from the wooden rafters over the stage. The remaining guests were crowded into three tiered balconies with cast-iron railings that surrounded the performance space. Garlands of calla lilies and cornflowers stretched along the railings. Night-light candles in china teacups were set into recesses of the stone walls throughout the venue. The acoustics of the room transformed the buzzing chatter of the guests into a melodious hum. Clare gripped William's hand as they found a spot on the second tier.

Instead of Mr Buckley walking his daughter down the aisle, they wove along each balcony, swamped by gushing excitement and thunderous applause as they moved. Enid's father walked one step behind her, guiding her elbow with one hand, dabbing his eyes and shining bald head with a ridiculously large white silk handkerchief with the other. The skirt of Enid's dress was so wide that, on the corners, she had to turn sideways to proceed, laughing all the time at the absurdity of it. Her blue-black hair had come undone from the elaborate style the hairdresser had conjured that morning; it collapsed about her shoulders under the crown of white roses that circled her head. It looked perfect. When Enid saw Clare, she hugged her old friend, kissed her forehead, before she was swept along by the current of well-wishers. In her wake, William put his arms around his wife, and she rested her head on his shoulder. He hated to think of not being there with her today; to imagine her standing alone in her silver taffeta dress, feet side by side in her white velvet Mary-Janes and new coat.

As Enid reached the stage, Seamus stepped forward, handsome in a seaweed-brown tweed suit that suited his dark colouring. He was an island man, with wild, black curls, and piercing blue eyes glistening out from under one bushy eyebrow. His right arm was in a sling from a surfing accident the week before, his cast covered in scribbled good-luck messages. The shaman who would lead them through the ceremony hushed the whooping from the audience. Silence descended as he guided them through each ritual before the couple pledged their vows: the lighting of their individual candles at the beginning and the united flame at the end; the binding of their hands together. As they exchanged rings, Enid's mother stood and sang 'She Moved through the Fair', her hands straight down by her side like a soldier. The white chrysanthemum posy on the lapel of her fuschia blouse glowed in the theatre spotlight.

> I dreamed it last night
> That my true love came in
> So softly she entered
> Her feet made no din
> She came close beside me
> And this she did say:
> 'It will not be long, love,
> Till our wedding day.'

William handed Clare his handkerchief and she dabbed her eyes carefully. He smudged away a gloop of mascara from her temple with his thumb and she gripped it for a second like a newborn. Seamus dipped Enid for a

Hollywood kiss and the wedding party jumped up to cheer in chorus, stamping their feet on the floorboards beneath them. 'Go on, Seamus, lad,' a heckler called from the back and his entourage whooped. As the newly married couple climbed down from the stage to lead their guests through to the reception hall, William and Clare stood in one shadowy corner of the balcony and melted into a long kiss.

Long wooden banquet tables stretched the length of the converted church where dinner was served; sunlight streamed through the stained-glass windows, dispersing prisms of coloured light on the white stone walls. A low river of green moss, pine cones and branches of fir trees ran down the centre of each table, interspersed with tea lights in green glass dishes and clutches of daisies. Each guest's name was handwritten in white ink on a pistachio-coloured envelope that rested in the centre of their moss-green linen table mat.

The hall reminded William a little of the place where he and Clare had been married. Though less beautifully preserved, the town hall in Islington was of a similar vintage. At their reception, the Turkish rugs were threadbare and the brass chandeliers missing the odd bulb, but they had been drawn to the character of the rooms and felt the hall was just the right size for their wedding. Fifty maroon velvet chairs had been placed in two semicircles which faced each other, creating a natural pathway between them. There was no seating plan, but everyone organically found his or her place in the circle. Before the ceremony, Clare had struggled with the idea of walking down the aisle without her father to escort her. When William suggested that they arrive together, she threw her arms around him, covered his face with kisses and said, 'I knew that there was a reason I was marrying you.'

Clare dressed and beautified herself in Flora's flat before the two sisters took a taxi together to the hall, where they found William and Stevie awaiting their arrival. Stevie wore a silver suit with drainpipe trousers that were slightly too short; one hot-pink sock and one black-and-white chequered peeped out above his white Chelsea boots. William wore a plum velvet blazer with deep red lining and black trousers with braces over a starched white shirt. He still wore the blazer now sometimes, on special occasions; he felt it brought him luck. When Clare stepped out of the taxi, William was confused for a moment; she looked so different from what he had expected. No white dress or veil or bouquet of flowers; instead, a sophisticated black chiffon dress that hugged her waist and kicked out to the knee, and a white velvet bolero over her shoulders. Her hair was swept up into a glossy bun, a single red rose behind her ear. She wore little white gloves, a short string of pearls, red glitter shoes and carried a white rose tied in a scarlet silk bow. Clare resembled no bride he had ever seen and looked all the more magnificent for it. They stood in silence for a moment, absorbing what was happening.

'Are you disappointed, William? Would you have preferred a blushing bride in white?' she asked, her voice barely audible over the traffic that rushed past.

William held her by the arms, afraid to pull her too close in case he ruffled her outfit, and leaned towards her until their noses touched.

'Disappointed? You are the most fantastic, most beautiful, most brilliant bride there ever was, and I'm going to march you into that hall right now before you realize how ridiculous it is that you are marrying a silly fool like me and change your mind.'

Stevie and Flora went ahead to put on the music; Flora tucked Stevie's shirt in and made him tie up his wild (then lilac) hair on the way. William and Clare waited outside for the opening notes of Michael Dees singing 'What are You Doing for the Rest of Your Life?' before Stevie opened the door and everyone stood to watch William, adorned in plum, and Clare, elegant in black, walk down the aisle together. When they reached the registrar, everyone drew their chairs together to complete the circle. There was no religious element to the ceremony, no prayers to a God they didn't believe in, no words written for them to repeat by people who had never known them. Instead, they wrote their own vows, simple and honest, but with enough love in them to draw a little tear from even Stevie's cynical eye.

Before the end of the ceremony, the registrar called on the guests to step forward if they had particular good wishes or any wisdom from their own marriage to share with the newly married couple; a few brave souls did. Clare's uncle surprised them both by digging deep into his gruffness to speak. He revealed that her father had told him that he knew Clare would grow up to be an amazing woman and that he hoped she wouldn't let the failings of her parents turn her against the idea of spending her life with the right man, should he come along. Uncle Jimmy said her father would be delighted to see that his wish had come true.

After the ceremony, Clare and William snaked around the semicircles of chairs to accept congratulatory hugs, then they all walked to the Crooked Billet. The function room had been reserved for them, and a buffet of potato and chickpea curry, moussaka and bowls of salad and rice prepared. Fairy lights were strung in garlands around the room and tea lights sat on the windowsills in recycled jam-jars, transforming the dingy space into something a little bit more magical. Stevie's band played, until the landlord threatened to cut the power, and they danced until the final note rang out. William's favourite photo of the day caught him singing with the band while Clare danced beside him. They looked so happy. Just as Enid and Seamus did today. Could they tether the island of their love to the mainland once again before it was lost for ever at sea?

Giving the final speech, Mr Buckley drew to a close on the subject of his daughter, his elaborate handkerchief close to hand. 'My last wish for Enid and my new son-in-law today is this: when you have a choice between winning a row or saving the day, save the day. Remember: cynics may win battles, but romantics win the war. To Enid and Seamus.' The guests all stood, and echoes of 'To Enid and Seamus' rippled about the room as glasses clinked.

Clare lost her balance as she stretched across the table with her champagne flute. She knocked over one of the green tea-light holders and extinguished the flame.

'I think the fizz has made me a little soggy,' she whispered to William.

She poured herself a full glass of water and nudged her empty flute further away to prevent her topping it up again too quickly.

While the bride and groom slipped away for photographs, a space was cleared for dancing. Seamus's family band of traditional Irish musicians needed little encouragement to launch into a rousing sequence of set dances. From nowhere, a semicircle had formed at the front of the room: an accordion, bodhrán, tin whistle and fiddle poised and ready to play.

'Ladies and gentlemen, "The Siege of Ennis".'

Enid's family and friends from England watched in amazement as Seamus's contingent rushed forward and began to form orderly rows in sets of four; they weren't to remain bystanders for long, however. Seamus's mother circled the room, canvassing and cajoling, until everyone was on their feet. William and Clare partnered up with Seamus's Uncle Niall and Aunt Audrey.

'Don't look so frightened,' Audrey laughed, as she swapped places with William. 'You stick with me, and Niall will look after your good wife, there.'

And, with that, they were off, Seamus's father calling commands in Irish from behind his accordion: *Amach! Isteach! Brostaigí! Brostaigí!* William had no idea what he was saying but allowed himself to be swept along by the beat. His and Clare's feet found the rhythm and followed the pattern as they moved in lines up and down the room, swinging around in circles, crossing partners and ducking under arms to meet the next row of four. He caught Clare's eye as a giant of a man spun her so fast in his arms that her feet left the ground; she was doubled up in laughter when she staggered back into position. This music didn't tolerate melancholia; it was just the tonic they needed.

For the last dance of the evening, the DJ played 'Careless Whisper' by George Michael; Clare and William sat together and watched Enid and Seamus slow-dancing in the centre of the floor while their friends linked arms in a circle around them. 'I'm not sure that DJ Cliff Seacrest has really listened to the lyrics,' William joked. 'Maybe that wasn't the best choice of song to end the evening.'

He stopped laughing when he saw Clare's eyes flood.

'William, there's something you should know.' She moved her chair closer to him and picked up his hand in both of hers. She started again: 'I haven't . . .' But she never finished her sentence, because Audrey and Niall interrupted her.

'Come on!' Audrey called. 'They're doing the going-away.'

She pulled Clare to her feet and on to the dance floor, where, two by two, all the guests formed an archway for Enid and Seamus to run through before they left for their honeymoon. As the DJ cranked up the volume for Cliff Richard to serenade them with 'Congratulations', the bride and groom were stopped every few feet by couples dropping their arms to trap them and smother them in final well-wishes. William and Clare locked hands and bobbed along to the music while waiting for the newly-weds to reach them.

'What were you going to say, Clare?' William shouted at her over the din. 'Are you okay?'

He was relieved when she nodded, smiling now once again.

'It was nothing. I was just going to say I haven't felt this happy in such a long time.'

Enid and Seamus drove away in his green Peugeot 205, tin cans and old soccer boots clattering from the exhaust and white balloons filling the back seat. The wedding guests stood waving until they had vanished from sight up the quays. Clare and William strolled alongside the river.

'I don't feel ready to go back to the hotel yet, do you?' Clare asked as she hesitated outside the welcoming glow of the Boulevard Café on Exchequer Street.

William pushed the door open and they found a table in the window, where they watched revellers cavorting through Friday night. Every so often, a flash of red hair would dance past and catch his eye, despite himself, but he tried his best not to react. They ordered two hot whiskies for a nightcap and shared a basket of hot, fresh bruschetta. Sitting as they once had many years before, shy but hopeful, William was optimistic, albeit a little wary of saying too much. The day had been perfect; he didn't want to spoil it now by talking once again about worries that had been too big to squeeze through their front door.

Clare leaned across the table and brushed a curl behind his ear.

'Oh, William, maybe we should just pack it all in and move to the south of France or something. We could open a *boulangerie*, or a *chocolaterie*, and descend slowly into middle age, plump and happy, while we live the good life. No Tube. No clients. No letters!!'

His stomach flipped a little at the thought of a fresh start with this woman; he savoured for a moment how beautiful she looked in her silver dress. What was he doing still scanning the streets for Winter when his incredible wife was right here in front of him?

'We should do it. Let's just go. Anywhere. What's keeping us in London, really? We could just go and start again.'

Clare pulled her hand back into her lap and sighed. 'William, you know it's not as simple as that. We can't just run away and hope all our problems get left behind. They would just come with us and set up camp in Provence, or wherever we were, and we'd feel even worse.'

He reached for her hand once more. 'I know it seems mad, but maybe a fresh start is all we need?'

She took a deep breath and squeezed his knee under the table.

'I hope so, William. I really do.'

'And maybe we could even think again about starting –'

'No!' she snapped. 'Don't even go there. We can't try

to make a baby into some kind of bandage to paper over the cracks in our relationship. We've only just –'

He held his hands up in a gesture of surrender.

'Okay, let's drop it for the moment, but I really want you to think about it. Not just for my sake. If you're really sure you don't ever want to have a child, then that's fine. I know we can have a great life together, regardless, but please be sure you aren't just saying no out of fear, or stubbornness, or lack of faith in me, because we would work it out. I know we would. People in much worse situations than ours manage every day.'

She busied herself pouring them glasses of water from a carafe.

'Okay. I hear you,' she replied. 'But can we please talk about something else? Let's pretend we're just two people on a date. Tell me things about you that I've forgotten I know. Let's not try to fix everything in one evening. Let's just be glad we're here.'

The waiter came and cleared the empty bruschetta basket. When he left, William nudged his glasses further up the bridge of his nose and asked, 'Have you ever read *Ulysses*? I tried to start a book club of the classics in college, but there wasn't much interest.'

Clare laughed.

'I'll never forget your face when I walked in. You looked like you'd been caught red-handed, stealing biscuits or something.'

He shook his head at the memory.

'I was so mortified. The rejection of no one coming

was hard enough to endure on my own, but to have a witness, and such a gorgeous one, well, that hurt!'

All of a sudden, the lights dimmed and the waiting staff meandered their way through the restaurant with a cake and sparklers, singing 'Happy Birthday'.

Clare leaned into William and whispered, 'How embarrassing. I would die if that was for me,' but the performance came closer until she was laughing in shock as they screeched, 'Happy birthdaaay, deear Clllllaaaaareeee, Happy birthday to you.' She stammered a protest but the head waiter made her stand up on a chair to blow out the candles. The restaurant cheered while she tried to modestly hold her skirt down as she climbed back into her seat.

'You absolute rotter! I can't believe you did that to me! It's not my birthday for five months!'

Clare was beaming, despite her embarrassment. Was this all they had needed all along? A little fun? A little time away from the pressures of playing out the self-inflicted roles of their marriage?

As they strolled back to their hotel, they were happy, arms entwined, feet in step, and after they turned out the light later that night, Clare fell asleep on her spot on William's shoulder and, for what felt like the first time in a very long time, she felt like she belonged there.

17.

The telephone ringing on the night stand seemed part of Clare's dream at first. Who could be calling at this time? She shoved William to wake him, and nestled further into her pillow. He groaned at her, but groggily picked up the receiver. The night receptionist told him how sorry they were to disturb them but there was an urgent call from London. William shook Clare awake. They had left the hotel number on their answering machine in case the hospice called about Clare's mother. It had to be them. 'Clare, wake up! I think it's about your mum.'

She sat up in bed, confused by the hour and the worry in his voice.

'What is it? What's going on?'

'I think it's the hospice. The receptionist is putting them through.'

Clare turned on the overhead light and pulled a blanket around her. William watched her as he held the receiver to his ear, impatient to know what was happening but afraid of what was coming. Why would something bad have to happen now? A man's voice slurred down the phone. He was shouting over the din of a noisy pub.

'Clare, is that you? It's me. Clare?'

'No, it most certainly is not. This is William. Her

husband. Who is this? What is this about? Why are you calling at this time of night?'

'Oh, it's you, is it? The cuckold! Well, you should know, *William*, that she doesn't want you any more. Not really. Why don't you just let her go? She's too good for you. I could give her the life she deserves. You're wasting her –'

William threw the receiver down on to the bedspread. 'It's for you,' he said, and walked into the bathroom, where he sat on the edge of the bathtub in the dark.

'What's going on?' Clare called after William as she scrambled across the blankets to reach the receiver.

Through the bathroom door, William heard Clare whispering under her breath before slamming down the telephone. He waited for her to rush to him, but the moment stretched on. That was when he knew she had been lying to him. He walked back into the bedroom and plucked his shirt off the floor. Struggling to button it with his fumbling fingers, he realized he had put it on inside out. Clare stumbled towards him, her feet tangled in the discarded sheets, and tried to stop him pulling on his trousers next.

'William, stop. Let me explain. It's not what you think.'

He staggered away from her, the red of his face deepening.

'How long have you been sleeping with him?'

'William, it's not like that . . .'

He raised his voice.

'If you don't tell me the truth right now, I will walk out of here, and I swear you will never see me again.'

He watched the tears start to stream down her face, but the sight of them repelled him now. How could he have been such a fool? His instinct had told him there was more to what happened with Maxi, but he just hadn't wanted to believe it.

'It was just the one time, I swear. He came down to collect me from Wales –'

'*From Wales?* He was with you that whole time? For –'

'*No!* He just offered me a lift home, and then we ended up having too much to drink and stayed an extra . . . It wasn't planned, William, I promise. I'm so sorry. Please . . . it just happened –'

'Is that the best you can do? Just stop it. You made a choice. I never thought you could become such a walking cliché. The fancy lawyer with the big car and the house in the country he bought with his trust fund. You just couldn't resist it, could you? You've been trying to crawl up that social ladder your whole life, and when he handed it to you on a plate you just couldn't say no. So much for us.'

The colour drained from her face; she sobbed, making big, gulping noises. William stormed around the room, picking things up and throwing them back down.

'You're like a total stranger to me. And the *lies* you've told. You must think I'm such a fool . . . A right cuckold, as your *boyfriend* himself said. You bare-faced lied to me and lived with it day after day.'

Clare sat down on the edge of the bed with her head in her hands.

'Maxi shouldn't have said that,' she whispered.

'*Don't say his name!*' William slammed his fist into the

pillow, which was still warm from where he had been sleeping moments before. She stood up, tried to put her arms around him, but he pushed her away with such force that she splayed across the bed. He stopped himself from reaching out to her.

'I wanted to tell you!' she cried. 'I did! But I didn't know if we could survive it, and I thought it was better just to try and put it behind us, because it was just that one time.'

He stood over her, his voice cold now.

'Why would I believe anything you say? You could just be confessing this much for now, until I find out the next grizzly detail. And anyway, Clare, *once is enough!* You've never had a one-night stand or slept with anyone you didn't care about.'

She knelt on the bed and tried to pull him towards her.

'William, please. Tonight still happened – the things we said we meant. Please don't give up on us now!'

'I'm not the one who gave up on us, Clare. If you knew how hard I've tried not to get pulled out of our marriage . . .'

He stopped himself before he said too much.

'What is that supposed to mean? William?'

'Nothing, it doesn't mean anything. I'm going home and, lest there be any doubt in your mind, *you* are not. Hopefully, *Maxi* will let you stay with him. I'm sure he'll be only too delighted.'

'No, William. Please don't go!'

Her shoulders heaved as she watched him, gulping in deep breaths of air.

William struggled into his socks and shoes, distractedly checked his blazer for his passport, clutched his satchel by its handle and walked out, leaving the rest of his belongings behind. Clare followed him into the hallway and shouted after him. The hotel porter delivering champagne next door looked away, embarrassed at seeing her in her nightdress, her distress.

William didn't turn around but called over his shoulder, 'Don't you dare follow me!'

Despite his fury, it was gut-wrenching to listen to her crying as he walked away. He kept staring straight ahead so she would not see the tears that were rolling down his face, too.

18.

After William left, Clare curled up in a ball on the floor of the hotel bedroom. She couldn't crawl back into the bed where they had lain together. Her mind flitted from rage at Maxi to anger at herself. Now that she was faced with the bleak consequences of what she had done, the thought of Maxi repulsed her. How could she have been so cavalier about her marriage? Had she felt so secure in William's devotion to her that she thought it would be possible to play out her experiment without any retribution? The last thing she had wanted to do was hurt William – what had possessed her? What upset her most was the realization that, inebriated as she was when she invited Maxi to her room, she could even then feel regret prickling along her spine, but she had forced her own hand. She was compelled to follow through and see what another life, another Clare, might feel like. Fraudulent. Now, she knew.

The claustrophobic hotel room overwhelmed her; she couldn't wait there until morning, driving herself more and more insane with thoughts of where William might be, cursing her mistakes. How could she have done this to him? Deep down, she knew that if their marriage dissolved now, it wouldn't be only because of what she had done, but she couldn't tolerate the idea of this being how things ended between them. She couldn't – wouldn't – bear the burden of that on her shoulders alone. Not when they had been so close to finding each other again. It was a shock to realize how much she wanted to save their marriage when faced with the reality of losing William for ever. For months, she had lived with one foot already out of their front door, and now she wanted to barricade herself inside. She tried to quieten the conflicting voices in her head. Was it just fear of the unknown that trapped her? Or did she really want to make her marriage work? Everything had become so confused.

Clare departed for the airport to wait for the first early-morning flight back to London. Maybe William was doing the same thing and she would see him there. Packing their suitcases, her heart was in ribbons as she folded his trousers and shirt, balled his stripy socks and laid them in his suitcase. She pulled on his discarded T-shirt and breathed in the still-living scent of him before slipping into the night, pulling both their cases, enveloped in her big blue jumper with the crooked white stars.

In the taxi on the way to the airport, the driver tried to coax her story from her. Where was she off to? What had brought her to Dublin? She tried to shut down his questioning with murmurs about 'some bad news from London' and 'being called home unexpectedly', and stared out of the window to avoid his eyes in the rear-view mirror. The streets were filled with people spilling out of pubs on Wexford Street into the pouring rain.

The drops cascading down her window blurred the lights and smeared the colours across the pane. She had stopped crying. For now. Watching the tears of the city sky streaking down the glass, it felt as if the heavens were crying for them, but she didn't feel she deserved their sympathy.

In the deepest, quietest part of herself, she knew that William was right. A part of her must have wanted this to happen, willed for something irretrievable and powerful to force them to stop the procrastination, desperate for redemption, rejuvenation, salvation. Her mind scattered thoughts like ashes in the breeze. How could she ever expect him to respect her again? To trust her again? How would she ever be able to respect herself? She rustled in her handbag for a compact, smoothed some concealer on the dark circles under her eyes and traced a ribbon of red across her lips. Little threads to keep herself sewn together for what lay ahead.

At the airport, she scanned the departures area for William, walking through Duty-free in a robotic state. What would she say if she found him? Would he cause a scene? Blank her? Was there any chance he would take her in his arms? Instinct told her no. It was going to be a long walk back from here to the couple kissing in the shadows of a wedding that day. If they could ever find their way. She hoped that her legs had the strength to carry her.

19.

William waited at the airport on a hard grey plastic chair, a brown paper bag containing an uneaten toasted cheese sandwich by his feet, a cardboard cup with the cold dregs of instant coffee balanced between his legs. The interval to board his flight felt interminable; he was too mentally electrified by the night's events to sleep and yet he felt physically demobilized by them. No flights were arriving or departing at this time; his only companions were other displaced travellers lost in transit. When he saw Clare on the escalator, struggling to negotiate it with their two suitcases, his heart leaped to call her name but his head silenced him. He crouched down lower in his seat, hiding behind the pillar that shielded him from her vision as he watched her scanning the departures lounge – for sight of him, he presumed. Seeing her like this, he felt as if he were witnessing his own heart walk around the airport in another body. The further away she walked, the smaller and emptier he felt. He did not trust himself to see her now; he was weakened by the weight of his damaged love, crushed by her crime.

Before a plan had fully formed, William was on his feet and darting for the exit, his ticket discarded with the remnants of his unwanted breakfast. As he burst through the revolving doors to escape the airport, the sun was just beginning to rise; light diluted the dark sky, turning it a moody blue. He was the only person waiting for the bus to the city centre; he was happy to climb aboard as the sole passenger and take a quiet, leisurely route into town while he collected his thoughts. He sat on the upper deck in the front seat and watched the city roll out before him through the wide pane of glass as the morning brightened. When he was little, he liked to sit in this seat with his dad and pretend he was driving the bus through the streets of Cambridge. It was a shadowy day when his father told him he wasn't sure his knees could take the stairs. They had to sit on the ground floor, across from a grumpy old lady wearing a pink plastic visor and steadying a tartan shopping bag on wheels. He didn't want his dad to be one of those old people who chatted about the weather and the graffiti in the town square. And he didn't want another little boy taking his place in the best seat in the house.

It struck him for the second time in as many days that the drive into Dublin offered a grim first impression of the city. He wondered if tourists were shocked by the towers of council flats, the suburban housing estates and the miles of concrete all around. Where were the lush green pastures of the Emerald Isle they had been promised? No doubt the picture-postcard island would reveal itself in due course; he would love to explore it properly one day. Maybe take a train into the west? How he wished that was what he was doing now, instead of unravelling his whole life into a pile of tangled wool.

He wanted to explore Winter's Ireland; if he was honest, he wanted her to show it to him.

He jumped off the bus at O'Connell Street and walked across the bridge over the River Liffey. The light on the water made it glisten in silver and he recognized why Dublin was considered so magical; you could feel the fairy tale spinning from the old stone of Trinity College, dancing up Grafton Street and scampering down the side alleys. It was painful to absorb the beauty of it all while he was feeling so broken. Especially given how happy he had been to walk these streets with Clare the day before. He walked with his head down, listening to Morrissey sing harmonious songs about disharmonious minds on his Walkman; it soothed him like a lullaby. Why do we take such perverse pleasure from sad songs? Do they make us feel less alone?

He didn't stay in the same Dublin hotel as he had with Clare. There was no need this time for room service, jacuzzis or opulent surroundings; instead, he found a cheap room in a backpackers' hostel on the quays. As he waited for the receptionist to register his details, a wave of nausea washed over him.

'Sir, are you okay? You look very pale. Can I get you anything?' The touch of the girl's hand on his arm made him jump.

'What? Oh, yes, no, I'm fine. Just a bit dizzy. Maybe some water. Thank you.'

He fished the ice cubes from the plastic tumbler she handed him and allowed one to melt on his tongue, flinching when the cold exposed a sensitive tooth. Grinding the ice with his back teeth, cold rivulets of water escaped down his throat, a delicate relief. When he saw the reality of his accommodation, he regretted his pragmatism; the room smelled of onions and a plastic sheet lay under the thin grey one on his bed. What past indiscretions had prompted that act of protection from the management? He looked out of the window at a yard full of rubbish bins and bits of old machinery. An ebony coat stand stood forlornly in the midst of it all. How could such prime real estate in the city centre have become so neglected? He pulled the margarine-coloured curtains closed and lay gingerly on the crinkling mattress; he would just rest his eyes for a moment.

When he awoke in the hostel later that morning, the glorious sunshine bursting through the thin curtain fabric disoriented him. Where had yesterday's downpour gone? He washed as best he could in the cracked porcelain sink in the corner of the room, draped his blazer over his arm and walked to the grocery shop next door to buy some essentials. Despite his foul mood, he welcomed the unexpected warmth on his face as he breathed in the air; it smelled so much cleaner than London's. An instant remedy. He purchased a double espresso from a coffee trike called Java the Hut, sat on a marble stone bench beneath a lime tree and watched the light skip across the glittering surface of the Liffey as the city symphony tuned up for another day. A brown plaque rested on the bark of a nearby tree. It read, '60,000 street and roadside trees inhabit Dublin city centre, with an average of 5,000 new trees planted every year.' He wondered who had been given the task of counting them; pictured a man walking the streets with a spiral-bound jotter, losing track and starting again at the beginning.

The shock of the previous night was waning a little, the reality of why he was still in Dublin dawning. Clare's confession sat like a ball of iron in his stomach, but he forced the image it conjured from his mind. He hadn't allowed himself to try to find Winter before but, now, well, things were different. In his bones, he knew that some prescient instinct told him that coming to her city would be revelatory. Wasn't that why he had felt compelled to tuck her Polaroid picture beneath the cover of the moleskin-covered notebook he always carried? From his breast pocket, he removed this now and stared at it; how the shimmering morning light infused it with energy!

Compared to London, Dublin was a village. He even knew the name of Winter's favourite pub; surely if he asked some questions at some of her old haunts, it would help narrow down the search? He wondered how long it was since she had moved; it sounded quite recent in her letters. And if her name really was Winter, the chances seemed high that someone would remember her. Perhaps it was madness to chase a ghost through this city, but what was the alternative? Go home to pace the flat all weekend, worrying himself into a knot, arguing with Clare? William's thoughts bounced back and forth in agonizing indecision, until a stubborn peace settled upon him. He could not endure another day of dithering and withering under Ned's relentless scrutiny. It gave him a momentary relief to think he could refine his approach; Dublin seemed a much less overwhelming haystack to find a needle in. Everything was becoming more real, and that was a good thing. He couldn't play this out in his mind much longer; he needed some answers. And Clare no longer stood in his way. Winter's letters had struck a nerve; he couldn't allow life to just happen to him any more. Wasn't that what Clare had been trying to tell him for years? Maybe the impetus to get him here was involuntary, but now that he had finally taken some action, he had to follow through.

First things first: he needed to buy himself some time. He marched down the boardwalk, eyes peeled for a telephone box, until one presented itself, just before the Ha'penny Bridge. He folded himself inside it; the smell of the rotting fish and chips on the floor took his breath away. As he lined up neat piles of ten-, twenty- and fifty-pence pieces on the metal shelf covered in sticker advertisements, he propped the door open a crack with his foot to let some air circulate. He dialled his own telephone number, wobbled to hear Clare's voice on the machine; he remembered how many times she had recorded the message before settling on this one. 'That's not what my voice sounds like, is it?' she'd despaired. She deleted it and started again, while he threw cushions at her to make her laugh each time. As he listened, he heard his own faint laugh in the background. To his ears, his voice sounded weak and watery as he spoke but, this time, there was no opportunity to re-do it.

'Clare, I don't quite know if you deserve this message but, in case you call the police or some such, I wanted to let you know I'm staying in Dublin for a few days. Please don't be there when I do come home. I'll find you when I'm ready.'

He hung up the receiver and strengthened his resolve for call number two.

'Dead Letters Depot, Miss Clarke speaking.'

William recognized her telephone voice and a strange nostalgia touched him.

'Marjorie, it's William. I need your help, but why are you in on a Saturday? I was just going to leave a message for you.' He paused, dreading the outpouring of scorn and derision to follow but, in its place, her voice softened into a conspiratorial whisper.

'Oh, sometimes I like to come in to water the plants, do a few bits. The weekends are long. What can I do? Shoot!'

He pictured her sitting alone there, paused to consider it, but garbled on, 'I don't have much time to explain, but I'm stuck in Dublin and won't be back for a few days. Can you cover for me if I'm not in on Monday? Maybe you can say –'

'Don't worry. I'll think of something. Leave it to me. Everyone will be in a tizz because twenty-five life-sized mannequins arrived yesterday evening and they've taken over the place!'

The beeps warned him that time was running out, and he fed his last two coins into the slot.

'Thank you, Marjorie. I mean it. I know I haven't been my best recently.'

'Don't you worry, ducky. Just get home safe to us, okay? And William?'

'Yes?'

'Anything you need, I'll be here.'

The line disconnected. William emerged back on to the street with the dawning realization of how much Marjorie must care about him. Why had he always been so hard on her? Relieved to have completed his tasks, he continued across the Ha'penny Bridge to begin his mission in earnest. Now that he was on his way, the enormity of his actions enveloped him, and the lack of a concrete plan. He walked in long strides, avoiding cracks in the pavement. Supposing he did find someone who knew Winter – how could he explain why he was looking for her? What if they told her a strange Englishman was hanging around town asking questions about her, someone she had never even met but who knew so much about her? She would probably call the police, he would definitely lose his job, and any chance of ever resolving things with Clare would be completely gone. If that was even what he wanted any more. He compelled himself to remember that this was the woman who had cheated on him. Anything else would be a lie. He thought about her earlier confession: the slip of the kiss. In his gut, he had known that there was more to it than she had told him. If he had been prepared then to accept the implicit knowledge of betrayal and reach out a conciliatory hand all the same, what had really changed now that it had been made explicit? Should he have sat down wearily on the side of their hotel bed and tried to reach an understanding? Could he have just redrawn the line under the whole affair in a heavier, more permanent ink and allowed their weekend of rediscovery to continue? Would she love him more or less for his forgiveness? He closed the door on this line of thought. Nothing could ever be the same now, because the truth could never be unknown. He could never unlearn that she had lied to him and that she had chosen to continue to do so when the opportunity to tell the truth had finally presented itself. It was her ability to live inside that fraud that really sickened him. And that was before he even let himself think of what she had physically done. He could never have stayed in that hotel room and lived with himself.

He turned right along the river until a stone arch enticed him into Temple Bar, where the cobbled streets had become thronged with shoppers and tourists enjoying the unexpected sunshine. He paused outside the Rock Garden and read the billings for that night to see if anyone he had heard of was playing, but he didn't recognize any of the names. Who knows, if he and Stevie had stuck at it, maybe the Bleeding Hearts might have played here themselves. He strolled down Crown Alley, where all the rock-and-roll kids hung around in awkward little groups in self-conscious poses. A lady sporting a vintage tuxedo, her hair gelled into a bleached-blonde quiff, was dragging a clothes rail heavy with retro band T-shirts and denim jackets down two steps to rest in front of the purple-and-white-striped walls of her store. William helped her position it, and she winked at him.

'Thanks, chicken,' she said.

He followed her back inside as he wriggled Winter's Polaroid picture from his pocket.

'Excuse me!' he called after her. 'You don't happen to know where I might find a pair of boots like these?' He ignored how foolish he felt as she absorbed the image then quickly looked him up and down.

'My wife,' he offered. 'She bought a pair somewhere around here a few years ago but lost them. I wanted to try and replace them for her. Her favourite pair, you see.'

She pulled out a pair of round gold-rimmed spectacles from under the counter and studied the picture more closely.

'Hhhmmmm, I can't say I've ever seen boots like them before,' she said, with a drawl. 'You're not in Nashville, ya know. I wouldn't fancy your chances.'

A teenage boy, resplendent in yellow denim flares, black polyester shirt and orange platform boots staggered through from the back room, the top of his Afro just visible above the huge cardboard box he was hugging.

'Alex! Just the man!' she exclaimed. 'Here, take a look at these. Ring any bells?'

He dropped the box with a slap on the concrete floor and leaned over to peer at the picture.

'What am I looking for?' he asked. 'Who's this guy?'

He nodded towards William, who jumped in to answer.

'I'm trying to find a shop that sells them, or used to, anyway. Any suggestions?'

The young man drummed his fingers on the counter-top, chewing on the question for a moment. A look of hard concentration on his face gave William hope, but it quickly vanished.

'Nope, sorry,' he said with a shrug. 'I'm going to get a breakfast roll, okay?' he asked the tuxedoed lady, as he headed for the door.

In every shop along the alley where William enquired, he received the same incredulous looks, hopeless shrugs, offers of alternatives. He was sitting on the steps of Central Bank, contemplating his next move, when the yellow-flared teenager from that morning strutted past, paused and turned on his heel to call back to him.

'Yo! Boots guy!' he hollered. 'I just thought of some-where! There is *one* place you could try . . . on Dame Lane. They do more costumes, but I *think* they used to do cowgirl stuff.' He held up his hands in question. 'Worth a shot?'

'Yes, yes, definitely,' William answered. 'Thanks so much!' but the boy had already resumed his parade down the city catwalk, leaving William to watch him walk away.

Dame Lane – hadn't Winter mentioned that street in one of her letters? With revived purpose, William paused at the pedestrian crossing, looked at his street map to find the way to Dame Lane and discovered it was a little alleyway running parallel to where he stood. He picked up the pace as he travelled along its curling pavement, looking through the windows of a taxidermist's, at the closed blinds of a beauty parlour and the lonely white walls of a gallery empty of art. He was relieved to find the lane so short and the shops so few as to eliminate any chance of him mistaking the place.

A bubblegum-pink clapperboard hung on the black railings of a stairway leading down to a basement unit. Curly white lettering spelled out the name Gúna of Una, above drawings of ladies' hats with legs sticking out beneath them that appeared to be doing the can-can. He climbed down the stairs, pausing to look into the window, past the jailhouse bars to the lair within. The interior looked as if it had been dropped into Dublin from a Hollywood movie set. Mirrors framed by strings of white lights stretched along one of the whitewashed stone walls. Black-and-white portraits of fifties starlets adorned the rear, looking down on a turquoise chaise longue scattered with voluminous velvet cushions in myriad shades of blue. Red and black feather boas dangled from the ends of white wooden clothes rails, kissing the plush peach carpet underneath. Instead of changing rooms, a hot-pink velvet curtain was draped across one corner on an ornate silver rail. A woman's head and shoulders were visible over the top as she wriggled into something metallic-looking; her feet peeped from the bottom, where her trousers gathered around her ankles.

When William pushed through the glossy black door, little bells tinkled and the aroma of vanilla essence was overpowering. It was obvious this shop was not a domain designed for the comfort of men. Enthroned in a purple velvet armchair behind a black marble counter, a woman looked out at him from under a ruby-encrusted pill-box hat that sat neatly on rolls of shiny ebony hair. Her face was powdered chalk-white with eyebrows drawn on in black, sweeping false eyelashes, two circles of blush on each cheek and a perfect pout of sticky redness. She appeared to be wearing a short wedding dress. When she spoke, her voice was a raspy whisper, as if it had become tired from too much singing in smoky jazz clubs.

'Well, now, are you lost or on a mission?'

She beckoned him towards her with a frosted-pink talon, and William stumbled down the last step into the shop, steadying himself against a glittering ladder of stilettos that wobbled perilously.

'Um, I'm not quite sure what you mean.'

'I *mean*, have you stumbled in here by accident? Or have you sought out a secret wonderland where a man of certain persuasions can find another identity?'

'Oh, gosh, no, well, I did come looking for you, but not for my own benefit, per se. You see, I have a friend who I think likes to shop here, or liked to, anyway.'

'Marvellous. She has excellent taste, and you would like to buy her a present! Come with me.'

She stood up and rested a hand on her hip as she sashayed into the middle of the room. She pointed at a red-and-white polka-dot footstool before ducking behind the pink velvet curtain herself.

'Wait here, I shan't be a moment,' she cooed over the top.

William hesitated before lowering himself on to the little seat, which brought his knees in line with his chin.

His eyes wandered around the twinkling room, lingering over the cacophony of fabrics and colours. He tried to imagine Winter here, trying on exotic dresses and assessing her appearance in front of the mirrors, but couldn't really picture her, just the shimmering daydream his mind's eye conjured up. He certainly couldn't imagine Clare here; there wasn't a pair of black trousers or a two-piece suit in sight. He reprimanded himself for the unfair comparison: Clare hadn't always been that way. Slowly, over the years, the flowery dresses and stripy jumpers had been muscled out by the uniform of work which eventually became the norm. He had to admit, though, it was exciting to think of the sort of woman who would shop here; it raised his expectations further of how glamorous Winter might be. He just couldn't shake the image of scarlet hair tumbling down the back of her white rabbit-fur coat.

He tried to ignore the muted conversation of the ladies behind the dressing screen, but they weren't being very discreet.

'I'm just not sure it's very flattering. I don't know if I want to draw that much attention to my backside.'

'Sweetie, it's not the dress's fault. That's just your shape. Embrace it. Shake it. Love it.'

He heard a firm slap, followed by a little squeal of laughter, before the owner of the bottom appeared in front of him.

'What do *you* think? Do you like it?'

He surveyed the woman wriggling in front of him and tried to work out which 'it' in particular he was supposed to be remarking on. Her baby-blue hair was teased into a beehive rising a foot above her pixie-like face. Little blue silk butterflies were scattered throughout, as if they had become trapped there and set up home. A pink fish dangled from a hook in each ear and dozens of strings of multicoloured glass beads encircled her throat. The dress itself appeared to be made of tinfoil on the top half, with chains of metal hoops resting on silver paper at the bottom.

'Well? Do you like it? If you saw me in a bar, would you want to talk to me? Do you think I look ravishing? I won't settle for anything less than ravishing. You hesitated. It's awful. I knew it. Una, get me out of this contraption.'

Una started adjusting the dress on her shoulders.

'Nonsense, he's just shy. Look at him, he's spellbound. Aren't you?'

'Oh, yes, quite. I don't think I've ever seen anything quite like it before.'

'But, do you *like* it?'

'I'm really not a very good judge of these things. I don't really know anything about fashion or . . .'

His words were left suspended as she flounced back behind the screen. She wrestled out of the dress and tossed it over the top of the curtain.

'I knew it. Una, it just won't work. Let's try again next week.'

Una scooped up the fallen outfit and smoothed out the panels as she nonchalantly reclaimed her seat behind the desk. William shuffled over in front of her again.

'You just lost me a big piece of business, mister. I hope you're planning on splurging, big time.'

'I'm terribly sorry, I'm just not really the right person for this sort of thing. And the truth is, I'm not actually here to shop.'

She picked up a hand mirror, turned away from him and fiddled with the net at the front of her hat.

'Well, we're not a spectator sport. So, if you'll excuse me . . .'

The pixie lady bustled past him. The jingle of the bells was violent as she slammed the door behind her.

'Please, I just wanted to ask you about my friend.'

'Sale first. Conversation later.'

'But that's exploitation. Surely, you can't charge me for asking a few questions. I just want to see if you can help me —'

'I think I'll take an early lunch, so, if you'll excuse me.'

Una reached under her desk for a gold-plated handbag with tassels around the edge and removed from it a single avocado.

'Okay, okay, I have . . . let me see' – he rustled in his blazer pockets – 'twelve pounds and seventeen pence. What can I buy for that?'

She sighed, spun back to the counter and opened a deep drawer underneath.

'Some fishnet tights. What size would you like, sir?'

William ran his fingers through his hair with frustration.

'This is ridiculous; I don't care what size. They'll be going in the bin as soon as I leave.'

283

'Oh, darling, there's no need to be so hostile. We just want to make sure all our customers have a wonderful experience here.'

She smiled at him as she wrapped them, first in pink tissue paper, and then white, before tying the package with black silk ribbon. William was convinced she moved as slowly as possible to aggravate him and waited impatiently for her to finish before shoving the beautiful parcel into the front pocket of his satchel. She pushed her chair back and crossed her legs, revealing some elegant stockings of her own.

'So, tell me about this *friend* of yours.'

'Well, it's a little complicated. I'm not entirely sure of her name but I believe she may be called Winter.'

'You *believe*? I thought you said she was a friend. A lot of ladies love this shop; I don't recall ever meeting anyone called Winter.'

'She's more of an acquaintance, of sorts, and, you see, I'm trying to find her, but I only have a few clues, like, for example, I happen to know that she loves this shop. And I think she might have bought these boots here.'

He held the Polaroid out to her; she glanced at it without taking it from him.

'Yes, I remember those boots; they were for a child, actually. Sat here for ages before someone with small enough feet came in and wanted to buy them.'

'Gosh, do you remember who you sold them to? Do you keep records of your sales?'

'Oh, darling, I wasn't even here that day. Maybe the

old owner, Gloria, might know her, but she lives in Canada now. I bought the shop when she left.'

William stood in silence.

'I'm sorry I couldn't be of more help, but at least you've got some lovely stockings,' she offered.

He turned to leave, but he had one more question, 'Why is the shop called Guns of Una? It seems a strange name.'

She laughed and shook a handkerchief at him. 'Not "guns", you silly man,' she cooed. 'Gúna – *gooooona* – it's the Irish for dress. Gúna of Una, and that's me – I'm Una.'

Humiliation complete, William climbed the steps back out on to the streets of Dublin with the tinkle of bells and laughter in his wake. It was so frustrating to have such a strong lead go cold, but the palaver had not been entirely in vain. He left with a stronger sense of Winter than before; the sketch in his mind was filled in with a little more colour. The more he knew, the more enticing Winter became.

20.

Clare arrived back in London after an interminable spell at the airport waiting for the first flight to take her home. When she eventually arrived back at their flat, she was disappointed to find the hallway dark and silent when she pushed the door open. William must have waited to catch their original flight home, after all, she thought. It was crushing to see the evidence of their departure littered around the flat; was this the last remains of their final happy time together? Two unwashed teacups upside down in the sink; the shoe polish left open on the mat from William's last-minute shining; the curlers she had removed scattered across her dressing table. She swiped them on to the floor in an angry blow. How had she allowed this to happen? Just when she had started to believe in their future again, everything had imploded. She couldn't face unpacking their luggage, seeing their clothes from the wedding crinkled and used before going to bed alone. Instead, she went back downstairs to wait for him.

Clare's hands shook as she spooned coffee granules from the canister on the windowsill and dropped them in a waiting mug. The boiling water splashed over the sides as she tried in vain to steady her hand. The more she willed herself to act normally, the more her body failed her. She placed the mug on the table, took the milk from the fridge. As she poured, a sour stench struck her. She cursed in frustration and threw the carton into the sink, watched the thick, curdled mess clog the drain for a moment before breaking apart under the force of the water from the tap she ran. She sat at the kitchen table. I'll just rest my eyes for a second, she thought, before a heavy sleep seized her, her head lying on her forearms on the table. In her dream, the telephone rang, in the distance at first, then louder, as her consciousness rose. As her eyes blinked awake, she heard William's voice, shot up straight and called his name. She ran into the hallway, the living room, listened for movement upstairs. 'William?' she called, into a vacuum. Had she dreamed it? As she walked back towards the kitchen, rolling the stiffness from her shoulders, the flashing red beacon of the answering machine caught her eye. She pressed play and William's voice filled the hallway once more.

He sounded a million miles away: sad, lost and lonely. She rewound the tape and played it through again. And again. And again. When she could bear it no longer, she lay on the living-room sofa, listening to Morrissey on the record player. It made William feel closer. Eventually, she felt ready to formulate something of a plan. From the basket of white paper that lay beside his typewriter, she pulled a sheet and wrote him a note.

William, my love,
    You don't know how much I wanted to be here when you came home; how hard it is for me to resist trying to

make you forgive me with pure strength of will. But I know that you deserve some time alone to process what's happened, much as it terrifies me to think of what conclusions you may reach.

What I did was indefensible but, I hope that, in time, you will see that, although it was awful, it may have been understandable; something so ugly and profound it would force me to confront how I feel, about us, but also about what my life has become. I was desperate, and behaved desperately.

For what it's worth, I want you to know that there is nothing between me and that man and, even if we don't survive this, there will never be anything between us again. I promise you. I think we both need some time to take stock of what's happened, but I want you to know I think we can move past this, if we both really want to.

Please don't close a door that we can't ever return through. Maybe things can never be the same again, but couldn't that be a good thing?

I am going to stay with Flora – please come and find me when you're ready.

All my love,
Your Clare

She folded the letter and left it on William's pillow, tidied away the curlers she had swept to the floor and filled a backpack with some things she might need. Before she left the house, she paused at the front door and thought for a moment before running back upstairs to their bedroom. From under their bed, she dragged out her old portfolio and knelt before it. The dust it unsettled made her cough as she brushed it clean with a discarded nightdress that lay at the foot of the bed. Without really understanding why, she tucked it under her arm to take with her. As she propped it against the back seat of her Mini, she felt better for having it there. A little piece of her from before she lost her way.

21.

While Clare was writing William her note, William was pounding back up Dame Lane as an onslaught of spitting rain attacked his hunched shoulders. Droplets on his glasses blurred his vision, but he was too frustrated to unclench a fist from either pocket to wipe them. Instead, he kept his head down, too stubborn to pull his hood up, and continued marching blindly, until he almost walked into a lamp post. Resting his forehead against the damp blackness of the iron, he emitted a low whine. A hand on his left shoulder blade made him start, and the force of his reaction startled the owner of the hand in turn. A young woman with a nest of messy fair hair escaping from a pea-green beret looked at him with conflicting expressions of curiosity, suspicion and concern. They began apologizing at the same time. Her accent carried the sing-song cadence of somewhere beyond the city, each sentence ending in a high note, leaving him confused as to which sentences were questions and which were statements.

'I'm sorry – I thought maybe you'd had an accident, or hurt yourself? I can't help myself. I'm a nurse, you see, and whenever I think someone might be in trouble, I have to ask, or else I'd be thinking about it all evening and worrying I'd read about them on the news. Everyone would say how the world had become such a terrible place that no one would stop and ask a fella if he was okay, too busy minding their own business . . . it would put me off my supper . . . Anyways, I'm just blathering on now, and I can see you're okay, and we're both getting soaked to the skin. You are okay . . . aren't you?'

William waited a beat beyond what was comfortable before he began to speak. He had just about followed what she was saying but, now that it was his turn to speak, her jumble of words seemed to have rendered him incapable of making any sense himself.

'Yes, I just needed a minute. Sorry, it must have looked a bit odd.'

'Well, it's a funny spot to stop with the heavens opening above us. As long as you're okay?' She tightened the belt on her navy-blue raincoat and tucked a few soaked tendrils of hair back under her beret as she skipped backwards into the flow of pedestrians.

'You should get yourself home, have a bath. Steam the damp out of you.'

Her face broke into a lopsided grin that changed her appearance completely. Her expression became illuminated like a starlet in a silent movie with no words to tell the world what was on her mind. He waved to her as she turned away, little rivulets of water trickling down the sleeve of his coat, before darting through the traffic that had stopped at the lights. He ducked under the archway of a market arcade and shook himself like a shaggy dog. A chuckle escaped him as he remembered his glee at the sunshine state he'd awoken to that morning. Was this his punishment for tempting fate? He let his eyes wander to the source of the clatter behind him. Market traders packing away their wares from stalls that ran in two lines down the centre of the archway. Little shops on either side were growing dark as shutters were drawn, signs switched off, lights quenched and doors locked. He strolled through the detritus of the Saturday sales: war memorabilia, trophies won at long-forgotten sports days, football matches or tennis tournaments, rails of vintage dresses, floppy hats and moth-eaten fur coats, tiers of twinkling fairy lights, costume jewellery, and candles being snuffed one by one.

Should he bring something home to Marjorie? To thank her for looking out for him? Perhaps also to make up for stealing back his Winter letter and allowing her to think she lost it. He idled at a stall with racks of vinyl records and battered hardback books naked without their dust jackets and chose a slim volume for her: *The Love Letters of War*. Her valentine-soaked heart would revel in it. Some of the traders smiled at him hopefully as he continued on and trailed past their displays, a last-minute sale before home time would finish the morning off nicely, but he didn't linger at any one spot for long. He could tell some people were tired and just wanted to pack up as quickly as possible, resigned to the fact that it would all have to be unpacked again the next day. An impatient teenager stuffed colourful woollen tights and patterned knee socks into black plastic bags with no care for the meticulous manner in which they had been hung and displayed that morning. A lady dressed in baker's whites carefully flattened cream cardboard boxes. A young man, worse for wear in a dirty shell tracksuit and unlaced trainers, watched her out of the corner of his eye as he leaned against a closed shop front. William hesitated and pretended to browse through an album of old stamps as he surveyed the scene. What would he do if the watcher grabbed the woman's cashbox of takings? At least he might be able to startle him before it went that far, if he timed it correctly. In what looked like a painful manoeuvre, she dragged a stuffed plastic crate from under the rose-patterned tablecloth. The young man made a start towards her and William rushed forward, too, just in time to hear him gargle at her, 'Let me do that for you, Mrs Gallagher, you don't want to be puttin' your back out again.' She smiled at him and turned to look at William, who was now standing far too close for comfort and, for the second time that day, an Irishwoman gave him a worried look and asked him if he was all right.

'Indeed, I just wanted to catch you before you closed up.' He smiled weakly and mumbled an ineffectual, 'Smells delicious . . . mmmm.'

As the chap lifted the crate, he threw William a suspicious glance.

'Shall I take them to the car for you, Mrs Gallagher?'

'That would be lovely, dear. I've left a bag inside for the young fella, so help yourself. Take the keys and you can pop them in the boot.'

William hovered at the edge of the stall, feigning interest in a display of eccentric umbrellas in a shop window.

'Now, what were you after yourself? I've only got

one spelt loaf left, but there's a dozen or so scones still up for grabs, and a couple of cream buns. The market's closing early today so I brought less than usual with me. Fancy them doing works on a Saturday, the busiest day of the week. Thoughtless –'

'I'll take a cream bun, please.'

'Right, was that it?'

'And the spelt loaf,' William gulped. 'And the scones.'

'Lovely. Fifteen pounds all in, so.'

William added the unwanted baking to the superfluous stockings in his satchel. He walked purposefully away towards the beckoning lights of the busier end of the market, wondering what he could possibly do with it all. He cursed himself for his own inability to just say no. It was nearly time for lunch. A steaming bowl of soup was just what he needed to recalibrate and make a plan for the rest of the day. He strolled up George's Street, nodding at the closed shutters of the Long Hall pub, to which he knew he would return, and turned up side streets that led back towards Grafton Street and St Stephen's Green. He thought of Clare remarking that Dublin was a lot like Manhattan, really; the way the city sat around the lush green park at its heart. It was ludicrous; Manhattan could carry Dublin around in its smallest pocket, but still, he understood what she meant.

He found himself a temporary home in the library bar of the Central Hotel, where the atmosphere reminded him of Christmas Eve. An open fire was roaring in the hearth. Chesterfield sofas and plush armchairs were scattered around on thick, rich carpets in sets of twos and threes; all the lighting came from lamps and tea-light candles in crystal holders. What a dangerous place to encounter on a damp day such as this; he might never leave again. A softly spoken waitress with wing-tipped tortoiseshell spectacles and two long auburn plaits trailing down her back brought him a bowl of country vegetable soup and warm crunchy rolls slathered in butter. He tried not to think of the brown-paper bag of bread hidden under his seat as he relished the comfort food, having already decided to leave the bag behind him when he left.

After the soup had warmed his bones, an Irish coffee with its whiskey kick seemed the only option. He sank back into a rust-red leather armchair and stretched his toes to within inches of the flames flickering in the hearth. Stress ebbed from the tension in the back of his neck down his spine and out through his aching legs before wafting with the smoke up the chimney. He decided that missing his flight had been worth it, for this moment's grace alone. He closed his eyes and felt he was hovering a few feet above the room as he tuned in to the sounds around him: clinking glasses behind the bar, the pages of a newspaper being snapped taut after each turning, a vacuum cleaner murmuring in the hallway, animated chatter from two ladies surrounded by shopping bags, their high heels temporarily abandoned, sipping gin and tonics. Clare would love it here. The thought sunk him in gloom. He wanted to be angry at her, to hate her, even, but every time those dark feelings bubbled inside him they burst before they grew real legs. Deep down, he knew that what she had done was just a terrible symptom of how wretched they had become, but that didn't mean he could make peace with it. And definitely not yet.

He pushed the memory of last night from his mind and turned his thoughts to Winter instead. Had she ever lounged here on a lazy Saturday afternoon? Sometimes, it's harder to surrender to indulgences of that nature where you live; there's always some small task to be accomplished. Library bars, even one as seductively comfortable as this, could never be his weekly ritual in real life. Obligations would get in the way and turn the whole business into a spate of guilty mental list-making as he catalogued all the other ways he could be – should be – spending his time. This sort of pleasure had to be reserved for holidays, or the occasional spontaneous moment. What a sad truth to confront. Perhaps if he and Clare had enjoyed more of this and fixated less on accomplishing things on their to-do lists, they would be here together now with Clare's feet tucked in beneath him. Perhaps. He wriggled into a more upright position, rummaged in his satchel for his notebook and flicked through the history impressed upon its pages that stretched back to the time before this calamitous period in his life. He pined for the innocence of his scribblings:

Potential birthday presents for Clare:

A first edition (if can afford) . . . but of what?
Weekend abroad (is this just present for me, though?)

Telescope for star-gazing (can you see enough stars
    through the smog in London?)
Fountain pen (too work-related?)
Cooking classes (too open to misinterpretation?)
Espresso maker? (too domestic?)
Lingerie? (again, present for me?)

Directions to Karen and James's: Overground to H'bury
and Is; change at Dalston Junction; turn right until giant
street mural and next left to No. 11 over the dry cleaner's.

Shopping:

Paella rice (medium grain; regular if none)
Pimms (and lemons/limes/cucumber)
Cardamom pods
Non-alcoholic wine for Mrs C
Pesto (green & sun-dried tomatoes)
Honey – squeezy
Green olives (some stuffed with cheese for C.)
Chocolate digestives
Sweet potatoes

To do pre-Christmas:

1. Bleed the radiators
2. Order wine hamper
3. Bag of clothes to charity shop
4. Replace lights on bicycle
5. Arrange night with Stevie and the band

6. Xylophone!!!
7. Secret Santa

He hadn't done any of those things and couldn't remember at all what the xylophone reference meant. Perhaps Clare's frustrations at his alleged inability to get anything done weren't entirely misplaced. At least he had seen Stevie, although not under the circumstances he would have liked. He scribbled from memory a list of people and places Winter had mentioned in her letters; how he wished he could lay all her letters out before him and scour them for clues. He remembered her old career promoting records in radio stations and tried to consider how useful that nugget of information was. How many radio stations could there be in Ireland? If he spoke to one of the DJs, they would know all the radio pluggers, wouldn't they? It was hard to gauge what sort of relationship she might have had with them without him having any insight into how the industry worked, but it was definitely a lead worth exploring. He caught the eye of the waitress and gave her the universal gesture to request the same again. As she placed the hot glass tankard before him on a tomato-red napkin, he asked, 'Odd question, but do you listen to the radio much?'

'At home, I do. It doesn't really work to have music playing in here, though, if that's what you're thinking?'

'No, no. I was just wondering about the local radio stations, what I should tune in to while I'm in town.'

'Well, I listen to some of the pirates myself, but the main one is 2fm. That has all the big DJs on it and is a bit more mainstream. Apart from Dave Fanning. He's deadly and plays great tunes after eight o'clock. Rock and alternative stuff, mostly. Would you be into that sort of thing?'

'Sounds great. Like the Irish John Peel? Where is the station itself? In Dublin, I'm guessing?'

'Yeah, in RTÉ, out in Donnybrook. It's not far from here but, if you're into it, the Roadcaster is outside St Stephen's Green shopping centre today. You can go see the legend Larry Gogan in action.'

His antennae twitched at the mention of Donnybrook; wasn't that where Winter had lived, over a cake shop? He could have kissed the waitress for mentioning it, as he wasn't sure he would have remembered it otherwise.

'The Roadcaster?' he asked, hopeful for more intelligence that could help him.

'Yep, it travels all over the country with Larry playing the hits and his Golden Oldies. You should take a stroll up and check it out. You can play a request for Maggie and the gang in the Central Hotel, and my ma might hear it.'

William gulped down the hot Irish coffee as quickly as the scalding liquid would allow before heading back out into the warren of Dublin. The rain had stopped and the wet cobblestone paths glistened under the pale watery sunlight that tried to break through. As he drew closer to the gates of St Stephen's Green, he saw a little crowd gathered around a big black-and-yellow bus that was pumping out 'Teenage Kicks' by the Undertones. He edged his way to the front, where one of the happiest-looking men he had ever seen was chuckling behind a clipboard and wearing giant yellow headphones. A beaming young woman wearing a black jumpsuit with a thick cerise-pink belt was holding the microphone for him while he shuffled through his papers. The music ended abruptly and the spectators all shared a titter as the DJ jumped and giggled himself at nearly being caught out. A voice of chocolate, so warm and friendly, boomed out from the speakers. This must be the legend Larry himself, thought William. Larry turned to a blushing middle-aged woman who was bursting with pride at the attention. She kept fluffing her ginger perm as she watched him, shifting her weight back and forth from one foot to the other.

'So now we're going to have our last Just a Minute quiz of the day. Who do we have here?'

'Oh, Larry, I'm Ursula, and that's my friend Carole hiding over there, but she's too shy to go on the radio.'

'What's that, Carole? Carole, come over here and help poor Ursula answer a few questions out of that.'

Carole turned scarlet and waved madly, as if the nation of Ireland could see her gesturing over the radio waves.

'It's no use, Larry. She'll murder me after.'

'Don't mind her, Ursula. We'll give it a go ourselves. Are you ready?'

'Don't ask me any hard ones, Larry.'

'We'll let the clock start, then, Eddie, and away we go.'

A clock started counting down and Larry jumped into action:

'How many in a baker's dozen?'

'Thirteen.'

'How many times did Johnny Logan win the Eurovision?'

'Twice. Oh, I love him, I do.'

'Name the capital of Germany.'

'G.'

'Finish this famous proverb: as happy as . . .'

'Oh, as you, Larry.'

The crowd started laughing, but Larry managed to keep going with the questions.

'What do you put on before you go to bed?'

'Perfume.'

'Can you divide 144 by 12?'

'Yes.'

'A stitch in time saves . . . ?'

'Nine.'

'What do vegetarians not eat?'

'Vegetables.'

'What do caterpillars turn into?'

'Dust.'

The alarm sounded, and the crowd gave a big cheer while Larry's assistant counted her score.

'Ah, they didn't suit you, Ursula, but how many did she get, Anne?'

'Only four this time, I'm afraid.'

'Aw, don't worry a bit, Ursula. You got a few sticky ones there, but you did great. What do we have for her, Anne?'

'A great prize – two tickets to see Twink in her new show at the Gaiety and a Cadbury's chocolate hamper.'

'Great stuff. Let's hear it for Ursula, and it's back to the studio for the Boomtown Rats. Hit it, Eddie.'

Carole and Ursula posed for a photograph with Larry before he escaped, but William managed to catch the attention of Anne before she jumped on board the bus behind him.

'Excuse me, do you have a second?'

'Hello there. We're not doing any more quizzes today, if that's what you're after, but I can give you a form to fill out if you'd like to have a request played?'

'That's okay. I was just wondering if you might know a friend of mine who works for one of the record companies.'

'Maybe, but it depends on what they do.'

'She's a plugger, as far as I know.'

'Oh, well, Larry would probably know her, then. He listens religiously to every new track that comes out. What's her name?'

'Winter, although that could be a nickname.'

'Ooh, that's unusual. Doesn't ring any bells but, if you wait until the end of the show, you could ask Larry himself, if you'd like to.'

William started backing slowly away as he realized that he couldn't really ask this DJ if he happened to know Winter and, if so, where she used to work, without looking pretty peculiar. Was this blind alley just indicative of the end results he would face from all his clues? The futility of his search seemed ever clearer, and he started to panic about what exactly he was hoping to achieve. Was he hoping that whatever magical force had brought the letters into his life would also help him find the woman who wrote them?

He told Anne he might pop back later and ran to catch the number 10 bus that would take him to Donnybrook village. He asked the driver to let him know when they reached his destination, then watched Dublin city roll by. Larry's quiz reminded him of the challenge he had taken at last year's depot Christmas party; he was called up on stage to name something he had found in the depot for every letter in the alphabet. The audience shouted out the letters and, flustered though he was, he managed to call out a discovery in response to each one. He ran through the list in his head until the driver gave him the nod as he pulled up outside a huge chapel. A, apple tree; B, butterflies; C, chandelier; G, gnomes; J, jalapeño peppers; K, kaleidoscope; M, marzipan; P, picnic basket; V, ventriloquist's dummy. William jumped off the bus, his mind a momentary blank for what he had had for Y, before it hit him as he waited at the pedestrian crossing. Y, yo-yo! Of course!

He walked along the high street, with its artisan shops and ornate streetlights, hoping he hadn't missed the bakery as he strolled past. All these shops looked as if flats could exist above them. Did Winter walk along here every day? Buy her groceries in that market? Pore over paperbacks in that bookshop? Find bunches of flowers for friends in that florist? Anyone here could have known her, could still know her now. Everyone spread a web of connections across the world they inhabited: acquaintances, friends, chance encounters. Surely some sticky fragments of Winter's time here must exist along this street.

A cake shop sat on a curved corner, its stained-glass door opening on to the connecting street. This must be the one. In the window, a display of wedding cakes blocked most of the interior from view, but he saw that the bakery stretched further along the street; a row of little tables for two with blue-and-white-check table-cloths lined a long window. Each table had a red bud vase in the centre that held a sprig of winter jasmine. His favourite flower. In fact, the only flower that held any emotional significance for him at all. When he was a little boy, every November, his mother would take him out into the fields at the back of his grandmother's house in Devon to gather armfuls of it. They seemed to herald that Christmas was coming. His granny filled the house with them; in vases of all shapes and sizes but in empty milk bottles and tall drinking glasses, too. Whenever he could, he took a bunch to her grave in Highbury.

He was disappointed to discover that the flowers were plastic, but then, it was the wrong season. Goodness, where would he be spending Christmas this year? Would he and Clare be apart? Where on earth would he go if they were? Stevie's house? Thoughts of Christmas Eve without Clare made a cold mist gather on his skin. If he couldn't imagine Christmas without her, what was he doing sitting in a cake shop in Dublin, trying to track down a ghost? Even as every iota of common sense told him to leave and go straight to the airport, however, he was incapable of surrender. An important, essential part of himself had committed to this quest and, whatever his better judgement told him, he could not give up now. He forced himself to focus; he had lost sight of why he had come here.

William approached the counter, ordered a chocolate eclair and a peppermint tea, immediately questioning their compatibility, before starting to quiz the silver-haired gentleman in a starched white shirt and royal-blue tie who was so elegantly preparing his tray. William wondered if the clientele came as much for his attentions as for the little pastries that, he later discovered, were made by the man's wife.

'I'm visiting from London and remembered my friend, Winter, saying she lived above a cake shop around here. I don't suppose it was this one, by any chance?'

The gentleman's voice was slow and soft, only just more audible than a whisper. William felt they were already participating in a shared confidence.

'I don't suppose so.'

'Oh? Any particular reason?'

'A very particular one. I've lived upstairs with my wife for twenty-five years and, although we've had all the seasons living with us through that time, to the best of my knowledge, they have never taken on any human form.'

William concentrated on stirring his tea, watched the colour darken within the thick, glass-walled mug.

'I see. Twenty-five years. It's a long time. You must be very happy here.'

'Oh, we've had our ups and downs. And we did try to

leave once. My wife, Sylvie, became poorly, and we made an effort to retire in the west, but it wasn't for us. Syl spent all day making cakes without any neighbours for miles to give them away to. I thought I'd never be able to suffer the sight of them again. So, we came back to work, and my daughter kindly let us take the reins again.'

'Did she mind the shop for you while you were away?'

'Yes, she took over the whole business and lived upstairs but, really, I think she was relieved not to have to keep going. She had loftier ideas than inheriting the family business and always hankered to move abroad, to a bigger city where something exciting could happen.'

William's teaspoon clattered on to the silver tray while he registered this news.

'So, all for the best, then? Did she make the move? America? Or closer to home?'

'No, she wanted to go to America, but her mother's heart was broken at the thought of her being so far away, so she settled for London. Syl still feels guilty about that. Maybe if she had just gone to America, things would have turned out differently.'

William kept his voice steady as his heart banged and thrashed inside his ribcage. He rested his clammy hands against the tiled countertop to steady himself.

'Did she not like it, then? What's she up to now?'

His confidant took off a pair of wire-rimmed spectacles and patted his brow with a white handkerchief before polishing the lenses.

'I'm afraid she's not up to anything. Things took an

unfortunate turn over there and she got herself into some trouble. We've never really been sure exactly what happened; dodgy boyfriend at the heart of it, though, of course. Anyway, she passed away and was found in a horrible little flat in Shepherd's Bush, and by then it was too late to ever know the whole story.'

He started coughing, and William struggled to find something to say, before stammering out, 'I'm very sorry for your loss, sir.'

The gentleman folded and refolded the napkins on the counter while William gathered up his tray.

'I don't really talk about it that much, have to put a brave face on it. I'm sorry if I made you uncomfortable. It hits you at the strangest of times.'

'Not at all, it's the comfort of strangers.'

'Quite. Let me know if you need anything else.'

The man turned and pushed through the glass doors to the bakery, where William saw him circle his arms around a small, homely lady, her white hair in a net and flour on her bare arm, the sleeves of a yellow cotton blouse rolled up to her elbows. She leaned into him, and they rocked together for a moment, until she stepped away to pull a tray of loaves from the oven.

William sat back at his table for two and forced the eclair into his dry mouth. He couldn't taste anything and swallowed it in two forced bites that caught in his throat. This man's daughter couldn't be Winter. The timing was all wrong. Winter lived in East London, not West. And the letters were still arriving. Unless she wasn't posting them, or had sent them a long time ago.

What if she had found her great love in the guise of some awful man who had taken her to live in Shepherd's Bush and destroyed everything? Would he ever be able to find out? He finished his tea and carried his tray back to the counter. The man smiled as he took it from him.

'You can see her on the wall as you leave, our Moll. I give her a wave every day when I lock the shop door. That photo was taken the day she left for London. In my heart, I think of it as the day she died.'

On his way out, William paused in front of a lavender-coloured wooden photo frame that held a black-and-white photo of the man's daughter. It was hard to tell what colour her hair was – maybe light brown, maybe red – but her skin was powder white, with dark lines smudged around her eyes. Standing to the side of the frame, with a giant rucksack on her back that shaped her like a snail, she wore an army jacket over a black frilly skirt and above tartan tights and army boots. The camera froze the moment in time: she had an enormous grin across her face and a pillow tucked under her arm. William gave her a self-conscious little wave before jingling the bell over the door as he exited into another downpour.

He wrestled his satchel into a better position on his shoulders and began walking towards the city centre. He didn't care if he was soaked to the skin, if he got lost, or even if he never found his way back to the hostel. With no regard for avoiding puddles or pedestrians, he ploughed onwards, past pubs welcoming damp Dubliners in for warming pints, and parents running with strollers, groceries hanging from the handlebars. Hordes of supporters were pushing through the gates of the rugby grounds, and William enjoyed being tousled along by the groups of lads, the excuse it gave him to push a little and be a bit rougher than he needed to. He stood on a bridge and wondered if the river below was a tributary that flowed into the Liffey. He assumed it must be. The raindrops exploded on the surface as the water raced along, and William wondered how deep it was, if anyone ever swam there in summer. He watched a red scarf being dragged by the current, until it became tangled in some reeds. A swan pecked at it and swam away in disappointment.

He marched onwards, resigned to the squelching discomfort of his soaked socks squeaking inside his shoes, and crossed the intersection to Wexford Street. He recognized it as the road that would take him back to the hostel. Stopping outside the window of Whelan's, he watched a group of musicians setting up in the corner for a session. The fire was glowing and the people already dotted around the bar looked happy to have escaped another rainy day in Dublin. It was tempting to join them, but he dragged himself away from the honey pot and strode on. There was only one destination left on his itinerary, before he subjected himself to a night of scratchy sheets and the constant fear of an intruder. He couldn't shake the feeling that Winter and the bakers' daughter may be one and the same. The thought made him feel a sense of despair that his limited acquaintance with Winter should not produce. His spirits were low, but he wasn't quite ready to give up on his ghost yet. He had always thought the Long Hall held the best chance he had of finding information that would lead him to Winter. For better or worse, he was pinning his last hopes there.

The Long Hall had emerged from Victorian Ireland with all the paraphernalia of the era still intact. The deep oak panelling, velvet upholstery, chandeliers and brass fixtures proudly held their place as modern times swept past the heavy red wooden door. The ruby walls and tapestry carpets whispered secrets as clocks from times gone by tick-tocked down the hours to last orders. When William arrived, a gentle hush hung in the air and there were just a few customers propped against the bar, waiting for pints of Guinness to settle. William mooched towards the last stool and hung his drenched coat on the brass hook underneath the bar. As he walked past the gallery of photographs hanging on the wall, he scanned the captions for Winter's name and the faces for anything he might recognize, but to no avail. The *Irish Times* was open on the polished bar, with a half-completed crossword facing upwards, a pen resting on top, as if it had been patiently waiting for him. He leaned over to read the unsolved clues as the barman wandered over.

'Help yourself. I've done all the ones I know. What can I get you?'

William felt compelled to order Guinness, although he wondered how it would mix with the Irish coffee, peppermint tea, vegetable soup and eclair he had already consumed that day. He spread the newspaper out before him and scanned the headlines without really absorbing any of the content. He didn't recognize many of the faces that were famous here. He struggled with the heavy black drink; it was too much for him, and he sipped from just below the creamy head. The barman saw him grimace and folded his arms across the bar in front of him.

'Will I put a drop of blackcurrant in that for ya? It sweetens it up a little and helps you get it down.'

William slid the glass back across the counter and the barman added a splash of dark purple cordial from a decanter under the bar.

'You here on business or pleasure?'

'Well, sort of a mixture of both. I just came to do some research for' – he sighed – 'for something I'm working on.'

'A book, is it? We get plenty of writers in here. Tucked away in corners scribbling in their notebooks, cursing reviews in the paper.'

'Not exactly, but I can see what attracts them. It's a great little pub. How long has it been here?'

'Since before the turn of the century,' he said, polishing wine glasses with a tea towel adorned with a map of Ireland. 'Wouldn't say it's changed much, either. It'll be heaving in a few hours but, I have to say, it's one of the few pubs in Dublin where, even when it's bursting at the seams, you can still have a conversation. People appreciate that, I think, not to be screaming at each other over blasting music or being blinded by lights. It's always fairly civilized in here, compared to some of the places I've worked.'

William glanced around the room, his eyes lingering once again on the framed photographs.

'A friend of mine recommended it to me,' he said. 'She used to come here a lot before she moved to London.'

'Aye, we get a lot of regulars all right. Same faces every week.'

'Do you ever remember meeting a girl called Winter?'

'Winter?' He slapped the tea towel over his shoulder. 'What sort of a name is that? I've met a Summer, and a Spring, too, but never anyone called Winter. That's a bit depressing, isn't it? There was a girl in my class in school called Nollaig, mind you, which is "Christmas" in Irish, but that's different. Winter? Her folks might as well have called her Rain or Cloudy.' He chuckled at the thought.

'So, it doesn't ring any bells?' William asked, without much hope.

'No, but I've only been here since I moved up to start college in September. You'd want to ask the boss man. He's been here since he was my age, and that wasn't today nor yesterday. He'll be in at some point later on. You'll know him when you see him. Six foot seven and bald head shiny as a new penny.'

William moved from the bar to one of a nest of round tables at the rear and waited for the landlord to make an appearance. He examined the glass in front of him and doubted a pint had ever lasted so long in this establishment before, but he was content to let the warmth of the bar dry out his clothes and to give his bones a chance to settle.

At the stroke of six, as if the school bell had been struck, the neighbouring businesses released workers into the streets, and it seemed many of them proceeded directly to the sanctuary of the Long Hall. Pints lined up on the grille behind the bar at various stages of completion, and the barmen performed a beautiful choreography as they danced past each other, switching between tasks with the efficiency and grace of men who loved their job and took pride in doing it well. Coats were abandoned on hooks and stands to dry off, ties were loosened or stuffed into pockets. One woman shook down her hair from a tight bun into waves of golden blonde that shimmered in the light from the chandelier. William wondered if she was standing there deliberately because it cast her in such favourable light. He envied the patrons the ease with which they immersed themselves in the atmosphere of a Saturday evening on the town; pined for the nights he, too, had spent with little to care about other than not missing the last Tube home. Who knew, though, what sadness lay in the hearts of these people? What strife awaited them at home, what darkness weighed down their shoulders. From where he sat, however, all he saw was merriment and the easy company of comrades celebrating their survival of another week. He tried to seem relaxed himself and not to start at every swing of the door, like a man waiting on his blind date to appear. Whiskey after whiskey was his short-term solution.

William looked around him and wondered how he'd

ended up sitting on his own in a pub in Dublin city with no idea where his wife was or what she was doing.

'Do you mind if we jump in here? Are these free?'

Two young women stood over him, laden with two umbrellas, a Dunnes Stores plastic bag of groceries and what looked like several coats, hats and scarves.

'No, that's fine. I'm by myself,' he answered. William stood up as they squashed all their belongings into the tiny space under the table.

'Thanks a million,' one of the new arrivals answered. 'This is actually our table, you see; we sit here every week. Normally, we try to get here early to snatch it up, or else we just hover menacingly until whoever is sitting here gets the hint.' She laughed. 'So, what's your name? I'm Winter and this is Ailbhe.'

William spat a mouthful of Jameson on to the table, narrowly missing the sleeve of one of the pair.

'I'm sorry, what did you say your name was?'

'Indra. Although it doesn't normally get quite that reaction. What did you think I said?'

'Sorry, I just misheard you. It's been a long day.'

Ailbhe, who was swathed in multiple layers of wool, rolled down the polo-neck of her black-and-white houndstooth dress and pulled her polished black bob out to perch atop. She seemed not to be wearing any make-up, but her complexion was pure peach. Her eyes were a very dark blue, and she looked at William in a knowing way that unnerved him. When she eventually spoke, her voice had a husky Northern Irish lilt that William thought she could surely make a career from.

'So, what brings an Englishman to a Dublin pub on his lonesome on a Saturday night?'

'Well, I've been in town all day, and I thought it might be nice to stop off for a drink before I head back to the hotel. I wasn't expecting it to be quite so busy, though.'

Indra looked the exact opposite to her companion. She had platinum-blonde hair cropped close to her head, a slinky black dress barely covering her toned, tanned body and a lot of make-up: dark green around her brown eyes, something pink and sticky on her lips.

William chose his words carefully; he could hear a slight slur creeping in.

'How do you two know each other? Been friends for long?'

Indra laughed. 'You could say that. She's my big sister.'

'Really?' William looked back and forth from one to the other. 'You look so different!'

'Meaning she's gorgeous and I'm not,' Ailbhe sighed, rolling her eyes.

'No, not at all, that's not what I meant.'

'So you *don't* think I'm gorgeous?' Indra shot back.

William scratched at his beard.

'That's not what I meant. You don't even have the same accent.'

'Well, we didn't grow up in the same part of the country. You see, our father –' Indra began, but Ailbhe cut her off.

'Indie, there's no need to go into all that, okay? He doesn't want to hear our life story. And I definitely don't want to tell it. Again.'

William stood up. 'I'm sorry, it's really none of my business,' he said. 'Can I buy you both a drink? Then I won't feel so bad about you keeping me company.'

Indra clapped her hands.

'That's a marvellous idea. What's your name?'

He told her, and she held out her hand to shake his; on each finger twinkled a different silver ring.

'Fabulous, William. I can tell we are going to be great friends altogether.'

William yelped as a sharp kick found his shinbone. Ailbhe reddened a little.

'Sorry, my foot slipped.'

'That was quite the delivery for a slippery foot.'

'It was meant for Indy. I'm sorry, it's just we have some things to discuss, and we weren't really looking for company.'

'You do realize that you came to join me, and not the other way around?'

'Well, we thought you might be leaving soon and didn't expect you to join us, really. Sorry, I didn't mean to be rude. No offence.'

'Ailbhe, stop it! Please don't mind her. She's a stroppy cow when she wants to be. We'd love to have a drink with you. One vodka and white, and one white-wine spritzer, please. With lemonade, not soda.'

'Tell you what, I'll get you the drinks and then find somewhere to wedge myself at the bar out of your way. Best of both worlds, eh?'

He edged away from the table and started squeezing his way to the service area, ignoring Indra's protests and

Ailbhe's sulky silence. In the mirror of the bar, he saw Ailbhe watching him from under her fringe while Indra berated her, gesticulating madly with her hands. What an odd girl. He didn't particularly want to spend the evening being prodded and poked by these two. It definitely wouldn't help him accomplish his mission. He caught the eye of his new best friend, the barman, and ordered their drinks, with another shot of whiskey for himself. He squeezed on to a bar stool in the corner that had become a coat depository and beckoned to Indra to come and collect their drinks so he wouldn't lose his spot. She teetered over in pink wedge sandals.

'Why don't you come back over and join us, eh? Ailbhe doesn't mind, not really. She was just worried she wouldn't get a chance to give me a lecture about college if we had company.'

'No, that's okay, I'm not really in the mood for conversation much myself. You two have a good night.'

As he pushed his stool back away from the bar so he could pass her the drinks, Indra put her hand on his forearm.

'You've very sad eyes, do you know that? They are ruining your whole look. I bet that you're quite handsome when you're happy. Maybe we can cheer you up.'

He jerked away, spilling some of the white-wine spritzer in his haste. 'I don't think so,' he answered, as he tried to steady himself. 'But thank you. Maybe see you later.'

Indra shrugged her shoulders and went back to Ailbhe, who was staring intently at the floor. There was a time, long before Clare, when William would have found it irresistible to try to solve the puzzle of girls like that, but not these days. He swirled the whiskey around in his tumbler and tried to zone out of the conversations swirling around him. His ear couldn't resist tuning into the odd phrase here or there, though. Little exchanges caught his attention, as if he were spinning through different frequencies on the radio dial:

'He clearly fancies you. Just admit it.'

'But darling, he's my fitness instructor. He has to be friendly to me, that's his job, to be friendly. I'm sure he's the same with everyone.'

'He's never put his arm around me – not once – and I'm pretty sure I've never seen him do it to anyone else, either, for that matter . . .'

'I just feel like she's deliberately excluding me. I mean, it was my idea to include the snow globe, and then she didn't even invite me when they went to pick it out. Now, she'll get all the credit again, but I suppose that's what she wants, really, isn't it . . .'

'He keeps spouting Latin at everyone, and it could be entirely made up, for all anyone else knows, but it's not like you can challenge him on it. The only Latin I know was our school motto, *Fortiter et suaviter* or something, but I'm not sure how you pronounce it, even if there was an opportunity for me to roll out "Strength and gentleness" in conversation . . .'

'I heard the funniest joke ever today: what do you call a cat with no tail?'

'A Manx cat.'

William was growing more and more inebriated. He hadn't eaten any dinner to line his stomach and fortify him for the quick succession of drinks he was consuming. With no sign yet of the landlord, he questioned what he was still hoping for. That a group of people would just start talking about Winter within earshot and he could casually join the conversation? He lost his balance when he tried to stand up from his stool, and the room swirled as he stumbled on the way to the bathroom. The fluorescent light in the small, wood-panelled room dazzled him at first, but he pressed his forehead against the cold tiles around the mirror and found a little relief. He gripped the sink, closed his eyes and breathed deeply, despite the heady mix of disinfectant, men's cologne and something damp and moist that permeated from the walls. He sat on the steel-blue pipes that bordered the perimeter of the room, holding his throbbing head in his hands. Every so often, someone stepped over him to go to the cubicle, but he managed to mumble that he was fine convincingly enough not to raise alarm. The din from the lounge sounded far away, and he wasn't quite sure how long he had been resting there when a tall, imposing figure who looked alarmingly like a professional wrestler nudged him with a steel-toe-capped boot.

'Everything all right in here? You're the last one.'

William scrambled to stand up. The room had stopped spinning, but his head was pounding.

'Gosh, I'm sorry. I must have dozed off. One too many, I think. I'm a bit of a lightweight these days.'

The man shrugged and picked up the bin, which was overflowing with paper towels, and let the door close behind him, leaving William to pull himself together. He splashed cold water on to his face and rinsed the fuzzy feeling from his mouth. That must be the landlord, but William knew he hadn't made the best first impression. It suddenly struck him that he had no coat, no bag. What if someone had stolen his satchel with his passport and wallet inside it? He would be stranded in Dublin. He rushed out of the bathroom, back to where he had been sitting, but all the stools were upside down on the bar and a cleaning lady was hoovering the carpet.

'Don't worry. I have your things behind the bar for you.' His barman friend from earlier walked past him with a tray of empty glasses. 'I thought you'd left without them. What happened to you?'

'I'm ashamed to say I fell asleep on the floor of the bathroom. Your boss woke me up.'

The barman laughed, shaking his head. 'I'm surprised he didn't throw you out,' he said, 'You're not in Temple Bar, you know.'

'It's very out of character, I can assure you. Is he still around? I was hoping for a word.'

'He's in the cellar, but he'll be back in a minute . . . Good luck. He's not the most pleasant at the best of times. Most of the time, I just try to keep out of –'

A clearing of the throat interrupted them.

'Who, may I ask, is not the most pleasant, Mr Fitzpatrick?'

The landlord stood before them, his arms crossed in

front of his black leather waistcoat and skin-tight white T-shirt.

'Oh, no one, boss. We're just talking about some eejit from the telly. This chap here was looking for a word. I'll be in the cellars if you need me.'

The landlord didn't look at William as he spritzed the bar top with furniture polish and wiped it down with a wet cloth.

'So, Sleeping Beauty, what can I do for you? We're officially closed, you know.'

William followed him as he worked. 'I was just wondering if you might know a friend of mine, a girl called Winter?' he asked. 'She used to drink here all the time. Long red hair? She told me to say hello.'

He gave a little snort. 'I find that hard to believe. I don't really socialize with my customers. And I never met nobody called Winter.'

William tapped him on the shoulder. 'Maybe it was a nickname. You sure you never heard it before?'

The landlord turned to William and looked him straight in the eye.

'Positive. Now, if you're done, the door's that way.'

William struggled back into his coat, grappled to open the solid oak door. He made two unsuccessful attempts before stepping out into his third rain torrent of the day. It was strangely refreshing after his hot and sticky collapse on the floor of the bathroom. He ran to a bus shelter to try to get his bearings and come to terms with this latest blow. He stood before a map of the city centre, tracing his finger along the path he believed would take him back to the unwelcoming stench of his hostel. Out of the dark night, a soft voice spoke to him.

'Are you lost, William?'

Ailbhe sat on the bus stop bench, reading a book by the light of a torch no bigger than a pen.

'Ailbhe! Hello, well, no, not really. I was just confirming my route. Where's your sister?'

'Oh, she got a better offer. I was just letting the shower pass before I walk home. Usual story with Indie, I'm afraid. I'm sure you would rather find her sitting here.'

He sat down beside her on the bench.

'Not even a little bit — honestly. I find your sister quite scary, and she told me I looked sad, which is actually the sort of thing that, if you weren't depressed beforehand, would certainly bring on a bout.'

Ailbhe smirked at him.

'Oh, don't worry. She says that to all the boys, even the jolly ones.' She paused. 'In fact, especially the jolly ones. She has this theory that, deep down, all men are sad about something and are looking for a girl to make them feel better, so she pretends to sense it inside them and uses it to reel them in. It's very effective, actually, if horribly manipulative. When we were living in London, it seemed to work even better for her with the English boys. All those repressed feelings.'

'Crikey. Such cynicism in one so young!' said William. 'And here I was, worried that I looked a complete pitiable wreck when I thought I was putting on such a convincing brave face.'

'Oh, no, don't get me wrong: you look completely

broken by life. It's just she would have said that to you, regardless.'

Ailbhe turned her attention back to the book she was reading, as if to end the conversation.

'Is that it? We're done here?'

'Why? Is there more?'

'Well, you perform such a casual assessment of my person and then just opt out of the conversation. That doesn't seem very fair.'

'I didn't mean to offend you. Anyway, you started it, looking for sympathy because Indie called you out. Looks like the rain is easing off now. I might make a run for it.'

William was suddenly a little panicked by the thought of confronting the failure of his Dublin expedition by himself, even if the alternative was this spiky lady.

'Wait, how about a bag of chips to warm us up? Loads of salt and vinegar? You can eat them walking home.'

'You're not walking me home. You could be a serial killer, for all I know, though I do admit I'm not feeling hugely threatened.'

He experienced the odd sensation of being slightly offended that she didn't think he had the makings of a serial killer in him but decided against insisting that he would be able to murder her if he wanted to.

'That's fine. I'm not suggesting anything untoward, just some chips. I really feel partial to a bag but have no idea where to find some and thought you might accompany me in the right direction.'

'You're standing across the street from a chip shop, William.'

She lost her icy aloofness for a moment, unable to resist a little laugh at his expense.

'Marvellous. Let's go. You can tell me about your time in London.'

They dashed across the street through the slow-moving traffic and joined the noisy queue of post-pub famished masses craving curry chips, onion rings and garlic dip.

'You never told us what you are in town for.'

'Well, I was looking for something – for someone, sort of. But it didn't really work out.'

'A girlfriend?'

'No, I had a chance encounter with someone, of sorts, and I remembered they mentioned the Long Hall so, when I happened to be in town, I thought I would pop in and see if the universe might cut me a break. Silly, really. She doesn't even live in Dublin any more.'

'Unfinished business.'

'Exactly.'

'What's her name? It's a small town – maybe I know her. Maybe I'm your moment of serendipity in Dublin.'

'You won't. I'm starting to wonder if she even exists. Maybe I imagined her, or my wife invented her as . . . Oh my God, could that be it?' William put his hands on her shoulders and gushed, 'What if Clare wrote the letters? What if, all this time, it was her? Trying to tell me things about her? Oh God, what if she knows I'm here? This could be a total disaster.'

'I'm sorry – you're married? What letters? You look like you've seen a ghost.'

William paced up and down alongside the steamed-up glass window of the chip shop and put his thoughts back in order. A man in leather trousers and a white vest threw a chip at him.

'Jaysus, stop fidgetin' man, you're twistin' me melon!'

William ignored him and rejoined Ailbhe in the queue, whispering now.

'No, no, that's crazy. It couldn't be. The details were too specific, and she could never get into my office, and Marjorie had one, and anyway, what would be the point? To test me? No, stop it, no. That's not it, I'm just freaking myself out.'

'Have to say, you're kind of freaking me out, too, at the moment.'

William stood in silence as she ordered two bags of chips, with salt and vinegar on both but extra salt on hers.

'Together or separate?' barked the man behind the counter.

'Separate. Definitely separate,' Ailbhe shot back.

'Do you not want some chips with your salt? You'll end up with really high blood pressure if you keep that up, you know,' said William.

'That's great advice, Dad, and you probably shouldn't have nervous breakdowns in strange cities, either, but hey, at least your cholesterol is okay.'

She handed him his chips and they bumped into each other as they both tried to leave at the same time. William stood back and held the door open for her.

'So, tell me about her – your *unfinished business . . .*'

'Well, her name is Winter . . . and she lived here for quite a while, before –'

'Ooh, how exotic, like the burlesque dancer?'

William stopped in the street and turned to face her.

'What do you mean? What burlesque dancer?'

'Winter! She's fabulous, like a white-witch character. She has this stage persona that's all about magic and casting spells over men so they do her bidding. She really works the Celtic thing – she looks like a model from a *Visit Ireland* catalogue. All red hair and pale skin and these piercing green eyes. I saw her at the Clapton Working Men's Club last summer, and it was frightening how good she was. Nothing tacky or sensationalist, just a proper vintage burlesque routine.'

William dropped his bag of chips and they scattered about his feet.

Ailbhe jumped out of the way and shouted, 'Dear God, what is it this time? What have I said now?'

He once again put one hand on each of her shoulders and locked eyes with her.

'Are you telling me that there is an Irishwoman performing burlesque under the stage name Winter, in Clapton?'

'Well, yes. Why? Do you think that's your girl? If it is, you have no chance, I'm afraid. She is stunning – I mean, terrifyingly beautiful. Way out of your league.'

Her voice was fading away as the reality of the situation sank in. All this time, Winter may really have been sitting – or dancing – on his doorstep. He kissed Ailbhe on the forehead and did a little skip as he set off for his hostel. So many thoughts collided in his head: how Winter had written of a new persona, of how far the feathers would take her, Clare seeing her in a costume. He couldn't quite believe it, but it looked like this god-forsaken trip had yielded some results after all. A burlesque dancer, though? Was it remotely conceivable that a woman like that would be interested in someone like him? He felt so pedestrian. The thing was, though, she *was* searching for someone like him. Her letters told him so. And was her burlesque costume any different, really, from the one Clare wore to court or the one he wore to the depot? Was it strange she hadn't mentioned her performances in her letters? No, he decided. She wanted her great love to understand her interior world; she didn't want him to be seduced by the sequins. He was sure that must happen to her all the time. She was looking for someone different.

When he got back to the hostel, he peeled off all his clothes and sobered up a little under the ice-cold spray of the rickety shower. He climbed into the abrasive sheets, which no longer bothered him, and stared blankly into the darkness while the city citied on outside his window. When dawn broke, he was still lying in the same position, not quite asleep, not quite awake. He now knew where he could probably find Winter, so that's what he would do – wasn't it?

Clare lay on an inflatable mattress dressed in grey pin-striped bedlinen in Flora's living room/kitchen/dining room. To call it open plan would be generous; there was very little open about that space. Fitting the mattress on the floor had involved pushing Flora's two-person pine-wood dining table against the wall and stacking the chairs on top. When Clare reached out to the right, she could touch the teak sideboard that stood against the magnolia wall. To the left, the thin brown carpet gave way to the lime-green linoleum that differentiated the kitchen from the rest of the room. Her hand crossed the border as she traced the diamond pattern on the floor with her finger. Looking around the room in the morning half-light, it struck Clare how much of a stranger her sister was to her now. All these vinyl records; when had Flora started listening to soul music, fallen in love with the blues? Who were all those letters from, bundled together on the windowsill? Somehow, she had managed to splash colour and personality across every available surface that the tired little flat offered. Most of it had been collected on her travels, she'd explained. The row of terracotta pots with the family of succulents she brought home from Crete; the curtains made from woven blankets were from India; the Murano glass bowls had been carefully transported in tissue paper from Venice. A stuffed pheasant perched on the sideboard, its beady eyes watching Clare where she lay.

Over the kitchen table, dozens of photographs and postcards told a thousand tales of her adventures overseas. What did these smiling faces mean to Flora? Were they strangers passing through, or had some of them come to mean more to her? Any one person in particular? For so long, Clare had judged her little sister's roaming to be irresponsible, flighty, feckless. When was she going to settle down? Commit to something? Even when Flora told her she had trained as a doula, Clare wouldn't take her seriously. She realized now that, while she had been berating her sister for the choices she had made, Flora was out in the world, squeezing every spectacular second from life, experiencing so much more than her sensible older sister. At what point had Clare decided that only the lifestyle she chose had any value? Why was it so important to her that others reflected and reinforced her behaviour with their own? As she waited for the city, and her sister, to wake up into a new day, she was pleased to realize that she wasn't jealous, she harboured no resentment. All she felt was a renewed optimism that the world was still out there. And that it wasn't too late to get to know her sister on an equal footing, as adults.

She heard Flora gently creak the door open and pause.

'Don't worry, I'm awake. Come in!'

'Sorry, sis, if I woke you. The night ran much later than I expected. That little baby was in no hurry to meet us, but he got there in the end.'

Clare sat up in her charcoal silk pyjamas and propped herself against the radiator with some pillows.

'I don't know how you do it, Flo. You must be exhausted.'

Flora stretched out on the tattered beige corduroy sofa, her two feet propped on the armrest, twisting her wrists back and forth.

'Oh, it's worth it. They called him Lennon Presley, after John and Elvis.' She smiled. 'That baby has a lot to live up to. When I left them, his dad was cradling him in his arms and singing "Heartbreak Hotel".'

'That's sweet.' Clare yawned and rubbed her sister's arm.

Flora's voice dropped a tone. 'So you don't still think I should train *properly* and become a midwife?' she asked, raising her chin to look out at her sister from under her fringe.

Clare flinched, pulled the duvet up around her knees.

'I'm sorry, Flora. You know I've only ever wanted what was best for you –'

Flora swung her legs around so she sat facing her sister.

'It's okay,' she said. 'Annoying as it can be, I'd rather have someone nagging me than no one caring at all. It was almost like having a proper mum.'

Clare stretched her back like a cat and let the silence sit between them. She stood up, bounced along the mattress to make her way to the kitchen, and put the kettle on. While she waited for it to boil, she rummaged through Flora's fridge, sniffing different containers and tossing some in the rubbish bin. After a moment, Flora spoke again.

'I was thinking about you tonight – you and William.'

Clare closed the fridge door but remained staring at it, nudging a fridge magnet from Reykjavik along the edge with her index finger.

Flora leaned on the back of the sofa, watching her sister. 'I think you'd be great parents, that you'd be a great mum. I wish the whole baby thing –'

'*The baby thing!*' Clare pulled open the one tiny cupboard over the sink, snatched two mismatched mugs and shoved them on the counter-top. 'Please don't, Flora. I always said we couldn't even consider it until we had our lives set up properly – a proper home, his career sorted. And he never got it together so, case closed, as far as I'm concerned.'

Flora stood up, pulled the sheet off the mattress and released the valve to deflate it. The trapped air escaped with a high-pitched whine while Clare slapped two tea-bags into the flip-top bin. Flora folded the mattress into a clumsy square in her arms, speaking again to Clare, but without looking at her.

'Are you sure you're not just using all that as an excuse? You were never keen, even before William.'

'And what if I am?' Clare snapped, as she started gathering her clothes together from where they were draped over the back of a kitchen chair. 'It's still all true, and do you blame me? We didn't exactly have a great role model for mothering, growing up, now, did we? I would rather not have any children than risk turning out like her!' She turned towards the hallway.

Flora pushed past her sister to block the living-room door and stretched her arms across the frame.

'*No!*' she shouted. 'I'm not having it. You're nothing like Mum! You've no reason to think you'd make the same mistakes she did. You looked after me when she couldn't. And she was sick.'

Clare tried to squeeze past her, but Flora wouldn't budge. Clare tried to calm down, shocked how quickly this conversation had turned; her heart raced as if a mouse had suddenly scampered across the floor. She forced her voice to become neutral.

'Stop it! She wasn't sick. She was a drunk, and still is. You and Dad always make excuses for her, but I protected you from so much of it. I have no idea how to be a good mother, because I never had one. The older I get, the more I see her in me, and the harder it is to stay in control.'

She dropped her clothes in a heap on the floor and sat down beside them, holding her head in her hands. She was too tired for this. Any time she felt even a semblance of normality, she was thrown off course again. Flora slid down the wall beside her and put her arm around her.

'I'm sorry for pushing,' she whispered, 'but can I just ask you something? If you could be sure that you wouldn't end up like her, if your relationship was strong, would you want a baby, then? Because it's a hundred per cent fine if you just don't think it's right for you, but if there is even a small part of you that wants it, you need to be very careful about your next move, because it's one of the few choices you make in life that can't be reversed if you leave it too late.'

Clare rested her head on her sister's shoulder. 'That's what William said too.' She sighed. Flora remained silent.

'Okay,' she said eventually. 'If I could wave a magic wand and fix everything, then, yes, maybe I would consider it, but I couldn't do it by myself.'

Flora squeezed her hand. 'You wouldn't be alone,' she said. 'William would be there, I'm sure of it. And me, too.'

She stood up, offered her hand to Flora to pull her up also, and said, 'You have to understand, Flo, that us staying together isn't the only possible happy ending for us. There are no plan Bs now . . . only plan As. Does that make sense?'

'It does,' she answered. 'But I can still root for you, though, right? I think William'll come through.'

'Maybe he will,' Clare said, 'but I've hurt him a lot. You don't know the whole story, Flo.' Flora's head whipped around to look at her sister but Clare ignored her arched eyebrows and continued towards the bathroom. She called back over her shoulder, 'Do you fancy taking a drive? I've been working on something and want to show you the results.'

One shower and two slices of peanut butter on toast each later, Clare drove her sister through Camberwell, Shoreditch and De Beauvoir Town until her Mini rattled to a stop in front of what looked like a derelict building in Dalston. Flora pressed her hands on the glass of the passenger window while she peered out.

'Come on! All will be revealed,' Clare said, as she jumped out of the car and hauled the rusty corrugated gate open.

She punched a code into a security box to release the cast-iron front door and led Flora inside. A long concrete corridor stretched ahead, with burnished black doors to the right and left, and a steel staircase curled upwards at the rear. Flora followed her sister as she ran up the steps two at a time. At the top, she produced from her bag a silver key attached to a ring of turquoise fluff as big as a tennis ball. With it, she opened a white panelled wooden door and swung it wide to allow Flora to enter first into the wide, rectangular room. One wall consisted purely of windows; light flooded the room and clouds of dust danced across the old floorboards under their feet. Bits of threadbare grey carpet still stuck to the perimeter of the room; the previous tenant must have had the vision to tear most of it away to find out what the original floor was. A paint-splattered butcher's block ran down the centre, and a Belfast sink, chipped and cracked, stood in the corner.

'It still has running water,' Clare announced, turning on the taps to demonstrate.

'Wow! What is all this?' Flora was wide-eyed as she walked across the room to look out across East London through the cracked windowpanes.

'It's my new studio!' she said, turning slowly on her heel to survey the room. 'I paid six months upfront and, tomorrow, I'm going to blow a small fortune on a new

easel and every oil paint they have for sale in Ferguson's.
I don't think I've felt so excited in a long time.'

Flora squealed and ran back across the room to throw
her arms around her sister. They spun in a circle, holding hands like they had as children, before collapsing on
the dusty floor, laughing.

'Tell me everything! Does this mean it went well
with your boss yesterday?' Flora asked.

Clare wiped the palms of her hands on her jeans.

'Oh, it was just what I expected,' she answered. 'I'm
just glad it's over. He said I can take the year and they
will hold my job open, but that "leaving at this point in
my career will have a serious impact on my ability to
make partner".'

A wrinkle of worry creased Flora's brow.

'Are you not bothered about that?' she asked. 'You've
worked there for so long. And that ladder was so hard
for you to get on in the first place. You're the first woman
they've even considered for partner, you said it yourself.
That's a big deal!'

It was Clare's turn now to put her arm around her
sister.

'Not as much as it should. I just know that, if I don't
take a break now, I probably never will. And, at this
point, the fear of working for ever at a job I don't love
far outweighs the fear of falling a few steps down the
ladder if I have to go back. I mean, have you seen my
porcelain sink?' She winked at her little sister. 'C'mon.
I'll treat you to lunch at Soup Opera.'

★

As they drove back to Flora's, Clare felt as if the spring sunshine was glowing from within her and spreading out across the city. She knew in her bones that this was the right thing for her to do, but worries about William tailed her like a thundercloud. They stood at a crossroads. A large part of her wanted them to reinvent their lives together; the other worried that they might need space from each other to be able to do that. Either way, she knew she had to forge her own path so that, whether they stayed together or not, in a year from now she could be happy, or at least happier. She knew that she couldn't keep blaming him or their marriage for holding her back. It was on her now, and she wouldn't let herself down, but she hoped she could find a way to save their marriage. And she already had one idea about how she could do it.

Flora was singing along with the Bangles' 'Eternal Flame' on the radio when Clare pulled the Mini over. 'Do you mind if we take a detour past the flat?' she asked. 'I need to pick up a few things.'

'Sure thing,' Flora said, and she smiled at her sister. 'My big sister, the artist. Who'd have thunk it, eh?'

Clare tapped out the beat of the song on the steering wheel. She liked the sound of that.

24.

Discovering Clare's letter, instead of her physical presence, in their home was mostly a relief to William, but he couldn't shake a tinge of disappointment that she had done as he had asked and left him alone. He couldn't, however, deny what a comfort it was to hear that she was staying with Flora and not with that man. It was too soon, he thought, to consider when he might see her again or what he would say when he did. For now, he had to follow through on solving the mystery of Winter, for both their sakes.

William had heard about the Clapton Working Men's Club but had never been himself. Stevie, who had led many a conga line there in his time, had told him it was a giant dress-up box for students, eccentrics, performers, voyeurs and the fabulous to dance, play, perform and mingle with many unlike-minded people. On the top floor, it still existed as a club for working East End men to socialize, play cards and pool, and listen to records on the original gramophone that had been preciously maintained since the club had opened in the sixties. These members had their own entrance, a private stairway to their rooms, which minimized but didn't eliminate entirely the opportunity to converse with lindy hoppers, drag artists and adherents to the current craze Shoreditch inhabitants had for dressing up as Hollywood stars and staying in character all evening. It was exactly the sort of club that Stevie had moved to London for, and his only disappointment came with the realization that, with this crowd, he would never be the most interesting or flamboyant person in the room. He made a valiant effort for a while, experimenting with dressing up in a three-tiered-cake costume, as a fearleader – which William later realized was a dead cheerleader – and trialled numerous creative ideas involving body paint, glitter and carefully positioned feathers. Eventually, however, he grew fatigued and decided it was far more intriguing just to go as himself; it was one of the few places where Stevie, dressed normally, didn't cause a stir. He had invited William along a few times to 'broaden his horizons' and 'set him free', but William had always resisted. He considered asking Stevie to accompany him now. He might even be able to pass it off as a symptom of his general malaise in response to recent events, a need to embrace the world that existed outside the marital home. He was sure Stevie would support him fully, however he wasn't quite ready to admit to anyone, even Stevie, about what he had been up to in Dublin. He decided to investigate quietly by himself to begin with and call for reinforcements later if required.

The number 48 bus dropped William at Clapton Pond, and he patrolled the avenues, looking for the right address. When he finally arrived at the venue, he almost walked past the entrance, it blended so perfectly with the residential houses along the street. A brass plaque adorned a white iron gate at the end of the driveway with the letters C.W.M.C. and an engraving of the happy/sad Greek-theatre masks connected by a snooker cue. He creaked the gate open and continued up a path that wound around the side to the rear. The whole building was much larger than the front exterior implied; the back garden revealed a world of wonder at play. Festoon lighting draped from the roof of the house through the branches of the trees. Oversized swings and hammocks rocked gently in the breeze as they waited impatiently for someone to fill them. A giant chess set sat on the lawn; the queens stood with their backs to each other, wearing lipstick, plastic sunglasses and baseball caps – the bishops, too. A dozen tutus of varying sizes were drying on a washing line; they looked rather disturbing as they danced in the wind, like discombobulated ballerinas. Tables and chairs painted in proud rainbow stripes were scattered around the garden, behind bushes and in nooks and crannies, to accommodate private mischief. The door of a shed painted scarlet was swinging open, and William could see that the interior was red, too: the walls and floors, sofas and chairs. He didn't dare to cross the threshold, but wondered what lay further inside, what activities were enjoyed there after dark. William felt a bolt of envy towards those who came here freely and weren't ashamed to act on their desires; something he struggled to do more and more as time passed.

The back wall of the house was covered in graffiti: giant flowers and kaleidoscopes of colour, peace slogans and dancing zebras. Perhaps there were all sorts of subliminal messages at play that William was innocently absorbing. The windows were covered in starry cloth that prevented him peeking at the interior, but in the centre of the back door sat a frame made of white lights and miniature crystal balls containing the programme of events. It offered the Sailors and Sweethearts Swing Ball, the Camping in the Countryside Sleepover, Hollywood Bingo, Fun and Funky Friday, The Cocky Horror Picture Show, Rock and Roll in the Hay . . . and there, in a cursive silver font, Winter Wonderland: Burlesque Revue. There was a photo of a lady in silhouette lying atop what looked like a giant block of ice with cascades of fiery red hair flowing over the edge. It had to be her.

The heavy black wooden door opened a crack and a head emerged, wearing what looked like the gusset of a pair of tights on top of it and very white powdered make-up. The man's lips were painted red, but so far only one eye had been decorated with elaborate make-up and false lashes; altogether, it gave him the appearance of a very disturbed china doll.

'You're not a journalist, are you? I don't even have all my face on.'

His voice was very deep, with a strong northern accent.

'No, no. I was just checking the listings. The burlesque show sounds interesting. I might come along.'

The character behind the door swung it open to reveal a black fluffy bathrobe with white fishnet stockings peeking out beneath.

'Oh, you definitely should. Those girls are just fabulous,

and they'll move on to other, bigger things soon, I can tell you. I've been the manager here for ten years now and they all move on in the end, but these girls in particular are far too good for this dump. You just can't get the talent, usually, to turn out a decent show. Do you perform yourself?'

For a fleeting second, William considered that this could be the in he needed, but caught himself before he opened up another Pandora's box of ridiculous behaviour on his part.

'No, no. I'll definitely come along to see one of the shows, though.'

'All right, then. Close the gate on your way out. We're keeping a low profile today. Bit of trouble last night.'

'Oh, what sort of trouble?'

He paused for a moment as he surveyed William further, and then the whole story came gushing out as his shoulders collapsed forward.

'Dolly Get-Your-Part On was whizzing around on rollerskates while under the influence and accidentally fell through the curtain while the Von Tramps were performing, and that horrible old queen Dixie Trix pushed her off the stage, and Dolly's wig came off, and the wheels were spinning underneath her while she tried to stand up, and she got madder and madder and pulled at Dixie's skirt for balance, and the two of them ended up rolling around the floor, with hair and lashes flying and pantyhose ripping, and then all the Von Tramps piled in and it became a bit of a free-for-all.'

He took a breath before he continued. 'Some fool in the audience called the police, which was completely unnecessary, as we always resolve these little matters ourselves, but when they arrived we were still serving – after hours – so now I'm in so much trouble you just wouldn't believe it.'

He sat down on the doorstep and held his head in his hands. William awkwardly patted his shoulder and mumbled something reassuring about first offences and extenuating circumstances. The manager patted his hand, nodding his head like a toy bobbing dog.

'Maybe a little sleep would help?' he suggested, as he peeled his hand away. 'I hope you get everything sorted.'

Turning the corner to follow the pathway out, he looked over his shoulder and saw the old dear wiping his eyes with one of the tutus as he collected them from the line. Winter's show was scheduled for the following Thursday, so William knew exactly where he could find her then. He could ask Stevie to come to the show with him, but the prospect of watching her perform made him terribly uncomfortable. Winter hadn't told him about it herself, and to go and see her on stage felt as if he were stealing something from her, something she hadn't chosen to share with him. Maybe he could see her afterwards? Or leave her a note. Or a letter? Yes! A letter was definitely the right way to contact her after all this time. His new friend could pass it on, perhaps.

Back on the 48 bus, William forced himself to consider why the club had affected him so much, why he felt so jealous of a life that could so easily be his. Had Clare been right all along? Had he just convinced himself that he was happy at the depot because he didn't think he deserved another chance to live a more creative life? Maybe he saw Winter as his portal to a second chance. He knew, though, that only he could set himself free. For too long now, he had been a passive observer in his own life. Could Clare ever support him if he tried again to succeed as a writer while she was still trapped in the snares of her job? Did they each need to start again as individuals to have the freedom to let go of their past selves? Maybe Winter had come for him so that could happen. Or maybe her letters would help him find his way home. Whatever the outcome, he knew he was close to the truth.

Two blue Basildon Bond envelopes sat on William's desk, one addressed to Winter, one to Clare. They waited like a pair of starched pillows anticipating a pair of tired heads. He traced his forefinger over one name and whispered it aloud into the deserted office space. *Clare.* How easily his pen had scrawled her name, how practised those letters in that order were by his hand, how effortlessly his pen nib scratched their shape. His fountain pen formed the word 'Winter' more clumsily; he had smudged the crossing of the 't'.

He felt compelled to read both letters again, hoped the words found at midnight were not so soaked in Jameson as to prove incoherent. Beyond the windows, a wet blackness was spilling across the skyline, an inkpot toppled on sheets of pale-grey paper. The office was too dark to award him a reflection; he looked beyond the glass out to a city hushed and shrouded in mystery. The city lights were blurred in silver rain as black cats raised black kittens in alleys more puddle than path.

In this enveloping gloom, it was hard to imagine sunlight could ever sweep this town, illuminate corners, coax it to shimmer. It was even more difficult to think of those two women with only their absence in common. Where was Clare tonight? Was she sitting hunched over a computer at work, pale face, tired from the longest of days, glowing in the electric-green light? Had she kicked off her stilettos and slipped her stockinged feet into the wine wool stockings she hid in her bottom drawer for nights when she worked late alone? Or would she have pulled her hair from its daytime knot, swapped a suit jacket for a leather one, carefully applied scarlet lipstick and absconded to a cellar bar to drink expensive white wine with the men from her office, or with one in particular? The thought made him want to race into the wet night and trawl the streets looking for her. Would she want to be found? He wasn't sure any more. It was less than a week since she had left him in Dublin, but what a difference those days had made.

Where was Winter tonight? Whenever his mind turned to her, splashes of vibrant, energizing colours shot through him: crimson, sunburst, shades of the sea. He imagined a scarlet head bent in laughter over clinking cocktail glasses, saw her huddled under an old-fashioned black umbrella held by another, a long, green scarf dancing behind her in the breeze. He could not summon her face. Sometimes, when he hovered in half-sleep, a flash of apple-green eyes forced him awake. Where did he draw them from? Could you fall in love with scarlet hair, green eyes and words on a page intended for someone who might not be you? Could that be enough? Words rising in a smoke plume that curled down your throat, a searching light exposing cobwebs and evaporating shadows. He extended his forefinger and drew circles in the condensation on the glass, his nail hidden by a blackened bruise. A set of Russian dolls, porcelain dolls, paraded across the windowsill. Marjorie's work, he presumed. He smeared his left hand across the pattern he had made, dried his palm on his corduroy trousers and turned back to the desk. The two letters glowed in the lamplight. He picked up his missive to Winter first.

Dear Winter,

Is that your real name? Since I've started reading your letters, the word has stopped meaning a season to me. Instead, it has become an answer to a question I did not know I had been asking. In my line of work, I endeavour every day to find resolution for undelivered letters, to help them find their homes. This is how your letters found me. In truth, it feels like something much more than a professional inevitability; that letters such as yours would always end up on my desk. It's quite the opposite, in fact. The unlikelihood of each one reaching me is staggering, even with my determined searching every day. For I have come to believe that they were intended for me – only me – and that some divine or magical force guided them to my anxious hands. This, of course, may not have been your intention. You may have hoped for so much more than me. You may have expected nothing at all.

I hope it doesn't alarm you to hear that I have been searching for you. For a number of weeks, I have pieced together the clues you laced through your letters, little lighthouses that have helped me find you. But, now that I have, I cannot imagine walking up to you in the street, mouthing this confession and surviving the shock it would give you.

Instead, I thought I would write these lines, explain where I have come from, introduce myself a little. Perhaps then we could arrange a time to talk, if it doesn't all feel too peculiar for you. I know this is highly unorthodox: I have had months of getting to know you; you have just these few lines. Maybe it will be too strange for you; I can understand if that is so, and will not trouble you again. I shall return your letters, and you can save them for someone else you feel should have been standing at the shore when they washed up in a bottle.

I hope you will choose to meet with me, though. Your letters have joyridden through the streets of my mind, and I long to meet the driver who disturbed my peace. I come with no expectations; I am not in a position to have any, other than a closing of a story that will otherwise haunt me. If you would like to sit with me a while, you can leave me a note at the Dead Letters Depot on Redchurch Street, letting me know where and when, and I will come to you.

John Donne once wrote, 'More than kisses, letters mingle souls.' I believe he spoke the truth.

Yours,

William Woolf

It was difficult for William to judge whether or not his letter hit the right tone. Would it frighten Winter to think that, in order to find her, a stranger had used private details she had innocently shared? His instinct told him no, that she would want him to reach out, that, on some level, Winter had hoped that the letters would lead someone to her. He squashed the lingering doubt that he may have projected more meaning upon this woman than was sensible and carefully folded it over on its original crease. He guided it back into the envelope before reaching for the letter to Clare.

My dear Clare, my wife, my friend, my heart,

I have lost you, and there is a great hole in my life where you should be.

Since I came home alone, I have allowed myself to fantasize that true love is not this difficult, hurtful, destroying; that if we were meant to be together, then none of this would have happened. I have dreamed of starting again with someone else who understands me, where the loving comes easy and I have an unblemished heart to offer. The road back for us seemed too hard; surely it would be easier to go on alone.

But I couldn't make it ring true. Even these terrible months of anguish are better than no you at all, for at least it means our story continues, and continue it must.

I could leave you for ever but you will never leave my heart. We can part, if we choose it, both leave this marriage, broken and bruised, try to build ourselves anew somewhere else. Or we can build our marriage anew together.

We had so many years of happiness before things went wrong. Surely it is naïve to think that nothing testing would ever come our way, that we wouldn't fail at some point. What you did? It makes me feel like you have become a stranger to me. I want to decide instead that it was the deed that was strange and not you – that I am still your husband. For I am.

We can come back from this, my darling Clare.

Please don't give up on us. Let us put the world to rights.

We should be together again.

All my love,

Your William

He lined up Clare's letter beside Winter's. Did he believe what he had written? Or was he fighting for her because he felt he should? Was his heart more deceitful, or his head? Could he really be so sure that Winter was just an escape pod? A fantasist reaction to a horrible reality? Was it just immaturity that made him believe in Winter? Or was it immature to think his love with Clare was valid only if it endured?

He flicked the desk lamp off and moved through the sleeping office with just the spill from the corridor light to guide him. As he passed Ned's desk, he paused to run his fingers over the final draft of the *Volume of Lost Letters* that awaited him there. One hundred and eleven pages. Forty-one letters, and the stories that accompanied them. To think, in a matter of months, the Supernatural Division would be immortalized for ever in hardback books. The name gave him pause: was it quite right? He ignored the niggling doubt. Just two hundred copies, initially, to be distributed to libraries across the country, but it was a start. He longed to show Clare, but had waited to show her the finished product, had planned to wrap it and present it to her as a fait accompli. He hoped he would still get the chance.

He couldn't resist taking a detour past the fourth floor, teasing himself with the sight of three new sacks awaiting his attention. He was tired, too tired to think of tackling one now. He knew that, if he started, he would feel compelled to empty them all. He turned out the light and left the room in darkness. On the landing, he paused as prescient instinct tingled; the idea that a letter from Winter could be lying there waiting for him was more than he could bear. His antennae were erect, his gut urging him onwards.

The contents of the first bag spilled across the floor. William raked through impatiently, allowing the envelopes to sieve through his fingers like flour. Nothing. He hastily shuffled them together and poured them back into the mouth of the mail sack. How his attitude towards these little mysteries had changed. No delicate hands now, or slow, respectful movements. All tenderness lay in reserve for just one type of letter. And there it was, buried deep down in the second batch. Brazen and shocking in its sudden appearance, as if he had summoned it out of sheer will. Goosebumps marched a slow beat down his spine. How had he known there would be one? Hadn't he wished and willed for one before, with no results? William felt a quiver run through him as he picked it up.

He slid his back down the pale-mint wall and leaned uncomfortably against the rickety cast-iron radiator. He could feel the cold metal hugging him through his clothes but did not wriggle away from it. He just wanted to read what she had written.

My Great Love,

Should I be posting this to you or handing it to you? Now that I've found you. Now that I must believe you have found me. These last few months have been a miracle. My mother said I was just the type to be swept away in a whirlwind romance. How that galled me. As if my fondness for you was born of nothing more than a romantic predisposition or lack of independent thought. When I think of all the secrets we have shared, the unravelling of old lives, the threading together of a new one, it feels like there is no good reason to wait. The only cloud that lingers around me is these letters. Why haven't I told you about them? Isn't it silly to think if you were he – the love – you would have found them somehow? Of course it is. Of course it is.

So why do I feel confused, writing this letter? I feel as if I am writing to a wish of a man and hoping the real man grants it. Is this one last chance for the universe to allow me to marry the wish and the reality both? Before I marry you, or him? Oh, how I hope it is you. I am in a muddle. On the last Saturday of April, I will don a white dress and my father will walk me down the little aisle of the chapel in Hoxton Square. I hope the right man will be waiting for me there. I have waited so very long for you.

Winter

The information slapped William like waves on a sailboat. Winter was getting married. Tomorrow. To someone else. And he knew where to find her. Was she hoping he would? Or was she just a nervous bride, full of anxiety as her wedding day drew closer? Imagine the shock she would get if he did try to intercept her at the chapel.

The Dead Letters Depot shrank around his shoulders. The walls and ceiling and floor inched closer until he was afraid to open his eyes, lest the room had become a cell with no windows, no doors. William scraped his back up the wall and stood. He returned, at a funereal pace, to the front door of his flat. The light was glowing from the hallway, even though he was sure it was off when he left that morning. He pushed the door open, and knew Clare had been and gone. The scent of cinnamon lingered in the air, but the rooms were too quiet for her to still be there. The flat sounded different when Clare was home, even when she was completely silent. He walked into the kitchen and saw a crisp white envelope sitting on the table; his name, written in Clare's handwriting, on the front. He turned it nervously over and back in his hands, unsure what to hope for inside.

Still standing, wearing his coat, scarf and gloves, his woolly fingers clumsily prised it open. He had to shake the contents free, and a folded sheet of dove-grey paper floated to the floor. William tore off his gloves and knelt down to rescue it from beneath the table. He stayed sitting there as he read it.

William,

I am more sorry than you can ever know. Please don't let all that we shared be reduced to that one awful happening. I don't know if we have moved too far away from each other to find our way back. Maybe we have grown into versions of ourselves that can't connect in the way we once did, but the memory of those two people gives me hope. Do you remember how it used to be? Do you believe our love can endure and heal the rift that has separated us? Before you decide, I've left you something in the living room that I made for us. Open your heart, William, and let me back in.

All my love,

Clare

William swallowed hard as he moved to the living room and cautiously swung the door open. A white sheet was draped over the window; his old super-8 projector resting on a pile of poetry books, e e cummings on top. He flicked the switch to let the film play, and the picture crackled into life. He knelt behind the projector as Clare's face glowed on the screen. It was their wedding day: scenes from the ceremony, the reception, the dancing, all edited together. It cut to William on a boat on their honeymoon in Sorrento; they were searching for the local resident dolphin and he was gesturing madly at Clare to where it swam behind her. She swung around too late to catch him and the camera wobbled as she lost her balance. To the Isle of Man, where Clare blew him a kiss from the back of a motorbike as she spun past along the cliff road. Next, William waved a bottle of cheap champagne at her as he climbed the rocky road to Edinburgh Castle, weighed down by a backpack and too many layers of clothes. The film cut to Clare and William dancing on a bandstand in Kent; he remembered Flora had filmed them when they went to a Carpenter family wedding. Memory after memory flashed before him. The final scene was Clare making snow angels outside his college bedsit on the night of their first date. The picture crackled and the screen turned to white.

William slumped on to his side on the carpet. A draught from the chimney danced a lock of hair across his forehead, but he did not brush it away. The sky was lightening before he finally creaked up to sitting. He spread four letters on the floor in front of him: two written to him, two written by him. Was what had gone before with Clare enough to see them through? Would he ever forgive himself if he let Winter go? He felt torn in two, with only blind instinct to guide him.

26.

William abandoned the idea of sleep and climbed out of bed still wearing his clothes from the night before. He pulled the curtains wide and stood in the flood of weak dawn light. He stripped the bed of all its linen and bundled it into the washing basket with the other clothes that had been discarded haphazardly throughout the room. He stretched fresh sheets across the bed and made it perfectly, collected the half-empty water glasses and coffee cups from the bedside locker and swept the floorboards with more enthusiasm than he had ever shown them before. Even under the rug. The bathroom was next; he scrubbed the tiles, polished the taps, tossed the hard, gnarled soap that rested on a ceramic dish shaped like a fish. He mopped the floor until it gleamed, slipping on the wet surface in his haste to move on. His cleaning frenzy carried through the living room, the kitchen and hallway; it shocked him to see how filthy the flat had become while he had been distracted by his calamitous affairs of the heart. He folded the sheet that had been hanging over the window in the living room and placed it on top of the projector; tidied both away in the upstairs cupboard. The film Clare had made rested on top. He reached out to touch it again before he returned downstairs to vacuum, dust and polish. He angled the sweeping brush upwards to disturb each of the cobwebs that had gathered in the ceiling corners of the kitchen. There would no longer be any evidence of heartache in this flat. It was time for a new beginning.

The final cleansing was of his own body; he stood beneath the shower spray and washed any last remnants of indecision away. He felt focused. Clear and confident. After today, there would be no unfinished business. William left the bathroom spotless, as if it had not been used, and returned to the bedroom to dress. He paused in front of his wardrobe while considering what would be appropriate to wear that day, idly flicked through the shirts that hung there, rifled through the pullovers and T-shirts on the shelf, before it came to him. He wrestled free a hanger that housed in plastic the plum velvet blazer from his wedding day and laid it on the bed. Nothing else would do. He dressed in black trousers, a white shirt, then eased himself into the blazer. It felt a little tight across his shoulders, but the buttons still closed. He looked at himself in the mirror as he smoothed the velvet on his lapels – how much had changed since the first time he wore it. How much he had changed.

William's socks grew damp inside his leather brogues as he stood in the park; the grass was doused in morning dew and long enough to creep inside the hem of his suit legs. Small mounds of freshly cut blades were scattered behind him, their fragrance drenching the air, but the perimeter remained wild and unmown. With both hands, he gripped the black iron railings that encircled the park, his knuckles white with the cold, blue veins transparent. Across the street, people peacocked in their wedding attire, adjusting their posture in new shoes, fingers fidgeting at hats with feathers. Spring flowers spilled from weather-beaten crates, ceramic pots, hanging baskets; ropes of daisies entwined the church gates; an archway of yellow roses bordered the door. Columbia Road Flower Market decamped to Hoxton Square, William thought, with a small smile of acknowledgement. A swing-band trio – double bass, saxophone and guitar – in turquoise linen suits performed acoustically in the churchyard. They followed guests in serenade as they passed by, encouraging them to sing along. It was a spirited ensemble, and their enthusiasm was contagious; William caught laughter on the breeze and watched folk clutch each other for photographs and scan the new arrivals for familiar faces. He recognized the manager from the Clapton

Working Men's Club walking up the path in a pristine double-breasted burgundy suit and pulled back into the shadow, lest he himself be seen.

William clenched and released his toes inside his shoes. A Volkswagen campervan spluttered to a stop in a cloud of black smoke, the horn beeping wildly as white balloons tied to blue ribbons strained to take flight from where they were tied to the door handles and rear-view mirrors. A cluster of guests in the porch cheered and applauded before the van struggled away, leaving a tall, slim man with a mop of golden curls posing shyly for photographs in its wake. This must be the groom. He wore a midnight-blue suit. As he turned to greet the arrival of a black taxi, William saw his silver silk tie fluttering in the breeze and felt as if it were tightening around his throat. Had Winter chosen that suit for him? It must be so.

The groom opened the passenger door of the taxi; the lady who emerged took William's breath away in a cloud of confusion. Were the gods playing a cruel joke on him? A fragile woman engulfed in a sea of moss-green chiffon, a long, red braid snaking down her spine, placed her hands on the groom's shoulders and leaned forward to whisper something to him. William watched him blush and pull her close into an embrace. His memory searched for her name before he called it to mind in a moment of clarity. Could that truly be Alice-Ann? His photographer friend from Clovelly? What a sonic boom to the soul! Haphazard realization buzzed inside him: was she the grandmother Winter had spoken of who had pursued her passions and inspired her so? Could he have solved this mystery all those weeks ago if he had trusted his instinct to tell Alice-Ann his story? He started coughing as a teenage boy, awkward in an old man's tuxedo, stood at the doorway and beckoned everyone inside.

'The bride is coming!' he heard him call to the stragglers.

William craned his neck to watch for a car turning into the square, knowing that at any moment it would appear. He counted slowly backwards from one hundred, looking from his feet to the corner of the street and back again. As the fifties petered out, a white Beetle spluttered into sight and slowly chugged to a halt outside the chapel. His discomfort mounted. Had he invaded someone else's dream uninvited? Gatecrashed reality while hunting a ghost? The satellite he had orbited from afar was drawing ever closer; the earth tilted beneath his feet and left him spinning. He could see wispy clouds of white and a flash of scarlet blur through the window as the wedding car slowed to a stand. He saw the bride look to the left; one hand paused as it reached to smooth a stray red curl behind her ear. William touched his beard, held his breath.

Their eyes met.

The usher opened the car door and a white lace glove reached out to him. He steadied the bride as she climbed out and smoothed the skirt of her gown. It was an old-fashioned dress, knee length, full skirt of lace, long sleeves, a silk bow at the nape of her neck. The scarlet hair he had long imagined erupted from a boxy hat with a white lace veil. On her feet, sparkling white cowboy boots. An elderly man, resplendent in top hat and tails, climbed from the car and walked slowly but with great presence towards her to take her arm. William watched the man he was sure must be Winter's father hand her a bouquet of yellow daffodils; she reached her hand to touch his face and he kissed her on the cheek. As Winter took his arm, she turned her gaze towards William.

Their eyes met.

William jolted at the flicker of recognition that passed between them. Alice-Ann approached Winter and a photographer ran from the chapel yard to capture the bridal party in the moment of arrival. Winter's face froze into a perfect smile as she looked directly into the lens, before linking her grandmother to the right, her father to the left, and crunching up the gravel pathway to the chapel door. William moved along the railing, feeling for the gate without ever looking away from her. The Beetle backfired as it spluttered away. Winter jumped and whipped her head back towards the noise.

Their eyes met.

William walked to the kerb and paused as a stream of traffic whizzed past him. He stepped backwards towards the railing once again. At the church door, Alice-Ann's fingers fluttered over the bride's dress as Winter adjusted her veil. She paused, turned, before lowering it. The traffic cleared and, with it, the congestion blocking the avenues of William's mind dissipated.

Their eyes met.

He was lost and found.

One Year and One Day Later

Clare lay on a battered dusty-pink velvet love seat in her studio. Kate Bush played on the record player behind her; it looked as if the cherry blossoms on the tree outside her window were swishing in time with the music. The radiator cranked and groaned as it tried to warm the cold, exposed brick walls that surrounded her. She pulled the patchwork quilt she had finally finished the weekend before around her shoulders and smiled in contentment. She loved how the fabrics felt as she ruffled them with her fingers; she was surrounded by memories.

Clare looked up at the sounds of footsteps on the stairs and glanced at her easel; a sheet covered the painting. Good. She wasn't ready to show him yet. Her swollen belly strained against the paint-splattered fabric of her smock as she turned. She squirmed back into a more comfortable position and rested the book she was reading on top of the bump with the cover facing her. She was tickled by how well it balanced there: *The Lost Letters of William Woolf*. Resting her head on the cushion behind her, she closed her eyes and listened to the footsteps drawing closer. As the door to her studio creaked open, she turned.

Their eyes met.

Acknowledgements

First and foremost, I would like to thank my literary agent, Peter Straus, for taking a leap of faith on both this novel and the writer within me. I am eternally grateful to him and the entire team at Rogers, Coleridge and White for their endless support and dedication.

Thank you also to:

- My superhuman UK editor, Jessica Leeke, at Penguin, who guided me so mindfully through my first editing experience.
- The indefatigable Jillian Taylor, and her amazing comrades at Penguin for the boundless energy they devoted to bringing this manuscript to life.
- My agent in America, Kim Witherspoon, of Inkwell Management, for introducing this book to a whole new world across the pond.
- Margo Lipschultz, Melanie Fried and my magnificent publishing team at Graydon House in America for their insights, support and enthusiasm.
- Michèle Roberts, an inspirational writer and my mentor, who gave me permission to think of myself as a writer for the first time and encouraged me to just keep going.

- The fellow writers in my writing workshop for their encouragement and feedback; Natalie, Francis, Deb, David, David and in particular, Marc Lee, for his reading of early drafts and ongoing belief in the work.
- My parents, Frank and Margaret Cullen. All they ever want for their children is their happiness; unconditional love such as this is a tremendous gift.
- My late grandmother Julia for passing down bravery in the blood, and to my siblings, Patricia, Ger, Frank, Mary and Lynda and the extended Cullen clan.
- Hans, Gaby and the Wieland family of Cliffoney, Co. Sligo, where the mountains meet the sea, and many of these words were written.
- Karen Connell, who has believed in all my mad schemes since we first met at school, not least of all, that I would one day write this book. I would be lost without her.
- To all of my incredible friends who have taken such joy in watching this book come into being. I love and appreciate you very much – you all inspire me in a million different ways.
- To you, dear reader, for crossing the threshold to the Dead Letters Depot.

My final words of thanks go to Demian Wieland. The book is dedicated to him; he watched over me tirelessly as I watched over these words. Thank you, Demian. This one's for you.

Reading Group Questions

1. The language of Winter's letters is quite distinct and poetic. What kind of image did they conjure up of Winter? Did she turn out to be what you expected? Why was William drawn to her and what do you think this says about William and the ideas he holds about love?

2. From the beginning we get to see Clare's point of view and her reasoning behind her actions. How did this help inform your thoughts on their marriage and the different actions they took? Did you feel any empathy for William or Clare? How did this change as the novel progressed? Did you end up feeling more empathy for one character than the other?

3. William tells Clare in the heat of an argument 'I just enjoy the company of a beautiful young woman at work. So what?' (p.83). Do you think Clare's reaction was justified? And when we later discover that she cheated with Maxi, how did it change your opinion of this incident?

4. Conflict between adult responsibilities and following your heart is an important strand in the novel. Discuss the different ways that Clare and William deal with this.

5. Clare's childhood is a constant shadow over her current life, in the choices she makes and the person she wants to be. How does this affect her relationship with William? Should William have been more understanding of her overall? Or was he justified in his feelings?

6. Flora suggests to Clare to 'let go of feeling disappointed and start imagining what a new future together could look like, you might feel better about everything and he might get his confidence back' (p.160). Do you think this advice applies to Clare? What would be the practical ways for her to take it on? Would changing her viewpoint ultimately change William?

7. Clare and William's relationship is affected by all the things they don't say to each other and the ideals they hold of how their relationship should be. What do you think these ideals are? How are the expectations they have of each other informed by this?

8. Letters, and the act of writing them, are a major part of the novel. How are they used as tools of change throughout the arc of the story?

9. There is a degree of ambiguity surrounding the ending, particularly between the final words of 'their eyes met. He was lost and found' and the little snippet we see a year down the line. What was your interpretation of this? What ideas do you think author Helen Cullen wanted to offer up about love and relationships? How does this feed into your own opinion of these themes? And, ultimately, did it affect how you thought the story should have ended?

10. The author hints at the era the novel is set in with the use of payphones and mentions of events around the world, conveying a sense of nostalgia and charm. Do you think it had that effect? How would the story have been different if it had been set in the present day?

The Lost Letters of William Woolf Playlist

1. Chet Baker – Old Devil Moon
2. David Bowie – Wild Is The Wind
3. Nina Simone – My Baby Just Cares for Me
4. The Cure - Pictures Of You
5. Kate Bush – Hounds Of Love
6. Beethoven – Moonlight Sonata
7. Culture Club – Karma Chameleon
8. Sonny & Cher – I Got You Babe
9. Madonna – Like a Prayer
10. The Platters – The Great Pretender
11. Leonard Cohen – Suzanne
12. George Michael – Careless Whisper
13. Michael Dees – What Are You Doing for the Rest of Your Life?
14. The Undertones – Teenage Kicks
15. The Bangles – Eternal Flame
16. The Smiths – There is a Light That Never Goes Out

A Q and A with Helen Cullen

On the Book

What inspired you to write this story?

It all began with that line of poetry from John Donne: *'More than kisses, letters mingle souls.'* When I first sat down to tentatively write the first word, of the first page, of the first chapter of what would become this book, those words leaped from my memory and the premise for the narrative was established. I wanted the book to meditate on the lost art and power of letter writing, and knew that letters would remain at the heart of whatever I wrote. I was also very conscious of wanting to explore the juxtaposition that often exists between the way romantic love is portrayed in the media and the arts, and the pragmatic reality of sustaining a relationship over a long period of time. I was interested in the idea of second chances, and if they always necessitate something, or someone, new or if they could be found in the life you already inhabit. All of these ideas, and more, formed the emotional infrastructure of the novel, and these questions became the scaffolding on which the narrative was built.

371

The letters and the backstories to them are so personal and important to the recipient. How did you find the ideas for them?

Placing this story in the Dead Letters Depot was the greatest gift I could unwittingly have given myself as a writer; it allowed me to pull on the threads of so many short stories in the form of the letters that arrived there. It is a world where magic and reality could collide and co-exist on a daily basis, a place borne purely of the imagination where the gritty examination of relationships could be interrogated whilst also allowing for the potential magical elements of life to play: the serendipitous, the fated, the charmed. As I walked through the streets of London or along the lanes at home in Ireland, I found inspiration for the letters in the depot everywhere: the David Bowie exhibition at the V&A, an abandoned silk glove at the foot of Benbulbin mountain in County Sligo, a biscuit tin of wedding photographs, a cabinet of medals at the Imperial War museum, a walk-through Columbia Road Flower Market, listening to 'Bloodflowers' by The Cure on vinyl. In myriad different ways, inspiration was drawn from the flotsam and jetsam of life that we bob along with every day, the overheard conversations and silent observations. None of these letters were based on actual people, but they still felt very real to me.

Music features heavily in the book. Why was it important to you that the book had its own soundtrack?

Curating the songs to accompany the narrative allowed me to indulge in the perfect intersection of my two great loves: music and literature. One of the most revelatory moments in my relationship with each character came with the realization of who their favourite artists were and what music they chose to listen to at pivotal moments in their lives. Knowing that William Woolf was listening to The Smiths as he strolled through Dublin city made the whole scene crackle with life for me; I could place myself in the very heart of him. Understanding that Clare's musical heroine was Kate Bush gave me insight into the longings she nursed in private, the artistic instincts that she was working hard to oppress. Discovering that Winter's favourite band was The Cure reinforced in me her melancholic disposition, and how art could articulate sadness for her in a way that was restorative, uplifting and, ultimately, joyful. There is little in my novel that is biographical or inspired by events from my own life. The one thing that is borne of my own bones, however, is the importance of music in the character's lives. My great gift to these fictional folks that I developed such empathy for was the music that has been the soundtrack to my own life so far.

Why do you think letter-writing is such a powerful way to communicate?

I believe that when we sit down to write a letter it changes how we express ourselves: we become more thoughtful, more considered. In this digital world that we live in, we can communicate with more immediacy and efficiency than ever before, yet so many of us are also more isolated than ever before. Technology can give us all a false sense of connection that really doesn't permeate to the heart of who we are or eradicate loneliness. If those other mediums were all to vanish overnight, and we became dependant on letters once again, I think we would all get to know each other in new and profound ways. Yes, we would communicate less, but what we said would matter more. It is only when you create the opportunity of writing a letter that all the things you have to say reveal themselves, safe in the knowledge that the recipient won't, and can't, reply immediately but will also have time to think and reflect about what they want to say in return. I worry that there are generations of people now who will never know the thrill of seeing a letter on their doormat, with their name written in the handwriting of someone who loves them. I believe we are really pining for these physical connections in our lives now and hope that we will have a letter-writing revival.

And finally, what's one thing you'd love people to take away from *The Lost Letters of William Woolf*?

The instinct that they will probably never regret writing *that* letter and the impulse to begin it.

On Writing

As a debut writer, how did you find the writing journey?

It has been a roller coaster! From the ups and downs of writing the first draft through to the unmitigated joy of finding William's story on bookshop shelves, it has been a learning curve that I know still has plenty of bend to go. Like so many people, my dream was always to one day write a book, and I sometimes still cannot believe that it has come true. I am so grateful to everyone who has helped make it a reality and to the readers and literary community who have shown me such kindness and support.

What's one thing you wish you had known before you started writing *The Lost Letters of William Woolf*?

That creativity happens when you create the opportunity for it. I've learned I don't need the perfect mood, environment, or practicalities to be the catalyst for inspiration – I just need to sit down, anywhere, and get to work irrespective of how I am feeling thirty seconds before. The words are usually always waiting patiently for me to just get on with it.

Who or what inspires you to write?

One of the great lessons I have taken from writing this book is that inspiration is present all the time, all around us, in the life we are living right now, even in the moments when it feels its dullest. I am always amazed and thrilled when I feel the little tingle that comes with recognizing a sign or moment that feels created by the universe just for you.

And finally, any tips for budding writers?

I think it is helpful to try to keep moving forward one word at a time without rewriting too much until you have a first draft. You can finesse and correct anything in the edit, but working out the story you want to tell until the very end will give you the perspective you need regarding what actually needs to be edited, and hopefully the confidence to do it.

Quick-Fire Round

What was your favourite childhood book?

There is no doubt in my mind that I am a writer now because of the foundations laid with my childhood reading.

I loved Enid Blyton and my mother introduced me to all of the classics she in turn had loved as a little girl: *Little Women*, Laura Ingalls Wilder's Little House series, the Anne of Green Gables books, the Chronicles of Narnia, *The Secret Garden*, *Heidi*, *Black Beauty*, *Alice's Adventures in Wonderland*. I remain eternally grateful to my younger self for absorbing all that those incredible stories have to offer.

Favourite music?

The soundtrack to my life is an eclectic one, but there are some artists who are permanent residents in my heart: David Bowie, The Cure, The Smiths, Suede, Kate Bush, Feist, Tori Amos, Jeff Buckley, Radiohead to name but a few. I still think the planet is mourning David Bowie; I know I am.

Favourite artist?

I feel so fortunate to have wonderful work by Jennifer Rosemary Hooper hanging in my home. Both her art and her friendship are blessings in my life.

A quote to live by?

As with so many of life's big questions, I can find the answer to this in a line of poetry from Seamus Heaney: 'Walk on air against your better judgement.'

The new book from

HELEN CULLEN

Coming 2020

Read on for a sneak preview . . .

Inis Óg, 2005

It was Christmas Eve.

Murtagh wore tan sheepskin slippers, broken down at the heel.

He shuffled backwards and forwards along the well-worn floorboards in the shadowy hallway of the Moone family home.

Smoothing his crown of tousled golden curls back from his forehead, he gently touched where his temples throbbed. Still damp from the rain, he hugged his Aran cardigan tighter and the wooden robin brooch on his lapel turned upside down.

The ticking of his wristwatch was amplified in the silence, its pearlescent moon face catching the street-light through the window and winking back.

The door to the living room remained firmly closed. Christmas waited inside.

The branches of the lopsided fir tree he had dragged home across the Gallaghers' field seven days before were weighed down by decades of tinfoil garlands that the children had clumsily stitched together with red wool. None would ever be thrown away, however tattered they became. Every year, as the Moones assembled to transform their island cottage into something akin to Santa's grotto, each child claimed their own creations with jealous possession. With ceremonial grace, their mother carefully unrolled their handiwork from the fraying white tissue paper that protected the decorations for the other forty-eight weeks of the year. One by one they were placed on the tree.

Over these festivities, as with all others, Murtagh's wife reigned supreme.

His Queen Maeve.

None of the children challenged the traditions; their mother had sewn them so meticulously into the fabric of their being.

Stitches that could not be outgrown.

How he loved her for this gift she bestowed upon the family: permission to remain childlike in their enthusiasms, never to become embarrassed by what they had once loved. 'You never have to lose anything or anyone,' she often said, 'if you just change the way you look at them.'

And yet he had lost her.

Even while he held her close.

Even with his eyes wide open.

Murtagh had woken that morning, once again, to an empty bed; the sheets were smooth and unruffled on Maeve's side. He had expected to find her sitting at the kitchen table wrapped in her hound's-tooth shawl, pale and thin in the darkness before dawn, a tangle of blue-black hair swept across her high forehead like a crow's wet wing, her long, matted curls secured in a knot at the nape of her neck with one of her red pencils. He had anticipated how she would start when he appeared in the doorway. How he would ignore, as he always did, the few moments it would take for her dove-grey eyes to turn their focus outward. For the ghosts to leave her in his presence. The kettle would hiss and spit on the stove as he stood behind her wicker chair and rubbed warmth back into her arms, his voice jolly as he gently scolded her for lack of sleep and feigned nonchalance as to its cause.

But Maeve wasn't sitting at the kitchen table.

Nor was she meditating on the stone step of the back door drinking milk straight from the glass bottle it was delivered in.

She wasn't dozing on the living-room sofa, the television on but silent, an empty crystal tumbler tucked inside the pocket of her peacock-blue silk dressing gown, the one on which she had painstakingly embroidered a murmuration of starlings in the finest silver thread.

Instead, there was an empty space on the bannister where her plum woollen coat should have been hanging.

Murtagh opened the front door and flinched at the swarm of spitting raindrops that assaulted him. The blistering wind mocked the threadbare cotton of his pinstripe pyjamas. He bent his head into the onslaught and pushed forward, dragging the heavy scarlet door behind him. The brass knocker clanged against the wood with the force of his effort; he flinched, hoping it had not woken the children. Shivering, he picked a route in his slippers around the muddy puddles spreading across the cobblestoned pathway. Leaning over the wrought-iron gate that separated their own familial island from the winding lane of the island proper, he scanned the dark horizon for a glimpse of Maeve in the faraway glow of a streetlamp.

In the distance, the sea and sky had melted into one anthracite mist, each indiscernible from the other. Sheep huddled together for comfort in Peadar Óg's field, the waterlogged green that bordered the Moones' land to the right; the plaintive baying of the animals sounded mournful. Murtagh nodded at them with empathy.

There was no sight of Maeve.

As he turned back towards the house, he noticed Nollaig watching him from her bedroom window. The eldest daughter, she always seemed to witness the very moments her parents had believed – hoped – were cloaked in invisibility, and then remained haunted by what she had seen. Over the years, Murtagh had monitored how understanding began filling her up from the tips of her toddler toes, and knew it would soon flood her eyes, always so questioning, permanently.

Born on Christmas Eve, twenty years before, she was the only one of their children who came into the world via Galway maternity hospital and not into the impatient arms of Máire O'Dulaigh, the midwife of the island. She resented it: how it made her feel less of a true islander. What was more, the specialness of her own day for individual attention, her birth day, was irrevocably lost in the shared excitement of Christmas. In retrospect, it had been a mistake, perhaps, naming her Nollaig, the Gaelic for Christmas, and further compounding the association. No nickname had ever stuck, however. She wasn't the sort of child who inspired others to claim her for their own with the intimacy of a given name.

'Born ancient,' her little sister, Sive, always said of her with bored disdain.

And Murtagh sympathized. Nollaig carried the weight of being the eldest with pained perseverance, responsibilities heavy like stones in her pockets that she had purposefully chosen for herself; no one needed her to supervise them. Her mother certainly harboured a silent resentment of it, felt piqued at the implication that she needed the support. It seemed only natural, if unfair, that Maeve and Sive gravitated more towards each other; the baby of the family shared her mother's wit and wildness and often expressed the irritation her mother tried to hide at Nollaig's sense of duty.

Murtagh waved at his daughter as he blew back up the pathway. Later, he would feel the acute pain of finally understanding the prescience his daughter seemed to have absorbed from the womb.

'How long is she gone?'

Nollaig was standing before the hallway mirror, her face contorted as she vigorously tried to brush her frizzy mouse-brown hair into shape. She scraped it together into a tight ponytail that thrust from the back of her head as if it were a fox tail.

'Ach, you should leave your gorgeous curls be, Noll,' her father cajoled, 'instead of fighting them.'

She smiled at him but slammed the mother-of-pearl hairbrush down on the oak sideboard.

'I don't have curls, I have Brillo pads,' she sighed. 'Did she say where she was going?'

Murtagh squeezed his daughter's arm as he continued into the kitchen. 'I'm sure your *mother* is just out for a walk. Happy birthday, love. Lá breithla shona duit.'

He placed a small copper saucepan of water on the range to boil and waved the invitation of an egg at his daughter. She nodded begrudgingly and curled into the green-and-gold striped armchair that sat in front of the stove.

'With your white nightdress, you could almost pass for the Irish flag,' he joked, and was gratified when she emitted a spontaneous snort of glee in response.

He watched the clock hand count three minutes in silence. Expected any moment to hear his soaked wife splash through the door. He was poised, ready to run towards her with a towel and hushed reprimands for her careless wandering, but the boiling, cooling, cupping, cracking and spooning of each egg passed uninterrupted. Nollaig yawned, stretching her arms and legs before her in a stiff salute.

'Why don't you go back to bed for an hour?' her father asked. 'We'll all have a proper breakfast together later.'

She eyed him with suspicion but acquiesced. 'If she's not back soon,' she said, sidling away, 'come and wake me. Promise? We'll go out and find her. Remind her it's Christmas Eve, for God's sake.'

Murtagh nodded, ushered his daughter out of the kitchen and watched her climb the stairs.

As soon as he heard Nollaig's room grow still, he pulled on waterproof fishing trousers over his pyjama bottoms, thick yellow socks and wellington boots. He struggled into a heavy jumper of itchy grey wool, impatiently yanking the sleeves of his nightshirt down from where they were caught at the elbows, and pulled on the olive-green duffel coat that remained his favourite, though long past its prime. It was eight in the morning now; the sun would not rise until closer to nine. As he reached into the cupboard under the stairs for a torch, he was relieved to find only one waiting on the shelf.

At least she's taken a light.

The beam from his flashlight showed him little but the safest path for his own feet, but he was glad of it as he waded through the inky blackness.

Come meet me, Maeve.

Show yourself.

Come meet me, Maeve.

Show yourself.

As he marched a beat down the long, narrow lane towards the pier, trailing his left hand along the stony walls covered in moss, he repeated his mantra.

Not another soul stirred.

What would call them from the warmth of their own homes to be drenched in this storm? When the weather enveloped the island in an angry embrace such as this, the isolation became almost unbearable. The elements made prisoners of the islanders, who could be convinced they had been swept out to sea, lost and untethered, never to reach the mainland again.

As Murtagh leaned against the weather-bleached clapboard sign that shouted the ferry times in bright-orange paint, the sky became diluted with the first strata of light.

The rain eased.

The darkness slunk away in a mood, but only by as little as it had to for dawn to be officially broken.

Perhaps Maeve was already at home, she in turn now worried for him.

In the watery winter sunlight that was more skimmed milk than golden honey, he trudged through the sand to retrace his steps, willing with each breath for his home to have sprung to life with the dawn while he'd been gone.

The sound of the twins arguing in the kitchen heartened him as he wiped his boots on the back-door mat. Eighteen now, they occasionally loomed before him as fully grown men. At other times, they were still the small boys who hadn't liked sharing the same supermarket trolley seat, letting their objections be known.

'How hard is to toast bread, Mossy?' Dillon said, scraping the charred surface of a cremated slice of soda bread into the sink. 'Every. Single. Time.' He enunciated each syllable with a violent scratch of the butter knife.

Mossy, nonplussed, stood drinking orange juice straight from the carton, ignoring the rivulets that dribbled down his chin. His face lit up as his father peered around the door.

'Da! Where were ye? What's the story with break-fast?' He shoved the carton back in the fridge, the lid discarded on the counter top.

'Yeah!' Dillon chimed in. 'Where's the feast Mam promised? We're half starved waiting!'

Murtagh swivelled his head around the kitchen. 'She's not back then? Your mother?'

The twins caught each other's eyes, Mossy's cornflower blues meeting Dillon's charcoal greys, before their gaze fell back on their father as he wrestled off his boots.

'Was she not with you?' Mossy asked, dragging his floppy blond fringe across his forehead and plastering it behind his ear.

Son Day, his mother called him. Tomás Moone, the pale, blond, waifish bookworm who inherited not only his paternal grandfather's name but his colouring and tem-perament, too. Son Night, his brother Dillon, with his ebony-black curls, high cheekbones and grey eyes, was unmistakably his mother's son. Named in honour of two of her heroes, Bob Dylan and Dylan Thomas, the artistic mantle lay heavily on his shoulders. He had the dream to be an artist, but not the driven determination. Dillon was never really interested in struggling, only in enjoying what came easily. Mossy was the one who worked hard, persevered conscientiously with any task until it was com-plete. Sometimes Murtagh wondered how each would have developed if their names had been swapped at birth, or if, with the christening, their fates had been sealed.

Nollaig reappeared at the kitchen door, dressed now in the white velvet pinafore and red polo neck she had planned to save for Christmas Day. 'Has Mam not resurfaced?' she asked, her face flushing.

Murtagh looked at the questioning expressions on the faces of his three children and shook his head. 'I better wake Sive,' said Nollaig, and pounded back upstairs.

Sive had turned sixteen that summer and relished her new, more mature-sounding number. Obsessed with the Manic Street Preachers, Placebo and Suede, she wore fandom like a uniform, her jet-black bob curled under her chalk-white-painted face like the Lego hair of the figures she'd played with as a child. Eyeliner rimmed her eyes in rivers of kohl black, the same dove-grey eyes she saw mirrored in her mother. Blood-red lipstick emphasized how little she smiled. Her clothes, usually striped, always sooty-black, battleship-grey or midnight-blue, she wore in layer upon layer, with garlands of silver stars draped around her throat. A full-length fake-leopard-print fur salvaged from a charity shop on Eyre Street in Galway city was her most prized possession. It was this she wore over her Emily the Strange nightdress now, as she reluctantly followed Nollaig into the kitchen. She pulled the coat tighter around herself when she detected the melancholy cloud that lingered in the air, the private smoke signals the twins passed from one to the other. Her father was busily burning sausages in the pan. She was surprised to hear him curse when the sizzling oil spat at him.

'So, what's the plan? Is Christmas cancelled, then?' Sive asked, checking the temperature of the coffee pot with the palm of her hand.

Murtagh poured her a mugful and scoffed. 'Don't be daft! We're just going to have a little fortification, and then perhaps we can all take a stroll and go and meet your mother. She's lost track of time, that's all.'

Sive reached for the mug and they both held it for a moment. 'So, a search party. That's what you're saying. Great!' She slumped in a chair at the kitchen table and elbowed Mossy to give her more room.

Her father turned back to the pan, his voice strained. 'That's not funny, Si. And it's nothing of the sort. I think we'd all just like to start the day together. And you know your mam – she'll be having a great time walking the roads and will be delighted to see one of us coming to meet her.' He put the ham that Maeve had prepared the night before in the oven and set the timer for noon.

Not long afterwards, as the rain started to pour again, the twins forged ahead towards the rusty shipwreck on the east of the island.

Nollaig and Sive elected to walk past the chapel, on to Tigh Ned's pub, and agreed to then carry on to the castle ruins if they hadn't found her first.

Murtagh set out for the lighthouse, convinced if Maeve was gone this long that must be the road she had taken. Although, the thought struck him, he did not know how long it had been since she left the house.

Why hadn't he insisted she come to bed with him? She was too restless, she'd said. Too full of the moon for sleeping.

They would reconvene back at the house after they reached their destinations instead of continuing on; the chances were their mother would be waiting at home when they came back, wondering where they had all gallivanted off to.

Nollaig and Sive returned empty-hearted first. Nollaig scraped the ashes from the grate in the living room while Sive set the kindling for a fire. They stood in front of it in silence, waiting for the others, warming their hands near the flames without feeling the heat at all.

The twins burst in next, Dillon's soaked fluorescent trainers squelching as he walked. When they saw the sisters were alone, they backed out of the living room without a word; Mossy climbed back under his duvet, fully clothed, his brown brogues dangling over the foot of the bed, and pretended to read a book of poetry by Keats. Dillon drained the tank of hot water in the shower, his discarded clothes a soggy pile outside the bathroom door.

When Murtagh's arrival wasn't accompanied by the fluttering sing-song of their mother's voice, Sive's eyes flooded. Nollaig snapped, told her to pull herself together and hurried out to the kitchen to speak to her father alone. The aroma of roasting ham percolated throughout the silent house, as if in spite. When the electric beeps heralded its readiness, Nollaig turned off the oven without even looking inside. She hoped her mother would be home soon to reprimand her for not taking greater care. Dinner was sacrificed to a God she wasn't sure she believed in as her father prepared to face the elements once again. Nollaig called her brothers and sister together and they divided up the island paths between them for a second search. Nobody spoke as they marched out of their cottage in single file, back into the storm.

Minutes of acute expectation bled into anxious hours of increasing alarm. By mid-afternoon Murtagh and his four children were wet, exhausted and turning on each other. In vain, their father encouraged them to eat bowls of lukewarm vegetable soup that he ladled out slowly. He choked his own down, spilling some on his cardigan, dropping his spoon on the floor tiles with a clatter. Nollaig caught his eye and he nodded.

'We need more help,' he said, as he eased himself up from his chair. 'I won't be long.'

Murtagh walked to Tigh Ned, where the islanders were gathering for hot whiskies and shepherd's pies before the evening mass. The lime-coloured plastic Christmas tree on the windowsill wore the wine-and-white Galway jersey, circled by pint glasses holding beeswax candles donated by the parish priest, Father Donal. The *RTÉ Guide* bumper Christmas edition stood on display by its side with a small laminated sign perched against it: *Not to be removed from the premises*. The air was heavy and moist as a result of the condensation rising from damp clothes and human bodies huddled together.

Murtagh spoke to Father Donal, whose white denim jacket sat stark against his black shirt and slacks, a sprig of holly pinned to his breast pocket. With head tosses and clicking fingers, Donal summoned a semicircle of islanders before draining his tumbler in one, crunching an ice cube with his back teeth as he delivered instructions.

The Moone children would come to the pub, eat some dinner there, no objections entertained. Murtagh himself was to wait at home for Maeve.

'In case,' Father Donal said, before correcting himself, 'I mean, for *when* Maeve comes back by herself.'

In groups of twos and threes, they dispersed, half-consumed pints of Guinness left resting on the grille in the hope of a speedy return.

And so Murtagh found himself pacing the floorboards of the hallway, fingering rosary beads in the pocket of his cardigan more out of superstition than faith. What little light had broken through that day had once again dissolved into darkness.

From the little window in the hallway, he watched the streetlamps flicker into life in quick succession as the cuckoo clock chirped four with inconsiderate glee. He shouted at it to stop its keening and then found himself apologizing to the little yellow bird. A knock pounded the front door.

Murtagh hid in the study for a moment, covering his ears.

He didn't want the news a knock like that would bring.

What he wanted was a hand to reach for that door that belonged to someone who could unlock it, walk herself in and wrap her arms around him.

He blessed himself with the ruby-red beads and opened the front door a crack. Father Donal stood on the doorstep, his denim jacket soaked through, his hands wringing a tweed peak cap. Over the priest's shoulder,

Murtagh saw Seamus McCann and Áine O'Connor waiting outside the gate, huddled under a huge canopied umbrella advertising Tayto crisps, their eyes focused on the laneway beneath their feet.

'Why don't they come in, Donal?' Murtagh opened the door wide and beckoned them with his arm, but the priest reached for it and held it in his own.

'Tell me, Murtagh. Your currach, is it still in the boatyard? When did you last have her out?'

Murtagh took a step back, the priest a step forward, still holding his arm.

'Only yesterday. Where else would it be? No one would be out in this weather. No one. What are you asking me that for?' He stood up straighter.

Father Donal squeezed Murtagh's arm tighter, his icy blue fingers exposed in black fingerless gloves. 'There's a currach caught in the rocks by the westward cliff. A few fellas are climbing down now to release it. Could you come with me, Murtagh? Just so we know it's not yours. To eliminate it.'

Murtagh shook away the priest's hand and pushed past him without stopping for his coat.

Father Donal hesitated before pulling the door closed behind them.

Murtagh threw his shoulders back as he repeated his walk from that morning to the pier. His name deigned him protector of the sea, and now he pleaded with the melanoid Atlantic for protection.

Father Donal, Seamus and Áine rushed behind him in silence, but no one tried to match his step.

At the boathouse, he found the door unlatched, and the discovery stuck the soles of his shoes to the sandy path beneath him. Áine stepped forward, gently swung the door wide and pulled the string to light the bulb that dangled from the ceiling. With a glance, she quickly knew what Murtagh's eyes would not believe, however hard they scanned and searched.

The boat was gone.

From the distance, Murtagh heard voices calling from the shore. Ignoring protestations from the priest to wait until he had learned more, he staggered down the sand dunes to where a cluster of men stood in a half-moon around a currach, their hunched shoulders turned away from him. As he approached, Peadar Óg, owner of the whining sheep, moved towards him. His clothes were drenched, his face red raw and freezing, eyes wet and wild.

'I'm sorry, Murtagh,' he croaked. 'It's Maeve. We have her. She was tethered to the currach by a rope. Her pockets . . .'

His voice broke.

'Her pockets were full of stones.'

He stood aside, and Murtagh dropped on his knees in the wet sand beside the boat. In the silver light, blue veins traced delicate pathways across Maeve's face, like tiny cracks in a porcelain vase. He traced a line over each one with his little finger while the islanders turned their faces away.

Father Donal began a decade of the rosary and, in quiet voices, each one joined in, even the ones who weren't believers.

In fact, theirs were the loudest voices of all, as with each 'Amen', the darkness crept closer.